A Guest of Honour

by the same author

Novels

THE LATE BOURGEOIS WORLD
OCCASION FOR LOVING
A WORLD OF STRANGERS
THE LYING DAYS

Short Stories

NOT FOR PUBLICATION
FRIDAY'S FOOTPRINT
SIX FEET OF THE COUNTRY
THE SOFT VOICE OF THE SERPENT

A GUEST
OF HONOUR

Nadine Gordimer

JONATHAN CAPE
THIRTY BEDFORD SQUARE LONDON

FIRST PUBLISHED IN GREAT BRITAIN 1971
REPRINTED 1971, 1972
© 1970 BY NADINE GORDIMER

JONATHAN CAPE LTD, 30 BEDFORD SQUARE, LONDON WC I
ISBN O 224 00510 3

PRINTED IN GREAT BRITAIN BY
LOWE AND BRYDONE (PRINTERS) LTD, LONDON
BOUND BY G. AND J. KITCAT LTD, LONDON

An honourable man will end by not know-
ing where to live.

—Ivan Sergeevich Turgenev

Many will call me an adventurer—and that
I am, only of a different sort—one of those
who risks his skin to prove his platitudes.

—Ernesto "Che" Guevara

PART ONE

A bird cried out on the roof, and he woke up. It was the middle of the afternoon, in the heat, in Africa; he knew at once where he was. Not even in the suspended seconds between sleep and waking was he left behind in the house in Wiltshire, lying, now, deep in the snow of a hard winter. The road to the village would be blocked, the dog ran over the soft fields breathing like a dragon . . . the kernel of the house was warm with oil-fired heating and the light from red shades, the silky colours of Olivia's things—the rugs, cherry- and satin-wood pieces—and the red earth pots, bits of beadwork, the two fine carvings they once found in the Congo. A few days ago he was in that house, packing to leave in the flat progression of practical matters by which decision is broken up into reality. *If you have any trouble with the boiler, for heaven's sake let Mackie look at it before you send to town. —What a pity you gave away your shorts. —There's no knowing if I'll be anywhere where I could dare appear in shorts, any more. —But your waist measurement hasn't changed by so much as half an inch—I know by your pyjama trousers, I use exactly the same measurement for new elastic as I always did.—*

Three months before, Adamson Mweta stood outside a steak house in Kensington and said to him, Of course you'll come back to us now! He had driven home, slowing down on the empty road that led through the fullness of a deserted summer twilight, at last, to the

3

house. Housing estates overrun villages all over England, but here the process had been reversed; the house had once been a manor (Olivia thought that, even earlier, it had been a priory) but in the nineteenth century the village was depopulated by the drift to industrialized towns, lost its autonomy, and died; the shop-cum-post-office had closed, the cottages had fallen down; the woods and meadows took over the fields, only a few houses remained, to be bought by the people whose longing for country life discounted the inconvenience of isolation. As Olivia said, it ought to have been a sad-feeling place but it wasn't; there was instead a renewal: the country had come back, bringing the reassurance of stubborn peace and fecundity, a beginning again. And they were only two-hours-and-a-bit from London, their daughters and their friends. He had kept up, since he finally left Africa ten years ago, a close contact with Adamson Mweta and the other leaders of the African independence movement. He spent a great deal of time going back and forth to London to advise them when they conferred with the Colonial Office, and to do what he could to smooth the way for various delegations that came to petition against the old constitution and to negotiate independence for their country. It was there, in this Central African territory, that he had been a colonial servant until the settlers succeeded in having him recalled and deported for his support of the People's Independence Party. He said to his wife, "Mweta's invited me to come back as their guest."

"Well, you ought to be at the Independence celebrations, if anyone is. That's marvellous." She used to make packages of sandwiches for Mweta to take with him when he cycled for miles about Gala province at weekends, speaking at meetings.

He said to Adamson Mweta before they parted the next day, "Olivia won't be able to come out to Independence, unfortunately—our elder daughter's expecting a child just round about that time."

Mweta said, with his slow shy smile that always seemed to grow like a light becoming more powerful, as his eyes held you, "You mean little Venetia? She going to be a mother?"

"I'm afraid so," he mumbled in his Englishman's way.

"Well, that's good, that's *good*. Never mind, Mrs. Bray will join you later."

"I imagine by the time she's prepared to trust the baby to Venetia the celebrations'll be over."

"That's what I mean—you'll be more or less settled by the time she arrives."

They were standing at the door of Mweta's taxi; there was a sudden uprush of feeling between the two men; the Englishman stood there, the small, quick black man took him by the biceps, hard, through his dark suit, as in his own country he would have linked fingers with a brother. Under the release of physical contact, he said to Mweta, "I don't know what we're talking about," and Mweta said, "You—I told you we expect you back, now."

"But what would I do? What use should I be to you?" He was so accustomed to effacing himself in the hours of discussion of constitutional law and political tactics (a white man, an outsider offering impersonal service for whatever it was worth)—a strong consciousness of his own being flooded him as if a stimulant had been injected into his veins.

"Whatever you like! It's all ours! We need you; whatever you like!" Mweta broke away and jumped into the taxi.

The pale stone façade with its stone lintels and sills worn smooth as a piece of used soap was directly on the empty road but the real face of the house was the other side. Sheltered by the building the garden was a grassy look-out over fuzzy colours of flowers, bees, and early moths to the long valley. He and Olivia gardened on summer evenings, not seriously, as she did during the day, but desultorily pulling out a tall rank weed here or there, for the pleasure of feeling its roots yield from the humus and bring up, in the crumbs clinging to that beard grown underground, a smell of earth rich as fruit-cake. They had laid flag-stones under the walnut trees for the white wooden chairs and table, so that it wouldn't be too damp. They drank whisky there, or even the coffee after dinner. Sometimes before the dusk wavered the wood away into the distance, he went out into the sunlight that collected like golden water in the dip of the meadows and shot a partridge. There was no one to bother about shooting rights. Afterwards as the evening faded he cleaned the gun almost by feel and the clean, practical smell of gun-oil conveyed the simple satisfaction of the task. Olivia played records with the living-room windows wide open so that the music came out to them.

This summer it was Stravinsky and Poulenc; she was of the generation and class that paid other women to knit and now that she herself was about to be a grandmother she made funny stuffed toys for nieces and nephews. She had a cigar box full of odd buttons, as a supply of eyes, but she put it away from her because one of the things she had hated when she was young was the show of dissembling older women made when confronted with something vital to them.

"I suppose we said many times we'd come back when they got their independence." She gave a small, self-questioning shrug, admitting the glibness of another kind of daily talk in another time.

"It's not because of what one said." But both knew that; in those days, the important thing was to give Adamson Mweta faith in himself by positing a future that was real because you, a white person with nothing personal to gain by it, showed you believed it would come about.

Gazing out across the valley and then calmly at him, she had her look of wanting to find out exactly what they were talking about.

He said, "Certainly I thought of going back, *then*. Hypothetically. Before we left. —Just as I knew we should have to leave."

"Poor Adamson, it looked pretty hopeless at times. And yet it's come so quickly. Ten years!" Ten years since they had been deported from the territory, ten years since she was a youngish woman of forty, and the girls were still schoolgirls. "Historically, yes, it would happen —but not to Adamson, and not to us?"

The house they had bought, filled with possessions that had been stored all the years they were in Africa, the garden they had made, spoke for them. It was not a house to be quitted.

"They expect you back," she said with pride.

"Adamson was in the flush of victory, all right. I think he'd have embraced Henry Davis." Davis was the settler M.P. who had been responsible, at one stage, for getting Mweta banished to the far Western Province.

"He naturally assumes you'll come out of exile." They laughed. But they were talking of Mweta; the strange shyness of twenty-two years of marriage made it impossible for her to say: Do you want to go? The passionate beginning, the long openness and understanding between them should have meant that she would know what he wanted. And in a way she did know: because it was for them a code so deeply accepted that it had never been discussed—one was available wherever one was of use. What else was there to live by? And so the question of what they were talking about really amounted to her hidden, pressed-down, banked-over desire to know whether this house, this life in Wiltshire, this life—at last—seemed to him the definitive one, in the end. Because she was suddenly realizing that it had been so for her. She was, after all (in the true sense of after all that had gone before) an Englishwoman. She had taken out of storage the furniture and family possessions that had been nothing but a nuisance to her when they left England together twenty years ago, and, putting them in place, inevitably had accepted the life the arrangement of such objects provided for, and her comfortable private income made possible. In the room they had decided upon for his study, the desk from her great-grandfather that had naturally become his—a quiet field of black-red morocco scratched with almost erased gold—was a place to write the properly documented history of the territory (Mweta's country) that had never been done before; not the boxwood Colonial Office desk at which one dealt with government forms and made the empirical scribbles of administration or politics, written one day and screwed into a ball the next.

In the scented, mothy evening she felt the presence of the house like someone standing behind her. She did not know whether he felt it too; and she could not try to find out because if it turned out that he didn't—she had a premonition, sometimes, that in middle age you could find you had lost everything in a moment: husband-lover, friend, children, it was as if they had never happened, or you had wandered off from them without knowing, and now stood stock-still with the discovery.

They watched the moths in the tobacco flowers. She said in her sensible, inquiring, Englishwoman's voice behind which generations of her kind had sheltered, "Did Mweta say how long?"

"It was very much a gesture! He was tremendously in the air!"

"No, but he'd already mentioned it yesterday, isn't that so? You misunderstood him yesterday. A year? Six months? —What?"

White people given appointments in African countries after independence were usually employed on contract. "Good Lord, I've no idea, I'm sure he hasn't either. It's all in the air."

Olivia went in to change the record and because it was, unexpectedly, Mozart—the harp and flute concerto—he lit a cigar to smoke while he enjoyed it. She wandered down to the herb garden and brought back a branch of dill; "There he is," she said. It was their owl, a youngster who had hatched out down in the field and was heard every night. She remarked that tomorrow she must pick the dill for drying. Everything was just as it was. But everything was changed. All had turned over in the barrel of the world and steadied itself again. She knew, if he didn't, that he was going.

It was night in Europe all the way. Dark rain in the afternoon in London when the plane took off, at Rome the airport a vast, bleary shopwindow shining blurred colours through rain. He hauled down his coat again to get out at Athens. The metal rail of the steps wheeled against the plane was icy-wet to his palm and in the streaming rain he did not smell the Aegean or thyme, as he had remembered from other journeys to Africa. Inside the airport under the yellow light the passengers sat down again on exhausted-looking chairs, bundled deep in their heavy clothing. An old woman with crinkly grey hair woke up at her post outside the lavatory and opened the door, smiling and grasping a filthy cleaning rag. He walked around to ease the cramp in his knees but there was a small circumference and within a few strides one found oneself back again at the shop, before which women and child passengers were drawn to gaze at embroidered aprons and *evzone* dolls. A girl of ten or eleven with the badges of the cantons of Switzerland sewn to the sleeve of her coat had exactly the look of Venetia at that age. He bought a postcard of brilliant blue sea and dazzling white ruins and tried to write, in what he could remember of Greek: Winter and darkness here but in Cambridge, perhaps, there's already spring yelling its head off? My love to you, James. Venetia had had a first in Greek, herself, only a year ago, and could laugh over the mistakes.

But that was the end of Europe. At Kano a huge moon shone and in a light brighter than a European winter afternoon the passengers made their way across the tarmac at three in the morning against the resistance of a heat of the day persisting all through the night as the sun persists in a stone it has warmed. There was a smell of woodsmoke; the men moving about beneath the belly of the plane had bare black feet. When the passengers climbed aboard again, their clothes felt hairy and the plane was airless. He put the coat away on the rack, apologizing, trying not to hamper other people in the general move to rearrange gear; the anticipation of arrival, still some hours off, aroused in them not so much common purpose as a spread of instinct, as in the lifted heads of a herd become aware of the promise of water. When the sun rose some slumped off into sleep, but women began to examine the plastic bags in which they kept their hats, and, as the hard beams of the sun struck into the cabin on hairnets, pale lips, and stubble, queues formed for the lavatories. While he was writing on the customs and immigration form, BRAY, Evelyn James, and the number of his passport, someone was reading his name over his shoulder; he flexed it awkwardly, not because he minded, but in mild embarrassment. The queue for the lavatory moved along a notch, he glanced up and the man, carrying a flowered sponge-bag, caught his eye with a tired vacant stare that changed to an expression of greeting. The woman who had dozed beside him all night communicating the intimate rhythm of her breathing but never exchanging a word, suddenly began to talk like a bird who has the cover taken off its cage. He wedged himself between the seats to recover the shoe she had lost somewhere over a distant desert; she laughed, protested apologetically, and shook cologne down into her freckled bosom. Dragging back the little curtain from the oval window, she looked into the dazzling glare of space and said, "Glorious morning up here!" and they discussed with animation the cold and sudden winter that was left behind.

As he did not have a window seat he did not see the bush and the earth red as brick-dust and the furze of growth along the river-beds: not until the plane had come to a stop on the runway, and they were waiting for the health inspector to come aboard. He unhooked his safety belt and leaned over to look at an angle through the bleary lens on the far side of the aisle; and there it was, tiny and distorted and real, bush, earth, exactly as it remained in his mind always, without his thinking about it. It was underfoot. It was around. A black man in khaki shorts (used to be a white man in white stockings) sprayed a cloyingly perfumed insecticide over the passengers' heads as a precaution against the plane harbouring mosquitoes and tsetse flies. The doors opened; voices from without came in on currents of air; he emerged among the others into heady recognition taken in at all the senses, walking steadily across the tarmac through the raw-potato whiff of the undergrowth, the fresh, early warmth on hands, the cool metallic taste of last night's storm at the back of the throat, the airport building with the five pink frangipani and the enclosure where out-of-works and children still hooked their fingers on the diamond-mesh wire and gazed. The disembarking passengers were all strangers again, connected not with each other but to the mouthing, smiling faces and waving hands on the airport balcony. He knew no one but the walk was processional, a reception to him, and by the time he entered the building over the steps where, as always, dead insects fallen from the light during the night had not been swept away, it was all as suddenly familiar and ordinary as the faces other people were greeting were, to them. Waiting to be summoned to the customs officers' booths, the companions of the journey ignored each other. Only the man with the flowered sponge-bag, as if unaware of this useful convention, insisted on a "Here we are again" smile. "You're Colonel Bray?" He spoke round the obstacle of a woman standing between them. "Thought I recognized you in Rome. Welcome back." "I must confess I don't remember you. I've been away a long time." The man had long coarse strands of sun-yellowed hair spread from ear to ear across a bald head and wore sunglasses that rested on fine Nordic cheekbones. "I've only just come to live here—from down South. South Africa." He made a resigned grimace assuming understanding— "My wife and I decided we couldn't stick it any longer. So we try it out here. I don't know; we'll see. I read you were coming back, there was an article in the paper, my wife Margot sent it to me in Switzerland, so I thought it was you. You were just in front of me when we got out in Rome."

"Yes, I suppose I won't know my way around when I get into town."

"Oh, it's still not New York or London, don't worry." The man spoke with an accent, and a certain European kind of resignation. They laughed. "Well, in that case, we'll probably bump into each other in Great Lakes Road."

"Please! Nkrumah Road."

"I said I should have to learn my way round all over again."

The man looked about quickly and lowered his voice. "This country can do with a few more white people like you, take it from me. People with some faith. Sometimes I even think I'm down South again, that's a fact. I've said it to my wife."

A young black man with sunglasses and a thick, springy mat of hair shaped to a crew-cut by topiary rather than barbering had cut through the crowd with the encircling movement of authority. "This way, Colonel, sir. Your luggage will be brought to the entrance, if you'll just give me the tickets—"

The other man, bobbing in the wash of this activity yet smiling at it in hostly assumption of his own established residence in the country, was talking across the black man and the exchange of pleasantries, tickets, thanks: "—at the Silver Rhino, of course, you remember the place. Any time—we'd be very pleased—"

He thanked him, listening to the two men at once and hearing neither, and followed the firm rump in white shorts past barriers and through the reception hall. "That's all right, officer, this is Colonel Bray." "I'm looking after Colonel Bray, no need to bother him." A youthful black official at passport control said uncertainly, "Just a minute. I don't know about this—" but the pale Cockney who was teaching him to take over his job said, "That's okay, chum, it's our ole friend Mr. Kabata." The luggage was not waiting at the flag-draped and bunting-swathed entrance, where a picture of a huge Roman emperor Mweta, in a toga, smiled as he did in the old photograph of the Gala village football team. Mr. Kabata said, "What's the matter with these people. Excuse me, I'll get a boy," and returned with the cases on the head of one of the stringy, splay-footed peasants who had always constituted the portering personnel. The porter addressed both men as *Mukwayi*, the respectful term become servile during the long time when it was used indiscriminately for any white man.

There was an official pennant on the Volkswagen. Beside him, Kabata's strong thighs filled the seat. "It's not too comfortable for a man your height, Colonel. The President will be expecting me to have come for you with the Mercedes, but, honestly, if I'd have waited to get it I would have turned up I don't know when. You know how it is just at the moment. Mrs. Indira Gandhi arrives this afternoon and yesterday it was United Nations and Sékou Touré." There were gilded arches over the old airport road to town; several men on bicycles wore shirts with Mweta's face printed in yellow and puce on their backs. He said, "All very festive," but it was distraction; he had the feeling of listening inwardly, watching for something else. The young man said, "You are from Gala district." "I *was*. Why, are you from there?" "From Umsalongwe. But my mother is a Gala. I have visited that place." "Oh have you? Recently or when you were a child? Perhaps I was still there then?" "I think they'll be very pleased to see you back there." He laughed. "I wonder if I'll get that far."

"Oh, you must make trip" the young man said proudly. "I do it to Umsalongwe in ten hours. The road is much improved, much improved. You'll see. You could make it to Matoko in, say, six or seven. My car is a little tiny thing, a second-hand crock." Near the bridge the women were going for water with paraffin tins on their heads. Advertisement hoardings had gone up, there was a cement works, smart factories put together out of jutting glassy sections and, in between, the patches scratched in the bush where women and children were hoeing crooked rows of beans and maize. The children (an excuse to dawdle, of course) stopped and waved. He found himself waving back urgently, bending his head under the low roof of the car, smiling and craning to hold their faces when they were already out of sight. The car was approaching, was carrrying him through the market quarter of the town. Under the mango trees, barbers' mirrors set up a flash in the shade, and live chickens lay in heaps with their legs tied. It was the mango season, and there were the saffron-yellow sabres of the pips, sucked hairy, everywhere where people passed.

The bird was on the roof of the round, thatched guest room in the garden of his old friend Roland Dando—a Welshman—newly appointed as Attorney-General. When Bray was delivered to the house there was no one at home but servants well primed to welcome him. They gave him the African cook's special lunch that he remembered so well: slightly burned meat soup with lots of barley, overdone steak with fried onions, a pudding frothy on top and gelatinous underneath, tasting of eggs and granadilla juice. Roly rang up to see if he had arrived, and explained again—he had done so in advance by letter—that he had an official lunch to attend. Bray's ears were filled with the strange echoes of exhaustion and, stoked up by the hot lunch, his body threatened to suffocate him with waves of heat. He went into the room kept darkened by drawn curtains and slept.

There was no ceiling and he looked up into the pattern of a spider's web made by the supporting beams of the roof. The underside of thatch that rested on it was smooth and straight, grey where it was old, blond where it had been replaced, and, like a tidy head, here and there showed a single stray strand out of place. The bird was probably balancing on the little porcelain conductor through which the electricity wire led to the light dangling above him. The bird was gone; he knew, almost as if the breath's weight of claws had pressed down the roof and now the pressure was released.

The sun had come round and the curtains glowed like the sky above a fire. The stale cool air of the room had heated; yet weariness receded, his head was left high and dry of it. There was silence and then he heard that there were voices in the silence droning some-where, breaking off for breath, laughing—not softly, but softened by being almost out of earshot. Not quite. A voice separated, wound nearer, there was the starting up of a hiss (a hose, he thought) and he made out a word: not just as a particular combination of articulated sounds, but a meaning: "later on," the compound word for this phrase, in the language that was spoken round the capital, and that he had never really known well.

He got up and went over to the main house for a bath. The sun in the garden was burning, dazzling, seizing. In the bathroom flies were buzzing themselves to death against the windowpanes. Roly was a bachelor and his house was the particular mixture of tranquil luxury and unchangeable dreariness that is a condition of households where white men live indulged in the sole charge of black male servants. The cistern of the lavatory drizzled into the pan constantly and couldn't be flushed properly, and the towels were stiff as a dress-shirt (Olivia had taken years to get people to learn to rinse the soap out of the washing), but an old fellow in a cook's hat put tea under the trees for him and carried off his crumpled suit to be pressed without being asked. A youth was cutting the tough grass with a length of iron bent at the end. Coarse and florid shrubs, hibiscus with its big flowers slut-tish with pollen and ants and poinsettia oozing milky secretion, bloomed, giving a show of fecundity to the red, poor soil running baked bald under the grass, beaten slimy by the rains under the trees, and friable only where ants had digested it and made little crusty tunnels. A rich stink of dead animal rose self-dispersed, like a gas, every now and then as he drank his tea, and he got up and looked around, as he had done so many times before, and with as little suc-cess, to see if a rat or mole were rotting somewhere. Whatever it was could never be found; it was the smell of growth, they had long ago decided, at Gala, the process of decay and regeneration so accelerated, brought so close together that it produced the reek of death-and-life, all at once. He strolled to the limits of the garden and climbed through the barbed-wire fence, but the grasses and thorn-bush on the other side (Dando's place was eight miles out of town) were too entangled for walking where there was no path. He listened to the bush and had the old feeling, in the bush, of being listened for. There were—or used to be—leopards on the outskirts of the town; Dando had once had his dog taken. He walked a hundred yards or so up the road, and, meeting a man on a bicycle, greeted him in the language that had come back to him as he lay in the room.

At six Roland Dando came home. He gazed anxiously from the car, as if, despite the telephone call, he were not sure if Bray had been safely received, but once he set eyes on him behaved as if they had seen each other a week ago. He was indiscreet, like many people who live alone, and brought back with him from the town—a child bulging with favours from a party—all the anecdotes and gossip of the Independence celebrations, producing, in a clinging fluff of supposition and rumour, bits and pieces of real information and opinion about Mweta's position and the sort of team he had gathered around him. Another tray came out under the trees, this time with whisky and gin. An old black Labrador with corns on his elbows stood slowly swinging his tail before Dando as he talked. Jason wouldn't bring home any golden fleece, believe you me (Jason Malenga was the new Minister of Finance); no, it wasn't a bad thing that the British Chief of Police wasn't being kept on, people always judged by the Congo, the idiots, but the African deputy, Aaron Onabu, was perfectly capable of taking over from that dodderer anyway; Talisman Gwenzi was first class, and a real Mweta man, David Sambata was an unknown quantity for Agriculture, what black knew a thing about agriculture, anyway; Tom Msomane was a corruption risk—there was reason to believe there'd already been something shady over a land deal for a community development—but he was from the right tribe, Mweta knew he couldn't attempt to hold the show together without at least three Msos in the cabinet.

Dando pulled ticks off the dog's neck and burst them under his shoe while he drank and dealt out judgements. Out of a kind of jealousy of the new young men from Britain and America who were so careful to show their lack of colour-feeling by avoiding tainted words and addressing people by polite forms, he recklessly used the old settler vocabulary that reflected an attitude he had had no part of, ever. Roly Dando could say what he liked: Roly Dando hadn't "discovered" the blacks as his fellows only yesterday. "Of course, Mweta has to hand out a job to everybody. Every pompous jackass from the bush who filled his pipe with tobacco bought with dues from the local party branch. They're all heroes, you know, heroes of the struggle. Struggle my arse. Edward Shinza's one of the few who did his stretch and got his head split open that time by Her Majesty's brave boys, and where's he—back in the Bashi Flats among his old wives, for all I know, no one even mentions his name."

"But Shinza's here for the Independence ceremony?"

Roly glared. "Nobody gives a damn where he is."

"But he is in town, now?"

"I don't know where the hell he may be."

"You mean Edward's not going to take part in the celebrations? That's not possible. He's not come up to town?"

"You can see he hasn't been given a cabinet post. I don't suppose he's going to turn up for the honour of standing in the crowd and waving a flag, eh?"

"But that's ridiculous, Roly. You know Shinza. He knows what he wants. I had the impression he'll be ambassador to U.N. Give time for Mweta to shine on his own for a bit, and any tension between them to die down. Of course he should have got Foreign Affairs. But that's between the two of them."

"You might ask Mweta, if you get a chance to talk to him, ask him if he isn't going to find a piddling little job somewhere, something with a decent label to it, for poor old Shinza, he was banging on the Colonial Secretary's door with a *panga* while Mweta was a snotty picannin singing hymns up at the mission school." Dando glowered pettishly over his third or fourth gin and ginger beer. He was given to putting himself on strange mixtures. He would drink one for several months and then switch, for similar good reasons (it was more digestible, it was less likely to produce an after-thirst) to another.

"Oh Mweta's not like that."

"You know Mweta. I know Mweta. But there's the President, now. If there's a father of the state, it's got to be him or no one."

"I certainly had the impression whatever tension there was had eased up, last time I saw Mweta in London."

"Yes, 'poor old Shinza,' that's what everyone says. Poor old Dando."

Dando did not explain the shift of reference. Perhaps he simply remarked upon his own getting older; undoubtedly he looked older. His
small nose showed unexpectedly beaky now that the skin had sunk
on either side.

Bray had a lot of questions, not all of them kind, to ask about other
people. Some of the answers were extraordinary; the two men quickened to the exchange of astonishment, ironic amusement, and (on
Dando's part) scornful indignation with which he told and Bray
learned of the swift about-face by which some white people turned a
smile on the new regime, while others had already packed up and left
the country. "Sir Reginald himself will present Mweta with a *buta*-
wood lectern and silver inkstand, it's down for Tuesday afternoon."
Dando was gleeful. Sir Reginald Harvey was president of the consortium of the three mining concessionaire companies, and it was common knowledge that, as a personal friend of Redvers Ledley, the most
unpopular governor the territory had ever had, he had influenced the
governor to outlaw the miners' union at a time when Mweta and
Shinza were using it to promote the independence movement. There
was a famous newspaper interview where he had called Mweta "that
golliwog from Gala, raising its unruly and misguided head in the
nursery of industrial relations in this young country." "—It's enough
to make your hair stand on end," said Dando; and enjoyed the effect.
The People's Independence Party, at the time, had taken Harvey's remark as an insulting reference to Mweta's hair; he still had it all, and
it certainly would be in evidence on Tuesday.

Bray repeated what had been said to him at the airport that
morning—that some of the white people still living in the capital
would be more at home down South, in Rhodesia or South Africa.
"Who was that?" "I don't know—one of the people from the plane—a
baldish fair man with an accent, I didn't catch the name. He'd recently moved up here."

"Oh Hjalmar Wentz—must have been. He and his wife took over
the Silver Rhino last year. I like old Hjalmar. He's just been to Denmark or somewhere because his mother died. We'll go in and have a
steak there one evening, they're trying to make a go of it with a charcoal grill and whatnot."

"What happened to McGowan?"

"Good God, they've been gone at least five or six years. There've been three other managers since then. It's difficult to do anything with that place now; it's got the character of the miners' pub it was, but it's very handy for the new government offices, not too overaweing, so you get quite a few Africans coming in. A genteel lot, very conscious of their dignity, man-about-town and all that, you can imagine how the white toughies feel about all those white collars round black necks in the bar. Hjalmar's as gentle as a lamb and he has to keep the peace somehow. Oh I'll tell you who's still around though—Barry Forsyth. Yes, and making money. Forsyth Construction. You'll see the board everywhere. They tell me he's got the contract for the whole Isoza River reclamation scheme—employs engineers from Poland and Italy."

Because of the mosquitoes, they moved into the house. The spiders came out from behind the pictures and flattened like starfish against the walls. There was no air at all in the living-room, and a strong smell of hot fat. Every now and then, while dinner was awaited, their conversation was backed by intensely sociable sounds—sizzling, scraping, and high-pitched talk—let in from the kitchen as the servant went in and out, laying the table. There was another large meal, and an exchange about a bottle of white wine between Dando and his cook, Festus.

"Of course I don't open wrong kind bottle. I know when is eat-e chicken, I know when is eat-e beef."

"Well it is the wrong one, because I told you this morning I wanted the round flat bottle put in the fridge."

"You say I cook chicken, isn't it? I look, I see the round bottle is red wine inside—"

"Pink. It's pink. I specially didn't say anything about the colour because I didn't want to muddle you up. I know how obstinate you are, Festus—"

They argued self-righteously as two old-maid sisters. Festus could be heard retailing the exchange, confidently in the right, in the kitchen; Dando, equally assured, went on talking as if without interruption. ". . . It's not an exaggeration to say that what they're having to do is introduce a so-called democratic social system in place of a paternalist discipline. You haven't replaced the District Commissioner by appointing a district magistrate. You've only replaced one of his functions. You've still got to get country people to realize that these functions are now distributed among various agencies: it's no good running to the magistrate if someone needs an ambulance to take him to the next town, for instance—and yet that's what people would have done in the old days, isn't it?"

"In bush stations there wasn't anything we weren't responsible for."

"Exactly. But now people have to learn that there's a Department of Public Health to go to."

"A good thing! A good thing for everybody! What a hopeless business it was, hopeless for the D.C. and for the people. Dependency and resentment hand in hand. Whatever the black magistrates are like, whatever the administration's like, it won't be like *that*."

"The magistrates are all right, don't you worry. A damned sight better than some of our fellows. I'm not worried at that level. The Bench doesn't change of course."

Bray laughed at Dando's expression; the look of weary, bottomless distaste in the wrinkled mugs of certain breeds of dogs.

"They'll die off, I suppose. There's that to be said for it. But God knows what we'll get then."

"I met Gwenzi's brother in London one day while he was at Gray's Inn; he told me he was going to be the first African at the bar here."

When Dando's opinion of someone was really low he did not seem to hear his name. "Don't think I don't know I've got some bad times coming to me," he said, as if taking up, in private, current talk about himself. "When I said yes to Mweta I knew it and every time I walk past the title on my office door I know it. The day will come when I'll have deportation orders to sign that I won't want to sign. Warrants of arrest. Or worse." He ate a mouthful of the left-over granadilla pudding, and there was the smallest tremor, passing for a moment through his head. "Poor old Dando."

"Anyone who's stayed on is a fool if he hasn't thought about that," said Bray.

"And I'll be instructing the State Prosecutor to act when I'd rather not, too. That I can count on. What if Shinza should make a bit of trouble at the next elections, what if he were to feel himself bloody well discounted as he certainly is, and start up a real opposition with all the tricks that he taught PIP, eh? What if he brought the whole Lambala-speaking crowd out in a boycott, with all the old beatings-up at the polls, hut burnings—you think I wouldn't find myself the one to put Shinza inside, this time?"

"Well, I know. But why on earth should it come to that?"

"I knew it when I said yes to Mweta. Poor bloody Dando. The blacks' dirty work isn't any cleaner than the whites'. That's what they'll be happy to note. But what their contented little minds will never know is that I knew it when I took the job, I knew it all along, and I'll say it now as loud as I'd say it then—"

"Who'll be happy?"

Dando refilled the brandy glasses again. "My colleagues! Those worthy fellows who've gone down South to Rhodesia and South Africa where they can feel confident they'll never have a black man on the Bench to give a verdict as biased as a white man's. —My colleagues, Tencher Teal and Williamson and De l'Isle!"

It was after midnight when they got to bed. Bray went to the kitchen to fill his brandy glass with water for the night. Cockroaches fled, pausing, from what they regarded as positions of safety, to twirl their antennae. A furry black band of ants led up a cupboard door to some scrap that had flicked from a plate. He stood at the sink, drinking cold water and looking at the avocado pear pip growing suspended by three matchsticks in the neck of a pickle jar of water on the sill. He was conscious of a giddy swing of weight from one foot to the other that was not of his volition; it seemed he had been standing there a long time—he was not sure.

He heard Dando, forced by the old Labrador into the garden, walking about outside the guest hut and talking reproachfully to the dog; and then it was morning and Festus's assistant was at the door with the early tea.

A helicopter snored over the celebrations, drowning the exchange of greetings when Bray was introduced to someone in the street, expunging conversation in bars and even speeches. Nobody knew what it was for—a security measure, some were satisfied to assume, while others accepted it as vaguely appropriate, the symbol of progress inseparable from all industrial fairs and agricultural shows and therefore somehow relevant to any public display. There was a moment in the stadium at the actual Independence ceremony when he heard it on the perimeter of the sky just as Kenyatta began to speak, and he and Vivien Bayley, the young wife of the registrar of the new university, sitting beside him, collided glances of alert apprehension—but although the helicopter did not exactly go away, it did not appear overhead, and supplied to the ringing amplification of the speeches only the muted accompaniment of the snorer who has turned over, now, and merely breathes rather audibly. Later it was discovered to have been giving flips at half-a-crown a time to a section of the population who were queueing up, all through the ceremony, at the nearby soccer field; a publicity stunt for an international cigarette-making firm.

Neil Bayley was the one to find this out, because of some domestic mishap or misunderstanding that made his arrival at the distinguished-visitors' stand very late. Bray was conscious of furious tension between the young couple at his side as he sat with the great stir of

tiers of people behind, and the space in front of him, before the velvet-draped and canopied dais, filled with press photographers and
radio and television crews, who all through the solemnities raced
about bent double on frantic tiptoe, snaking their wires, thrusting up
their contraptions, manipulating shutters and flashlights. It was as if
with all made splendidly ready for a theatrical performance, a party
of workmen with their gear had been left behind. This activity and
the risen temper along the back of a silent quarrel beside him provided the strong distraction of another, disorderly level of being that
always seemed to him to take away from planned "great moments"
what they were meant to hold heady and pure. Here was the sym-
bolic attainment of something he had believed in, willed and worked
for, for a good stretch of his life: expressed in the roar that rocked
back and forth from the crowd at intervals, the togas, medalled
breasts and white gloves, the ululating cries of women, the soldiers
at attention, and the sun striking off the clashing brass of the bands.
Or in the icecream tricycles waiting at the base of each section of an
amphitheatre of dark faces, the mongrel that ran out and lifted its leg
on the presidential dais?

Mweta had the mummified look of one who has become a vessel of
ritual. But once the declaration of independence was pronounced he
came, as out of a trance, to an irresistibly lively self, sitting up there
seeing everything around him, a spectator, Bray felt, as well as a
spectacle. Bray was half-embarrassed to find that he even caught his
eye, once, and there was a quick smile; but Mweta was used to having eyes on him, by now. He talked to the elderly English princess
who sat beside him with her knees peaked neatly together in the
Royal position curiously expressive of the suffering of ceremonies, and
Bray saw him point out the contingent of Gala women, their faces
and breasts whitened for joy, who were lined up among the troops of
musicians and dancers from various regions.

And yet when that ceremony was over, and in between all the
other official occasions—State Ball, receptions, cocktail parties, banquets, and luncheons—a mood of celebration grew up, as it were,
outside the palace gates. He attended most of the official occasions
(he and Roly saluted each other with mock surprise when they met in
the house, half-dressed in formal dinner clothes every night) but the
real parties took place before and after. These grew spontaneously

one out of the other, and once you had been present at the first, you got handed on to all the others. He really knew only some of the people but all of them seemed to know about him, and many were the friends of friends. Dando took him to the Bayleys; but Neil was a friend of Mweta, and Vivien was the niece of, of all people, Sir William Clough, the last governor, who had been a junior with Bray in the colonial service in Tanganyika. The Bayleys were friends of Cyprian Kente, Mweta's Minister of the Interior, and his wife Tindi, and Timothy Odara, one of the territory's few African doctors, whom Bray, of course, knew well. Through each individual the group extended to someone else and drew in, out of the new international character of the little capital, Poles, Ghanaians, Hungarians and Israelis, South African and Rhodesian refugees.

After the State Ball there was a private all-night party in a marquee. Roly Dando had promised to drop by, and of course Bray was with him. Many other people Bray had seen at the ball streamed in in their finery: they had contributed to the arrangements for this party. Cheers went up from the people already present who had not been at the ball; they had decided to dress for once, too, and the two groups of women mingled and exclaimed over each other, everyone began to talk about what the ball was like, champagne came in, a Congolese band whipped up their pace, and the absurd and slightly thrilling mood of the State Ball and the cosy gaiety of the party swept together. The tent was filled with chairs and divans borrowed from people's houses, and flowers from their gardens. Someone had put up a board with a collage of blown-up pictures of Mweta—speaking, laughing, yawning, touching a piece of machinery with curiosity, leaving, arriving, even threatening. The trouble everyone had taken gave a sense of occasion to even the wildest moments of the night. Vivien Bayley, queenly at twenty-six, with her beautiful, well-mannered, disciplined face, came to hover beside Bray between responsible permutations about the room to make sure that this young girl was not being bothered too much by the attentions of someone older and rather drunk, or that young man was not being overlooked by the girls who ought to be taking notice of him. Bray surprised her by asking her to dance, swaying stiffly to a rhythm he didn't know, but nevertheless keeping the beat, so that they wouldn't make fools of themselves among the complicated gyrations of the Africans. "I'm so glad you dance," she said; he was ashamed that he had asked her only out of politeness. "Neil won't—I think it's a mistake to let oneself forget these things because of vanity. Tindi Kente is a wonderful dancer, wonderful, isn't she—just like a snake brought out by music, and sometimes he'll try with her. He loves to flirt with her when Cyprian's not looking, but get her doing her marvellous wriggle on the floor and he just stands there like Andrew, dragging his feet." Andrew was probably one of her children; being accepted with such immediate casual friendliness by everyone was rather like being forced to learn a foreign language by finding oneself alone among people who spoke nothing else: it was assumed that he would pick up family and other relationships merely by being exposed to them.

Someone called to Vivien and they were drawn away from the dancers to a crowded table. A young woman leaned her elbows on it and her white breasts pursed forward within the frame of her arms. "Have my glass," she said, as there were no spare ones to go round. She went off to dance, holding in her stomach as she squeezed past and balanced her soft-looking body. The heat was heightened by drink and animation and the glass filled by the long, narrow black hand of his neighbour was marked by the fingerprints of the white woman who had relinquished it. "You don't remember me? —Ras Asahe, I came to your place in England once." The young man said he was in broadcasting now, "so-called assistant to the Director of English Language Services."

"And how's your father? Good Lord, I'd like to see him again!" Joseph Asahe was one of Edward Shinza's lieutenants in the early days of PIP.

"He's old now." It was not the right question to have asked; what the young man dismissed was any possible suggestion that he was to be thought of in connection with Shinza. His clothes, watch, cufflinks were those of a man who feels he must buy the best for himself, he had the Mussolini-jaw quite common among the people in the part of the country he came from but those hands were the lyrical, delicately strong, African ones that escaped the international blandness of businessmen's hands as Bray had marvelled to see them escape the brutalizing of physical hardship. Convicts broke stones with hands like that, here.

They made conversation about the radio and television coverage of the celebrations, and from this broke into talk that interested them both—the problem of communication in a country with so many different language groups. "I wonder how much use could be made of a radio classroom in country schools, whether it couldn't help considerably to ease the shortage of teachers, here, *and* maintain some sort of standard where teachers are perhaps not very well qualified. I'd like to talk to somebody about it—your man? I'm not keen to go straight to the Director-General—"

"It won't make much difference. They"—Ras Asahe meant the whites—"all know that after the end of the year they'll be on contract, and that means they'll be replaced in three years. Not that they ever made an effort. Sheltered employment all these years, what d'you expect? You don't need ideas, you don't need to move out of your chair, you simply go on producing a noise out of the magic box to keep the natives quiet—and now, boom, it's all gone, including the only incentive they ever had, their pension. They're pathetic, man; certainly they haven't much to offer when they look for jobs with the BBC. They're just not going to find any. They *want* to go, they're longing to, you can see they can't stand the sight of your face when you're working together—which makes things very pleasant, you can imagine—" A slim little white girl slipped between them and took up Ras Asahe's hand with the gold-metal watch-bracelet as if it were some possession she had put down—"Save me from Daddy Dando."

"—I could give you a dozen examples of the sort of thing that happens—the ceremony this afternoon: like a horse-race, man—the arrangements were exactly what they used to use for the charity Christmas Handicap, what else do they know? Suggest what you like, they just talk it away into the cigarette smoke, nobody even listens." The girl was there in their conversation like a photograph come upon lying between the pages of a book; Bray was not sure whether she was child or woman: thin collar-bones, a long neck with a face hardly wider, pale and sallow, a big, thin, unpainted mouth, black hair and glittering, sorrowful black eyes. She wore a dress made of Congo cloth.

"Suppose at the end of the year they were not put on contract? What about the golden handshake—wouldn't it be cheaper, in the end?"

"Not if there's no preparation of replacements being done in the meantime. I tried two years ago to initiate a pilot scheme to send local people away for training in broadcasting techniques—nothing doing. If I had to take over the English-language services tomorrow, you know what I'd have to do it with—a bunch of Lambala and Ezenzeli speakers from the vernacular sections and some refugee schoolteachers from South Africa."

The girl sat and saw nothing, like an animal out of breath, holed up against danger.

Bray had to rise to be introduced to a big woman marking time on the edge of the dancers with the American, Curtis Pettigrew: she was a West African whom Timothy Odara had married since Bray saw him last. She spoke with an American intonation, too, and in her flamboyant national dress, dragged round her as if snatched straight from the brilliant bolt on a shop counter, she seemed in every way twice the size of the local African women, who were usually kept at home, and showed it. Pettigrew was hailed by someone, and Bray and the woman were left facing each other like the dancers; she put her hand on his arm. While they moved off, she said, "Guess what my name is?" and when he looked embarrassed—"Same as yours, I believe. Evelyn." "But they call me James." "I should damn well hope so. Well, I've picked someone my own size at last tonight. We could just sweep the others off the floor." She maintained contact all round her as they danced, talking over his shoulder to this one, putting out a broad calloused brown foot in a gold sandal to nudge that one in the calf. "Get her to sing," Dando called out proudly. "Not tonight, Dandy-Roly, I'm on my best behaviour." "That's what I mean!" "Would it embarrass Evelyn if Evelyn sang?" she asked Bray. "Not in the least. What sort of thing?" "Well, what'd you think? What do I look as if I'd sing?" She had the self-confidence of a woman of dynamic ugliness. "Wagner?" A snort of pleasure: "Go on! I've got a voice like a bullfrog. It's terrible when I sing the old chants from home but it's not so bad in English—English is such a rough-sounding language anyway."

Vivien Bayley's urgent face took up conversation in passing, "—that's Hjalmar Wentz's daughter—you were sitting with."

"The Oriental-looking little girl with Ras?"

"Yes, lovely creature, isn't she? Margot would only let her come if I promised to keep her wholesomely occupied. You didn't leave her with Ras?"

He moved his shoulders helplessly. The dancers were falling back round a Polish agriculturalist who was teaching a gangling English-man and two young Africans an Eastern European peasant dance. The Congolese band had no idea what music would do, and produced a stomping crescendo; then one of the Poles played the piano, and Neil Bayley moved in on the drums. The undergraduate form of self-expression that emerges where Englishmen want to give themselves to celebration imposed itself for a while. Someone left, and reappeared with another case of champagne. The wine was warm, but an early-hours-of-the-morning rain came out like sweat, and coolness blew in on necks and faces. Later the Odara woman sang the new national anthem in a beautiful contralto, her big belly trembling under the robe. The young bachelors romped and the tousled girls, passing close by, or smiling suddenly at people they weren't aware of, gave up the scent of cosmetics and perfume heated on their bodies. Then there was breakfast at the Bayleys'; a thinning of faces, but some had kept reappearing all through the night in the changing light, and now, against the rippling pink-grey sky behind the Bayleys' veranda, over the smell of coffee, a curled blonde head with gilt hoops in the ears, shining straps that had worn a red track on a plump white back, Timothy Odara's starched and pleated shirt-front and dead button-hole—all had the melodrama of circus figures. They said good night to each other in the bright slanting sun and the Bayley children were already out on the grass in their pyjamas, riding bicycles.

In a few days the faces had lost the stylized, apparition-quality of that first night, the night of the Independence Ball, and become, if not familiar, at least expected. A young woman was in and out the Bayleys' house, sometimes adding to, sometimes carrying off with her the many children who played there. She was Rebecca, Rebecca Edwards, like a big, untidy schoolgirl in her cotton shirt and sandals, the car key on her forefinger jingling harassedly. She was always being sent to pick up people when arrangements went wrong; she came for Bray one afternoon in an old station wagon littered with sweet-papers, odd socks, and Dinky toys. It was she who had given her glass to him that night at the Independence party; the Pole who had danced the *gazatska* became the man with whom he gravitated to a quiet corner so that they could talk about the curious grammar-structure of Gala and the Lambala group of languages. The atmos-phere at the parties was what he thought it must have been at gath-

erings described in nineteenth-century Russian novels. Children
swept in and out, belligerently pleasure-seeking. Babies slept in dark
rooms. Food was cooked by many hands. Invitations were measured
only by how long the beer and wine lasted out. He felt himself the
middle-aged relative, a man of vague repute come from afar to the
wedding, and drawn helplessly and not unenjoyably into everything.
It was, in a curious way, an extension of what he was at the official
receptions, where many people had little idea who the white stranger
was, sitting in a modest place of honour; and once, at a press dinner,
Mweta's reference to the presence of "one of the fairy godmothers"
who had been "present at the christening and had returned for the
coming-of-age of the State" went, thank God, unnoticed as a reference
to himself. It became his Independence story; as the story of the cigarette company's helicopter was Neil Bayley's, related again and again
while the private drama between husband and wife that had made it
pass unremarked at the time was quite dropped out of the context.

Bray asked everywhere about Edward Shinza; certainly he was not
in evidence at any official occasion. Bray felt he must be somewhere
about; it was difficult to imagine this time without him. It was his as
much as Mweta's. But no one seemed to have seen him, or to know
whether he was, or had been, in the capital. There were other faces
from the past; William Clough, the Governor, lifting his bristly eyebrows in exaggerated greeting at Mweta's banquet, the way he used
to do on the tennis court in Dar-es-Salaam. "James, you must come
and say hello to Dorothy before we leave. I daren't say dine—we're
homeless, you know—"

"Uncle Willie's Independence Joke," Vivien said. "Produces a
hearty, man-of-the-world laugh from Africans."

"The kind of laugh they've picked up from people like Uncle Willie," said Neil.

Still, the Cloughs pursued Bray through Vivien. "Aunt Dorothy
says her secretary's been trying to get hold of you. They want you for
drinks on Monday. I'd go if I were you, or she'll tell everyone in London you were buttering up to the Africans and didn't want to see
them." He laughed. "No, it's true. She says that about me, to my
mother. And she knows quite well that we'd never see each other in
London either."

The Cloughs had moved into the British Consulate for the last week or two before their departure, a large, glassy, contemporary house placed to show off the umbrella thorn-trees of the site, just as in an architect's scale model. The consul and his wife had been swept into some back room by the presence of aides, secretaries, and the necessity to keep their cats out of the way of Lady Dorothy's dog. There was some sort of scuffle when Bray arrived—he saw the consul's wife, whom he had met briefly, disappearing upstairs with her head bent consolingly to a Siamese. Flower arrangements were placed everywhere, as if there were illness in the house.

"Well, the job is done, one asks nothing more but to fold one's tents. . . . . He's a good chap, if they'll let him alone, he's learnt a lot, and one's done what one could . . . if he keeps his head, and that one can't be sure of, not even with him, mmh? Not even with him." An elderly servant came in with a silver tray of glasses and bottles, and Clough interrupted himself to say with the sweet forbearance of one who does not spare himself, encouraging where others would give way to exasperation, "It would be so nice if we could have a few slices of lemon . . . and more ice? —Yes, all I've said to Mweta, again and again—make your own pace. Make your own pace and stick to it. He knows his own mind but he's not an intransigent fellow at all—well, of course, *you* know. Some time ago—a word in your ear, I said, you'd be unwise to lose Brigadier Radcliffe. Well, they've been clamouring away, of course, but he's refused to touch the army. Oh, I think I can say we've come out of it quite good friends." It was a modest disclaimer, with the effect of assuming in common the ease with Africans that he believed Bray to have. He looked pleasantly into the martini jug and put it down again patiently. The elderly servant who brought ice and lemon had the nicks at the outer corner of the eyes that Northern Gala people wore. "That's perfect. Thank you so much."

Bray greeted the servant in Gala with the respectful form of address for elders and the man dumped the impersonality of a servant as if it had been the tray in his hands and grinned warmly, showing some pigmentation abnormality in a pink inner lip spotted like a Dalmatian. The ex-Governor looked on, smiling. The servant bowed confusedly at him, walking backwards, in the tribal way before rank, and then recovering himself and leaving the room with an anonymous lope.

"I'll pour Dorothy's martini as well, maybe that'll bring her. If only one could be transported on a magic carpet . . . anyway, we shall have three months in London now, with perhaps a week or two in Ireland. What've you been doing all these years in your ivory tower in Wiltshire? Were you a golfer, I can't quite remember . . . ?"

"It was tennis . . . and afterwards we took the girls for beer to the old Dar-es-Salaam hotel with the German eagle?"

Dorothy Clough came in and Clough cried out, "Does it fit? Come and have a drink with James—"

"My dear James— it must be a hundred years—"

"We've had a crate made to transport Fritzi, and she's been trying it on him."

"My niece Vivien found a carpenter. She has the most extraordinary contacts, that girl. It's very useful!"

William Clough took a pecking sip at his martini. He said with gallant good humour, "Reposting was child's play compared with this. One has had to learn how to camp out . . . I'm sure it's terribly good, keeps the mind flexible."

"Denis thinks your angle lamp's been left at Government House, did he tell you?" Dorothy Clough sat forward in her chair, as if she had alighted only for a moment.

"For heaven's sake, let them have it, it's someone else's turn to burn the midnight oil there, now—wha'd'you say, James . . ."

Roly Dando asked with grudging interest about the visit. "He's never been sent anywhere where there was anything left to do," he said. "Clough only goes in for the last year, after self-government's been granted and the date for independence's been given. An early date."

Bray was slightly embarrassed by gossip, when quite sober, and said hesitantly, smiling, "The impression was that he and his wife were slipping away quietly after the field of battle."

"Since he arrived eighteen months ago there's been damn all for him to do except go fishing up at Rinsala."

At the Pettigrews' house that night, Dando's voice came from the group round someone basting a sheep on the home-made spit: ". . . damn all except go fishing with his secretary acting ghillie. . . ." Rebecca Edwards had just told Neil Bayley that Felix Pasilis, the Pettigrews' Greek friend, was furious with her because she'd forgotten some essential herb that he wanted for his sheep—"If I were Felix I'd make you go back home and get it, my girl," Neil said, and the look of inattentive exhaustion on her rather heavy young face moved Bray in fellow-feeling to distract attention from her, saying, "My God, I'm afraid I behaved like a child at Cloughs'! I showed off by making a point of speaking to the servant in Gala." Neil and Rebecca Edwards laughed. "Poor Uncle Willie." "He was quite a nice young man in Dar-es-Salaam. He took Swahili lessons conscientiously and he certainly spoke it better than I did." They laughed at him again.

Everyone was gathering round for servings from the roast sheep, and the fair stocky man from the airport signalled a greeting with a piece of meat in his fingers. "Wentz, Hjalmar Wentz, we met on the plane."

"How are you? Roland Dando said we probably should be seeing you at the Rhino." They moved off with their plates of food, and Wentz said to a woman settled in one of the canvas chairs, "Margot, here is Colonel Bray."

"No, no, please stay where you are."

In the fuss to find somewhere to sit he saw the light of the fire under the spit running along the shiny planes of the woman's face as it did on glasses and the movement of knives and forks. Bright hair was brushed up off a high round forehead and behind the ears, in a way he associated with busy, capable women.

"Try some, Margot, it's wonderful—"

"Aren't I fat enough—" But she took a tidbit of crisp fat from her husband's fork.

"To tell the truth, this's the first time for a week we've had time to sit down to eat. Honestly. Margot's had to be in the kitchen herself from six in the morning, and some nights it's been until ten. She literally hasn't sat down to a meal. . . ."

"Oh, not quite . . . I must have had hundreds of cups of coffee. . . ."

"Yes, with one hand while you were busy stirring a pot with the other. The cook went to the Independence ceremony and we haven't seen him since—just for the afternoon, he said, just to see the great men he's seen in the papers—well, what can you say?"

"We felt it was his day, after all." The woman showed a well-shaped smile in the dark.

Bray asked, "How on earth have you managed?"

She gestured and laughed, but her husband was eager to break in, holding up his hands over the plate balanced on his knees—"A hundred and twenty-two for dinner! That's what it was on Thursday. And yesterday—"

"Only a hundred and nine, that's all—" They laughed.

Bray raised his beer mug of wine to her.

"What about my assistant cook? You mustn't forget I've got help," she said. Wentz put down his glass beside his chair, to do the justice of full attention to what he was going to say. "Her assistant cook. I got him from the new labour exchange— I thought, well, let's try it, so they send him along, five years' experience, everything fine."

His wife was listening, laughing softly, sitting back majestically for a moment. "Fine."

"Five years' experience, but d'you know what as? —You know the barbers under the mango trees there just before you get to the second-class trading area?"

"Our son's comment was the best, I think. 'Mother, if only Barnabas had worked for a butcher and learnt to cut meat instead of hair!'"

"Well, here's to three crazy people," said Wentz, excitedly picking up his glass. "Everyone knows you must be crazy to come of your own free will to one of these countries."

"Colonel Bray isn't going to run a hotel." She had a soft, dry voice and her accent was slighter than her husband's.

"I'm not as brave as you are."

"Oh, how do you know?" said Wentz. "We didn't know what we were going to land up doing, either."

She said quietly, "We certainly didn't think we'd be the proprietors of the Silver Rhino."

"Anyway, that's another story. —I heard you were going to the Ministry of Education?" said Wentz.

"Oh, did you?" he laughed. "Well, perhaps I am, then. I should think the bar of the Silver Rhino's as good a place as any to learn what's really going on."

"If you want to hear how much ugliness there is—yes." Mrs. Wentz had the tone of voice that sounds as if the speaker is addressing no one but himself. "How people still think with their blood and enjoy to feel contempt . . . yes, the bar at the Silver Rhino."

"Our son Stephen is looking after it tonight. It's amazing how he deals with those fellows—better than I do, I can tell you. He keeps them in place."

"We promised him a liberal education when we left South Africa, you see." Mrs. Wentz had put down her food and she sat back out of the light of the fire, a big face glimmering in the dark, caverns where the eyes were.

"He's at Lugard High, taking the A levels," said Wentz, innocently. "—You're not going to finish?" The white blur of her hand moved in a gesture of rejection—"You have it, Hjalmar."

It rained and people felt chilly on the veranda and drifted indoors. There was a group in loud discussion round the empty fireplace where the beer bottles were stacked. ". . . banging on the Governor's door with a *panga* when the others were still picannins with snotty noses . . ." Now Dando had the sulky outraged attention of a young patriot from the social welfare department, the glittering-eyed indifference of Doris Manyema, one of the country's three or four women graduates, and the amused appreciation of a South African refugee whose yellow-brown colour, small nose and fine lips set him apart from the blackness of the other two. In the light, Margot Wentz's head was the figurehead of a ship above the hulk of her body: a double-chinned, handsome dark blonde, the short high nose coming from the magnificent forehead, water-coloured eyes underlined with cuts of fatigue deep into each cheek. With an absent smile to Bray across the room, she took up, for a moment, an abandoned beauty. When he joined the group, they were listening to her. "We don't have to argue; we can take it that colonialism is indefensible, for us, no? You think so, I think so—right. But the forty-seven—" "Forty-eight"— Timothy Odara's eyes were closed; leaning against the wall he kept his lips drawn back slightly, alert. "—I'm sorry, forty-eight years you were under British rule, digging their mines, building roads for them, making towns, living in shanties and waiting on them, cleaning up after them, treated like dirt—now it's all over, you really think there was any way at all you could enter the modern world without suffering? You think there was someone else would have given you the alphabet and electricity and killed off the malaria mosquito, just for love? The Finns? Swedes? The Russians? Anybody? Anyone who wouldn't have wanted the last drop of your sweat and pride in return? These are the facts. From your point of view, as it luckily lasted less than two generations, wasn't it worth it? Would anybody have let you in for nothing? Anybody at all? Wouldn't you have to pay the price in suffering? That's what I'm asking—"

"Oh you make the usual mistake of seeing the life of the African people as a blank—and then the colonialists come along and we come to life—in your compounds and back yards."

She was shaking her head slowly while Odara was speaking. "All I'm saying, don't wear the sufferings of the past round your necks. What does independence mean—I don't use 'freedom', I don't like the big words—what does your independence mean, then?"

"The past is useful for political purposes only" said Hjalmar, as he might have said: she's right.

Someone said, "Watch out for the man from the CIA." "Down with neo-colonialism."

"Of course, Curtis," said Hjalmar. "But if you have to do it by keeping that forty years or whatever sitting at the table with you and your children—ach, it's not healthy, it makes me sick. What do they want to hear how you had to go round to the back door of the missionary's house?—"

Mrs. Odara had joined the group, ruffling a big, silver-nailed hand through Curtis Pettigrew's crew-cut hair. "Oh God, Timothy, not that again."

"—Let them hold up their heads naturally in their own country without having to feel defiant about it!"

Odara laughed. "But it always comes down to the same thing: you Europeans talk very reasonably about that sort of suffering because you don't know . . . you may have thought it was terrible, but there's nothing like that in your lives."

Bray saw Margot Wentz put up her head with a quick grimace-smile, as if someone had told an old joke she couldn't raise a laugh for.

"Well, here you're mistaken," her husband said, rather grandly, "we lived under Mr. Hitler. And you must know all about that."

"I'm not interested in Hitler." Timothy Odara's fine teeth were bared in impatient pleasantness. "My friend, white men have killed more people in Africa than Hitler ever did in Europe."

"But you're crazy," said Wentz gently.

"Europe's wars, white men's killings among themselves. What's that to me? You've just said one shouldn't burden oneself with suffering. I don't have any feelings about Hitler."

"Oh but you should," Mrs. Wentz said, almost dreamily. "No more and no less than you do about what happened to Africans. It's all the same thing. A slave in the hold of a ship in the eighteenth century and a Jew or a gipsy in a concentration camp in the nineteen-forties."

"Well, I had my seventeenth and eighteenth birthdays in the detention camp at Fort Howard, the guest of Her Majesty's governor," said Odara, "that I know."

"Her two brothers died at Auschwitz," Hjalmar Wentz said; but his wife was talking to Jo-Ann Pettigrew, who offered blobs of toasted marshmallow on the end of a long fork.

"For God's sake, Timothy, stop baring your teeth and sink them into something." Evelyn Odara spoke to her husband as no local woman would dare; yet he ignored it, as if turning the tables on her with his countrymen's assumption that what women said was not heard, anyway. He said angrily to Wentz, directing the remark at the wife through the husband, "What did *you* get in return that was worth it?"

Margot Wentz said, looking at no one, "That one can't say." She waggled her fingers, sticky from the marshmallow, and her husband took his handkerchief from his pocket and gave it to her.

It was the evening when Bray, Neil, Evelyn Odara, one of the South African refugees, the Pettigrews, and a few others set off for the Sputnik Bar. While Bray was standing about in the group with the Odaras and the Wentzes, Jo-Ann Pettigrew, having failed to get him to eat her last marshmallow, put it in her mouth and signalled to everyone there was something they must hear. "Rebecca's been to the Sputnik and she says it's terrific now. They've knocked out a wall into that sort of yard thing and they have dancing. With girls laid on."

Neil said, "Hey? And which one of us's been taking Rebecca to the Sputnik?"

Laughter rose. "Well, why don't we all go, that's what I want t'know." The young Pettigrew woman was always in a state of enthusiasm; her long curly hair had sprung out, diademed with raindrops, because she had done her marshmallow toasting outside over the spit fire. She was an anthropologist, and Bray accepted this as an explanation for her passion for arranging excursions, on which she carried her baby tied on her back, African style.

"*Who* was it? Out with it!" There was a roar again.

"No, no—well, Ras took her—"

"Oh Ras, was it?"

"Sputnik Bar, eh?" "So that's it, now."

Rebecca Edwards came in from the veranda, smiling good-naturedly, inquiringly, under the remarks shied at her. She said, "There're bulbs like you see in films round the star's dressing-table, and they light up and spell INDEPENDENCE HURRAH."

In great confusion, there and then they decided to go. Dando refused and Vivien had to go home to the children, and Rebecca Edwards protested that hers were alone too. Neil insisted that Bray must come; he was one of those people who, late at night, suddenly have a desperate need of certain companions. But when Neil, Bray, Evelyn Odara and the South African got down to the second-class trading area, the others hadn't arrived. They went into the Sputnik Bar for a moment, meeting music like a buffeting about the head, and then someone said that he thought the arrangement had been to meet at the railway crossing. There began one of those chases about in the night that, Bray saw, Neil Bayley fiercely enjoyed. They went all the way back into town to the flats where the Edwards girl lived—Neil stood on the moonlit patch of earth in front of the dark building and called up, but there was no response. They stopped somewhere to give a man a lift; he was caught in the lights, hat in hand; only his clean white shirt had shown on the dark road. He answered Neil with a liberal use of *Bwana*, as a white man would expect if he were to do such a thing as stop for a black one on the road, and when he got into the car beside Bray and the South African, sat among these black and white city people like a hedgehog rolled into itself at a touch. Bray, back in this country once more, again aware of his own height and size and pinkness almost like some form of aggression he wasn't responsible for, knew that the fellow was holding himself away from contact with him. The voices of Evelyn, Neil, and the South African flew about the car; they passed the shadows of the mango trees in the bright moonlight, lying beneath the trees like sleeping beasts; a donkey cropping among broken china on a refuse mound; the colours on

the mosque almost visible, the silvered burglar grilles on the elaborate houses of the Indian sector. The second-class trading area had
been laid out long ago and haphazardly; shops cropped up suddenly,
streets met, the car plunged and rolled. All was shuttered under already bedraggled flags and bunting, black and deserted except for the
bars—little shops crudely blurred with light, juke-box music and the
vibrancy of human movement and noise.

Bray offered to be left outside the Sputnik in case the other members of the party turned up. For ten or fifteen minutes he strolled in
the street whose vague boundaries were made by feet and bicycle
tyres rather than the strip of tar considered sufficient by the white
city council of the old days. The cement verandas of the Indian shops
were quays in the dust; snippets of cloth had been swept off them
everywhere—that was where the African men employed by the Indians sat at their sewing machines during the day. The shutters and
chipped pillars were plastered with stickers of the flag and Mweta in
a toga. Young boys peering above the paint that blacked out the
shop-front entrance of the Sputnik picked at the stickers on the
breath-gummy, manhandled glass and giggled at Bray. The doorway
was constantly blocked by befuddled men making to get out and undecided men looking in.

How confused our pleasures are, he thought, and walked slowly up
the street again, past a man who had got as far as the clustered bicycles and lay sprawled in the warm dust. The unmade road level had
worn so deeply away from a shop veranda that the cement platform
was the right height for sitting on. The din from the bar was companionable, like a reassurance that there was life going on in the house,
and he smoked a cigar, releasing the fragrant, woody scent in the air
stained with those old smells brought out by dampness—urine and
decaying fruit. After ten years, the light of the town was still not big
enough to dim the sky; there was no town for thousands of miles big
enough for that. Ropes and blobs of stars ran burningly together; he
let himself grow dizzy looking. Then Bayley's car came back, and
they decided to give up hope of the rest of the party and have a
quick beer before going home to bed. The old part of the bar, a shop
furnished with benches and rough eating-house tables, was full of the
local regulars sitting over native beer and taking no notice of the
band pressed deafeningly into a corner. In the new beer-garden—a

yard more or less cleared (the dustbins still stood overflowing) and set
out with a few coloured tables with umbrellas over them—there were
some bourgeois Africans with women, and a couple or two dancing;
Evelyn Odara waved at someone she knew. Bottled European beer
was being drunk here. Neil had friends everywhere, and went in
search of the proprietor, a handsome, greedy-faced young black man,
ebullient with plans for making money. He settled down with them
and brought, in answer to Neil's insistence and insisting, for his part,
laughingly, that they didn't exist—three of his "girls" to join them.
"You'll do the kids a favour. Just about this time the police comes
along on a round, and they're not supposed to be here alone, you see
—this town's backward, man." Beer arrived with the girls—"No, no,
its a pleasure to have you and your friends in my little place. Of
course, it's not nicely fixed up yet . . . we wanted to have some night
life for the celebrations. I'm paying the band alone twenty pounds a
night, I'm gonna have a posh bar out here with whisky and ice for
the drinks, everything nice . . . for high-class trade from town, you
understand."

The three women were cheaply smart, with the shine of nylon
tightly stretched over plenty of sturdy black leg. They had the rather
appealing giggling pleasure in being dressed up for the part, of those
who haven't been in the business long. They were pretty, with
straightened hair, painted eyes, and purplish-painted lips. But the
coloured bulbs that spelled out INDEPENDENCE HURRAH had been fused
by the rain, and were not working.

It was true that Edward Shinza was not in the capital; given the
past, this absence could not have been more pointed. For Bray himself, it was an absence somehow always present.

The drives home at night on the dirt road to Dando's were punctuated by the death-thump of nightjars who sat stupidly in the path of the car and then rose too late to escape, just as they used to on the roads at Gala. In daylight their broken bodies were slowly ironed into the dust by tyres passing and repassing over them. He and Olivia had kept a log-book of bird life in and around Gala; it had bothered them to think how, since there was no way to avoid killing these birds in the dark, one gradually got accustomed to it, so that the thump of their bodies against the car went unremarked as the shot of hard-back beetles striking the windscreen. One didn't even notice, any more, that the dead birds were beautiful with their russet and black markings. They had tried to make a study of the nightjars' habits, one summer, to determine what it was that made them partial to the roads; came to the conclusion that lice under their wings caused them to try repeated dustbaths. Yes, Africa *was* a kind of study, then, with detached pleasures and interests, despite his involvement in politics.

During the week of the celebrations it was difficult to get into town without being held up somewhere by a right of way cleared for some dignitary or other. Traffic officers in white gauntlets zoomed arabesques on their motorcycles, soldiers in well-ironed khaki blocked the road and held back children, women, idlers and bicycles; sometimes a band came tootling and mildly blaring in the vanguard, and there were always flags. Then came the Daimler or Mercedes with the President of this or the Prime Minister of that, deep inside; often it was only after his car had gone by that one realized who it must have been, the kernel of so many supernumerary, black, bespectacled faces emerging from the identical perfect grooming of dark suits and snow-white shirt collars. Once it was the English royalty with her grey-permed lady-in-waiting, and once Mrs. Gandhi; and, while in the car with Vivien Bayley, Bray was even held up by Mweta himself. The Bayley children climbed out onto the roof and bonnet of the car to cheer, Mweta was in his orange toga in his open car, he was borne past with the unseeing smile that already, in a few days, he had learnt to sweep across faces become all one, to him. Vivien said sadly, "Magnificent, isn't he? Ours is the best-looking of the lot."

"I wonder if he's enjoying it. He's certainly carrying it off just as we always expected he should."

"What's he say?" she said.

"I haven't spoken to him, really—not where one could talk properly."

As usual, a traffic policeman drew up the rear of the entourage with a figure-of-eight flourish about the empty road and the traffic broke loose again, hooting at sluggish and dazed pedestrians. The Bayley children fought and struggled to get back into the car through the windows, pulling at each other's legs; shy black children looked on, one giggling nervously behind the thumb in her mouth. A young woman swung her baby onto her back, tied it firmly in her cloth, and put a small child on the luggage rack of her bicycle before wobbling off while keeping up a shouting, laughing exchange with a woman on the kerb. Bulging cartons tied with rope were loaded onto heads, bigger children took smaller ones on their backs, a group of young men on bicycles lounged and argued and the bells of other bicycles trilled impatiently at them. An advertising jingle from a transistor radio held intimately to a young man's ear as he walked, rose and tailed off through the people. "I want to give the little girl my flag," said Eliza Bayley. "Well, hurry up about it, then. No—the rest of you stay where you are."

They watched the fat little white girl, usually belligerent with her own kind, go up as if to the platform at a prize-giving, and hand to the black child with the thumb in its mouth one of the small, flimsy flags hastily printed in Japan in time to catch the Independence trade. People were tramping and drifting past the obstacle of the car. "Are *they* enjoying it?" said Vivien. There had been a sports rally, and a police band and massed school choirs concert, as well as the rather peculiar historical pageant that had gone on for hours at the stadium. Tribal dancing and praise-songs alternated with tableaux of Dundreary whiskered white men showing chunks of gold-ore to splendidly got-up chiefs; it had all to be kept vague in order not to offend the tribal descendants of Osebe Zuna II with a reminder that the old man had given away the mineral rights of the territory to white men for the price of a carriage and pair like the Great White Queen's and a promise of two hundred pounds a year, and in order not to offend the British by reminding them that, at the price, they had got the whole country thrown in. Schoolgirls bobbing under gym frocks and helmeted miners epitomized the present on much safer ground.

Bray and Vivien speculated about the celebrations in the African townships and villages. "Beer-drinks? Big barrels of it . . . and meat roasted, and a place cleared for dancing—" Vivien transposed the fountain of wine and the village square of Europe. In the back of the car the children were quarrelling; the little girl was self-righteously boastful about her gift of a flag. "How I do dislike Eliza sometimes," Vivien said in an undertone. Self-doubt, that he thought of as the innocence of intelligent people, often gave a special beauty to her face. She was candid not in the usual sense of being critical of others, but of herself. "D'you think she'll feel it?"

"She will."

"That's something one never imagines. That you can feel the same sort of antipathy towards your own child as you would towards anyone else. In a way, won't it be a relief to get older and to have made all these pleasant little discoveries, once and for all."

"Oh but I've reached that stage, long ago!" He was amused and perhaps slightly flattered that the girl should forget they belonged to different generations.

"It must be a relief."

"One can't be sure. There may still be shocks."

"But you don't think so?" —A statement more than a question. He had the feeling she was talking about marriage, now: her own; and his, that she knew had lasted twenty-two years—people talked of Olivia and himself linked in the same breath, as it were, but it was as a combination of two intact personalities rather than the anonymous, double-headed organism, husband-and-wife; perhaps it was something she attained to, not very hopefully, with her Neil.

"Well, no. But some people get angrier and somehow wilder as they get old. Take Tolstoi. Some of the late Yeats poems—it seems to me old age must be like that for quite a lot of people. More often than the evening-of-life stuff. Good God, which would be worse?"

She said, as if it were all much more serious for her, "I don't think I've read them. Except one. About an old man—"

" 'The devil between my thighs'—that one?"

"Yes—but surely sex is the least of it. There are other things one'd like to be sure to be done with."

"What about the things one'd never conceived of. Even the simple hardening of arteries could turn you into a grasping hag who'd suspect the people she used to love of stealing out of her purse."

"But can you imagine it ever happening to you?" They were stopped by a red light and she turned to look at him, a young woman's face just beginning to take on the permanent expression of the emotions and self-disciplines that were making over her features in their likeness.

"Of course not"; and his middle-aged calm, that was in itself an acceptance of such horrors to come, belied the reassurance of his words. She smiled.

Dando suggested they should eat at the Silver Rhino—he came, with the air of putting an end to something, from the kitchen, where there was the question of whether or not dinner had been expected to be provided at the house that evening. "Who's on, who's off, hopeless chewing the rag about it." They had a drink in the garden, and put on their jackets to go to town as soon as it got dark. Festus was loading his bicycle onto the luggage grid on the roof of the car; he, at least, was going to some sort of festivity. "What's it, Festus?" Dando asked, when Bray inquired.

It was a "boxing fight" at the stadium. "I must come half-past seven."

"I know, I know, don't panic. You'll be there."

The black man sat in the back of the car in a white shirt and grey pants, smelling of carbolic soap. He repeated, nevertheless, "Half-past seven."

"I hope you'll be in as good time with breakfast tomorrow as I'll get you to the stadium tonight."

Festus gave him a look registering the intention to answer, but in the meantime rolled down the window and yelled out. A faint cry went up from the servants' quarters. Festus bellowed; and this time the youngster came running to open and close the gates behind the car. As the headlights threw a bright dust-opaque ramp into the sky, Festus took up Dando. "When I'm don't come, you tell me."

"Just be sure you remember you've eight miles to ride after refreshment, that's all."

"I say: tomorrow we know."

Bray turned and offered a cigarette over his shoulder. Festus took it, but without the complicity of a smile against Dando; he had the preoccupation of someone off duty.

After they had dropped him not at the stadium but at a street corner that he pounced upon (clutching Dando by the shoulder to make him stop the car) in an intention clearly held all along but not conveyed, Dando drove to the Great Lakes Hotel instead of the Rhino; he thought he must have left his glasses there, over lunch. The Great Lakes had been built several years before by the biggest gold-mining company because there was nowhere suitable to entertain principals from Britain and America. It was designed, down to the last doorhandle and ashtray, by a prizewinning contemporary British architect who had never been to Africa; the lacy cement lattice that served in place of walls between the public rooms and the patio had not provided for the acute angle at which rain swept in during the wet season; the thick-carpeted boxes of bedrooms depended entirely upon air-conditioning for ventilation and kept out the perfect, sharp air of the dry season. The patio was now partly glassed in, the rain-damaged raw silk had been replaced with nylon; the hotel was no longer beautiful but had adapted itself for survival, as a plant goes through mutations imposed by environment.

Some sort of official cocktail party was ending as they arrived and the lategoers had got as far as the patio round the pool, standing about in suddenly intimate groups talking still in the voices of a crowded room. The tiny pennants of the country's own new airline stood among wisps of lettuce in the Golden Perch Room; Dando and Bray passed through to another bar, with greetings and snatches of talk catching at them. Roly Dando's running commentary was carelessly loud enough to be heard by anybody, had they been listening. No one was. Heads lifted, eyes turned to follow, faces were glazed with the cosy daze of sundowner time. ". . . Raymond Mackintosh, no less. I wonder what he's crawling up Norman's arse for now. Look at it. —Well, Raymond, here's to your first million. —Hullo Joe, hasn't the steak gone down yet?" A black man waved with an important smile, looking up from the depths of a conversation that brought him forward in his chair, knees wide, trousers straining, to confer with the white man opposite him. "—Joe Kabala was here with Stein at lunch, as well. The milling company. Going to be the first black one on *that* board, wait and see. A lovely champion of private enterprise, keeping the seat warm for white capital investment and raking in the director's fees. He's starting to eat smoked salmon, I saw it myself. . . . —Hadn't you better be going home to your children?" Rebecca Edwards peered round a rubber plant at the sound of Dando's voice. She was drinking beer with Curtis Pettigrew, obviously come straight from work, with untidy paper carriers from the supermarket dumped beside her. "The dinner'll be dried out again, Curtis. It's all right for a bachelor like me to come home when I please."

They were waylaid by an FAO man and Father Raven, who ran the refugee education scheme at Senshe. Bray had already been out there and at Bill Raven's request had made some notes, at odd times at home in Dando's rondavel, for a simple course in economic administration. "You don't happen to speak Portuguese? The Zambians have dumped a batch of Frelimo chaps on us"—Raven was half-thrilled at the dilemma. The FAO man offered to take Bray to see the experimental farm he was setting up in the South; "If I'm still around, I'd like to go with you."

He went off after Dando, who was up at the bar having an argument with his friend Coningsby, the manager, about the Austro-Hungarian empire and the character of Franz Josef. Dando was accustomed to knowing more about any subject than the person who took him up on it, and in the absence of better intellectual stimulus, enjoyed the advantage in a grudging way; Bray remembered that this

was what had happened to men who lived in a restricted circle and
read a lot. The bush mentality was not what people thought; it could
take the form of a burning compulsion to explain to somebody—
anybody, the driver of the road transport, the district vet—the work-
ings of the Common Market or Wittgenstein's theories.

Bray always found bar-stools uncomfortable—he was too big to accommodate himself without prodding someone with his shoulder or
knee—and he was best off with one elbow on the bar and the rest of
him turned towards the room. He drank whisky and watched them
all. It was a daydream from the past, with incongruities that made it
of the present. A small party of white people out to dinner came in,
the patina of well-being on heads fresh from the hairdresser, faces
shiny from a second shave. Laughter, the worldly kind that causes
quiet paroxysms beneath well-fitting suits, had taken a huddle of
three white men sitting farther up the bar counter as they said to
each other urgently, "Wait—wait—" and then added a twist to the
anecdote that set them off again. A black man in an American tartan
jacket was with another in a dark-blue suit, talking to him without
looking at him, his mind elsewhere. Orange fingernails scratched up
cashew nuts; a woman who called everybody "sweetie" protested because there was no olive in her martini, protested again when the
barman was reproached. Two more black men came in and looked
over the heads conspiratorially, haughtily, then saw the raised finger
of the man in tartan and broke into the sort of hearty formalities of
hand-shaking and back-slapping that the white men would have
winked about before, but that now simply brought a momentary distant look to their eyes.

The occasion for the party with the ladies was clearly the need to
entertain a tall, blond young man from out of town to whom they all
listened with the bright show of attention accorded to wits or experts.
He was what is recognized as a Guards officer type, perhaps a little
too typical ever to have been one. Not so young as all that, either; his
small, handsome, straight-backed head on broad shoulders had lon-
gish, silky hair thinning on the pate, and when he smiled his teeth
were bony-looking. He had a way of bearing down with his nostrils
and drawing air audibly through them, to express exasperation or
raise a laugh. Certainly his friends found this irresistible. His diction
was something no longer heard, in England, anyway. Most likely explanation was that he must have taken part in amateur theatricals

under the direction of someone old enough to have modelled himself on Noel Coward. Amateur theatre had been popular among the civil servants and settlers; even Olivia had once appeared in one of those dusty thrillers set in Lord Somebody's country house.

". . . Oh Lord yes. Her father's getting right out too. *Right* out. The place at Kabendi Hills has gone. Carol's heart-broken over the horses . . . to Jersey, I think. . . . Chief Aborowa said to me last week, there's going to be trouble over the culling—some of these chaps've had that bloody great government stud bull the department's spent a fortune on—and I said, my dear chap, that's *your* worry, I hope there'll be a couple of billion gallons of sea between me and your cows and your wives and the whole damned caboodle. . . . 'I don't want Pezele near my stool.' I said don't be a damned fool, Aborowa—as soon as I see him alone there's no nonsense, I talk to him like a Dutch uncle, we were drinking brandy together—"

"—Priceless!" One of the women was so overcome she had to put down her glass.

"—Heavens, that's nothing—Carol buys old Aborowa's wife's corsets for her."

More laughter.

"His senior wife. Poor old baggage, she doesn't know where the bouz begins and the derrière ends. Colossal. Such a dear old soul. I don't know what she'll do without Carol, they adore Carol. Yes, buys her corsets for her, bloomers, I don't know what . . . Special department at Harrods, for the fat ladies of circuses or something . . ." He drew breath through pinched nostrils while they looked at each other delightedly. "I don't know who's going to replace *that* service when we go, I can tell you, central government or provincial authority or what the devil these gentlemen're going to call themselves. M'lord Pezele—great fat Choro gentleman from the Eastern Province, he is—comes along in his brand-new jeep (I've been requisitioning for four years to get our jalopies replaced, but no dice), he stumps into the Great Place: 'My appointment with Chief Aborowa is at nine-thirty' —he's looking at his watch. Thinks he's at the dentist. And there's the old man over at his house, looking forward to a nice chat over a nip."

The black man with the friend in the tartan jacket said pompously to the black barman, in English, "The service is very bad here. I asked for ice, didn't I?"

But no one was listening except Bray.

". . . happy to get eight per cent on short-term investment instead. Five years is all they work on in these countries, you know."

Dinner music had started up in the dining-room, and the trailing sounds of a languid piano came from a speaker above the bar.

"Oh there'll be no difficulty whatsoever, there, that we're confident. . . ." The white businessmen, now that they were serious again, had the professionally attentive, blandly preoccupied faces of those men, sitting in planes and hotels in foreign countries, who represent large companies.

". . . your odd Portugoose wandering in from over the border . . . wily fellows, your Portugooses, but my boys always managed . . . now get this straight, Pezele, when I'm gone you can stew in your own *uhuru*, but while I'm doing my job . . . political officer, is he?—then tell him when he can read English well enough to understand other people's confidential reports that'll be time enough to get his sticky fingers—" The blue eyes, dilated fishily with vehemence, caught Dando and Bray on their way out of the bar with a half-smile of acknowledgement of the empathy counted upon in every white face.

"Moon, June, spoon," Dando was saying, "who in the devil wants that drivel? I must speak to Coningsby. It's even relayed in the lavatory. Can't hear yourself piss in this place."

The Silver Rhino was a short way out of town, built, like most of the hotels of these territories in the colonial era, on the Great North road that goes from country to country up through Central and East Africa. Ten years ago it had been a place where white people from the town and the mines would go for a weekend or a Sunday outing; there was fishing nearby and a tame hyrax and caged birds in the garden. But now the capital was spreading towards the old hotel, the lights of scattered houses were webbed in the bush, there were street names marking empty new roads, several Ministries had moved out that way. Bray heard that the site for the new university was to be there. "Yes—but that's all changed again," said Dando, sitting to the steering wheel as if it were the head of a reckless horse. "The university'll be on the west slope of the town, most likely. And now that they've put up a hundred-and-fifty-thousand-pound Ministry of Works, it's finally occurred to them that all government buildings ought to be in one area. So they're going to build another Ministry where the others're going up. A thousand acres, just below Government House and the embassies. Which is what could have been seen by anybody except a specially imported town planning expert, in the first place."

"What's going to be done with the building here?"

Dando accelerated, providing a flourish to his answer. "Raise battery hens in it, for all I know. Poor old Wentz. He doesn't have much luck with his investments. He's still in some sort of mess over the title deeds to the hotel—I keep promising him I'll go over the papers with him, he's in the hands of that bloody fool McKinnie, remember McKinnie and Goldin? He came up here and bought the place and signed the agreement, and then when his wife and family followed, there was some damn fool clause he should never have agreed to. They nearly didn't get possession."

"Good God. They had to leave South Africa because of some political trouble, didn't they?" Bray had the mild interest of one who is passing through.

"Don't know about *had* to. She was nervous and wanted to go—Hjalmar's wife. She's Jewish—he got her out of Germany in thirty-six, you know, though he's not a Jew himself. Smuggled her over the border. It's a terrible story. Of course he wasn't allowed to marry her in Germany. He couldn't even tell his family, couldn't trust anybody. Just disappeared, with her. Incredible story. You wouldn't think Hjalmar would have the guts, but he did it. He could have been in a concentration camp along with them if he'd been caught."

A string of coloured bulbs was looped from pillar to pillar on the Silver Rhino's familiar old wide veranda. Africans sat about on hard chairs drinking beer. Some were accompanied by women, who were, of course, accompanied by babies. Little children played with empty beer bottles and climbed the low veranda wall. The telephone booth that had always been there had a large portrait of Mweta, surmounted with a gold rosette, pasted on the door; people had scribbled numbers on the margin. Inside the hotel the mouldering butterfly-wing pictures had been replaced by some rather good Congo masks and the walls had been plainly whitewashed—otherwise it was all much as Bray remembered it. In the dining-room there was a hooded construction like a wishing well for grilling meat over an open flame, but it was not in use that night and the steaks came from the kitchen. Since Bray was last in Africa there had been the advent of the deep-freeze, and now he found himself eating these steaks everywhere: large, thick wads of meat that, once cut into, had the consistency of decomposing rags. "She usually makes a mushroom sauce, something special," Dando grumbled. "All these places are the same, they start off all right." Hjalmar Wentz had seen them—probably it would be impossible to go there for a meal without involving oneself in a visit to the Wentzes—and he came over to the table. He wore cotton trousers and a green knit shirt wrinkled round his chest and held out his hands apologetically. "Good God, you must excuse me—I wanted you to come and have a martini or something first, but what goes on here . . . I can't tell you— The chamber of commerce is having a lunch tomorrow and this morning when I got the crayfish from the station we found it was all bad. The lot. Margot's concocting something else, a miracle of the loaves and fishes . . . is that wine all right? Roly, I want you to try a Montrachet I found . . . but that's steak, eh? Well, we can't offer you crayfish tonight. But next time, remind me, you must try it . . . so light and dry." He sat and drank a glass of wine with them, and they talked British politics; he would lose the thread, reluctantly, now and then, and look about him in the necessity to be elsewhere, and then return irresistibly to the talk. When the coffee came he said, "Oh Margot wants you to have coffee with us, later. With luck we'll be out of the kitchen by ten. Come to our palace. Roly knows." "Stephen in the pub?" said Roly. "He may be. I'm not sure. The barman ought to be there tonight." The waiters had been looking anxiously at him for some time; he hurried off.

The bar was stifling, with the cool, sour undersmell of liquor. A fan made a mobile of tiny Viking ships, the sort of thing sold in airport shops, bob slowly like unevenly weighted scales. "How old are you, young man?" Dando called out to a plump, fair boy with a dent in his chin. Apparently it was an old joke; Stephen Wentz smiled and showed off a little as he put down a bottle of brandy and two fancy goblets. "Old enough to know what you like, Mr. Dando." "Hjalmar's son and heir. All these bottles will be his, some day." Hjalmar Wentz appeared with the embarrassed air of someone who has just taken his leave; he spoke to the boy. Dando held his brandy glass like a bird between two hands. "I've just been telling that son of yours I'll have to report you to the police for employing a minor in a bar." "Never mind, you should see the trouble we have sometimes to keep out the babies on backs."

"We saw them outside," Bray said. "It looked very homely."

"That's Margot," Hjalmar was expansively confidential. "They love to come here. She goes around giving the kids sweets. All the other hotels, of course, they're trying to get them to leave the kids at home."

Most of the Independence-week visitors had left but the bar was half-full with the regulars, a mixture of white and black, some of whom obviously had come in together. Smaller fry from the staff of visiting dignitaries were quartered at the Rhino—a Senegalese secretary, two men from the Ivory Coast—and there were newspapermen and a Filipino couple working for a United Nations demographic commission (Dando pointed them out) with friends from the Ghanaian Embassy. One or two of Mweta's junior lieutenants in routine administrative jobs mingled with these cosmopolites, but Dando remarked, "They're still at the dedicated, puritanical stage, in the government—first'll come the bribery and the purges, then'll come the normal drinking in pubs, along with ordinary mortals like ourselves. They'll settle down." He was greeted by many people; even Bray saw faces that he had come to know, by now. But they did not join anyone; Dando, sitting in damp shirt-sleeves in a stifling bar in this company, was contentedly meditative, for once; like a man at home in the chatter of his own kitchen. A little later they were summoned to the Wentzes' flat. There was something strongly European about the little living-room they entered, despite the transparent lizards on the walls and the nondescript, locally made furniture. It was the table that did it: a round table with a heavy, curlicued central leg, and a yellow cloth falling flounced, a lamp in the middle. Within the circle of its light there was a European interior, an interior contained by the early darkness of winter afternoons, the wet, tapping winds of winter nights. But the windows were wide open to lukewarm darkness and the ear-ringing racket of insects.

Coffee and a black-rich chocolate cake with a bowl of whipped cream stood on the table. Dando ate three pieces. Margot Wentz had the calm of preoccupation or exhaustion. She seemed hardly aware of Dando and Bray, beyond the necessity to feed them, and it was unlikely that she had known, earlier, that they were in the hotel. She gave a wavering smile now and then, in answer to one of the guests, but she did not seem to hear her husband although he talked on, relating anecdotes that drew upon and assumed her participation, and quoting her opinions as if she were confirming them.

"A schnapps with the coffee," he insisted, and although Bray wanted no more to drink Roly Dando said, "Ah, lovely," and Hjalmar, still blond and handsome in a sun-toughened, run-down way, began to shuffle about the room opening cupboards and fussing like an old man. "It's aquavit, should be here . . . where now . . . I'm half a Dane, you know, it's my national whad'you-call it, tipple, yes. . . ." Good God, what only isn't pushed in here. . . ." Piles of torn-off envelopes with stamps fell to the floor, curled-up photographs, bank deposit slips, box-top free offers of this and that. He began to look behind the volumes of philosophical and political works that filled rickety bookshelves; there were books all over the room, Shaw and O'Neill and Dos Passos and Auden, in English, Hesse, Hauptmann and Brecht and Rilke in German, psychology in German and English —a quick glance established that this was the remnant of the once-indispensable library of people young in Europe in the Thirties who had not had the money or the space to add to it, nor the strength of mind ever to leave it behind.

"What is it that you want, Hjalmar?" Margot Wentz said suddenly in a ringing voice, patient and strong. She had her back to him.

"No, it's all right, the aquavit, wasn't there a bottle still from Christmas, the one Vibeke—I'm just—wait a minute—"

She got up with the determined sleep-walking gait of someone who has the plan of cupboards, nooks, niches, and their contents clear in her mind as a cross-section of an anthill under glass, and took a bottle from behind a stand of gramophone records in worn covers. "Here you are, Hjalmar."

He went on marvelling over how he had thought it was here or there, he knew he had put it somewhere, and she continued to stand for a moment, looking at him as if waiting for the whir of some piece of clockwork to die down.

Their daughter, Emmanuelle, slipped in and cut herself a piece of cake. "Yes, I know you," she said directly to Bray when her father began the introductions; the night at the Independence party, when she had sat like a small animal holed up against pursuit and had not so much as acknowledged the presence of the middle-aged stranger talking to Ras Asahe, was suddenly presented as a shared intimacy. She deliberately cut the cake at an angle, apparently to avoid the filling, careless of the fact that she had spoiled it for the next person. She sat nibbling little broken-off pieces, holding them in long, thin, sallow hands. Her hunched shoulders showed deep hollows above and below collar-bones on which the greenish slippery skin shone in the heat. In a way she reminded Bray of one of those pictures of Oriental famine victims—all eyes and bones; but her legs under the short shapeless dress were beautiful, the thighs slender but feminine, the kneecaps round.

Stephen was straightening the books his father had disarranged. "Oh, ma, I've got the name of the stuff to kill those things."

"What things?" said his mother, not turning.

"Those things that are eating the bindings."

"Silverfish," she said.

"You can get it from the chemist. It's called Eradem, you just sprinkle it on the shelves."

She said, "He knows how to stop them being eaten up but he never opens one."

Wentz was talking to the two guests but the interjection came from him like a voice taking over a medium. "What time has he got. You know he hardly gets through the schoolwork."

"That's right."

His attention hung in the air a moment, probing her; then he took up again the discussion of the new university, disagreeing with Bray that the concentration ought to be on the sciences, in particular engineering.

"Well I don't see how any one of these new African universities is going to find enough students of a suitable educational level to fill places in half-a-dozen different faculties," Bray was saying. "The sensible solution would be for those countries linked by geographical, economic, and other ties to plan a kind of federation of higher education, each university concentrating on one or two faculties, and drawing upon all the territories for students. Here, I think the university should start off by offering degree courses in engineering and medicine only. The people who want to read the humanities have Makerere and Lusaka to go to. That way you could build up first-class teaching staff and equipment, instead of spreading the jam so thin and lowering standards."

"Then you'll still have to have some kind of interim programme—I don't know . . . something between the school and the university. For the general level of education of your youngsters—also the ones who are going to go to the universities in neighbouring countries, nnh?"

"No one's questioning *that*," Dando said. "It's a recognized principle—a school of further study or some such."

"But what's against combining it with the university, then? That's what they're really doing, by lowering the entrance qualifications here. You just take a little longer to go through your degree course, that's all. But if the university would specialize, Colonel, then you've got to have this extra school or whatever, another foundation, another administration, just for the people who are going to study law or languages somewhere outside."

"What's needed is technologists, mining engineers, electrical engineers, my dear Hjalmar, not a lot of patriotic idiots writing theses on African literature!" Dando exploded.

"If I want to read law, I don't know where I'll go," Stephen said, pleased.

"Not law, for you," Hjalmar said. "If you've got to get out, you can't practise law in another country. That's the way to get caught."

"Come on, Hjalmar, you drop-out, you could do some teaching at a college preparing people for university, you could contribute something to the nation."

Wentz poured Dando another glass of aquavit. "Kant and Hegel for the graduates of the mission schools." Smiling at himself: "If I remember anything to teach."

"If you can teach, you should," Bray said. And added, turning to Margot Wentz, "Why do we say that with such certainty, always? How does one know what is right for other people to do?" She took it with a considering smile, like an apology. She said quietly to her daughter, "And how was your cocktail party?"

The girl shrugged and looked into a distance.

"The trade commissioner for the People's Republic of China, wasn't it?" said Hjalmar, for the guests, knowing perfectly well what it was. "Very elegant. With paper lanterns and fireworks. Yes!" He pulled a comically impressed face, as at the feat of a precocious child.

Emmanuelle suddenly grinned delightfully. "You should've seen Ras bowing from the waist. Everybody bowing from the waist. A eurythmics class. A man's invited Ras and me to some youth thing in China. He had a long talk with me—through an interpreter of course. Asked me how I'd broken free of neo-colonialist influence. I didn't know what to say."

Her brother said to her, "Why does Ras always say 'longwedge' for 'language', he talks about African 'longwedges'? Sounds so funny."

"Go to hell." Emmanuelle sat up straight.

Stephen laughed, protested. "No, really, why does he . . . I mean it sounds . . . I always notice it. . . ."

She was raised like a cobra, her small head ready to strike. "Get back to your beer bottles."

His half-afraid, uncomfortable laughter made him writhe; but she was the one who left the room, ignoring everyone. "Hi, Emmanuelle, where're you going?" Dando called. "Aren't you going to play the flute for me tonight? What have I done to you, my beauty? Come here!"

"Not Emmanuelle," said Margot Wentz.

"She's good, she's good," Dando said to Bray.

"Yes, you must hear her another time," her mother said.

"But there's no one to teach her, here, that is the trouble," Hjalmar said. "She's really very talented. She plays the violin, too. She gets it from Margot's father, it's rather nice, she was named for him, too. Emmanuel Gottlieb, the physicist, you might have heard of . . . ?"

Margot Wentz waved away the possibility.

"You should hear how she can play African instruments, Colonel Bray," Stephen said. "That little hand-piano thing? What she gets out of it! The thing you play with your thumbs."

"You know Ras Asahe, from broadcasting?" said Hjalmar. "He's going to do a programme with her playing local instruments. I don't know what it's about. He has all sorts of ideas."

"I used to know his father," Bray said. "They're a bright family."

Everyone was rather tired. There was the sort of silence that winds up an evening. Hjalmar Wentz looked quickly at his wife, and then slowly from Dando to Bray. He spoke in a low tone, a gesture to the presence of the boy, Stephen. "One doesn't know quite what do do, in these circumstances. You saw tonight. He takes her about everywhere. He must be at least twelve years older; a man of the world. Normally one wouldn't hesitate to put a stop to it. If he were a white man. But as it is, it's awkward. . . . As soon as Margot says anything to Emmanuelle, she thinks . . . As if, with us, that would ever come into it!" His face was full of the hurt his daughter had no doubt not hesitated to fling at him.

Stephen proclaimed his presence. "Emmanuelle'll use anything to get her own way."

But Margot Wentz had the closed, dreamy face of one who is angry to hear private matters put before strangers. They spoke of trivial, friendly things for a few minutes before leaving.

The invitation to lunch with Mweta came with a telephone call from Joy Mweta herself. Bray had already talked to her at various receptions and they had danced together—for the first time in all the years he had known her—at the Independence Ball. "You know where we're living now, of course?" she said in her cheerful, chuckling voice, and they laughed. The newspapers had made much of the fact that until the day the President moved into what had been the Governor's Residence, he had continued to live in the little three-roomed, tin-roofed house in Kasalete Township which had been his home ever since he and Joy came to the capital from Gala. "Is it a formal lunch?" She was a little scornful— "Adamson just wants to see you. At least I hope it will be only you. My baby says to me, mama, why do all these people come and live with us?"

"Which baby is that? Telema?"

"You're behind the times! Telema's in standard six. And Mangaliso's nearly ten—the one that was born after you left. The baby's another boy, Stanley, he's two-and-a-half."

"Good work, Joy. How's Stanley's Gala? I need someone to practise on, someone not old enough to be too hard on my mistakes."

"Oh what do you think! Do I talk English to my children?"

He had the use of the Bayleys' second car, now, so he drove himself to the Governor's Residence—nobody remembered, yet, to call it the

Presidential Residence. There had always been some sort of attempt at a characterless formal garden on the entrance side—pot-bellied palms and beds of regimented annuals—but he was pleased to see, while he was stopped at the gates for the sentries to check his bona fides by telephone with the house, a family of women, children, and cooking pots whose presence was given away by a thread of smoke coming from the shrubs behind the guard-house. Perhaps they were even kinsfolk of Joy or Mweta; Bray wondered how Mweta would deal with the rights of the extended family, in a house obviously large enough, on the face of it, to accommodate one and all.

Of course, it didn't look like a house; at least, not in Africa. He felt this with a chill, for Mweta, as Vivien's old Renault gritted over the raked gravel to the entrance. It was neo-classical, with a long double row of white pillars holding up a portico before a great block of local terracotta brick and mica-tinselled stone, row upon row of identical windows like a barracks. The new coat-of-arms was in place on the façade. The other side, looking down upon the park as if Capability Brown had been expected but somehow failed to provide the appropriate sweep of landscaped lawn, artificial lake, pavilion, and deer, was not so bad. The park itself, simply the leafier trees of the bush thinned out over seven or eight acres of rough grass, was—as he remembered it—full of hoopoes and chameleons who had been there to begin with, anyway. It had been saved because one of the first Governors had wanted it to simulate the conditions of the local golf-course —he practised his drives from the double-staircased terrace.

A black man in the white drill, gloves, and red fez worn by domestic servants at colonial residences opened the door, and a young, top-heavy black man wearing blue pin-stripe and a white carnation ushered Bray to a private sitting-room. He was Mweta's new secretary, but there was also a young white man hovering with an aide-de-camp's social ease. Bray had heard about him: formerly a P.R.O. at the biggest mining house, who had been taken on mainly to protect Mweta from the availability to his people that had characterized him as a party leader. They still expected simply to be able to walk in and talk to Mweta; no black secretary could hope to withstand the importuning of women from the Church of Zion or old peasants with a grievance, when such people were told that it was now necessary to apply in writing for an interview with the President.

"What luck for me, Colonel Bray, I'm Clive Small, my aunt Diana Raikes used to be a friend of your wife's, I remember her reading out a letter from your wife just before you left this country that time—most impressive. I think it was one of the things that roused my interest in the place—I was a student, still." The young white man's red-tanned forehead was gilded with hair bright at the brow-line and temples, he had the well-cut lips and slightly bushy, antennae-eyebrows of a man attractive to women. He wore skin-fitting linen trousers and a gay pink shirt, and gently took over from the elderly African butler the preparation of the martini jug. "You know I like to fuss with this, Nimrod. We've got a new division-of-labour system going in this department."

"The President will be with you in a few moments, sir." The secretary turned from Bray to Small in an exchange of the casual, cosy asides of people who breathe fumes of power and palace intrigue so habitually that these seem to them an air like any other. "Did you prevail?"

The black man heh-heh'd that things couldn't have gone otherwise: "Well, what could he say? 'We very much regret'—all that kind of thing."

"The big man will be de-lighted. Just wait. De-lighted. And Douglas? I'll bet his nose is ninety degrees out of joint. Mm?"

When Mweta came in, they stood aside, flanking him, smiling as if they had produced him.

He wore the sensible if stylistically confused tunic that had been adopted by the Party, years ago (somewhere between a Mao blouse and a bush jacket) but there was something turned-out about him. He came to Bray before Bray could approach. Their hands held fast, they almost swayed, smiling, Mweta laughing up at him, and the two others standing there, smiling. "About time. About time," Mweta kept saying. "Always across the room, in the crowd! I just catch your eye, and then there's another face there."

"It's strange to be stopped on the road and see you go by, waving at us all."

Mweta hunched his shoulders and laughed like a boy who has had to show off a little. "But it was always for you, if you were there, James, you know that, it was certainly for you."

The butler was carrying round a tray with Mr. Small's martinis,

c

and a glass of orange squash for Mweta. Yet Mweta's voice and spirits rose, in the talk and laughter, just as if the alcohol were rising in his bloodstream as in the others'. He had always had this self-intoxication, this flooding vividness that was at once what brought people to him and what their presence released in him. Years ago, he would turn up in a village on his bicycle and before he'd got his breath back from the ride there would be a group around him, and his voice quickly heard above the others, holding the others. Later his face gleamed wet with excitement when he would talk for two hours to some football ground holding a crowd tight as cells in one organism, a monster speaking his name as if booming from the mouth of a cave: MWETA. He developed the technique of long pauses, space for swelling, echoing, wavering response. They yelled; he took it; he began to speak once more. Once Olivia had been overcome— "There's something horrible—it's as if they coax some precious secretion from him —like ants stroking captive aphids."

The secretary, Wilfrid Asoni, had the beaming professional ploy of making the President's interests his own. "Mr. President, it seems we can thank Colonel Bray for the services of our friend Clive, here. Oh indirectly, I mean, but just the same."

"Oh your sphere of influence, again, Mweta," said Bray. "Imagine how it's going to be, operating internationally—I wonder if U.N. realizes."

"No, no, yours, James."

"Well, even if you think so, don't tell them. You mustn't be too friendly with a has-been like me."

"But you were, how shall I say, born out of your time—"

"—deported out of it, anyway, wouldn't you say, sir," Small slipped in, through laughter.

"—You're now at last where you belong, *now, now,* building the state with us. Isn't that so? Of course!"

Their raised voices and laughter brought the high, overlarge room down to comfortable size. Blue cigarette smoke hung a haze over the view through the french doors of the bush in the park, retreated into the heat-haze of midday. Now and then Bray's attention drifted out there in counterpoint to the talk; the shimmering tremble seemed to spread through his own consciousness, smoothing, soothing, wavering it away into a state of suspension; the small happiness of warm cli-

mates. Into the close male company came Joy Mweta, followed, or
rather preceded, circled, and assailed by several of her children and a
prancing dog. For a few minutes there was pandemonium in the
room; Bray had not seen two of the children before, the third had
been an infant when he left the country: they wore white socks and
the eleven- and ten-year-old had already lost the shyness of African
children and talked confidently to their elders, demanding and complaining; only the little one clung to his mother's hams and peeped
round suspiciously. Mweta spoke to them in Gala and they spilled
out onto the terrace; then the dog showed a preference for the shade
of the room, and the carpet, and the littlest boy rushed in again to
get him out. His brother and sister followed; Clive Small swung the
little one round. "By the legs! By the legs!" the others begged. "Your
mother's made that taboo, Mangaliso, she's afraid I might drop you
on your head and you'll be bottom of the class ever after."

"I'm thirteenth and there are thirty-five in our class," the child vol-
unteered to Bray.

The smallest climbed onto Mweta, a wet-lipped little creature,
breathing heavily, with round, exposed nostrils and round eyes that
make a reproach of every black infant's face.

"I haven't told you," Bray said, "I'm a grandfather. I got a cable
only this morning. Venetia's had a daughter."

"Venetia!" Mweta was shaking his head. "You remember I used to
take her for a ride on the back of my bicycle? —And she used to
make posters for us," he said to Joy, whom he had married after Venetia had gone to school in England. "Yes, this little girl was a very
young supporter of PIP. Posters announcing the date and place of
meetings and so on. And slogans. Clive, she once showed such a poster to the Colonial Secretary—who was it, then, James? That's right
—he was here after the first London talks with Shinza, that time—
and he went on a tour of the Gala district, of course"—everyone
laughed—"to see where all this independence nonsense started, and
to see what sort of fellow this Bray was who didn't seem to be stopping it—and while he was in the *boma* that day and he went home
to the D.C.'s house for lunch, he asks this little girl, the D.C.'s daughter, what's that nice picture you're painting, and Venetia says, it's not
a picture, it's a poster, look! What's it for, little girl? Can't you see?
she says. For the PIP rally, of course!"

Bray was nodding and laughing.

"She was proud of her painting. Eh?" said Mweta. "Why not?" And they all laughed again, and drew from Bray his version of the story, with interjections from Mweta, who grew more excited with every flourish.

"Years afterwards," Bray said, "Venetia took me aside and asked me, very seriously, to tell her the truth: was it partly through her that I got kicked out? She said that ever since she'd grown up she'd begun to think about it and have it on her conscience."

Mweta's eyes narrowed emotionally. "Venetia! She must come here with her husband, eh, James. She should have been with us for Independence."

"What about a photograph?" Small said to Asoni. "Wilfrid's dying to try out his new camera, sir."

They all straggled onto the terrace; the heat seemed to foreshorten them, their voices rang against the façade of the house. Bray and Mweta stood together, Bray stooping and embarrassed, Mweta smiling with a hand on his arm. The dog ran across the picture. The secretary took it again. Then there was one with Joy and the children; they put their feet together and folded their arms.

"We're getting a swing and slide," Mangaliso said.

"*And* a jungle gym." The little one spoke to Bray for the first time. "The Princess said it."

Joy laughed. "Yes, the Princess was full of good ideas. She was telling me everything I should do. She said we should wall off a part of the garden and make it specially for the children, with swings and so on. You know, I mean she is used to living in this sort of place. She said you must have somewhere your own—specially for kids."

"Oh they got on like a house on fire," Mweta said. "Joy knows all the secrets of Buckingham Palace."

"Nonsense, she doesn't even live there."

"And the wife of the Chinese Ambassador, they were great friends too. She speaks English quite well."

"She wants me to come to Peking and speak about African women." Joy challenged him, smiling at Bray.

"Joy was always a great asset," Bray said.

"That's what *I* tell him."

The children had pulled off their shoes and socks and the close fuzz on the baby's head was full of grass. A guilty wet patch had no sooner appeared on his trousers before the heat began to dry it again. One of the white-suited domestics hovered in the shadow of the house with the announcement of lunch, but could not find an opportunity to catch anyone's attention. The secretary and the P.R.O. were fiddling with the Polaroid camera. Then the picture emerged, and everyone crowded to see. By now the party had been joined by a woman with blonde baby-hair drawn up on top of her head in thin curls. Like many women, she bore the date of her vintage year in the manner of her make-up: the pencil-line of the Dietrich eyebrows on the bald fine English skin above each blue eye, the well-powdered nose and fuchsia-pink mouth. She wore navy blue with a small diamond brooch somewhere towards one shoulder. Bray was introduced to Mrs. Harrison with the quick, smooth exchange of people who have learned the same basic social conventions in the same decade and country. Mweta and Bray and Joy were gossiping about the Independence celebrations; the children were jumping up round Wilfrid Asoni and Small, reaching for the camera. "Wait, wait, Mangaliso—do you want your picture taken? Not even with Bimbo?"

Mrs. Harrison's high clear Englishwoman's voice sailed in: "Children—I wonder who's been borrowing my *sécateur*? Do *you* know, Mangaliso? I should think Mangaliso might know, wouldn't you, Telema?"

The children dropped to earth, cut down. They stood there, wriggling, turning their feet on the grass, looking at each other. Under her eyes were made plain the shoes and socks tossed about, the wet patch drying between the little one's legs.

"Mangaliso!" said Joy.

"I shall give you a pair of *sécateur* for your birthday," the woman said to the child, "but you must be sure not to borrow mine. I need my *sécateur*, you know."

He smiled at her, frowning, pleading to be out of the limelight; he had taken the pruning-shears, but he didn't know what "*sécateur*" meant.

"That's a good boy," Mrs. Harrison said. "Mrs. Mweta, I'm afraid if you don't go into lunch cook's soufflé will be a pancake. He's in quite a state."

"Oh my goodness—what time is it? We were having a photo—

Adamson, we must have lunch." She was laughing and bustling, confused. The children were sent off, with some difficulty; Mrs. Harrison was standing in the sitting-room, her eyes taking some sort of private inventory, when the party filed through. Then they had to wait a few minutes for Joy, who had taken the children to their quarters. She came back giggling and apologizing and fell in with Bray. "They can't understand why we don't eat together any more."

"Well, can't you, sometimes? When you're alone."

"Never alone!" she explained, with a slight lift of the shoulders to indicate Small and Asoni. "Even if there're no visitors."

"You're not letting that Mrs. Whatnot run the place?" Bray said accusingly.

She laughed at him. "No, no, there's a cousin of mine from home, and my sister-in-law's little sister. They've come to help. You know, during the celebrations there were some days when I never had time to see the children at all." She had dropped her voice, perhaps because the atmosphere of the cool dining-room, as they entered, was so different from the noisy family party on the terrace. Her large, matronly but still young body took the chair at the foot of the table subduedly. Mweta took the head with something like resignation, as if it were the conference table. Behind each person a servant stood. Mweta did not even seem aware of their presence, but Joy would catch the smooth inattention of one or another, now and then, and half-whisper something in the local language. There was smoked salmon. And a cheese soufflé, and cold duck. Mweta, while talking about American foreign policy, carefully removed every vestige of the thin layer of aspic that covered the meat. "I really don't see it matters whether it's due to having got overinvolved in Vietnam, or whether, as this authority you've mentioned says, America's reached the end of an outward-looking phase and must concentrate on problems at home, or because, as some of my ministers have it, she has found influence hard to buy even with dollars. If America wants to withdraw" —he put up his palms—"all right, she's strong enough to do it. If she says to the hungry, no wheat unless you can pay, right, she does it. And the old scare story about who's going to fill the vacuum—not interested any more. But *we* can't do that. The only surplus the African states have got is a surplus of debts and need. We're struggling. We're forced to buy maize from South Africa, this from that country, that from the other, we are tied together like a three-legs race with all sorts of people. The economic structure of colonial times trips us up all the time. Of course we have to help each other. —But mind you, that doesn't mean we always understand each other's problems. It doesn't mean I must let myself be told by the OAU how to run this country, eh?" He looked at the dome of pink mousse being offered at his elbow and said to his wife, "I thought we were going to have ordinary food in the middle of the day—wasn't that decided, from now on?"

"Yes, I know—"

"No fancy things. Just a bit of fruit."

"Yes, Mrs. Harrison says it is fruit—made of fruit."

He hesitated and then plunged the spoon with a squelch and put a dollop on his plate. "What am I to Obote? The lime for the cement he'd have to pay a third again as much for if he had to import it from somewhere else. What's Nyerere's health to me? The low tariff for our goods at Dar-es-Salaam—"

"That's what I wanted to ask you, Adamson—what are the prospects for Kundi Bay?"

"Better ask Mr. Small about that. He's just been there water-skiing." Mweta smiled and shovelled up the last of the pudding.

"Well, I can't give you an expert opinion on its prospects as a harbour, but I was telling Mr. President it certainly has great possibilities as a resort. The beaches are better than those on the Mombasa stretch, far more beautiful. Marvellous skin-diving and goggling—what you need is to interest Mr. Hilton in putting up one of his hotels."

"It's within a hundred miles of the game park at Talawa-Teme, another tourist attraction," Asoni announced to Bray. He murmured agreeably in polite English response; he and Olivia and the children had camped there at Kundi, once, when it was nothing more than a fishing village, though it was said to have been used as a harbour for slavers early in the nineteenth century, and there were the remains of a small fort. Just before Independence a team of Italian experts had been out to examine the possibility of building a harbour big enough to handle tankers and large merchant vessels. "When's the report to be published?" His voice dodged round the starched sleeve of a servant.

"Oh it's being studied," said Mweta, with a smile that closed the subject. Joy Mweta was saying, "I want Adamson to build a little house down there. The children have never seen the sea. Just a small little house, you know?"

"The only thing was, I got absolutely eaten up by tsetse fly, my arm was like a sausage. No, not the beach—on the road, the road from the game park."

"—But that will be eliminated," Asoni said, "they will be eradicated. It has been done in the North. The department has it in hand. Anything can be done, today. We are living in the age of science. The mosquito has gone. The tsetse will go."

"It will be paradise." Mweta gave one of his famous gestures, one hand opening out the prospect over the table, the long room, the country, and laughed. As they rose from their chairs, he squeezed Bray's arm, hard, a moment.

After coffee in the sitting-room Mweta took Bray to his study. The Harrison woman had come in a convention of apology glossing firmness, to speak to Joy Mweta about something, and Joy had gone to her at once with the half-nervous, prideful air of a favoured pupil summoned by the headmistress. Clive Small said as Mweta passed, "By the way, sir, I'll take care of those people from Fort Howard if the call comes through."

"And Wilfrid knows about it?" He turned, and he and Asoni exchanged a few words in Gala. "All right. But please, if the chief's brother insists . . ."

"No need to worry, I'll handle him like a butterfly," said Small, tightening his handsome mouth. He saluted Bray gaily. "Hope very much to see you again, sir." .

The corridors of the place were paved with echoing black and white tiles. Mweta held open the door, first, into a men's cloakroom. When Bray came out of the lavatory Mweta was standing there waiting for him; they might have been on some London railway station. Bray was amused, with the touching sense of finding the friend, intact, behind the shifting superimpositions of a public self. One did not have to say, confronting the portrait in the toga, is this what he is now? The figure in the toga, the sacred vessel on the velvet-draped dais, they were all simply this rather short man with his head thrown back, in full possession of all these images. He did it all the way he used to jump on the bicycle and pedal to the next village and the next.

Yet the study was oppressive. Heavy curtains made a maroon, churchy light. An enormous desk with a leather top. Leather chairs. A sofa upholstered in something woolly with a tinsel thread running through it. It might have been the office of a company director; it had all been furnished for him by someone who saw him as another sort of tycoon, a black villager who found himself, by political accident, nominal supra-chairman of the mining companies that *were* the country. It probably had been done, indeed, by somebody on loan from the Company—who else would there have been who had any ideas of how a top man should be set up? But this speculation came from hostility towards the room; perhaps it was merely the way the Governor had left it, like the rest of the house.

Mweta hesitated at the big chair behind the desk but walked away again. He began to walk about the room as if they were waiting for someone. "I never dreamed it would be so long. Every day I wanted to phone and say come over . . . ? I felt worried about it, eh? You wouldn't believe me but there isn't a half-hour—every day—there hasn't been a half-hour—when there wasn't something that had to . . . somebody to see . . ."

"But that's how it must be," Bray said, from the sofa.

"Yes, I know. But if you're here, James—"

"Doesn't matter who's here."

"I suppose so." His eyes disowned the jolly, officially welcoming tone of lunch, that kept creeping back in intrusion.

Bray said, "You're the President."

"But not with you."

"Oh yes." Bray put himself firmly in his place.

Mweta looked deserted. He had the strange combination—the smile affirming life, and in the eyes, the politician's quick flicker. "I don't even know where my books are. I think they must still be over at Freedom Building."

"I was up there to have a look at the old place on Friday." The shoddy block behind the main streets of the town, leased from an Indian merchant, had been PIP headquarters from the years when all they could afford was one back room.

"Well, Freedom Building is over at parliament now!"

"Of course it'll be seen to that the Party machine doesn't run down," Bray said.

But Mweta had not forgotten the polite English way of making a warning sound like an assumption. He laughed.

"How could that be?"

"Well, I'm glad to hear it. Specially in the rural areas. People could feel nearly as remote from what goes on in parliament as they did when it wasn't their government, you know."

"That's what I've got ministers of local government for. And I'll still see as many people as possible, myself. I want to tour the whole country at least every few months, but already I've had to take on this fellow . . . at Freedom Building people used to come and see me any time of the day or night, and sometimes when Joy got up in the morning she found someone already sitting in the yard. . . ."

"He's essential, I should say. For the time being, anyway. People will get used to it. They'll learn to understand."

"Oh he manages very well. But it's not what I want."

"What's she doing here—the Englishwoman?"

"She was here before—she did the flower vases, things like that," said Mweta. "And for the celebrations, Joy wanted someone, she wasn't sure she could manage."

"Everything went off splendidly," said Bray. "Not a hitch anywhere."

"Let's go out there." Mweta stood up in the middle of the room as if he were shedding it. They took the first door from the corridor into the park and fell into strolling step together, over the rough grass and under the sprinkled shade, as they had done, walking and talking, years ago. Mweta was smaller and more animated than Bray, and seen from the distance of the house, as they got farther away their progress would have been a sort of dance, with the small man surging a step ahead and bringing up short the attention of the taller one. They paused or went on, in pace with the rise and fall of discussion. Mweta was telling a story that displayed the unexpected shrewdness of Jason Malenga, the Minister of Finance, about whom Bray had heard many doubts expressed, not only by Roly Dando. "Of course if I'd kept Foreign Affairs for myself, Tola Tola would have been the one for Finance, but it was decided I couldn't hope to do it."

"No, how could you." No mention of the obvious choice of Shinza.

"Well, others have tried. In any case"—they exchanged a look—"Tola Tola's always there if Malenga needs advice." Again, in spite of the silence over Shinza, so much taken for granted between them brought a qualifying remark: "If Malenga would ever admit it."

They dismissed this with smiles. "What I might do"—Mweta gave way to the urge to seek reassurance for the rightness of decisions already made—"in a few months time—next year—if I reshuffle, I'd give Tom Msomane the Interior, shift Talisman Gwenzi to Finance, perhaps a double portfolio, let him keep Mines—" Bray's silence stopped him. "I know what people say about Tom. But he's a chap who can handle things, you know?—he's shrewd but he can pick up a delicate situation without smashing it. He's got, you know, tact. And for the Interior—problems of refugees, deportations, and so on. You should see the file. Just waiting for the celebrations to be over, and then they must be opened." He gave a rough, nervous sniff. "I am thinking seriously about Tom."

Bray said, "But for the Interior. Doesn't he take too personal a view? Won't he be inclined to settle old scores?"

"Well, maybe, that may be, but being in office, the responsibilities and so on. I think he'll be all right. Sometimes you have to take one risk against another."

Bray didn't know whether Mweta was inviting a question about Mso support, or not. His face was screwed up, momentarily, in a grimace against the sun or his thoughts; perhaps he felt he had made enough confessions.

"I'd rather see him safe in Posts and Telegraphs, myself."

Mweta nodded to acknowledge the joke, rather than in agreement.

"Adamson, you never thought about Shinza—for Foreign Minister?" He phrased it carefully that way, but Mweta was quick to take it up the way it really was—"Look, I'm prepared to do something for Edward because"—he shook his head wildly as if to get rid of something—"because he thinks he taught me everything, and—because the past is the past, I'm not the one to try to get away from that. —But what it can be, I don't know, that's my trouble."

"He's a brilliant man."

"You still think so?"

"Oh come, you know so."

"James," Mweta said, making it clear this was to please him, "what can I offer Shinza? You think an under-secretaryship or something like that? Because that's all I've got. And it wouldn't be what *he* wants. He wants to change the world and use me and this country to do it for him, never mind what happens to the country in the meantime. I can make him an under-secretary—that's all."

"You can't do that."

Mweta opened his firm lips and closed them again without having spoken.

"I should be inclined," said Bray, hearing himself come out more gently pontifical than he had wished, "to find him some special position not directly involved in actual government, but recognizing his claims to elder-statesmanship-out-of-office. Mm? I should have thought he'd have done darned well as representative at U.N., for instance. For a start." He remained old-maidishly composed while Mweta stared at him in bitter astonishment. "Our ambassador to United Nations? Edward Shinza? After what he said? After what he said to the Commonwealth Secretary? His so-called minority reports at the last conference, not six months before Independence? After what we've had from him?"

"Make him spokesman for the majority and you'll see. You talk as if he'd started a rival party."

"He acts as if he has! A lot of people think it would be better if he had! Come out in the open!" Mweta began levelling with his heel a trail of fresh molehills on the grass. "—What a nuisance, these things — If he stops sulking away down there at home, well . . . It's up to him. . . ."

"I hope you're not going to let him sulk."

"You've been to see him, James?"

"I don't know if I'll get the chance. I couldn't believe he wouldn't be here for Independence."

Mweta shrugged; appealed suddenly. "We're going to talk every few weeks like this. We'll make it a regular thing." They had turned back towards the house, rising red and solid out of the hazy, unassertive shapes of the bush.

"But my dear Adamson, I shall have to go back pretty soon. I was thinking of next week. You're all getting down to work again now. Time the guests left."

Mweta stopped again. "Back? But you are back."

"I don't know what I could do, if I stayed," Bray said, smiling.

The conventions would make it easy for them both; whenever they reached this point they had simply to go on following his polite pretence that he had never thought of himself as anything but a visitor, and Mweta's polite pretence that a place had been provided for him as something other than that. It was so easy, very tempting—he looked at the ugly house looming up in their way—one could walk round the past they had inhabited, as one does round a monument.

"No, no, now don't—" Mweta said with some difficulty, as years ago he would have said of someone from the Colonial Office: "They mustn't come their English with me." He said grudgingly, "What is it you're doing over there in England, really?"

"Yes, it's a very lazy sort of life, I suppose, it's quite astonishing how well one takes to doing very little—" Bray turned the question to an accusation, cheerfully admitted; making it easy for the other man—it was part of the game.

Mweta didn't answer, implying that this sort of waffle could not reach him. But he didn't do much better, himself; in the cross voice that disguises lack of conviction, using the hearty "we," he said, "What nonsense to talk about going next week. We can't allow that."

They turned to other things. Mweta wanted to discuss the Kundi harbour report, after all, now that they were alone. He watched Bray's face when he came to the points about which he himself was particularly worried. There was the old sense of seeking correction of his own assumptions and findings. Then they found themselves back at the house again, with the young men in attendance, Joy going in and out, and the Harrison woman pouring tea. Telephones rang, the secretary brought in a cable, Mweta was called away and Bray waited to say good-bye to him. When he returned the convention fell quickly into place again; it was all *bonhomie*, playful scolding and exaggeratedly graceful regrets, plans, and promises— "We don't want to hear this talk about England, ay?" "All right, not a word about England." "I've told him, England's for old men to go back and die in, ay?" Joy would phone again; they would be meeting at a reception the following week, anyway. Mweta's lively hand was firm on his shoulder. Yes, that was fine, Bray said. (He would be gone by then; his flight was already booked.) Mweta insisted on coming out onto the steps of the entrance. He looked young, quick, beaming, waved his hand with a pause, like a salute, and then turned away inside at once. Already he existed like that, for the future, in Bray's mind. He would have rejected with distaste any suggestion that Mweta had been a protégé, but he did have, that day, the sense of relinquishment with which, as an interested party, an older person sees a young one launched and going out of sight.

For some reason he had not given Olivia an exact date for his return, though his seat on the plane was booked; he was thinking he perhaps might stop off in Spain for a week, on the way. He had never really had a proper look at the Prado.

Three days before he was to leave a letter came, delivered by hand. Mweta asked him to accept an immediate appointment as special educational adviser—a newly created post—to investigate the organization of schools, technical schools, and adult education projects in the provinces, beginning with the largest, the northern province, Gala. He stopped himself from reading it through again. He passed it over to Roly Dando.

"Someone thought that one up quickly," Dando said.

They roared with laughter, not because anything was funny, but because Bray was moved and excited in a way that couldn't be acknowledged. Shut away there behind a Great Wall of responsibilities, echoed by sycophants, surrounded by the jailers of office, Mweta had torn out of the convention: Mweta hadn't believed any of it for a minute.

Dando couldn't keep his mouth shut. "Bray's been offered the Ministry of Pot-hooks and Carpentry, is that it—oh yes, but what he'd really been angling for was Pectoral Development and Backscratching, well, so I've heard." People laughed but understood that there was something in it; appointments were being handed out every day as the administrative changeover took place and various development plans got off to a start. Most of the appointees were unpronounceable names and black faces that the white shopkeepers and mine officials had never heard of before. But in law, agriculture, public health and education, there were many white men: foreign experts, and a few familiar faces, like that of Colonel Evelyn James Bray, who, in the old days, had shown themselves more concerned with the interests of the Africans than with the life of the white people in the colony. Among the group in which Bray moved in the capital, friends of friends passed through on their way to new projects or jobs in different parts of the country; there was much talk of the finance, equipment, staff or lack of it, that people expected to manage with. Bray was simply another one of them, not quite sure how he would set about what he was supposed to achieve, given no assurance of any particular resources being available to him. Most people thought that this job of his had been an understood thing all along; no one seemed to remember that he had been going home. The drinking party that Roly Dando had arranged as a send-off became just another gathering out at Dando's place.

The day the letter arrived, a fierce stab of uncertainty had come to Bray when he returned to the room in the garden with it in his pocket. If it had come only three days later, he would have been gone. It would never have brought him back.

Mweta was in Nairobi at a meeting with Kenyatta, Kaunda, and Nyerere, and he did not see him again. When he had talked to the Minister of Education, discussed the terms of reference of his job and settled that he would go to Gala within two weeks, he wrote to Olivia. He told her he "suspected" the job had been created specially in order to offer him something; he did not need to tell her that it was one that needed doing and that perhaps he might be able to do better than most people—she would know that as well as he did. He poked fun at it a little, and said that he'd promised to undertake a trial period of six months or so, long enough to have a good look around and write some sort of preliminary report. He was to get a government house—back to the old "basic furniture supplied." By the time he'd made sure it was habitable, and that he could get on with some work there, she would come out and join him. Surely Venetia could be trusted to manage the baby by herself, by then? —The only thing he did not tell her was that he had had his seat on a flight back to England when Mweta's letter came.

PART TWO

Bray bought himself a second-
hand Volkswagen from someone "getting out" and drove north to take
up his appointment. He left the capital on a low grey morning that
would lift to a hot day; Roly Dando had gone to work but Festus in
his cook's hat and the garden boy stood by to watch him go. Vivien
Bayley had brought a present of whatever Penguins she could find at
the local bookshop: *Diary of a Nobody, The Three Caesars, Stamboul
Train, Les Liaisons Dangereuses, The Plague—* "Well, I always think
you want to read things you know when you're living away somewhere, alone." They were in a basket on the back seat with a bottle of
whisky and some files that had come up from the Ministry of Education at the last minute. He drove out through the main street of the
town and saw Mrs. Evelyn Odara trying to park her car outside the
new post office and several other people whose faces were now familiar to him, going about their daily business. The vendors of wooden
animals were polishing them under the flame trees; the unemployed
were hawking plastic bags of tomatoes. As the town ravelled out towards the gold mines lorries swayed past him filled with concrete
pipes and building materials, stiff pig carcasses from the cold storage
and rattling crates from the brewery. Then there were the landscaped
approaches to the mine properties themselves, all flowery traffic round-
abouts, signboards, and beds of cannas and roses, and then the
stretches of neat colour-washed rectangles of housing for the African

miners, a geometric pattern scribbled over by the mop-heads of paw-paw trees, smoking chimneys, washing lines, creepers and maize patches, and broken up by the noise and movement of people. In twenty minutes it was all gone; he passed the Bush Hill Arms, its Tudor façade pocked with wasp nests and a "For Sale" notice up (someone else "getting out"), and then there was nothing at all—everything: the one smooth road, the trees, the bamboo, and the sudden open country of the *dambos* where long grasses hid water, and he saw at last, again, the single long-tailed shrike that one always seemed to see in such places, hovering with its ink-black tail-plume like the brushstroke of a Chinese ideograph.

He drove all morning and met not more than a dozen cars and the top-heavy bus that apparently still did the journey from the Tanzania border twice a week. Where there were African villages, a few bicycles and stragglers appeared on the road. Bags of charcoal leaned here and there on the edge of the silent forest. People lived deep inside this environment as if it were a house; their individual shelters were flimsy. He kept remembering—no, experiencing—things like this, that he had forgotten. In England, sometimes, over the years, he had had dreams that seemed to happen in this country, but it wasn't this country at all; and even conscious recollection was nothing but psychological memory—something selected to match the emotions engendered in a particular place at specific times.

Dando's house, left behind, was no more present than Wiltshire. He enjoyed a kind of freedom that he knew would last only until his recognition of his surroundings passed into unthinking acceptance, and he could no longer hold back and view them as the past revisited or a present not yet broken into.

He called at the White Fathers' Mission at Rungwa River, but Father Benedict was away and he could see that none of the younger ones knew who he was. The swallows still twittered in and out of their mud nests in the refectory, where he was given tea. A loud clanging that he knew so well came from a length of iron suspended from a tree and beaten with a stick, announced the end of school and the hot peace was invaded by yells and the muffled stampede of bare feet. The Fathers were good enough to sell him a couple of gallons of petrol, one working the hand-pump with a grin, his rosary swinging, the other standing by with his hands folded into the sleeves of his cassock and his big, blueish, celibate's feet placed close together in their rough sandals. The Fathers were shy as young girls. The African schoolboys scuffled and chattered at a distance, and when he called out a greeting, laughed and called back.

There were large villages near the road in this part of the country, smoking up through the forest. The cultivation of land by lopping off the branches of trees and burning them round the trunk, for potash, made druidic circles everywhere. New signs pointed into the bush: "Freedom Bar," "New York Bar," "Independence Bar"—crooked letters in English painted on bits of wood. But the generation that had grown up in ten years was as poor and dull-skinned as their fathers had been.

He had had the intention to spend the night at the old Pilchey's Hotel at Matoko, the usual half-way house. He arrived there earlier than he had thought he would; he was half in mind to drive on but did not know if the government rest-house that used to be at the cattle dipping station, sixty miles north, was still open. The tarred road was long left behind and the ugly little red car looked, as he got out and smoothed his rumpled shirt into his trousers, as cars always did up here. The undersides of the mudguards were rimmed with clay and the fender was plastered with the broken bodies and strange-coloured innards of dead insects.

Heat and silence fell upon him. He tramped over the cracked veranda and looked into the dark of the hotel: a smell of beeswax and insecticide, no one in sight. He knew where the bar was and the sound of his own footsteps accompanied him there, but the door was locked and he felt sure the ship's bell that hung beside the name "Davy Jones' Locker" was purely decorative. Back he went to the veranda; there was no main entrance, but screen doors all over the place that gave out long-drawn, dry squeaks behind him and led to a deserted dining-room with fan-folded table napkins and dim green corridors of closed doors. A child's cot piled with old pillows and the broken marble from an old-fashioned washstand stood where the corridor turned; there was a tray with two empty beer bottles and glasses on the floor.

He went back to the veranda and stretched out his heavy long legs from a chair. He knew this hour; everyone was asleep. If he sat for any length of time he himself would fall into an afternoon sloth.

There were borders of orange lilies in the garden, and the same huge sagging aviary, like a heavy spider's web, behind which blue cranes and guinea fowl pecked at their own feathers in some affliction induced by confinement. He could see their jerking, worrying heads. The farming land was good around here, and when the white farmers got merry in the bar it used to be the thing to bundle one of their number in with the birds. A vast sense of unreality came over him. He noticed a brass bell-push, gleamingly polished, and stuck a forefinger at it, not expecting anything in the way of response. But after a while a very young waiter appeared, with a red fez and a tin tray. He asked for a cold beer and was told *Doña* was sleeping; the bar would open now-now. "Is it still *Doña* Pilchey?" Yes, *Doña* Pilchey was sleeping. This was not Gala country yet, but the local language was related. He spoke to the boy in Gala and was understood; they agreed that the luggage should come out of the car even though he couldn't have a room until *Doña* Pilchey woke up. Was the kitchen locked? No, it seemed the kitchen was open. The youngster would make him some tea in the meantime.

While he was drinking it, the shadow of one of the big trees fell across the veranda and seemed to bring a breeze. The heat of the afternoon turned, as it did quite suddenly; one of the guinea fowl began to call. He was no longer used to driving for hours at a stretch. His big body was restless with inactivity. He walked off nowhere in particular, though he knew this road that led from the main road to the Matoko *boma* about two miles away. The red sand was pleasant to tread on—he had not walked at all, really, in the month in the capital, except in the streets of the town; no one walked—and the coarse sleek grass leaned beneath its own weight on either side of the road, as high as his shoulders. Scarlet weavers with black masks flicked up out of it and hung upside down at the entrance to their nests. A rough driveway marked with whitewashed stones and aloes curved up to a small schoolhouse on a rise and down again. He took the little detour to give some sort of shape to his stroll. There was the school garden—a patch of maize and beans, some staked tomatoes— the length of dangling iron that was the school bell, and, as he walked past the open doorway, the schoolmaster himself sitting at work. The man jumped up and at once started apologizing as if guilty of a grave breach of hospitality and respect. "No sir, I am very sorry, sir, I was just taking the chance to get a little study—" Bray greeted him in Gala, giving him the form of address to be used by respectful pupils towards the master, to put him at ease.

The man was shyly delighted and immediately brought out all he had to offer—the school register, the exercise and text-books of the pupils, all the time explaining and answering Bray's questions in a slow, anxious way. A pupil who had been sitting with him at the deal table where he was working sat, unable to go on, her hand on her place in a book, listening and smiling faintly in greeting. She looked like a grown woman, but irregular schooling often meant that African schoolchildren were far older than whites. The schoolmaster himself was very thin, black and pigeon-chested under a woollen pullover. His two-roomed school was seven years old; there were some desks but the smaller children, the schoolmaster explained, still sat on the floor. Some of the children who lived far away stayed in children's huts in the village and walked home at weekends. "This year we are sixty-five" he said, "our biggest year so far. And twenty-one are girls." He proudly showed a single poster on the damp-mapped walls: OUR LAND—a smiling miner working down a gold mine; smiling fishermen hauling in a catch; a smiling woman picking some crop. Population statistics in green, revenue figures in red. "From the Education Department. Oh yes, we are beginning to get nice, nice things. I am filling in the forms. Now we will get them. I wish you were here when the children are in school, they would sing for you."

Bray had been sung to so many times by black schoolchildren. "Another time, I hope."

"My wife teaches the choir. She also teaches the first and second grade." The young woman was smiling, looking up from one to the other.

"I thought you were one of the young schoolgirls!" Bray said, and they laughed.

"Well, I am teaching her for her Standard Six exam. She goes next month to town for it. She has had four children, you see, her studies were interrupted. But I teach her when I can. She wants to write the teacher's exams eventually."

"It's lucky for you that you married a teacher." Bray tried to draw her into the conversation.

"And I am working for my O levels, the Cambridge Certificate," the schoolmaster said, with the urgency of a man who has no one to turn to. "I have here the English paper—not the one I will have to write myself, you understand—"

"I know—a specimen."

"Yes, the paper written by the students in 1966—you understand. I have a difficulty because there are some words not possible to find—" He went over to the table and brought a small, old, school dictionary.

"I see—well, that wouldn't have the more unusual words, would it—"

The wife swiftly helped him to find the paper and his exercise book. He went down the paper with his eyes, lips moving a little. Bray noticed how tight his breathing was, as if he had a chest cold. "This one word here—here it is, 'mollify' . . . ?"

Bray wanted to laugh, the impulse caught him by the throat as a cough rises; he took the examination paper to play for time, in order to pretend, out of the "civilized" courtesy of his kind, that uncertainty about the meaning of the word was something anyone might share— and this in itself was part of the very absurdity: the assumptions of colonial culture. He read, "Write one of the following letters: (a) To a cousin, describing your experiences on a school tour to the Continent; (b) to your father, explaining why you wish to choose a career in the navy; (c) to a friend, describing a visit to a picture gallery or a film you have enjoyed."

The schoolmaster wrote down the meaning of "mollify" and showed those questions, ticked off in red ink, that he had been able to answer. "This will be the third time I try," he said, of the examination.

"Well, good luck to you both."

"When she goes for the Standard Six she takes our choir along for the big schools competition. Last month they won the best in Rongwa province. Now we don't know—but we hope, we hope." The schoolmaster smiled.

He was shown the football field the pupils had levelled; a little way behind was a mud house, shaped European-style with a veranda held up by roughly dressed tree-trunks, which must have been where the schoolmaster and his family lived. An old woman was doing some household chore with pots, outside, in the company of two or three small children. The schoolmaster said, "If there was someone I could ask, like I ask you—" but he was embarrassed to appear to grumble and began to talk about his pupils again.

Bray, feeling as he had felt a thousand times before in this country, the disproportionate return he was getting for a commonplace expression of interest, said, "What do you feel is your biggest problem at the moment?" and was surprised when, instead of turning again to his expectations of the Education Department under Independence, the man took time to think quietly, in the African lack of embarrassment at long pauses, and said, "We have to make the par-ents let the girls come to school. This is what I have been trying to do for years. Our girls must be educated. I can show you the figures—in nineteen-sixty-five, no nineteen-sixty-four, yes . . . we had only nine girls, and they left at the end of two years. Yes, two years. I cannot persuade the parents to keep them on. But I try, try. I go to the par-ents myself, yes, in the country. I talk to the chiefs and tell them, look, this is our country now, how can the men have wives who are not educated? There will be trouble. We must have the girls in school. But they don't want to hear. I went to see the par-ents, I talk to them. Yes, well, this year we manage to keep twenty-one girls and some are in the Standard Three class already. I talk to the people slowly." The man smiled and took one of his gasping breaths; his hand took in the bush, his suburbia. "I go and tell them. I've got my bicycle."

Bray remembered that things were different now, even at Pilchey's. "Why don't you come up to the hotel this evening—I'm staying the night. We could talk some more."

The schoolteacher had the suddenly exhausted look of a convalescent. He screwed up his eyes hesitantly, as if there must be something behind the invitation that he ought to understand. "At what time, sir?"

"Come up after supper. We'll have a beer. And your wife, too, of course."

The man nodded slowly. "After supper," he repeated, memorizing it.

When Bray got back to the hotel Mrs. Pilchey was at her desk in the bar, doing accounts. Her big head of thick, reddish-blond hair had been allowed to fade to the yellow-stained white of an old man's moustache. She looked up over her glasses and then took them off and got to her feet with the pigeon-toed gait of heavy, ageing women. "I thought it sounded like you, when the boy told me." Sex had died out of the challenging way she had had with men; it was bluff and grudging. They had never liked each other much, in the little they had known of each other, and extraordinarily, the old attitude fell into place between them as if the ten years didn't exist. There was laughter and handshaking. "A big *Bwana* with grey hair at the sides, and he can talk Gala. Well, there didn't used to be any white hairs—but I thought, that's Colonel Bray! No, well, I heard you were out, anyway, so I'm not as clever as I fancy myself—"

He said, "So you're carrying on alone? Olivia and I heard when Mr. Pilchey died."

"Five years," she said. There were pencil caricatures of Oscar Pilchey behind the bar, done in an attempt at Beerbohm's style. "I don't think he'd have been able to stand it if he'd been here now."

Bray had sat down at the bar. "It's a tremendous job for a woman on her own."

"I don't know about that, I've been in the hotel business twenty-five years, as you know. But to cope with it the way it is now, it's enough to drive you nuts, that I can tell you."

"Shouldn't you have someone to help you—a manager or an assistant?" He asked for a gin and tonic and she tipped the bottle where it hung upside down over its tot measure and prepared the drink with a kind of grim insolence of practised movements that was in itself a contempt for those for whom it was all very well to talk. "You can't get anybody to do anything. *They* don't care. They want to be rich. They want to learn to fly aeroplanes. That's what I get told by one of my kitchen boys, yes, I'm not telling a lie. He doesn't want to scrub the tables, he can go to town and learn to fly an aeroplane now."

Bray smiled. "And who told him that?"

"You're asking me!" But her quick freckled hand, doing what had to be done, wiping the wet ring left by the ice bucket, made it clear that she knew that he knew quite well. "I can only say, since last week I can't sack any one of these fine pilots out of my kitchen without asking the Ministry of Labour first. You know that, of course? Published last week. I got a circular from the hotel-keepers' association, though what they think they're going to be able to do about it —I must get the permission of the labour officer in my area, whoever that is, I don't know, and what the gentleman whoever-he-is knows about my business—"

They both laughed; her accusation of what Bray was, of all that he had been, he and his kind, was laid out flatly between them along with the plaster Johnny Walker and the S.P.C.A. tin for small change. She sat down again at the set of books beside her glass of beer.

He said, "I can sympathize; it must be hellish difficult for you."

She didn't believe him; it was all very well for people like him who hadn't had to make a living, who were sent out by the British government for a few years and took sides with the blacks because they didn't have to stay and live with them if they didn't want to. But she went on, letting him hear it all. "My old Rodwell, Rodwell that worked for Oscar from before we were married. They come here the other day to ask him to show his Party card. I ask you! All he knows is he's the best-paid cook in the country; twenty-five years he's been running his kitchen here. Party card! And they turn nasty! They wouldn't think twice about beating him up on his way down to the compound at night. He says to me, *Doña*, what can I do—? The bunch of thugs." She wouldn't say "the PIP"; by the refusal to name names she was able to say what she pleased without being provocative. There was a curious kind of intimacy of insult in their chat. He said of the new powers the Minister of Labour had taken on himself, "The trouble is there's danger of unemployment rising, just at present."

"Well, a lot of people are selling up—if you can find anyone to buy. When these pilots and other gentlemen come back hungry looking for their jobs they'll be in for a big surprise. The Quirks have gone, last month. Johnny Connolly says he'll send his cattle to the abattoir at Gala if he can't get rid of the dairy as a going concern. Lots of people."

"Oh I'm sure farmers are nervous. But I don't think it's a few white people leaving that means much to the labour position. It's the inevitable hiatus between now and the time when the development plans get going—the harbour at Kundi's coming, I understand. And the draining of the swamp land round the Isoza area. There aren't *more* unemployed people, now, than there were under the colonial administration; it's just that they naturally have the feeling they've done with living in the villages at subsistence level and there's a danger they may flock to the towns and the mines, where there's no hope of work for them, really. It could be the old story of peasants without skills leaving the land."

"Well exactly, what do they know," she said, "all these years they've had their cassava and their goats and their beer. And happier than we are, believe me."

There was the sound of cars drawing up and voices from the veranda. The two waiters went in and out the bar with orders which she dispensed deftly, the smoke of the cigarette in the corner of her mouth making her keep one eye narrowed. Moving about, she had the big head and pouter chest dwindling to unimportance of the caricatures on the wall. In between times she returned to her accounts, looking down her cheeks at the figures she ticked off while talking to Bray. He asked directly, "Do Africans come here now?"

"It's the law," she said, as directly. "My boys serve them if they come. It's very few; they like their own beer, of course, in their *khayas*, that's what they want. . . . They sit on the veranda and as long as they behave themselves, that's all right. They know they've got to behave themselves."

"And do the farmers still put chaps in the aviary on Saturday nights?"

She laughed and put down the pen, shaking her head in pleasure. "Oh those were the good days, ay? My, what a night we used to have sometimes. And Christmas and New Year! What a lot of life our crowd here used to have in them. Oscar used to say never again, never again. And every time—good God, ay? Ah, that's all gone, now."

She had cast disgruntledness, blood back in her face, moisture of laughter in her eyes—the brief jauntiness of an old dog remembering to wag its tail. He was touched, as always, by a sign of life; but even in the odd moment of warmth she kept in her face an aggression of pride and inferiority: not that *he* and his kind had deigned, had known how to enjoy themselves!

When he had bathed and changed for dinner she bustled into him in one of the passages, jingling keys. "Sure you got everything you want? Towels, soap—all right? I never know, these days." He reassured her. The white men were still drinking on the veranda, and the bar was comfortably full, too. Darts were being played and the news was crackling over the radio. There were no black men. The dinner gong had been sounded up and down the corridors, verandas and annexes that made up the complex of the hotel, and the lights were on in the dining-room, but no one made any move to go and eat. He did not feel like sitting in there on his own. But on the veranda he knew no one except perhaps one face—a man with a head of blond bristles catching the light like the fine hairs on a cactus; probably Denniston, who used to be in the mounted police. He ordered a drink and watched the frogs keeping an eye on the humans with pickpocket wariness while snatching flying ants that fell to the veranda floor from the light. Mrs. Pilchey's cat came to stalk the frogs in turn, and he chased it away. For the first time, he felt an interest in the stuff from the Education Department that was lying in the car; the little school and the schoolmaster roused him to it. He felt some stirrings of purpose towards this job that was not real to him because he was not sure what it ought to be. He had accepted it in his mind as taken on "for his own reasons": not to be questioned, for the time being, but about which there must be no illusions of objective validity. He went to the car for the file; he could just glance over it while finishing his drink before dinner.

As he walked back to the veranda, the schoolmaster was standing on the steps in an army-surplus overcoat, hat in hand. Bray had the impression that he had been waiting about in the shadows, perhaps not sure, among all the white men's faces heavily blocked out of the dark by the streaming light, which was the one he sought. "Oh good . . . splendid . . . this's my glass, I think—" and they sat down. He ordered the beer that the other said he would have. "I don't know whether I ever introduced myself, Bray, James Bray—and yours . . . ?"

The schoolmaster cleared his throat and leaned forward. "Reuben Sendwe. Reu-ben Send-we." Then he nodded in acknowledgement of this identity and sat back again.

He was, of course, used to being summoned and talked at; Bray knew that being able to drink up at the hotel wouldn't change that. One could perhaps only make him forget himself. Bray began to talk about *him*self, about how he had worked in the British administration, been district commissioner in the Gala district, and then become "unpopular"—as he put it—with the Colonial Office. "But that's all ancient history, not of much interest"—he wanted to know more about the school, about schools and teaching, generally, in this district. Sendwe had got what secondary school education he had at the mission at Rungwa. Naturally he knew Father Benedict. "The Fathers told me this morning that the government is going to take over the school. What do you feel about it?" Sendwe said, "I wish, sir, I knew

how much money our government has got." "Yes, money—? Go on."
He licked his dry lips, "If our government has plenty money, then we
must take over all the mission schools. If we did not have the missions when I was small, there was no secondary school for me. The
English government had only that one small school at the *boma,* you
know? But if there is the money then it is the best thing for all education to be the same, for all children to get the same chance. And then
you see, our government can't think, all right, there is a mission
school there, near that village or that village, so why must we build
another school—you know what I'm saying?"

"Oh yes, exactly—"

"That was what the English government did, but our government
must not now do the same. That is why we must close the mission
schools. Not because the Fathers are not good men. *I* don't say that.
Nobody of our people says that. The Europeans mustn't say we are
throwing out the mission people; we must have our own schools in
our country, that's all. I just want to know if we have got money."

"I think you have," Bray said, "but not the teachers, that's going to
be the trouble. I hope you can persuade the mission teachers to give
over the running of their schools to the government, but to stay on
and teach. Even then hundreds of teachers will have to be recruited
from somewhere—somewhere outside."

"If we have got the money," he said, with satisfaction.

"Does the Education Department help you with your own studies?
Where do those lessons you showed me come from—a correspond-
ence course?"

He shook his head and coughed. "I pay myself . . . . From London."

The veranda was emptying and cars were driving away although a
hard core of drinkers remained noisily in the bar. Mrs. Pilchey came
bearing down across the veranda with authority. "Doesn't anybody
intend to eat tonight?" she said at large. She was level with Bray and
he half-rose politely. "I certainly do. Shan't be too long."

Sendwe was standing up. She looked at him. "Well, how did the
sheep go down?" she asked in her loud voice. "Oh, you know Mr.
Sendwe, Mrs. Pilchey—" "Of course I know Sendwe." The schoolmaster's hand went out for his hat and clutched it automatically from the
chair. He stood there in the overcoat and, the way the veranda globe
shed its glare, his eyes couldn't be seen at all in his thin black face.

He said, "Oh madam, I should come to thank you. It was very, very nice. But I was sick since then."

She kept the stance of someone waylaid. "Celebrations too much for you were they?"

"I have a very bad cold" he said. And as she was going he took courage and appealed. "The children were very, very happy with the meat. I thank you very much."

"That's okay," she said briskly, on a rising note, and was gone with the heavy tread, listing a little to one side, of one who has been too many years on her feet.

He sat smiling. "It was a whole sheep," he said. "The hotel gave it to the school for Independence. Oh it was a very nice present. Oh the children were happy." He coughed again, took some beer, and went on coughing. When he had recovered his breath, Bray said, "What about dinner, now? What d'you say?"

"I have had a meal."

"Oh, are you sure? You don't feel like something else, now?"

"No, I don't feel hungry ever since I have this cold again." He was still breathless from the coughing bout.

Bray said, "Are you doing something for it?"

"I went again to the clinic. They say I must go to the hospital for tests." He mentioned the name of the TB hospital in the capital. He held up three fingers. "I was there for seventeen months three years ago. But they cured me. It's only about two, three weeks now I've got this very bad cold. I don't feel hungry."

"I see. Well then, let's have another beer." But they did not sit down again. "When will you go?"

The man smiled. "It's very far."

"But you shouldn't wait."

"When I write the O levels," he said. He seemed suddenly confused by the feeling that the visit was over and he did not know the right way to conclude it without leaving without what he had come for. "Sir, I want to ask if you can write to me about my young brother. He wants to learn farming—European farming. He's working there at Mr. Ross's farm and Mr. Ross is good, he teaches him while he's working there. Now for a long time he wants to go to the farmers' school, we heard about it. If you can please send to me the papers for him—I can help him to fill in everything . . . to apply . . . . If you can just send me the papers . . . ."

Bray explained that he was not going to the capital, but north; but he would arrange to have particulars about the agricultural college sent. The figure in the army overcoat plunged into the darkness, bisected diagonally for a moment by the light cast by the hotel. Bray turned to the dining-room, where some men were eating and talking with the gusto of old friends getting together. The thud of the waiters' bare feet shook the boards; he ordered a half-bottle of wine and propped up, where he could glance at it, a report picked out at random from the file he was still carrying about with him. Already he was falling into the bachelor habit of reading while he ate. While he remembered, he made a note to send the schoolmaster an Oxford dictionary.

So that was starting all over again; he was half-amused, half self-contemptuous. The man was so desperately poor in everything—what was there that he didn't need? Olivia said, "Kindness is ridiculous." She had meant here; then. She had had to organize jumble sales so that the charitable white wives could provide a clinic for African children, while the mines were paying dividends of millions a year to shareholders in England. She had had to put on white gloves for opening charity bazaars; out of the newspaper pictures taken when they arrived in London in the sensation of their recall from the territory, had looked a civil servant and his lady disconcertingly like the class and kind of couple on whom white settlers had depended so long.

After dinner he went off to his room past Davy Jones' Locker and the flushed faces there—a large Englishman with the administrator's gait of a man eternally carrying papers under his arm.

He lay in a bed that, like nearly all hotel beds, was too small for him, and read. Mrs. Pilchey's clip-on bed lamp had a broken neck and he turned on the bulb in the ceiling. It shone at a point just between his eyes. He read through everything there was in the Education Department's file; very little, in terms of something to go on. In most places figures were not analysed properly, and the frequent "unforeseen circumstances" that caused a high percentage of failures, or the abandonment of modest experimental schemes, were never explained. When he turned out the light the silence was deep, deeper; as if the night measured the distance he already had come.

He spent his first week in Gala occupied with what he described in letters to England as housewifery. The house, vacated by an accountant declared redundant under the new system of administration, had no cook and no curtains. He stayed in the local hotel while word-of-mouth brought applicants for the post, and the Indian tailor consented to make the curtains. Mr. Joosab was distressed at Bray's choice of material, but Bray and Olivia had always liked the maroons and blacks, the oranges and browns, and the gnomic texts in Swahili or Gala printed on the cloth local women wrapped round themselves and their babies—he didn't have to bother with considerations of what was or was not considered suitable for a D.C.'s house, this time.

The broad main street that was Gala had been tarred along its high-cambered middle but the rose-tan earth remained in a wide border down either side, splotched, pocked, and sometimes blotted out in deep shadow from the mahogany trees that hung above it. Gala was an old place as colonial settlements go; and even before it became a British outpost, Tippo Tib had established one of his most southerly slave depots there—to the north of the village there was the site of his Arab fort. Walls had fallen down in the village but trees remained; too big to be hacked out of the way of the slave-caravan trail; too strong to be destroyed by fire when British troops were in the process of subduing the population; revered by several genera-

tions of colonial ladies, who succeeded in having a local by-law pro-
mulgated to forbid anyone chopping them down. Their huge grey
outcrops of root provided stands for bicycles and booths for traders
and craftsmen; the shoemaker worked there, and the bicycle and sew-
ing-machine repairer. There was a slave tree (the trade had been conducted under it as lately as a hundred years before) that the same
English ladies had had enclosed in a small paved area and railing,
with a plaque quoting Wilberforce. It was down in the part of the village where, Bray found, the beginnings of industry had started up
since he last saw the place. Young workers from the fish-meal plant
and lime works hung about there, now, playing dice and shedding a
litter of potato crisp packets.

His big figure in the grey linen bush jacket and trousers he had
found for himself in the capital moved busily back and forth across
the road from sun and shade in and out of the interior of the shops.
The familiar smells assailed him—calico, paraffin, millet, sacks of
dried *kapenta* with the tin scoop stuck among the musty little fish;
the old feel of grains of spilt sugar and maize meal gritted between
the soles of shoes and the cracked concrete floors. In the tailor's shop,
sweetness of cardamoms hanging about the bolts of cloth and shiny
off-cuts of lining. The same framed pictures of Edwardians with long
cigarette holders and shooting sticks; a photograph of Mweta in his
toga beside the old one of the Queen. Mr. Joosab and his son, Ahmed,
were almost the first people from the old days whom Bray spoke to.
(The hotel had changed hands; there were black clerks in the post office, now.) Joosab was a pale fat man in shirtsleeves, with a tape measure worn like an order over his waistcoat. His soft laugh was nearly
soundless; he stood there with Ahmed, who was thin, dark, and had
grown up—as Bray remembered the mother—with that obsessed,
slightly mad look that comes of having very black eyes with a cast.
"The Colonel, it's the Colonel, you have come back to us . . . ."
Joosab's bright gaze darted, brimmed and danced like an embarrassed girl's. "My second son, Ahmed . . . you don't remember the
Colonel (he was a small child, eh, Colonel) . . . Colonel Bray? Of
course you remember! The District Commissioner, and Mrs. Bray—
oh what a nice lady!"

The thick glossy straight hair seemed to rise and sink on the boy's
head in a speechless response of embarrassment.

"Well, the Colonel . . . my, we'll be glad to have you back. I've often said to my wife, we don't have a gentlemen like the Colonel, again! Oh Mr. Maitland, he came when you left, he was a nice gentlemen, oh yes. And then Mr. Carter, and then there was Mr. Welwyn-Jones. But not a long time, I think he was only here about fifteen month . . . oh the Colonel . . ."

"And how've you been, Mr. Joosab, how are things going?"

He was still laughing soundlessly, spreading his smooth hands like a member of a welcoming committee. "Oh *all right,* yes, I can say all right"—he suppressed a coquettish little shrug, as if he had almost let slip a secret— "of course things are a bit unsettled, business has dropped off a bit, oh that's only natural, of course, Colonel. I'm not complaining—you understand? Our community supports the government a hundred per cent. We are contributing to Party funds—last year more than five hundred pounds. And we have the assurance of the President—oh yes, we have had that. Of course a lot of people have gone—you know, the old Government people, all gone. Oh I know how they feel, I can imagine. Dr. Pirie and Mrs. Pirie, gone back to England, sold their place. He built a lovely house a few years ago, on the lake, when he retired, you know. But of course they don't want to stay now, naturally . . . . Why should they . . . Up in your house"—he meant the D.C.'s residence— " there's Mr. Aleke now, with his wife and seven or eight little children. Yes. The place looked perfect when you and Mrs. Bray were there, Colonel—the garden, it was wonderful! Mrs. Bray's garden. And what was the other lady— Mrs. Butterworth? Oh yes, what a nice lady. You know I made the first pair of ladies' slacks for her? I said, but Mrs. Butterworth, madam, I never made for ladies. But she was a lady who like to get what she want, you know. You can do it, she say, you can do it! And Mr. Playfair. He won the golf championship again this year. He's still here, and Mr. Le Roy, and the Andersons up at the club—Mr. Anderson's still the chairman of the committee, they're putting on a show there, this month. I think it's Mr. Parsifal again who arrange it, you know he's a very clever man—" He related all the details of the activities of the white community in which he had never had any part. "Oh there's quite a lot from the old days," he promised. "You'll see, Colonel—" It was not that he had forgotten that these were the people who had demanded that the Colonial Office have Bray removed, but that he remembered only too well—it was his way of dealing with events, to shield himself and others from danger by bowing in all directions at once.

Most of the white tradespeople in the village greeted Bray with professional cheerfulness overlaying a certain stony-facedness. They had not forgotten either; but someone would be getting his custom. He had no particular awareness of his "position" among them; the past in relation to Mweta and Edward Shinza and the country's future meant something to him, but the past in relation to his difficulties with the Colonial Service and the settlers was simply an outdated conflict in which each side had acted—fair enough—according to their convictions in a particular historical situation, a situation that no longer existed. Not objectively, and not for him; he had been away, and come back clear of it. The fact that he was sent to his old district did not seem of any particular significance to him except that it sensibly took advantage of the fact that here he knew the language and the people; he did not see himself as coming back to a place from which he had been driven out—of what relevance to the present was that sort of petty triumph?

But for the residents who had stayed behind, he had not come anew, but returned; he, about whom ten years ago they had held a public meeting in that same hotel where he was now staying, he, whom they had petitioned the Governor to remove from office. On the first Saturday morning in the village, he realized this; a bother, more than anything else. They came into town to do their shopping as they had always done and he moved, alone, among them. They greeted him, even stopped to talk, women with their baskets, or men with carriers of tinned beer hooked between thumb and forefinger, making use of the conversational conventions of the English background they shared with him, so that the first pause became the opportunity to say, "Well, Alcocks' won't keep a chicken for me if I don't hurry up and fetch it" or "Robert'll be cooling his heels outside the post office—I'd better be getting along," but they made him (not vain and therefore the least self-conscious of men) aware that they were *confronted* with him. He bore them no grudge whatever. Which, he realized with slightly exasperated amusement at himself and them, was insufferable, if it should be found out.

In a first letter to Gala, Olivia had written, "I suppose it was strange to see the old house!"—but he had not even gone so far as to take a walk up the road to the ugly residence that existed in his mind not as a place so much as an interior life hollowed out by experiences that had been dealt with there. One day he would go and see Mr. Aleke's "seven or eight" children playing in the garden, and tell Olivia about it.

As he went in and out of the Fisheagle Inn he was sometimes arrested, from the veranda, by the sight of the lake. The sign of the lake: a blinding strip of shimmer, far away beyond the trees, or on less ·clear days, a different quality in the haze. For a moment his mind emptied; the restless glitter of the lake, the line of a glance below a lowered eyelid—for it was not really the lake at all that one saw, but a trick of the distance, the lake's own bright glare cast up upon the heated atmosphere, just as the vast opening out of pacing water to the horizon, once you got to its bush-hairy shores, was not really the open lake itself at all, but (as the map showed) only the southernmost tip of the great waters that spread up the continent for six hundred miles and through four or five countries. It was then, just for a moment, that this symbol of the infinity of distance, carrying the infinity of time with which it was one, released his mind from the time of day and he was at once himself ten years ago and himself now, one and the same. It was a pause not taken account of. He went on down the veranda steps, intent on buying some bit of equipment for his house.

He was able to move in by the second weekend. Of course he had presented himself to the people at the *boma*. He'd had a talk with Aleke, the first African District Commissioner—but they didn't call them D.C.s any more, they were known as Provincial Officers. And he'd seen Sampson Malemba, the local Education Officer, who happened to be an old friend, principal of the African school when Bray was in office. Aleke was just the sort of "new African" the settlers would dislike most: fat, charming, his Mweta tunic hitched up by solid buttocks, he spoke fluent informal English, lolled behind his desk like a schoolboy, and was seen chewing a piece of sugar-cane while having his shoes shined under the trees. The settlers were at home with the conventional pompousness of half-educated Africans —men in undertaker's suits, bespectacled, throat-clearing; they recognized the acceptable marks of civilization in this caricature of an image of themselves, even if they were beer-drinking farmers in crumpled shorts. It remained to be seen if Aleke were to be efficient, into the bargain; from the little Bray had heard, it was likely. He said cheerfully he didn't know what he could do for Bray—he had been asked to "do everything necessary to facilitate," etc., and it was up to Bray to tell him what that might be. "Could I have somewhere to work— that's the main thing." Aleke found this very funny. "I mean can you spare me an office and a share in a typist—I'm sure you're short-staffed." "An office! Naturally! But the typist isn't very pretty, I'm afraid. I'll introduce you." He rang a bell and in came a typical second-grade male clerk with an old man's bony back and an adolescent face drained of vitality by home-study courses. "Mr. Letanka. He will be helping you all he can." When the clerk had gone, Aleke was still amused: "So there you are. But I have applied for a really efficient and beautiful secretary, first priority, so maybe our standard will improve."

Aleke urged him to get settled into his house before "we get down to anything serious"; it was an amiable enough way of postponing the problem of not knowing what to do with him.

The moving in didn't amount to much. The various purchases he had made during the week stood dumped about in the living-room. Mr. Joosab had been good enough to send his son and one of his daughters over to put up the curtains. Stretched across the windows they looked like tablecloths; they didn't meet. And when they were drawn back they sagged skimpily. He didn't know what exactly was wrong; he thought of Olivia and smiled. He had a young servant called Mahlope, which meant in Gala, "the last one of all," who was already wearing the long white apron to buy which he had at once requested money the moment he was engaged. He had covered the concrete floors of the house with the inevitable thick layer of red polish in preparation for Bray's arrival and the two men spent the Saturday afternoon arranging—with sure instinct for the placing of one of the government issue morris chairs, the utilization of an old brass picture hanger to hold the bathroom mirror high enough for Bray to see himself shave—the unchanging white-bachelor household that was as old as settlement itself. Mahlope put a tattered embroidered doily under the leather frame that held a picture of Venetia with a blurred little mummy, her new baby; and set down the whisky, gin, a bent opener and glasses in their permanent position on what was listed in the house inventory as the "occasional" table. Already the kitchen smelled of paraffin, on which the refrigerator ran, and the living-room of flea powder, for a house that stood empty for more than a few days always became a playground for fleas, and Bray had had his ankles bitten through his socks while simply visiting the house.

He had begun to wake up early again, as he used to do in Africa. The servant was about, chanting under his breath, from half-past five. Bray ate his first Sunday breakfast in the garden on a morning scented with woodsmoke. It came back to him—all, immediate, as with the scent of a woman with whom one has made love. The minute sun-birds whirred in the coarse trumpets of flowers. Delicate wild pigeons called lullingly, slender in flight and soft of voice, unrecognizable as the same species as the bloated hoarse creatures who waddle in European cities. In perfect stillness, small dead leaves hung from single threads of web, winking light. A tremendous fig tree was perhaps several trees, twisted together in a multiple trunk twenty feet up and then spreading wide and down again in a radius of interlaced branches. Little knobbly figs fruited all over it, borne directly on the old, hard wood of the trunk. Skinny wasps left them and fell into the jam. He felt an irrational happiness, like faint danger. He dragged a rickety trestle table ringed with the marks of potted plants, under his tree, and wrote letters and read the papers Olivia had sent, sybaritic in the luxury of being alone.

But the afternoon was long. In the air were the echoes of other people's activity; the distant plock of tennis, the swirl of arriving and departing cars at the other houses in the road, the sky ringing like a glass with the strike of church bells distorted aurally as the lake, from the hotel veranda, was distorted visually. There was a kind of thickening of the background silence, a vague uproar of Sunday enjoyment from the direction of the African township away over to the east. He thought he would look around there; he hadn't, yet. Of course, he had known it very well when he was D.C., he had spent a lot of time down there; too much, for some people's liking. But he knew that it had changed since then, grown; and there was a whole new housing scheme and a hostel for the industrial workers.

Raw red roads led off through the trees. People were strolling, pushing their bicycles as they talked; women held their children against their skirts as he passed, boys laughed and threw mango pits at each other, there were little groups of religious sects holding meetings under the trees, young couples in their best clothes and old men hauling wood or charcoal on sleds, Sunday no different from any other day, for them. The bright little new houses looked stranded in the mud; the forest had been cleared for them. There were some trampled-looking patches of cassava and taro and a beached, derelict car or two. The houses had electric light and children were playing a game that seemed to consist of hitting the telephone poles with sticks. They yelled defiantly and gaily at the white man in the car.

He saw the hostel on the rise that had been a kind of buffer, hiding the black village from the white; a modern, institutional building around which stalls and hawkers' carts had collected like hovels without the palace walls. But he turned instead down into the old town that he remembered, and plunged along the unmade streets among close shacks, donkeys, dogs, and people. The old town was filthy and beautiful; in this low-lying ground palms grew, giving their soaring proportion to the huddle, and lifting the skyline to their pure and lazy silhouette. The place stank of beer, ordure, and smoke. The most wretched hovel had its setting of sheeny banana leaves, with a show of plenty in the green candelabra of pendant fruit, and its pawpaw trees as full of ripening dugs as some Indian goddess. Green grew and tangled everywhere out of the muck, rippled and draped over rotting wood and rusted iron. Romantic poverty; he would rather live here, with the rats under the palm trees, than up on the rise in those mean, decent cubes already stained with bare earth: that was because he would never have to live in either. A little naked boy waved with one hand, clutching his genitals with the other. An old man took off his hat in greeting. Bray knew no one and knew them all. There was an anonymity of mutual acceptance that came to him not at all in England and hardly ever in Europe—in Spain, perhaps, one market morning among the butting bodies and smiles of busy people whose language he didn't speak. It wasn't losing oneself, it was finding one's presence so simply acknowledged that one forgot that outwardly one moved as a large, pink-faced Englishman, light-eyed and thick-eyebrowed behind the magnification of glasses, encased yet again, as in a bubble of another atmosphere, in the car. He drove slowly round with unselfconscious pleasure, not quite sure where he was going yet feeling that the turns he took were familiar ones, the way past the houses of people he once visited or knew. And then he came out at the nameless stretch of communal ground where the bus sheds were, and goats sought discarded mango skins, and women and children sat contentedly under the trees.

It was here, in this space to which people drifted on a Sunday, that the drumming came from, the drumming he had heard over in the town. There were little shops blaring jazz, with open verandas on which men stood or sat drinking. In the open ground in front of one was a wall-less thatched shelter beneath which tall drums were mounted over charcoal embers. When Bray's car came to a stop, it was in the middle of a pause; a young boy was using a goat's-skin bellows to flush the embers into heat to make the drums taut. Only one drum was keeping a dull beat going so that the rhythm could be taken up at any point, at any time. The undertone thudded gently through the chatter round about and the jazz. Bray just sat in the car in the midst of it all. Babies broke away and staggered onto the clearing, to be pursued and snatched up by older children. Others cried or were suckled. The women talked absorbedly and gazed about, alert to the children, but they had the smiling air of women who are spectators of their men. Some of the men were drinking, others stood together, fallen away from the centre of their activity. Somebody got on his bicycle and rode away; someone else arrived. The undertone of the drum was counterpointed by a louder beat, breaking over it from another drum; the drummer, putting an ear low, was not satisfied with the quality of the resonance and the counterpoint died away. The drummers were absorbed in tending the drums and did not speak to or look at the drinkers or anybody else. Their faces and hair were powdered with dust. They ordered the boy about and his strong pointed elbows moved in and out over the bellows; red eyes opened and closed in the charcoal. But with the brief counterpoint that was taken up and died away again, a middle-aged man with clips on his trousers had begun to tread, alone, in the clearing. Another joined him, and then another. Slowly, what had gone slack between the drinkers and the idlers was pulled close again; the drums were drawn in, the men were drawn in; there was an ever-mounting yet steady and serene jumble of movement and drums, shuffle, pause, and beat, that in all its counterpoint of sound and movement was yet the sum

D*

of one beat, experienced as neither sound nor movement, the beat of a single heart in a single body. It was not orgiastic or ecstatic, but just a Sunday afternoon dance; Bray lifted his long legs out of the car and stood leaning an arm on the boot, among the onlookers. People seemed to know who he was. A remark passed between them now and again; he asked a question or made an observation, as one does, out of proximity. An old man confirmed that the bars were fairly new. A young man waited for the old one to move on and then dismissed all that he had said: this bar was three years old. And the dance was an old-style thing that the old-fashioned people did. If I were you I'd be dancing, Bray said. The young man looked derisive and a woman laughed. The stamp and beat came up through Bray's feet and theirs as if they were all standing on deck over an engine room.

A black Mercedes with the flourish of new officialdom about it drew an admiring acknowledgement of turning heads. It had stopped short, suddenly, in the middle of people. Bray was surprised by the approach of one of the white-collared, dark-suited passengers, who had jumped out and was hurrying over with long strides before which way was made for him. "Are you all right?" Before Bray could answer, the face of the mayor was thrust out of the back window of the car, and the voice called across in English, "Have you lost yourself, Colonel? Can we help?"

Bray had met the mayor a few days before, with Sampson Malemba. "No, no, just passing the time." And then he thought it polite to go over to the car. "Thanks all the same." "Sure you're okay?" The mayor, a large man with his hair parted in the centre over his unmistakably Gala face, was dressed for some official occasion; or maybe he was simply enjoying paying visits in his handsome car, accompanied by relatives or friends dressed in their best.

Little boys raced behind the car while it swayed off gracefully. People were grinning at Bray, as one who had brought them distinction. Someone said, "That's the biggest car in Gala," and the old man, who had appeared again, said, "The mayor, you know who it is? The mayor!" The women giggled at his slowness. "He knows, he knows." There was no envy of the mayor, with his splendid car manifesting his favoured position; only pride.

It was still light when Bray got back to the house and he wandered about the garden and then out across the bush perhaps in response to some faint promptings of habit reaching out from the life in Wiltshire —he and Olivia exercised themselves as regularly as city people did their dogs. The bats were beginning to fly over the golf-course and the club-house was already swelling orange with lamp-shaded light. Sunday evening: most of the white community were there, drinking after sport. He had put up his name for membership, again; the secretary's face, when he filled in the form, was flat with the effort to disguise astonishment. But it was not a gesture of bravado, let alone a desire to rub his countrymen's noses in the "triumph" of his return. He had always done things whose directness was misunderstood; it was not even the "hand of friendship" he was extending—simply an acceptance that he was living in Gala again, among these people, and did not regard them as outcast any more than he had shared their view, in other times, that the Galaians were beyond the pale of the community. When Olivia came, she might want to use the club swimming pool, anyway; the only one in the district. One had to make use of what there was. And then, of course, since Independence, the club had made the usual gesture of such dying institutions; the mayor had been made a member, *ex officio,* and so had Aleke, as P.O. —not that he supposed they had ever put a foot in the place.

There were thirty or forty cars parked under the trees; an Alsatian dog barked behind the closed windows of one. Excited by the darkening twilight, white children shrieked as they ran about the lawns. The building was adaptable; could be a real asset. As Bray went up the steps and heads were lifted here and there at the veranda tables outside the bar, he was thinking that it would be perfectly adequate for an adult education centre. In the smaller rooms the trade unions could hold night classes for apprentices, Sampson Malemba could run literacy courses, and the big dining-room could serve as a hall for performances by school choirs and so on.

He greeted a few people he knew. A beautiful blonde with a child on her hip and one by the hand stood patiently at the reception desk while her husband and another man, in club blazers, could not tear themselves away from the high emotion of companionship that comes from victory on court or course. Bray begged pardon past them, but they did not see him—except the children, whose blue eyes, wide in the moments before sleep, followed him to the notice board. His name was up, all right, but there was no seconder's beside it. Broken bursts of singing sounded like a party going on; the repetition of the opening bars on a piano made him realize that it must be a rehearsal in progress: the theatrical production Joosab had mentioned.

He began that week to tackle a programme he had worked out for himself. Long talks with Malemba made it clear that it would be senseless to base a report and recommendations on existing schools and available figures for children of school-going age. The province was huge; a whole European country could fit into it. The last census was seven years old, and had scarcely pretended to accuracy. You couldn't simply divide off the map into suitable chunks and allot a certain number of new schools to each, such-and-such a number of educational facilities to the square hundred miles. Sampson Malemba wanted a large new secondary school at Gala itself; but what was needed was a careful coordination of educational facilities over the whole province, from primary to school-leaving at least at the English O level, with provision for late starters and others, not suited by potential or opportunity to academic education, to be diverted to technical colleges of an elementary kind. "How many children in the primary schools of the province can be expected to be at secondary school level in, say, five years? Enough to fill the places in a new secondary school? More than we'll have places for? So many that it would be better to have a new secondary school somewhere else?" But Sampson Malemba couldn't answer that; "Exactly. It will depend on how many new primary schools we need and can get." And that in turn depended not only upon how many children were in school, but how many could be in school. "And how many teachers we can hope to claim from the general pool." "Ah, that's the trouble." Malemba was always happiest to agree. But Bray had decided that if he himself was to be any use at all, he must combine a down-to-earth acceptance of limitations with a certain obstinacy; he must assume they would be overcome.

He set out to go through the whole province, district by district and village by village, visiting schoolmasters and headmen and collecting the facts. He intended to make his own census of children of school-going age and youths, already in some form of occupation, who were still malleable enough to benefit from something more than a smattering of literacy. He didn't see how he could begin to consider what ought to be done next until this was done. He began with Gala itself and its satellite villages, and meant to move out in a wider radius each day, each week, until he had covered the whole province from the lake to the Bashi Flats. He would return home every night so long as that was possible, then, as the circles carried him further from the centre, he would spend each night at a point convenient for the range of the next day's inquiry. Malemba went with him round about Gala itself; it was all rather like a school inspection, with the inevitable assembly of children, the anxious formality of teachers—and at the end of the visit a sense that politeness had dissipated any real contact with the giggling, expectant faces of the children, turning blindly to the sun of attention, and the half-educated, poorly paid teachers garrulous or tongue-tied with their inadequacies. He came home each day that first week with a sense of the deadness of what was passing for education in these bare schoolhouses with their red earth playground stamped hard by the children's naked feet. The children were squirming with life and the cold grease of third-rate instruction by rote staled in their minds, day by day. He wrote in his notebook: *If all M's government can do is extend dingy light of knowledge we brought, not much benefit.* He felt that *he* himself was not qualified to find the radical solution that was needed; neither was the Ministry of Education, with its advisers, the capable English don who had been headmaster of a famous public school thirty years before, and the American on loan from a Midwest university's African Studies programme. They were all men for whom the structure of education was based on their own educational background and experience; even he himself, who had lived in Africa so long, tended to think of needs in relation to the educational pattern familiar to him, and to fail to do so in terms of the child for whom what was taught at school did not have the confirmation of being part of his general cultural pattern at home. What was needed was perhaps someone with a knowledge of the latest basic techniques of learning. Someone who could cut through the old assumptions that relied so heavily on a particular cultural background, and concentrate on the learning process itself. That should be freed to form its own correlation to a relevant culture. "Write a letter to a friend describing a trip abroad with your aunt"—he thought often of the schoolmaster at Matoko.

To get to the fishing communities farther up the lake he left his car at the fish-freezing plant at the southern tip and went by water, hitch-hiking, more or less, on the cumbersome, home-made boats of the independent fishermen. Some of them were traders rather than fishermen, really; they went where the *kapenta* were running, and then sold them by the eighty-pound sack wherever on the lake they were scarce. Boundaries were ignored by these boats; they put in wherever there was a likely village, and the men aboard spoke Swahili as well as Gala—Swahili had come down, hundreds of years ago, from the East Coast and was the *lingua franca* of the lake, even though the inland people, so far south, did not speak it. Locked in the middle of the continent, the lake villagers had something of the natural worldliness of seaport inhabitants, and the sense of individualistic independence of those whose range takes in the tilting, glittering horizon forever receding before the boat. They laughed and joked and talked fish prices around Bray; his Gala was so good again, now that he was speaking it every day, that he could take part in the talk and even pick up the Swahilisms that crept into it. Hour after hour he sat on his berth of sacks of dried *kapenta*, exchanging his Karel I's for their pipe tobacco, the boat dipping and lifting over the immense glare of the lake. His English face turned stiff and red and then, as if some secretion of pigment, that had ceased functioning in the years he had been away, began to be produced by his body again, his arms and hands and face became richly burnished and the face in the shaving mirror was a holiday face. No matter how animated the talk was, the voices were lost out on the lake as completely as a dropped coin ingested by the waters. To him the scape—radiance of water and sky, a kind of explosion of the two elements in an endless flash—was beautiful, with the strange grip of sensuosity of place, of something he had never expected to see again. *This* was it. One couldn't remember anything so physical. It couldn't be recaptured by cerebration; it had to be experienced afresh. The fish eagles gave their banshee whistles, a sound from the dark side of the sun. Now and then the water boiled with the tails of churning shoals, rock-bream feeding on *kapenta*, tiger fish snapping at rock-bream, fish eagles and gulls hovering, swooping and snatching. To his companions, the place was a condition—weather, luck (with the fish), distance to the next objective. His mind idled; did this add another meaning to the theory of aesthetics that held that beauty was an incidental product of function? Beauty could also be another way of reading circumstances in which a function—in this case fishing for a living—took place. One of the men put a finger to the right side of his nose and cleared the left with a sharp snort, into the lake. The water, that same exquisite pale element through which the fish shone, bore the snot flushed efficiently away.

On shore, there were whole communities of several thousand people where the children didn't go to school, just as (Aleke complained when Bray got back to Gala) the men didn't pay taxes. "While you're about it, up there, perhaps you could think of something we can do about that." Aleke spoke in the dreamy humour of a man slightly dazed with problems. "The government tells me that after the miners, those fellows are the biggest money-earners in the country, but they don't want to know about income tax. All you can get out of them is that they've always paid hut tax. Income tax is something for white men to pay. Must they become white men just because we've got our own government? Good God, man, what sort of thing is this independence!" Thinking of the fishermen, Bray laughed rather admiringly. "Well, they're self-employed, illiterate, and extremely shrewd—quite a combination for an administration to beat." "I mean, how can you assess their earnings? It's not a matter of keeping two sets of books. It's all in here"—Aleke poked a finger at his temple—"what auditor can get at that?" "Organize them in cooperatives," Bray said, still amused.

"Well, there is the big trawler company."

"Yes, but that's a foreign company, the men who work on the trawlers are just employees. I mean the people who fish and trade for themselves. Oh, it'll come, I suppose."

"Those people? They don't want to hear from us what's good for them!"

"Never mind, Aleke, the president favours free enterprise." They both smiled; this was the way in which Mweta gave poker-faced reassurance to the mining companies, without offering direct affront to members of the government who feared economic colonialism.

"D'you bring any fish?" Aleke asked, shoving papers into drawers; Bray had walked in as he was going home for lunch.

"Didn't think about it! But I'll remember next time. What does your wife like? I saw a magnificent perch."

"Oh she's from town, she wouldn't touch anything out of the lake.

But I won't have the kids the same. I told her, they must eat the food that's available, there where they live. So she says what's wrong with meat from the supermarket?"

"I'll bring you a perch, next time."

"Yes, a nice fish stew, with peppers, I like that." He had taken up a nailfile and was running the point under the pale nails of his black hands as if he were paring a fruit. "I'm full of carbon. I have to do my own stencils, even. I shouldn't really go home to eat today, the work's up over my head, man. Honestly, I just feel like driving all the way and kidnapping a decent secretary from the Ministry." Grumbling relaxedly, he left the offices with Bray; one of his small sons had come down on a tricycle to meet him and was waiting outside, nursing a toe that had sprung a bright teardrop of blood: while they examined the hurt the drop rolled off the dusty little foot like a bead of mercury. The boy had ridden against the low box-hedge of Christ-thorn that neatly bordered the *boma*'s entrance. All *bomas* in the territory had Christ-thorn hedges, just as they had a morris chair to each office and a standard issue of inkpots. "Look at that," Aleke said in Gala. "It's gone deep. What a plant."

"Why not have it dug out, get rid of it," said Bray.

Aleke looked uncertain a moment, as if he could not remember why this was unlikely. Then he came to himself and said in English, "You're damned right. I want this place cleared."

"You could have mesembryanthemums—ice-plant," Bray said. But Aleke had the tricycle, hanging by a handlebar, in his one hand, and was holding his child under the armpit with the other, urging him along while he hopped exaggeratedly, "Ow, ow!"

You had only to leave a place once and return to it for it to become home. At the house Bray came through the kitchen and asked Mahlope to fetch his things from the car; Mahlope had a friend sitting there who rose at once. Bray acknowledged the greeting and then was suddenly aware of some extraordinary tension behind him. His passage had caused a sensation; he made an involuntary checking movement, as if there were something shocking pinned on his back. The face was staring at him, blindly expectant, flinching from anticlimax. The anticlimax hung by a hair; then it was knocked aside: "Kalimo!" The man started to laugh and gasp, saved by his name. The face was one from another life, Bray's cook of the old time, in the

D.C.'s house. The salutations went on for several minutes, and then
Kalimo was in perfect possession of the occasion. He said in English,
"I'm here today, yesterday, three day. No, the boy say *Mukwayi* go
Tuesday, come back Friday. I'm ready." Bray's eyes followed into the
labyrinth of past commonplace the strings of Kalimo's apron, tied
twice under his arms, in the way he had always affected. "How did
you find me?"

"Festus he send me. He send me say, Colonel he coming back, one
month, two month, then go to Gala. I'm greet my wife, I'm greet my
sons. They say where you go? No, I'm go to Gala. Colonel him back.
No, I go. I must go."

They began to talk in Gala, which was not Kalimo's mother tongue
—since he came from the South where he had first begun to work for
the Brays many years ago—but which, like Bray, he had learned
when he moved with the Brays to Gala. They exchanged family news;
Bray fetched the picture of Venetia's baby. The pleasurable excitement of reunion hung over his solitary lunch, with Kalimo bringing in
the food and being detained to talk.

But later in the afternoon, when he had sat for an hour or two writing up his notes on the lake communities, he came to the problem of
Mahlope: what was to be done about Mahlope? Kalimo had taken
over the household as of right; Bray felt the old fear of wounding
someone whom circumstances put in his power. It was out of the
question that he should send Kalimo away. He belonged to Kalimo;
Kalimo had come more than a thousand miles, out of retirement in
his village, to claim him. The thought appalled him: to cook and
clean for him as if his were the definitive claim on Kalimo's life.

He went into the kitchen where Kalimo, hearing him begin to move
about, was making tea. Bray had seen Mahlope through the living-
room window—put out to grass, literally: swinging at it with a
home-honed scythe made of a bit of iron fencing. "Kalimo, did you
talk to Mahlope about the job?" He spoke in Gala. "*Mukwayi?*" "I
took on Mahlope to look after the house, you see."

Kalimo made the deep hum with which matters were settled. He
had got older; he drew out these sounds now, like an old man in the
sun. "Mahlope will be for the garden, and to clean the car. I am your
cook. And he has the washing to do. We always had a small boy for
the outside work."

"Yes, but I'm not the D.C. any more, you must remember. And I'm here on my own. This isn't the big house, with a whole family. I don't need more than one person to look after me."

Kalimo swilled out the teapot with boiling water, measured the tea into it, poured on the water, and replaced the lid, carefully turning it so that the retaining lip was in the right place.

"One person to cook and wash and everything—just for me."

"Does *Mukwayi* want cake with tea, or biscuit?"

Of course, Kalimo would have baked cakes, put the household on a proper footing, against his return. He made Bray feel the insolence of teaching a man his own business, of so much as bringing up the subject.

Kalimo carried the tray into the living-room. As he put it down he said, "I have always looked after you. Cooking, washing, outside—it's the same for me."

Bray said, "You are not tired?"

He had sat down at his table. Kalimo looked down at him, and smiled. "And you? *You* are not tired."

"All right. I'll explain to Mahlope. We'll keep him until we can find him another job. You can make use of him—the garden, whatever you think."

After dinner he wrote to Olivia. *Well, you won't have any doubts about how I'm being looked after from now on; Kalimo has turned up. He heard through the grape-vine—took him a month to get here, by bus and on foot. I'm embarrassed but suppose I'm lucky. The bad old good days come back.*

Shinza. Edward Shinza. Even the occurrence of Kalimo was a reminder. He ought to go and see him; it was easy to assume to himself that he thought of it often; he did not, in fact. The work he was doing, unchecked by distraction or interruption, filled his mind. In the capital, work would have been compressed into a few hours a day, jostled by other demands and the company of friends. But now although he was often conscious of being alone—alone at night, with a Christmas bee dinning at the light, and the bare furniture taking on the waiting-room watchfulness of a solitary's surroundings; alone in the garden, reading letters and papers at his table under the fig tree —the interviews, the paper-work, were a preoccupation that expanded to take up the days and long evenings. Dando had just writ-

ten again and asked among other things, whether he had seen Shinza
—Dando's writing was so difficult to read and covered so closely the
sheets of thin paper that his were the sort of letters one put aside to
read more attentively another time. Roly would have gone off with a
bottle to get drunk with Shinza long ago, by now. He throve on dissatisfactions, paradox and irony. He would have made himself welcome with a man at his own funeral, if that were a possible occasion
for friendship and solidarity. Whenever Bray saw himself coming into
Shinza's company once again, he felt suddenly that there would be
nothing to say: he was brought back by Mweta, now he was working
for Mweta. It was better to concentrate on such practical matters as
the possibility of resuscitating the old woodworking and shoemaking
workshop in the town and expanding it to become a sort of modest
trades school. He discussed this with Malemba. The Education Department had abolished these rural workshops on the principle that
everyone was to get a proper education now; the black man was no
longer to be trained just sufficiently to do the white man's odd jobs
for him. "But what about mechanics and plumbers, if you're going to
raise the standard of living? And you're still going to need village
carpenters and shoemakers for a long, long time in communities like
this one where people haven't yet completely made the changeover to
a money economy and buying their needs in the stores. If we can
train people in crafts that will give them a living, we'll have *some* alternative to the drift to the towns. It's a better idea than labour
camps, eh?" Malemba, Bray saw, would be glad to have the suggestion come from him; Malemba himself thought it unrealistic for the
government rural workshops to have been closed, but did not wish it
to be thought, in educational circles in the capital, that he was a
backward provincial when it came to demanding higher education
for the people. Malemba was not a sycophant but he needed a little
stiffening of confidence; it was one of the small satisfactions that Bray
had set himself to find worth while, to see that through their working
together, Malemba was beginning to gain it.

Yet he said to Aleke, "I'd like to look in on Edward Shinza one of
these days." He was in Aleke's house—his own old house—on a Saturday afternoon: there was no exchange of invitations for drinks and
dinners between officials as there had been when officialdom was
white, but Aleke had said, "Why don't you come over to my place?"

and so clearly meant the open invitation that Bray had taken it up as casually and genuinely. The radio, as always, was playing loudly on the veranda. Some of the seven children pushed toy cars through tracks scratched in the earth of the tubs where Olivia had once grown miniature orange trees.

"The road's very bad that way, they tell me," Aleke said, lazily, though not exactly without interest.

Bray realized that he had brought up the subject because, although he would go and see Shinza openly, would tell Mweta so himself—indeed Mweta would expect him to seek out Shinza—he had some cautious reluctance to have Aleke reporting that he had visited Shinza. It should be established that it was not a matter of any interest to anyone except himself.

Mrs. Aleke brought tea and was sent away to fetch beer instead; she tried to clear the veranda of children, but Aleke was one of those plump, muscular men whose self-confidence, apparently made flesh, exerts a tactile attraction over women and children. His small sons and daughters ran back to press against his round spread thighs. He spoke of his wife as if she were not there. "She's a woman who can't get children to listen. The same with the chickens. She chases them one way, they go the other."

"They're naughty." She looked helplessly and resentfully at the children.

"We used to hear *my* mother's voice." He fondled the children; it was easy for him. When he had had enough he would pick them off himself like burrs. She said to Bray, "And your wife is coming here? This place's dead. There is nothing in the shops, I wish I could get away to town, honestly."

But she was drawn, like the children, to her husband, though she did not quite touch him. He shooed them all away, just as easily, with a gesture of demanding air.

Bray felt a small rankling in himself for having put his acquaintance with Aleke momentarily on a footing of caution. Why should Aleke even think of him in terms of political manoeuvre? Telling Mweta what he thought was one thing; anything that might be construed as political action was another, and something he set himself outside from the beginning of his return. This disinterest was only confirmed by the right to look up an old friend, whoever he might be.

The unease—living alone one became too self-regarding—had the effect of making his plans turn out to take into account the Bashi Flats —Shinza's area. He went off one morning, meaning to go through the mountains where the iron-ore mine was, on the way, and to take a week over it. He remembered that Shinza liked cheroots, and called in at the *boma* as he left Gala; there was a new box in the desk Aleke had allotted him. The office door opened on someone who had been about to open it from the other side—a young white woman stood with her hands, palm open, drawn back at the level of her breasts. He smiled politely and then saw that she knew him; it was Rebecca Edwards, of Vivien's house in the capital. While he rummaged for the cigars, she explained that she had come up to work for Aleke. "Roly said he'd written to you, so I told Vivien not to bother." Of course there had been something in Dando's letter—an illegible name. "Was there anything I could have done for you?"

"Oh no, you know how they are down there. The whole network has to be alerted everytime somebody moves."

He left a good-bye message with her, for Aleke. "He must be triumphant. He's been threatening to storm the Ministry and carry off a secretary."

"I came quietly," the girl said, with her good chap smile.

It had rained in the night and the elephant grass was matted with brilliant dew. He could hear his tyres cutting the first tread of the day into the wet packed sand on the road; his blunted sense of smell revived to something of the animal's keen nose. Bamboo, rocks, lichens—they stood out fresh as a rock-painting doused with water. Ten miles or so from Gala he picked up a young man who was trudging along with a cardboard suitcase. There were other people here and there on the road, women with bundles and pots, barefoot country people criss-crossing the forest and the grass in the ordinary course of their daily lives as clerks and shoppers move about the streets of a town, but this man in shirt-sleeves with new shoes spattered with mud was, at a glance, outside this activity: Bray stopped just ahead of him, and he got into the car without a word. "I'm going to the mine—that direction. How far're you going?" "That will be all right."

The presence in the car changed the mood of the morning; the sensuous pleasure of it sank back. The sunlight was empty upon a heavily charged object: the man breathed quietly, his lips closed with a small sound now and then on something he had not said aloud, and Bray saw, out of the corner of his eye, curly lashes slow-blinking and a line of sickness or strain marking the coarse cheek. His trousers were very clean and had the concave and convex lines of having been folded small in a suitcase. Once he took the ball-point pen out of his shirt-pocket and clicked the point in and out in a beautiful, matt-black hand.

Bray did not know whether the youngster was merely paralysed by the social proximity of a white man—so often the old dependencies, the unformulated resentments, the spell in which even the simplest of confrontations had been held so long, struck dumb—or whether he did not want to speak or be spoken to. Yet his presence was extraordinarily oppressive. Bray tried Gala; the young man said, without response, "I am returning home." How long had he been in town? "Two months and seventeen days." Bray did not want an interrogation; the man accepted a cigarette and Bray let the motion of the car and the focus of the passing road contain them dreamily.

The iron-ore mine was a purplish-red gash in the foothills before the pass. A sandcastle mountain of the same colour had been thrown up beside it, bare of the green skin of bush and grass that hid this gory earth on the hills. A new road led to it; on a nearby slope, a settlement was drawn and small figures were set down here and there, moving thinly. As the car came nearer they became the demonic figures of miners everywhere, faces streaked with lurid dirt under helmets, gumboots clogged with clay—the dank look of men who daily come back from the grave.

"I'm going to call in on someone who has a place about three miles on . . . ?"

"Yes sir."

Bray had thought he would get off at the mine; that was what was understood—but it didn't matter. "Just tell me when we get near your village." The young man heavily waved a hand to suggest an infinite distance, or indifference. They drove to the cattle ranch that had been remote fifteen years ago, when George Boxer settled there. Now there were a mine and telephone wires, over the hill. Boxer was still there, still wearing immaculately polished leather leggings, and attended by three Afghan hounds lean and wild in locks of matted hair. Boxer was one of those men whose sole connection with the world is achieved through a struggle with nature. The affairs of men did not engage his mind. Men themselves, white or black, had a reality for him only insofar as they were engaged with him in that struggle. Whether the man who searched with him for a lost heifer or worked with him to repair a fence was black or white was not a factor: the definitive situation was that of two men, himself and another, in conflict with dry rot in a fence-post, or with the marauding leopard who, too, was after the heifer. He had not joined in the settlers' hue and cry against Bray ten years ago for the same reason that he hadn't joined the exodus of settlers with the coming of independence: it was not that he had no feelings about colour, but that he had no communion with human beings of any colour. Circumstances—Bray's circumstances, then—had made Boxer look like a friend simply because he was indifferent to being an enemy, but Bray had always known that this appearance had no more meaning in its way than that other, physical, appearance of Boxer's—he wore the clothes, maintained the manners and household conventions of his public-school background not as if these were the manifestations of a place in a highly evolved society, but as if they were the markings, habits, and lair with which, unconscious of them (like any hare or jackal), he had been born.

Bray was directed down from the house to one of the cattle camps to find Boxer. While they were talking, looking at Boxer's two fine bulls that he had bred himself, Bray forgot his passenger. Boxer began to walk Bray up to the house past the car: "There's someone I'm giving a lift." Boxer glanced at the passenger, swept aside the pause—"I'll get something sent down to him. You'll have lunch, of course." But Bray insisted that tea or a drink was all he could stay for. They went into the living-room-cum-library that Boxer had panelled in the local mahogany; it was dimly like a headmaster's study, although the reference books were agricultural. The tea-tray had a silver inscription, the inherited English furniture was set about as Bray now remembered the room. They talked about the mine. "Any chance of a find on your property? I suppose you've had it prospected?" Boxer took a can of beer out of a cabinet filled with tarnished decanters. "I don't have to worry. There's nothing. The Company's gone over every inch. At one time I had it all planned—there'd be a vein here; how much I'd be paid out; the twenty thousand acres I'd had my eye on to buy down on the Bashi Flats. Kept me amused many nights. Awake, anyway."

The books on cattle breeding had pushed the *Mort d'Arthur,* the *Iliad* and Churchill's memoirs to the top shelves but there were book-club novels and *The Alexandria Quartet* in paperback accessible among the farming journals, and some seedpods and a giant snail-shell lying among rifle cartridges on a tray. —Bray remembered George Boxer's wife, a black-haired woman with green eyes, pretty until she smiled on little, stained, cracked teeth. They had had a son; just entered Sandhurst, Boxer said, as if reminded of something he hadn't thought of lately.

"Why the Bashi?" Bray asked. "I shouldn't have thought it was the place for cattle."

"No, no, that's the point—it's a lot of nonsense about the low altitude and so on. I've gone into the whole business thoroughly for ten years, I've collected sample pasture, recorded water supplies, collected every kind of tick there is all over this country. And you can take my word, there are *no* fewer tick-borne diseases up here than on the Flats, it's exactly the same problem, and the natural pasture is infinitely better. If the water-conservation scheme goes ahead—the flood-water diversion one, I mean—I think one wouldn't have to supplement feed at all, not even in August-November, before the rains. You could keep your pasture going right round the year. And you'd have no problem about watering your cattle. You see, at the moment, when the floods recede, everything drains away quickly to the south."

"But I've seen ground water there right through the dry season."

"No, no, you haven't. Not clean water. Swamp soup, that's all. You can't go through the winter on that. That's why you get the big cattle migration every year, and that's how foot-and-mouth has spread, every time there's been an outbreak. Pick it up on the Angolan border and trek it back to the Flats in November." He drank beer and tea indiscriminately as he talked—his was the dehydration of fatigue, he had been up all night with his cattlemen and the dogs after a hyena that had killed three calves in the last month. The elegant dogs had cornered and killed it; it had not needed even a final shot. They lay and panted around him, their film-star eyelashes drooping over unseeing eyes, too nervously exhausted to sleep with them closed. But Boxer was fired with the chance—not to communicate but to expound aloud, reiterate, the tactics, successes and reverses of his year-in, year-out campaign in the calm bush where, through the windows, as the men talked they could see his cattle move, cropping singly, stumblingly, or driven—far off—flowing in brown spate close through the thin trees. He took Bray to a bathroom where, in aspirin bottles in the cupboard, there were labelled specimens of all the varieties of ticks to be found in the country—"All that I've been able to identify, so far—" He made the reservation with the objective modesty of scientific inquiry. Many of the ticks were alive, living in a state of suspended animation for months without food or air. In the disused bath, silverfish moths wriggled; Boxer turned a stiff, squeaky tap to flush them out. There were peeling transfers of mermaids and sea-horses on the pink walls of this laboratory.

Boxer showed no interest or curiosity in Bray's return to the country or his activities now that he was there. But Bray was quick to see that some use could be made of George Boxer's knowledge, if one could find the right way to approach him. No good suggesting that he offer his services to Mweta's agricultural planning committee— human contact on any abstract level reduced him to cold sulks. "If you come into Gala sometime—I mean if you're coming anyway— perhaps you would talk to the people doing the animal husbandry course we're hoping to set up. We want to get the old craft schools going again on a new basis—a modest trades school, of course with practical farming techniques lumped along with anything else that's useful. I don't see why it should be left to agricultural colleges—even if we had one. It might fit in with your own line of inquiry—the chaps could collect grasses and stuff from the places where they run their cattle."

"Oh Gala. I don't think I've been more than once since Caroline left—Caroline's in England."

"Well, when she gets back, no doubt you'll find yourself coming to town again, and then—?"

"Must be more than two years. Time flies. I don't suppose the place has changed. Amazing; don't know where the days go to. When did you people come back?"

"Olivia's following. I've been here—yes, I suppose it's more than three months. She was supposed to come as soon as Venetia's baby was born—"

Boxer looked round the pink walls, over his neat bottles of ticks. "Her bathroom," he said. He meant the wife with the bad teeth. "What in the world d'you need two bathrooms for." A comfortable feeling of understanding, based idiotically, Bray felt, on misunderstanding, encircled them. Olivia *was* coming; how quickly three months had gone by.

It was absurd to bother to set things straight with Boxer. They went on talking in the tacit ease of men who have drifted the moorings of family ties.

When Bray got back to his car, his passenger had gone. Boxer called a servant; the meal taken to the man had been eaten. They looked about for him but he was not to be found. Bray felt slightly rebuffed, as if there had been some sort of response expected from him that he had failed to understand. "He wasn't a very forthcoming passenger," he said, with the defence of a philosophical irony. "Probably just out of clink," Boxer said. "Head was shaved, eh, I noticed."

Bray went over the Bashi Mountain pass, thumping on the worn springs of the car through sudden U-shaped dips into stream-beds, shuddering over rises covered with loose stones. He spent the first night in the old government rest hut at Tanyele village. Under the mopane trees pink and mauve flowers bloomed straight out of the sandy soil, without visible stem or leaf, as if stuck there by children playing house. At first he thought of them as irises (irises in bloom round the lily pool in Wiltshire) but then they fell into place as the wild lilies that Venetia and Pat used to pick when, as small girls, they had the treat of being allowed to go on a tax-collecting tour with him. He heated himself a tin of curry and rice; there had used to be an old cook attached to the rest-house who wore a high chef's hat and made ground-nut stew on a Primus.

He woke next day to the gentle tinkle of goats' bells and went to visit the local schoolmaster. Everybody seemed to remember him; he drank beer with Chief Chitoni and his uncle, the old Regent who had kept the stool warm when Bray was D.C., and was presented with a fierce white fowl and some sweet potatoes. At a decent distance from Tanyele, he untied the fowl's legs and let it loose in the bush; someone appeared among the trees and he hoped it was not a Tanyele villager. Then he saw that it was, in fact, his passenger, still carrying his cardboard suitcase. Bray smiled; the other did not seem to feel any bond of acquaintance, but climbed into the car once more as if they had met by appointment. At the next night's stop, he insisted on sleeping in the car and kept himself aloof from the people of the village. His shoes were grey with dried mud, now, broken in to the form of his feet, and when he moved his arms, a strong, bitter blast of sweat filled the car. But it was as if whatever had been locked inside him now escaped, harmless, a pungent dread. The stink was nothing; that dark, depersonalized, vice-hold of presence had become a tired, dirty body that had walked a long way in the sun. On the third day he suddenly asked Bray to stop the car; Bray thought he wanted to relieve himself but after disappearing among the trees for a moment or two he came back and said, "I stay here, sir." There was a charcoal burners' camp nearby.

Bray spent two more days criss-crossing the higher part of the Flats from village to village on rough tracks. The exhaust pipe kept falling off the car and was repaired in various ways in every village. On the morning of the sixth day the Volkswagen was poled across the river and the silent motion, after the perpetual rattling of the car, was a kind of presage: Shinza was on the other side. In the light, sandy-floored forest he came upon movement that he thought, at a distance, was buck feeding; it was women gathering sour wild fruit, and they turned to laugh and chatter as he passed.

The trees ended; the scrub ended; the little car was launched upon a sudden opening-out of flowing grass and glint of water that pushed back the horizon. He had always felt here, that suddenly he saw as a bird did, always rising, always lifting wider the ring of the eyes' horizon. He took off his glasses for a moment and the shimmering and wavering range rushed away from him, even farther.

The dabs and shapes of hot blue water gave off dark looks from the endless bed of soft grasses. Small birds flicked like grasshoppers from the feathered tops. There was a smell of space, here. Thousands of head of cattle on this plain; but they were lost specks, no bigger than George Boxer's ticks in the grass. The road was terrible; the violence of progress across calm and serenity could only be compared to the shock of a plane hit about by airpockets in a clear sky. Herdsmen stood to watch, unmoved, speculative, as he negotiated runnels cross-furrowed by the tracks of the sleds used to drag wood. Ilala palm began to appear in the grass, the flanges of the leaves open like a many-bladed pen-knife. Feeling his way through the past, he drove, without much hesitance at turnings, to Shinza's village. A new generation of naked children moved in troops about the houses, which were a mixture of the traditional materials of mud and grass, and the bricks and corrugated iron of European settlement. Some of the children were playing with an ancient Victorian mangle; Belgian missionaries from the Congo and German missionaries from Tanganyika had waded through the grass all through the last decade of the nineteenth century, dumping old Europe among the long-horned cattle.

Shinza lived now (so he was directed) behind the reed wall of a compound set apart like a chief's—in fact, it turned out to be part of Chief Mpana's quarters. Inside were various mud outhouses and an ugly brick house with a pole-and-thatch veranda, and scrolled burglar-proofing at the windows like that of the European houses in the suburbs of the capital. There were no children in here. It was very silent. An old woman lay on her side in the sun, completely covered by cotton rags except for her bare feet. Bray had the feeling that if he touched her with his foot she would roll over, dead.

As if he were in a deserted place, he wandered round instead of knocking at the door. He looked in on a dark, dank hut that held nothing, in its gloom, but two motorcar tyres and an old steel filing cabinet beside a pile of rotting sleeping mats. As he turned back to the sun, a man appeared, tall, small-headed, in grey flannel trousers and a sports-coat, like a schoolmaster or a city clerk. "Yes?" he said rudely, not approaching.

"Is Edward Shinza here, d'you know?"

The man did not answer. Then he approached to look over Bray more closely. "You want to see Shinza?"

"They tell me he lives here, now. Is he around?"

The man stood, refusing to be pressed. "I don't know if he's here."

"Could you perhaps ask, for me?"

"You want to see him." The man considered.

"I'm an old friend."

"I don't know. I'll see if he's here. At the moment."

The man went into the house but Bray had the impression that he left it again by a back door; he saw someone come into vision a moment, crossing the yard. Bray stood in the sun. The old woman did not stir. There was a smell of hides. The man came back. "Come on."

They went into the house, into a sort of parlour with a wasp's nest in the corner, and volumes of Hansard on a sideboard. The man waited in silence beside him like a bodyguard. They sat on the hard chairs for long minutes. The gloom of contrast with the sun outside lifted. Then Shinza came in, hands in the pockets of a dressing-gown, barefoot, feeling for a cigarette. But it would not be the first cigarette of the day; the immediate impression was not of a man who had just got up, but of one who had not slept at all.

"So you decided to come and see me anyway."

Edward Shinza, smiling, his nostrils open and taut, unmistakable. "James . . . you Englishmen, you do what you want." He made a face fearful of consequences, but exaggerated into a joke.

There's something different (Shinza had Bray's hand casually, he held the matchbox between thumb and first finger at the same time): it was a tooth, a broken front tooth—that was it. Shinza now had a front tooth broken off in a curve, already so long done that it was smooth and rounded like the edge of any other tooth. He lit the cigarette and then looked at Bray, head drawn back, and said, still making fun of him, "You know it's nice to see you, James, it's nice, it's—I should make a speech, honestly, I'd like to—" He deliberately ignored the dressing-gown, as if it were the way he chose to dress. He told the onlooker, in Gala, to leave but return in an hour, apparently careless of the fact that Bray could understand what was said.

But when he turned back to Bray and said in English—the remark was a paraphrase of one of Mweta's slogans before large gatherings —"So you're helping to build a nation, ay . . ." Bray thought that he had intended him to know that in an hour he expected to be rid of him, like any other guest.

"Weren't you the one who taught him speech-making?"

Shinza was light-coloured for a Gala; he tenderly rubbed his yel-

low-brown breast where the gown fell open. A few peppercorns round
the nipples, like the tufts that textured the skin of his face, sprouting
from the surface pocked and cratered by some far-off skin affection,
childhood smallpox or adolescent pimples. The furze ran together
over the curves of the mouth, making a vague moustache. It empha-
sized the smile again, under the wide, taut nostrils. "A good teacher.
But I didn't teach him how to shut people up. He learnt by himself.
Or perhaps others help him; I don't know." He made the mock-fearful
face again, as if it were something Bray would recognize.

"Ah, come now—it was visualized as a one-party state from the beginning, you'd always said the—what was it you called it—?"

"Kiddies' parliament," Shinza fished up, dangling the phrase detachedly; a smile for it.

"Kiddies' parliament—that's it—the kiddies' parliament Africans
think reproduces Westminster in their states was not going to waste
time and money in this one."

"Of course, and I was damn well right, man. And now your boy
would like to see me choose a fancy name and start an opposition
party to draw into the open all the people around him he's afraid of
—a nice, harmless little opposition you can defeat at the polls by that
unity-is-strength speech-making I taught him. Or by getting his
Young Pioneers to beat up voters—it always looks nicer than turning
on people who've made PIP and put him up there in the Governor's
house, ay? —Why do we stand?" He dumped on the table the clean
washing—faded check shirts, crudely embroidered sheets—that was
laid on an ugly brown sofa, and spread himself with careless luxury,
flexing his neck against its back with the chin-movements of a man
aware that he has not shaved.

There were so many ways by which they could have arrived at this
point. Bray had been aware of it as to be approached through layer
by layer of past associations, present preoccupations, the half-intimate
trivia with which one mind circles another before establishing on
what level they are to be open to one another, this time. But they had
fallen through tentativeness at once; nothing stood between them, no
protection. They might have opened their mouths and begun to speak
out of the unsaid, as a man addresses a dark room. Bray said, "From
the day I arrived, I tried to talk to him. I'd thought—if you and he
weren't hitting it off—you might go to United Nations for a time."

Shinza watched him, lolling in a kind of faint, distantly bitter amusement at a spectacle that ceased to concern, a mouthing figure in an action from which the sound has been cut off. "Oh yes, United Nations," he said kindly.

Bray sat down on the sofa.

Shinza continued to bear with him, smiling.

It was a powerful indifference, not listless. A lion fixes its gaze on no object, does not snap at flies. Old Shinza. But he's not old at all, fifty-four or -five, about a year older than I am. Bray was aware of the vigour of Shinza's breast, rising and falling, the strong neck shining a little with warmth—a body still a man's body and not an old man's, although the face for years had had the coded complexity of experience and drink.

"I got the impression that there were things between you I wasn't supposed to know about."

"Of course, James, of course. How else could Mweta explain? Of course; ter-rible things—" He began to laugh and put his hand on Bray's knee. "He didn't want to have me around. That's all it is. It sounds so silly, ay, how could he say to you, I don't want Shinza. I-don't-want-Shinza. Shinza's big black face in the papers. Shinza's big mouth open in the cabinet. Shinza asking questions when I make my deals with the mining companies. The British. The Americans. The French. Why. How. How much. *And who for.* Better have that mister what'sisname, the young Englishman who jumps about licking, a nice, friendly dog, you pay him and he makes bow-wow, that's all. No Shinza asking damn questions. Before, he used to ask *me* what questions to ask. Now he's the one who has to give answers."

"Shut people up?" Another meaning to the phrase that had fallen casually, earlier, suddenly opened. "You said something just now—what did you mean exactly?"

Shinza was stroking his neck under his unshaven, lifted chin, smiling, giving him one ear. He righted himself and smiled at Bray. Then all expression died. He said, "Oh, bush stories, like the chap you had in your car."

"That youngster? The one I picked up?"

Shinza kept the moment suspended, watching without much interest, from an inner distance.

Bray was rushed by unmatched thoughts; *had* he mentioned the boy to Shinza? He said, at once conscious of the idiocy of it, "But he hardly had a word to say for himself."

"Yes, shut up. He'd been shut up." Shinza made a point of the broken-toothed smile at his smart play on words.

Two months and seventeen days.

He's probably just out of clink.

"Where?"

"Oh Gala, of course. You know District Chief of Police Lebaliso. And the Provincial Officer, Aleke. Of course you know them."

"What was the charge?"

"Charge? What charge? No charge; no trial. Just taken inside."

"And what'd he done?"

"Worked at the fish-meal factory."

Bray made a sudden, uncontrolled gesture for Shinza's attention— and Shinza gave way, calmly: "Spoke to the other chaps about pay and conditions and so on. Told them something of how the fishing concessions with the company work. The time the government renewed the concessions for another five years—you know . . ."

Mweta's minister had renewed the contract with the British-Belgian trawling company under terms that transferred a percentage of the stock to the government, but left the wages of the workers at the level of colonial times.

Bray sat forward clumsily, his hands dangled between his knees.

Shinza stuck another cigarette in his mouth, spoke round it, standing up to thrust for the matches in the dressing-gown pocket. "There were a few little meetings down in the township—the men from the factory and the lime-works fellows. The trade-union steward didn't like it. The Young Pioneers didn't like it."

"They arrested the boy?"

"I suppose you call it that. They took him away and locked him up; they had a lot of questions to ask, it took two months or so, and now you gave him a lift home." Shinza finished it off abruptly, like a fairy story for a child.

"More than two months." About the time he had arrived in Gala. "I never heard a word."

"No," said Shinza, biting off the end of a yawn, "not a word. From Lebaliso? From Aleke?"

"Whose responsibility would an order like that be? Who signs?

E

There's no preventive detention law in this country now."

"Oh well, there's the tradition, from the old days of the Emergency." There was the growing feeling that Shinza was closing the conversation.

"But whose orders?"

Shinza said patiently, boredly, "Lebaliso. Aleke."

"I'd like to talk to the boy."

"He's had enough 'questions,'" said Shinza.

"It's possible that Mweta doesn't know," Bray said.

Shinza laughed. Bray was standing about; he did not know where to put himself, he heard his own shoes creaking. Shinza's legs were thrust before him under the dressing-gown, the eyes held in a disgusted, amused sympathy. Bray said, "I mustn't take these away with me again"; he put the box of cigarillos on the washing. "Your old brand."

Shinza got up, the situation now on his own terms. "God, man, I love those things. I smoke these damned cigarettes nowadays, someone brings them in for me. Can you get me some more of those, James? I'd like a case, send them to me from England, eh?" When his man came in he ignored him and sauntered Bray through a kitchen and out of the house to another house, a mud-and-thatch one.

"The beer she makes isn't too bad," he said by way of introduction to a young woman who scuttled behind the dirty curtain that divided the house into two rooms. He called after her and in a moment she came back with a clean dress on and her feet hobbling into shoes. "She's just had a baby," he said, in Gala. "Where's your son, Talisa, show off your son," and she laughed and answered in the spirit of the dialogue before a stranger, "Why can't you let him sleep, why do you have to look at him all the time?" "You're jealous. I've got a lot of children, one more doesn't matter to me. —It's her first," he said to Bray, and went behind the curtain, where there were laughter and argument, and he came out tugging the dressing-gown straight with one hand, crimping his eyes as he blew cigarette smoke upwards to keep it away from the tiny baby he held, wearing only a little vest, in his other hand. It was pink-brown, faintly translucent, with minute hands and feet stirring, and a watch-sized, closed face. The girl took the cigarette out of Shinza's mouth as she gazed at the baby, and with the first finger of his other hand he delicately traced the convolutions of its ear, whose lines were still compressed from the womb. It peed in a weak little arc, like the squirt from some small sea-creature disturbed in its shell. Shinza laughed, making lewd remarks, almost tossing it to the mother, while she was joyously fussed and embarrassed and bore it away behind the curtain, where it burst into surprisingly powerful yells that rivalled its father's laughter. He moved about looking for a cloth. The mud room smelled coolly of fetid infant, beer, woodsmoke. There were clothing, cooking pots, newspapers, a radio, a brand-new perambulator of the kind you see in European parks—the decent disorder of intimacy. A trunk with labels from Southampton docks, San Francisco, and New York (Shinza was of the generation that got scholarships to attend Negro universities in America; Mweta was born too late for that and went straight into politics from school) had a lace mat and fancy coffee service set out upon it. Shinza grabbed a garment of some kind and mopped his chest, tossing the rag into a corner. A kitchen table with an old typewriter was his desk. There was a packing-case of books in disarray; behind it, the only adornment on the walls, a football-team group—Nkrumah, cross-eyed Fanon, mascot Selassie, Guevara, a face among others that was Shinza himself: a meeting of Afro-Asian countries in Cairo, the beginning of the Sixties. Shinza saw Bray looking, and said, "Rogue's gallery." He was smoking one of the cigars; he had the authority, pitched here in this mud tent, of a commander in the field.

They drank home-brew and talked general politics in a distracted fashion, for Shinza was twice called out (in the sun, men waited like horses, moved away to speak with him), the girl and baby were about. None of these things was allowed to interrupt the talk, not because Shinza was giving Bray his full attention but because all that passed between them was peripheral, to Shinza.

The second time Shinza returned to the hut, Bray stopped him as he came in: "How far did it go with the boy?"

Shinza made a pantomime of jerking his head, blinking. "What?"

" 'Questions,' you said. Enough 'questions'?"

Shinza kept the cold butt of the cigar in his mouth. "Oh you know what questions amount to, James."

"Do I?"

"And after all, Mweta's your man, you have certain ideas about him, about us . . . ."

Bray hardened in the indifference as flesh contracts in a cool breeze.

"Questions've got to get answers. Somehow. If not one way then the other. You know."

"I want to know what happened."

Shinza said, explaining to a child, "James, his head wouldn't answer, so they put their questions on his back."

"I see."

"You can see the questions on his back. You want to see them? I'll fetch him for you." As if to get it over with, he became whimsically determined, now, to have Bray examine the exhibit. "I don't want you to believe any wild stories from the bush—I'll fetch him and you can look. No, no, you stay, I'll fetch him for you."

Bray was left standing alone in the presence of Shinza's things. The girl was quiet behind the curtain—it seemed that she was listening; she did not come out.

Quickly Shinza was in the room again, marshalling the youngster ahead. The boy gave no sign of recognition—Bray's greeting died, irrelevant. Shinza said in Gala, "Bend over." He lifted the boy's shirt. The boy stood, legs apart, hands braced on his knees. He did not look round. From his waist, narrowed by the weight of his body falling away from the spine, his back broadened to the muscles under the shoulder, yellowish round the waist, powder-grey in the shallow ditch on either side of the vertebrae, stale brown over the muscles and shoulders. The pores of the skin were raised, grainy with hardened sebaceous secretion that had not been released by fresh air and sun for a long time. Skin that had lost its gloss like the coat of an animal kept in confinement; Bray knew that skin; had not seen it since the days when he was on the magistrate's bench, as D.C., and prisoners had come before him. In the house in Wiltshire, such things—the reality of such things had no existence.

He was so awakened by the fact of the skin that the weals that had healed across it, tender, slightly puckered strips with the satiny look of lips, scarcely gave up their meaning. Scars, yes, wounds, yes, the protest, the long memory of the body for all that is done to it—the anger of pimples, rough patches, all recording, like messages

scratched on the bark of a tree. The small depression in the rib cage,
low down on the left-hand side, for instance: where did that come
from? A congenital deformation? A stunting of the bone through
some early nutritional deficiency? —He ran his finger over the braille
of a scar—then took it away, burned with embarrassment. The boy
remained bent, an object, as he must have been made to bend for the
blows themselves. Some of the scars were no more than faint marks
left paler than the surrounding skin, blending into it, forgetting, soon
to link imperceptibly with the other skin cells. *That* one must have
gone deep and gaped on the flesh, to have had to make such a thick
ribbon of scar tissue to make it whole. Suddenly he saw the pattern of
the blows, sliced regularly across the back as the cuts in a piece of
larded meat. On the calf-muscle of one strong, rachitically bowed leg
another pale slash showed through the sparse hairs. Bray described it
in the air an inch or two away from the flesh, looking at Shinza: and
that?

"Somebody missed," Shinza said. His lips lifted, the parenthesis of
surrounding beard moved back; he showed his teeth a moment, and
then the grin sank away as the lips slid down over the teeth again.

It might have been an old scar from some innocent injury—a fall,
an accident—unconnected with the prison at Gala, but Shinza had no
time for such niceties of distinction. Bray saw that to him all wounds
were one; and that his own.

"What could they get from him that was worth this."

And now Shinza really grinned, putting his palm on the boy's rump
as on a trophy. He said with the pleasure of being proved right,
"Good old James, just the same as ever."

Bray said in Gala, "Why doesn't he get up—" and Shinza, recalled
to something unimportant, gave the rump a friendly clap and said in
English, "Okay. That's it."

The boy pushed his shirt into his shorts. Bray wanted to say something to him but when he looked at him the boy at once fixed his eyes
on Shinza.

"Well then," Bray said, "what did he have to keep to himself that
would make him take this?"

"James, James. You see a hero behind every bush, when you come
back here. He told them whatever he knew as soon as they took him.
Right away. Without a scratch. But they had some questions he

didn't know the answers to. It's a method; if someone won't talk, never mind why, you're not expected to know why—let him have it. It's routine."

"We know. Of course it's happening all over the world. But in what sort of places."

Shinza said, "This place, James." And he gave a short laugh and added, "Ay?"

Bray said, "It's still possible Mweta doesn't know."

Shinza considered an academic question; "Not about this one, no —keep up with every little instance, you can't expect that." To the boy, "All right."

The boy looked at Bray at last, and gave him the polite form of leavetaking, in Gala. Shinza recalled him and tossed over a packet of the cigarettes he had put aside for the cigars. The boy took them without a word and left.

Bray said, "The thing to do is to take a statement. A statement made before both of us."

Shinza was looking at him almost with fondness. "Those days are over."

"You give up too easily, Shinza." Bray took on in mock submission the naïveté imputed to him. He waited for Shinza to accept this form of refutation, to begin to speak.

"Oh yes," Shinza said, "I'm just a lazy bastard, rusting away. Plotting. No, no, not plotting, rotting. Whatever they like to think, it's up to them. A case for lung cancer. Some say liver. —Tell me, how's old Dando? And the old crowd, in London? I hear from Cameron now and then, if you ever see him, tell him where I am we use the talking drums, that's why I don't write." The girl came out with the baby, now wide awake again, and they sat, lordly, drinking more beer and talking the sort of joking nonsense between old friends that admits a third presence.

Shinza left open no way that led to himself. But leaving, Bray said, "I'll be back." It hung in the air, a remark in bad taste. Of course Shinza understood that he meant to see Mweta; but Shinza was merely lingering politely at the reed fence, smiling, his attention cocked, like a dog's ears pointed backward, elsewhere. "You making a long stay this time?" he remarked absently to Mweta's guest.

"If I thought I could achieve anything."

Shinza ignored the question implied. "What's it again, James— schools? Wha'd'you know about schoolmastering."

"I'm working with Sampson Malemba on the schools, for one thing —looking at the whole educational system, really; technical schools, trades schools, that's what's needed, too—a modest start with adult education for the new sort of youngsters coming along with a bit of industry going, now, in Gala itself."

The lime works. The fish-meal factory, where his passenger came from.

Shinza nodded.

Bray said suddenly, "Anything you need, Edward . . ."

They stood there at a distance for a moment.

"Oh well, the cigars—you said you'd get them for me from England. That'd be fine, you know." Shinza was smiling.

With his hands dragging down the dressing-gown pockets so that his muscular buttocks jutted along as he walked, he disappeared into the house where Bray had waited for him. Bray did what he had to do; went to the school in the village, drove on twenty miles to the White Fathers' Mission school, turned, at last, back along the road he had come and passed without stopping the children still making a hobby-horse out of the old mangle, the goats, the bicycles, the mud houses, and the reed stockade where Shinza was. But Bray got through it all with blind attention, holding off a mental pressure that built up, waiting for the gap through which it would burst. The wobbling of the gear-shaft in his palm over the terrible road became the expression of a trembling of his hand itself, suppressed. Two months and seventeen days. Back here only a few months and already it's begun—the beating up, the putting away. An old story. No wonder Shinza couldn't resist the opportunity to sneer at his reaction. He had never counted himself among those whose radical liberalism amounts to no more than an abstract distaste for coercive methods. He had never before found himself out in that particular kind of dishonesty. Over the years he had accepted—at a distance—some ugly facts if, unfortunately, they appeared unavoidable to gain the social change he believed in. He struggled to set aside the vision of the boy's back. He'd forgive a great deal to see achieved the sort of state that Shinza and Mweta had visualized together for the country.

But the "questioning" of the boy stood between Shinza and Mweta.

And himself? Would he forgive himself? Perhaps this agitation of his was a matter of not wanting to get his own hands dirty. That was his kind of dishonesty. Let it be done if it must be, but not by me, let me not put my hand to it, not by even so much as a signature at the bottom of a report on education. Was that it?

Yet he had an impulse to go straight to the capital at once; to Mweta; as if that would do away once and for all with ambiguities: his own as well as those of what had happened. —Aleke? He ought at least to talk to Aleke first, get the facts straight. Aleke must have been the one to take authority, to sign. He saw Aleke and himself, moving in and out about houses, *boma*, village street in Gala, entwining waving antennae when their paths crossed, senselessly as ants. But Aleke would never have shut a man away on his own initiative; then was it Aleke taking orders from Lebaliso? Aleke and Bray laughed at Lebaliso, a jerky little man who had taken over from Major Conner, whose batman he had been in the war. Lebaliso was a nonentity; Aleke certainly was not: both would do as they were told. Aleke was an efficient civil servant, independent but not. politically minded or politically ambitious. If an order came from the capital, and it did not touch upon the day-to-day smooth running of his local administration, he would simply sign. Easy-going, confident, sitting on his veranda working at his papers among the noise of children, he knew what he was doing and presumed the people up there at the top knew what they were doing, too. After all, the government was PIP. On the solid convictions of people like Aleke governments come to power but are never threatened; Aleke would never change his mind about Mweta, or anything else.

Mweta had given Justice to Justin Chekwe; Bray didn't know him well, but Roly Dando called him a Gray's Inn pin-up boy—"Who knows what really lies under that nylon wig, I sat next him at dinner and caught him admiring himself in a soup spoon—" Dando talked so much: "Once you've been given Justice, you don't have much to do with justice any more. You keep the peace the way the big boys want it kept. Same with the Attorney-General's job—a pair of Keystone Cops, Justice and I, really, that's all. He'll be all right, I suppose, so long as Mweta stays on the straight and narrow." He would phone Dando as soon as he got home; and decided as suddenly that it was not the thing to do. The house had a party line and anyway the local exchange would hear every word. He recoiled from Roly's ventriloquist patter coming out of the distance.

While Bray was with Shinza he had felt like an adult reluctant to believe that a favourite child has lied or cheated. He was afraid, in Shinza's house, that Mweta *did* know. But now—alone to the horizon of gentle grasses with no sign from another human except the flash of a paraffin tin carried on a woman's head—he felt there was the possibility that Mweta really did not know, that the size of this unwieldy country with its communications that dwindled out in flooded tracks and ant-eaten telephone poles made it feasible for people to take the law into their own hands while behind the red brick façade of the President's Residence, telephones, telex, and the planes coming to the airport down the road brought Mweta closer to Addis, New York, and London than to this grass-inundated steppe, soughed down under the empty sky.

In the pass (driving directly now, he covered in one day what had taken him three) the confidence went again, as unreasonably. Rough, dark-flanked mountains enclosed the road and himself. Shinza had another kind of confidence, one that Bray was provoked by, not just in the mind, but in the body, in the senses; Shinza moved in his immediate consciousness, in images so vivid that he felt a queer alarm. A restlessness stirred resentfully in the tamped-down ground of his being, put out a touch on some nerve that (of course) had atrophied long ago, as the vagus nerve is made obsolete by maturity and the pituitary gland ceases to function when growth is complete. Shinza's bare strong feet, misshapen by shoes, tramped the mud floor—the flourish of a stage Othello before Cyprus. He was smoking cigarettes smuggled from over the border; friends across the border: those who had cigarettes probably had money and arms as well. And the baby; why did the baby keep cropping up?—Shinza held it out in his hand as casually as he had fathered it on that girl. He did not even boast of having a new young wife, it was nothing to him, nothing was put behind him. . . .

The man will change his life, Bray thought burningly. Mweta became no more than the factor whose existence would bring this about, rouse it into being. Shinza might as well have been thirty as fifty-four. No, it wasn't that he was an ageing man who was like a

E*   ⟩ 129 ⟨

young man—something quite different—that he was driven, quite
naturally, acceptedly, to go on living so long as he was alive. You
would have to have him drop dead, to stop him.

The house in Wiltshire with all its comfortable beauty and order,
its incenses of fresh flowers and good cooking, its libations of carefully discussed and chosen wine came to Bray in all the calm detail of
an interesting death cult; to wake up there again would be to find
oneself acquiescently buried alive. At the same time, he felt a stony
sense of betrayal. Olivia moved about there, peppermints and cigarettes on the night-table, her long, smooth-stockinged legs under
skirts that always drooped slightly at the back. A detail taken from a
painting, isolated and brought up close to the eye. He suddenly tried
to remember what it was like to be inside Olivia's body. But he could
not. All that he produced, driving through the scrubby forest alone,
was the warm reflex of a beginning erection in response to the generalized idea of the warmth inside women, any woman. His mind
switched to Mweta again, and his body shrank. He ought not, he was
perhaps wrong to question Mweta about anything. He had made it
clear from the beginning that he would not presume on any bond of
authority arising out of their association because he saw from the beginning that there was always the danger—to his personal relationship with Mweta—that this bond might become confused with some
lingering assumption of authority from the colonial past. I mustn't forget that I'm a white man. A white man in Africa doesn't know what
to see himself as, but mentor. He looks in the mirror, and there is the
fatal fascination of the old reflection, doesn't matter much, now,
whether it's the civil servant under a topi or the white liberal who
turned his back on the settlers and went along with the Africans to
Lancaster House. If I don't like what Mweta does, I'd better get out
and go home to Wiltshire. Write an article for the *New Statesman*,
from there. He almost spoke aloud to himself. He wished Olivia
would be at the house in Gala, when he came back. He suddenly felt
alone, as he might have felt cold, or tired. He began to write a letter
to Olivia in his head, telling her to make up her mind and come
quickly. He felt he missed her very much.

He would have liked to get back to Gala the next night—could
have done it, prepared to drive through the night until one or two in
the morning—but he stuck reluctantly to his original intention to

make a loop on his return so as to include the Nome district. On paper, it was the site of a resettlement scheme; the people were poor and apathetic, one came upon them laboriously picking about some task in the forest with the dazed faces of those who are underfed from the day they are no longer suckled. Some villages had no school hut at all. Filthy and silent, children appeared from the forest and sold him those mushrooms big as plough disks that grew at this time of year. Their cool flesh gave off a soothing cellar-smell; the depressing odour of luxury in the midst of human poverty that he always recognized as peculiar to Africa. Here in the forest there were extravagant left-overs from some feast of gods—huge mushrooms, lilies blooming out of sand—but no ordinary sustenance for the people.

He drove the last lap back to Gala in a complete preoccupation of the will to get there, tense for any change of rhythm that might indicate trouble in the car, crossing off the hours and miles with each look at his watch. When at last he turned into the main street and the mahogany trees swallowed him in their well-deep shade and quiet he saw the shops were shut—it was Sunday. He went to the office just the same; Aleke might be there, doing some work. But there was nobody. The Christ-thorn had been dug up. He could hardly go to Aleke's house—his own old house—and confront him in the midst of the Dinky cars and the children. The same old sound of Sunday drumming thudded faintly through the afternoon. The gleaming backs of cars huddled round the club. A car turning into the entrance paused as he drew level and the occupant was grinning at him invitingly, importantly. Broughton, the secretary, mouthing something at him. He rolled down the window and grimaced politely to show he couldn't hear. "You don't answer your phone. I've been trying to get you all week. Your application's been approved by the committee. Henderson seconded it. So there you are, I knew you'd be pleased but you've been the devil to get hold of." They were blocking the entrance and the man gestured and drove in, expecting Bray to follow, his face bright with the readiness to resume the barely interrupted chat.

Henderson was the owner of one of the two local drapers' shops: preparing the ground against Olivia's return, thoughtful man. Bray drove on down the quiet dirt road past the half-hidden houses, past a male Gala "nanny" wheeling a white child, and the children and dogs of one of the black administrative officials who had moved into government houses, bounding round a meeting of flashing new bicycles. His eye separated from the other greenery the towering, spreading outline of the fig tree; nothing has changed, nothing has changed. And all the while, when everything was as it is now, the boy had been shut up in the prison in the bush outside the town.

Mahlope had cut the grass on the verges of the road before the house. Aprons were spread stiffly dried on the hibiscus hedge. Bray had a revulsion against entering the empty, closed-up bungalow where all he would meet were the signs of his own occupancy. His sense of urgency was thrown back at him, an echo.

He began to lug his things out of the car and dump them on the grass. The soft questioning of children's voices rang through the sunny quiet; he looked round and saw a woman and three small figures coming across the half-cleared scrub between his house and the one from which he was pleasantly isolated. Their heads were wrapped in something—towels. But everything—the club secretary's happy interest, people with their heads wrapped up in towels—was simply part of the distance that had been put between himself and the life of this familiar place by what he had heard existed there, beneath these appearances of which he himself was part.

It was the girl, Rebecca Edwards, again, with three of the numerous children who overran the Bayleys' house in the capital. Soapy trickles ran from under the turban down her temple and cheek. Bray said to the children, "Been swimming, eh?" and the smaller one clutched his mother's thigh. She wiped away the soapy tear. "Oh, it's awful to worry you—you see there suddenly isn't a drop of water, and I'd just put this stuff on our hair . . ." Another tear ran down and fell on her bare foot. "If we could stick our heads under the garden tap—" "Heavens, come to the bathroom. I'll open the house." She and the children all wore cheap rubber-thonged sandals. They trooped in behind him, driving away the silence with their squelching footsteps and displacing the emptiness with their invading bodies. He pushed open the stiff bathroom window, he turned on the taps; there were exclamations of relief when the water gushed out—"It's even hot," he said, and left them to it.

There was unopened mail addressed in familiar hands, newspaper rolls; the cardboard folders of notes and papers, as he had left them:

DISTRICT, SCHOOLS, POPULATION UNDER 18. He put a carbon between two sheets of paper and rolled them into the typewriter. He began a letter to Mweta; and then pulled out a cheap blue pad, the only kind you could buy in Gala stores, and began to write by hand, a letter or the draft of a letter. Before he could touch any of this again—the folders and notes—before there was any point in going on, he must have an answer from Mweta. The stammering, repetitive questions of a small child whose need for expression runs ahead of its vocabulary came muffled from the bathroom. He tore the wrappers off a couple of newspapers and rolled them the opposite way to flatten them. What he wrote, what he was saying to Mweta was not about the boy at all. . . . *the whole opposition between you is false, I don't believe it's based on any real difference of approach at all, but you have pushed Shinza into the position where if he is to do anything at all he must oppose you, and not in a negative way. He must set up something against what you are setting up without him. If you behave differently in power from the way you did before, so of course would he. . . . If you had him with you, now, both of you would be facing the same problems of adjustment, and there's a pretty good chance, taking into account the closeness of the old association, you'd come to the same sort of solution. Don't you see? To put it at its worst, it would at least ensure a kind of complicity . . . at least you'd avoid finding yourself in the position where you'd have to do some of the things you'll find you have to do now. . . .* Rebecca Edwards and her children came to thank him; with an abstracted awareness of bad manners, he realized that he hadn't even asked how she came to be making for this house; where she had come from.

"Did you find somewhere to live? You're not still at the Inn?" She explained that she had moved into the house across the scrub, was sharing it with the agricultural officer, Nongwaye Tlume, and his wife. "I don't mind, there's a kind of extra kitchen attached to that rondavel outside. Anything to get out of the hotel, anyway, it was costing me such a lot of money." The children's hair was rough-dried and spiky, hers was combed out neatly like a wet dark fringe all round. Her bare big forehead and the wings of her nose shone faintly from the ablutions. She had yellow eyes, like a pointer he had once had. The four went off the way they had come, through the scrub. Poor thing; there was some story there nobody bothered to ask—she and her children could have stayed in this house instead of the Fish-eagle Inn while waiting to move in to the Tlumes', he should have thought of it. Probably that was something of the kind that Roly had expected of him. . . . *I can't believe Shinza would have made a move to oust you, standing beside you as it were. No moral reason, but because there's always been something secretive in his nature, some pleasure in being behind the scenes, recognized for his importance only by a few people in the know. . . he likes to be the face you can hardly make out between the other faces, but there. . . . And he has a laziness about people—you know that—he can't be bothered with the continuity of day-to-day contact, shaking hands and grinning crowds. He's essentially a selfish and withdrawn man—I mean success would become vulgar to him, he would always have left that part of it to you. . . .*

Kalimo arrived back and cooked him some supper. Afterwards he stood under the fig tree in the dark, smoking one of the big cigars he didn't allow himself too often. There were bats at the fruit, the most silent and unobtrusive of creatures, torn-off rags of darkness itself. He wondered with whom he could take the traditional refuge of dropping in for a drink. Not the club, the new member taking up his rights. Not Aleke. He could go to that girl, Rebecca Edwards, one of the group in the capital. But he and she would have nothing to talk about; his mind was blank of small talk. He leant against the tree and the cigar burned down to a finger of firm ash. Ants ran alerting a fine capillary tree of nerves over his back.

He went inside and wrote to his wife, suggesting that she make up her mind and fly out within the next two weeks. He had to go to the capital in any case, and this would mean that he could meet her and drive her back on the same trip. After he had signed, he wrote: *All our reasons for your not coming seem to be simply because we can't put a name to why you should come.* It was a love letter, then. He scored it out. He wrote, experimentally, *All our reasons for your coming seem to be defeated by some unknown reason for your not coming.* He felt he did not understand what he had said. He did not stick down the envelope. He put it with the pages he had covered for Mweta; about Mweta.

In the morning, he left the pages there. At least until he had spoken to Aleke. At least until then.

Aleke and his new secretary were starting the day with a cup of coffee when he arrived at the offices. It was an atmosphere he had known all his life—what he thought of as "all his life," the years in Africa. The offices still stuffy but cool before the heat of the day, the clerks talking lingeringly over their shoulders as they slowly began their to-and-fro along the passages; the time before the satchel of mail came in. Aleke filled his pushed-back chair and questioned Rebecca Edwards with the banter of a working understanding.

"You didn't forget to stick in Paragraph B, Section Seventeen, eh, my girl." She leaned against the windowsill, cup in one hand, cigarette in the other. "I did not." Of course, she could be counted on to take work home over the weekend; Aleke said it himself: "You're an angel. And will you get that file up to date by Friday? Cross your heart?" He had for Bray the smile with which a busy man greets one who has been off on some pleasure-trip. "Well, how was the bush? Get through all right?" There was chatter about the condition of the road. "Mr. Scott said to Stanley Nko, 'The best thing would be for the Bashi Flats to secede. . . .'" (Nko had taken over from the white Provincial Manager of Public Works, Scott.) Quoting, Aleke was immensely amused at this solution to the problem, and they all laughed.

"Could I have a word with you, Aleke?" Bray asked.

"Oh sure, sure."

Rebecca Edwards tactfully made to leave at once. "Here, here, don't forget these—" A file was waved at her.

Aleke got up, took the lavatory key from its tidy nail, and went off for the daily golden moment, saying, "Be with you right away—if you want to listen to the news—" He gestured at the transistor radio on his desk.

Aleke was washing his hands with *boma* soap, drying them on the strip of *boma* towel.

"I gave a young fellow a lift," Bray said.

Aleke began to nod and turned smiling at a story he could guess—"Long as he didn't bash you over the head. It's getting as bad as down in town. What'd he take off you? Some of these fellows from the fish factory—I don't stop for anybody, any more, honestly."

"Yes, from the fish factory—but he'd just come out of prison. He'd been inside more than two-and-a-half months. No trial. No charges laid. Here in Gala, in Lebaliso's jail."

Aleke sat down at his desk and listened to something he knew instead of guessed. He put out his hand and switched on the fan; he probably did this every morning at exactly the same time, to ward off the heat as it came. His face was open to Bray. "You know about it," Bray said.

"Lebaliso kept me in the picture."

"So it was Lebaliso's decision?"

"We'd been keeping an eye on that fellow a long time. Shinza's chap."

Bray said, "What d'you mean, Shinza's chap?"

"There're a lot of Bashi working here now. Shinza sees they make a nuisance of themselves now and again. In the unions and so on."

"Aleke." Bray made the attempt to lift the whole business out of the matter-of-fact, where Aleke let it lie like a live bomb buried in an orderly garden. "Aleke; Lebaliso shut up a man for two months and seventeen days."

"From what I was told, this one was a real trouble-maker. I mean, it's not my affair, except that what's good for the province concerns me. From that point of view, I'm expected to keep an eye on things. If there's likely to be any trouble, I just like to know what I'm expected"—in mid-sentence he changed his mind about what he was saying—"well, I must be kept more or less in the picture."

"And what you see is Lebaliso taking the law into his own hands."

Aleke was friendly, tried to invoke the amusement at Lebaliso he and Bray had shared. "Of course I said to him at the beginning, the magistrate's the man to go to with your troubles. Not me. Anyway it seems something had to be done about that fellow. They wanted to know a bit more about him."

Bray said, "Was Onabu the one who was interested?" Aaron Onabu was Chief of Police, in the capital.

Aleke agreed rather than answered. "I suppose so."

Bray said, bringing out each word steadily, "And I never heard a word from anyone in Gala."

"We-ll, you've had other things to do but think about old Lebaliso up there—" The hand waved in the direction of the prison, behind the trees, behind the village. "We've all got enough on our hands. But this girl, Bray—I'm telling you, my life is different now. When I want something, it's there. If I forget something, she's remembered. And give her anything *you* want done, too. If you want your reports typed. She'll do it; she's a worker, man."

Bray watched the fan turning its whirring head to the left, the centre, the right, and back again, the left, the centre, the right, and back again. He wanted to ask: And are there others up there—with Lebaliso? But the telephone rang and while Aleke's warm, lively voice rose and fell in cheerful Gala, he felt the pointlessness of pursuing this business through Aleke and, signalling his self-dismissal, left the room.

In his office he set himself to put some order into the files he kept there; they were constantly being moved back and forth between the *boma* and the house. The office was not exclusively for his use and Godfrey Letanka, the clerk, came carefully in and out. He gave him some typing to be done; he couldn't bring himself to take advantage of that girl. The heat grew and filled the small room; he stood at the window and looked across the village muffled in trees. At twelve o'clock it was alive with bicycles taking people home to the African township for lunch, black legs pumping, shouts, talk, impatient ringing of bells. He went out and the sun was dull, behind cloud, on his head; he had the feeling that he was not there, in Gala, really: that he had lost external reality. Or conversely that he carried something inside him that set him apart from all these people who were innocent of it, uninfected. What was he doing among them? He dropped at Joosab's a pair of pants with a broken zip; Joosab stitching, moulding layers of interlining upon a lapel, the naked bulb over his sewing machine, Mweta on the wall. Joosab's brother-in-law and mother-in-law had just been to Mecca, and the brother-in-law was in the shop, wearing his white turban. "Home again, Colonel." Joosab celebrated the two travellers, one from the bush, one from the pilgrimage, in vicarious pleasure. "Your tuhn will come, your tuhn will come, Ismail." The brother-in-law was generously reassuring from the bounty of his importance. "More than fifteen year now, I been thinking next year and next year . . . but seriously, Colonel, I have plans to make the trip." At the general store, where he had to pick up a cylinder of domestic gas, changes were in process: a cashier's turnstile was being set up at the new EXIT ONLY—a second door formerly blocked by rolls of linoleum and tin baths. Already men and women in the moulded plastic sandals that were now worn by all who could afford shoes were shoving and shuffling for a share of supermarket manna—a free pocketcomb with every purchase above two-and-sixpence. An old crazy woman who wandered the streets of Gala had somehow got in behind the turnstile and was singing hymns up and down the lanes of tinned food and detergents.

He took a detour past the prison instead of going home. He thought there was a track that led round the hill behind the hospital to the prison road. It was as he remembered; followed by the yapping dogs of a squatter family, he came out upon the road and saw it up ahead, like any military camp or prison in Africa, a bald place with blind low buildings exposed to the sun. He did not know what he expected: there was a new, very high fence of diamond mesh wire, barbed on top, rippling tinny light; the new flag drooped. He had been inside many times, while he was D.C. He knew the hot, white courtyard and the smell of disinfectant and sour manioc. No political prisoner had been kept there, during the British administration; they had been sent to detention camps in the various emergencies. He had seen those, too; encampments set down in remote places where no one lived, and, inside, the weeks, months, years, passed in heat and isolation. People had been beaten in them; died of dysentery. A commission of inquiry hadn't healed them or brought them back to life. His agitation on the journey from the Bashi suddenly became something inflated. It sank out of an abnormal glare; he considered it dispassionately. He had looked on that scarred back; but was it really something so inconceivable, for Mweta, for himself—for anybody who had ever ventured out of Wiltshire? His hands had shaken— over that, a commonplace horror?

To condemn it was as much the centre of his being as the buried muscle that pumped blood in his breast. But to tremble virginally at the knowledge that it happened, here under his nose . . .

Part of common knowledge. The air we breathe; I have lived my whole life with that stink in my nostrils. Why gag, now? You work with the stink of violence in your nose just as a doctor must work within the condition of disease and death.

The screw of noon turned upon everything. It held in the breathless house when he sat down to the lunch Kalimo had burned. (Kalimo was much less efficient than he had existed in memory, in Europe; or was it just that Kalimo was older, old? —Bray noticed a bluish ring like the ring around the moon demarking the brown iris from the red-veined yellow of the man's eyeballs.) The more he thought about confronting Mweta the more urgently doubtful he became about his own purpose, and beyond it the shadowy matter— like the area of darkness over a suspect organ in an X-ray plate—of his own authority. If the affair of the boy were an example of abuse by some official making free of new-found power, the conversation with Aleke in itself might be enough to put a stop to this particular incident; Aleke would pass the word to Lebaliso, and Lebaliso would be afraid to act again to please (presumably) some local PIP lordling. The intervention of Mweta might go one step further and ensure the censure of Lebaliso. But there would continue to be other such incidents about which nobody would hear, about which there would be nobody to pass the word. The only way they could be counted upon not to happen at all would be if things were to go well enough, long enough, in the country for a code of efficiency to supersede the surrogate of petty power among administrators and officials. Then only the sort of abuses, involving profit rather than flesh, that are tacitly time-honoured in the democratic states of the West and East, would remain. And for the country to go well enough, long enough, Mweta needed the help of Shinza.

But if what happened to the boy was what Onabu ordered, from the capital?

If such things were part of the regular activities of the Special Branch, State Security—whatever name such an organization chose to go by? His mind went cold with refusal. Yet he had lived so long, and so long here, among white and black, that he half-knew it could not be otherwise. And if that were so, then more than ever what was pointed to was that the country could not afford to have Mweta make an enemy of Shinza.

Mweta was in a neighbouring state on a few days' official visit. Bray could not see him at once. He did not post the letter he had written him; the one to Olivia, either. He went about the house and the *boma* and the broad, shade-dark main street that was Gala like someone who has packed his belongings and sent them ahead to some unknown destination. He kept away from the few people—the Alekes, the Tlumes—he had got to know. One lunchtime on his way home he stopped for a beer at the "native" bar near the vendors' trees. Young men from the industries were there; the elite of Gala, with money coming in regularly every week instead of intermittently, from the occasional cash crop. Old men sat alone at dirty trestles over a mug of home brew, blear and tattered, turning coins and snuff from cotton tobacco bags in that miserly fingering-over with which the aged spin out time left to them. The young ones drank European bottled beer from the local factory and he listened to them arguing about soccer and the price of batteries for radios. Some wore PIP badges as others wore buttons given away by a soft drink company. They ignored him suspiciously; one of the old ones shifted on his seat in a gesture of respectful salute.

At the turn-off to the road where his house was he caught up with Aleke's secretary, trudging along in the heat. Above big sunglasses her forehead shone damp and white. She said, "It's only another hundred yards," but got into the car. "The clutch's gone on my old faithful—going to cost me fourteen pounds." "It's madness to walk in this heat. I can always give you a lift to work."

She said, "Well, I didn't want to force you to go up and down at eight and twelve and so on, just because of me . . . I mean, you don't have to keep office hours, do you . . ."

The house was cool, stuffy, dim, empty; Kalimo had drawn the curtains against the heat, thin and violently coloured as flags against the light. It was true; he didn't have to keep office hours, his job was his own invention, he was responsible only to himself. Those were the conditions he had wanted, in order to make himself useful. The small clink of a cup replaced in a saucer and the faint screech of his knife accompanied him at table in the dim room. Well, there was no reason why anyone else should have to walk in the sun, just because he did not have to be back at the *boma* or anywhere else, at two; while he was having coffee he sent Kalimo over with a note and the Volkswagen key, telling the Edwards girl to use it. Kalimo said, "The *Doña* she very please, she say thank you, she must fetch children, thank you."

He carried some work out under the fig tree; while compiling his own reports he had also sent to England for whatever literature on education systems in underdeveloped countries was available. A tome dealing with Latin America was among the stuff that had arrived while he was at the Bashi. He set himself to read and take notes; the unfamiliar Spanish names provided grist for the tread of his attention, gone smooth and glassy: he plodded on in heat thickening the atmosphere like gelatine setting a liquid. The garden was a bad place at that time of day. The white of the sun under cloud moved a welder's flame along the outlines of branches and skinny leaves and thrust into the nerve that throbbed, a Cyclopean eye, between his eyes. Yet it was too much trouble to move indoors. At half-past four, since that was the time colonial officials had come home, Kalimo brought tea, and Bray asked for cold water as well. It hurt his teeth and seemed to touch the nerve achingly in that third eye. He left the books under the tree and went into the shrouded living-room, the calm decision coming to him matter-of-factly as he entered: he would go to the capital tomorrow. He lay down on the sofa, whose loose cover hitched up under his weight, and smoked a cheroot. His mind was blank of what he had read. He slept; and must have been asleep more than two hours.

He was waking up in a cooling, darkening room from which the day was withdrawing in a pinkish darkness reflected from one of those brilliant sunsets outside the veranda. The air was mottled with rose and dark like the inside of an eyelid. A shape moved in the room. She was putting the keys down on the table without a sound, keeping her eyes on him so as not to wake him. She stopped as a child does in the game of "statues," as he saw her. There was a ringing in his ears—the ringing of crickets all round the house, from the garden. He put out the dark shape of his arm—to receive the keys; a gesture of apology.

And then, with a second's hesitation, she turned with that sideways movement of the hips with which a woman moves between pieces of furniture, came over, and took the forearm—not the hand—in the strange grip of consolation, a kind of staying. As if he were falling asleep rather than waking, he saw with great awareness and clarity what he had scarcely taken in at the time: her hands drawn back, palm open, her breasts offered by the involuntary gesture of backing away, the first day he walked into her as he opened the office door and she was standing there behind it.

They were looking at each other but the faces were concentrations in the half-light, not to be made out as features. He said, "Sit down," and turned his forearm in her grip to take her wrist and press it towards the sofa.

"The door was open," she said, sitting there beside him. Darkness was running together all over the room. A mirror of lemon-coloured light hung in the doorway.

"I don't know when I've had such a headache."

"Oh did you? The humidity was terrible about three o'clock."

"The Volksie behave itself?"

"It was a blessing. The children were way over the other side of town, at the Reillys'."

He would get up, turn on the lamp, offer her a drink. While he thought this he was taken by such desire that his whole body felt swollen with it, the awful undifferentiated desire that he hadn't felt since he was an overgrown youth.

In spite of this, he was not one; he kissed the mouth and caressed the flesh with the skill of experience, got up to make sure Kalimo was not in the house and to lock the doors, and stood there a moment, looking down at the glimmering shape of the body that he had unwrapped from its disguising clothes, the prototype at once familiar and a marvel. He remembered to ask her whether it was all right, and the voice said in the dark, "No," trusting him. He began to make love to her, they began to make love to each other fiercely and while his body raced away from him—extraordinarily, he was thinking of Shinza. Shinza's confident smile, Shinza's strong bare feet, Shinza smoking cigars in the room that smelled of baby. Shinza. Shinza. He brought a small yell of triumph from her; and again.

She took up her clothes by feel and went to dress in the bathroom. For him, with the light, there sprang back the sofa, table of untidy papers, bookcase with its huddle of books tented on one shelf and its spike of invoices and spare light bulbs. A cockroach ran under the rug. He pulled on his trousers and shirt and went to the kitchen for water for drinks. But she came out and said softly, plainly, "What about your boy? I'd better go." She meant that the servant might already have noticed the darkness and the locked door; if anyone saw her now he would put a face to the unusual circumstances.

She was gone before there was the necessity for some sort of show of tenderness, of a change in their acquaintance as strangers. She was gone down through the garden and, he supposed, across the empty scrub. He heard the dogs bark at her approach; she was home already. He realized that he had made love to her without seeing her face. He was alone again in the quiet house; and now remembered that it was Kalimo's evening off to go to church; otherwise the old man could so easily have come battering at the door. The moon had come up and shone upon the books he had left in the garden as it does upon the stones in a graveyard.

He banged the Bashi dust out of his suitcase and put a few things in it again. He tried to put through a call to Roly Dando but after an hour the exchange rang back to say there was no reply. He took a lamp and changed a worn tyre on the car. Flying ants came to the light and shed their wings like soapflakes underfoot. There was the smell of his sweat, and, as he worked, very faintly, that other odour. He had a shower and at ten o'clock felt very hungry and put together

a strange meal out of all the small souvenirs of past meals that Kalimo hoarded in the refrigerator. He left early, getting up before light.
The trees of Gala had not yet come to life with birds, but the main
street was not quite empty. An old man rested on the post office
steps, his day's journey already begun, patiently digging a jigger
from his big toe.

Bray reached the capital by lunchtime next day and did not go to
Dando; instead he went straight to the Silver Rhino and took a room
there. "No difficulty about that," Margot Wentz said dryly, and, keys
in hand, flung open the doors of empty rooms and rondavels for him
to choose from.

"Of course things'll pick up again, it'll pick up again now." Hjalmar
Wentz was awaiting their return to the office, watching their faces as
they appeared. His wife ignored the remark. "Don't go in for lunch,
eat with us," Hjalmar put in, and she said to Bray, "Of course, you remember where to come—just down the passage here, to the right.
You don't mind waiting till about two? I can't get out of the kitchen
before then."

Hjalmar seemed in a state of happy alarm over his arrival. They
went into the bar and he appropriated an order of Danish beers
meant for someone else. The bar was full, even if most of the rooms
were empty. The fan on the low ceiling churned voices that it seemed
had not stopped since Bray had left the capital last time. "If the
Czechs can turn them out at five pounds a thousand, there's nothing
in it for us. . . ." "He used to be down in Zambia, with the R.S.T.
crowd, little plump Scotsman, you remember . . ." ". . . played to a
five, but that was when I was a lot younger . . ." ". . . yes, but what's
the point, you can't·work on less than twenty-five per cent, a waste of
time . . ." ". . . at head office in Nairobi, I said, you might get away
with that sort of attitude . . . stupid bastard . . ." White men in
bauxite, in road construction, in mining equipment, in technical aid,
textiles and tin, black men from Agriculture, Public Works, Posts and
Telegraphs—the Ministries down the road. The black ones were more
carefully dressed than the white and most spoke a back-slapping,
jolly English instead of the local language. They were youthful and
good-looking, with their little ears, round black heads, and black
hands, among the bald pale heads and drooping, gin-flushed ears. "I
was at his home yesterday, my dear chap, I know him well, ever

since we were at teacher-training in Salonga . . ." ". . . very incon-
venient, the wife said to me, 'How was it Mr. Mapira didn't see you
at Chibwe's place'—oh yes—there's nothing you can keep from a
wife, good Lord—" ". . . have a chat with the Minister next week,
yes that's what I intend . . ." ". . . these garage chappies, man, something should be done about them, I mean they charge a person what
they like. . . ."

The tiny Viking ships of the mobile above the bar spun slowly in
the sluggish draft; Hjalmar was plunged into an account of the Silver
Rhino's finances and the terms of sale under which the place had
been acquired. His voice burrowed through the babble with the
obliviousness of a man for whom everything around him is a manifes-
tation of the problem that possesses him. He could never sell so long
as the legality of the original sale was not settled, meanwhile the first
mortgage wasn't met and the bank refused to give a second mortgage
because of the dispute about ownership. The builder was "getting impatient" over the alterations he had done when they took over; everything would be all right if the brewery would advance money in exchange for a share, but now with the new legislation the breweries
weren't supposed to advance to people who were resident aliens and
not citizens of the country.

Living alone, remote from the demands of friendship for the past
few months, Bray had become unaccustomed to this European intimacy, this steamy involvement in other people's lives. All he could do
was prompt with the sort of brief questions that enabled Hjalmar
Wentz to unburden himself—though it was an unburdening only of
the facts: Bray could sense that they construed a kind of front—
"Margot and I think . . ." ". . . all we really need, then, is, say, another year to get straight"—out of a more private struggle that could
not be talked about. Wentz was saying, after a pause, "The thing to
do, I suppose, would be to talk to Ras Asahe. . . ." The haggard,
handsome Scandinavian face seemed to be waiting, as if for a blow.
The cuts of strain slashed across the cheekbone under each eye. "He
has an uncle on the board—you know." All large white companies
had a token black man on their boards. "A word from there, and everything . . . well. It would get us out of a hole for the meantime."

"Yes, if the brewery were to be persuaded—"

Wentz was still waiting, ready not to flinch. He said, "But Emmanuelle is not easy to deal with. My wife—Margot—we don't know how Emmanuelle would react. And apart from that, what would it look like, I mean to the man? Up till now, we've never encouraged it, this friendship with Emmanuelle."

Now that he had delivered the slap himself, he was in some way released. "How do you think things are going?"

"I should ask you. I'm too far away from the centre."

Wentz opened his hands at the room, interlocked them under his chin. "What? This? The black ones have got the government jobs they wanted, and the white ones are in business as usual—*they* are happy, nothing's changed. He's been very clever. You should hear them: what a marvellous chap he is, what a stable government . . . Oh he's been very clever. When you think what they said about him before, eh? All that business about flight of capital is forgotten, they want to stay put and get good quick returns. Of course the honeymoon isn't over. I only talk about what I see. The black people—after all, who are they, here?—the people who have moved up into admin- istrative power, the white-collar people who aren't somebody's clerk any more, and the mine workers who are moving up into the jobs they could have done before and were kept out of because of the white man. So I say it's going very well. *He's* doing very well. What it's like for the rest of the country—I never get farther than the vege- table farm where Margot gets the stuff for the hotel, I drive there with the van twice a week, and that's what I know of the country!" He laughed at himself. "What's happening up there?"

"Well, there's a bit of industry beginning around Gala itself—but the new agreement over the fishing concessions leaves the whole lake area just as it was, and the Bashi Flats need about everything you can name before one could think of resettlement schemes there— roads, control of flood waters—everything."

Hjalmar objected. "The royalty on the fishing rights is increased by about twenty per cent, I think. The money's not all going out of the country any more."

"But wages in the fish industry haven't gone up one penny. Of course there's the Development and Planning Commission— something may come out of that, for the lake people. And the Bashi —they need it even more. But the potential of the fishing industry is *there* for the taking. . . ."

"Schemes, commissions, plans—well, poor devils—it's their affair, isn't it," said Hjalmar Wentz. "It's not for you and me, it's not our life, they have to work it out for themselves." He took a deep breath and held it a moment: his eyes were following the movement of someone across the room, and then he gave an anticipatory smile as his daughter came up. "Emmanuelle, you remember Colonel Bray? He's staying with us this time—" She was saying with the inattentive correctness of one performing an errand, "Someone called Thomson-Waite is here to see you. He has a black attaché case with initials. The hair in his nose is dyed by nicotine." "Good God, Emmanuelle." Her father laughed, showing her off to Bray. The girl, perfectly serious and distant, bit at a hangnail on her thumb. "So you can decide whether you will see him or not. I should say he comes from a bank or a health department; he's sniffing about after something." "Oh God. I better go. Did you put him in the office?" Hjalmar went ahead of her with his head thrust before him anxiously. Bray saw him look round to ask her something but she had turned away through the tables.

Bray had a shower and sat in a broken deck-chair in the garden, waiting for lunch. He read in the morning paper that Mweta had returned from his state visit. Unity had been reaffirmed, useful proposals had been made, the 50-million-pound hydro-electric scheme to serve the two countries jointly had been agreed upon in principle . . . the leading article questioned the economics of the scheme, as opposed to its value as a demonstration of Pan-African interdependence. *There is no doubt whatever that this country sees its destiny always as part of the greater destiny of the African continent . . . no doubt that President Mweta, the day he took up the burdens of office, has taken along with responsibilities at home the ideal of an Africa that would present an entity of international cooperation to a world that has so far signally failed to resolve national contradictions. But we must not waste our own resources in order to foster cooperation across our borders. We have, in the lake that forms our northern border, a potential source of electric power that renders unnecessary any such scheme in the South, a scheme that by its nature would place our vital industrial development ultimately at the mercy of any instability that might manifest itself in our neighbour's house. . . .*

Hjalmar's daughter walked right past him across the grass with Ras Asahe, deep in low-voiced conversation. They ignored the figure behind the paper; living in a hotel, the girl carried her private world about her in the constant presence of anonymous strangers. A piping scale climbed and descended; she must have a recorder. The pair settled down somewhere on the grass quite near, and he heard Emmanuelle's clear, decisive voice: "Somebody told me it was just like a sneeze" and the man's deep, derisive voice: "Good God, that's how you whites prepare girls. If you'd been an African, you'd know how to make love, you'd have been taught."

"Oh you're so bloody superior, you've got the idea nobody else knows how to live."

There was silence. Then Bach on the recorder, piercing, trilling, on and on, up and up, sustaining high notes in a gleeful, punishing scream.

At the round table in the Wentzes' quarters the chaps of Margot Wentz's heavy white arms hung majestically over the dishes as she served. She had powdered her face but the smell of hotel gravy clung about her. Every now and then she gazed on her son Stephen as at a gobbling pet dog at his dinner-dish, half affectionate, half repelled. He had his father's blond handsome face, blown up to the overgrown proportions of young white men born in Africa and forced by sport and the sun, like battery chickens. Hjalmar Wentz kept arching his eyebrows and blinking, fighting off a daze of preoccupation. He gave in to laughter against himself: "The fellow who approved the plan for the servants' rooms just stamped it without looking. He was going back to England anyway, couldn't care a damn. The whole thing is against municipal regulations, there aren't enough air bricks—can you imagine, the water main is connected in such a way we haven't been paying for the water used down there?"

"I told you I could smell drains or money." All the tendons and muscles of Emmanuelle's brown hands showed with anatomical precision as she buttered a piece of bread.

"What you going to do?" Margot Wentz said.

He appealed to Bray: "What they tell me I have to, eh? Get the builder along and discuss it with the inspector."

"Have some more salad, Colonel Bray? No? —What builder?" Margot Wentz put down her fork and waited for the answer with the patience of one who knows all the answers she can expect.

Her husband gave her a quick glance. "Well, Atkinson—who else?"

"I don't think Atkinson will work for us again, Hjalmar."

Stephen was holding out his plate for another helping of meat; he shook it impatiently, wanting to speak but occupied with the surveillance of what he was getting. "Knock out a few bricks, what's the big fuss?"

"The water. The regulations." His mother laid out the facts gently.

"Agh . . . it'll be a year before they send someone again, and if they do, well, there're the air bricks, you knock out a few bricks, that's all—" The boy was cutting up food, spearing it, now he stopped his mouth with it while his sister, her hands idle on the table, said, "Close your eyes and wait for them to go away, Hjalmar." Her own narrow black eyes acknowledged Bray's presence a moment, the pupils seemed actually to contract closed, falling asleep, and then come to life blackly liquid again, and, just as he was thinking how the girl never smiled, she smiled at him, the brilliant, vivid, humorous smile of a deep self-confidence.

Lunch broke up abruptly among the preoccupations of Hjalmar, his wife, and the son; Stephen was summoned by the barman, a coloured man with a strand of silky black moustache. "The trouble is you're too soft with these guys. Someone's only got to say he comes from the water board or something . . . it's not the *end of the world* . . . ?" Stephen's lingering reproach was sympathetic, directed from the door. The barman showed the servant's facility for pretending not to hear when in his employer's quarters. Bray felt oddly grouped with him as the man stood there easing his feet in shoes that had cut-outs to accommodate bunions. Hjalmar swallowed his coffee because Margot Wentz reminded him that he had to be at the station in half an hour; she explained to Bray, "If you're not there when the train comes in, they just take the stuff out of the refrigerated truck and dump it on the platform in the sun."

"Where've you got the invoices?"

"All right, all right, it'll come to me in a minute—" She got up to follow an instinct that would lead her to the point at which, in the morning's tread up and down between corridor and kitchen, storeroom and office, she had set down the papers.

Emmanuelle went over and kissed her father on the forehead, for her mother's benefit. Margot Wentz, picking up glasses to look over the invoices she had found in her handbag, paused as the girl pushed aside with her lips the strand of bright hair that stretched across the baldness; there was on the older woman's face a groping recognition; and then she turned away in herself and with a hitch of the nose to settle her glasses, peered down at the invoices.

Although Hjalmar was in a hurry he made slow progress with Bray down the passage, talking and pausing to make his point. It was the railways, now; a high incidence of accidents since Africans had been taken on as engine drivers. Bray said, "Drinking seems to be the trouble." Hjalmar Wentz found it absolutely necessary to place on record in some way the assumptions, the misrepresentations that threatened all round. He invoked Mweta without name, the touchstone of a personal pronoun on which the voice came down with passing emphasis, signally, instantly understood. He said passionately, "Of course they are drinking. They have to show somehow to themselves that the new life is good. How do these whites think their great-grandfathers behaved when they first got wages for a week's work in a factory in Europe, eh? These Englishmen—their great-grandfathers were getting drunk on cheap gin, and they turn up their noses at the Africans. . . . But *he* knows how to go about it, *he* knows the thing to do. Now he makes it an offence to drink before you go on duty, one drink and you're out of the job. Sensible, reasonable. You'll see, soon, eh, the men themselves will impose a code of behaviour—the railways won't be any worse than before."

Bray went to the public booth on the veranda to telephone Mweta's private secretary, Wilfrid Asoni. But he was "not available"; Clive Small, the PRO, came to the telephone as a substitute. He was enthusiastically pleasant; he was sure the President would be delighted and so on—"Do you think it's possible for me to see him tomorrow?" Small would certainly do his best; as Bray knew, of course, the Big Man had only just come back—Small would leave an urgent note for Asoni—there was all the confident sycophancy of the professionally agreeable in the voice. Then Bray phoned the Bayley house, but was relieved that there was no one home; he did not want to go about among the group of friends until he had seen Mweta. He had half meant to mention to Hjalmar Wentz that it was not necessary to tell Roly Dando he was there, he would do so himself tomorrow. Well, he had said nothing. He decided to leave it all to chance, and even took the car into town to do some shopping; as always, when you lived in a remote posting, there were small comforts that were exotic to the general stores at home. And then it was an event to walk into a bookshop again, even the rather poor one here, stocked mainly with last year's best sellers and James Bond. He bought himself a paperback Yeats, a book of essays by an African professor of political science at an East African university, a reprint of Isaac Deutscher's *Stalin*—everything come upon was a treasure. For a half-hour he forgot why he was in the capital. He bought a stapler and a couple of ball-points that seemed an improvement on the usual kind, trying them out on the recommendation of a pretty little African shopgirl with a crêpey black pompadour and painted eyes. There were children's books on display and he almost bought a couple of Tin-Tin—for the children, the girl and those little boys, one at either hand of Rebecca Edwards, coming across the open ground between his house and the Tlumes'. But he put the books back on the stand. He collected all the copies —three weeks old—of overseas newspapers and journals he didn't subscribe to, and came out laden.

When he got back to the Silver Rhino there was a message from the President's secretary's office. There was an appointment for him at eleven-fifteen tomorrow morning. Hjalmar Wentz, who had taken the message, showed the opposite of curiosity—in fact, Bray felt overestimated by Wentz's determinedly laconic discretion, which assumed that Bray's position was all along some confidential, influential one, for which the banishment to the bush on a vague educational project was a front. "Oh—by the way, if Roly comes into the bar, you won't say I'm here, will you? I'm going to ring him tomorrow, but I don't feel particularly sociable at the moment, it would mean a heavy-drinking evening if the two of us get together—"

"Good thing you said so. I'll warn Stephen."

His daughter lifted the counter-flap of the office and walked through. Her jutting hip-bones pegged a skimpy cotton dress across her flat belly, she carried a music-case of the kind that children swing. "Emmanuelle, if you should see Mr. Dando, don't say anything about Colonel Bray being here."

"I never see Mr. Dando," she said fastidiously.

Bray laughed, and her father was forced to smile, admitting: that's how she is.

Bray took a beer to the same rickety deck-chair in the garden, his back to the bar and the hotel. Suddenly two sticky hands smelling of liquorice pressed over his eyes, and the chair was jiggled and bumped amid giggles. Vivien Bayley's children ambushed him, while Vivien, grown pregnant since he saw her last, stood waiting by, smiling for it to be over. "Enough now. You've given James a surprise. Now let him get up. Enough, Eliza! *Enough!*"

He gathered a couple of the children by arms and legs, and came over to her, limbs agitating in all directions. He dropped them on the grass, and kissed her. She had the neglected air—forgetful of herself —of a child-bearing woman. "We saw you at the traffic lights at the railway bridge. They insisted."

The children were yelling, "Caught you, caught you!"

"I phoned when I arrived, just after lunch."

"I'd gone to pick them up at school. Neil'll be thrilled. He's just been to Dar-es-Salaam for a week and it's so flat to be home again. James, you're looking slim and *beautiful*, and as you see—" They laughed together, over her.

"I've sweated it off, Christ, it's been killing sometimes this month."

"Well, I know, but mine isn't the kind that will melt, I'm afraid."

"Oh, it'll be shed all at once one day, though, and no keeping off bread—" Their liking for each other came alive instantly, as it always did, the pilot flame turned up by meeting.

She carried him off for dinner; that was the way it was, in the capital, nothing had changed. Homeward traffic was thick in the hour after the shops closed; an hour later, and the streets would be those of a country town, warm and empty in the dark. They passed Mweta's residence with the sentries in their boxes. In the Bayleys' garden Vivien brought him up to date, while the children ate their supper on the grass. The Pettigrews had been posted to Beirut, and were pleased, Jo-Ann would do some work at the university there; David Rathebe, the South African refugee, had disappeared for two months and reappeared, he was supposed to have been in Algiers; Timothy Odara had been offered the Secretaryship for Health, but Evelyn had made him refuse because she wanted him to take up a post-graduate research scholarship in America. They hadn't seen much of Mweta and Joy, though the children had been to a birthday party at the Residence last week; Joy had got rid of the flower-arranging Englishwoman and was much happier, running the place very competently in her own way, with the help of that nice sensible woman, an aunt of hers, who had been housekeeper for twenty years or so to the General Manager of one of the gold-mining companies. Mweta was certainly being very successful in wooing foreign capital, at the industrial level, if not on the international money marts; there was even going to be a Golden Plate dinner where white businessmen could meet the President at a cost of a mere fifty pounds a ticket, money to go to the university scholarship fund.

Neil Bayley came home and was the centre of tumbling, shouting children. He still looked more like a student than a registrar. It was natural for him to deal with a number of different people and situations at once; he plunged into greetings for Bray, shadow-boxed his son, patted his wife on the backside: "How-you, girlie? Good God, I've just been acting father-confessor to a gorgeous, red-haired eighteen-year-old peach-of-a-thing . . . if you . . . bloom'd come off if you so much as . . . They're told they can come to me to discuss any problem so long as it's not sex, religion, or politics, James."

After a lot of wine at dinner Bray felt the desire to talk mastering him. He wanted to talk about Shinza, to bring the figure of Shinza, barefoot in his dressing-gown, up over their horizon; to see what Neil would look up and interpret it as. He talked round the figure in his mind, instead. What were the rumours of Mweta's difficulties with some of the Ministers? Any idea of the basis? "Paul Sesheka's always given a bit of trouble, from the beginning, as you know," Neil said. "And there's been some talk lately about Dhlamini Okoi lobbying for him—the allocation of funds vote, and so on. A lot of squabbling about that because inevitably, everyone wants to be able to say they've done this and that for the development of the area they come from. Everybody wants to be the brown-eyed boy back home, because he's got them a cotton ginnery or an abattoir. Nobody wants to leave it to the development planning commission to decide which area needs what. Yes, Okoi and Moses Phahle've been showing signs of making ready to attach themselves to Sesheka, as if the pilot fish's going places—but I don't know, I can't see Sesheka really threatening Mweta, do you? I don't see him lasting five minutes with Mweta, I don't think he has the stuff. He wavered badly over this hydro-electric scheme, now. You must have read that? First he pressed the P.M. to go ahead, he "regretted" that so little was being done to demon-

strate the practical friendship and brotherhood and so on with neighbouring African territories. Then he suddenly changed his mind and
put forward the claims of the lake for a scheme of our own—which
wouldn't be a bad idea, if it weren't for the fact that we'd have to
bear the whole cost alone, whereas the other scheme's a shared one
and anyway the finance is already assured, America and West Germany and France are paying—"

"That's the line the morning paper took, I saw."

"I know. Just coincidence. I don't think Sesheka has any influence
there. That's just Evan Black wanting to keep the circulation up by
being provocative."

Vivien said, "Unfair, Neil. You know Evan thinks the people up
north are being forgotten."

"But if it were someone more forceful than Sesheka, would Mweta
have to worry?" Bray asked.

Neil belched, shaking his head, and when he could speak: "Aha!
But that's another story, James. That's always something to worry
about; if it were to be a Tola Tola, for instance, even if there isn't any
genuine grievance for him to climb up by."

"You don't think there's any genuine grievance?"

"No I don't. By genuine grievance I mean that Mweta would have
to be failing to make use of what is available to him for this country."

"Hjalmar tells me industrialists are paying fifty pounds just to dine
with him."

Neil grinned. "My God, he's a glutton for punishment, old Mweta."

They talked of Bray's work and Bray told an anecdote or two about
Gala—how his name had been up at the club for weeks until the
bold draper seconded it. Vivien was in conversation with a friend on
the telephone; she came back after a while and said, "Did you know
Mweta's going to speak over the radio at midnight? Apparently it's
been announced every hour all afternoon."

Neil opened another bottle of wine. "The contract's been given to
the Chinese. France, West Germany and America have called off the
loan. Or they're going to build both dams—the lake one as well. My,
my. We can't go to bed."

Vivien looked at Bray. She said, "He's tired, he's driven hundreds
of miles."

He was feeling embarrassed for Mweta. Why midnight? Who advised him about such things? Perhaps he didn't know that Hitler used to choose odd hours of the night or early morning for his speeches, entering through the territory of dreams, invading people's minds when blood pressure and nervous resistance are at lowest ebb. "Certainly midday would be a pleasanter time to report back on his dam."

"Joy says he's never in bed before three, anyway."

Neil began to scratch his neck restlessly. "Shall we phone Jennypenny and Curtis and get them to join the vigil?" Vivien said mildly, since nothing would stop Neil if he felt the need of company, "We haven't seen James for months, I want to talk to James. Rebecca writes she's got a house quite near you?—thank heaven she's out of the hotel. I do think your Aleke should have seen there was somewhere for her to live before getting her up there. What sort of man is he? You know, with Rebecca, people just exploit her." She looked for reassurance.

Bray was saying, "Half a house. She's sharing with some people—" while Neil gave his short laugh and said fondly, "Poor old backwoods Becky, we must write to her."

"But Aleke—you think he's all right?"

"Darling, of course he'll make a pass at her, if that's what you mean." Neil cut across. "What else do you expect? She has that effect, our Becky."

Defending her against Aleke, Vivien said, "It's not right that this idea should've somehow . . . she's quite the opposite, if you really know her—she doesn't try for men at all. But it's just a kind of awful compassion . . ."

Neil said aggressively, "Oh really, is that what you females call it."

"Oh I know you don't like the idea. That there could be anything about you." She was talking to her husband, now; slowly they were beginning to pick up words like stones.

Bray felt unimportantly ashamed of his casualness. But all he said was, in the same tone, "Aleke's a good chap to work for, I should think. Her children have got in to the local school."

At midnight Mweta's voice filled the room. They sat dreamily still, not looking at each other. Vivien's right hand was pressed against the side of her belly to quiet the only movement in the room, stirring there. Mweta announced the immediate introduction of a Preventive Detention Bill.

It was all there, set out again in the morning paper. As he read he heard Mweta's voice, as if it were addressed to him. Emergency regulations had been invoked to bring the Bill into force immediately without the usual parliamentary procedure. The step had been "taken with the greatest reluctance" but "without any doubt of the necessity." "I would be betraying the people, the sacred trust of their future, if I did not act swiftly and without hesitation. . . . Certain individuals have begun to gnaw secretly at the foundations of the state which the people have laid down so firmly through their work and dedication. Certain individuals are incapable of understanding the transformation of personal ambitions, petty aims, into the higher cause of securing the peace and progress of the nation—a cause that even the humblest people of our nation have shown themselves equal to in the short time since we have had our country in our own hands. Certain individuals are ready to destroy the general good for the sake of petty ambitions. They are weak and few, and so long as you trust and support your leaders, you need not fear them. They are small as ants. But they are also greedy as ants; if we say, oh, it's only a few ants, we may wake up one day and find the floorboards collapsing beneath all we are building. We must take the powers to stop the rot before it starts, to act while there is still time to turn these people from the mistakes they have fallen into, and to show them where their true interest, like yours and mine, really lies—"

The paper reproduced across five columns the picture of Mweta smiling from the doorway of the plane as he arrived back in the country a few days before, and the leading article, suppressing the question mark, pointed out that there was no cause for confusion and alarm; the President would not have left the country if he had not felt fully in control of the situation.

The waiters shouted to each other as they went about the rondavels at the Silver Rhino, banging on the doors to deliver early morning tea and newspapers. (Between finger and thumb, Bray pinched off a couple of ants that had quickly found the sugar.) A boiler was being stoked up. The off-key musical gong that was played up and down corridors and garden to announce meals drew close and faded, as the girl's recorder had done the day before. Footsteps clipped over the concrete paths with the purpose of morning. The taps on the washbasin began to creak and fart as the plumbing was taxed. Bray was taken by the flow of these things—bathroom ritual, clothes put on, breakfast eaten—and brought to the point where, five minutes before eleven-fifteen, he had the door opened to him under the portico with the white pillars to which he had come a number of times in his life: to pay respects as a D.C. newly appointed; to plead for Mweta's release from confinement; to answer the complaints made against himself by the white residents of Gala province.

Out of the trance of commonplace that had brought him here, Bray in the waiting room of the Presidential Residence became intensely alert. He could feel the rapid beat of his heart in the throb of the hand, on the chair-arm, that held the cigarette burning away. He distinguished the quality of the room's silence, and the displacement of his own presence there, like the rise in the volume of water when some object is lowered into it. At the same time he was going over rapidly and fluently, in words instead of those surges of imagery and emotion with which a meeting is usually rehearsed, what was to be said. He was possessed with the calm, absolute tension of excitement. It was the first time for a very long time. He opened the windows above the window-seat and the park out there—thin trees standing quietly in the heat, a pair of hoopoes picking on the grass—existed within a different pace, like a landscape seen through the windows of an express train.

The secretary, Asoni, came in quickly. "You understand, Colonel, if it had been anybody else it would have been out of the question today, as I said to Mr. Small. There is really no time for private interviews. . . . We are only just back, and now this other—" The sides of his mouth pulled down, proprietorial, brisk, impulsive. "If it had been anybody else I couldn't . . . but I have just managed to fit you in . . ." It was the manner of the waiter, exacting dependence on his goodwill for a decent table. Small looked round the door: "I'm fascinated by the splendid work you're doing in the North." It had all the conviction of a stock phrase; simply substitute "in the South" or "the swamps" or wherever the individual had happened to have been since Small saw him last. "I know the Big Man's longing to see you, nothing would induce him to miss that, though he's up to his ears. Unfortunately, it'll just have to be rather brief, alas, I'm afraid."

Bray was not forthcoming with any assurance that he would not prolong the visit. Chatting, the two of them escorted him out into the corridor, where they were held up by the passage of a giant copper urn or boiler being shuffled along on the heads and arms of workmen. Wilfrid Asoni turned, with a theatrical gesture to Small.

"What in God's name d'you think you're doing?" Small stood his ground before the procession. The men lost coordination under the burden, and their gleaming missile swayed forward. "Why wasn't that thing brought through the service entrance? The kitchens—why don't you use the kitchen door, eh? Who allowed these men to come this way?" Servants and explanations appeared. The kitchen doors were too small. "You can't just bring men through the Residence, you know that. *You* know that perfectly well, Nimrod. Good God, anybody just walking through the place, anybody who says he's a workman?" He and Asoni looked to each other. "That's security for you, eh? —Well, get the thing *out of the way,* get it in *here,* come on, come on . . ." The men backed off through the double doors of a reception room in a bewildered posse, to let Bray and Asoni and Small pass. The two had lost interest in Bray. "Fantastic!" "You're certainly right, Clive." "But seriously, eh?" "That's Colonel Onabu's security, yes." "Well, I know who's going to hear about *that.*" "I *hope* so. I certainly hope so." "I'll be on that telephone in five minutes. Unless you'd rather do it?" Wilfrid Asoni slipped into the President's study and closed the door on his own voice switched to the official calm of the doctor entering the ward of an important private patient. He appeared again at once and opened the door for Bray absently. Bray caught a brushing glimpse of his plump sculptured face, the eyes set in the black skin smoothly as the enamelled eyes of ancient Greek figures, already turned to the piece of importance he shared with Small.

Mweta was on his feet behind the company director's desk, leaning forward on his palms. There was always the second, on first entering his presence, like the pang of remembering the first sight of someone with whom one long ago fell in love. He came round with that smile —a toothpaste-advertisement smile, really, in the associations of Europe, but in Africa the smile of a boy come upon on the road somewhere, biting into sugar-cane—and took Bray's hands in his elegant dark ones. A kind of current of euphoria went through the two men. "If you'd said to me, who'd you like to be there when you get home, James would have been the answer. Oh but it's tiring, eh, James?— years ago, you didn't tell me, you didn't warn about that. From the moment the plane arrived, three, four meetings a day—and the lunches, and the cocktail parties, the dinners— And twice it happened there was something special to discuss before a conference— the only time was before breakfast or after midnight."

"Well, you've always had the stuff it takes. All those miles on the bicycle; that was the right preparation."

"Anyway, we got what we wanted. And this is one of the times when a tied loan is an advantage, eh, all the equipment and materials and skilled manpower comes from the financing countries. They're paying and their men'll see to it that the job is done. No throwing up your hands over this delay and that. No defaulting contractors to blame, while we pay. D'you know we'll get six thousand kilowatt hours a year, when it's fully operative. We could sell to the Congo, Malawi—Zambia, even—who knows, it's possible they'll get out of Kariba. Our lake scheme in the North was just one of those dreams, you know, nice dreams we had before Independence. It's not a proposition, compared with this. The main thing is money—it's exactly twice as hard to get money for a scheme that benefits a single state as it is to get the same money to benefit two. And you've got to try for it alone. I can tell you, James, it's all the difference in the world, it's the difference between going as a beggar and going as statesmen. That's one thing I've learnt."

There was a tea table near the woolly sofa, now, with a couple of black leather airport chairs for talks less formal than those conducted across the desk. They came to rest there.

Bray said, out of the warmth and ease, "That seems to have gone off splendidly. But what bothers me is the other. Last night." It seemed a piece of cruelty to speak. Mweta's eyes winced. He folded his arms to recapture the ease. "I don't understand, James."

"Doesn't it bother you?"

Mweta's eyes continued to flicker. He said, smiling, "You heard what I said."

"Oh that. What you had to say. But what you think about it? The real reasons why you've found it necessary? I wasn't coming to talk to you about this at all—"

Mweta made an eager, dismissing gesture; Bray came to see him because he was Bray.

"No—I had a reason"—a rebuff for them both—"there was a young man I picked up on the road to the Bashi last week. I discovered later that he'd been in detention at Gala prison for almost three months—he didn't need to wait for your new law. I was going to talk to you about him, I didn't know whether you knew, though of course I could tell that Onabu knew, this sort of authority—I don't know what to call it—came from up there, from Onabu. . . . But that's not what matters. I mean, it matters enormously in itself, but there's something much more important, and now, since last night, even more important. The boy, the Detention Bill, they're the effect."

Mweta sat back in himself, arms still crossed, in the determined, flexed attention that Bray knew so well. His face had smoothed momentarily as if he were to be let off; then the flick in his eyes came again. Bray was aware of it all the time.

"—That's not what matters. Because it seems clear to me that what happened to the boy, the Detention Bill—they're inevitable, essential, you can't do without them, your reason being what it is—"

Mweta came in quickly but distrusting: "Yes, my good reason. I'm not going to stand by and let this country be ruined by trouble-makers."

"What do you call trouble-makers, Mweta?"

"You get people who see Independence right from the beginning as a free-for-all. Grab what you can . . . They're always there. You have to deal with them. You know that. I don't like it, but I have to do it."

"You're better off than most, here. You've got a good chance of giving people what they lack."

Mweta said, "James, that's not the point. You could give them all a house with electric light and a clean-hands job and you'd still have trouble from some people."

"Then there's something else that's bothering them."

Mweta gave a little snorting smile. "You're quite right, it's power, that's what they want. Somebody wants power and there's only one way for such a person to try and get it. He must use every poor fellow who'll listen to him, he must stir them up with talk they don't understand, so they'll be only too ready to believe we've bamboozled them, too, and from this it follows so easily to convince them that if this country isn't the Garden of Eden, that's got nothing to do with their inadequacies and our difficulties. —James—we'll clean up that young rubbish and show the people behind them it's no good. You can believe me. I don't want the Detention thing a day longer, after that."

An irritable spark like static electricity ran between them. "There won't be an after that. You'll need to keep that bill forever, if you don't do something about the reason why you need it in the first place. If you'd do that you wouldn't be obliged to 'deal' with it. The way you have to deal with it now. This way you don't like, Mweta—"

Mweta was about to answer and did not. He smiled at Bray to shut him out. "Well, go on."

"I believe some of those ants of yours are nibbling under their own benches in the House."

Mweta's mouth moved and settled.

" 'They are being watched,' " Bray said, "Well and good. And who else? Who else is being watched? And why? Mweta, why? What for? I can't help feeling convinced that if you'd given him a ministry there'd have been no trouble. From him. He'd have dealt with the trouble."

"He's the one who's always made it," Mweta said. Then suddenly, like an actor going out after his audience he turned shining eyes and eager-hunched body, all gathered up in a stalking intensity and burst out, beguiling, gesturing—"Shinza! From the day of self-rule he began to turn his criticism on us. From that day. Always looking at me and shaking his head inside. Whatever it was we were discussing.

F*   ⟩ 161 ⟨

No trust any more for anybody. He made up his mind he had to watch the rest of us the way he used to watch *them*. Yes! You remember? At the talks in London, he was always the one would come out and say, afterwards, 'I don't think so-and-so means what he says, he's playing for time.' 'So-and-so's going to do what the Colonial Secretary says.' 'This one must be made to back down. . . .' He watched them for us while we were too busy thinking what point to make next. He found out things I hadn't noticed, often he was right, he could warn you. But among ourselves! Our own men! In the Central Committee, among the ministers! How can you work like that? James, James"— his voice dropped to patient reasonableness, soft and dramatic—"I can tell you, his eyes were on the back of my head. I ask him something—I went to him as I always did, you understand—he was my father, my brother—he listens with a smile on his face and his eyes closed." Mweta was standing over Bray. He hung there, paused, breathing heavily, gasping, almost, like a man about to sob, deserted by words. " 'I hadn't understood the issue properly.' 'Did I realize who I was dealing with?' —With his eyes closed. To smell me out. Yes, like he did the Englishmen in Lancaster House, making the noises in the throat and looking like they're falling asleep just when they're ready to get you. It was mad, eh? All right. I said to myself, he's your father, your brother. *All right.* But let him come out in the open. Let him speak what he thinks at the time for these things, like anybody else. This is a government, not a secret society. Open your eyes and look at me, Shinza. But I kept quiet. A long time, a long, long time. Did I ever say anything to you? That last time in London? You never knew what it was like. I was ashamed, you understand, I didn't want you to know how he was behaving. I didn't want to believe it myself. But I can't think about myself any more. If I do, I must get out"—he strode to the window and flung away the park, out there, rippling in the still heat—"We're not in the bush in Gala any more, with nothing but each other. Eight million people are in this country. I can't be tied by the hind leg like a cow. When Clough and the British Chief of Staff met for the defence agreement and the question of a base on the southern border came up, Clough starts outlining what he 'believes' I'd agree to, and, my God, it's clear to me that he's got a pretty good idea before where we'll make a concession and where we'll stick fast—the missile base question, for example. Clough obviously knew we were going to bargain with that, he was prepared, he made no bones about it—and so I said to him—that is, I made a point of raising an objection to something that we really had no objection to at all, just to see what his reaction would be. And he came out with it just like that: 'But I understood that this would be acceptable to your government.'—From *where* did you understand, I said. Who gave you to understand? Of course, he got out of that one somehow. But later on I asked him, alone. 'I was given to understand.' He looked at me as if I was mad, as if I didn't know. You can't blame him. Who gave you to understand? —*He* had had talks with Clough: 'Of course, Shinza knew my predecessor well.' It was often useful to chat beforehand. Much progress had been made quietly, in the past. And so on. What could I say? Well, that time no damage was done. Luckily. But that's the kind of thing. Look at the minority report he put in. And that's something you knew about. You know what you thought of that. Yes, well, a bit tactless, that's what you said to me. But you're not one to say much, and I know you were worried, whatever you said. I have eight millions on my hands, James, and I can only look after them my own way."

"You've forced him into a kind of opposition that isn't there, between you."

Mweta's hands dropped, swung helplessly. "Not there! If you give him *that much*, he'll swallow your arm. You only think of him years ago."

"Yes, he has changed," Bray said. "But you know I've seen him."

"No," Mweta said. "No, I tell you I didn't know."

It was the first time, the first time since he was that boy with a guitar, on a bicycle, that Bray didn't know whether Mweta was speaking the truth.

"When?"

"That was where I was going—last week, on the Bashi road."

"Oh. I see."

"No you don't see. I wrote something to you—didn't send it, the business about the boy bothered me. . . . But I wanted to tell you, I can't believe Shinza would make a move to oust you *if he were with you*. If you were still in it together. The differences you had in the Party, just before independence—that's not to be taken as conclusive. He'll fight you there because he believes that the Party should stand

for certain things, the Party shouldn't take account of the government's limitations, even if they're enforced by circumstance: that's
what the Party's there for, in a state like this one. To keep in front of
the government the original idea of what Independence should mean,
to oppose that idea all the time against the government's acceptance
of what is expedient, consistent with power. The dialectic, in fact.
That's what his opposition within the Party really means."

"Oh we all know about his early Marxist training. His six weeks in
1937. We've heard all about that from him a dozen times. We all
know he was the intellectual of the Party while we were the bush
boys. We've had all that."

Bray said, "What I'm getting at is there's something in him that
would always make him want to be a power, but not *the* one . . .
that's more or less what I said. You'd distrust a moral reason why I
think he wouldn't threaten you, just as I should myself. . . . But this
isn't a moral reason, it's a matter of temperament. Temperament exhibited and proven over a long, long time. . . . He wants only to be
known to the few people in the know. That's enough for him. He enjoyed helping to 'make' you; why didn't he employ the same energy
to make himself?" (He thought, do I touch on vanity there; no,
Mweta knows he didn't need making in any sense implying inade-
quacy.) "Because he hasn't the will to lead, really, he doesn't want it.
He didn't want it. It's a weakness, if you like, a kind of arrogance.
Let someone else be out there handled by the crowd."

Mweta had the weary obstinacy of one who is following his own
thoughts. "He'd have done exactly the same in my place."

"If he were with you," Bray said, "If you were together, Mweta . . .
you'd both be in the same place. He'd be seeing things from where
you are, and that makes all the difference. Power compromises," he
added, with a gesture of embarrassment for that sort of phrase. "He
wouldn't have so much fire in his belly if he were sitting at table in
this house."

Mweta folded the fingers of one hand over the knuckle of the other
and pressed it, testingly. Bray suddenly saw that he was fighting for
control, holding together some trembling part of himself. I have hurt
him, I hurt him by so much as acknowledging the other one's existence. They couldn't change the relation in which they had stood to
each other, he—Bray—and Mweta; he must have endorsement from

me, that is my old role. Anything else is betrayal. It was stupid; and Mweta was not. But the boy on the bicycle; when Mweta's with me he can't get away from the boy on the bicycle. *The President* wants love and approval, unrelated to the facts, between us. When it comes to us.

Bray felt a hardening distaste for the arrogant bare feet, the cigar at the centre of the broken-toothed grin in the thick beard. He said, "If I were you I'd send for Shinza. Now."

Mweta's voice cracked his own silence. "But you disapprove of preventive detention. If Shinza came in with me you'd see both of us backing it." He gave a cold and patronizing laugh.

"There'd be no need."

Mweta was looking at the big frame he knew so well, as if for a place where it would give. "You think so? What about Shinza's crowd? They'd follow him? —There'd always be need." He got up and walked round the desk, glancing at the papers there like half-recognized faces waiting to attract his attention; turned abruptly and came and stood near Bray's chair. "I've got no message for Shinza," he said.

"I'm not a messenger."

"But the best thing you can do is make him understand that what he's doing isn't any use. He's not going to bring it off, whatever he thinks he's aiming at. He's making a fool of himself. Or something worse. Really James, if you are worried about Shinza, tell him to leave it alone, don't encourage him."

It was a hit. "Encourage?"

"As you said, the friendship of the old days, and so on."

"I didn't say, Mweta," said Bray, gently. "And the past—well that's what it is. You two, you and Shinza, it's a matter of state, now, and I can't have any part in it. I can only tell you what I think about you two; but that's all. What I think, what I believe, urgently believe."

"All right, all right. All the same, when you see him you'll tell *him* what you think."

Bray said, "Don't you want me to see Shinza?"

Mweta said sadly, with a touch of the politician's deftness at the same time, "James, I would never tell you what you should do. Good God."

But I ought to know it—what I should do. "I'm your visitor here."

Mweta said emotionally, "You're home."

Bray said, "What happens when the Party Congress comes up? Next month?"

Mweta was still chairman of PIP, and Shinza, as a regional chairman, was on the Executive.

"We meet. If he comes."

"How do you mean?"

Mweta waited a second and then said, "He's not always at his place, these days. So they say."

"But he'd come for the Congress, of course." Bray's tone changed; he made it sound almost as if he were joking: "Maybe you'll have it out, then. Eh? Something very down-to-earth about Party congresses. —Tell me, what sort of people are you going to detain with your new Act—are they all kids like the fish factory one I picked up? What do you hope to hear from them?"

"That's Onabu's affair. He's got men who know the right questions."

"All the fish-factory lad did was explain the fishing concession to some people at the hostel. Of course the Union found this annoying. Or out of order, or something. But it hardly seems to call for two months and seventeen days in jail. Time to ask a great many questions."

Mweta said, "Well, all that will be looked after now, thank heavens, local police people won't be able to do what they like. There are proper provisions and checks in the Act—Chekwe worked it out with Dando very carefully. —That silly boy wasn't badly treated?"

Bray said, "He was beaten. There doesn't seem much point in testifying to that, now. —You don't really mean that every time a workman grumbles this is at the instigation of Shinza? Granted, his ideas may influence the Bashi people in our part of the country. But what about people elsewhere? Can everything that bothers you be laid at his door?"

"That's what the questions are for—to find out whose door. And if it's Shinza's—you wouldn't believe it?"

"I'd have to. It wouldn't change my belief that it didn't—doesn't need to happen. You don't have to make an enemy out of Shinza."

Mweta was shaking his head against the words as they came at him. "Believe me, James, believe me."

Yet he didn't want Bray to go; there was always, between them, the sense of being held in a strong current. Out of it, in opposition, they floundered, and were drawn back.

Bray said suddenly, "You're not going to arrest Shinza?"

"If that should ever be necessary it would be a bad day for us." It was parenthetic, a private reference to the old triumvirate: himself, Bray, and Shinza.

Bray felt a useless resistance and alarm: Mweta retreated, out of reach, into the old relationship, as if what the President did was another matter. Bray was led, stumbling and reluctant, to talk of other things: "And Aleke? What do you think of Aleke?" "Oh, quite competent, I think." "A bit easy-going, mm?" "Oh . . . I can't fairly judge that. It depends what you want of him, anyway. He's got a good civil-service temperament." "Exactly, exactly. That's just what I mean. But he gives you what you need?"

Bray stopped, and smiled. "I don't know whether I'm doing what you need from me."

"But how's it going, James?"

Bray kept the smile, answering slowly and politely. "I've covered the whole province. I've made my own census of the educable population, you might say, a pretty broad age limit. Now I must collate the stuff and write a report. That's it, more or less. It should be a fairly accurate sample guide for the rest of the country. Once it's done, it'll be easy to do the same sort of thing for the other provinces, the work could be allotted to local people. Then I shouldn't have to spend more than a few weeks in each. I don't know how much longer I'll need to stay in Gala; I'll see Kamaza Phiri."

"Good, you'll see Phiri . . ."

"He wrote with some suggestion that I ought to put what he calls pilot schemes into operation in Gala. Before moving on. I'd written him a note on an idea I had for a technical school of a kind. I thought we might take over the club"—they both laughed—"but I think I'd better do what I have to do to complete the report—I'd better move off to the other provinces soon."

Mweta said, "But if Phiri wants to set up something in Gala. There's no hurry to leave Gala."

"Sometimes I feel I've never been away; but that's when I'm alone, you know. It's something to do with the atmosphere of the place, the smell of it and so on. But my old house and the *boma*—they leave me cold. I suppose leaving the old life the way I did . . . Sometimes I feel I've never been away; sometimes I feel I've never come back."

"I don't think you should be in any hurry. Is the house you're in all right, there? We really ought to be able to get you a decent house, James. If you hear of any people who are leaving, any settler's house you know about, you must write—the government could buy a house like that for you."

"Oh the house is perfectly all right for my purpose. There's a magnificent fig in the garden."

"There should be a really nice house for you and Olivia. It worries me. Not one of those British shacks. She can't come to live like that."

"There's nothing wrong with the house! For a few months, it's perfectly adequate. I don't know whether Olivia will come, now. She's hung on so long, you know."

"Don't be in a hurry," Mweta said, looking at him, open. "You know, it's a funny thing, all these years—I always thought of you as if you were still there, in Gala. And even when I went there; I expected you. I think of you in Gala. Like myself. I'm in Gala, too. That was the time"—he drew first his lower lip under his teeth, then his upper lip. "Now I must rely on Simon Thabo." Thabo was Provincial Minister for Gala. "You can't talk to him, James. If I send for him he says to me, don't concern yourself, Mr. President, everything is under control. You know how some Africans are, James, you know how we are? He has certain ways of saying things, certain words he repeats. And he always talks in English, the special English he learnt at that public administration course run by the mission down in Zambia. I say to him, don't tell me what the police chief said, saluting in front of you, don't tell me that. Tell me what people said, what you heard. . . . I could get more from five minutes' talk with you, James, than I get from all his reliable sources and what-not."

Bray thought of the boy who had been locked up, while he was living in the house with the fig tree less than five miles from the prison. "I'm in the dark."

"Thabo is not a person you can talk to," said Mweta. "With you there, I . . . I know that whatever you say to me, you have this country"—his fingers knocked at his breast—"inside—and you will see, you will see, I can't let personal feelings in this. And you won't either. I have to know what's happening there. From someone who understands."

—Shinza. Shinza. "I didn't even know that Lebaliso had people in jail," Bray said.

"It's a big country. Impossible to prevent these things. Little police-men feeling big. We will learn." He meant it, in spite of his Detention Act. Bray watched him. He said, in a rush, "James, we are disappoint-ing you. Good God." Bray sheltered for a moment, like a match alight between his palms, an idiotic vanity; conscious that it was so: prime ministers and presidents as confrères now, and still he turns this way. To me. Mweta was saying, "You must help us, James. We need you, just like always." That's why he is where he is; the politician's unfail-ing instinct for taking up the advantage he's put you at. Bray was fas-cinated, as a man who knows he has had a lot to drink does not real-ize that the judgement is arrived at under the influence. He answered what was not at issue; Mweta could regard it as a code: "If only this education thing of mine makes sense." And Mweta let him talk. "After all, I'm not an expert, I go by what I see to be necessary, a very home-made pragmatism, and the shortcomings of education as I know it. Must it be a white-collar affair? Do the lake people need to pro-duce lawyers? What about literate fishermen, able to run their own co-operative from top administration to control of spawning grounds? If we've got nothing, if we're starting from scratch, then can't we escape the same old educational goals? I wish I knew more. I feel the an-swer lies somewhere in educational techniques as much as in organi-zation. I don't know enough about them."

The talk turned to the fishing communities Bray had visited. Bray criticized the terms of the new concession without further mention of the boy who had been detained for doing so, and Mweta listened with that flickering of the eyelids of a man to whom words are whips, blows, and weapons, taken on the body and given on the bodies of others. He agreed that the concession was hardly an improvement on colonial times, so far as direct benefit to the fishermen was concerned, but argued that the increased royalty made it worth while. "Five years, James. Five years is nothing. By then we'll be in a much better position to take over the fishing industry not as an isolated thing, but as part of the whole development of the lake country. I'm hoping for a fifteen-million loan or a new road up there, some of the money com-ing from the company itself, and the rest from the countries the com-pany represents. Then none of our surplus fish will go up the lake for small profits, but down here and to the markets in the South."

"The fishermen have to wait."

Mweta said, at one with him, "I know. But that's what we are having to do all the time—strike a balance. I don't want anybody to have to wait a whole generation, that's all. That's the aim I set for us."

"The pity is that there will be preventive detention to deal with impatience."

"James," Mweta said. He was seated again; he leant forward and put his hand on Bray's big knee. "It will not be used for that. I promise you. It was not intended for that." He sat back. His face shone like the faces of black schoolchildren Bray had seen, tense with effort and enlightenment.

Bray felt the corruption of experience; perhaps things happen here as they do because we bring from the old world this soiled certitude that makes anything else impossible. He said, "Once the law is there, there's no way of not using it."

In the old days they would have sat down to stew and bread and strong tea supplied by Joy, or not eaten at all until there was time for such a meal, but Mweta must have had to accept along with the turning of night into day on planes and the suitability of any hour as a working hour, the stodgy snacks that fuelled that sort of life. They had sandwiches and coffee on a tray; washing down the triangles of bread like labourers they discussed Mweta's ministers, Mweta confiding doubts and Bray making observations that neither would speak of to anyone else. Mweta still wanted Talisman Gwenzi for Finance, he was a better economist than Jason Malenga and generally much shrewder, but who else would there be for Mines who understood as Gwenzi did that looking after Mines was purely a matter of a grasp of international finance, on the one hand, and handling local labour relations on the other—it wasn't a knowledge of ores and mining techniques the Minister needed, all that was the affair of the companies. "If I had two more Gwenzis!" Mweta said enviously, "Just two more!" "One for Finance and one for Foreign Affairs, eh?" "That's it." And Gwenzi had pushed ahead the Africanization ideal magnificently —and put the onus on the companies. In two years, through intensive training courses devised and taught by the companies, all labour up to the level of Mine Captain would be African. Mweta swallowed his coffee. "A few years ago we weren't even trusted to use dynamite down there." They both laughed. "—Of course there may have been other reasons for that." "Last time I was here Phiri was talking about training people for mining administration at the School of Further Education." "The trouble is once you start a course like that, you're going to get a lot of teachers resigning from the ordinary schools. They've got the basic education to qualify—and of course what an administrative job on the mines will pay compared with what you'll get as a teacher . . . I think something like a Mine Secretary would get twice as much as a school headmaster . . . ? We can't afford to drain our resources in one place to fill up in another." "The best thing to do would be to channel people off at high-school level—have scholarships for the school-leavers to go on to the course at F.E., just as you have scholarships for teacher-training."

Mweta crunched a paper napkin into a ball and aimed it at the wastepaper basket. "Time, again, time. In the meantime, we've got to keep the Englishmen." Mweta called all white men Englishmen: South Africans, Rhodesians, Kenyans, and others who sold their skills up and down Africa. "Talk to Phiri about it, though, it's an idea."

Mweta's mind moved among problems like the attention of a man in charge of a room full of gauges and dials whose wavering needles represent the rise and fall of some unseen force—pressure, or electricity. He spoke now of the move he had taken a few weeks before, the surprise expulsion of the leader in exile and group of refugees from the territory adjoining the western border of the country. These people had been living in the country since before Independence; in fact, one of the first things he had done when he got responsible government as a preliminary to Independence was to insist that Jacob Nyanza, David Somshetsi, and their followers be given asylum. He couldn't receive them officially, for fear of the reactions from their country; but they had a camp, and an office in the capital, financed by various organizations abroad who favoured their cause. Outwardly, he maintained normal though not warm relations with the president of their country (there was an old history of distrust between them, dating from the days when Mweta and Shinza were seeking support from African countries for their independence demands); from time to time there had been statements from President Bete vaguely threatening those "brother" countries which sheltered their neighbours' "traitors." Mweta explained how it had become impossible to let Nyanza and Somshetsi stay. Of course, he had publicly denied President Bete's assertion that Nyanza and Somshetsi were acquiring arms and preparing to use the country as a base for guerrilla raids on their home country. . . . He turned to Bray, pausing; Bray gestured the inevitability. "They didn't care any more" Mweta said. "They didn't even take the trouble to conceal anything. Nyanza flew in and out and there were pictures of him in French papers, shaking hands all round in Algiers. They kept machine guns in the kitchen block the Quakers built for them at the camp—yes, apparently there were just some potatoes piled up, supposed to be covering—" He and Bray had a little burst of tense laughter. "So there was nothing else I could do."

Bray took out a cigar and held it unlit between his lips. And so Nyanza and Somshetsi had had to move on, over the border to the next country, to the north-east, a country which was not part of the new economic federation which was about to link their country and Mweta's.

"I saw Jacob Nyanza. Nobody knows. I saw him before they went. He was always a more reasonable chap than Somshetsi." Mweta stopped; of course, he would have hoped that Nyanza, if not Somshetsi, would understand. But apparently it had not been so. Bray lit the cigarillo and Mweta followed the draws that burgeoned the blunt head into fire. He did not smoke or drink: influence of the Presbyterian mission where he had gone to school. "You saw what Tola Tola had to say at Dar-es-Salaam?" Bray's lips opened and closed regularly round the cigar. He nodded.

"It was good, eh?"

Bray said, smoke curling round the words, "One of the best speeches there."

"This morning there's a call to say he's going to Copenhagen, Stockholm, and Helsinki." In the House some of Mweta's most important front-benchers had questioned the expenditure of the Foreign Minister on travel and produced a log-book of his journeys, showing that since Independence he had been in the country for only a matter of weeks. "Yes, if I had another Gwenzi," he said. "Albert is busy broadening the mind, isn't that what you say. If someone invited him to drink a glass of iced water at the North Pole, he'd go. It's very difficult for me to do anything. He gives me his good reasons . . . you know? And of course he is capable. They listen to him—" He meant in the world outside. Albert Tola Tola was also an Mso, the only one with a key cabinet post; what Mweta really was discussing was the fact that Tola Tola, capable or no, could not be replaced without betraying the electoral pact with the Mso, and could not be kept without agitation from Mweta's men looking for a good reason to have him out. And beneath this tacit acceptance of facts was another that could not be taken for granted—if Tola Tola were given another portfolio, did Mweta believe that he would become one of the ants? Did Mweta fear there was a possibility of a disaffected Tola Tola being drawn to discuss his grievances with others—Neil Bayley had mentioned the Minister of Development and Planning, Paul Sesheka, Moses Phahle, and Dhlamini Okoi. Tola Tola was a brilliant man; sophistication had taught him the showmanship of the common touch as a formidable substitute for what Mweta had naturally.

Bray was able now to talk about the Bashi Flats as an issue apart from the question of Shinza—Shinza or no Shinza, there must be roads, there must be an energetic move to make the Bashi less like another country in comparison with the area round the capital and the mines. "The trouble is there's nothing there," Mweta said.

"No, nothing in terms of what is exploitable, what's attractive to foreign capital. But the people, Mweta."

"Unless there's a mineral discovery of some kind—there's a geological survey due out there in the next few months, Swedes—the only thing is cattle. And even then. I mean they come down on the hoof—what slaughter cattle there is."

The Flats were one of the few parts of the country not infested with tsetse fly, the carrier of the cattle disease trypanosomiasis, but cattle were used mainly in the traditional way, as a form of wealth and capital possession within the tribes. Bray said, "You'll have to change all that. Get beef cattle-raising going there on a commercial basis. Then you'll be able to stop importing meat from the South. And it'll be uneconomic to have the stuff coming down on the hoof—you'll have a good reason for building roads."

Mweta began to make notes of their conversation. "I want to come out there with you and have a good look round. I'll fly to Gala next month some time and we'll go up. And then later in the year we'll go to the lake. Perhaps I can bring Joy and the kids, if Olivia's there they can have a holiday for a few days while you and I—there's that house for me, you know, I've never seen the place—" The fishing company had presented the President with a "lodge" on the lake, at the time of Independence. "In the meantime, James, you will write to me, ay? A letter every now and then. Let me hear. We mustn't lose touch."

He insisted that Bray stay in the capital for the rest of the week. "You'll come to the dinner. The one with the white businessmen. I'll tell Asoni." Mweta threw back his head and his shoulders heaved loose with laughter. "You know what they wanted to know? If they must build a special lavatory for me." Years before, when some minor royalty came to the territory, PIP had made political capital out of such unpromising material as a "comfort station" for the Royal Highness, quick to point out that this small building cost more than the type of house provided for an African family down in the native town. While they laughed Bray remembered it was Shinza's idea; Shinza had a sure instinct for the concrete issue, however unimportant, and knew how to make his opponents look absurd as well as reprehensible.

When he got back to the Silver Rhino and went to the reception desk for his key, he stood there, the man who finds himself on stage in the middle of a play he knows nothing about: Hjalmar Wentz and his daughter were passing and repassing one another excitably in the cage formed by counter, desk, and safe. Hjalmar faltered, greeted Bray, but the girl was in a high passion: "Just wish to Christ you wouldn't go on about the war of the generations, that's all. Things you read in the English papers. It's got nothing to *do* with the generations." Hjalmar's thin-skinned blond face was red along the cheekbones and under the streaks of yellow hair on the dome of his forehead. Her black eyes shone with the glitter of an oil-flare on night water, her breathing sucked hollows above her collar-bones. She shuffled a pile of letters together and walked out; Bray caught the musky whiff of anger as she lifted the flap of the counter and exposed her little shaved armpit, licked with sweat.

Emmanuelle had heard about her parents' plan to ask Ras Asahe to intervene on their behalf with the brewery. "God knows who told her," her father said, and Bray saw that Hjalmar must have told many people besides himself. The impossible thing was that she wasn't angry because they'd thought of using Asahe, but because they had hesitated to do so, been afraid to suggest it to her . . . she was furious about that. She had raged at them for "driving everybody crazy" when they knew all along something could be done. She had said to her father, "Your scruples make me want to vomit." He said to Bray, "Of course children must assert themselves, it's inevitable, and in each generation the form that opposition takes is always impossible for parents to understand."

Bray had heard the girl's reaction to that. He said, "You'll be able to go ahead and see what you can do through Ras Asahe, anyway," but he was aware that the practical aspect was something Hjalmar Wentz looked at without recognition now. The red faded patchily from his head as his hands touched about the familiar objects on the desk.

The girl was doubled up in one of the sagging deck-chairs in the garden. Bray tried to walk quickly past so that she would not have to pretend not to see him, but she said, in the rough sulky voice of a child making amends for bad behaviour, at the same time unable to disguise her lack of interest in the trivial preoccupations of other people, "How was your shopping?"

He stopped, to show that everything was all right between her and the world. "Oh I wasn't looking for anything special, you know."

She was picking at some invisible irregularity beneath the skin of her upper arm, picking at it with her nail and then cupping her hand over the dark, smooth knob of her shoulder. She said, "They are ridiculous. Oh *nice* . . . but that doesn't change it—ridiculous. They shouldn't ever have come to live here—a gesture, that's all. My father's so romantic. Everything he's ever done was a romance." While she spoke she scratched at the grain of skin until whatever it was was lifted off, and a dark and brilliant eye of blood sprang against the flesh. She squinted down and put her mouth to it tenderly.

Bray said, "Even Germany?"

"Particularly Germany." She kept sucking the blood and then looking at the place. "He can't manage ordinary life at all, and she can't stand that. And who blames her. What's the point of shambling around from country to country. What's the point of being saved from gas ovens, for that."

He laughed at her, but she suddenly became shocked at herself, if he would not be. "We're such bloody yahoos, my brother and me. I'm just as bad, in my way. That's another thing. My *mother* wrings her hands because we've grown up wild in Africa, *so uncultured*, without the proper intellectual training of the Europeans who wanted to murder her."

"And you think you're wild?"

"D'you think we'd survive, if we were like *them*."

There was this continual presence of people brushing against him, like so many cats weaving through his legs. And they were all so brimful of assertion and demand, eyes turned upon you, car doors banging, entrances and exits opening and closing the aperture of your attention as the pupil of an eye reacts to light and dark. The impulse to express this to someone glanced off with the flat remark to Vivien Bayley: "I hardly realized how solitary I've been."

Before he could get in touch with Roly Dando, Dando telephoned. "Didn't get a wink of sleep the night you arrived, I hear." Bray, standing in the veranda telephone booth beneath the picture of Mweta, on which scribbled numbers had encroached, smiled at the aggressive cackle. "I gather you haven't lost any. The President tells me you and Chekwe did a good job." "Oh bloody hell, Bray. I can always be counted on to do a good job. Not so bad as it would be if I hadn't been here. That's all I ask, lad. That's as much as I expect of myself."

At dinner at his house, he said, "That's how I'd define the function of the law in any country you'd like to name, today. That's what the principle of justice has come to—you control how far the smash and grab goes. Settle for that. Better regularize it than allow the rule of law to be lopped off and carried aloft by the dancing populace, ay? So you have your immigrant quotas in Britain, so the British won't turn on the blacks next door, and you have your censors back in the newspaper offices in Czechoslovakia, so the Russians won't come back instead." He drank a mixture of lemon juice, soda, and a white spirit in a bottle without a label. "Popococic gets it for me—slivovitz. The Yugoslav trade commissioner. Pure spirit's less trying on the kidneys. That's what's really on my mind these days—believe me, your ideals only function when you're healthy, they only give you any trouble when everything's working well inside. I've got this damn prostate thing, getting up to pee every hour and if I'm caught out somewhere having to stand with one leg round the other to hold it in." His face was petulant with dismay and consternation at a machine that refused to work properly. He had got thin; his voice, for the size of that shrinking head, sounded bigger than ever. The old Labrador lay panting between them on the grass. At the bottom of the garden the gardener and a friend were playing *chisolo* on a board scratched out of the red earth, a gramophone screeching very faintly behind the urging grunts and cries with which the stone counters were encouraged to progress from one hole to another.

"You can have an operation, Roly." The twigs of the thorn-trees on the close horizon ran hair thin, jet and hard as if the pink sky had cracked intricately, like a piece of fine china.

"Yes, I know, you wait and see what it's like. I'd pack up and go off to sit on my arse somewhere, but what's the point. All countries are the same. We're all backward people. Might just as well stay put where I am instead of taking up a new lot."

"Whose idea was the Detention Bill?"

Dando showed that the question was irrelevant: "Cyprian Kente's I suppose. Has a lot of ideas. Or a gift for coming out with what others don't want to be the first to say. Mweta has an unspoken thought, Kente brings it right out loud where it can't be suppressed, you see."

Kente was the Minister of the Interior. "Mweta mentioned only you and Chekwe."

"Call in the scribes. We've got the right words. I was able to get in *my* word, anyway. There's a clause that the Act's got to come up for renewal every year. That's my little clause."

The cicadas began a chorus of doorbells that no one would ever answer. Bray said, handling both Dando and himself gently, "And it will be renewed every year. Long after everyone's forgotten quite what it was for in the first place."

"Well, wha'do I care. It's my conscience clause, laddie. *I put it there*. The temptation of virtue, justice, if anyone should like to fall to it. Available. You see what I mean." His cheek lifted with a twinge of inner discomfort. The Labrador got up slowly and put its snout on his knee, but was pushed away.

"And Mweta says he won't keep the Act a day longer than he needs it."

Dando's restlessness produced an irritable delight at Bray. "The humanitarian at the court of King Mweta. Oh shit, James. You're the one who said to me anyone'd be a fool if he thought he could take my job without doing things he didn't like."

"Any other reason you know of besides Shinza?"

"No. Not really. You can't take Sesheka seriously. A bit of nuisance with out-of-works—not unemployed, strictly speaking, they trek in from the lands to town. . . . But you know how many Bashi are in industry, road-building, railways. Always have been. Nearly a third of the labour force. Shinza's opposing the PIP unions through them, very definitely so."

Bray said, "Preventive detention to deal with that?"

Dando put his hands on the rests of his chair and heaved himself out. "He's no green boy like ours. It's a small start. He's got friends outside and maybe friends inside as well—there are people who'd perhaps be prepared to take a ride on his back. He's been treated like dirt, mind you— Just a minute."

He tramped off in his schoolboy sandals to the shelter of a hibiscus hedge and against the insects' shrilling Bray heard him piddling slowly and loudly.

Festus came round from the back of the house with a bowl of fresh ice. He took the opportunity of Dando's absence coupled with the evidence that he was also in hearing distance, to accuse. "Why *Mukwayi* doesn't stay with us this sometime?" He withheld the ice until Bray answered.

"I didn't know I was coming, Festus, I tried to phone . . ."

The excuses were accepted and the ice put down, in the convention, invented by white men long ago and become, curiously, part of the old black man's dignity, that his "master's" concerns were his own.

"Kalimo goes all right?" he said severely. Bray had written to Dando to thank Festus, when Kalimo turned up. They chatted a moment, falling into the local tongue, which Bray spoke with some hesitancy, helped out with a word here and there supplied by Festus. Making in his throat the deep, low exclamations of pleasure and politeness, he collected an empty soda bottle or two and went off as Dando appeared.

"—Yes, poor bloody Shinza. Poor bloody Edward." Dando looked tranquil now. He began to pour fresh drinks.

"He's got a new young wife and a baby," Bray said with a smile. "He's flourishing."

"The old devil!" Dando was delighted; he himself took new life from the thought.

And cigarettes from over the border; and a house in Mpana's compound. But Bray didn't say it. It was none of his business. Dando said gleamingly, "D'you tell the good news to Mweta?"

Bray said, watching him, "I told him to send for Shinza. Even now."

"If he ever sends for Shinza now, it won't be on a gilt-edged card."

Bray said, after a moment, "I thought that was the one thing you'd jib at—touching Shinza."

Dando put his drink down patiently, gave a short, sharp, instructive laugh. "I work for Mweta, my boy."

Bray got back to the hotel very late from Dando's; it was impossible to spend an evening there without drinking too much and he had to drive with conscious carefulness. He saw a pair of eyes, two feet above the roadside: a small buck, feeding. The cold smell of heavy dew was voluptuous through the car window.

Hjalmar Wentz was still up. In the stuffy office that had no direct access to a window or door, the odours that his wife had swept and scrubbed and banished from the public rooms of the hotel collected in unstirring layers—smoke, insect repellent, boiled cauliflower, spilt beer. Hjalmar's head shone under a lamp; as always he was surrounded by invoices and newspaper cuttings. He had confided to Bray, once: "I know of a refugee in London who's been able to live off his files of cuttings. People pay him to consult them. A professor from the University of Budapest, had to get out in Fifty-six."

He said to Bray in the confidence of the night, "The other day— did Emmanuelle say anything? Margot saw her talk to you in the garden."

Bray lied, quoting Turgenev. "'An honourable man will end up by not knowing where to live'—that was more or less it."

A look of shy, weary pleasure crossed the face like a hand. "Good God. She's strange, that girl of mine. But you know who'd told her about Ras Asahe? Stephen. Her brother. *He* told Margot. Usually Emmanuelle doesn't get on with him at all. That terrible mutual antagonism of brother and sister. Thomas Mann only dealt with the re-

verse side of it in his incest themes—" The lie was life-giving, and he
kept Bray from bed, their voices sounding through the small-hour
deadness of the hotel like the conversation in people's dreams, the secret activity of mice, and the steady jaws of cockroaches.

The House was sitting that week; there had been no need to call an
emergency session. He walked in on the second reading of the Detention Bill. It was difficult for a man his size to be unobtrusive; as he
stooped quietly along the polished wooden pew-wall that divided the
visitors' gallery from the members, several faces on the floor flashed
aside in recognition. The beautiful chamber, panelled in wood from
the Mso forests with its watermark of faint stripes, was murmurous as
a schoolroom. It smelled like a church. There were one or two in
togas—among the cabinet, Dr. Moses Phahle and little Dhlamini
Okoi, fine Italian shoes showing beneath the robes—but most of the
members wore formal Western clothes with the well-being and assurance peculiar to black men. Roly Dando's narrow white face barred
and marked by thick-rimmed spectacles and toothbrush moustache
was a fetish object set among them.
With the sudden change of atmosphere from sun and traffic outside, these impressions came to him like the tingling of blood in a
limb coming to life. Through the susurrus there was the voice of
Kente, Minister of the Interior, an order paper crunched in his fist.
". . . What ordinary, peaceful citizen has anything to fear? What is
this 'web of intimidation' that the Honourable Member for Inhame
speaks about? Where does he get his language from? It is clear to us
in this House that it has nothing to do with the realities of life in this
country. It is clear to us that it comes from overseas, the Honourable
Member has been reading too many spy stories—this House is no
place for James Bonds and Philbys—"
He got some of the laughter he wanted, but not much; though
hardly anyone had escaped the evangelism of James Bond, many had
not heard of Philby. The Speaker, sitting lop-sided against his tall
chair as if his curly white wig weighed him down, had his attention
caught by Cyrus Goma, now member for one of the north-eastern
constituencies, already half-risen from his seat. So Goma had adopted
the toga; while he spoke he settled the free end of it like an old lady
putting her shawl straight, fastidiously, his jutting chin held jackdaw
style towards one shoulder—just as Bray remembered it—his face

tight, eyes screwed up, while his voice remained soft and reasonable. "We have accepted the necessity of this Bill. That is one thing. But we must not allow ourselves to think that people who are worried about it, who have grave doubts about it, are something to poke fun at. I suggest to the Honourable Minister of the Interior that such people are sincere; they should not be ridiculed. A Preventive Detention Act is no laughing matter. We did not laugh when the British imposed one on us." There was a sudden contraction of attention in the House. "We did not laugh in the camps in the Bashi—" Someone called, "Yes, Bashi!" "—and at Fort Howard." He paused a mere instant, but it was just long enough. "Howard!" "Bashi!" "Howard!" The Speaker called the House to order. Cyrus Goma swayed slightly and began to speak again, reasonably, softly. "Our President didn't laugh when he spent seventeen months shut up there. He suffered because it was necessary to win our freedom. If we must accept that it is now necessary for us to introduce preventive detention, that is no occasion for laughter."

There was a distrustful hush; momentary. A spatter of hard-palmed applause that, as it sought to assert itself, was pressed out by a kind of rise of temperature in the House. On his feet, someone shouted, "If you want to cry for traitors!" The assembly seemed to fuse in hostility, presenting a bristling corporate surface, the back of some huge animal rippling at Goma. But from the direction of the hand-clapping someone else took the floor, a young man, hippo-faced with minute ears, who rested a tapering, ringed hand on his huge backside. His English was strongly accented. "Can the Minister explain why the Bill was not fust put before the Central Committee? Correct me, but as far as I am aware this is the fust time it has not been done. The Party has not approved this Bill because the Party was not informed about it. Is the Central Committee going to be a rubber stamp, just to come down *like that* on decisions already made by the Government? Is that it?"

Cyprian Kente smiled, taking the House into his confidence at the naïveté of the question. "The Honourable Member is aware that this was a decision taken by the President under Emergency Powers."

The huge schoolboy figure was obstinate.

"The President is also the President of the Party. Did he consult his Central Committee. That is what I am asking."

Mweta, clear-faced, with the immediate, calming authority of a man who appears always to take everyone's point of view seriously, rose in place of Kente. "I would like to reassure the Honourable Member, because I know the devotion he has brought to the Party ever since he was one of the outstanding organizers of Party youth. I share with him the concern that the People's Independence Party—which you, and I, and all of us made—should continue to carry out through this government the policies it has hammered out of the will of our people. In urgent response to certain information, I took the step of introducing a Preventive Detention Bill without having had the opportunity to present the Bill to the Central Committee. But I would like to point out that I took this step in full consultation with the Cabinet. And out of the eight members of the Central Committee, five are members of the cabinet." A triumphant hum of assent; he cut it short, modestly, continuing, "When this measure is presented to the Congress of the Party next month, I have no doubt that it will have the endorsement not only of the remaining members of the Central Committee, but also of Congress as a whole, granting a country-wide mandate for what was in the first place a majority decision by the full representation of the Central Committee in the Cabinet." The stir of disagreement on the back benches was tramped out by the applause of well-polished shoes drumming the floor. Mweta's supporters beamed and overflowed confidence. Carried by it, he did not allow himself to be swept away, but swiftly turned the momentum towards the dissidents: his voice rose clear out of the clamour. "In this first year of our nationhood we stand together in a way that perhaps will never be repeated. In the years of our children and our childrens' children, if God blesses our country with the peace and stability we are striving for, the business of running this country may be no more than a piece of efficient administration by professionals. But we are brothers in arms. We are the people who demanded freedom when we didn't have more than one pair of pants. Yes, we are the people—Cyrus Goma, the member for Selusi, myself, many, many faces I see here—who sat in prison together not because we wanted to destroy but because we wanted to create a new life for the people of Africa. We are the people who made the struggle and the same people who are now doing the governing. We are the first crop. That's what the people who used to run us call it. And it's true that they sowed the dragon's teeth of colonialist repression and up we came, a generation breathing fire. . . . We have learned the hardest way since our schooldays what unity demands from us—and how, without it, nothing, *nothing* that is any good to any of us, can be gained or kept. Small doubts and differences—we respect them in each other. They are family opinions. They don't touch the fact that we are one. . . ."

Cyrus Goma with his hand blinkered against the side of his face, his eyes turned to Mweta, and on his face the expression of a man who cannot be reached. Dando looking bored. Bray moved out ahead of the press of people as the House adjourned for lunch; only the journalists preceded him—one small black man in a paisley waistcoat had already gained one of the streamlined glass telephone booths and was mouthing away. President calls for unity: of course. Bray stalked slowly down the flowered drive to the visitors' parking ground and had to pause, not knowing for a second whether to jump back or forward before a mini-jeep swivelling out of the members' car park. The driver was the huge young man who had brought up the question of the Central Committee. Braking, he bounced himself so high he almost hit the canvas roof, and coming down, gave an open-and-shut grin at the plight of the two near-victims, Bray and himself.

Bray was to meet Neil Bayley for lunch. An Italian who had drifted down from the Congo had opened a pizzeria just behind the Central African Stores—it was filled with the younger white people of the town; no African would pay six shillings for a circle of charred dough smeared with tomato and anchovy. When the small white population tired of eating pizza, the Italian would have to open a fish-and-chip shop, where the Africans would patronize him. But for the present it was evident that this was the place to go in a town where there was nowhere to go; under the bunches of raffia onions and the blare of "Arrivederci Roma" pretty secretaries from ministries, embassies, and missions and men from other ministries, embassies, and missions (Conferences are great places for picking up birds, Neil Bayley remarked) were occupied in the early moves of sexual attraction, most easily established across a table. Like everyone else, Neil Bayley and Bray drank the house wine in Coca-Cola glasses, and Bayley's big river-god's head with the red-blond curly beard gazed out in pleasure across the room between his bursts of intensely lively concentration on what he was saying. "Yes, yes, of course, Goma's a subtle bastard, and when he opens his mouth he's not only speaking for himself, you can count on that. What others can't say because they're in the cabinet, our Cyrus says from the floor."

"He managed to get them to imagine themselves shut up in Bashi and Fort Howard again, this time by their own people . . . in one sentence . . . and the pause was just calculated. . . . Then before anyone could put a finger on what he was saying he brought up Mweta's seventeen months, the great example of sacrifice . . . a paragon of loyalty!" Bray laughed with admiration.

"Oh he slips the knife between the ribs while appearing to give a pat on the back."

"It was a good piece of cape-work. Quite something to watch."

Neil Bayley presented a handsome, chin-lifted profile to the room, waving the carafe for more wine. "Tastes a bit metallic, ay? Matured in genuine old paraffin tins. —Oh he'll have a long life in politics, that boy."

"He's had a long one, already. He was national organizer for a while, when Shinza was Secretary-General."

"Is that so? I didn't realize. James, you're a walking archive—archives? How would you say it? Have some more. But Mweta can wrap them all up in a neat little parcel."

"Yes, he did that," said Bray.

"He's convinced you he needs preventive detention," Bayley said, his splendid pink face gleaming with wine—half a question, half a determination.

"Mweta's a strange man."

"How d'you mean, James?" Bayley had a passion for springing the lock of confidence; it was part of his "technique" with women—they became fascinated by the man who had made them give themselves away—but he enjoyed exercising his persuasive, bullying, blackmail skill with anyone.

Bray arranged the olive pits on his plate: first in a row of nine, then in two rows, one of five and one of four. He smiled.

"What d'you mean? You believe him and you don't want to? You don't believe him and you do want to? Come on. You must have all the facts. Come on, now, James."

He gave Neil Bayley the look of an older man, smiling, keeping a younger man waiting. Bayley looked sceptical.

"He calls for an act of faith."

Neil Bayley raised his golden eyebrows. He decided it was meant satirically; so that was what it became. Bray slipped out of his hands under cover of the exchange: "Interesting. Interesting. His early training with the White Fathers." "It was the Presbyterians. He's not a Catholic." "Oh of course. This wine has a touch of carbide . . . Nepenthe. Lethe. I'm gone. I swoon."

Roly Dando and a man with a white crew-cut, young face, and frowning smile, appeared peering over the crowded tables and their low-lying smoke. "Come on, mop up the vino on your chins and let us take over." Dando introduced his companion, an American jurist who was on his way home from South Africa and Rhodesia, where he had been an observer at political trials. He had the conscious naturalness of the distinguished in unsuitable surroundings; anyone but Roly would have given him frozen Dublin Bay prawns and Chablis at the Great Lakes Hotel. "What're you doing here with old Bray? Run out of popsies?" Dando and Neil Bayley genuinely bristled towards each other, although Dando was the old seal, long outcast from lordship of the harem by the young bull smiling down at him with strong white teeth and shining lips. Bayley found the war-time sexual slang quaint: "bint," "popsie"; he had been a small boy evacuated to the country with a label round his neck, while dapper Captain Dando (there was a photograph Festus kept dusted on Dando's mantelpiece) carried his cane under an arm through the streets of Cairo. "Just showing James the field, Roly. Of course you've played it, no interest to you." Dando disapproved of American usage, the American idiom, especially in the mouth of the registrar of a university. But the visiting jurist gave a concupiscent chuckle, anxious to be simple and human.

"And how did you find South African justice, Mr. Graspointner?" The river-god was not only handsome and amusing, he also knew who Edward Graspointner was (Institute for Advanced Study, Princeton, author of standard works on international law) and he knew how to introduce a subject on which he himself was prepared to expand eloquently.

"Well, I must say that I found the conduct of the court unexceptionable. It was something of a surprise. It was an open court. It was an impartial court—although, as you know, some of the accused were white, some coloured. The judge was an Afrikaner. But the conduct of the court was equal to the highest standards of jurisprudence as we

G

know it anywhere in the free world. Justice was done according to the law."

"According to the law. Ah yes. But what of the law, Mr. Graspointner? The laws of the Republic of South Africa are unique in the world for their equation of the legitimate aspirations of the majority of the population with crime, with treason. Legitimate aspirations as defined in the U.N. Bill of Rights. Would you agree?"

"Broadly, yes. That is so."

"Then was what you saw justice, or a going through the motions of justice? A lot of wigged heads jumping through the hoop. Is justice a piece of machinery or an ethical concept? Does the promulgation of a law make that law just? Can justice be done through it? I thought the answer to that question had been given at Nuremberg."

"It was not given at Nuremberg. It has never been given anywhere," Dando said, with testy patience. "For the simple reason that there is no such thing as international law in the sense of an international standard of justice. International law is a code for Interpol, for refugee-swopping and spy exchange, for boundary blood-feuds and squabbles over airspace and the three-mile limit for herring fleets. Justice is an empirical affair arranged by each country in order to perpetuate a particular social system. You should know that. Bill of Human Rights! Why not the Sermon on the Mount? Good ringing phrases, man."

"Of course I met a lot of troubled people down there. Very, very troubled about just that issue, Professor Bayley—"

"What a human climate to exist in! Could you live in a place like that?" Neil Bayley's thighs rolled apart, his arms fell wide, he seemed to make free of the whole black continent, the muddy banks of the Niger and the Congo, the forests and the deserts, the shy Batwa and shrivelled Bushmen, the lovely prostitutes of Brazzaville and the eager schoolchildren of Gala. "Could you, Graspointner?"

"Well, I don't know. One mustn't be too hasty about this. One person told me his *raison d'être* was to stay there in opposition, just be there, obstinately, even if he couldn't do much to change things. I'm not a revolutionary, he said. I haven't the courage to risk prison. But I can't let them get away with it unwitnessed. I have to stay and oppose in my mind. It's my situation; I haven't any other that means anything."

"Disgusting!"

"Of course, in daily life, he admitted . . . you develop a certain insensitivity . . . you let things pass that . . . eh?" The American turned to draw in Bray.

Bray offered, "I read something the other day—every nation has its own private violence . . . after a while one can feel at home and sheltered between almost any borders—you grow accustomed to anything." And he thought, where did I get that from? Somewhere in Graham Greene? Why do I keep turning to other people's opinions, lately, leaving myself out.

Neil Bayley stood up, blocking the waiter's path. "Yes, thank you *very* much. At least one can choose one's own violence. They're not all equally vile, that's the point. And I won't have it that we're all equally culpable. Flabby sentiment. So you could live there, James, a white man, and 'oppose in your mind'?"

Dando said, "Don't be more of an academic idiot than you have to, Neil. Of course he couldn't live there. Christ, he was being run out of this country by the British while you were still—"

"—Yes, yes—a snotty-nosed piccanin having his backside striped in Exeter, Devonshire." Bayley knew Dando's pejorative in all its variations. They laughed; a noisy table in the loud room. Bayley sat down again for a glass of Dando's wine and Bray was given a fine cigar with the jurist's initials on the band. "I have a friend gets them in from Cuba, God knows how. The band's put on in Tampa, I guess."

He thought, I have a friend, too, who likes cigars.

He had to leave the company to pick up a borrowed dinner jacket and trousers for the Golden Plate dinner from the wife of the secretary to the Minister of Development and Planning—resourceful Vivien had arranged it. Gabriel Odise's wife was a social welfare worker and the offices of her department were in the old part of the town, the strip of human habitation along the line of rail that once was all the town had been. A few old *mupapa* trees humped their roots out into the street, there; there was the cod-liver-oil smell from sacks of dried *kapenta*, and the strange sweet reek of dangling plucks in a butcher's. A pair of Congo prostitutes, heads done up like bonbons in turbans, sat on the kerb giggling down at their painted toenails and gold sandals, and looked up smiling, as he stepped past. They wore the *pagne* and brief blouse that bared a little roll of shining brown middle, making local women look dowdy and respectable in their cheap European dresses. The internal staircase of the Social Welfare Department was stained and splashed with liquid in which ants had died and dust had dried, and the wall alongside it bore witness to the procession of people who hung about the place, for one reason or another, enduring by scribbling not the obscenities of the literate, but the pot-hook names and signature flourishes of the semiliterate. People sat tightly on one or two benches; the rest squatted on the corridor floor and moved their legs and bundles stoically away and back again to make way. While he waited among them—the only white person—he glanced down out of a window and saw in the courtyard at least another hundred and fifty people gathered on a ground worn bare by feet and bodies, under trees shabby as lamp-posts with the rub of human backs. Those in the corridor watched without resentment as he was beckoned in to Mary Odise's room ahead of them. She was a pretty girl with the air-hostess neatness that African woman often assume with responsible jobs; as she let him in, her eyes went in quick tally over the crowd, with the look not so much of assessing numbers as of estimating the weight of what lay upon them, there on their impassive faces. A diagnostic look. She had a pink rose in a glass on her desk; the worn floorboards were scrupulously clean and there was the taint of baby-sick and dirty feet that can never be scrubbed out of rooms where the poor and anxious are received. The courtroom in Gala used to smell like that.

He tried on the dinner jacket and measured the pants against his side, waist to ankle. She took good-natured pleasure in the fact that they would seem to do. "The tie! I forgot to ask about the tie."

"I can easily buy one. It's extraordinarily nice of you . . . you're sure your brother doesn't mind?"

"He has two and never wears them. They used to be working clothes, for him—he's got a band, they're playing at the Great Lakes Hotel. They wear silver jackets now, with blue lapels—terrible! And the dry cleaners here don't know how to do them. He'll just have to give them away when they get too dirty." She folded the suit expertly and put it in a strong paper carrier that bore the legend: I've Been Saving At The Red Circle Supermarket.

"Very overworked, Mary?"

She was fastidious to avoid the gushing complaint that was a convention among white colleagues.

"Not really. You can only see a certain number of people in one day. And if you try to rush it, you can't help them. I'm attached to the Labour Department now, and I get all these people referred to me from the Labour Exchange."

"So many old women and children—don't look particularly employable, to me."

"They're not looking for work. They're looking for relations who come here from the bush on the chance of getting jobs. They don't know where the person they're looking for is, they don't know where he works—if he works. What are you to do? They have no money. You find them sleeping down at the bus depot. The Labour Department doesn't know what to do with them. They send them to me." She gave her gentle, sympathetic laugh. "I've suggested setting up a shelter—there's the old market building, for instance, I thought of that. But the Chief Welfare Officer points out that we'd be taking responsibility for them . . . they really shouldn't be here. They'd just stay on endlessly, some of them. It's a headache."

"What on earth do you do?"

Mary Odise had trained as a social worker in Birmingham, where she had investigated the wife-beating, child-neglect and drunkenness of the people who had brought white civilization to her country. At one of the Independence parties he found himself sitting with her and she mimicked for him an Englishwoman, pouring out the sordid tale of her woes, who once said, "I don't feel so ashamed with *you*, dearie, as you're a blackie."

She was professional. "Give them bus fare and try to persuade them to go back home. But now we issue bus chits instead—they were taking the money and hanging on. Yesterday my junior found out some of them have begun to sell the bus chits." She was laughing softly as she showed him out. As the door opened there was a listless surge in the corridor: eyes turned, bodies leaned forward. He was stopped on the stairway by an old man with a piece of paper so often folded that it was dividing into four along the dirt-marked creases. A garbled name on it looked as if it might be that of a building firm; he shook his head, pointed at the queue in the corridors, and gave the old fellow half-a-crown. He was careful not to speak a word in Gala or the local language. To these poor country people, by long experience, whiteness was power; if it were to be made accessible to them through their own tongue, how would he escape the importunity of their belief? Next thing, I'll be making an ass of myself, trailing old people round to find wretched yokels who are hawking tomatoes somewhere.

The trousers were a little short. He looked at himself in the damp-spotted mirror on the door of the wardrobe in his room. He had forgotten to buy a dress tie, after all; but Hjalmar would have one. Yes; and it was a beautiful tie, finely made of the best ribbed silk, with a Berlin label still in it. Emmanuelle laughed. "Nobody wears those butterflies any more. Ras will lend you his. It's just like two pieces of black ribbon, crossed over in front." Ras Asahe was with the Wentz family; drinks were on the round table under the drawn-down lamp. There was the atmosphere of solicitude and consideration that comes after a successfully resolved family upheaval: Asahe must have been approached about his uncle.

"Sure, if you want to pop over to my place?"

But Bray was quite satisfied with the tie he had. Hjalmar was laughing loudly at Asahe's description of an exchange with the director of broadcasting programmes in English, whose deputy he was. Apparently the man was a South African—Asahe imitated the Afrikaner accent: like many educated men in the territory, Asahe had been to university for a time, down South, as well as having worked in broadcasting in England. ". . . It happens to be standard BBC pronunciation, I told him. 'Hell, man, well it's not standard *our* pronunciation.' —I won't be surprised if the rumour goes round from him that I'm a neo-imperialist. . . ."

Hjalmar kept glancing at his wife to see if she were amused. She held her eyebrows high, like an ageing actress. Emmanuelle was inwardly alight, flirting with her father and even her brother, calling her mother "darling"—for the benefit of Ras Asahe or perhaps to present for herself a tableau of family life as she imagined it to be for other people.

It was a warm, singing evening with the moon rising on one side of the sky while a lilac-grained sunset had not yet receded into darkness on the other. There was the smell of boiled potatoes given off all over Central Africa, after nightfall, by some shrub. By the time he got to the tobacco sales hall where the Golden Plate dinner was being held, it was dark. He had not wanted to go, really—Mweta embarrassed him slightly by the invitation—but the cars converging on the grounds, the white shirt-fronts and coloured dresses caught in head-lights, and the striped canvas *porte-cochère* with its gold-braided commissionaires created a kind of simple anticipation of their own. The warm potato-smell and the mixture of black and white faces in the formally dressed herd pressing to the entrance were to him evidence that this was not just another municipal gathering—this was Africa, and this time Africans were honoured guests, being met with a bow and a smile. There was a satisfaction—naïve, he knew; never mind—in this most obvious and, ultimately, unimportant aspect of change. It did not matter any more to the Africans whether white people wanted to dine with them or not; they themselves were now the governing elite, and the whites were the ones who had to sue for the pleasure of their company. Fifty pounds a head for a ticket; he waited in line behind a rusty-faced bald Englishman and a lively plump Scot with their blond wives, and a black lady, probably the wife of some minor official, who had faithfully assumed their uniform of décolleté and pearls. She smelled almost surgically of eau-de-Cologne. The African Mayor and the white President of the Chamber of Commerce dealt jointly with the receiving line, dispensing identical unctuousness.

The tobacco sales hall had been decided upon because not even the Great Lakes Hotel's Flamingo Room was big enough to accommodate the guests expected. The bare walls were entirely masked by red cotton; an enormous coloured poster of Mweta hung amid gold draping above the dais where the main dignitaries were to sit; stands of chemically tinted lilies and gilded leaves stood between long tables and at the four corners of a specially constructed dance floor like a boxing ring.

The perfect reproduction of municipal vulgarity was softened by a homely and delicate fragrance of tobacco leaves, with which the building was impregnated and which prevailed, despite the smell of food and women's perfume. Bray was conscious of it when his mind wandered during the speeches. The Mayor spoke, the President of the Chamber of Commerce spoke, a prominent industrialist spoke, the chairman of the largest mining company spoke. Through grapefruit cocktail, river fish in a pale sauce (*Tilapia Bonne Femme*, in the illuminated lettering of the menu), some sort of beef evidently brought down on the hoof from the Bashi (*Boeuf en Casserole aux Champig-*

nons), he sat between Mrs. Justin Chekwe, wife of the Minister of Justice, and Mrs. Raymond Mackintosh, wife of an insurance man who was one of the last white town councillors left in office. The white matron, like a tourist proudly determined to use her phrase-book sentences to demonstrate how much at home she feels, leant across him to say to the black matron, "Mrs. Mweta looks so young, doesn't she? What a responsibility, at her age. I'm sure I wouldn't be able to cope. Doesn't the hall look beautiful? One doesn't realize how much really hard work goes into these functions—you should have seen our chairwoman, Mrs. Selden-Ross, up a ladder hammering nails into that material." She added in a lower tone to Bray, "We begged it all from the Indians, you know." Mrs. Chekwe, sullen with shyness, her neck and head propped up on the bolster of flesh held aloft by her corsets, did not know what to do with the fish, since, unlike the more experienced Bray and Mrs. Mackintosh, she could not overcome repugnance and eat it. She murmured, "Oh yes," and again, "Oh yes?" varying the tone to a polite question. For his ten minutes' attention to Mrs. Chekwe, he thought he might do better by talking in Gala, but decided it might be misinterpreted, on the one hand (Mrs. Mackintosh) as showing off and sucking up to the blacks, and on the other hand (Mrs. Chekwe) as patronage and the inference that her English was not good. However, he knew she came from the Northern Province and he managed a not too halting chat with her about the changes in the town of Gala and the whereabouts of various members of her family. Mrs. Mackintosh was talkative, one of those spirited colonial ladies—"It'd take more than this to throw *me*": she was referring, of course, to her problems as a member of the ladies' committee, but she gave him a game look that swept in present company. She did not know who he was; the curious fact was that people like him and her would not have met in colonial times, irrevocably separated by his view of the Africans as the owners of their own country, and her view of them as a race of servants with good masters. They were brought together now by the blacks themselves, the very source of the contention, his presence the natural result of long friendship, hers the equally natural result of that accommodating will to survive —economic survival, of course; her flesh and blood had never been endangered—that made her accept an African government as she had had to accept the presence of ants in the sugar and the obligation to take malaria prophylactics.

He had been placed at the main table, but right at the end—a name fitted in after the seating plan had been made up. The industrialist spoke of the huge new assembly plant for cars (a British-American consortium) that would employ five hundred workers, and said how stable government and "sensible conditions" for foreign investment were attracting capital that turned its back on neighbouring territories with their "impossible" restrictions on the foreign ownership of stock and "wild demands" for nationalization of industry; "here industry and the nation will go forward together." Sir Reginald Harvey, chairman of the gold-mining companies, spoke in a tone of modest, patriarchal pride, "allowing himself" boldly to say that the mining industry, whose history went back to before the turn of the century, "brought to this part of Africa the first light of hope after the centuries-long depredation and stagnation of the slave trade. On the basis of the auriferous rock discovered then, in the eighteen-nineties, the modern state of today has been founded. . . ." It was not even necessary for him to mention that forty per cent of the national income came from the mines; everyone in the hall was aware of that as unquestioningly as they knew the sun would rise in the morning. The mining industry was continuing to open up new fields of endeavour . . . there had been a temporary setback at the old Mondo-Mondo mine—but the tireless research, on which the company spent over a million a year in its efforts to better mining techniques and raise production, might soon make it possible to overcome these difficulties and reopen the mine . . . the mining companies and the nation would go forward. . . .

Applause was regular and vociferous, descending on cue as each speaker closed his mouth. Black cheeks gleamed, the blood rose animatedly in white faces while in the minds of each lay unaffected and undisturbed the awareness that what the industrialist had said was, "You'll use our money—but on our terms," and what the chairman of the gold-mining group had said was, "We don't intend to reopen the Mondo-Mondo mine because our shareholders overseas want big dividends from mines that are in production, not expansion that will create employment but take five or six years before it begins to pay off." The director of the cold-storage company, whose butcher shops all over the country had served Africans through a hatch segregated from white customers until a PIP boycott three years before had forced a change, charmingly insisted that the black guest across the table from him accept a cigar. "Put it in your pocket, then. Smoke it at home when you feel like it." Mr. Ndisi Shunungwa, Secretary General of the United Trades' Union Congress, who had once said, "They got in with a bottle of gin and a Bible—let's give them back what they brought and tell them to get out," solicitously fished under the table to retrieve the handbag of the wife of the Director of Medical Services. A plump and grateful blonde, she was apologetic: "Oh I am a nuisance . . . oh, look, you've got all dusty on your arm. . . . Oh I am . . ."

Mweta spoke very briefly. From where he was seated, Bray was presented with the profile, the high, round black brow, the little flat ear, the flash of the eye beneath womanish curly lashes, the strong lips that were delicately everted in speech. All who worked together for the country were countrymen, Mweta said. "From the earliest days of our struggle" he had never thought of citizenship as a matter of skin colour. If it was wrong to profit by the colour of the skin, it was also wrong to discriminate against a colour of the skin. He understood "this dinner was the most expensive meal any of us here has ever eaten." There was laughter; he smiled briefly, but he was serious, candid, a man who had lived until less than a year ago in a tin-roofed, two-roomed, black township house: "—but the cost is really much higher even than that, the price of this happy meeting has been paid over more than fifty years by the labour of the people of this country and the energetic foresight of those from outside who had faith in its development."

Loud music unfurled over the talk and clink of plates, and the harrassed stump of sweating waiters. Joy Mweta was steered out onto the dance floor by one of the white men. Voices rose in adjustment to the noise; the Congolese band played their particular hiccuping rhythm, marked by South American rattles and clappers. Every now and then the trumpet blurted like a shout of obese laughter. Some of the white men began to drift together as they did at club dances, and the black men were drawn to the male camaraderie of whisky and business talk. White wives went off to the cloakroom close as school-girls, and came back with faces animated by a good laugh about the whole affair. Black wives sat patiently, born to endure the boredom and neglect of official occasions. Dancing with a dutiful Bray, Mrs. Mackintosh was made careless now by gin and tonic. She giggled at the red bunting that covered the walls. "Bummed it from the coolies, my dear. They cheated the poor bloody native for so many years, they can afford to give away something now."

He danced with Evelyn Odara. She dragged him off to be introduced to an elegant girl he had noticed passing with unseeing eyes the African wives dumped like tea cosies and the white women watching her with their men, a white dress and dangling glass earrings making her black satin skin startling. Doris Manyema. But he had met her before, during the Independence celebrations. She had just been appointed the country's cultural attaché at United Nations; she received congratulations with guarded, confident disdain—it was as if one could look at her only through glass, this beauty who would take her place neither in the white man's back yard nor in the black man's women's quarters. She was going by way of Algiers; they talked of Ben Bella and Boumedienne for a few minutes and then a young white man who had been waiting for an opportunity to join in, meanwhile looking at her nipples touching against the inside of her dress and touching at his own blonde moustache in a kind of unconscious reflex, passed some remark about Tshombe's death. "I lost my bet he'd get out of prison there. I worked out the chances—you know, how many times he'd survived by the skin of his teeth before—fed 'em to a computer. Marvellously wily fellow, he was. I'm in insurance—actuary, you see," he said, a disarming apology for talking shop. Doris Manyema did not look at him, saying to Bray, "I hope Tshombe rots in hell." "Oh come now." The young man, jollying, bridling sexually. "I just took a sporting interest." Her long eyes looked down along her round cheekbones, her small nose distended slightly at the nostrils. "We don't share the sporting instincts of you people. Your blood sports of one kind and another. They only kept him alive that long because of Mobutu. Otherwise he ought to've been thrown in a ditch the way he did with Lumumba." The young man asked her to dance and led her off by the elbow, golden sideburns very dashing. "A handsome couple," Evelyn Odara said, with her man's laugh. She was draped like a solid pillar in florid robes; Ndisi Shunungwa's rimless glasses were flashing as they did when he made a political speech, but he was dancing with his apologetic blonde, smiling down sociably with his head drawn back from her, while she had on her face the circumspect, wide-eyed look of a woman who is dancing with her pelvis pressed against a strange man. As the evening went on, roars of laughter came from the groups of hard drinkers; they began to forget the presence of Africans and tell their obscene stories. The black men gathered here and there and spoke in their own language, *pas devant les enfants*. In the men's room, one of the white men standing beside Bray took a quick look round and said to a companion, "Thank Christ it's gone off all right, eh, Greg? Jesus, but it's heavy going with these chaps. And one mammy I had to push round the floor— I'm telling you, I needed to go into low gear to get that arse on the move."

The confusion of noise was interrupted suddenly by the band stopping. People broke off talk and looked around. There was some sort of stir; people began to crowd up; a different kind of buzz started and was hushed again. Mweta with Joy was parting a way through the guests, his guitar in his hands. That was how Bray saw it: his guitar. But of course it was not that guitar, it was simply one handed over from a member of the band in answer to a suggestion or request, maybe even Mweta's own sudden idea. Anyway, he was walking almost shyly, Joy by the hand and the guitar in the other, with the look of half-anticipation (he had loved that guitar) and half-pride (he had liked the pleasure village people took in the performance) he used to have when he got off the bicycle and the guitar slid from his back. Without any announcement, quite naturally, they stepped up onto the dais and he began to play, while she brought her hands together once or twice, straightened her young, slack, motherly body in its schoolgirlish pink dress, smiled, and then began to sing with him. Their voices were soft and in perfect harmony. They sang some banal popular song from an American film of the Fifties.

The whites applauded thunderously; delight came from them: perhaps it was an unconscious relief at seeing this black man of all black men in the old, acceptable role of entertainer. The Africans merely looked indulgent; after forty years of being told when to come and go, when to stand and when to take your hat off, a black president himself decided upon procedure. Then Mweta handed his wife down from the dais, gave back the guitar and left the hall through an avenue of people who surged forward spontaneously under the bright glance of that black face, that smile of vulnerable happiness.

He thought of how he had said to Bayley of Mweta, "He calls for an act of faith." What he had really meant was it takes innocence, a kind of innocence, to ask for an act of faith. He was talking to the Director of Information, who, as the first black journalist in the territory, had come to interview him years ago when the summary recall to England had just been announced. "What was worrying me most, I was worrying you would notice that I had no shorthand at that time . . ." They laughed, in the convention that the past is always amusing. But he was experiencing a clenched concern for this being that was Mweta, a contraction of inner attention, affection and defensiveness on behalf of Mweta, defensiveness even against himself, Bray. He was hyperperceptive to the world threatening to press the spirit of Mweta out of shape—white businessmen, black politicians, the commanding flash of Ndisi Shunungwa's rimless glasses, the OAU—his mind picked up random threats from memory, newspapers, and the actuality around him. There must be one being you believe in, in spite of everything, one being!

The band inflated the hall with noise again. At once the guests were deafeningly set in motion, drinking and dancing.

Next morning when he was on the road back to Gala trees and bamboo clumps came at him monotonously and his mind settled upon the past few days as if they had been lived by somebody else.

A hennish anxiety, last night.

Write to me. Write to me. We must keep in touch. About Shinza, of course; go back to Gala and keep an eye on Shinza. Don't forget to *keep in touch* about Shinza.

Call for an act of faith: it takes innocence. Bunk. It's an act of incipient Messianism—oldest political trick in the world.

I suppose so.

There was a salutary aftertaste in jeering at himself for being taken in.

PART THREE

Beneath the fig tree he sat day after day compiling his report. There was no more rain; at night the stars formed encrustations of quartz across the sky, bristling light, and the smallest sound rang out. Kalimo laid ready a fire of logs on which the dried lichens were frilled medallions of grey and rust.

In the imposed quiet of Gala he found himself held in a kind of aural tension—something cocked within him, as in an animal in the dream that is grazing. Listening; he would raise his head from the papers and the hum of the tree's proliferate and indifferent life— rustling, creeping, spinning, gnawing, crepitating, humming—did not lull him. Gala had the forest village's eerie facility of covering everything, of swallowing everything, sunk out of sight by the closing in of a weight of green. Down under the mahogany trees the same foreshortened black figures went. No sound from bare feet in the dust; voices flitted like birds caged by the branches. Slave raids, punitive expeditions of Portuguese and English—the wake of perpetually renewed foliage came together behind them. The distant clangor and grind of the small industrial quarter was muffled out in the same way. Nothing happened in the open in this small, remote, peaceful cross-road. All change was a cry drowned by the sea of trees. A high-pitched note, almost out of range. (In a noon pause, one morning, he experienced in fantasy this same quiet of sun and heavy trees existing while things went wrong—he saw a car burning, bleeding bodies far down under the shifting shade-pattern of the trees. It lasted a vivid moment; his skin contracted—it seemed prompted physically, like the experience of *déjà vu*—a rill of cool air had got between his damp shirt and warm back.)

He began at once to spend a lot of time down at Sampson Malemba's house in the old township.

Kamaza Phiri had made available an immediate grant to get a technical school going. Bray had said to him, "You realize that what Malemba and I are doing is a bit of mouth-to-mouth resuscitation on the old government workshops your department closed? The whole thing's contrary to policy." Phiri's palms expanded, tea-rose coloured. "It's an experiment for the purposes of the Bray Report"—the side of Bray's mouth went up in amusement at the term—"I'm prepared to go along with it."

Sampson Malemba was filled with a meticulous enthusiasm. He was making a round of the factories to talk to people about what initial courses were most needed. He had written off to Sweden for prices of machine-shop equipment. "Why Sweden, Sampson?" But at the table in his kitchen with its flowered oil-cloth he had done his homework; "The agreement—you know. The loan the government got: there's a balance of credit there for agricultural and industrial machinery."

They had a plan for small village centres to be run as ancillaries to the main one in Gala itself—each chief was to be asked to build a large hut where basic equipment would be provided by the scheme for the teaching of shoemaking, carpentry, and, most important, maintenance and simple repair of the motorized farming equipment the agricultural department lent to these communities. Malemba had had a brilliant idea: mechanics in the two local garages would be paid to give night classes in the villages, or, if these were too out of the way, weekend courses. The great problem for every branch of instruction was to find people qualified to give it; but if one let oneself be deterred by that, both were sanguinely aware nothing could be done in Africa at all. The garage mechanics were the sort of model makeshift solution to be tried for in every instance—they spoke the language, and although proper apprenticeship as motor mechanics had never been established for Africans under colonial rule, they had, while working for *Bwana*, became skilled all the same. In Gala they had kept the cars and tractors of the white community going for years; their own community had had neither.

Another problem was a place to house the centre. Bray felt fairly strongly that it should not be in the old African quarter or even in the new housing and hostel area, but in the "town" itself. It was important for ordinary Galaians to make a stake, firmly, in what had always been the white man's and was now the white man's and the black officials' preserve. He wanted the people who merely came into town to work, buy, or comply obediently with one or another of the forms of administration that ruled their lives, to establish once and for all that they belonged there, too. The club, the Sons of England Hall, the Princess Mary Library—they had passed by these for too many years. He wanted them to claim the town at last. He did not say this in so many words, as he went to see various people with a view to finding premises. (It was not for nothing, after all, that he had once been a civil servant.) But in the apparent simplicity of his approach—as if this were a routine matter of no unusual significance —there was something that, in spite of, perhaps because of, the old, innately unaggressive manner that many of them remembered in him from before, roused that unforgiving resentment towards one who always seems to have the moral advantage. His audaciousness was of the quiet sort, too, a joke played upon him by his background, producing in him a parody of the stiff upper lip. He approached the secretary of the club, even though he and Mweta had laughed at the very idea; one had to give the club members a chance. It was rather like the chance Dando had to give parliament to rescind the Preventive Detention Act. He suggested to the secretary that the disused billiard room—the generation of billiard players had died off, the squash courts were popular now—might be used for adults' secondary school classes Sampson Malemba himself intended to teach. The billiard room had a separate entrance from the club complex's general one. The classes would be held at night only. Then there was the big barn or shed that, as he (Bray) remembered, was put up to house the pack (years ago there were drag hunts in Gala and someone had brought out from Ireland the hounds who had died, one by one, of biliary fever; but not before they had bequeathed the occasional U-shaped ears that still appeared, in the odd generation of local curs). That shed would make an adequate workshop for fitting and turning classes, and as it was well away from the main building, would not interfere with members' activities in any way.

"You see we're going to be a bit like one of those big universities, with their faculty buildings distributed through different quarters of the city," Bray said in gentle self-deprecation. He and Sampson Malemba—sitting inside the club for the first time in his life—caught each other's eye and smiled.

But the secretary seemed afraid that a smile might give away the whole club to the black victors as a wink at an auction sale knocks down a job lot. He said, weightily, "I understand." He would, of course, put the matter before the committee—Bray must write a letter, setting out the facts, etc. "Yes, Mr. Malemba will do that—the scheme is under his department." Again, the secretary "understood"; but he could tell them straight off (and here he did smile, the beam of regrettable bad news) that the billiard room was jam-packed with scenery and props, the dramatic and operatic section had claimed it years ago, he couldn't even get his boys in there to clean up the place. And that barn—"You do mean the one down near the compound, just by the seventh tee?"—that barn was where the green-keeper kept his stuff, the mowers and so on, and, to tell the truth, some of the caddies dossed down there; "I know about it and I don't know about it—you know." He became expansive with conscious good nature now that he was disposing of his visitors. "Perhaps we can enrol the caddies," Bray said, feeling like a jolly missionary. The secretary was a big fellow whose thighs rubbed together as he left his chair; his short hair was so wetted with pomade that he had always the look of one who has just emerged from the shower. He laughed along with the black man, although he had not actually spoken to him apart from the initial introduction. He ushered them out with an arm curved in the air behind their shoulders. "Colonel, have you mentioned your scheme to any of the people here? I mean, just in the course of conversation?" It was the reasonable, flattering tone he might have used to encourage a member who had a good second-hand squash racket to dispose of; he knew Bray hadn't so much as had a drink in the bar since he'd been told his membership was approved. And Bray murmured, straight-faced, "I haven't been much in Gala lately, I haven't had a chance, really . . ."

In the car he said, "What a mistake about the caddies. The golfers will take it as the knell of doom: now we are going to take away their caddies and *educate* them."

"I would like very much to put them in school." Malemba was dogged. "Those kids know nothing but to smoke cigarette ends and gamble with pennies."

"Good God! The caddies will see their doom in us, as well. They'll be at the barricades along with the members, defending the place with golf-clubs."

There must have been an emergency meeting of the club executive. Within a week there was a letter in the mail brought up by messenger from the *boma*. Inside, the communication itself was addressed to The Regional Education Officer, Mr. Sampson Malemba, and marked "Copy to Colonel E. J. Bray, D.S.O." The members of the Gala Club, while always willing to serve the community as the Club had done since its inception in 1928, felt that the club buildings and outhouses were inappropriate and unsuitable as a venue for adult education classes. The purpose of the Club was, and always had been, to provide recreational facilities, and not educational ones, whose rightful and proper place was surely in schools, church halls, and other centres devoted to and equipped for instruction. Therefore, it was with regret, etc.

He phoned Sampson Malemba, who had one of the few telephones in the African township, but there was only a very small child repeating into the mouthpiece the single inquiring syllable, "Ay? Ay? Ay?" With the mail was a note from Aleke, beginning dryly, "I hear you're back." He had not been to the *boma*, it was true; he had all his papers at home, and for the present Malemba was the only official it was necessary for him to see. Anyway, Aleke invited him to supper that evening; to look me over, to see how well I was managed, in the capital? He thought, I wish I knew, myself.

When he walked up the veranda steps of what had once for so long been his own house, the first thing he saw was the girl. Rebecca Edwards—she had her back to him. She was pouring orange squash for the cluster of barefoot children, black and white, whose hands and chins yearned over the table top, and she turned, jerking her hair away where it had fallen over her face, as the other people greeted him. She said gaily, naturally, "Welcome back—how was everybody?" not expecting an answer in the general chatter. It was all right; he realized how he stonily had not known how he would face the girl again, not seen since that twilight. Of course it was because of her that he had not gone to the *boma,* it was because of her that he had arranged for the mail to be sent to him every day. He *had not wanted to be bothered* with the awkward business of how to treat that girl. The days that had elapsed had restored the old level of acquaintanceship. Or the incident was as peripheral to her as it was to him; her friends in the capital hinted as much, in their concern about her.

Sampson Malemba was there (his shy wife hardly ever came to such European-style gatherings, even if they were held by Africans); Nongwaye Tlume, the agricultural officer, and his wife; Hugh and Sally Fraser, the young doctors from the mission hospital; and Lebaliso, dropped in an uncomfortable old deck-chair before the guests as if by a gesture of Aleke's, saying, *There,* that's all he is—a bit of a joke with his 1914–1918 moustache aping the white man he replaced, and his spit-and-polished shoes—brown and shiny as his cheeks— giving away long apprenticeship in the ranks. Malemba and Bray at once began to talk about the letter. Over beer, and with the comments of the company, it appeared much funnier than it was. In fact, the first sentence in particular, the one about the Club having "served the community" since 1928, with its still inevitable assumption that the "community" meant the whites only, made them laugh so much, with such an exchange of wild interjections, that one of the smallest children (a Tlume offspring) crept up the steps towards the noise in dribbling-mouthed fascination, and then rose swaying to its feet like a snake charmed before music. Rebecca Edwards picked it up and cuddled it before the trance could turn to fear.

"And where do you go from there?" Fraser asked; he looked like a stage pirate, black curly hair, and hairy tanned forearms, a touch of beer foam at his lips.

"What do you say, Sampson?" Bray challenged.

"We'll have to consider."

"There goes the schoolmaster!" Aleke's remarks were amiable, critical, a hand rumpling his guest's hair.

Hugh Fraser rolled his eyes. "Let us preserve for ever the venerable, ivy-covered walls of the Gala Club, steeped in the history of so many memorable Saturday night dances, and so many noble performances of Agatha Christie."

"No, but really, James?" Aleke said lazily. He kept cocking an eye-brow at the Tlume infant, and slowly, it slid from Rebecca's lap and crawled to his leg.

"It'll have to be the Gandhi Hall, next. Don't you think, eh, Sampson."

"Simple enough. Get an order to commandeer whatever premises you need." Everyone laughed again in acknowledgement of the context of Sally Fraser's remark—the aura of Bray's friendship with the President.

"Oh, I'm not an Aleke or a Lebaliso!"

The policeman took it as a compliment, chuckling round to the company, pleased with himself: "Now Colonel, now Colonel . . ." Aleke half-acknowledged the feint by pulling a face. At that moment his wife said that food was ready and he announced, "Aren't I the cleverest damn P.O. there has ever been in Gala district? You know who cooked? My secretary, here. Yes"—she was smiling, shrugging it off, as he hooked an arm round her neck—"I get her to cook, too." "Nonsense. I gave Agnes the recipe, that's all." "She's been here the whole afternoon, making dinner for me," Mrs. Aleke said calmly. "I gave you the afternoon off, didn't I, Becky? I'm the best boss you've ever had, aren't I, Becky?"

Bray had not bought anything for the Edwards children but the Bayleys had. He was able to say to the girl now, "Vivien sent some things for you—a parcel. I'm sorry I haven't delivered it yet."

"Oh it doesn't matter. I can send one of the children." She extricated herself gently from Aleke's big forearm.

Next day he went to see Joosab. There could be something in the club secretary's suggestion that one might "mention the scheme in the course of conversation"—if not with Gala Club members, then with a member of the Indian community. Joosab said nothing; his large black eyes in wrinkled skin the colour and texture of a scrotum kept their night-light steadiness through Bray's outline of the scheme, the confidence about the white club's refusal, and what he knew was coming: the suggestion that the Gandhi Hall and the private Indian school of which it was part could provide premises. Although the Indians of Gala were mainly Moslem, like many such communities in Africa, they claimed Gandhi for the prestige he had brought to India and the third world in general, and perhaps also had some vague notion—in the uncertainty of their own position among Africans—

that the Mahatma's condemnation of caste and race prejudice might somehow soften incipient African prejudice against themselves. Of course the hall and school were in what was known—according to colonial custom by which the whites had placed various races at different removes from themselves—as the "bazaar," a small quarter, not more than a few streets, behind the Indian stores on the fringe of the white town. "But this will be a good thing, don't you think, Joosab— to break down these worn old distinctions of who belongs where, which are taking so long to die . . . ? Your people would be setting an example to the Europeans that should make them think again . . . and it certainly couldn't seem less, to the Africans, than proof of your good faith as citizens of this country . . . . Don't mistake me, either —we hope any Indians who are interested will take any course that may be useful, Joosab—"

Bray had never called him "Joosab" before, without the prefix "Mr."; the tailor was aware that if it had been dropped now, this was not because of the distance that other white people put between himself and them by not granting it to him, but because it had come to these two men that they had known one another a long time, and through many changes.

He smiled, "All our people have received education, Colonel. Since the first days, we have had our own school."

"I know. In fact, I'm counting on getting some teachers from you . . . I intend to see Mr. Patwa about that."

Outside the shop, one of Joosab's grandchildren was sitting on a gleaming new tricycle, ringing the bell imperiously while being pushed along by a ragged little African male "nursemaid"; every time the boy straightened himself, grinning, panting, the small girl screamed at him in furious Gujerati.

Permission came from the committee of the Indian school for the Gandhi Hall and the school wood-workshop to be used by the adult-education scheme, with the provision that this should not interfere with ordinary school hours or days of religious observance. Bray was writing a letter of thanks for Malemba and himself, sitting in his usual place under the fig tree. One of the Edwards children appeared —he didn't know whether it was a boy or a girl, they all had the same cropped hair and shorts. A clear, girl's voice asked for the parcel for mummy. Rebecca Edwards was in her shabby car in the road

with the other two children. She waved apologetically. He carried
out the Bayley present and they chatted at the car window; inside,
her boys were blowing up a plastic seal and giant ball, their swimming trunks tied round their heads—it was Sunday morning. He said
to them all, "Water is the natural element of this family. I associate
you with water."

She smiled, looking at her children. "I like your new office; I always see you sitting there when I pass. Like Buddha under the sacred
banyan. But what a good place to work. Certainly an improvement
on the *boma*."

"Well, it was you who pointed out to me that I was superfluous at
the *boma*."

"*I?* But I've never done anything of the kind?"

"Don't worry—and now I'm grateful. It's magnificent, my fig, isn't it.
Now that it's cooler it's a perfect place to be."

She was quick to be alarmed and embarrassed. The blood died
back from her face, leaving only a brightness in the eyes. "But when
did I say it?"

"Oh never mind. You were being considerate and excused me for
not thinking to give you a lift when your car was in the garage."

"Oh then—but you misunderstand—"

"Yes, I know, one sometimes hits on a little truth, just by mistake."
She was soothed, if slightly puzzled. Nothing was said for a few moments, they simply paused quietly with the morning sun on their
faces, as people do, outdoors. "What happened about the Indians?"

"We're getting the Gandhi Hall so long as it isn't on high-days and
holidays. Fair enough."

"Oh *that's* good."

He said, "Poor devils. What could they say. They hope it may
help."

She shook her head interrogatively, making a line between her
eyes. "Of course it'll help. It's a start for you."

"Help them. If things should look like going badly for them sometime."

"They're all right, though? Nobody's said a word about them?"

He said to her, "They see what's happened round about. Kenya,
Uganda. Rumbles in other places. Everywhere they kept out of the
African movements in order to keep in with the Colonial Office, they

hesitated to give up a British nationality until it wasn't worth the paper it was declared on. When I was here, before, they refused to let the PIP branch hold meetings in the Gandhi Hall, and the bigwigs on the Islamic committee never failed to inform me of the fact. Now they're going to allow a lot of bush Africans in where they've never set foot before—it's in the same sort of hope, although their situation isn't exactly a reversal of what it was . . . there's no alternative power now, it's the Africans or nothing. But the instinct's the same. The instinct to play safe; why does playing safe always seem to turn out to be so dangerous?"

"It's unlucky." She said it with the conviction that people give only to superstition.

He laughed. But she said firmly—she might have been reading a palm, "No, I mean it. Unlucky because you're too scared to take a chance."

"It's unlucky to lack courage?"

"That's it. You have to go ahead into what's coming, trust to luck. Because if you play safe you don't have any, anyway."

"It's forfeited?"

"Yes."

"Well, you're right so far as the Indians are concerned . . . whatever their motives for giving us the hall—whether they had decided to give it to us or not, it's not going to count if things go wrong."

He saw in her face that she suddenly thought of his connection with Mweta; that recognition that always embarrassed him because it seemed to invest him with a sham importance. "Why do you say if things go wrong?"

His tone was quick to disclaim. "A profound cycle of change was set up here three or four hundred years ago, with the first of us foreign invaders. We're inclined to think it comes to a stop, full circle, with Independence . . . but that's not so . . . it's still in process— that's all. One mustn't let oneself forget. And as for the invaders—we still don't know whether, finally, the remnants will be spewed out once and for all, or ingested. So far, the states that go socialist become the most exclusively African, the capitalist ones have as many or nearly as many descendants of the invaders as they did before. Not surprising. But it can all alter . . ."

"My people went to settle in England—my parents," she said. "I

don't know . . . I feel I'd be too lazy, you know? I'm not talking
about washing dishes—I mean, to live another life."

"Where were you before here?"

"Oh, Kenya. I was born there, and my brother. When he was replaced he went down to Malawi, and when Gordon—my husband's
contract wasn't renewed we pushed off to Tanzania, to begin with.
Clive was born there." She dangled her hand over the child's nape,
and he wriggled it off. He said, "Is *he* coming to swim with us?"

"Silly-billy, we came to pick up the present from Vivien, you know
that—" The children began to clamour to open it. When she drove
off they were worrying at the wrappings like puppies wrangling over
a bone. She turned to smile good-bye; she was getting a line of effort
between her brows.

He went back to his fig tree and sat there before the notes, reports,
and newspaper cuttings that awaited him. He lighted a cigar and
flicked away ants that dropped from the branches and crawled over
the lines of his handwriting. There was the problem of the bottleneck
that would arise if, in the zeal of getting every child to school, the
output of primary schools exceeded the number of places available in
secondary schools. It was comparatively easy to build and staff primary schools all over the country; but what then? Kenya. He saw
that he had made a note: For every child who wins entry into secondary schools in Kenya, four to five fail to find a place. He wrote, in
his mind but not on the paper before him. There must be a realistic
attempt to turn primary-school leavers towards agriculture, where for
the next two generations, at least, most will need to make their lives,
anyway. His eye ran heedlessly as one of the ants down the table he
had made of the number of teachers, schools, and government expenditure on education in comparable territories. There was a letter
from Olivia, with photographs: Venetia's baby lay naked, looking up
with the vividness of response that is the first smile. Shinza had held
the pinkish-yellow infant in one hand. The third page of Olivia's letter, lying uppermost, took up like a broken conversation: *not at all, as
you might expect, one of your own over again. A different sort of
love. You know, it's closer to the ideal where any child, just because
it is a child, makes the same claim on you. I feel freed rather than
bound.* He contemplated with fascination that distant landscape of
the reconciliation of personal passion and impersonal love, of attach-

ment and detachment, that had been her liberal-agnostic's vision of
grace. As it turned out, grandmotherly grace. His wife was nearly
his own age; they had married during the war. A few years younger
than Shinza. Her attainment was the appropriate one, matched
step by step to the stage of her life; he felt a tenderness towards
the blonde slender girl with the small witch's gap between her front
teeth, who had become this—it was like the recollection of someone
not heard of for many years, of whom one has asked, "And what happened to . . . ?"

There was a note from Mweta in the mail, too. The plain typewrit-
ten envelope had given no indication of who the writer might be, and
when he opened the sheet inside and saw the handwriting it was with
a sense of the expected, the inevitable, rather than surprise. Mweta
hoped the grant "was enough"; he urged again—what about a decent
house? When was Olivia coming? He had thought he would have a
letter by now, but perhaps Bray had been on the move again, about
the country? "We mustn't lose touch."

Every time Bray met the fact of the letter on the table he was
gripped by a kind of obstinacy. The letter was a hand on his shoulder, claiming him; he went stock-still beneath it. His mind turned
mulishly towards the facts and figures of his report: this is my affair,
nothing else. This is my usefulness. He would not answer the letter;
his answer to Mweta would be no answer.

A day or two later he was writing the letter in his head, accompanied by it as he walked across the street in Gala. *You know me well
enough to know I cannot "move about" the country for you: I can't
inform on Shinza to you, however carefully we put it, you and I. You
can't send me in where Lebaliso can't effect entry, I cannot be cour-
ier-cum-spy between you and Shinza. I did not come back for that.*

The letter composed and recomposed itself again and again. Once
while he was tensely absorbed in a heightened version (this one was
a letter to make an end; after it was sent one would get on a plane
and never be able to come back except as a tourist, gaping at lions
and unable to speak the language) he met the Misses Fowler at the
garage. He had not seen the two old ladies since his return from England, although he had made inquiries about them and meant to visit
them some time. They were trotting down from the Princess Mary Library with their books carried in rubber thongs, just as they did ten
or fifteen years ago, when they used to lunch with Olivia at the Resi-

dence on their twice-monthly visit to town. Disappointed in love during the war-before-the-last, they had come "out to Africa" together in the early Twenties and driven far up the central plateau in a Ford (Miss Felicity, the elder, had been an ambulance driver in that war). They grew tea on the slopes of the range above the lake and were already part of the landscape long before he had become D.C. of the district. Miss Adelaide ran a little school and clinic at their place; they saw courtesy, charity, and "uplift" as part of their Christian duty towards the local people, although, as Felicity freely confessed to Olivia, they would not have felt comfortable sitting at table with Africans the way the Brays did. When the settlers met at the Fisheagle Inn to press for Bray's removal from the *boma* because of his encouragement of African nationalists, the Fowler sisters rose from their seats in dissent and protested. Apart from Major Boxer (who had done so by default, anyway), they were the only white people who had defended him.

Adelaide did most of the talking, as always, taking over Felicity's sentences and finishing them for her. They were mainly concerned with Olivia—she was at home in Wiltshire, wasn't she? She would be there?

"Are you going over on a visit?"

"Oh, no—we're—"

"You must have heard that we're leaving," Adelaide stated. "Surely you've heard."

It seemed necessary to apologize, as if for lack of interest.

"There are so many things I don't seem to hear."

"Well, I don't suppose you see much of them," Felicity said, meaning the local white residents.

"Oh, it's all right, everything is quite amicable, you know. —I've so often thought of coming to see you, and then I kept promising myself, when Olivia comes—"

Adelaide's old head, the thin hair kept the colour and texture of mattress coir, under a hairnet, tremored rather than was shaken. She said firmly, "Our time has run out. We are museum pieces, better put away in a cupboard somewhere."

He said, "I should have thought you would have been quite happy to let it run out, here. You really feel you must leave your place? I think you'd have nothing to worry about, you'd be left in peace?"

Felicity said, "We've had these inspectors coming—Adelaide had to guarantee that we'd not lay anybody off, in the plantation, you know. And they have a new native inspector for the schools—he wanted to know if I was following the syllabus and he—"

"There's nothing the matter with that, Felicity." Adelaide spoke to her and yet ignored her. "But we're too old, James. You can't stay on in a country like this just to be left in peace."

They chatted while Bray's tyres were pumped and his battery topped up with water. He promised to write to Olivia and tell her the Misses Fowler were coming. He saw that Adelaide's books were Lord Wavell's memoirs and a Mickey Spillane.

They went off down the street under the trees, Adelaide with her white cotton gloves and hairnet, Felicity in her baggy slacks and men's sandals. Old Adelaide (they used to call her Lady Hester Stanhope, they used to laugh about her, he and Olivia) was not a romantic, after all. She had not been a liberal and now she was not a romantic. The old girls hadn't wanted to sit in their drawing-room with Africans, but now they did not expect to be left in peace there. They had recognized themselves for an anachronism.

By such encounters as this, remote from him, really, his mind was tipped. Again, the letter was mentally torn up. Thrown to the winds. What sort of priggish absurdity did he make of himself? The virginal drawing away of skirts from the dirt. I am not-this, not-that. What am I, then, for God's sake? A boy scout? Clapping my hand over my backside? A vast impatience with himself welled up; and that was something new to him, too, another kind of violation—he had never before been sufficiently self-centred to indulge in self-disgust. There had always been too much to do. But now I refuse, I refuse to act. Because it's not *my place to do so*.

He thought again: then go away, go back to the house in Wiltshire. Finish the damned education thing. May be some use, can't do any harm. What you set out to do.

Yet like the gradual onset of a toothache or a headache came the recurrent tension that he was going to see Shinza, couldn't stop himself, would one day find himself calmly making the small preparations to drive back to the Bashi. He would go to Shinza again, and he would know why when he got there.

T he Tlumes, the Edwards girl and her children, the Alekes and Bray—they drifted together and saw each other almost every day without any real intimacy of friendship. Gala was so small; the Tlumes and the Alekes, along with a few other officials' families, were isolated from the black town; Rebecca, because she was a newcomer living under conditions new to the white community, and Bray, because of the past, both were isolated from the white town. Bray often shared the evening meal at the Malembas down in the old segregated township, but also he sometimes would be summoned by a barefoot delegation of Edwards and Tlume children to come over and eat at the Tlume house across the vacant piece of ground. And the Alekes' house—his own old house—by virtue of its size was the sort of place where people converged. His bachelor shelter, without woman or child, remained apart, the table laid for a meal and shrouded against flies by Kalimo's net.

They were all going to the lake for the day, one weekend, and he found himself included in the party. An overflow of children and some picnic paraphernalia were dumped at his house as his share of the transport; the children sang school songs to him as he drove. On arrival, the company burst out of the cars like a cageful of released birds and scattered with shouts and clatter. Bray and Aleke were left to unpack; Aleke had brought a scythe in anticipation of the waist-high grass on the lake shore and took off his shirt while he cleared a space as easily as any labourer outside the *boma*. He had sliced a small snake in two—a harmless grass-snake. He put it aside, in schoolboy pleasure, to show the others, and, wiping the blade with a handful of grass, stood eyeing Bray amusedly. He remarked, "So we're getting rid of Lebaliso."

"You're what?"

Aleke lowered his young bulk into the cut grass and took one of the two-week-old English newspapers Bray had brought along. "The note came yesterday. He doesn't know yet. Transferred. To the Eastern Province. Masama district." His interest was taken by a front-page picture showing people in androgynous dress—boots, mandarin coats, flowing trousers, leis and necklaces, waxwork uniforms—and a few elderly faces in morning coats and top-hats, advancing like an apocalyptic army, under the caption PEER'S SON WEDS: WEDDING GUESTS JOIN VIETNAM PROTEST MARCH.

It was Bray's turn to watch him. "Aren't you surprised, then?"

Aleke smiled; it seemed to be at the picture. Then he looked up. "No, I'm not surprised."

"Well I am!"

Aleke's big face opened in a laugh; he was tolerant of power. If Bray could go to the capital and have the ear of the President, well, that must be accepted as just another fact. Of course Aleke, too, in his way, wanted to do his job and be left alone.

Bray said, "Well, it's a good thing, anyway." Aleke was amiably unresponsive. He lay back on one elbow, his thick hairless chest and muscular yet sensuously fleshy male breasts moved by relaxed, even breathing. He was rather magnificent; Bray thought flittingly of old engravings of African kings, curiously at ease, their flesh a royal appurtenance. "Of course he might just as well have got promotion for his powers of foresight. Still, that youngster should have brought an action against him."

They fell silent, turning over the pages of the papers. Bray was reading a local daily that came up from the capital twenty-four hours late. Gwenzi, Minister of Mines, appealed to the mine workers not to aspire "irresponsibly" to the level of pay and benefits that the industry had to pay to foreign experts; the experts would "continue to be a necessity" for the development of the gold mines over the next twenty years. A trade union spokesman said that some of the whites had "grown from boys to men" in the mines; why did they have to have paid air tickets to other countries and special home leave when they "lived all their days around the corner from the mine?" The Secretary for Justice denied rumours that a ritual murder, the first incident of its kind many years, was in fact a political murder, and that an inquiry was about to be instituted.

Cut grass swathes glistened all round; the voices of the women, calling in children, came sharply overhead and wavered out across the water. Winter hardly altered the humidity down at the lake; the air was so heat-heavy you could almost see each sound's trajectory, like the smoke left hanging in space by a jet plane.

After lunch, Nongwaye Tlume got talking to some fishermen and borrowed their boat. It was too small to hold all the children safely; Bray intervened, and had to take two of the younger ones, with Rebecca in charge, in a pirogue. Aleke and his seventh child slept in an identical glaze of beer and mother's milk.

The big boat went off with cheers and waves, pushed out of the reeds by splay-footed, grunting fishermen. Bray paddled the rough craft scooped out of a tree-trunk with the careful skill of his undergraduate days. He kept close to the shore; his load seemed tilted by the great curve of the lake, rising to the horizon beyond them, glittering and contracting in mirages of distance. They had the sensation of being on the back of some shiny scaled creature, so huge that its whole shape could not be made out from any one point. The other boat danced and glided out of focus, becoming a black shape slipping in and out of the light of heat-dazzle and water. The faces of the brown and white children and the girl were lit up from underneath by reflections off the water; he had the rhythm of his paddle now, and saw them, quieted, with that private expression of being taken up by a new mode of sensation that people get when they find themselves afloat.

The girl had half-moons of sweat under the arms of her shirt. Her trousers were rolled up to the knee and her rather coarse, stubby feet were washed, like the children's, by the muddy ooze at the bottom of the pirogue. He realized how solemnly he had applied himself to his paddling, and the two adults grinned at each other, restfully.

The children wanted to swim; everywhere the water was pale green, clear, and flaccid to the touch, gentle, but too deep for them

H

where the shoreline was free of reeds and followed a low cliff, and with the danger of crocodiles when the pirogue came to the shallows. Bray struck out for a small island shaved of undergrowth six feet up from the water to prevent tsetse fly from breeding; the children were diverted, and forgot about swimming. But when he slowly gained the other side of the island, there was a real beach—perfect white sand, a baobab spreading, the boles of dead trees washed up to lean on. The girl grew as excited as the children. "Oh lovely—but there can't be any danger here? Look, we can see to the bottom, we could see anything in the water from yards off—"

He and the girl got out of the pirogue and lugged it onto the sand; it was quite an effort. Their voices were loud in this uninhabited place. His shorts rolled thigh-high, he waded in precaution from one end of the inlet to the other; but there were no reeds, no half-submerged logs that might suddenly come to life. "I think it's perfectly safe." The children were already naked. She began to climb out of her clothes with the hopping awkwardness of a woman taking off trousers—she was wearing a bathing suit underneath, a flowered affair that cut into her thighs and left white weals in the sun-browned flesh as she eased it away from her legs. She ran into the warm water, jogging softly, with a small waddling fat black child by one hand and a skinny white one gaily jerking and jumping from the other.

He had stretched himself out on the sand but stood up and kept watch while they were in the water, his short-sighted gaze, through his glasses, patrolling the limpid pallor and shimmer in which they were immersed. The black baby was a startlingly clear shape all the time, the others would disappear in some odd elision of the light, only a shoulder, a raised hand, or the glisten of a cheek taking form. Where no one lives, time has no meaning, human concerns are irrelevant—an intense state of being takes over. For those minutes that he stood with his hand shading his eyes, the most ancient of gestures, he was purely his own existence, outside the mutations of any given stage of it. He was returned to himself, neither young nor middle-aged, neither secreting the spit of individual consciousness nor using it to paste together the mud-nest of an enclosing mode of life. He smoked a cigar. He might have been the smoke. The woman and children shrieked as a fish exploded itself out of the water, mouth to tail, and back again in one movement. He saw their faces, turned to him for laughing confirmation, as if from another shore.

She brought the children back and stood gasping a little and pressing back from her forehead her wet hair, so that runnels poured over neck and shoulders, beading against the natural waxiness of the skin. "It's—so—glorious—pity—you—didn't—" She had no breath; undecided, she went in again by herself, farther out, this time. He felt he could not stand watching her alone. It would be an intrusion on her freedom, out there. He sat with his arm on one knee, vigilant without seeming so, sweeping his glance regularly across the water. That wet, femininely mobile body, tremblingly fleshy, that had stood so naturally before him just now, the sodden cloth of the bathing suit moulding into the dip of the navel and cupping over the pubis, the few little curly hairs that escaped where the cloth had ridden up at the groin—so this was what he had made love to. This was what had been there, that he had—"possessed" was a ridiculous term, he had no more possessed it than he did now by looking at it. This was what he had entered. Even "known," that good biblical euphemism, was not appropriate. He did not know that body—he saw now with compassion as well as male criticalness, as she was coming out of the water towards him a second time, that the legs, beautiful to the knee, with slim ankles, were thick at the thigh so that the flesh "packed" and shuddered congestedly. She stretched out near him; she was sniffling, smiling with the pleasure of the water. No one was there except the two small children. He said to her as he might have said in a meeting in another life, "I'm sorry about what happened."

The words lay with the sun on her closed eyelids. After a moment, she said, guardedly, "Why?"

He felt culpable of having heard her talked about in the capital. He didn't answer at once.

"Because it's as if it never happened."

"Then that's all right," she said. She lay quite still; presently she sat up and asked for a cigarette, bundling the towel round herself with a complete lack of vanity.

"It's almost like the beaches at Lake Malawi."

"Is it? I never ever got to Malawi. We were going there on local leave the year I was kicked out, so it never came off. We used to picnic here with my children, years ago."

"This beach?" she said.

"Oddly enough, I've never been to this particular beach before—didn't know it existed, till we found it today. —Farther along, we used to go, up past Execution Rock, you know: on the main shore."

"What's Execution Rock?"

"You don't know the legend? Well, closer to us than a legend, really. The Dolo, the tribe of the paramount chief around here, used to have a trial of endurance for their new chief-elect. Before he could take office he had to swim from the mainland to the island. If he managed it, he would be rowed back in triumph. If not, he was supposed to be carted off and executed by being thrown from Execution Rock. That part of it's never been done in living memory, but the channel swim was still carried out until very recent times—the predecessor of the present chief did it. He was still alive when we came to live here."

She said, "Is your wife as attached to this place as you are?"

He smiled, half-pleased, half-misunderstood—"Am I so attached?"

She did not want to presume on any knowledge of him. "But you've come back."

"I can't go explaining to everybody—but how difficult it is when people impose an idea of what one does or is. . . . And others take it up, so it spreads and goes ahead. . . ." (He realized, with quick recovery, that while he was ostensibly speaking of himself he was suddenly doing so in paraphrase of thoughts about her, the image of her as presented by their friends in the capital, that he had steered away from a few minutes before.) "Coming back's a kind of dream, a joke —we used to talk about my part after Independence like living happily ever after. Mweta was in and out of jail, I was the white man who'd become victim, along with him, of the very power I'd served. I was a sort of symbol of something that never happened in Africa: a voluntary relinquishment in friendship and light all round, of white intransigence that can only be met with black intransigence. I represented something that all Africans yearned for—even while they were talking about driving white people into the sea—a situation where they wouldn't have had to base the dynamic of *their* power on bitterness. People like me stood for that historically unattainable state— that's all." He thought, am I making this up as I go along? Did I always think it? —I did *work* with Mweta, in London, on practical things: the line delegations took, proposals and memoranda and all the rest of the tug-of-war with the Colonial Office. "But the idea persists . . . Aleke thinks, now, Lebaliso's been removed at my pleasure.

I can see that. He tells me this morning about Lebaliso being given the boot as if remarking on something I already know." He gave a resigned, irritated laugh. Of course, she would be not supposed to know about Lebaliso—Aleke's typist. But it gave him some small sense of freeing himself by refusing to respect the petty decencies of intrigue. He knew nothing about Lebaliso's transfer, and had as little right as she to hear it before the man did himself. "There was a young man— Lebaliso beat him up, in the prison here. He was being detained without being charged. I found out by chance."

"I suppose Aleke thinks you told them—the President."

"But of course, I did. And now it's assumed that all I had to do was ask the President to remove Lebaliso—and it's done!"

"Just the same, the President must have thought that you thought it would be a good thing. I mean, he's known you a long time. Whether you asked him or not."

He instructed himself. "I'm responsible for Lebaliso's removal, whether I want to be or not."

"But you think it's a good thing he's going? Then why does it matter?"

"There's a Preventive Detention Act. What he did's been legalized, now. The principle on which he could've been removed seems somewhat weakened."

She drew up her big thighs, so that, knees under her chin, they hid her whole body. She was removing sand from between her toes. "Perhaps Mweta did it to please you," she said. At the same moment they noticed the children had disappeared into the bush. "Where've they got to?" There was the rambling cadence of small voices. They both made across the heavy sand. He carried back the skinny little white boy, she had the black one, indicating in dumb show how the fat rolls round his thighs outdid the cheeks of his bottom. The child lay looking up at her with the lazy pleasure of one to whom being carried is his due. "I believe you've got a grandchild?"

"Yes, a girl." They smiled. "It seems very, very far away."

"You've never seen it," she said.

"Oh, photographs." He gave a little demonstrative jerk at his burden. "This is yours—I ought to know by now, but there are so many always—" Although the boy was dark-haired, as she was, he was completely unlike her, yet with a definitive cast of face that suggested a marked heredity—black eyes under eyebrows already thick and well shaped, berry-coloured lips with a dent in the lower one: there was a man there, despite the poor little legs dangling from scabbed bony knees, and the cold small claws hoary with dirt-grained chapping. Her children were neglected-looking, stoically withdrawn in their games and gaiety as children are when they must accustom themselves to constant and unexplained changes of background and ever new sets of "aunties" and "uncles."

"He's Gordon all over again," she said, as at something that couldn't be helped. "Not just the looks. The way he speaks, everything. It's funny, because he's been with me all the time, I don't think Gordon's lived with us for more than three or four months since he was able to walk."

"They were worried about you, at the Bayleys'." He was careful how he phrased it. "Whether you'd be happy working for Aleke."

"Aleke's a darling. He really is, you know. It's all a lot of bluff, with him. He likes to think he's driving me with a whip. Good Lord, he doesn't know some of the people I've worked for. There are some bastards in this world. But I don't think a black could ever be quite like that."

"Like what?" The children were playing at the water's edge again, and he and the girl strolled along the beach.

"Get pleasure out of making you feel about *so* big. I mean they're as casual as all hell, they borrow money from you and you never get it back—things like that. But they don't know how to humiliate that way."

"—Not Aleke?"

"Oh yes—my first pay check. But that he did pay back. Last month again, and now he's not so prompt. I don't mind—that house is really too expensive for them, you know. There's too much room for relations and they all have to eat, even if it's only mealie porridge. Agnes's bought a washing-machine, as well. They're paying off for furniture."

"Still, it must put your budget out somewhat."

She threw away a piece of water-smoothed glass she had picked up. "Aleke! You know what he said—but quite seriously, helping me, you know—when I said that I must have the loan back this month or I couldn't pay my share of the Tlume household? He would speak to the Tlumes for me, he would explain that with the move, and so on, and the car repairs, I'm rather short. . . ."

"You'd better not tell the Bayleys."

"Oh but Aleke's fine. I remember once, in Rhodesia, Gordon turned up and found I couldn't take any more of that old horror I was work-ing for, Humphrey Temple. He wouldn't even let me go to pick up my salary. He went up to the offices himself, walked straight into Temple's room and demanded an apology. . . . Nobody in that office even had the faintest idea who this cocky man was. . . ." She laughed. She said, returning to the Bayleys' concern, "It's all right here, for me. At the beginning, I thought I'd just have to pack up and give in. Go back. I felt I'd been mad. . . . But that was just the usual panic, when you move on."

"It is isolated. Won't you be lonely?" He almost added, quite natu-rally, "—after I'm gone," not in the sense of his individual person, but of the presence of someone like himself, a link between the kind of life that had existed for white people and created these remote centres, and their future, different life which had not yet cohered.

"I didn't think about that. You know how when you think only about getting away—that seems to solve everything, you don't see be-yond it. And then when you are—safe . . . it turns out to be the usual set of practical things, finding somewhere to live, looking for a school . . . But it's better, for me. You know how nice they all are, down there. I love those people but"—she looked away from him, out over the lake, then took refuge in a kind of deliberate banality—"I—got—sick—of—them." There was the pause that often follows a half-truth.

The tempo of their communication switched again. They talked about the lake, and his journeyings round about. "You realize how hard it is to grasp change except in concrete terms. In Europe if you had been away ten years and then come back, you would *see* the time that had elapsed, in new buildings, landscapes covered with housing schemes, even new models of cars and new styles of clothing on people. But there's nothing that didn't look as it did before—the lake the same, the boats the same, the people the same—not so much as a bridge or a road where there didn't use to be one. And yet every-thing has changed. The whole context in which all this exists is differ-ent from what it has ever been. And then, on top of it, I went to see an old friend . . . a contemporary of mine, you see, and in *him* you could see the ten years—grey hairs, a broken tooth, the easy signs that make you feel you know where you are. But he turned out to have a new-born son—there was a baby born the same time as I got a grandchild!"

"Nothing so extraordinary about that," she said, inquiringly amused.

"But confusing," he said, also laughing.

"I don't see why. Perhaps he's a grandfather as well."

"Oh, I'm sure. Several times over. He had many other sons, as I remember."

"Oh, an African."

"Have you ever heard of Shinza—Edward Shinza?"

"Can't remember. I suppose so. A political leader? I usually know the names of the cabinet ministers but after that I give up. You'll find I'm an ass at politics, I'm afraid. Not like Vivien."

"He's an old friend. He was the founder of PIP."

She said, "You know everybody."

"Yes," he said, "that's the trouble."

"Let me paddle on the way back, will you?" she said. "My God, this lake is wonderful. It makes all the difference."

"To what?"

She looked for a moment as if she did not know, herself. "To living here." Sunburn highlighted the flanges of her nostrils and her cheekbones, and her lips looked dry—she seemed to have brought no make-up with her with which to make repairs. It was true that there was a deliberate lack of flirtatiousness in her. It was almost an affront. Her yellow, lioness gaze rested on the children.

That evening when the whole party was back home, he walked across the vacant ground to get rid of the bits and pieces children had left in his car. She was playing chess on the veranda with Nongwaye Tlume; they had a modern gas-lamp that gave an underworld, steel-coloured light. She dumped the miscellany on a chair and walked with him through the garden which had no fence and was marked off from the scrub only by a few heads of zinnia and the shallow holes and tracks made by children. "I taught Nongwaye to play but now he beats me regularly. When I grumble he says it's an old African custom, to beat women—but he's so westernized he does it at chess." Strolling, chatting, her arms crossed over her breasts, she

ended up nearer his house than the other one, and came in for a
drink. "Is it too cool to sit under the fig?"

"No, no, I'd love to sit under the famous fig."

He had a little candlestick with a glass mantel. It lit the fissures
and naves of the great tree like a lamp held up in a cave; even at
night the bark was overrun by activity, streaming with ants and bor-
ers indentured for life.

"You seem to get on very well in the Tlume household." It interested him that a woman who appeared to have little or nothing of the
liberal principles and fervour that would make the necessity a testing
virtue, should find living with an African family so unremarkable. She
apparently had been brought up in the colonial way, and had lived
her life in preserves on the white side of the tracks, wherever she had
been.

She said, "They just are very nice people. I was lucky. It's a hell of
a risk, to share a house."

"You haven't found them rather different?—you know, in the small
ways that count rather a lot when you're living together."

"Well, it is another thing, of course—when you live with people.
For the last year or two I've been working with Africans and then in
our crowd at the Bayleys' there were African friends; but I've never
lived with them before. But as I said this afternoon . . . at the time, I
didn't think about anything . . . and I had to get out of that hotel
and the chance came up. . . . Of course it is a bit different—there's
not much privacy in the house, we really do all live together, I mean,
it's not the arrangement of these are my quarters and those are yours,
that I'd assumed. They just take it for granted; we eat together, people wander in on you all the time. . . . But at the same time there *is*
a kind of privacy, another kind. They never ask questions. They simply accept everything about you." When he came back out of the
house with their beer, she said, "Of course, Gordon's up in arms. I
wrote to tell him where we were and, naturally, *that* brought a letter
from him. I got it last week—what sort of educational background for
his children and all that. He nearly had a *fit*. Whenever he gets all
concerned he writes these sort of lawyer's letters, so snooty and silly.
He sees us sitting in the yard eating mealie porridge out of a big pot
—you don't know Gordon's imagination." She laughed derisively but
almost proudly.

"Where is Gordon?" he said, as if he knew him.

"I hate to tell you." Half confidential, half enjoying an opportunity
to shock. "In the Congo, with that old bastard Loulou Kamboya"—
she saw him trying to place the name—"no, not a politician, just an
ordinary crook. Well, extraordinary. Gordon met him in a bar in
Zambia, Loulou goes all over the place in his black Mercedes. Gordon went into the souvenir business with him. Loulou's got a 'factory'
making those elephant-hair bracelets. He supplies all kinds of hideous
things—fake masks and horn carvings. He wanted to get down to
South Africa to make contacts in the curio racket there, but of course
they wouldn't let him in. So Gordon went for him. There was going to
be a fortune in it, they were going to have a network over Africa from
east to west and north to south—you know. I don't know what's
happened—it seems to have faded out. In this last letter Gordon says
he's taking a job on the Cabora Bassa thing—the dam. He worked on
Kariba, of course: that was when I went to Salisbury. He's an engineer when he has to be. —If you ever want any elephant-hair bracelets, I've got a surplus stock."

He would be like the Tlumes and never ask questions—that is,
questions that were intrusive. But she had introduced the subject
of this man, the husband; he seemed hardly more than an anecdote. Bray said, "Well, at least he isn't a mercenary. When you said
Congo—"

"Oh, I'm sure Loulou's done his share of gun-running, but that
really would be too profitable to let anyone in on. Gordon Edwards
wouldn't be included in that." It was a kind of parody of the solid
suburban housewife's plaint that her husband was always bypassed
by promotion. He was entertained by this sturdy dryness that he had
not seen in her before. She began to tell him anecdotes about life in
the capital, involving Dando, people at the various ministries and the
university, both of them laughing a good deal. They were the stories
of an intelligent secretary, background observation; if there were any
that were the stories of an intelligent mistress, she didn't include
them. He walked her home across the scrub again and gave her a
good-night peck on the cheek, the convention between the men and
women of the group to which he and she had belonged, in the capital. She was a courageous and honest girl and he had the small comfort of feeling he had put things right between them. He had a distaste for false positions. Even tidying minor ones out of the way was

something. He did it as he would tidy his table when there seemed no way of tackling what he really had to do. When he met her during the week, buying icecream for the children, he offered to take them all to the lake again at the weekend—he wanted to have a talk to the people at the fish-freezing plant.

But she telephoned on Friday night—Sampson Malemba was in the room with him, they were working—and said that the children had been asked to a party and were "mad keen" to go, so— It didn't matter at all, he'd take them another time maybe (he had always the feeling even while he spoke of everyday plans, that he might be gone, quite suddenly, before they were realized). Then he thought he might have sounded a little too relieved at not having the bother of the outing, and added—"Of course, you come along if you want to—if you've nothing better to do? I have to go, anyway." She said she'd let him know on Saturday morning, if that was time enough? He felt the reciprocal tolerance of one preoccupied person towards the preoccupations of another.

Malemba sat waiting with his head tilted back, tapping a pencil on his big yellow teeth; it was a question of money, money, again now. There was an old police compound—a square of rooms round a courtyard—that they could acquire very cheaply and convert into classrooms at the cost of a few hundred pounds. The existing grant was already earmarked for other things; Malemba said, "If you wrote and asked for more?

"To whom?"

He looked at Bray and shrugged.

Yes, he had only to ask Mweta; he said, "Suppose I were to write to my friend the American cultural attaché, down there. They're keen on educational projects. Of course, they like the big ones that show— like the university. But lecture rooms—that's the way to put it—it might just ring the bell for us."

He heard her coming through the screen door of the veranda while he was finishing breakfast. She was wearing men's blue jeans and her rubber-thonged sandals, and was pleased to be in good time. She looked very young—he did not know how old she would be, round about thirty, he supposed. Kalimo had carefully tied up with string saved from the butcher's parcels a package of food: "What's inside?"

Bray asked, and Kalimo counted off with a forefinger coming down on the fingers of the other hand— "Ah-h loaste' chicken, eggs with that small fish in, ah-h tomatoes, blead, sa't, litt'e bit pepper. No butter. You must buy butter." It was the picnic he had always prepared, down to the stuffed eggs with anchovy, that Olivia had taught him to make, and the paper twists of salt and pepper. "Don't bother with butter, it'll just melt" the girl said. He stopped on the way out of the village and bought a bottle of wine instead.

She had a small radio with her, and when he had warned her she might have quite a long wait for him at the freezing plant—"Not the most attractive place in the world to hang about in, either"—she had taken something to read out of his bookshelves, more with the air of wanting to be no trouble than anything else. It was pleasant to have company in the car; she lit cigarettes for them both and the dusty road that climbed down through the mountains was quickly covered. So far as he had taken notice of her at all, he had always felt rather sorry for the girl whose life overlapped the lives of others but was without a centre of its own. Now she seemed like one of those hitch-hikers who let the world carry them, at home with anybody in having no home, secure in having no luggage, companionable in having no particular attachment. She might have flagged him down on the road, just for the ride. He left the car in what shade he could find at the fish factory; the trees between the buildings and the rough wharf had been hacked down and the dust was full of trampled fish entrails hovered over by wretched dogs and flies. He saw her at once settle down to make herself comfortable, opening the doors of the car for a draught, and hanging the little radio, aerial extended, from the window.

There had been a dispute at the fish factory reported in the papers the week before; some sort of dissatisfaction over the employment of what were termed "occasional" workers—it was not very clear. What *he* had come for was additional data on the number of families and the extent of the area they were drawn from, as represented in the records of men employed on the company's trawlers; there was some discrepancy, in his notes, between the educational needs of the population based on the number of workers who, although scattered, could be considered local, and the actual size of this population—which might be much less, if the workers in fact came largely from commu-

nities much farther up the lake and left their family units behind. Lake
men had a migratory tradition that pre-dated colonial settlement;
they had gone where the trade was, where the fish ran. It was sometimes difficult to find out to which community they belonged. For
themselves, unlike other groups whose home ground was twice defined, once by tribal tradition and again by the colonial district system, they belonged, as they would say "to the water," a domain
whose farther side, away up in other territories of Africa, they had
never seen.

The freezing plant section had the morgue atmosphere of men in
rubber aprons hosing down concrete floors, and sudden reminders of
blood and guts that no hygiene could do away with entirely. He saw
the white manager for a minute, a man seamed, blotched and red-
dened from a lifetime of jobs like this, dirty, but routine as a city office, in the wilderness, in the sun. He was handed over to a grey-eyed
coloured man with uplifting texts in his office. The records were not
too satisfactory; Bray asked if he could talk to one of the shop
stewards—the union records might make more sense. The clerk became vague and left the room—"Just a minute, ay?" He came back
with the composed face of an underling who has passed on responsibility. "The manager says we don't know if he's here today, they
doesn't work Saturday, only if it's overtime." Bray had seen that some
people were working. "Yes, some are working overtime this morning,
but I don't know . . ." Uneasy again, the clerk took him down to the
cleaning and packing floor. He seemed to have the helpless feeling
that Bray would single the man out instantly; in fact, one of the section overseers, a big, very black man standing with gumboots awash
where the fish were being scaled, looked up alertly and caught the
clerk's eye. He came with the matter-of-factness of one who is accustomed to being summoned. Bray introduced himself and the man said
with almost military smartness, "Good morning, sir! Elias Rubadiri,"
but couldn't shake hands because his were wet as the fish themselves.
Scales gleamed all over him, caught even in his moustache, like pail-
lettes on a carnival Neptune. They went out into an open passageway
to talk; oh yes, there were union records. But the man who kept them
wasn't there, they were locked up. Where? Oh at his house, that
man's house. Could one go to see him, then? —The scales dried
quickly out in the open air, he was rubbing them off his hands, shed-

ding them. "He's not there. . . ." There was that African pause that often precedes a more precise explanation. Bray switched to the intimacy of Gala, and the overseer said, "You know, the other day . . . he got hurt on the head."

Then they began to talk. Rubadiri was one of those half-educated men of sharp intelligence, touchy with whites yet self-assured, and capable of a high-handed attitude towards his own people, who appear in authority all over the place after independence is achieved. PIP was kept alive by such people, now that the old brazier-warmth of interdependency that was all there was to huddle round had been replaced by the furnace blast of power. There was no sense in the dispute—that was how he presented it to Bray. The old men and women who were employed by the fish-drying "factory"—"those sticks in the sand with a few fish—you'll see out there"—were not capable of any other work. They did not keep regular hours of employment, they were sick one day, they started only in the afternoon the next, they had pains in the legs—he laughed tolerantly. "It gives them something to do, the money for tobacco." Of course, the company did own the fish-drying, it had been there, a small private concession that they had bought up along with some boats and the use of this landing stage when the factory was started. It produced a few thousand bags of dried fish a year, that went to the mines—but that demand was dwindling because even before independence the mines had almost abandoned migratory labour and workers who lived with their families were not given rations as compound workers had been. For the rest of the market, the company had the fish-drying and fish-meal factory in Gala, as Bray must know, where the whole thing was done by machinery. So these people here—his hand waved them away—"the company just lets them stay." The union that had been formed when the factory started didn't recognize them.

When he began to talk about the "trouble" of the previous week he took on a closed-minded look, the look of a man who has stated all this before a gathering, repeated it, perhaps, many times, with a hardening elimination of any doubt or alternative interpretation.

"Now some people come along and say, the fish-dryers work here, they work for the same company, why aren't they in the union? They say, they are paid too little, it's bad for us if somebody accepts very low pay. How do we know, if there's trouble, if one day we strike, they won't be brought in to do our work?" He lifted his lip derisively and expelled a breath, as if it were not worth a laugh. "Of course they know, the same time, that's all rubbish. How can women and old men do our work? All they could do is wash the floors! They don't understand the packing, and the freezing plant machinery."

"Why do these others bother about them, then?"

"Why? Sir, I'll tell you. These are people who say they are PIP, but they are not PIP. They want to make trouble in the union for PIP. They want to make strikes here. I know them. They only want trouble."

"They're not lake people?"

He looked surly. "They are from here. But they have got friends—there"—he stabbed a finger in the air—"in the factory in Gala, there in town— I know."

"So there was a row," Bray said.

"Trouble, trouble, at the meeting. Some of our people want to expel them from the union. Then there was fighting afterwards . . . trouble."

"And you—do you want them expelled?"

He smiled under his ragged moustache at Bray, professionally. "PIP doesn't have to be told to look after the workers here. They must change their ideas and see sense."

Bray talked to him a little longer, getting some useful information about the origins of the trawler and factory workers; it turned out that Rubadiri himself had his wife and family not in the immediate area, but in one of the villages farther up the lake.

Bray knew that he had kept the girl sitting in the car nearly an hour, but when he made out the racks of drying fish looking like some agricultural crop stacked in the sun away over the far side of the jetty, he went up quickly to have a look. It was true that it was more like some local fishermen's enterprise than part of a large, white company's activities. Just a bit larger—not more elaborate—than any of the home-made fish-drying equipment you saw wherever there were huts, as you went up the lake shore. The usual racks made of reeds and bound with grass, on which split Nile perch and barbel were draped stiff as hides, yellowish, rimed with salt, and high-smelling. The ground was bare, the verge of the lake was awash with tins and litter, and certainly no one was working. But of course it was Saturday. Naked children and scavenging dogs were about; then he noticed that a series of derelict sheds under one rotting tin roof were not storage sheds at all, although they stank like them, but were inhabited. There were no windows, only the dark holes of doorways. Faces loomed in the darkness; now he saw that what he had taken for rubbish lying about were the household possessions of these people. There were no traditional utensils, of clay or wood; and no store-bought ones, either—only the same sort of detritus as scummed the edge of the lake, put into use, as if these people lived from the dirt cast off by a community that was already humble enough in itself, using the cheapest and shoddiest of the white man's goods. There were no doors to the sheds. He felt ashamed to walk up and stare at the people but he walked rapidly past, a few feet away, in the peculiar awe that the sight of acquiescent degradation produces in the well-fed. The malarial old lay about on the ground outside, legs drawn up as if assuming an attitude for traditional burial. Vague grins of senility or malnutrition acknowledged him from those black holes of doorways, gaping like foul mouths. He saw that there were no possessions within, only humans, inert, supine, crawled in out of the sun. A girl with the lurch of a congenitally dislocated hip came out with the cripple's angry look that comes from effort and not ill-temper, and put on a beggar's anticipation. A crone looked up conversationally but found it too much effort to speak.

He went back round the freezing plant to the car and said to Rebecca, "Come here a minute. I want to show you something."

They walked rapidly, she subdued yet curious, glancing at him. "Christ, what a smell—" They passed the racks. He took her by the arm and steered her along the line of sheds. His grip seemed to prevent her from speaking. She said, "But it's horrible." "I had to show you." They spoke under their breath, not turning to each other. The crippled girl, the crone, the quiet children watched them go.

Back at the car she burst out. "Why doesn't someone do something about them? Who are they?"

He nodded. "I just wanted to be sure I wasn't somehow exaggerating. I mean, this is still a poor country. Life in the villages isn't all that rosy."

"But this! In tribal villages they may not have the things they have in town, but they do have their own things, you can see they are *living*. In that place they have nothing, Bray, nothing. No necessities for any kind of life."

"Just what struck me. They're somehow stripped."

"How do they keep alive at all?"

"They're fish-dryers." He began to tell her the story while they drove away and left the place behind them.

At last he said, "Well—let's find somewhere to eat," and slowed down to consider. She gave a little shudder: "Somewhere beautiful."

"Where we were the other day?"

"Oh, lovely." But when he stopped along the lake shore track and prepared to settle, she looked uncertain.

"Isn't this the place?"

She said, "I thought you meant the island—"

"All the way over to the island?"

"Never mind, this's fine—"

"Well, if you're in no hurry to get back, I'm certainly not. Wait—let's see if I can find a boat—"

She kept protesting, but she couldn't disguise her hope. There were two pirogues, much patched with tin, dragged up among the reeds. A fisherman was picking over a net. There was a short exchange of cheerful greetings in Gala and then they were given the choice of craft. They took the one that seemed to ship the least water, and they had two paddles this time. Their progress was erratic but she was determined to do her part, flushed and self-forgetful in a way that was unusual in an attractive woman. Once they were past fourteen they were never free of a nervous awareness of how they must be appearing; he had seen it in his daughters.

She was right. The island, the beach, were worth the trouble. She was proprietorial with pleasure. "Have you ever seen such perfect sand? And look—a back-rest, and you can face the water—" They had a swim first, undressing and dressing again without false modesty, each not looking the other's way. Then Kalimo's lunch was unpacked. "Have one of the eggs with little fishes in it, come on." They ate greedily, and drank the warm red wine. She really was too fat-thighed for those old trousers, now that she had eaten they were drum-tight over the belly, as well. What did one mean by an "attractive" girl, then? Was her face pretty? It was a square, ruddy brown-skinned face, he did not like such broad jaws, when she became middle-aged she would be handsome and jowly. She had a good forehead, in profile, under the straight black hair—her hair was very black. And, of course, lovely eyes, those yellowy, lioness eyes. No, "attractive" meant just that—a drawing power that had nothing to do with the beauties and the blemishes, the disproportions and symmetries existing together in the one woman. She used no perfume but the warm look of the tiny cup formed by the bones at the base of her full neck made you want to bury your face there where the body seemed to breathe out, to smoke faintly with life.

They lay down on the sand, side by side; she had taken one of his cigars and was enjoying it. Every now and then, to ask a question or make a point, she raised herself sideways on one elbow, a hand thrust up into her untidy hair, the other hand half beneath her body, covering the falling together of her breasts in the neck of her shirt. Whatever she was, she was not a coquette.

"How long is your contract—with Aleke?"

"Eighteen months."

"And after that—you'll go back?"

"Where?" she said. He was thinking of the capital, it was a habit of mind for him to think in terms of some base. "I don't know what it'll be. Maybe we'll go to South Africa. Because of Cabora Bassa."

"It's in Mozambique, miles from anywhere."

"But he'll be working for South Africans. He'll be paid in South African currency. But perhaps I'll just renew—another eighteen months here. We'll see. Anyway I want to put Alan and Suzi into a boarding school."

"But not in South Africa."

"Well, yes. I don't fancy the idea of Rhodesia. And they can't stay here much longer—" She was anxious not to hurt his feelings—she saw all occupations in personal terms—by suggesting that his great plans for education in the country were not good enough. "It's just that, with the schools newly integrated, the standard *has* dropped like hell, and, you know, one can't let one's children come out of school half-baked."

"Of course. For the time being only the African children benefit, while the white ones are at a bit of a disadvantage. But you wouldn't really consider sending them to South Africa?"

She said again, "Oh I don't know, they say the schools are good."

He saw that she was thinking of the money; there was a chance
that there would be money in South Africa, to pay for them. Under
the surface, her life was laid on bedrock necessities like this, that
made luxuries out of scruples as well as emotions. But he said, gently,
"Here you are all living happily with the Tlumes. And you'll send
them there, to be brought up in the antiquated colonial way, to consider that their white skin sets them above other people."

She smiled, slightly embarrassed and defiant. "Well, what about
me? It was like that in Kenya. It's only while they're at school; they'll
grow out of it again."

"Not everyone can be as natural as you," he said.

She turned on her elbow again. "I don't quite understand how you
mean that."

"You cling to reality," he said. "They couldn't condition you into
the good old colonial abstractions—a nigger's a nigger and a white
man's an English gentleman. You obstinately stick to other criteria—I
don't know what they are, but they certainly aren't based on colour."

"It's a big fuss about nothing. If that was all you had to worry
about . . ." She dropped her head, rolled back. Perhaps she was
thinking about her "other criteria"—what they were. Perhaps she was
dissatisfied with them—with herself. It was easy to decide for her
that necessity ruled her life with beautiful simplicity, even where it
was makeshift and compromised. What criterion was there for this invisible man to whom she was married but with whom she never
seemed to live? And the obliging reputation she had among husbands
of the little group left behind in the capital? He felt again as he had
the first time they had been on the island beach, only this time she,
this young woman, was present as he was in the state of immediate
existence, curiously quiet and vivid, unmediated by what they both
were in relation to other people and other times.

The fish eagles hunched indifferently on a dead tree out in the lake.
If he tried to follow their gaze over the water, his own faltered out,
dropped in distance; theirs was beyond the capacity of the human
eye as certain sounds go beyond the register of the ear. She said, "Not
as if they were ever going to be South Africans."

"It's a contradiction of your realism, you know. You can't be realistic without principles—that's just the convenient interpretation, that
the realist accepts things as they are, even if those things express an

unreal situation, a false one. You're the one who should see over the head of that situation, and instinctively reject it even as a temporary one, for your children. That's the practical application of principle."

She mumbled into her crossed forearms, "I'll remember that." —He saw from the movement of her half-concealed cheek that she was smiling.

Ah yes, how nice to set oneself up as the mentor of a rather lonely young woman, to explain her to herself. "We'd better move, soon."

She said, preoccupied, "And how long have you still got?"

"That's up to me."

"Your contract's with yourself." She was generously envious.

"Very convenient. And only I know what the terms are. Or I ought to."

"Then you probably do."

"Do I?"

"Oh yes. People do. We know all about ourselves. Al-ll about it." She was scratching her scalp and paring the collected road-dust from beneath her nails, concentratedly, as if she were alone. He thought defensively, how very natural she was; he had always liked so much Olivia's fastidiousness, her almost awesome lack of little disgusting personal habits. Olivia could never have gone to bed with someone who picked his nose. . . .

They lingered on the island, and on the shore when they returned and paid for the use of the leaky pirogue, chaffing with the bandy-legged fisherman in his athletic vest and torn pants. He seemed surprised at being paid at all; so far as he was concerned, he was busy with his net and they were welcome to his boat in the meantime.

But once he saw the money in his hand, he must suddenly have thought of something he wanted to buy, for he looked at it smiling, as if to say, what use is this to me? He said to Bray, in Gala, can't you give me two-and-nine more? Bray didn't have the change but the girl did, and they paid up, amused. So the drive back was started well on in the afternoon, and it was slower going, climbing the pass instead of descending it. They had just come out onto the savannah when Bray felt that there was a puncture. They changed the tyre without much trouble but did not get back home till well after dark. "This's one of the times when one would like a good little restaurant to ap-

pear magically in Main Road, Gala." She said something about having to get back to the children, anyway; but when they drove along
under the weak, far-apart street-lights of the road where they lived,
she seemed to forget her concern, and came into the house with him.
Kalimo had the fire lit; the ugly room was perfumed with the soft, dry
incense-smell of *mukwa* wood. They had bought a couple of bream at
the lake, and wanted to cook them over the wood-ashes, but Kalimo
carried them off. "Don't fry them Kalimo, for heaven's sake—grilled
not fried—"

She laughed to see him trying to prevail. "If you are worried about
the children . . . ? You could dash over now? Kalimo won't be ready
for an hour if I know him."

She went as if she had been intending to do so, but he saw that she
wouldn't have gone if he hadn't said anything; and she was back
within ten minutes. She had put on lipstick and her hair was brushed
back, lank from the lake. She herself had the look of a child fresh
from the bath. "Everything all right?"

"Oh Lord, yes. Fed, in bed. Trust Edna Tlume for that." She had
brought a packet of marshmallows: "For afterwards, with the coffee.
Don't you love them toasted?"

When Kalimo came in to clear the table he looked disapproving;
she was squatting before the fire, watching carefully while the pink
sweetmeats swelled on the end of a fork, wrinkled and slightly blackened. "Try one, Kalimo" she waved the fork at him, but he stumped
out—the kitchen was the place for cooking.

She smoked one of Bray's cigars. It was half-past ten by the time he
heard Kalimo lock the kitchen door. She was resting her head and
arms on her knees. He stroked her hair; such a banal caress—it did
for dogs and cats, as well. She jerked up her head—in repudiation or
response, he didn't wait to understand—he put his face down to that
small cup of bone at the base of her full neck and was at once
launched, like the wooden cockleshell upon the lake, on the tide of
another being, the rise and fall of her breathing, the even, hollow
knock of her heart, the strange little sound of her swallowing.

She was smiling at him, slightly sadly.

"How long can you stay?"

"As long as we want."

He began to kiss her, for last time as well as this time, and he pressed his palm protectively on her belly and the round hardness of her pelvis in the tight, worn old jeans that didn't become her. It was all understood, between them. He undressed her and took her to his bed in that bare, male room which he had never shared with a woman; at once a schoolboy's room and a lonely old man's room, the room left behind him and the room somewhere ahead of him in his life. But the narrow bed was full again, he was full again, and it was all there, the body that had run shaking into the water, the big legs shuddering, the breasts swaying. This time he saw every part of it, watched the nipples turn to dark marbles rolling in his fingers, found the thin, shining skin with a vein like an underground stream running beneath it, where the springy soft hair ended and the rise of the thigh began, had revealed to him the aureole of mauve-brown skin where the cheeks of the backside divided at the end of her spine. All this and more, before he hung above her on his knees and she said with her practical parenthesis, "It's all right" (knowing how to look after herself, trusted not to make any trouble) and she reached up under his body and took the whole business, the heavy bunch of sex, in her hands, expressing the strangeness, the marvel of otherness, between the two bodies, and then he entered all that he had looked on, and burst the bounds of his body, in hers.

She was a woman full of sexual pride. She said, "You had a lot of semen." His mouth and nose rested in her hair, smelling the dank, flat lake water. Beneath one instant and the next, he slept and woke again; his hand left her humid breasts and trailed, once, down the trough formed by the rise of her hip from her rib-cage, as the strings of a guitar are brushed over as it is laid aside.

They put out the light, now, and in the dark he began to talk. It was the old story; the unburdened body unburdens the mind. Hence the confidences betrayed, the secrets sprung, beans spilled, in beds. He was aware of this but talked to her just the same; about Shinza. "—I have this unreasonable idea that when I see him again—I will know."

"That's what I thought. About you and me. If—*if*—it should come to that—again—I thought, then I'll know."

"What?" he said, teasingly. His sex lifted its blunt head and gently butted her, a creature disturbed in its sleep.

"What we would do," she said.

He drove to the Bashi that week. At the European-style house in Chief Mpana's compound, the man in clean grey flannels and polished shoes was summoned by a child. He said that Shinza was sick. Bray said that he was sorry; could he go over and see him in his house, then?

"No, he's sick."

But surely, just to greet him? What was the illness?

He was asleep. He was asleep because he was sick.

"If I wait a while?" Bray said.

The man had eyes like the inside of a black mussel shell, opaque and with a membranous shine, as if they had been silvered over with mercury. Although his face was lean, the lids were plump and smooth. He said, "He's sick." It was the contemptuous obtuseness that had done so well for colonial times; the white man could be counted upon to turn away and leave you alone: dumb nigger.

"If he knew I was the one who was here, he would want to see me."

"He's sick."

Bray went back to the car and smoked one of his cigars. There was a big box for Shinza on the seat. He should have left them for him, anyway; he was on his way back to the house with the cigars in his hand when he had an impulse to skirt it and go to the big hut where Shinza and the girl and the baby lived. Only children were about in the yard. The door was open, and before he knocked softly he saw, with a wave of familiarity, the deal table stacked with papers, the trunk with the coffee set displayed, the family group of leaders askew on the wall—then Shinza's girl, Shinza's wife appeared, carrying the baby, no longer pinkish yellow; it had taken on colour as a pale new leaf does. She greeted him shyly, formally. He apologized; and how was Shinza feeling?

She said, "Oh? Oh he is all right," suddenly speaking in mission schoolgirl's English. "But I thought he was ill in bed?" She stood and looked at him for a moment, deeply, startled, caught in his presence as in a strong light. Then she went over and closed the door behind him. It was dim and secure in the room; the thatch creaked, an alarm clock ticked. Hardly able to see her, he said, "What's happened to Shinza?" His voice sounded very loud to him.

She leaned forward—"He's away again. Don't tell anybody."

"Over the border?"

She grew afraid at what she had done. "I think so."

He said, "Don't worry. I'll go quickly. If anybody sees me, I'll say you wouldn't let me see him. It's all right."

The baby's arms and legs, where he lay on her lap, waved like the tentacles of some vigorous underwater creature. She said, "Must I tell him you came?"

"If you don't think it will get you into trouble with him."

"I'll tell him."

The baby gave a little shriek of joy. He whispered, "Your son's a fine boy," and took the cigars back with him, in case she decided to forget that he had come.

The new chief of police had arrived; a man from the Central Province, but a Dendi, one of the Gala-speaking tribes. "Ex-middleweight," Aleke said, "Once had a go for the title about ten years ago, they tell me."

"Punch-drunk?"

"Oh no, no he's all right up there." Aleke laughed.

Rebecca told him, "The new police chief's been in to ask for you." "Really? What should he want me for?" The next time he was at the *boma*, she put her head around the door quickly—"He's here again." A few minutes later Aleke's voice mingled with another in the corridor, and Aleke brought in a man as tall as Bray himself, with the flat-nostrilled but curved nose that the mingling of the blood of Arab slavers with the local populations had left behind. Evidently the nose had not been broken although the whole face had a boxer's asymmetry. Aleke went off. "I'll tell the boy to bring you tea."

"I'm glad to know you are here in this district, Colonel, it's an honour."

"And you—are you pleased with your new posting?"

The exchange of genialities went on.

"Oh yes, well, you get accustomed to this moving about. We are still reorganizing, you know. The country is young, isn't it so? Well, I'm just getting organized—there are always little things, when you take over. But I don't think I'll have trouble. There will be no irregu-

larities from now on. From now on everything will be"—he spread
his fingers and jerked his hands apart—"straight—right—" And he
laughed, disposing of peccadilloes.

"I've heard of your reputation in the ring," Bray said. "I'm going to
have to ask you to come along and give us some tips at the centre.
We're going to have various recreation clubs there, as well."

"Oh, a pleasure, a pleasure, if I can fit it in—this job of mine is
really full time—you never know when you can count on being free
for a few hours, just to take it easy—" The affability of a man making
promises he knew he would not be asked to fulfil.

And the girl had said, *perhaps Mweta did it to please you*. There
would be "no irregularities, now"; also to please me? There wasn't
anything else the policeman could have come to see him for. Bray sat
in the worn chair at the desk that was not really his, and took off his
glasses to rub his eyes. His hands pushed the skin back from the sides
of his nose over the cheekbones, pressed up the slack of his neck,
lifted the eyebrows out of shape. Shinza was over the border; with
friends, there; again. The wife said that: again. Shinza goes back and
forth over the border, and perhaps they know about it—he saw the
pleasant, battered face of the policeman who replaced Lebaliso—
perhaps they know, and perhaps they don't. Mweta would be
wounded because no letter came. It would be so simple to take a
sheet of paper and write: you were right about Shinza not being at
home, he goes and comes across the border, his wife says. You may
have some ideas about who it is he sees over there.

He was very short-sighted and taking off his glasses had the effect
of drawing the world in towards him as a snail does its horns. The
greenery outside the window was blurred. The titles of the reference
books on the dusty shelf—trade directories, an ancient Webster's—
were illegible to him. He sat in this visually contracted world, obstinately, doing nothing. But his mind could not be held back; it was
after Shinza, ferreting down this dead end and that, following and
discarding scraps of fact and supposition.

He had told Rebecca he hadn't been able to see Shinza because
Shinza was ill; everyone else was vague about his purposes and des-
tinations, anyway. She spent a lot of time at the house, now. At first
she came only at night, disappearing from the Tlumes' after they had
gone to bed, coming across the scrub with her little pencil-torch, and

being escorted home by the hand through the dark trees at two or
three in the morning. The nights were so blackly brilliant then, the
stars all blazing low together like a meteor tail, and the cicadas and
tree-frogs silenced by the chilled air; they could hear each other
breathing as they quickly covered the short distance. When he came
back the fire was fragrant ash, the room warm; each evening con-
sumed itself, and left no aftermath. Then she began to come to eat
with him and would stay the night, leaving only just before Kalimo
unlocked the house in the early morning, and before "the kids burst
in" to her room up the road. She told him that as it grew light she
and Edna Tlume would sit and drink coffee together in the kitchen
—Edna got up very early to do her housework before going on duty
at the hospital.

"What do the Tlumes think?"

"Oh they are very discreet. I told you. They don't think anything."

In spite of himself, he remembered the ease with which they talked
of her, from hand to hand, down in the capital.

"D'you know what Edna said? 'After all, where is your husband? A
girl must have a man.' It was so African."

She was standing at his table, where he sat with his papers. He
drew her in and pressed his face to her belly through the stuff of her
skirt, then pushed up her sweater and took out her breasts, releasing
the warm breath of her body that was always enclosed by them. She
had a way of standing quite still, with patient pleasure, while she
was caressed. He found it greatly exciting. He had not thought her
body beautiful at first but as it became familiar it became imbued,
transparent, with sensation—it was the shape, texture and colour itself of what was aroused in him.

She moved unremarkably into the empty house with ordinary
preoccupations of her own; cobbled at children's crumpled clothes,
sitting on the rug before the fire, wrote letters in her large, sign-writ-
er's hand, did things to her hair, shut up on Sunday afternoons in his
bathroom. She brought over her sewing machine and began to re-
make the curtains. "When your wife comes she'll have a fit, seeing
these awful things."

Olivia had written saying that she really promised to come, now,
by November—it was the shy, culpable letter of a spoilt little girl
who knows she's been exploiting the will to have things her own way.

November was a long way off, to Bray. All time concepts seemed to be stretched; or rather, unrealizable. Next week and November were both equally out of mind. He did not know where he would be, any time other than the present. He did not know what he meant by that: *where he would be.* There was a growing gap between his feelings and his actions, and in that gap—which was not a void, but somehow a new state of being, unexpected, never entered, unsuspected—the meaning lay. He sat in the same room with the girl and wrote to Olivia, saying with affectionate reproach, November was about time, but it was a pity she was missing the winter, which she might have forgotten was so lovely, in Gala. There was nothing in the letter that touched upon him. All the easy intimacy it expressed was extraneous; the thin sheets lay like a shed snakeskin retaining perfectly the shape of a substance that was not there. He folded the letter and put it in the envelope.

Rebecca was doing some typing for him; that was inevitable. She looked up, mouthing a word; then focused, giving a quick faint smile. He said to her, "Edward Shinza was away when I drove to the Bashi."

She had often a slight air of apprehension when he began to talk to her, as if she were afraid she might misunderstand—even in bed in the dark he would sense it.

"He was over the border. It's not too difficult to come and go across the north-west border there, in the Bashi. Miles of nothing, the Flats run out into half-desert, there's only the one border post on the Tanga River. That little wife of his more or less told me he's been before.—Don't look so worried!" Her face had gone broad, smoothed tight of expression.

"I'm wondering if it isn't Somshetsi he goes to see. You remember about those two? —Mweta expelled them a couple of months ago because old President Bete accused him of allowing them to set up a guerrilla base on our side of the Western border."

"And if he's going to see them . . . ?"

He drew a considering breath; his waist was as slim as it was when he was twenty-five but like many muscular men of his height, he had developed a diaphragm-belly—it could be drawn up into his expanded chest, but there was no ignoring the fact that it pouted out over his belt when he forgot about it. He shifted the belt. "There's a piece in one of the English papers. Apparently Somshetsi and Nyanza

have split. Somshetsi's the man, now. He denounced Nyanza for wasting funds and not taking advantage of opportunities for furthering
plans of liberation and so on. Whatever's behind that, if Somshetsi
could see any chance of a change here, a change that would allow his
group to come back and base itself here, why shouldn't he be very interested? Where they are now, they're the width of a whole country
away from their own. No possibility of any attempt to infiltrate.
Where they are, there's no common border with their country. Shinza
could be their chance."

All her comments were half-questions. "If he really means to make
trouble here."

"What I'm thinking is that if Shinza had retired to raise another
family he wouldn't be slipping over the border to Somshetsi."

"What could he get out of it?"

"I don't know." His mouth was stopped at the point of hearing himself say aloud, Shinza might get support, through Somshetsi, from
other sources that would like to see Mweta out; might get arms,
might form some sort of alliance with Somshetsi—Shinza! A flash of
absurdity. Shinza and Mweta belonged in the context of the fiery ver-
bal wrangles at Lancaster House, with the conventional sacrifices and
sufferings of an independence struggle with a power that, in contrast
to the settlers who believed it existed to represent their interests, was
simply choosing the time to let go. Shinza was better suited to the
role of President to Mweta's Prime Minister, than to intrigue in the
bush.

There was a small knock, low down, on the screen door of the veranda. Rebecca called out, "Yes, Suzi?" The children never ran in
without knocking carefully; he wondered whether she had trained
them, or whether they had some sort of instinctive delicacy or even
fear of finding out what the grown-ups assumed they were not supposed to know. The little girl's voice was muffled.

"Come inside and tell me. I don't know what you're talking about."

The child banged through the door and rushed to her mother with
some complaint about the boys.

"Don't take any notice. They're just silly."

"I'm goin'a tell them they just silly."

Rebecca smiled in culpable alarm to him. "Oh no, don't tell *them*.
It's a secret, just for you and me."

The child's indignation calmed as he called her over and gave her a cigar-box of mahogany-tree beans he had collected for her from the tree outside Sampson Malemba's house. "Someone must make holes so's I can make a necklace."

He was very polite and courteous with children; the perfect uncle, again. "I haven't got the right tool to drill holes, Suzi, but I'll get them done for you down at the Gandhi School, if you can give me a little time."

The little girl said confidently, "My daddy will do it for me when he comes." The children seemed to have no sense of time; they spoke of their father as if he were part of their daily life.

When the child had gone she sat with her hands between her spread thighs, staring at the typewriter. She turned and said, "You'll be going down again now." She meant to the capital; to Mweta.

"That I will not."

"No?"

"No."

She had not followed properly, lagged somewhere: she looked stoically forlorn. He noticed only that, not knowing any particular cause, and came over to touch her absently, gently; there was so much in each other's lives into which they did not, would never inquire—never mind, he could offer the annealment of the moment. He stroked a forefinger across her eyebrows, drawing them there above the strong lashes always tangled together a little where upper and lower met at the outer corners of those eyes, the colour of tea, today. None of her children had her eyes.

"It would be fatal," he said.

He walked away from her. He felt, almost accusingly, you would have to have known me all my life to understand. But he went on talking, as if he were talking to Olivia, *who would feel exactly as he did;* except that he didn't talk to Olivia any more, even in letters. While he spoke he was aware of an odd, growing sense of being alone, like coldness creeping up from the feet and hands. And while his matter-of-fact, steady voice was in his ears he thought suddenly—an urgent irrelevance, striking through his consciousness—of death: death was like that, the life retreating from the extremities as a piece of paper burns inwards towards the centre, leaving a cold ring of grey.

"I understood perfectly what I was doing . . . when Shinza and Mweta started PIP it was something I believed in. The apparent con-

tradiction between my position as a colonial civil servant and this belief wasn't really a contradiction at all, because to me it was the contradiction inherent in the colonial system—the contradiction that was
the live thing in it, dialectically speaking, its transcendent element,
that would split it open by opposing it, and let the future out—the
future of colonialism *was* its own overthrow and the emergence of Africans into their own responsibility. I simply anticipated the end of
my job. I . . . sort of spilled my energies over into what was needed
after it, since—leaving aside how good or bad it had been—it was already an institution outgrown. Stagnant. *Boma* messengers, tax-collecting tours—we were a lot of ants milling around *rigor mortis* with
the Union Jack flying over it. . . . But now I think I ought to leave
them alone."

She was sitting very straight, as if what he said drew her up, held
her. "Why is it so different? You must know what you think would be
the best, the best government, the best—"

"For them—that's it. Why should I be sure I know? Why should I
be sure at all? It was different before. That was my situation, I was in
it, *because* I was part of the thing they were opposing, *because* I
could elect to change my relation to it and oppose it myself—you
see? Now I should be stepping in between them—even if it were so
much as the weight of a feather, influencing what happens, one way
or the other—it would still be on the principle of assuming a right to
decide *for them.*"

She was indignant on his behalf. "Mweta wants you to persuade
Shinza! But if they ask you!"

"That doesn't change my position, if Mweta wants to make use of
the temptation held out to me, if it suits him to—"

After a moment, she said, "What about people who go and fight in
other people's wars. Just because they believe one side's right. What
about something like the Spanish Civil War."

He smiled, rubbed his nose, lifted his head as if for air. "The distance between the International Brigade and the mercenaries in the
Congo, Biafra . . . !"

She began to type again, slowly. The taps were hesitant footsteps
across the space that separated them.

"The trouble is, I mean—you are so—you *are* in it. You don't care
about anything else, do you?"

"Oh, everybody 'loves' Africa."

"You live in your beautiful house stuck away in England as if your life's over. I mean, nothing awful ever happens, you read it all in the papers, you drive away from it all in your nice car, like some old—"

"Retired colonel."

There were almost tears in her eyes, she had not meant to say that; affection came over him as desire.

"This is the place where everything's happened to you. Always."

"There was the episode of the war."

"You never talk about it," she said.

"This's the continent where everything's happened to you," he said.

"Oh well, I was born here. No choice."

"Dear old colonel, dreaming of the days when he was busy foment-ing a revolution behind the *boma*."

"You're here. You love that man, that's the trouble," she said with a kind of comic gloom.

"Which man?" he said, making a show of not taking her seriously by appearing to take her very seriously.

"Well, both of them, for all I know. But Mweta, I can see it. And so all that stuff about interfering and so on is counted out. You are tied to someone, it goes on working itself out, like a marriage, no matter what happens there are always things you still count on yourself to do, because after all, there it is—what *you*'d call your situation. Stuck with it. What can you do? You'll forget what people say, what it looks like, what you think of yourself. You simply do what you have to do to go on living. I don't see how it can be helped."

He held in his mind at the same time scepticism for her "uplifting" notion of that higher, asexual love (a hangover from some Anglican priest giving the sermon at the Kenyan girls' school?) along with a consciousness of being flattered—moved?—at her idea of him as ca-pable of something she saw as unusual and definitive; and the presence of Mweta, Mweta getting up behind his desk.

"You'd be off like a shot to tell Mweta that Shinza does cross the border, and that what he probably does there is make contact with Somshetsi."

She scarcely waited for him to finish. Her head cocked, her full, pale, creased lips drawn back, the line pressed together between her eyebrows—"Yes, yes of course I would. It's natural!"

"I don't much believe in that sort of love," he said, as if he were talking to her small daughter.

"Oh well, that's English. It must come out somewhere—this idea you mustn't show your feelings."

"My dear little Rebecca, the English have become just about the most uninhibited people in the world. You haven't been to England for a long time; love is professed and demonstrated everywhere, all the kinds of love, all over the place. It's quite all right to talk about it."

"I've never been. —But just the same, you don't come from that generation, Bray—ah yes, the old taboos still stick with you—" They lost what they had been talking about, in teasing and laughter.

After they had eaten, she was crouched at the fire and suddenly read aloud from her book: " 'People have to love each other without knowing much about it.' "

He was searching through a file and looked up, inattentive but indulgent.

She was leaning back on her elbow, watching him. "So you see."

Then he understood that she was referring to himself—and Mweta.

They (he and she) had never used the word, the old phrase, between themselves, not even as an incantation, the abracadabra of love-making. "What's the book?"

She smiled. "You remember the day you went to the fish-freezing plant? I took it before we left." She held out the exhibit; it was Camus, *The Plague*—one of the paperbacks that Vivien had given him when he came to live in Gala.

Already a past in common.

What am I doing with this poor girl? To whom will she be handed on? And why do I take part in the relay?

He was teaching her the language—Gala. His method was a kind of game—to get her to start a sentence, a narrative, and if she didn't know the right word for what she wanted to say, to substitute another. She would start off, "I was walking down the road—I went on until I passed a little house covered with . . . with . . ." "Come on." "With . . . porridge . . ." They laughed and argued; if the sentences were not simply ridiculous, they might turn into bizarre comments on the local people, sometimes on themselves.

He fished for a cigarillo in his breast pocket and went to sit in the

I

morris chair with the lumpy cushion, near her. She hitched herself over and leaned her back against his legs. He said in Gala, do you have to go home tonight? She answered quite correctly, looking pleased with herself as the words came, no, tonight I am going to—could not find the word "stay"—sleep at the house of my friend. And tomorrow? And yesterday? He tested her tenses and the terms of kinship he had been teaching her over the past few days. Yesterday I stayed at the house of my cousin, tomorrow I am going to my (mother's brother) uncle, the day after that I am going to my brother-in-law's, and on Friday I am going to my grandmother's. "Very good!" he said in English, and switched back to Gala—"And after that will you come back to your friend?" She was an apt pupil; she remembered the one term she had not used: in Gala, there was no general word for "home," children had to use the word for parents' house, men referred to "the house of my wife," and women referred to "the house of my husband." "Wait a minute . . ." She went over the sentence in her mind—"Then I will go to the house of my husband."

She had it right, paused a moment, smiling in triumph—and suddenly, as he was smiling back at her, an extraordinary expression of amazement took her face, a vein down her forehead actually became visibly distended as he looked at her. This time the game had produced something unsaid, with the uncanny haphazardness of a message spelled out by a glass moving round the alphabet under light fingers.

She tried to pass it off by saying, ungrammatically, in the *non sequitur* tradition of the game, my husband is away from home in the fields.

Then she said, in English, "I had a letter from Gordon. He might come to see the children."

"So he's coming."

"I only heard a few days ago. You never know with him, I'll believe it when he arrives. That's why I haven't said anything. But then this afternoon Suzi said that to you about the beans—"

"When?" he said.

Now that she had confessed she was unburdened, at ease, almost happy. "This next week. If he does."

But he knew she knew that the man was coming—the day, the date. He said, "What will you do?"

She said, "He'll probably stay at the Fisheagle Inn. Edna really hasn't a bed for him."

She would have arranged everything; after all, she sewed curtains against the arrival of Olivia.

She spent the night at "her friend's." She lay in the bath, her body magnified by the lens of water, and, while he gazed at her, said dreamily, "I don't suppose Olivia will ever know about me."

"I suppose not."

"You wouldn't tell her?"

"Probably not."

"I don't know—I would have thought you are the kind of couple who tell everything."

We were, we were. "You're anxious about Gordon?" Still dressed, he sat on the edge of the bath; her brown nipples stuck out of the water, hardened by the cool air, the weight of her breasts when she had suckled children had stretched the skin in a wavering watermark. It was a young (she was only twenty-nine, he knew by now), damaged body, full of knowledge. "Oh Lord no."

"Somebody might be kind enough to tell him. I suppose everyone knows. The whole village." He had never thought about it before; it might be a scandal, for all he knew, among what was left of the white locals. If no one had seen the pencil-torch and the two figures crossing the piece of bush in the early hours of the morning, then it was unlikely that Kalimo had not gossiped to other servants.

"I don't think so." She was thinking of the loyal Tlumes, the Alekes; the white people she really knew only as the parents of children who were at school with hers. "He lives in a world of his own. Just every now and then he remembers our existence. You'll like Gordon, you'll see. He's a very likeable person. Everyone does."

She might have been talking of an old friend, rather a character. He said, "I'll believe in him when I see him."

"Oh I know." On an impulse she got out of the bath and streaming wet, with wet fingers, undid his shirt and pants and pressed herself against him, a contact at once nervously unpleasant and yet delightful.

Early in the morning he woke with a fierce contraction of dismay, it seemed because Kalimo was at the door and she was still there— they must have overslept. His clenched heart swept this knowledge into some other anguish, left from the day before. Kalimo opened the door but did not bring in coffee. In fact, it was much earlier than coffee-time, and he had come to tell Bray that there was someone to see him. Bray half-understood, and forgot the girl, calling out, "Kalimo, what on earth is it all about—say what you mean, come here—" And Kalimo opened the door and stood facing the bed, after one quick glance not seeming to see, either, the woman stirring. "*Mukwayi*, he say he the brother of your friend, there—there—"

Outside the kitchen door, under the skinny paw-paws in the strangely artificial light of dawn, a young man stood hunched against the chill.

Shinza wanted to see him. "At Major Boxer's place! He's there now?"

"Yes. Or you can tell me what day you are going to come. He will come there."

He watched the man off, one of those figures in shirt and trousers who are met with on all the roads of the continent, miles from anywhere ahead, miles from anywhere behind, silent and covering ground. The red sun came up without warmth behind the paw-paw trees, as between the fingers of an outstretched hand. It struck him full in the eyes and he turned away. He walked round the front of the house and stood under the fig. As many arms as Shiva, and dead-still, always stiller than any other tree, even in the calm and silent morning, because its foliage was so sparse, in old age, that air currents did not show. It was surrounded by its own droppings; fruit that had dried without ripening and fallen, dead leaves, grubs and cocoons. She came out of the house dressed, looked once behind her and then came over to him.

"I may go off, today or tomorrow, for a day. No, not to the capital. *He* wants to talk to me—from the Bashi."

As she went across the rough grass he was struck by the subdued look of her, and called softly, "Rebecca!" She paused. "All right?" — Of course, Kalimo had walked in on them; he must know anyway, but all the same . . . She nodded her head vehemently, the way her children sometimes did. It was only when he was on the road that the thought crossed his mind that he had not noticed whether Kalimo showed any particular attitude in his manner when he served breakfast. Kalimo's proprietorial dependency had belonged to Olivia and himself as the couple, the family; yet he had not, even by the quality of a silence, asserted Olivia's presence-in-absence. Perhaps in some subconscious way even Kalimo found Bray's presence different, in relation to himself, from what it had been before—he remained a servant, but although nothing was changed materially for him the emotional dependency between ruler and ruled was gone. With the dependency went the proprietary rights, also the concern. Or maybe Kalimo was just older, and seeing Olivia as part of a past.

Because of the iron-ore mine, the Bashi road as far as Boxer's was kept in fair repair. There were the usual work gangs making good in the dry season the pot holes and washaways of summer, and every now and then he was waved onto a detour by a barefoot labourer prancing with a red rag on a stick, but he still reached the farm by two in the afternoon. He was slightly dazed from having driven so long without a stop. Boxer's polished leggings shone in the sun. "I don't know what the old devil wants." He absolved himself at once of any association with Shinza or anybody else. "But it's all right with me, if you've got doings with him. Take your time. He came to see me once to borrow money!" It was one of the few things that could make Boxer laugh: the idea that he might have any money lying around to lend. He was also making use of the dry season—to put up some new farm building. Bray had to look at a consignment of pre-cast concrete blocks that couldn't be laid properly because they were all out of true. "Bloody things taken from the moulds before they're dry!" The blocks came from the new factory at Gala; Bray had to promise to complain.

Boxer went on with the job of sorting out the usable blocks, calling, "Where's that boy? I don't know where milord is himself, though I know he's arrived because I saw his father-in-law's car down over at my dam—but he's left someone here to look out for you." His face reflected emotions that had nothing to do with what he was saying—annoyance at each fresh evidence of misshapen cement, distrust of the judgement of the two black cattlemen who were working under his eye. The scout had disappeared. "Oh well, must've gone to fetch him. You can go along into the house. I don't mind. Pour yourself a drink or ask in the kitchen for some tea."

One of the Afghans followed Bray back to the house. The signs of division of the rooms between the various functions of the household

during a previous occupancy—the Boxers as a family—were becoming completely overlaid by the single-mindedness of an existence so
perfectly contained by the preoccupation of cattle breeding that it
really had no diversity of functions to be reflected. The living-room,
going the way of the bathroom that Bray remembered from last time,
was slowly losing the character of its old designation as phials of vac-
cine, pamphlets on feeds, dried specimens of pasture grasses had settled among the tarnished silver and the Staffordshire dogs, and three
pairs of boots, still encrusted with summer mud, had found an obviously permanent home on a small red-gold Shiraz next to the sofa.
It wasn't that nothing was put away in the right place, but there was
no longer any place in the house that was not appropriate for anything. Bray opened the liquor cupboard and took a can of beer from
among bottles of bloat medicine. He heard a car and took out a second can. The beautiful male dog that looked so humanly feminine—a
kind of inversion of anthropomorphism—got up gracefully within its
fringes of fur and barked beside Bray at the door as it saw a black
man get out of the car. Shinza wore a gay shirt flapping over his trousers, sandals that he had to grip with his toes as he walked. There
was an almost West African swagger about him. He ignored the noise
of the dog and came up the steps to the veranda and the open living-
room with the air of self-conscious disingenuousness that was instantly familiar—film actors, sports champions, they came at the TV
camera lazily, like that, fresh from some triumph or other. The car
was a big old American one, all snub surfaces gleaming under dust,
lying heavily on its worn springs.

"That's a very grand affair."

Shinza was grinning, coming in to Bray's greeting. "Well, in those
days you were generous to your Tribal Authority, you know. Chief
Mpana was one of your big men."

"So you married Chief Mpana's daughter?"

"You know her, you've met her!" Shinza put his hand on the head
of the dog, murmuring something admiring to it, and it growled and
wagged its feather-boa tail.

"Yes indeed I have, she's a charming girl. You're lucky."

"The car's not in all *that* good condition." Shinza laughed, sat himself down and glanced with a guest's mild interest round Boxer's
room, seeing it as one of those white men's lairs that even he, who
had lived in Europe and America, sometimes found inexplicable.

"How is she? And the son?"

"It was nice of you to come and see her."

"Unfortunately you'd gone out to get cigarettes."

Shinza's flash—a gap-grin of admittance, mutual acceptance—at once converted the casual atmosphere to another voltage. He waited while Bray poured the beer, but with an air of having got down to the ground between them. "That hasn't been worrying me." Bray made a face questioning the wisdom of such trust. "I know I had nothing to worry about. But I wanted to have a talk with you—you know, I want to tell you a few things, I want to show you—" He closed his teeth under open lips, his hands round the beer mug made, half-comically, a gesture of directing an invisible head to face something. "That's all. A lot of things we decided a long time ago. Not only in London. Before that, right at the beginning, eh, here at home. What's happening to all that, eh? What's happening to it, James?"

His voice mastered the questions rhetorically. The half-insulting, preoccupied reserve that had discounted Bray's presence when they talked in the house in the Bashi might never have existed. Now an old intimacy was taken for granted just as easily as it had been taken for dead. Shinza could move among examples, anecdotes, and private thoughts without bothering about sequence, because the links were there, in Bray's mind as in his own. He accused, demanded, derided —speaking for them both. "Kayira sits in the House of Chiefs—that old criminal who raped a child a few years ago and told the judge it was his right as a chief. Those ignorant old men were going to be stripped of their 'rights,' of all their forms of parasitism, and made to stand on merit—but have you heard a mention of abolishing the House of Chiefs? No, you've only heard that the House is going to be enlarged so that those fat men in blue suits can spread themselves comfortably. —Painted, you know. Made nice. Mweta still talks about the need to forget tribal differences—that's how it's put now, you don't say abolish tribalism because you might make the fat old men shake—but all the time he's improving the House of Chiefs. Because they're going to sit there—as long as he's where he is. Mweta likes to make speeches about the time when we each had only one pair of pants—the trouble is, he doesn't remember that we also knew, then, what we wanted. We were going to make this country over from top to bottom. Right? Turn the whole thing over, just like you kick an anthill, and make new lives for all those people running about not understanding where they were going. Right, James? But what are the signs? Reginald Harvey tells him that unless the gold price rises the company can't think of opening marginal-production mines, and he takes it without a word. Well, not without a word, Harvey's got plenty of words, Harvey's only got to mention that the company can get a far bigger return by expansion in South Africa, and *he* falls over backwards to say how he appreciates what a favour the company's doing by earning dividends here at all. But was that the idea! —Oh yes, I know, within two years all work up to the level of mine captain will be Africanized. So what? What sort of window-dressing is that if new jobs are not being created at the same time. We move up into the seats of the expatriate whites, and go on earning dividends for them when they go back 'home' to retire? Was that the idea? Christ, James, what were we talking about all those years, if it was for this? He handles the English and Americans like glass— because we need foreign capital. But if you keep going to the old places for it you keep on getting it on the same old terms. A child should be able to see that. And the profits are geared to *their* economies, not ours. The great new sugar scheme we've heard so much about—what's it amount to? They'll get sugar at a preferential price, while we could be growing rice instead and getting a better price in the open market. We're exporting our iron ore at their price and buying back their steel at their price. We're still selling our cotton and buying their cloth—the Czechs offered to send us the technical aid for a textile mill, but the tied loan he got from the Japanese for the cotton gin stipulates they get the whole crop. So we're back where we were. Wearing the cloth they make and sell back to us. We could have had the same as Nyerere's got—a textile mill as well as our cotton gin, a textile mill set up by the Chinese, all the know-how we want, and the whole thing financed interest-free. What's he afraid of? He'll only play the game with the devil he knows, eh? Apart from one or two big schemes that aren't off the paper yet, and a couple of bad new contracts for the expansion of existing industry, like the deal with the fishing concessionaires, a useless thing if ever there was one, a mess—apart from that, what've we got?—The Coca-Cola bottling plant and a factory for putting transistors from Germany into plastic cases, because our labour's cheaper than Europe's, and they get a bigger profit when we buy the radios? Are we only educating our people to need the things *they* sell? Good God, are we to pass from exporting raw materials only to bottling, assembling—never making?"

"It's a slow start, yes."

"A start! Where's it headed for?" Shinza waited as if for the echo to die away. "It's not the start we planned at all. He's forgotten! Forgotten what this country meant to do. What we promised. Bush politicians' big promises. Now let them bottle cold drinks while they wear out their freedom shirts." He gave a bellow of a laugh. "Couldn't you sit down and cry?" he said. "James, couldn't you howl like a bloody dog?"

"Shinza, I suppose I'm naturally more detached about it than you —" And then in the raw atmosphere Shinza had stripped down between them, he said aloud what he was thinking— "It's a terrible clarity you have . . . you know . . . ? But perhaps it's easy . . . perhaps you expect too much too quickly, because you're not in the dust that's raised, you haven't had to do any of it—I see that in myself now that I'm stuck with this education project. Mweta's had only a few months."

"—Yes, and the twenty per cent of the budget that was going to go into education, how does it look so far? You're penny-pinching to get anything done, eh? Meantime another thirty thousand kids are starting to draw their sums in the dirt in our so-called schools. And soon another fifteen thousand youths will leave half-baked and wander off to the towns."

"It won't be more than twelve per cent of the budget, certainly."

"A few months! James, we know that a few months is a long time for us. PIP has become a typical conservative party—hanging on wherever he can to ties with the old colonial power, Western-orientated, particularist. It's a text-book example. *His* democracy turns out to be the kind that guards the rights of the old corporate interests more than anyone else's—the chiefs, religious organizations, precolonial nations. Foreign interests. All that lot. In seven months you show which way you're going. It's right from the start or it'll be never. Look around you. This continent, this time. You don't get years and years, you don't get second chances."

It was said coldly, an accomplished fact; and yet also a strange mixture of threat and concern. At the same time as his argument carried Bray with him, the presence of Bray brought out in him an old responsibility for Mweta.

"I don't agree he's done as badly as you think. But the general direction—"

Shinza was watching him, fishing a cigarette out of the sagging breast pocket of the holiday shirt made of Japanese cotton, and the recognition of the admittance he had drawn from Bray—now appearing—grew beneath the control of his face as Bray was speaking.

"—The way he's going, I'm inclined to agree about that." Bray made a gesture of impatient self-dismissal. "I'm sure it's not the way it should be. If you and he meant everything—then. I must judge by what was visualized then. The sort of state you had in mind, that I believed you to have in mind when I"—his voice disowned him, as it always did, fastidiously, when it came to defining his part in a struggle he did not claim his own—"decided to go along with you. It's true—what you were absolutely clear about was that coming to power wasn't going to be a matter of multiplying the emancipated, while the rest of the people remained a class of affranchised slaves—" He referred with a smile to the phrases from Fanon. "It's never been put better."

"—That's been forgotten. And something else we got from Fanon: 'The people must be taught to cry "Stop thief!"' "

"I don't remember . . . ?"

"Look it up," said Shinza. "Look it up."

"It's a long time since I read him. —I wonder now if you were clear enough in your minds about how to go about getting what we were so sure you wanted. The less simple objectives remained very much in a sort of private debate between you and Mweta—"

"—And you," Shinza said.

"—A handful of others, not even a handful. It couldn't be helped. Everything was hell-bent on the business of organizing PIP purely and simply as a force that would get independence. How many people could be expected to see beyond that. Well it's an old story, not worth discussion—one of the results of the policy we"—he was suddenly speaking of himself as part of the colonial administration—"had of discouraging political parties until such time as they burst forth as mass movements—and then in due course they could be counted upon to become potentially violent and could be banned in the interests of law and order . . . . But the effect was to make parties like PIP miss out the vital stage of their function as political schools and ideological debating forums, a means of formulating the blind yearning to *have* into something that would hold good beyond the"—his hand spiralled through the air—"grand anticlimax of paper freedom. That really wasn't touched on—a practical means of taking hold not of the old life out of the white man's hands, but a new kind of life that hasn't yet been. It just wasn't touched on. Only among ourselves. And at the back of the minds of even the most intelligent and reasonable people there's a vague intoxication of loot associated with seeing the end of foreign rule. Loot of one kind or another . . . it doesn't have to be smashing shopwindows, you know. Even the imponderables can be loot. 'We'll shop around when the time comes.' "

"Maybe." Shinza made the concession of one who does not agree. "Maybe I should blame myself. I should have seen."

"What could you have done, with things as they were?"

"I should have seen what *he* was."

Bray gave a little snort of a laugh. "I always say the same thing. It always comes round to the same thing. It should have been both of you. It *was* the two of you. One didn't know what originated with which one—of course always granting the influence of your trade union experience. One couldn't foresee how *he* would develop after a split. Or how you would, for that matter."

"I've always known what we were going to do. Nothing's changed at all with me. I was just too damned lazy, I suppose . . . you've got to give yourself a kick in the backside sometime." He put his hands behind his head, smiling, making his words ambiguous by the easy gesture.

"You definitely don't consider starting a new party?"

Shinza was shaking his head before the words were out. "I've told you. PIP is this country—just as he says, PIP made it. Everything must come from PIP. He would like a purified party, of course, degutted like the bloody fishing concession. PIP is the party I started."

"It was meant as a leading question," Bray said.

"I don't hide from you. You see it all exactly as I do, you haven't changed either, it's just you've got the same polite nice way of speaking you always had, really nice, covering it up . . . James! But if you

had to choose between Mweta and what happens to this country—
Good God!"

"He said more or less the same to me." It was dryly, gently set
aside; he smiled.

"With one essential difference, of course, whatever *he* decides for
this country must be right." Shinza stretched his toes like fingers and
clenched the leather button that held each sandal.

"No, no—just the implication that I would do what is usually
known as 'anything'—in other words, something that went against my
grain—because it might help." Still the old maid, setting the mats
straight, he thought.

"Help? What?" said Shinza. "To hold the country together almost
exactly as it was before? To keep the sort of status quo the Europeans
call stability—the stability of overseas investment, the stability of
being so poor your feast comes once a year when the caterpillars
hatch on the mopane? But we want an instability, James, we want an
instability in the poverty and backwardness of this country, we want
the people at the top to be a bit poorer for a few years now, so that
the real, traditional, rock-bottom poverty, the good old kind that
'never changes' in Africa, can be broken up out of its famous stability
at last, at long, long last, dragged up from the shit—"

How demandingly, alive, they both reached out—he and Mweta.
Bray said, "I must tell you, he may have some idea about your going
over the border. He mentioned something—before I came to see you
again. I didn't take much notice at the time."

"Borders! Doesn't mean anything in the Bashi," Shinza said. "People are wandering over after their goats, every day. You forget we're
the same people on both sides."

"If I can imagine what you're doing there, it's reasonable that he
may."

Shinza was drawing and swallowing smoke with absent appetite.
Once a cigarette was lit it remained in the side of his mouth until it
burned down to his lips.

Bray said, "What's it all about—Somshetsi and Nyanza?"

"The usual thing, in exile." The glance held, direct, as if to prevent
Bray's mind from venturing off this chosen interpretation of the question. "They haven't been getting on too well . . . . Nyanza's always
been a pretty easy-going chap, sitting back and waiting for the fruit

to fall. When Mweta said go, he just went straight to Somshetsi"—he jerked his bearded chin—" 'pack up'; never occurred to him to make a bit of fuss, to let a few friends know . . . . I mean they could have played for time, there could have been denials, protests to the High Commissioner for refugees at U.N.—"

They grinned. "Considering the way they were scrupulously observing the conditions of hospitality," Bray said; and waved his own provision aside.

Shinza said matter-of-factly, "Well, that's about it. Somshetsi thinks Nyanza will just make himself comfortable wherever he gets pushed off to next. Somshetsi wants to get going. He doesn't see himself dying in bed with the grandchildren round. Of course there's help to be found if you show you're moving."

"Not much you can do if you're the width of a whole country away."

"No, that's true." Shinza agreed with detachment.

"I can see what you can offer—promise—Somshetsi, but I don't quite see what he has worth offering you."

There was the understanding between them of people who are both lying; Shinza's flexed bare yellow toes with their thick, uncut nails; the silence, strangely easy. With tremendous effort to break free: "Unless you're thinking of going in for a guerrilla war."

"And then?"

It was being drawn out of him; Shinza wouldn't say it for himself. "I suppose—you could give him a leg up over the border, he could bring the arms from outside, you could do things together. Just as the South African and the Rhodesian guerrillas do, through Zambia. Only more successfully, I should think. It would depend whether you're prepared to use violence."

Shinza's head nodded, hearing a lesson by rote. Then he said, "I like to know I have a chance to win."

Perhaps he referred to the hopelessness of starting a new party, perhaps—he gave a half-comic shudder—he implied that he couldn't win a guerrilla war if he were so unwise as to start one.

"You're going to turn up at the Party Congress?"

"Turn up? It sounds like a dance hall." He rose from the base of the spine, straight-backed. "I'm on the Executive. Still. I'm going to be there."

"Bravo!" —How easily I fall whichever way he aims.

"And you're going to be there?"

The answer came pat, in the same mood. "I'm a Party member. I suppose I still am? But of course I don't belong to any delegation I know of."

"Oh he'll see to that. You remind him." Shinza said in a satisfied way that made Bray uneasy, "Good God, I wanted to talk to you, you know, James? It's all right, all right. I knew it would be all right. You can't be fooled."

"Shinza, I just have a—well—mad hope. About the Congress. You may be able to do something about the—direction. That's the place."

"Well, come and see. Come and give us a hand." Shinza was not good at being hearty; he gave his smoker's wheezy laugh at himself. "Come and be frog-marched out with me, it'll be like the old days."

The dog had got up and stood swaying its plumes in the veranda doorway. Boxer appeared, making his approach exaggeratedly fore-warned by grunting as he mounted the steps, sighing and whew-ing; the dog was puzzled. Boxer spoke to the black man sitting in his living-room with the offhand, demonstrable ease of one whose forms of intimacy, if they exist, are thereby defined as something far removed from this. "You flourishing, Shinza? Of course. What's the grass been like this year? Of course, you're bored by cattle, I know. But your father-in-law—he must have a nice five or six hundred head, eh? One never can get at the figure. But those chaps down there have got size-able herds, all right. I wouldn't mind a share. Was there much red-water this year? It's been a bugger, here. I've lost fifteen or sixteen of my beasts."

Shinza didn't rise; challengingly casual, by white men's standards —but he made a real effort to talk to Boxer about the things that interested him. Shinza, unexpectedly, knew quite a lot about cattle; as he did about everything one doubted in him. His attitude towards Boxer reminded Bray of that of a grown man visiting one of his old housemasters; a combination of kindliness and slightly resentful pity, with the consciousness of having outdistanced the teacher beyond even his understanding. When Shinza had gone off in Mpana's old car, Boxer said innocently, "Now let's settle down and have a drink. I hope to Christ you didn't give him anything. He's much too grand to pay back."

"But I thought you'd refused him a loan."

"You're damn right I refused. Donkey's years ago. He wanted money to start the political business—their party—*you* know. But Mpana, that other old devil, he once asked a bull off me, for stud— no wonder his herd's so flourishing. Never saw a penny. I'll go down there one day and look over his heifers and say, look, old man, I recognize my daughters in your house—you know the sort of thing, he'd appreciate it."

He had to spend the evening with Boxer. A long-interred loneliness —born not so much of solitude as of single-mindedness—stirred to weak impulse in the man. Cloudy bottles of wine bought from the Lebanese importer on some rare visit to the capital were brought out and opened without comment (Boxer, like Shinza, had a certain delicacy) but in a sense of occasion. Boxer talked incessantly as usual, with lucid precision and even with style, of his animal husbandry, pasture ecology, and his extraordinary observation of the strange form of life manifested in ticks—a description of the sub-life of the silence and patience of parasitism. He was oddly changed without his hat; his forehead, half-way up where the hat rested day in and day out, was white and damp-looking, creased as a washerwoman's palm. Real nakedness belongs to different parts of the body in different people; here was where his nakedness was, in this exposed cranium, luminous as the wine went down and produced a sweat. Never mind the ticks—he himself appeared to Bray as some strange form of life. Bray listened with the bored fascination with which once, just before he left England, he had sat with Olivia through a space film, his own sense of life lying strongly elsewhere.

He was writing to Mweta when he looked up just as the yellow dress that he knew so well became visible, approaching through the scrub. She was hidden and appeared again, nearer; he stood up to wait. Just this way sometimes, in the early mornings or evenings, he kept dead still while a female buck that probably fed on the golf-course during the night moved silently, quite near. But his body had associations of its own with the yellow dress, robust but no less tender; there was a surge of pleasure that he would press against her in a moment, when they met. And then she came hurrying out onto the garden grass and there was a check—something different about her—as if she had sent someone else, smiling, in her place. As she reached him he saw that, of course, her hair was pulled up and tied back. He said, "Darling, I was hoping you'd notice the car was back, as soon as you got up—" and as he put his hand out behind her head he was suddenly checked again, and this time of her volition as she stopped dead a foot away from him, her palms raised for silence or to hold him off, her face bright, conspiratorial, pained and yet half-giggling. "They're just behind me—the children, Gordon. We're coming to invite you to drinks for him tonight. I've told him I've been doing typing for you in the evenings. It's all right."

His body died back first, before his mind. He said, "Why bring him here, Rebecca?"

She was gazing at him, passionately, flirtatious, giggling, ablaze. He had never seen her like that. "The children, you ass. They keep on talking about you. It's obvious we're running in and out your house all the time. It'd look funny if we didn't come now."

"My God, why didn't you say when he was coming. I could have stayed away for a few days." He withdrew into what she had called his "elderly" voice, meaning, he knew, in her generous and unresentful way, that it put the distance of social background, education and assurance, rather than age, between them.

"Oh don't be *idiotic*." She pleaded, tears like tears of laughter standing hot in her eyes. "It's perfectly all right. You don't *know* him. He'd *never* think anything. He's not like that. He's very attractive to women. It never occurs to him that I could ever look at anybody else. I've told you. He'll away again soon. It's quite *all right*."

She stood there, a schoolgirl about to stuff her hand into her mouth to stifle a give-away of hysterical guilt before authority. He was amazed at her as much as angry at himself for in some way appearing to himself as a fool. He was about to say, And what we think—my dear girl, doesn't it occur to you that I don't really want to meet him —but the children running like puppies before the man burst into chatter, almost upon them, and a voice that he thought of immediately as somehow Irish in its effortless persuasiveness was making an entry, talking, talking— "—That's a tree for a tree-house, Clivie, now! That's what you call a tree! You could build one big enough to put a camp bed in, there—" "And a stove, to cook—" The skinny little girl jumped up and down for attention. "I'll show you—I always climb it!" —The smaller boy scrambled ahead, ignoring his mother and Bray. "Don't you say good morning to James, don't you say good morning?" She caught him up and held him struggling— "Leave me! Leave me! Leave me!" She laughed, imprisoning him vengefully, while he kicked and blazed at her, his black eyes fierce with tears.

"Becky, for God's sake—why does it have to be mayhem and murder wherever we walk in."

She dropped the child, laughing at its huge rage and at the reproach. The little boy trying half-fearfully to kick at his mother's shins always had had the definitive cast of features that in a child shows a strongly inherited resemblance. Now Bray saw the face that had been there in the child's. The husband was surprising; but per-

haps he would have been so however he had materialized, simply because he hadn't existed for Bray at all. He was unusually good-looking in a very graceful and well-finished way, rather a small
man—but, again, that was perhaps only from Bray's height. Five foot
ten or so—tall enough to stand sufficiently for male pride above Rebecca. He wore young men's clothes elegantly, tight beige trousers
belted on the hips, a foulard tied in the open neck of his shirt. Rebecca in her yellow dress and rubber-thong sandals looked shabby
beside him. He wore a small bloodstone on one of the little fingers of
his strong, olive-coloured hands and his face was smoothly olive-coloured with the large, even-gazing shining black eyes of the little boy,
and the dull-red fresh mouth. On the man the face had a C-shaped
line of laughter just marking the end of the lips on either side, and
fine quizzical spokes at the outer corners of the eyes. His dark hair
was prematurely silvering, like an actor's streaked for distinction. He
was saying, "I suppose you're used to all this racket my crowd kick
up. I think Becky's let them run a bit wild, she's too soft. Yes—I'm
going to have to tan your bottoms for you—" He turned with a mock
growl on the children, who shrieked with laughter, the little one still
with tears undried. "—But that's a marvellous tree there you've got
for a tree-house, I don't think I'd be able to keep my hands off it,
even if I didn't have any children around, I'd have a little retreat of
my own up there, electric light, and pull the ladder up after me—"
And Bray the good-humoured friend was saying, "Oh I make do
with this old thing on the ground, as you see—" while Rebecca in the
same blazing, flirtatious, exaggerated way she had used with him,
attacked— "Gordon, for heaven's sake! Don't put the idea into their
heads! At least leave Bray in peace with his tree, you don't know how
he loves his tree—"
While they all went on talking in this friendly ease he noted the
slip—even she with all her apparent skill, born of long practice. For
a woman to use a man's surname like that couldn't be mistaken as
formality; it was a tell-tale inverted intimacy, sticking out, so to
speak, from under the hastily made bed. He felt some small satisfaction in catching her out. She said, "I'd better leave you two, much as
I like your company—Aleke needs his secretary. I'm about half an
hour late already." "Phone the fellow and tell him you're taking the
afternoon off," the handsome man instructed. "D'you want me to do

it?" "Oh no Gordon, I can't, he gave me yesterday and tomorrow's the weekend anyway. Everything'll be piled up for Monday." He shrugged. "Well get cracking then, if you got to go, go—" She put her head on one side: "Keys?" He tossed car keys to her; she missed, they both ducked for them. "No wonder my sons can't play cricket—" He gave her a pat on the backside. "Shoo! And no damn nonsense about overtime or anything. D'you hear? There are people coming at six. D'you hear me?"

She ran, turning her head back to them, nodding it like a puppet's. Her thighs jerked as they did the day she came out of the water, on the island.

The children were climbing the fig tree and pelting each other with its shrivelled fruit; they had never behaved like that before, either— subdued little creatures, running in with a sidelong glance and saving their fierce quarrels and boastful games for when they were living by some law of their own away from the awesome grown-ups. By contrast, Bray's daughters had been such self-assured children, perfectly composed in conversation with a visiting Colonial Secretary at nine or ten, politely offering an opinion to an African nationalist over lunch at fourteen. Like their mother, they could talk to anybody and kept their distance from everybody.

The husband stood about with the instant and meaningless friendliness of the wanderer. This way he was at home in the bars and hotels of Africa; a man who, since he never stays anywhere long, assumes the air of the familiar personality at once, wherever he is. This way he would stand about in conversation with the garage proprietor in a remote Congo village where (as he was relating to Bray) his car had broken down, just as he now did with the middle-aged Colonel for whom his wife did a bit of typing. He was "crazy enough" to have business interests in the Congo—"But I've had the fun and games. I've pulled out. There's still money to be made there, mind you. But the Belgians have moved back in such a big way and they push everybody else out . . . the Congolese wide boys would rather work with the devils they know than with devils like me. They would." (Shinza's old saw about Mweta coming up again in a new context.) "I know a chappie—Belgian chappie—who's back for the fourth time. First he had a natural gas concession up in the Kivu—the volcanic lakes, there's a fortune lying there for someone, someday, if you can

live that long. Then he was in industrial diamonds in the Kasai, they
were going to break away and he was all set to get a consortium to
finance their diamond industry when they kicked out Union Minière."
He gave his slow, relishing smile, sharp yet humorously worldly, the
teeth good. "Don't know what it was the third time round. Now he's
in the currency racket between Lubumbashi and the Zambian border.
He told me he feels 'useless' in Europe. Here he says people want
help to keep things going—they'll take it whatever way they can get
it, and they know you don't get it out of the goodness of someone's
heart. While the Russians and the Chinese and Americans are each
watching to see what the other one will give, you have to go on living."

"You think of us as devils?" Bray said.

Present company was waved away. "You know as well as I do.
White men don't hang around in Black Africa for their health or anybody else's. Wherever a vacuum comes up, there are the boys who
won't hesitate to fill it. Good God, you should just meet some of them
the way I do. —Okay that's enough—out of that tree, now. And clear
the mess you've made on that table—James'll never let you put up a
tree-house if you drop things on his papers—" He grinned at his own
audacity, always confident it would be well received, at once took
command again: "Wha'd'you think of it, putting Becky in that sort
of accommodation, though? If they need her they must damn well
find somewhere for her to live, eh? There must be a house in this
place. And if there isn't, they must find one. That's the way it is—you
want somebody's services, you have to be prepared to pay for them.
I told Aleke straight off, yesterday: you need her, you find her a
house."

"I think Edna Tlume's quite a help, in a way." It was impossible to
make any remark that did not have, to his own ears, an absurd innu-
endo.

"Oh that woman'd do anything for Becky. But the point is the
house is a slum. Two rooms and no bathroom of her own. Can't live
like that. I said look, if I had one week, I bet I'd find a house—your
government's prepared to pay for it?" The children stood around the
man proudly. "See!" Suzi thrust out her dry little hand with its blackened encrustations where Rebecca applied wart-remover to the middle finger. She was wearing a bracelet made of threaded mahogany
beans, shook it up her arm with a sudden feminine gesture.

The children had cleared away the fruit they had pelted onto the table. He blew brittle leaf webbed in dust and spider-spit from his letter. It had gone completely from his mind. The little troupe chattered off the way Rebecca always appeared and disappeared, through the thin-leafed trees. The letter came back. He asked Mweta not to forget to arrange for him to be invited to the Party Congress. He mentioned what progress was being made with the education centre. "It could turn out to be rather like the workingmen's clubs in Britain in the nineteenth century. Here in these country places where men are beginning—though of course they don't put a name to it—to have a new consciousness of themselves as something more than units of labour, they are ready to take anything that's going: may come in useful. Whether someone gives judo classes or explains the different ways of dealing with the law of supply and demand . . . I wanted to suggest to the local PIP branch that they might use the centre as a place for a more general political instruction than the sort of hip-hoorah stuff that comes out of party meetings. It would help combat unruliness, too. I would always rather go on the assumption that above people's heads is higher than the people who instruct them are likely to believe."

The style and reasoning of such letters was something he picked up with a pen. It functioned of itself. For a lifetime—lying suddenly in his mind, the word associated with advertisements for expensive Swiss watches: lifetime. The habits of a lifetime. He felt himself outside that secure concept built up coating by coating, he was exposed nakedly pale as a man who has been shut away too long from the sun. The girl presented herself face-to-face, fact-to-fact with him, a poster-apocalypse filling the sky of his mind. Thought could crawl all over and about her, over the steadfast smile and the open yellow eyes and in and out the ears and nostrils. He sat for a moment exactly as if he had swallowed an unfamiliar pill and waited for the sensation of the drug to unfold itself. Then the telephone rang in the house. It was Malemba in great excitement: the lathes from Sweden had arrived. He went to borrow a truck (the obliging Indian traders again), pick up Malemba, and fetch the machinery from the road-transport depot.

The gathering at the Tlumes' house was unlike the usual absent drift towards the Alekes' or the Tlumes' for an hour after work, when often one of Edna's relations or some subdued minor official, new to his Africanized job, sat without speaking, and children wandered in and out with their supper in their hands. There were even one or two faces that didn't belong; a telephone engineer Gordon Edwards had travelled with, and the blonde receptionist from the Fisheagle Inn. She was the one who had brought the thigh-high skirt to the village (there was a time-lag of a year or so between the beginning of a fashion in Europe and its penetration to the bush) but she sat in this mixed company with those famous thighs neatly pressed together as a pair of prim lips. The doctors Hugh and Sally Fraser from the mission hospital were there with a young Finn who had just walked down from West Africa—his rucksack leaned against the wall. He wore a shirt with the face of some African leader furred and faded by sweat and much washing, and was prematurely bald on top, like a youthful saint in a cheap religious picture. Sampson Malemba had changed into his best dark suit after the dirty business of loading and unloading machinery. Aleke was wearing a brown leather jerkin with fringes —Gordon's present; how did he know just what would sit splendidly on Aleke's powerful male breasts? But there was the impression that Gordon Edwards acquired things that remained in his possession like clues to the progress of his life if one could read them: he happened to be here at a certain time, and so picked up this, happened to be there, and so was around when that was available. And in the same fortuitous fashion, it fell out that these things suited this one perfectly or were exactly what that one would like.

Alekes, Tlumes, Frasers—all accepted Bray's presence with Gordon Edwards without a sign. It might have been agreed upon, it was such a cosy, matter-of-fact conspiracy of friends: he did not quite know whether he was chief protagonist or victim? Everyone was so gay. Sometimes he felt as if *he* were a deceived husband; Rebecca wore a new dress (another present?) and when he danced with her had the animated, lying look of a young girl. Who could believe, as she had implied, that that lithe and handsome little man didn't sleep with her? Physical jealousy suddenly weakened his arms so that he almost dropped them from her. Between chatter she expected him to lip-read —"I'll try and come early one morning." He murmured, "No, don't." She pulled a face, half-hurt. She said, "Let's go to the lake again. *You* suggest it. On Sunday." A family party. He felt himself smiling, the cuckold-lover: "All right, I'll be host." Gordon Edwards danced again

and again with the tall refined tart from the Fisheagle; he must be
the reason why she was present. Perhaps, then, he was staying at the
hotel after all? It was impossible to say to Rebecca, does he sleep in
this house? Idiot, idiot. He saw himself amusedly, cruelly, as he had
done so often since he had come back here, where all should have had
the reassuring familiarity of the twice-lived, the past. Aleke took over
the Fisheagle blonde; his large, confident black hands held her softly
as he did his children's pigeons, she kept her false eyelashes down on
her cheeks, she had moved from the shelter of the settlers' hotel into
the Tlumes' house as if on a visit to a foreign country. Agnes Aleke
was wearing the wig Rebecca told Bray she had ordered by post and
looked like a pretty American Negress. She talked to the Finn about
her longing to visit the cities of Europe, holding her head as a
woman does in a new hat. To him they were battlegrounds where the
young turned over rich men's cars and camped out in the carpeted
mausoleums of dead authority, not her paradise of shops. " 'Nice
things'?" he said in his slowly articulated Linguaphone English.
"Here you have the nice things—the shape of the trees, the round
sun, these beautiful fruits"—he was balancing on his knees a mango,
caressing it. She flirtatiously patronized his lack of sophistication—
"This shirt? You got it in Africa? Who's that president or whatever it
is?"

The Finn squinted down at his chest and said as if putting a hand
on the head of a dog that had accompanied him everywhere, "Syl-
vanus Olympio."

"But alas, *assassiné*—he's dead." Bray turned to Agnes, giving her
the advantage.

The Finn said unmoved, "Never mind," in a tone that implied he
was a good fellow anyway, dead or alive, in fact better than some
who were still about, perhaps in this room.

Agnes's patronage collapsed into the African internal feminine giggle that paralysed her, and, by a quick glance, infected Edna. This
uninhibited and inoffensive amusement at his expense, along with a
lot of beer, melted the Northerner. He began to dance wildly, but
preferred to do so on his own. He was so thin that the only curve in
his entire form was the curve of his sex in the shrunken jeans.

The immigration officials had impounded his money at the frontier.
Bray said, "That's quite normal, any country'll do it—he hasn't a re-

turn ticket. They have to protect themselves in case they get stuck with him here."

"So we'll have to be keeping him in pocket-money in the meantime." The Frasers considered him, parenthetically.

"Oh he won't have any great needs."

Aleke smiled and remarked to Rebecca, "We can write to immigration? The mission would give a guarantee for him, ay? Maybe we can get them to release part of the money."

"That would be marvellous," Hugh Fraser said. "He must report to the Police Commissioner, by the way, while we're in town."

"But I don't think the Commissioner is." Aleke looked undecidedly at Bray for a moment, and then said to him in the far-away manner with which he referred to such matters, "There was the rumour of some trouble up at the iron-ore mine."

"Oh? What sort?"

"Nobody knows how these things start, until afterwards. Something about overtime."

The union had just agreed to a forty-eight-day cool-off period before any strike would be recognized. "Striking?"

"Apparently."

"We heard a truckload of local PIP boys'd been seen driving up the Bashi road," Fraser said. "We'll know tomorrow when the broken heads start coming in to the hospital. Ota, better not knock yourself out, old son, you may have to start work sooner than you think."

"That's okay. I rather bandage heads than bury." The light, light blue eyes that had emptied themselves of Europe turned with neither compassion nor judgement on Africa. His rib-cage heaved under the freedom shirt and he began to dance again.

"Where'd he get it, anyway?" Rebecca said.

"A man give it to me," he said. "I stayed in his hut, it was a small place, banana leaves on the roof, but it's cool inside. At the end of the time, you know, he say, it's not a new shirt—but he give it to me."

"We must get him a Mweta one now that he's here. Not secondhand. We can afford it." Rebecca's new comradely way of talking to Bray. Not entirely new; it was rather the way she had been when she was odd-woman-out in the Bayley set in the capital, rather the way she talked to the men there. The usual concealment of the whereabouts of another kind of relationship existing within the general company, maybe. Her other new manner—the oblique flirtatiousness

—also showed under the surface now and then. Speaking not to him but at him, she asked, "Wasn't there a strike at the fish factory not long ago?"

"Oh they're a difficult lot. Always something simmering there. But that was settled, that other business." Aleke answered for everyone.

Bray felt her attention on him. He said, "All's peaceful on the lake. We should take advantage of it and go down. What about Sunday?" Everyone was enthusiastic. "I'll bring the food. Kalimo will get busy. No, no—it's my party." "What's the spear-fishing like?" Gordon wanted to know from him at once. "I hope to God you've got my gear up 'here?" he added to Rebecca, and she said, indulgent, pleasing— "All in the brown tin trunk. All intact." "I've never tried, but it should be good." "We'll have a go, anyway, eh? You've got a boat?" "There are pirogues everywhere and anybody'll let you use one."

"You won't *need* it," Rebecca assured enthusiastically. "There are millions of fish. They were swimming in and out my legs. You don't need to go miles out into the lake. They're everywhere round the island."

The husband began to question her closely and patiently, as one does when making certain allowances for personal characteristics one knows only too well. "If she's once had a good time in a place, she exaggerates like hell, this girl."

Her eyes shone, brimmingly; it was her way of blushing, and she pressed back her square jaw before the two of them. Gordon Edwards turned to appreciate her with Bray. "Have you ever seen anyone so much like Simone Signoret? Have you ever? The set of that head on the thick neck? The shape of the jaw?"

She did not look at him. She flew out appropriately, animatedly, at the husband. "She's fat and middle-aged. She's got a double chin!"

"Bunk. I just hope you'll age the way she has, that's all. Consider yourself damn lucky."

He wasn't sure who Simone Signoret was—an actress, of course, but he and Olivia hardly ever saw a film. "Well, I hadn't really noticed . . ."

"That old bag!"

They laughed together at her indignation.

He was living at the Tlumes' all right; he would appear, talking already before he entered, at any time of day—the perfectly brushed, white-streaked hair, the olive, tanned skin, the black eyes resting confidently round the room. He treated everyone as if he had known him all his life and decided unquestioningly into what part of his own established pattern of relationships with the world each person would fit. So Bray, in whom he had been quick to recognize a long-time professional wielder of authority just as he would impartially have recognized the particular usefulness of a currency smuggler or a doctor who wouldn't be unwilling to help out with an abortion, was at once assumed to be the ally for various decisions to be taken up not so much against Rebecca as sweeping her unprejudicedly aside.

"No sense at all in sending Alan and Suzi off to some school while the little one stays at home. They're all still at an age when they need their mother and a proper family life. What's the point of a woman having children if she doesn't bring them up? She was so mad keen for babies. It's a crazy idea to uproot them again for a few months— it just depends how long it takes for me to arrange things, and she joins me. What's the point of having to pack up all over again, in the meantime? The trouble is, wherever she finds herself she begins to arrange things as if she was going to be there forever. *This* place. I mean, have you ever heard . . . ? I find her landed here like a bird on a bloody telegraph pole. I should have done as I wanted in the first place, and sent her to her mother in England. 'She didn't want to be so far away.' But what could be farther from anywhere? Camping out with the locals, not even a bathroom of her own. This's no place for my boys to grow up. Becky tells me proudly they're learning to speak Gala. Where in the world are they going to need to speak Gala, for Christ's sake? Who's going to understand their Gala?" He laughed, "In England? In France? In Germany? How would I get around with Gala instead of French, and my bit of Portuguese I've picked up—I was in Angola for a while, you know, one of the best times of my life, as it turned out"—he smiled, showing his charming, slightly translucent-looking teeth, a man with no regrets, and offered at least half the story— "Good God, just the other side of Benguela, the spear-fishing! It looks like Greece—bare yellow rock and blue sea. Not a tree or a blade. I was doing a contract for the harbour at Lobito. Every weekend we used to go off across the desert and pick our bit of coast. *Garoupinhas*—like that. Well, I learnt Portuguese among other things. I can make myself understood . . . and now

there's a contract for Cabora Bassa, the dam—you know? The French
and Germans are going to build it for South Africa and the Portuguese. I get on well with Continental engineers—we've worked together before. I'm tempted to go back to engineering. For a while, anyway. So my Portuguese'll come in handy again, in Mozambique. You
find yourself stuck in the bloody hot bush, miles from nowhere, it
helps if you can chat the local storekeeper or the police, they'll do
things for you. I like ice in my drinks . . . This may be a particularly
hot spot in other ways"—the understanding was that this was between themselves, not for Rebecca's ears—"you've probably read
about the terrorists' threat to blow up the thing while we're busy on
it. Well, I don't want to die for the South African and Mozambique
governments any more than I want to die for anybody else. The
blacks or the whites—they're not getting this one. Personally, I don't
think there'll be a chance for them to come near—the whole thing'll
be guarded like a military installation. You can trust the South Africans for that. Nowhere's what one can call safe, anyway. I wonder
about here. The strikes going on up at the iron mine. I know these
countries; once they start with labour troubles, it's sticks and stones
and they don't care who it is who gets in their way. One road out and
a small plane twice a week—one mustn't forget that. D'you think it's
all right? Well—I trust you to know that if ever it looks as if it's
going wrong, you'll tip her off and see that they go without waiting
for trouble to come. I know you'd do that?"

"Of course."

"Because you can see how Becky is—she never believes that anyone would do her any harm. To come to the *bundu* in the first place
—just mad. Well, if you want one of the good-looking sexy ones you
settle for having to do the thinking yourself, don't you? Can't have
everything—" His daughter had come up to him and he wound up
the visit, talking of the mother but playfully transferring the reference
as if it were applied to the daughter, hooking her ragged strands of
hair behind her ears with his first finger, turning her meagre urchin's
face to rub noses with his own. "Is that all you've got to wear, your
brother's old pants? Lovely bird like you? Shall we go and buy you a
decent dress?" She did not speak, only nodded her head vehemently
to everything. It was true that there was something shabby and de-
prived about Rebecca's children. Bray had a curious loyal impulse to

distract the father's attention from this by changing the subject. "What sort of equipment have you got for the lake—you don't mean diving suit and oxygen and all that?"

And so Gordon Edwards insisted, at the lake on Sunday, that he try spear-fishing with him. There were several pairs of goggles, flippers and three spear-guns. He found a strange and delightful engulfment, freed from association with anything else he had ever experienced. He caught only one small fish, while the other, of course, expertly got quite a catch, including a Nile perch weighing about fifteen pounds. Once they met underwater, the two men, coming up to face each other at the end of the gliding momentum of their webextended feet. He met the smile behind the goggle-plate, the wetdarkened hair, the undulating body; the encounter hung a moment in that element.

"Well, how'd you like it?" She was waiting for them when they came back.

"Oh wonderful. I felt like a fish *in* water—"

Nothing would persuade Aleke or Tlume to go down. "And these're the guys who shout about other people exploiting their natural resources, ay, James?"—Gordon Edwards, cocking his head at them. Aleke said from under a hat, lying in the shade, "My country needs me. Life too valuable."

The Frasers' rumour was borne out. While they were all at the lake that day a party of PIP thugs drove through the workers' quarters on the bald hillside at the iron-ore mine and kicked over the Sunday cooking fires that were going outside nearly every house, burned bicycles, and in one case, killed somebody's tethered goat. Aleke related all this later—when they got back from their picnic there was an urgent message for him from the new Commissioner of Police, Selufu, to come to the mine. There was a moment when Aleke half-suggested Bray should go with him but it was no sooner broached than both of them, for different reasons, let it pass, as if it had not been serious. Perhaps Aleke had been told to let it be seen that Shinza's old friend had, in fact, some quasi-official status in the interests of Mweta; perhaps he merely had been told to make Bray feel important. . . . On the other hand, if he had no directive from above, maybe the moment the words were out of Aleke's mouth he had wondered whether an uncertain quantity like the Colonel should be allowed an inside view of difficulties in the district. They had never talked again about the boy Lebaliso had beaten in Gala prison.

But down at the *boma* next day Aleke, his fan turning from side to side all morning although the winter weather was pleasant, talked about Sunday's affair rather as if it had been a rowdy football match. He was critical of such behaviour but described it with gusto. "One old woman was worried as hell about her sewing machine—she ran out with it on her head, I don't know where she thought she was going—and a fellow"—he always called PIP militants "the fellows" —"made a grab at her more out of devilment than anything. A policeman grabbed *him*, so she puts down the machine and she starts punching and kicking the fellow while the policeman's holding him. . . . You've never heard such a carry-on. And the women are always the worst . . . our women! Nothing gives me a headache like one of those old mothers when she starts yelling."

The PIP "fellows" had gone to the mine with the purpose of supporting the union officials' decision (made against the decision of the miners themselves) not to start a wildcat strike. They said they wanted to hold a meeting at the mine—"to let them know that not only the union but PIP expects them to go to work," Bray supplied. "Exactly," Aleke said. "The fellows say it was going to be a peaceful appeal to loyalty and so on. And nothing would have happened, man, if the moment the lorry arrived at the compound everyone hadn't started shouting, specially those old ones. . . ." A few heads had been broken; not enough to create an emergency at the Mission hospital. "You're lucky, Aleke, when I was doing your job, I'd have had them all up before me in court next day."

"Don't I know it." Aleke offered good-natured professional sympathy. Although he described the night with such laconic detachment, he and Selufu apparently acted efficiently. Selufu arrested most of the PIP fellows and they had been remanded for preparatory examination by the Gala magistrate. It was all as it should be; Bray allowed some inner tension to relax. Of course he wondered about Shinza—there in the area of the mine the week before the proposed strike. Well, Shinza would see that the PIP militants at least had been arrested.

Mweta's letter came back promptly; Bray certainly would be invited to the Congress—under what label, he didn't say. As Bray

knew, the Congress was going to be held in the capital this time.
(There was already much criticism over this move; it had always
been held in the small village of Yambo, on the border of Central
Province and Gala, where just after the war the first successful political demonstration and the first arrests by the British administration
had taken place.) Mweta ignored the fact that Bray hadn't written
the letters he had wanted from him and simply said, as if there
had been no silence of rebuff in this area of their relationship,
he wondered what Bray thought about the dispute at the iron
mine?

He wrote at once from under his fig tree that what interested him
was the pattern emerging from disputes like those at the fish factory
and the mine. In both cases it was the same: an issue raised by the
workers was not backed by their shop stewards and other union officials, who were also PIP officials. The issue in both cases was an
agreement reached between the union and the employers which apparently was not acceptable to the workers as a whole: in the fish factory, the status of so-called casual labour (and Mweta knew, he had
told him himself, how those people were employed and lived); at the
mine, a question of rates of pay for overtime. It seemed clear that PIP
interference in the unions was in danger of defeating the function of a
trade union itself—to represent the workers' interests as against those
of the employer. This was what could happen where the interests of
the employer and the state appeared to coincide, and the government, in turn, was the Party. It led to labour unrest without union
leadership which had the confidence of the workers sufficiently to be
able to control them. "If you destroy the unions, you need the police
—more and more police. At the beginning. In the end, of course, it's
peaceful, because the workers have no more rights to assert. State and
employer, knowing what's best for the economy, decide what they
need and don't need. And there's a name for that, too." Taking his
tongue out of his cheek, he remarked that he would look in on the
court when the PIP militants appeared; it was a good thing for the
Party that they had been arrested and committed for trial.

She came early one morning that week, but not so early that Kalimo was not about somewhere. She closed the bedroom door quietly
behind her and he heard a hoarse morning voice, his own: "Lock it."

She was dressed ready for work, with a file under her arm. The room was dim and a bit musty from the night, his clothes lying about, the private odours of his body. The sun pressing against the curtains emblazoned their emblems of fish, cowrie, cockerel and coffee-bean like flags and they threw rich garish glows across the room. He propped himself up in bed on one elbow but did not let himself become fully awake. She smelled of cold water and toothpaste, her heart beat lightly and quickly with the energy of one who is already up and about. His had still the slow heavy beat of sleep. With his abrasive beard and night body-warmth he blotted out this surface dew of morning hygiene and found her underneath. With closed eyes he took off her freshly-put-on clothes, tugging and fumbling with blunt fingers. It was not a matter of undressing her, it was a matter of baring her sexuality, as one speaks of baring one's heart. She went down into the banked-up, all-night warmth of his bed and took him in her mouth, the soft hair of her head between his legs. In an intensity that had lain sealed in him all his life (dark underground lake whose eye he had never found) barrier after barrier was passed, each farthest shore of self was gained and left behind, words were reunited with the sweet mucous membrane from which they had been torn.

She took a clean handkerchief from his drawer, dipped it in the glass of water beside his bed and wiped herself—face, armpits, sex. She didn't want to meet Kalimo or Mahlope on the way to the bathroom. She dressed.

"I'll get up and see if it's all clear."

"I'm going the golf-course way—the car's down near the fourth hole. Said I had to go early to do some work I brought home and didn't do last night."

"It's all right—I hear them in the kitchen." For these practical whispers words would do.

She was gone.

She had not been with him more than half an hour. It was strangely like the very first time she had come. The very re-enactment itself was the measure of the difference: a ritual that had once been gone through in ignorance without remotely knowing what its real meaning could come to be.

He walked into town because he had to use the perfect coordination and balance in his body. Coming down into the long main road under the splendid trees he had a vivid sense of all the things he enjoyed; riding through light and shade in Wiltshire or years ago at Moshi in Tanganyika, finning along in slow motion on the bed of the lake last week—it was all one with an awareness—every minute detail leaving a fresh pug-print—of this road, this place. Everything was immediate and verifiable on a plane of concrete existence. The precise spiciness of the dry season when the dust had not been wetted for several months; the ting of bicycle bells plucking the air behind him; two children wearing only vests and passing a mealie-cob from mouth to mouth; the crows cawing out of sight. An ordinary morning that was to him the sunny square: the last thing the condemned prisoner would ever see, and would see as long as he lived.

The courthouse was part of the old administrative building where people came to collect pensions and pay taxes. Outside a group of ancient women were smoking pipes. Their bodies, bare from the waist except for beads tangled with their dugs, rose snakelike from the coils of cloth in which they squatted. They did not speak. Clerks, hangers-on, young men in white shirts and cheap sunglasses brushed past them. He went into the room that still smelled like a schoolroom; he himself had once sat up there on the rostrum and fiddled with the carafe covered with a glass. On one of the benches among other people, he was the only white man. His two neighbours talked across to each other behind his shoulders, not rudely, but in the assumption that he couldn't understand what they were saying and therefore wasn't there. They were discussing a debt owed to one or both of them; clearly they were such close friends it didn't matter which. They had the same cowboy jeans imported by local Indian stores, the same sort of Japanese watches with a thick gilt band, the same topiary skill of the open-air barbers had shaped their dense hair into the flat-topped semblance of an *en brosse* cut. The three tribal scars on each cheekbone were worn with no more significance than a vaccination mark.

PIP Young Pioneers solidly filled the first two rows of benches. Most could scarcely be called youths any more. The adolescent force that lingers heavily beyond its season in those whose hopes have not been realized was in their postures and restlessness. They gazed and shuffled, brazen and sullen. Some wore PIP forage caps, others wore the torn sweatshirt of the family's idle son, and one had a transistor radio with him that a court orderly with creaking boots came across to warn him not to use. He continued to hold it to his ear now and then, just not turning the knob, under the orderly's eyes.

The usual beggars and eccentrics who had nowhere else to feel themselves accepted along with other people, were deep in blank preoccupation; an old man had the worried, strainedly alert look that Bray knew so well—a kind of generalized concern in the face of the helplessness of all black people before the *boma* and the law. He wondered who the country women outside were; probably relations of men from the mine who were involved in the case. There were other, "respectably" dressed men and women from the African townships who must be relations, too. The familiar atmosphere of resignation and fear of authority that sat upon country courtrooms and made one the innocent and guilty was stirred by the arrival of the accused filing into the dock just as the slow whirling into action of the ceiling fans, set in motion at the same moment, began to slice the stale air. The court was full and faces kept peering in the windows from a gathering crowd outside. There was even the straggling boompah of a band out there—abruptly silenced. The eleven accused were too many for the small dock and like people whose seats at a theatre have been muddled up, they shifted and changed places and at last some were given chairs in the well of the court. A special detail of Selufu's men had come in with them, and ranged themselves round the visitors' gallery. The court rose; the black magistrate came in and seated himself before the carafe. He was an ex-schoolmaster and lawyer's clerk from another province and now and then he used an interpreter to translate for him into English when he was not sure that he had fully appreciated the nuance of some expression in Gala. Bray had met him at Aleke's; a cheerful, intelligent man who appeared morose on the bench.

An Indian lawyer from the capital had come down to conduct the defence. The men in the dock moved out of their stoic solidarity to get a good look at him; probably they had not seen him before. The indictment was read. He stroked back the shiny hair at his temples as he listened, as if he were still ruffled from the journey. In his quick, soft, Gujerati-accented English he asked at once for the trials to be separated: that of the nine men who were accused of trespassing and wilful damage to property to be heard independently of that of the

K

two accused of assault and an offence under the Riotous Assemblies Act. The request was granted; the cases were remanded until two separate dates a week or two ahead. The attorney objected that there was not sufficient time to prepare the defence; the cases were postponed still further ahead. Bail was renewed for the nine, but refused for the other two. The Young Pioneers creaked their benches and make tlok! noises in their throats like the warning notes of certain birds. More faces bobbed at the windows. One of the pair who had been refused bail was a slim young man whose bare neck had the muscular tension of a male ballet dancer; he kept twisting his head to look imperiously, frowning like Michelangelo's *David*, round at the crowd. Whenever he did so there was a surge in the two front rows, the force there shifted its weight in precarious balance between his look and the stolidity of Selufu's policemen.

The lawyer was objecting to the refusal of bail; the prosecutor was adamant. The magistrate appeared not to be listening to either; he confirmed that bail would not be granted. That was all.

As the prisoners went out, making use of their numbers by making a slow progress of it, they began to sing a PIP chant and the two who were going off to the cells yelled slogans, the old slogans of pre-Independence days. Bray allowed himself to be carried and hindered by the courtroom crowd. Women in their church-going clothes opened their mouths calmly and ululated. The magistrate banged his gavel and was resigned to being ignored; he mouthed what must have been an adjournment and walked out. Another case was to be heard and the exhibits, including a bicycle with one wheel missing, were carried in while the police moved along the rows of benches and were held adrift, clumsily bobbing. It was difficult to tell whether the movement through the door was people pressing in or the court being cleared. It was not an angry but a strangely confident crowd, talking and shifting about in possession. The ululating women stood where they had risen from the benches, and swayed. It was like being caught up in a dance with them; he was taller than anybody and as he was pressed and shifted he could see everything, the PIP claque taking up the prisoners' chant and moving their heads like hens as they urged themselves through the people, the bewildered face of the old beggar, the young men turning vividly from side to side. He wanted to grin: a bespectacled white totem, waving ridiculously about on the wake of backsides swinging their cotton skirts magnificently as bells. Slowly the whole crowd, and he with it, was drawn through the door as water circles the hole in a bathtub.

Outside, the three-man band whose evangelical beat derived from the Salvation Army was banging away falteringly. The PIP contingent went into discussion among the spectators and lingering courtroom crowd. There was a coming and going of individual PIP men, racing between the gathering and the office of the court; everyone was waiting for the nine to appear after completing bail formalities. When they did come out, rather sheepish, like people disembarking from a journey before the eyes of friends, the whole crowd was moved from the old-fashioned open verandas and yard of the building by the police. There was a momentary loss of direction when they might have dispersed; and then someone made for the piece of open ground on the other side of the road, next to the Princess Mary Library. The band tramped across, playing. The PIP Young Pioneers began an impromptu meeting; he waited a moment, beside the uneven pillars of the tiny, tin-roofed parthenon the ladies of the British Empire Service League had raised, to listen. The speaker stood on a wooden crate that had been abandoned by some shopkeeper and not yet carried off bit by bit by people looking for firewood. PIP had brought freedom and people who did not obey the orders of PIP were fools . . . there was nothing in the country that was not the business of PIP . . . PIP had not got rid of the white man to be told what to do by black men who were just as bad. . . . You were not allowed to talk about something that was in the courts but he would still tell everybody this—people who defied the trade unions defied the government, and PIP knew what to do with them.

He began to walk away and stepped round a scuffle that had kicked up—sudden blows between young men, and stones flying. He was in the path of one; it got him on the side of the neck: his hand went up with the involuntary movement of slapping a fly. A woman passerby gasped, "Oh sorry, sorry, *Mukwayi* . . ."

The sting drew no blood. He had caught the stone as it fell into his open collar; he pushed it into his pocket.

There were several irritable incidents in Gala that day. Not all appeared to be concerned with the trial, but were released by the roused confidence of the courtroom crowd that affected the atmosphere of the village as a heat wave affects the citizens of a cold country.

"They ought to be rounded up and put to work on the roads," Mr. Deal at the supermarket said to him confidentially, wrapping the pound of ham that he had bought. "Lot of hooligans and no one to give them the language they understand, any more. All they've learnt is how to thieve better. You wouldn't believe it if I told you my losses since I've converted to self-service. This place just isn't ready for it— you've got to have civilized people."

A small girl trader had ranged her few undersized tomatoes on the pavement. He was buying some when Gordon Edwards came by and at once suggested they have a beer at the Fisheagle. No black face had yet dared appear in the inside bar at the Fisheagle; the patrons were talking about golf and a European motor rally that had been shown on TV the night before.

Gordon Edwards told an amusing story about a friend of his who, after serving in the Mozambique channel on a patrol ship whose purpose was to intercept ships carrying cargoes for Rhodesia, had resigned and himself become a successful middleman in the sanctions-breaking business, getting out tobacco and taking in machinery. While Edwards talked his eye kept wandering to Bray's neck. "Something's bitten you."

His expression implied that he was unaware of it. The small stone lay among the other kind of currency in his pocket as the fact of what had happened in the early morning lay in his mind among the ready pleasantries of small talk.

The nine men were found guilty and fined. The other two never came to trial at all; on the special intervention of the President the case against them was dropped.

Almost every day, there were reports of disturbances in one or other of the provinces.

Everyone who could afford a TV set continued to watch the syndicated programmes from America and England—sport, popular science, old Westerns, and (if they were white people) the interminable serialization of *The Forsyte Saga*. Edna Tlume had hired a set and the full complement of the household was generally to be found in the darkened Tlume-Edwards living-room during the hours when the station in the capital was open. There was a news round-up once a day (Ras Asahe was the commentator for a while) but the station could not afford a permanent team of cameramen and reporters to film live events at home. The dim room—blaring with music and barking recorded voices, smelling of grubby children, curry powder from cheap meals, and Nongwaye's medicated tobacco—where a football game in Madrid was being played or a trial of Vietcong refugees was flickering into focus, was more real than what was happening in the neighbouring province and the next village. The heavy green of Gala hung shutting that out.

As his bulk blackened the doorway Rebecca would get up quietly from her canvas chair and slip away from the audience; everyone else remained absorbed. He and she were seldom bothered by the children now; he sometimes thought—and at once forgot again—he ought to remind her that they shouldn't be allowed to become addicted to the box. She sat with her children resting against her, each one in physical contact with some part of her, the littlest sometimes falling asleep in her lap; what they drew from her, then, was enough and more to counteract what passed before their eyes and skimmed their understanding. There was fellow-feeling with them; he knew that steady current of her body, its lulling and charging effect. No harm could come while one breathed in time with that flesh.

The husband, Gordon Edwards, had gone away again. He had not found out if she had slept with him—never would, he knew even as, at the moment of putting aside her legs with his knee and entering her body himself, he would think of it. It was not in her eyes, anyway, as she lay as she sometimes liked on top of him and looked into his face as only lovers do, her face open to him. She complained that because he was short-sighted his eyes were intensely blank in passion, he was concealed from her. "I can't ever see what you're thinking."

"I'm not thinking then." But she was the one with secrets. Yet her lioness-coloured eyes (browner with the pupils dilated) were not secretive. The flirtatious animation she had put on like some curious form of reserve when the husband was there was gone, too. She had been clever to come to him that one morning, so that there was no question, once the other had left, that they would have to find a way to come together again: it was already done, they had never been anything else but together, beneath the convenient collusion of friends and circumstances. Yet there was nothing "clever" in her, in those eyes. She was simply *all there,* nothing withheld, nothing reserved, not even her secrets. So there was a stage you could reach where even the relationships each had with other people belonged to the relationship with one another. That could contain everything, encompass everything, not resignedly but in a fine sort of greed. If I'm too old for virginity of any kind to be anything but ridiculous in me, then allow that so must she be, in her way, too. It wasn't, after all, naïveté that enabled her to improve the curtains against the arrival of Olivia.

He wrote to Olivia about the strikes, lock-outs, and the confused expressions of dissatisfaction that, in the bush, took the form of tribal wrangling. He did not suggest to her that this atmosphere was the reason why she should not come. But neither, in their letters, any longer wrote as if she were coming. He did not wonder why she, for

her part, should have dropped the idea, because—he realized quite
well—it suited him that she had done so so tacitly. He wrote her
about cattle slaughtered in vengeance, huts burned, the proposed
amendments to the Industrial Relations Act that would make strikes
illegal for teachers and civil servants. She wrote about the beautiful
officer's chest, circa the Napoleonic wars, that she and Venetia had
found in a village antique shop, and a jaunt to London to see a play
about the incestuous homosexual love between two brothers that
couldn't have been shown while the Lord Chamberlain still had the
right of the blue pencil. Their younger daughter Pat had been home
on a visit from Canada. Venetia and her husband and baby spent a
lot of time in the house in Wiltshire; photographs of the baby, laughing on flowery grass, were enclosed. He kept coming upon them in
the broken ashtray in the sideboard which Kalimo had considered
safe keeping, and was wedging them round the edges of the frame
that already held a picture of Venetia and the infant, on an afternoon
when Rebecca came in all smiles and relief to tell him that it was all
right, her period had turned up after all. She had been nearly a week
overdue. She took off his glasses and kissed him frantically, grate-
fully; "Though if it ever did happen, I could go to England. I always
think that."

He poured tea for her and stroked her hair. "England?"

"It's illegal to have something done here."

So there was no child from him this time; but there could be, any
time. He could see that she was afraid of it and accepted being
afraid. She had told him she couldn't take the pill because it made
her get fat.

Sampson Malemba and his wife were coming to supper. It was
taken for granted that Rebecca was in the position of the woman of
the house, now. She helped Kalimo when he would allow it; Kalimo
kept Mahlope firmly confined to outdoor work—Mahlope's vegetable
garden supplied the Tlume and Aleke households as well as its own.
Mrs. Malemba (much too shy to call any white person by his first
name or to invite anyone to call her by hers) would come to Bray's
house if he asked the Malembas alone. She was content not to talk at
all except for her extremely polite responses to offers of food and
drink, and as soon as there was a mew from the bundle of infant she
always had with her she would disappear into the kitchen to feed or

tend it. Rebecca managed to draw her out a little; Rebecca was a woman whom other women liked, anyway, but these days it was easy for Bray or her to be nice to other people. They had awakened together in the morning and, when everyone parted for the night, would be going to sleep together in his narrow bed; this was the source of an overflowing generosity of spirit.

The adult-education-centre-cum-trades-school was going surprisingly well. Sampson had clerks from the *boma* running literacy classes for older people in the townships. Bray had persuaded the most unlikely people among the white community to teach various skills at the Gandhi Hall workshop; white people, in a skin-wrinkle of apprehension hardly interpreted, were beginning to feel that perhaps it wasn't a bad idea, so long as it didn't cost you anything, to make a gesture of cooperation towards the blacks who were running the show. He also quietly counted on the ordinary, unconfessed pleasure anyone takes in demonstrating what he knows. The Americans had supplied a couple of surprisingly useful workers as well as money— not Peace Corps people, but Quakers of some sort—who were teaching fitting and turning, motor winding and various other skills that fitted in with the needs of the beginnings of light industry in the Gala area, and they took their jeep into the country to teach people how to use and maintain the heavy agricultural machinery that was available on loan from Nongwaye Tlume's department. Even Boxer had come down for a week and enjoyed talking uninterruptedly, in an intensive course on animal husbandry. The Americans had a tape recorder and the whole thing was preserved for use again and again; as Boxer spoke in Gala, it could be played to and understood by people in the remotest village. Boxer stayed with Bray; Rebecca had had to keep away, of course, not even an early morning visit was possible. Boxer was up at five and moving about his room. He brought with him that old-maidish bachelor cosiness which he assumed he and his host shared: there was the feeling that he thought it would be ideal if they could live together permanently. He was the sort of man in whom sexual desires die early; perhaps he was already impotent? He talked about Shinza without prompting: the continuing trouble at the iron-ore mine was due to the meddling of "his lordship," coming from the Bashi in his "pa-in-law's" car and getting at people. The Mineworkers' Union secretary had come from the capital to see what was up, but who would listen to him?—they were all Mpana's crowd, and they would listen to whomever Mpana told them. And Mpana told them to listen to his son-in-law, his lordship Shinza. Boxer gave the facts as a piece of local gossip.

The morning Boxer left she came at lunchtime and they made love. The lunch table waited, draped in Kalimo's mosquito-net cover. She said while they ate, gay to be rid of the visitor, "Why's he such a depressing man?"

"Because he's a vision of myself without you."

She laughed with pleasure and indignation. "You! Ever like him!"

"Everybody has a private vision of what he could be at the other end of the scale, the very bottom. Nobody else recognizes it, only oneself."

She was filled with curiosity. "Extraordinary that you should ever think of yourself in terms of *him*. The private vision must also be the most unlikely thing that could ever happen. Quite crazy."

"But haven't you got one?"

"Have I? I don't know." After a moment she said, "Oh yes. After all, I left the capital because of it." And now she was sombre, dreamy, while he was talkative and hungry.

The centre was perhaps even achieving something useful; he worked on at it with Malemba in spite of all that was happening. It continued to exist and to take up daily action while the context—of the country and of his mind—in which it had that existence was broken up and riding at different levels, swirling and giddying. The practical working intimacy with good solid sensible Sampson Malemba, the attentive faces gathered at the Gandhi Hall or the converted police compound, the Quakers' jeep carrying the momentum of its own dust to villages down on the lake savannah or towards the Bashi—all this purposefulness was taking place on a land-floe on which people moved about their business unaware that their environment had broken free and was being carried, a house riding upon a flood, the furniture still in place and the pot-plants in the windows. What one does oneself every day is real, he thought; she was sitting on the bed under the reading lamp, picking hard skin off her little toes ("It's my winter layer peeling off—in the summer when I wear sandals all the time I don't get it").

He woke in the small hours of the mornings and his mind punched the facts out of the clarity of darkness. Shinza always had been able to count on influence with the advanced sections of the community, the workers, through his connections with the trade unions. On the side he also had had a useful pull on tribal loyalties through his relationship with the Paramount Chief's family—he was a nephew, if Bray remembered correctly. It was mainly because of him that the Lambala-speaking people—an offshoot of the Gala, distributed widely through the Bashi country—had been kept within PIP from the beginning. With his marriage to Mpana's daughter he must now greatly have extended his support, and taken into his influence not only Mpana's considerable following at home but also the scattered thousands who had always formed a large part of the labour force all over the country. Mpana was the man who, in Bray's time, had been appointed Tribal Authority by the colonial government when it deposed the Paramount Chief, Nagatse, for intransigence and support of the nascent PIP; with Independence, Nagatse had been reinstated as Paramount Chief and Mpana found himself once again an ordinary chief with a souvenir of better times—his battered American car. Well, Shinza drove that car, these days. It was a logical enough alliance, marriage apart. Mpana and his people certainly would not forgive Mweta the demotion; however far removed from theirs Shinza's cause was, if it opposed Mweta, it would serve their own.

And Shinza? Nagatse had been one of his converts, his "enlightened chief" who wasn't afraid of a nationalist movement. Mpana had been one of the "good government boys," a stooge Shinza made fun of, which was his sharp and generous way of despising. Family feeling would hardly change that; but no doubt expedience did. Shinza had curious friends, everywhere, these days.

Sometimes as he lay awake among these facts it seemed to him that Shinza's roster of friends now constituted a stark assembly—in assessment, in the dark. He placed Mweta before them. He could not decide what Mweta would do, should do. If I were Mweta—but the point was, he was not. He tried to rid himself of lifelong preconceptions, discard the last hoary virginity. But there was always another and another—if he could come to the end of them! His mind was freed by the night. If there was a revolution to let people out from under intimidation, exploitation, and release them from the chalk circle drawn by the wrong sort of power, how far could the revolution go to protect itself and what it gained for people? How far, before it slowly picked up the rubble of the same walls and weapons it had smashed; began to use them against what it called the counter-revolutionaries? What were counter-revolutionaries? The enemies of the revolution, or revolutionaries who thought the revolution was being betrayed? Shinza and Mweta had both identities dubbed on them, each by the other. Shinza believed that Mweta had betrayed the principles of the revolution, and was its enemy; Mweta believed the same of Shinza. And *he* wanted them both to be wrong. He wanted to believe that together, neither would sell out the new life more than the daily attrition of human fallibility in power made inevitable. He defined it precisely as that to himself, to hold his ground that what he believed was flatly reasonable.

Sometimes, as the dead silent interval (minutes? hours?) between the cessation of night-sounds and the beginning of predawn sounds was invaded by a shrill unison of birds chipping away the dark, the hard-edged facts in his mind arranged themselves differently. The importance of Shinza's alliances sank; Mweta had only to reinstate Shinza beside him, placate Mpana with some provincial office, disengage PIP's domination of the trade unions—it could be done. And Shinza had said, "I like to know I have a chance to win." With his roster of allies—Mpana; perhaps even some of Nagatse's people; a following in the trade union movement whose strength and numbers one couldn't assess; that wild business of Somshetsi over the border —could he have any real chance?

But this was choosing to ignore, behind closed eyes where everything was present at once, other facts, boulders of facts. Tom Msomane, the Minister of Labour, said one day that industrial unrest was not based on "real demands" but "agitation," and the next day was at pains to cover up this implication that there was political dissatisfaction among the workers. How many of the strikes and disputes were blown on by Shinza's inspiration? One could be crediting him with too much or too little. And what was the sense of thinking that all Mweta had to do was lift PIP's heavy hand off the back of the unions —Mweta believed that the way to expand the economy quickly for the benefit of the workers themselves, and everybody else in the country, was to support investor-employers by guaranteeing a docile labour force.

Surrounding this firmament of facts that could not be reconciled was its own atmosphere—emotion like the layer of spit an insect wraps round the great concern of its existence, its eggs: he resented Shinza because he thought Shinza was right, and he resented Mweta because he could not admit that Mweta was wrong. And at the same time (four o'clock, now, five?) he was ready to turn over, like a tombstone, his own judgement, and find there beneath only the sort of things that lie under stones.

He would get up and go to pee in the stuffy bathroom. He used the basin, running the water softly as a flush in order not to disturb her with the noise of the lavatory. Once he suddenly remembered with obstinate urgency something Shinza had said—". . . people must be taught to cry 'Stop thief!' " What was the context? Shinza had said, look it up. He padded down the passage to the living-room and turned on the light. The ashtrays were coldly full. There were raisin stalks in the fireplace and a cup of scummy coffee on his table. He was naked and knelt, dangling, the wet touch of himself against his own ankle, searching through the government-issue bookshelf. He had brought Fanon to Africa with him, after all. The pages of the paperback had gone the colour of the shaded nicotine stain round a cigarette butt. He found the place: " 'Stop thief!' In their weary way towards rational knowledge the people must . . ." He went back a few lines, for the sense. ". . . yet everything seemed to be so simple before: the bad people were on one side, and the good on the other. The clear, the unreal, the idyllic light of the beginning is followed by a semi-darkness that bewilders the senses. The people find out that the iniquitous fact of exploitation can wear a black face, or an Arab one; and they raise the cry of 'Treason!' But the cry is mistaken; and the mistake must be corrected. The treason is not national, it is social. The people must be taught to cry 'Stop thief!' In their weary road towards rational knowledge the people must also give up their too-simple conception of their overlords."

He went back to bed and lay again, awake, with her head on his arm and her leg slid up between his; if she rose anywhere near the surface of consciousness she moved her lips against the hair of his chest. All the hours of these nights when he was in turmoil he was also in the greatest peace. He was aware of holding these two contradictions in balance. There was once a crony of his mother's who used to say gleefully of anyone who found himself suddenly subjected to extraordinary demands—Now he knows he's alive.

He wondered if she had known what she was saying.

He saw the silver aerials of the two police jeeps lashing along through leaves and brush, full of Selufu's men. He was coming home in the afternoon from a village that would one day be in the suburbs of Gala. That was how one got to know what was going on: one saw something, heard something. He mentioned it to Aleke when he called in at the *boma,* and Aleke must have telephoned Selufu once he was out of the room. Anyway, by next afternoon everybody knew what had happened. A labourer on the construction of the railway, now within forty miles of Gala, had been killed. The other workers downed picks in protest against working conditions; they threatened the Italian foremen. One of these drove to Gala half through the bush, half on forest track. When Selufu's policemen got to the construction site they found that the people of the village of Kasolo, nearby, from where casual labour for this stage of the construction was recruited, had carried the dead labourer home for burial and in a kind of mourning frenzy gone straight from the funeral to join forces with the strikers. The foremen had locked themselves in the railway car they slept in; a freight car had been burned and equipment had been tipped into the river.

"Things are hotting up a bit before the Congress," Aleke offered, as if that were simply to be expected. He and Bray and Rebecca were drinking tea to give some purpose to their standing about in Aleke's office. Now, while Selufu was without the best men of his small force, some obscure trouble had started between the Young Pioneers of PIP and the workers at the fish-meal and lime factories, down in the industrial area of Gala town itself. It spread to the townships after working hours, and there was even a triumphant roving gang who wandered through the town and the main street. Rebecca had encountered them driving home; she repeated, "I hooted and they sort of parted to let me through, yelling all the time, but I don't think it was at me." Perhaps she wanted to be told she had been foolhardy, or insouciantly bold; what she questioned was her own behaviour rather than the gang's. He said to her, "Well, you should have been able to make that out?" pretending to chide her as her instructor in the language. "All I could hear was something about 'we are coming' "—she repeated the phrase in Gala, for confirmation.

"People like a bit of excitement, that's all, that's the impression I got this morning." Aleke had been called to the township to drive around with the mayor, Joshua Ntshali. Selufu was no fool and thought that a show of civil service and civic authority might not only disguise his shortage of police but even suggest that the presence of policemen was not necessary. "Quite a few people were home from work for no reason—we saw them standing about outside the houses, they ought to've been out of the way at work by that time. —People who've got nothing to do with the fish-meal factory or the lime works. One said he'd taken the day off because his wife and mother didn't want to stay home alone. Another one's wife wouldn't let him go because she was afraid he would get into trouble in town. And so on. It's ridiculous. Josh gave him a lecture that covered everything from how to keep a wife in place to his responsibility for the health of the famous city of Gala. Turned out he was a cleaner at the abattoir."

But there was more than excitement at the hostel, the big new block on the hill that once separated white Gala from the native town, keeping it out of sight. "If these youngsters are out-of-works who attach themselves to the Young Pioneers what are they doing living there?" Bray asked. The hostel was supposed to accommodate unmarried men who were employed in industry and public works.

"That's what I said to old Ntshali. It's a municipal affair. That hostel is full of people who haven't any right to be there—they have no jobs, they just move in and share the rooms of their relations who are working in the town."

"Then PIP should disown them."

"PIP doesn't disown any of our people," Aleke said.

"My dear Aleke, PIP can and does—what about the iron miners who defied the union?"

Aleke granted it with a smile, passing no judgement. "That hostel's a bad idea anyway, whoever it was thought it up."

"Of course. Too much like a compound. It was planned by people who still thought in terms of migrant workers." He added, for Rebecca, "—The last white village board, before Independence; it was their baby."

"Yes, I suppose so," Aleke said. "How do you go about getting

everyone to know there's going to be a curfew tonight, in a place that
hasn't got a newspaper? Selufu insists we need a curfew for a day or
so."

Rebecca said, "The radio?"

"Well, no . . . I don't know." Aleke and Bray both knew the objections to that; one didn't want to publicize over the whole country the
impression—hardly borne out—that Gala was in a state of emergency.

He looked at Aleke. "Of course, it'll probably be in the news
service—curfew imposed and so on." But that was different from
broadcasting an injunction to the people of Gala, a warning that
everyone else would hear.

"Selufu wants a van with a loudspeaker to go round."

"That's certainly the best."

"But he hasn't got a police van to spare—they're all up in the bush
at the railway."

"What'll you do?" Rebecca said. She came and stood beside Bray.
They were looking out across the neat *boma* garden (hibiscus had
been planted where the Christ-thorn had pierced the toe of an Aleke
child) down the slope of the town half-hidden by the cumulus of ev-
ergreen, where a part of the market with its splotches of vegetable
colour, a top-heavy, faded yellow bus with its canvas flaps waiting at
the open ground of the bus depot, the yard of Parbhoo's store with its
Five Roses advertisement on the roof, and the comfortable, squatting
queue of women and babies outside the clinic, were all in the frame
of vision. The usual bicycles and pedestrians moved in the road, bicycles bumping down over the bit where the five hundred yards of tar
that had been laid in front of the *boma* ended and there was a rutted
descent to the dirt. He had the feeling—parenthetic, precise—that
they were both suddenly thinking of the lake at the same time. The
lake with its upcurved horizon down which black pirogues slid towards you. The lake still as a heat-pale sky.

Aleke said, "Borrow PIP's, I suppose. They're the only people
who've got one ready fitted-out."

For some reason or other Rebecca wanted him to come to the
Tlumes' for lunch—usually she was busy fetching the children from
school and feeding them, unless they happened to be going home
with school friends and she could come to him. He agreed without

thinking about it, anyway, because he had had a call at the *boma* about noon from Joosab, and had to go off and see him, knowing before he got there what the urgent and apologetic summons would be about. Sure enough, I.V. Choonara of the Islamic Society was in Joosab's tailor shop. There among the ironing board, the sewing machine and the counter with its long-beaked shears attached to a string, the two elderly gentlemen "expressed the worries of the community" about the Gandhi Hall and School. He was giving his twice-weekly class to the local PIP branch there—the economic basis necessary for Pan-African aims. The Islamic committee members wondered whether it was wise to have these young men gathering at the Indian school just now. . . . What they really hinted was that they wanted to close the school and workshop to the adult education centre while there was disturbance about. He was not surprised; though he privately doubted whether this PIP class would have been likely to turn up anyway, for the time being. Several Indian stores in town had kept their wooden shutters down, he'd noticed that morning.

At the Tlumes' Rebecca and the assortment of black and white children she had brought home from school were already at table. There was lemonade and a cake. "They insisted you must be here"; he realized that it was her birthday, not one of the children's. "Didn't I know when your birthday was?" She laughed—"I think I once must have told you. When I wanted to know your astrological sign." "Mine's a fish," the little one, Clive, said.

He could kiss her for her birthday, in front of the children. Although she was apologetic for making him suffer the noisy and not very palatable lunch-party she was rather happy and flattered at being the centre of the children's attention. They had presents for her —drawings and painted plaster-of-Paris objects made at school. Clive reminded that Daddy's present was on top of the wardrobe. A fancy-wrapped box held a transparent stone on a silver chain. The kind of thing that comes from Ceylon and is set by Indian jewellers in Dares-Salaam or Mombasa. Suzi made her put it on and all through the meal it dangled where those breasts of hers were pressed against their own divide in the neck of her dress. She must have kept the parcel specially to open on her birthday.

Whether Selufu had sent for them or not a reinforcement of police from other posts appeared round the town in the afternoon. Dazed and dusty, they stood with the faceless authority of strangers on the street corners, outside the African bar, at the bootblacks' and bicycle menders' pitches in the gigantic roots of the mahogany trees of the main street, under the slave tree in the industrial end of town. He was about everywhere, trying to find something decent to buy Rebecca, and there was nowhere he didn't come upon them.

What could one find in Gala? He even went back to Joosab's to ask whether any of the Indian shops, who had had nothing to show him but Japanese cottons, didn't have some elegant silk sari hidden away against the marriage of a daughter. But there was nothing; not even a good bottle of French perfume at the chemist's—"no call for that." In the end he bought her a leather suitcase produced from a back room in the gents' outfitting corner of Deal's supermarket; it was the only beautiful thing he could find in Gala, must have been there for years, too expensive to sell—standing wrapped in a cheap travelling rug since before he left, ten years ago. He carried it to the Volkswagen, not entirely satisfied, but it was better than nothing, and had to halt before crossing the road while the PIP loudspeaker van went past. A buried voice bellowed forth in a terrific blare that could not fail to be heard but whose sense could not be made out. Frank Rogers, owner of the bottle store, the Fisheagle Inn, former mayor of Gala, and once one of the organizers of the move to have the D.C. recalled, stood waiting beside him. Rogers' teeth had gone the same rusty yellow as his golden hair. He grinned. "Not walking out on us again, Bray, are you?"

"Farewell present for one of my staff at the education centre."

Of course, everyone knows Bray's got a woman—first he took up with the wild men among the blacks, now he comes back to find himself a floozy, safe from any trouble at home. That's the big attraction for white men like him—do what you like, the blacks don't care.
—He knew that old rumours about his keeping black women had been revived, the moment he had come back to Gala—all hankerings after their own back yards were projected by indignant whites onto those who shared their colour but not their politics. Would the undoubted existence of a white mistress prove less of a smear than the mere fabrication of a black one? It would have been amusing to know if a white mistress were considered a lesser or greater sign of degeneracy.

And would Olivia, in her way, mind a black woman less than this white one? (She knew of the lovely black girl he had been so attached to in Dar-es-Salaam, before his marriage.) Would she find a black girl more understandable, in him? Not because she thought black women didn't count on her level, but because she herself had found many of them beautiful, and could well imagine a man might find in Africans certain qualities that Western women had traded for emancipation. It would be interesting to know that, too; but there again, he never would. Olivia would never know about this girl, never suffer. This fact seemed incontrovertible while at the same time he was living with the girl, had no plan or thought that did not assume her presence. The idea of "giving up" the girl didn't exist; and yet there was the equal acceptance that Olivia would in some way remain unharmed, untouched, embalmed in the present. All his life he had lived by reason; now unreason came and paradoxically he was resolved; whole; a serpent with its tail in its mouth. An explanation? The point was that he didn't feel any necessity to ask an explanation of himself. None at all.

Tom Msomane's Permanent Secretary for Labour flew to Gala to look into the Kasolo railway affair, landing on the airstrip near the prison watched by bare-bellied children. But by then the whole thing was settled. Three men who were alleged to be responsible for throwing government property into the Solo River were awaiting trial and the rest had gone back to work; only the Italian who had bounced through the bush for help refused to return. The Permanent Secretary was welcomed by a big beer-drink at Kasolo village, where he made a speech telling the villagers how the railway would bring more money and work to the district.

Caleb Nyarenda was a guest of the Alekes while he was in the area. He was a small, bushy-haired lively man who belched a lot behind a neat hand while he drank strong tea and told anecdotes from the days when he had been a burial society collector in the capital. Perhaps he still had too much of a professionally tactful no-farther-than-the-door manner with people; he remarked that the Kasolo villagers had been very friendly, but "no one came forward to tell me what was really going on. 'Oh that business last week' "—he showed how they waved it away—"—after all I didn't come up for a wedding."

"Well, they were just pleased to see you, that's all," Aleke said. "People like to think the government takes notice of them."

"Heaving one of those great big earth-eating things into the river, that's some way to get noticed!" Nyarenda laughed, looking round for confirmation.

Someone mentioned the Italian foreman, who was still in Gala, sitting all day on the veranda of the Fisheagle Inn, dark glasses observing without being observed, the cross round his neck gleaming on the curly-haired breast in his open shirt. Bray could speak a little Italian and made a point of being friendly if he happened to pass. The foreman told him he was going to hitch a lift to the capital as soon as he could get his things from the site; then he was going home to Foggia, and the company could sue him if it wanted to. "He says the Virgin Mary saved his life once, but you could never be sure she would do it again. '—Do it in time, again' was what he actually said."

"That's the man who pushed my trolley round for me in the supermarket yesterday." Agnes Aleke wore the wig and eye make-up, reserved for special occasions, all day while the Permanent Secretary was there, not out of a desire to attract him but to set some sort of standard for the remote Northern Province.

"Didn't he realize you were government property?" Nyarenda was quick.

Agnes stood with her hand on her hip. "All I can tell you, that's the first time in my life a white man ever offered to carry anything for me."

"And the blacks?" Edna Tlume said in her soft voice.

"Oh *them*. Don't talk about them. You don't even expect it of them."

While the banter went on, Aleke turned, in conversation aside with Bray, to the Kasolo villagers again. He had accompanied Nyarenda, of course. "They want a dam there, I'm told, but they wouldn't discuss it with him. I asked why but they said he's an Mso, why should he tell the government to make a dam for the Gala? Naturally, he'll see that dams are built for the people where he comes from." Aleke shrugged and laughed.

"But why didn't *he* bring up the subject?"

"How's he to know what they want?"

Aleke's system of leaving well enough smoothed over; if order were restored and the people had had some pride in entertaining an important representative of the government even if they had no personal confidence in him, why turn their attention back to their dissatisfactions? Well, if the dam were discussed and then not built, Aleke would be the man who'd have to deal with the resentment.

Gala township calmed down, too; Mr. Choonara consented to have the Gandhi School opened to the use of the centre again. At the iron mine there continued to be trouble of one kind and another. The phosphate mines in the Eastern Province threatened a wildcat strike. One broke out among the maintenance depot workers and drivers of the road transport company, which carried mail and newspapers to Gala. For a week Gala was without papers, and letters were long delayed. In spite (or perhaps precipitated by the silence?) of irregular mails, Rebecca got a letter from her husband. He had apparently changed his mind about boarding school for the children; he had entered them for a school in South Africa.

"That where he is?"

"He wrote from Windhoek, but the school's in Johannesburg."

"And the little one?" Bray said. With the father's face; surely too young for school—only five years old.

"He'll stay with Gordon's sister. For a while. That's more or less the idea. She's got twin girls his age. —So's Gordon can see something of him."

He said to her, "Didn't he ask you to come, too?"

She had a shy, cocky way of concealing a danger once it was over. "Yes, he wanted us all to leave—but I've explained, I can't break a government contract, and there's the money—and the money from the house, too, I can't just leave that here, all in a minute. . . ."

"What house?"

"The house in Kenya—my father built a house for us when we got married. It was sold last year and we managed to get the money out and bring it here. But you can't get money transferred from here to South Africa, now."

"Oh my God." He saw her stranded in Johannesburg: Gordon Edwards ensuring the ice for his whisky far away in the Mozambique bush; himself unreachable. It was one of those prescient visions of destitution and abandonment that come in childhood at the sight of a beggar asleep in the street.

"What does he say?"

"About me?" Her voice slowed. "But I *told* him. I couldn't come. I ought to finish my contract. At least I can't leave unless Aleke can get somebody else."

Her full, square jaw set but her eyes were exposed, held by him, like hands quietly lifted at gunpoint.

They went on to talk about the practical details of the children's departure.

That night at the end of love-making she began to cry. He had never seen her cry before. The tears, released, like his semen, trickled into her hair and the hollow of his neck. He put up his hand to make sure and his fingers came away wet as if from a wound he had not felt. She didn't bury her head or hide her face; she was lying on her back within his arm. He thought of the little boy, and said, "I know. I know." He smeared the tears against himself. Because she was not a woman who wept, she became for a few moments just like those others he'd known, who did, and there was nothing to offer her but the usual comfort—he kissed her eyes and ran his tongue over the eyelids. She said, "He's so independent, but all the same . . . little, isn't he?"

He brought her an aspirin and a glass of water and she slept, snoring a bit because of the weeping. A process of dismemberment began to take place in him. She would go with her children. He would tell her. He held her and the current of her body carried him, as if nothing had changed, finally to sleep.

In the morning they overslept and it was impossible to begin to talk. She could not come to him in the evening; Nongwaye was away in the bush and Edna was on night duty, so she had to sleep at home with the children. He went over for supper and again there was no chance—it was Friday and the children were allowed the treat of staying up late. He and the girl played musical chairs with them. She was full of private jokes and was happy and when the children had gone to bed it was not the time to make her sad again. She was happy because Edna's mother was coming to look after the family next day, and he had promised that they would go alone to the lake. Every day made what he had to say more difficult. Driving to the lake brought back each time a renewal of the first time they had been there alone together. They went to the island—these days they took the spear-fishing equipment with them—and she got her first fish. It was spring; the heat that built up over the two months before the rains was beginning, and he had to drag up the pirogue and balance it against the rocks to make shade—the baobab was not yet in leaf. Even then, the stasis of one o'clock was formidable. Drawn up into their covert of shadow they talked in the mood of animated confidence that, for them, went with being at the lake. At one point she said, ". . . and when I was miserable—you know. It really was that I hardly mind at all. It's awful, isn't it. I look forward to you and I . . . not having them around, just . . . The trouble is I want to burst with joy at the idea of us being left alone—" and for a moment he did not quite realize what she was saying—he had forgotten, in the familiarity and pleasure of the day, what it was that had to be said by him.

And so it was not said; there was no need for it.

The children left Gala by car with the United Nations husband-and-wife medical team who were on loan to advise on the country's health services. They were old friends of Rebecca from her time in one African country or another, and were returning to the capital after a trip to the lake communities. In the capital, Vivien saw the children off in the care of a friend of hers who was travelling on the same jet to Johannesburg.

In the last days before her children went Rebecca was sometimes sad, and wept again—but perhaps this time really because of the parting from them. They were too excited by the importance they assumed and the prospect of flying to their father to have much emotion left—and now and then, when they were babbling all at once about Johannesburg and what "we" were going to do there, there would be a moment of vacancy in the face of one or the other, and the remark—"Silly, Mummy won't be there yet." They seemed to believe—or had been told by her?—that she would be following soon. Perhaps it was true, and she had not told him.

Edna Tlume was found sobbing in the Volkswagen after the children left; she had gone there to be alone, and had to be brought out and comforted. Her starched uniform was crushed as if she'd been violated and the ink from the two ballpoints she kept with the scissors in her neat nurse's pocket had leaked a stain. She said to Bray while Rebecca went to fetch a lemon for tea, "Don't tell her—I would never leave my children, never. Don't tell her."

It was not necessary to creep out of his house back to her rooms at the Tlumes' before it was light, now. Gordon telephoned from Johannesburg when the children arrived; it was a radio telephone call, the reception very poor, but sufficient for her to understand that all was well.

They sat under the fig, afterwards, she with her sandals kicked off and her feet up because they were swollen from the heat. "He wanted to be remembered to everyone—the Tlumes, and you."

He said to her, "He asked me to see that you and the children got out in good time, if ever I thought it necessary."

She was tranquil. "Oh? Well now there'll be no need for that." She put out her palm for his, and their hands hung, loosely clasped, between the two chairs.

PART FOUR

The Luxurama Cinema was owned by Ebrahim and Said Joshi, second generation of a family of Indian traders who came to the capital before the railhead. A Joshi brother was usually in the foyer at all performances, making sure the unemployed African youths did not push their way in without paying, but neither was to be seen the day of the opening of the PIP Congress and the expanse of red and green tessellated floor quickly being blocked out by feet in sandals and polished shoes, figures in trailing togas, in Mweta tunics, in dark suits and even in suits with a metallic sheen, and the intense gathering of voices in place of the apathy of cinema queues, gave the place the air of forced occupation. Fish lit up in ornamental tanks (the Joshis claimed theirs "the most lavish cinema in Central Africa") sidled along the glass and gasped mutely at their beaded streams of oxygen, like the playthings of a vanquished people, left behind in panic. The popcorn machine was not working; the soda fountain had been taken over by a committee of Party mothers with hired urns for tea.

Out in the street women's organizations in various quasi-uniforms —the only uniform thing about their dress was its combination of red-and-black PIP colours—sang full strength. One of the Young Pioneer groups had a tea-chest band going. Now and then, shouting Party slogans, holding their flags and banners tottering above people's heads, these celebrants surged into the foyer and made it impossible for lobbying delegates to make themselves heard, or for traffic to move up- and downstairs to where the secretarial committee responsible for the agenda sat in the mezzanine. Press cameras rose like periscopes out of the crush; flash bulbs puffed and caught faces in sudden lightning. A countering surge of impatience rather than the efforts of Party stewards sent the singers and chanters giddying back into the street among children, icecream tricycles, and the motorcycles of the police.

The heat of October—the white settlers used to call it suicide month—held siege outside, but the Luxurama was air-conditioned; in this refrigerator smelling of smoke and chewing gum Bray heard every word fall, suddenly clear of the noise and thick-headed humidity. Mweta walking in to give his opening address matched the mood of confidence Bray felt all around in the quick eyes white against black faces, the tense composure of people who hold ready within them, untouched as yet by any blight of counter opinion, the speeches they have prepared, the points they are going to send home. And Shinza was up there somewhere on the stage among the Executive and Central Committees; slowly the face detached itself; the beard, the way of looking up easily, not out into the auditorium but to one side, as if some invisible confidences were being made to his inclined ear. There he was.

Mweta's tunic had the variation of a small-patterned scarf in the neck; it made a reddish blur from a distance under the lights of the stage, and made one aware of his face among all others even when one was not looking at him. His skin shone; he was healthy and handsome. He began by speaking in his warmly confidential way of the instability of the government machine which was taken over less than a year ago, with the repatriation of the colonial administrative staffs greatly increasing an already chronic shortage of manpower. The country's skills always had been largely provided by expatriates because the colonial power had "thought it unnecessary" to develop the skills of the local population—that was the well-known policy of colonialism. "We were not 'prepared' for independence by the white man and when we fought for it and won, we took our country into our bare hands." From the very first day the fact had been faced that much of the administration and skilled labour would have to continue to be done by expatriates—with the difference that "we are the employers, and they are our employees, now: we pay the piper and call the tune." Considering this difficult, this dangerous, this precarious state of the country when it fell at last into the hands of its rightful owners, how did it look now?

Mweta broke off and looked out and around into tiers of spread knees and faces that he must have been able to half-see in the dimness of the house lights beyond the glare that enveloped him on the stage. He bared his face, a Sebastian to many arrows. And seemed to pluck them, harmless, from his flesh, in advance: yes, there had been certain difficulties, labour troubles in industry and public works, all of which were really the direct consequence of the colonial legacy, the problems shelved and shirked under colonialism, always put aside for another day. "That day is ours"—he switched suddenly to his football-stadium, mass-meeting voice, so that for a moment it was too much for the microphone, and the phrase flew back and forth about the walls—"that day is ours and it has to be dealt with by us just as if the government had created those problems instead of inheriting them. It is easy to please people for the time being, to put something into their hands and send them away happy—for a little while. But what happens when they come back with hands outstretched again, and this time you have nothing to offer, because you have strained the country's economy beyond its resources?" The needs of economic development, at this stage, must prevail over all others. The welfare of the country as a whole was what the government had in mind when it did not, could not and would not accede to the demands of the mineworkers, which were not based on the economy of an independent, developing country, but harked back to the economy that had existed in colonial times. It was understandable that this confusion could arise in the minds of the workers . . . and of course in this country everywhere there were individuals ready to take advantage of the confusion for their own ends. But "the PIP government has to stand tall and look over the heads of its people." The PIP government was settling industrial disputes in the way that served the long-term interests of the workers better than they perhaps could realize—in fact in *their* best possible interests, as well as those of the country as a whole. "During the European war, the British government in the U.K. took special measures, including forbidding the right to strike, in order to keep up industrial output. We are at war, too—with the underdevelopment of our country, with backwardness and poverty. I will never take the easy way out, if it means losing that war. I will never put myself in the position where the people of this country must be turned away empty-handed."

On the last syllable of the high-sounding phrase he produced his usual trick of confronting himself with another concrete accusation—there had been another problem that had had to be dealt with in these first few months. He had given a full statement to the nation at the time, but of course he would always regard it as a special responsibility to account to the Party for what was done in the Party's name. A Preventive Detention Bill had been introduced; a measure to put a stop to any underhand attempts to throw the country off balance at the time when it was still finding its feet. As he had already pointed out, in certain sections of the community impatience for the fruits of freedom could temporarily overcome the people's natural good sense. They were then in danger of falling victim to those sly disruptive forces that appeared all over the new Africa, trying to persuade people to sabotage themselves. It was easy to fan grievances; easier than to satisfy them through hard work and the controlled and orderly growth of the country. "When we have built our state we shall be able to tolerate the quibblers and the plotters as harmless madmen and we won't need preventive detention. It is a temporary measure for our new kind of state of emergency—an emergency not of unrest but of the necessity to get on with the job, unmolested by pests."

There had been a third problem, and this one also was not this country's alone, but common to emergent Africa. Often there was instability and unrest in neighbouring states; stable and peaceful countries found themselves in the position of having to play host to refugees "of one kind and another." These refugees knew perfectly well that they enjoyed the shelter of the country on the strict condition that they did not abuse it. No country could tolerate the presence of "plotting foreigners who violate the right of asylum by bringing arms into the country, and by using the ordinary, peaceful activities of the people as a cover for a traffic in weapons." Fish trucks transporting food from the lake to the capital had been used in this way by refugees. He would not allow anyone to "conduct a war at our expense." These people had been told to leave; and they could consider themselves lucky that they had not been tried in a court of law. The decision about whether such exiles should be tried for bringing in arms lay with the Attorney-General, and he would not fail to act if such incidents occurred again—other refugees could take note.

In spite of "all these troubles we were heir to when we took over" the country's prestige today stood high, both among its fellow African states and in the rest of the world, and, what was more important, the people could see their hopes taking shape in daily life. Africanization was going ahead. In the civil service, nearly half the customs officials were now African. African Provincial Officers had replaced all white District Commissioners. Sixteen African magistrates had been appointed. The command of the police force was in the hands of an African—a reflection of the unity and loyalty of the country that he did not think any other new state could match. In two or three years, even the commander of the army would be "one of our own people."

A new Apprenticeship Bill would see that the private sector of industry played its part in training youth as artisans. Of course the biggest step forward had already been taken—in two years, under the training scheme that had been put into operation immediately with the cooperation of the mining companies, all labour in the mines up to the level of Mine Captain would be African. He was happy to be able to announce for the first time, to this Congress, that he had just been told that the Minister of Education and the Minister of Development and Planning had made successful arrangements for the International Labour Organization to set up a management-training project in the capital. The specific aim would be to train Africans to bridge managerial gaps in commerce and industry, and take over middle-level and senior jobs now held almost exclusively by foreigners. A further aim would be to help expand the economy by motivating more Africans into business. The project would last five years, at the end of which time the United Nations experts would have phased themselves out. The United Nations Special Fund would bear eighty-five per cent of the costs, and the government the remaining fifteen per cent.

He had a way of waiting patiently for applause to end, his mind apparently already moved on ahead to what he was going to tell his audience next; but he gave a quick, wide smile of acknowledgement before he began to speak again. It was education now—"the whole position of education is being urgently reviewed with the object not only of making a full ten years' schooling available to all children, but also of finding a new approach that will cut through the psychological barriers that colonial schools created in the education of our children by relating the learning process only to foreign cultures and putting the idea into their heads that they were being offered a smattering of something that didn't really belong to them." Then he turned to the development of natural resources—the successful negotiations for the vast hydro-electric scheme meant that "our children will know a life of plenty while we ourselves are still alive." It also meant, since it was the joint project of two African states, that the country had taken the first important initiative in Pan-African cooperation, the building of a third world of African achievement, by Africans, for Africans, in Africa. In industry, the foreign mining companies' investment over the next five years would be between thirty-five and forty million pounds. This was the answer to those people, still thinking in terms of dreams before independence became a concrete reality, who "talked nationalization" at this stage. There could be no talk of nationalization in an underdeveloped nation.

He raised both palms to stem applause. This first Congress since the Party had come to power was perhaps the most important one in the Party's history. PIP had become, in effect, the government, and was itself responsible for carrying out the mandate it had been given by the people—it was no longer in the position of putting pressure upon others to do this or that. This called for certain changes. The Party could no longer be set to perform the old functions, the old activities of the struggle for freedom—these had become outdated and wasteful in some instances. It must realign itself in accordance with the functions and activities of a party firmly in power, a party that was not not only the inspiration of the people, but the consolidation and backbone of the government it had put in power. This was the spirit in which, as President, as leader of the People's Independence Party, he had called for this Congress so soon after Independence, sooner than the Presidents of most countries would have cared to report back. He knew that now, just as in the early days of the struggle for freedom, he would find the Congress vigorously adaptable, and ready to offer "the courage and collective wisdom of a truly African leadership gathered from every corner of the country."

The general applause first swamped the different currents of reaction. Then, as the various forms of applause became distinguishable from the general, they also became indicative of the differing forms of the reaction itself, as the instruments of an orchestra are indistinguishable in the crescendo in which they all are sounded, but can be identified when it dies down and some fall silent, while others sustain a theme or variation in which they at once become recognizable: the voice of the oboe, the collective plaint of the strings. Part of the hullabaloo was simply polite—everyone's hands must be seen to move when the President has spoken—and died out, leaving the hard palms of a large section of enthusiasts to keep a heavy brass going, getting louder, backed by the muffled regular stamping of feet on the cinema carpet. This deafening, obliterating racket stirred the dust of an unrest in other sections; men who had been sitting merely resisting any show of accord since they had given their token acknowledgement of the speech, began to move about in their seats, to twist their heads around them, to surge subterraneously towards another solidarity, in opposition.

Bray rested his neck back against his seat for a moment. The air-conditioned spaces were filled with turmoil like the wheeling and counterwheeling of birds. He had the impulse to make contact; to spin a filament between himself and Roly Dando, sitting up there on the stage with his arms akimbo and his ankles crossed under the conference table, the position he had taken up in unconscious defensiveness at the moment when Mweta had referred to his powers as Attorney-General. (Like a member of a private bodyguard, a thug; little Dando.) —Or to catch Mweta himself, straight in the eyes, believing for a moment that Mweta could make him, Bray, out, from that distance. The few remarks about an education plan were almost word for word what he had written to Mweta; they came back to him from the public rostrum, an oblique claim on his anonymous presence there in the crowd. The Secretary-General—Justin Chekwe was Secretary-General of PIP as well as Minister of Justice—was beginning the interminable business of welcoming and introducing representatives of political parties who had come from other countries as observers. Spatters and squalls of applause followed the names: enthusiasm for the TANU man from Tanzania, the UNIP man from Zambia; a half-hearted acknowledgement for the Nasser delegation with their

L

cropped crinkly shining hair, pleasant smiles and trancelike squint-
ing gaze—the country people did not know quite who they were and
for many of the others who did, they were too Left to be given the ac-
colade. In the usual way, Mweta was elected President of the Congress and it was moved that the election of the Party President, office
bearers and committees would be held at the final session.

Attention had drawn in momentarily as this formality was gone
through: it was as though everyone ran his mind's eye over the limits
of the battleground, confirmed in the contours of time. Two and a
half days in which to persuade, to rally, to group and regroup, trade
favours, call in old scores and tot up new ones. In the pale-nailed
dark hands scribbling notes and the unctuous, closed, hearty, determined or uncertain faces were embodied all the intentions gathered
from townships, villages, lake, flood plains, road-side stalls, Freedom
Bars, that cohere slowly in the interstices of daily life. Between
ploughing, drinking, herding, labouring, loafing, dreaming on rush
mats or iron bedsteads, arguing in wattle-and-mud church halls,
lounging over pin-ball machines and planning over second-grade
clerks' ledgers, the formulation comes into being. I want. You want.
He wants. We want. *They* want. The conjugation of human will. Because of it some of these heads about him were lit up within with a
private scene in which this face ousted that and this name took away
from that a prefix of office. Somewhere in the agenda there was the
plan of campaign to be decided; he had some idea of it in advance—
he must have a proper look before the sessions started in earnest. Already, while other formalities of procedure were being got out of the
way, Mweta's address was being sifted away into this memory and
that—slotted, categorized, the intention extracted and the verbiage
discarded. What was Shinza making of it? A thickly built man beside
Shinza hid him from view most of the time.

At the lunch break Bray hung about near one of the fish tanks; his
white face couldn't be missed anyway. The delegates had the gaiety
of boys let out of school before work has even begun; no one got farther than the chatter of the foyer. Several old PIP campaigners came
up to greet him—Albert Konoko, once treasurer (not an entirely honest one but he was long ago relieved of the post and the early "irregularities" forgotten), old Reverend Kawira from the Ravanga district
with his stick and his dog-eared briefcase, Joshua Ntshali, the mayor

of Gala—"We should have made arrangements to come down together—why didn't you give me a tinkle? Plenty of room in my car —some cold beer, too"—the one or two Indians who survived at del-egation-level from the small band who had supported PIP openly from the beginning. People threw cigarette ends in the tank and with his rolled-up agenda he lifted out one at which a fish had begun to nibble. "Poor fish." Shinza stood there. Shinza was good at private jokes derived from other people's absent moments. "You know Basil? Basil Nwanga." He had with him the heavy young man with the tiny hippo ears who had almost run Bray over outside the House of As-sembly one day. They recognized each other, grinning. "I heard him put his word in, in the House, not long ago." Nwanga went off after a few moments with the air of one who had been curious for an intro-duction, got it, and knows he mustn't intrude. "Are you going to eat?" Bray said.

"Where're you staying?" Shinza considered.

"With Dando."

"Oh. Well there's a café down the road. The one near the post of-fice. I'll meet you in a few minutes."

As Bray was leaving Roly Dando came up level with him, but left the distance of two or three people in between. As white men, there was a tacit feeling they shouldn't appear to stick together in any sense; a feeling based, in any case, below its social meaning, on the private inkling that their positions had become very different, al-though they were old friends. Roly said, "Having a good time?" His face was small with gloom. He had changed so much; the sexually spritely, dapper Dando of ten years ago really existed only as one re-membered him; this was the aged, middle-aged face, completely re-moulded by disappointments, desires and dyspepsia, that is more characteristic of a white man than his skin. No African ever trans-formed himself like that.

The shops run by Greeks had always been called "cafés" although they had little enough in common with the European institution from which they took their name. The one near the post office sold the usual fish-and-chips over the counter, for consumption in the street— a relic of the days when black people were not allowed to sit at the tables—and still served the staple frontiersman diet of eggs, steak, and chips. Shinza was already there drinking a glass of some bright synthetic juice that churned eternally in the glass containers on the counter. He held up a finger to settle an important question: "Steak and eggs? Sausage?" "Yes, sausage, I think." Between them on the table was the usual collection of bottles, like antidotes kept handy— Worcester sauce, tomato sauce, bleary vinegar. "Could almost have been old Banda himself in some places, ay," Shinza said; Mweta's address was between them with the sauce bottles.

Bray smiled. "For example?"

Shinza fluttered his hands over the table impatiently. " 'This is the answer et cetera to those who talk of nationalization.' '. . . no sense in talking nationalization in an underdeveloped country.' That's just what the mad doctor himself tells them in Malawi."

"Not quite as bad. *He* always says you have to accumulate wealth before you can nationalize—something like that. 'Nationalization as national suicide.' No—Mweta's was more Senghor's line."

"Senghor?" Shinza grinned at him to prove it.

"Oh yes. Senghor once said it—very much the same as Mweta. He rapped the trade unions over the knuckles and wrote an article saying there was no point in nationalization for an underdeveloped country."

"Ah, I remember what that was about. Yes, I suppose it's possible he did. . . ." Shinza gave his snort, acknowledging himself a man of no illusions. "He's always had it in for socialist-minded unionists. D'you know when that was? That was before sixty-one. When he was fighting UGTAN's demands for the development of a publicly owned sector in the economy. He was busy calling the union boys a hypocritical elite and a lot of other names." He nodded his head significantly at the parallel he saw he had stumbled upon there.

"I haven't had a good look at the resolutions yet. How've you done with the secretarial committee?"

Shinza pressed his shoulders back against the uncomfortable formica chair and his pectoral muscles showed under his rather smart, long-sleeved shirt. He wore no tie but the shirt buttoned up to a pointed collar and there were stitched flaps to match on the breastpockets. The outfit ignored as fancy dress togas or paramilitary tunics (he had worn a Mweta tunic during the days of the independence struggle, so this was a sign that, for him, there was no dilly-dallying in the past) and disdained the terylene-and-wool prestige of the new black middle class. He said—one who knows his chances don't look too good, but prefers to ignore this—"We submitted that the position of the Party in relation to trade union affairs be re-examined, but that was chucked out. *But*—so was the Young Pioneers' one that the Party should support the government 'in its efforts to consolidate the unions against disruptive elements in their ranks.' A little bird told me that's how it went. —I like that one, don't you? I *like* that. As one disruptive element to another." They laughed. "But we had a lot of smaller stuff—resolutions here and there that'll give more or less the same opportunities . . . we had an idea the big one wouldn't make it onto the agenda. . . . We've got quite a few that will do."

"How did the committee manage to squirm out of the big blast?"

"Oh you know—the old formula: all matters that would come under that heading were actually being dealt with separately under other resolutions, so there was no point. Well, we'd thought of that, too. . . . And the Young Pioneers must've been asked to go easy and give in on theirs. No need to have Congress discussing what they're allowed to get away with every day, after all."

Shinza ate quickly and almost without looking at what was on his plate. He cleaned it with bread, like a Frenchman.

Bray paused often. "I see the business of challenging Mweta's power to appoint the Secretary-General of the Trades Union Congress is coming up. How'd you manage that?"

"That's a resolution from the Yema branch—"

"—Yes, so I noticed." At Yema there were railway workshops and phosphate mines; the Party branch was one of the oldest established, started by trade unions organized by Shinza years ago.

Shinza gave his breathy chuckle; released his tongue with a sucking sound. "That was a tough one. They said it was a matter for the UTUC congress itself, not the Party Congress. But as it happened"—he raised his eyebrows and his beard wagged—"several other branches sent in exactly the same resolution . . . so . . . It made things difficult for the committee. They were forced to hear us."

"I was surprised."

Shinza nodded slowly.

"It could be very important," Bray insisted; either a question or a statement, depending on the way Shinza took it.

"It could be—" Shinza was gazing off in absent curiosity at the waiter clearing the next table, and then his eyes came slowly back to Bray and were steady there, his nostrils opened slightly, and tensed.

"You knew about the ILO thing," Shinza said, after a pause, watching Bray saw through his overdone sausage.

"You're not impressed."

"That's what's happening here. Management schemes. A training centre to make a petty merchant class. They'll learn how to get extended credit from the white importers and how to keep a double set of books for when the tax man comes." He tipped back his chair. "Everybody's happy because they think what's behind it is to get the Indians out. As if that solves anything. They think it's a stroke of genius meant to avoid that stupid situation in Zambia when the Indians were told to sell and it turned out there weren't any Zambians who had the money to buy or knew how to run a business. But anyway whatever they think, it's beside the point. It's not the race or the colour of the shopkeeper that needs changing. All middlemen are by nature exploiters; Africanizing the exploiting class isn't going to solve our problems."

It was not necessary for him to say he agreed, there; Shinza knew. "The training might come in useful for other things—running small retail co-ops and so on."

"We should have had something like the Tanzanians got—the ILO's establishing a national institute of productivity in Dar. Even the Ugandan scheme would have been better than this management thing. Small-enterprise training could be adapted along cooperative lines. They've got a fishing and marketing business going on Lake Albert, a carpentry shop in Kampala. Not bad. But you get what you ask for. That's set down in the policy of this sort of international aid —naturally; they can't go on and work against the policies of countries. So we've got a scheme that's for Africanizing an old, free-enterprise society." He turned round the bread-plate with the bill. "Well —let's get on, I suppose. How much's mine?"

"You can pay for me tomorrow."

They screeched the chairs back. Shinza let Bray go through first and said as he passed, "You better not eat with me too often." He stopped to buy cigarettes at the counter. He joined Bray in the glare of the street, putting on big dark glasses so that the secrecy of the beard was reinforced and his whole face was obscured. "Nobody here calls me 'boy' any more. Is it freedom or just I'm getting old?"

"You are not getting old," Bray said. "You may be older, but you are not getting old, I can tell you that."

Shinza pushed his shirt in under his belt, smiling. As they walked he took a match, broke it in two, and probed in his mouth. "My teeth are going."

Shinza, despite his sophistication, remained very African; if you lost your teeth, it was in the nature of things: he probably would not think of going to a dentist to have the process delayed. But Joshua Ntshali had prominent gold-filled teeth; it was simply that for him—Bray—what Shinza did was significant. There are people in whom one reads signs, and others, on the surface equally typical, whose lives do not speak.

"Why shouldn't we eat together?"

Shinza said nothing, threw the match away. "You stay at Dando's place. He might not like it."

"Poor Dando." Roly, too, was an old friend of Shinza's. He was about to say: Dando spoke to me about what happened to you, months ago, the moment I arrived. He got drunk and lamented you. "He's a functionary these days."

"That's so. They might not like it."

He wants to know whether I'm seeing Mweta.

"I don't think my presence anywhere compromises me."

"You don't think." It was not a suggestion that Bray was innocent of the facts of life; it was said almost bitterly, an accusation, a challenge. "But it has, it does, it will. *We* think."

He was faintly riled by the imputation that he fell short somewhere. His defence was, as always, to get cooler and cooler, give more and more evidence of being what he was accused of. "We? You and Mweta?"

Shinza laughed, but it was not a laugh that let Bray off.

Before they reached the cinema Shinza left him with the remark that he had to see someone. "I'm at Cyrus Goma's place," he said.

"Old Town?" The African quarter had always been called Old Town.

"Mm. I think it's number a hundred and seven, main road. Just by the Methodist Church."

"Oh I know."

"The dry cleaners' on the corner will give a message. A Mrs. Okoi. Take the number."

"Dhlamini's mother? I remember her." Dhlamini Okoi was Minister of Posts and Telegraphs; Mweta had just taken Information away from him and made it a separate portfolio.

"That's it. It's really the old Gomas' place I'm staying."

The secretarial committee had been careful to place no big issue on the first afternoon's agenda. The question of the participation of women's organizations produced hard words from the few women delegates—formerly they had attended congresses on a branch and not a regional basis—and they wanted their rights back. (This must have been the reason for the militant female singers outside.) The resolution that "strenuous" efforts be made to build up the State's own diplomatic network instead of continuing to rely on services provided by the former colonial power was the sort of thing that gives an opportunity for people to ride their hobby-horses through—in terms of party politics—an unmined field. Conservative or radical, everyone wanted the country to have its own diplomatic representation; the resolution satisfied patriotic principles even though the government didn't have either the money or personnel to carry it out. A resolution on the Africanization of social amenities, put by the Gala Central Branch, turned out to be Sampson Malemba's baby—Sampson hadn't said a word about it, coming down in the car. But there was no question which particular institution he, personally, had in mind when he spoke of the "white social clubs with valuable amenities, still existing in small towns where such things are not available to the community as a whole." There was one instance he knew where the "dogs' kennels were refused for a community centre workshop." A chest-hum of laughter stirred, rose aloud against him. Malemba looked slowly surprised; he explained that this was no ordinary doghouse. This time the chairman had to call Congress to order. Heads went down at the press table and ballpoints scribbled. Sidelights of Congress: the white editors would transcribe the anecdote into European connotations—Congress Puts White Clubs in Doghouse—and Africans would be puzzled and rather offended at the choice of issues publicized. The women were in splendid form after the vindication of their right to attend Congress in full force. If the chairman evaded one pair of commanding eyes he looked straight into another. A large woman with a turban in Congress colours and a German print skirt down to her ankles cited the "powder rooms" of shops and garages as amenities to be

Africanized. She spoke in her own tongue with the English phrase mouthed derisively. There were lavatories and water taps in these "powder rooms" but the keys were for white ladies only. If white women could put powder on their faces in there, why shouldn't African women be able to go in and wash their babies?

After this, the resolution that wine and liquor be taxed more heavily to discourage excessive drinking wasn't given the serious attention it perhaps deserved. The delegate who spoke to it had the facts and figures all right; fifteen times more liquor had been imported last year than in 1962. And this at a time when the European population was thinning out. The country must be careful not to follow the example of places like Madagascar, where one year liquor held second place of all imports, to the disadvantage of much-needed machinery and equipment. There was more laughter but faces were dutifully straightened when someone invoked the example of the teetotal president. Mweta himself grinned broadly in disarming self-parody of a strong-man showing his muscles. The resolution was carried and ended the day's proceedings and as they edged slowly out into the aisles Bray's neighbour remarked confidentially gaily, "And now we all go off for a beer."

He was back where he started, in the rondavel room at Roly Dando's. He lay on the bed and looked at the light hanging from the ceiling beam and the combed pattern of the thatch. Bluebottles bumbled hopelessly against the fixed central panel of the window and never found the open sections. They thudded and bounced against the unresisting, invisible barrier; at the drowsiness that overcame him. Behind closed lids in the swarming red-dark of himself she was there with her square-jawed, innocently belligerent face, the face of a woman who has always to fend for herself, some draggle-teated female creature whose head, above a well-used body, remains alert for her young. She suggested many things to him. Also an early Greek, in the inevitability that hung about her life. An Iphigenia who would have understood that Agamemnon must trade her for a favourable wind. He thought, perhaps it's that she's a commonplace girl, really, someone very limited, with courage but not the intelligence to use it for herself, and I'm just a middle-aged man enjoying the last kick of the prostate. It was a phrase he and Olivia used tolerantly, of friends'

L*

affairs; he had forgotten who coined it. (He saw the girl's breasts with the marks on them, her meaty thighs really too heavy for trousers.) It could happen to oneself, like cancer or a coronary; like dying. One connected it only with other people, but it could come. —Well, if this was what it was, no need to be tolerant—envy was more appropriate, if the superiorly tolerant ones only knew.

But Olivia would know that, too. Olivia had great intelligence; in the second sense as well, intelligence of everything: the body, too. At the beginning—for years, in fact—they had had that between them; Venetia and Pat, the young matron and the would-be actress, were made out of what had seemed unsurpassable intimacies. Olivia must remember them; but he was living them. For her, with her, they belonged to the past. The body has a short memory. His had forgotten her long before he began to make love to the girl. What had happened to Olivia and to him now seemed as useless to question as the result of an air crash; he was the survivor. He was aware of the sexual arrogance of this interpretation . . . a bird called out, persistently, overhead on the roof and he opened his eyes with a sense of having heard exactly that note before. He bunched the limp pillow behind his neck and set himself to read through the Party Congress agenda slowly, making faint pencil crosses here and there.

Roly Dando had had his operation and no longer interrupted the evening drinking with trips to the bushes, but the look of some annoying inner summons that twinges of the bladder had brought to his face had become permanent. With poor Dando, with everyone he met in the capital, Bray felt his own well-being must announce itself for what it was; that it would be as easily recognized, in its way, as the dark-ringed eyes of the adolescent masturbator. But Dando said nothing. The distance between them was difficult to analyse. Whether it was a matter of sexual energy, of age, of changing political and personal directions, was something that could not be separated from the atmosphere of the garden, which was not as it had been, although they sat there together just as they had always done.

Dando, too, had noticed that Mweta's intention to take to himself the right of appointing the Secretary-General of the United Trades Union Congress was coming up on the PIP Congress agenda. He dismissed Bray's surprise that it had got so far. "There isn't anything that isn't Party business. I suppose Shinza drummed up so much support, the secretarial crowd couldn't avoid it. Just as by bringing the whole trade union affair under fire at Congress, Shinza can't avoid showing his hand. He must have good reason to believe he's going to be Secretary-General again himself, if it's left to UTUC elections in the old way."

"Mweta's shown his hand too. If he's going so far as to bring in a new act just to keep Shinza out of the unions."

"Oh it'll only be a proclamation, you don't have to bother with a new act. The old Industrial Conciliation Act allows for it, it's a piece of good old colonial legislation, tailor-made to keep the blacks in their place. It'll do perfectly now." Dando drained the bottom of his glass, where the gin had settled, and pulled the skinny tendons of his jaw wryly.

"If Shinza became Secretary-General of UTUC again it would provide a perfect opening."

"For what, man, for what?"

"If Mweta would see it. A perfect opening to take Shinza back into the fold without loss of face. Shinza would have taken the step out of 'retirement' himself, he would have the one key position outside government; Mweta could simply put out his hand without patronage and without humbling himself in the least, and take him in. And the solution to labour troubles, the end of the split factions in the unions, at the same time. He would have a strong government then, all right."

"With Edward Shinza breathing fumes down his neck."

Bray smiled. "He isn't drinking these days."

"It's not brandy I'm thinking of. The revolutionary spirit."

"No harm in a bit of that."

Dando settled back for attack, his chair a lair. "I should bloody well hope so. I should bloody well hope there *is*. I don't know what mugs like me've wasted our time for on this continent if the ideas we brought to it haven't any harm in them for the set-up the blacks took over from the whites."

"Well, there you are."

"Here I am, all right." Dando's look lunged hit-or-miss round his garden; caught, his old dog cautiously wagged its tail. "But Mweta isn't going to have any continuing revolution stuff pressed on him by Edward Shinza or anyone else. When he talks about building on solid foundations and so on he means just that—not the peasants' toil and all that, but also the two-bricks-high capitalist state that was already under way here. He may put on a few decent outbuildings of state-owned enterprise here and there, you understand—but there'll be no change of style in the main structure. It'll look a bit like a Swiss bank—or perhaps a West German one's better. The extended family will have their huts in the grounds and they'll get quite a few pickings from Golden Plate dinners, they'll be better off than they were before, mind you, and they won't mind. Mweta genuinely believes that's the best he can do and he'll certainly do it the best way it can be done. A little black *Wirtschaftswunder*. If he let Shinza near at all—if he let him climb up by way of UTUC, he knows quite well what he'd have on his hands—the risk of the trade unions setting up in opposition to the government. That's what Edward Shinza's after, that's his comeback by constitutional means, that's what he's going to try for, and our boy knows it." He poured another drink for Bray as if to stop his mouth.

"I can't see it. I don't think Shinza'd stand a chance. If he's making a bid for power through the unions, it's to put himself in a position where, as I said, Mweta can recognize he needs him, as he always did. It's strange, even now when he talks against Mweta, sometimes with pretty strong resentment—he has a kind of concern, a feeling of responsibility, for him; still. Anyway—feeling or no feeling—I don't see he'd stand a chance of the other thing."

"Why in God's name not? Don't you see? Do I have to spell it out, Bray? You know UTUC and the Party have always been virtually the same thing, all these years until now. They both drew members from the same class, they had a similar intellectual formation—as far as political methods and social and economic attitudes were concerned, there wasn't any major difference between them. Some of the leaders of both were even the same people! Look at Shinza himself—first chairman of PIP and at the same time Secretary-General of UTUC. And Ndisi Shunungwa and a bunch of others. In spite of this, a situation could have developed early on where although they were in double harness the one could have pulled ahead of the other, eh?—you could have had the situation where a labour organization comes into conflict with a less progressive-minded political party. It didn't happen—it couldn't happen then because of two factors: the country wasn't free of outside political domination and it hadn't reached a certain level of industrialization. Eh? But now it's a different story. We're independent, the front line's not at Government House any more. In theory, UTUC ought to give purely professional considerations priority, now—they ought to go for corporate trade unionism. But UTUC is also virtually an integrated trade union, eh, part of the state, supposed to carry out the state's policy and aims—wasn't there even a clause to this effect in UTUC's constitution? I'm damn sure there was. UTUC's the representative of the workers and the junior civil servants, but it's also a kind of strong arm of the state department of labour—and that's a hell of a balancing act to bring off, my lad. UTUC's become a two-headed calf and there's Shinza's chance to make the killing. All he has to do is set himself up as champion of the rights of the workers against the state's domination of the unions and subordination of the welfare of the workers to the demands of the state. He's doing it. Look at his inspiration." He chopped his up-ended palm on Bray's agenda, with its marked resolutions. "He's done it with a dozen wildcat strikes all over the country. They listen to him on the quiet and defy their own union officials because the contradiction with its built-in dissatisfactions is there already—the two-headed calf."

"You've given the answer yourself!" He had been scratching the surprised dog energetically behind the ears while Dando talked, waiting an opening. Now he gave the dog a final thump. "You say that before Independence, even if the trade unions had found themselves in conflict with a less progressive-minded party, they couldn't have set up a successful opposition because the country hadn't reached a certain level of industrialization. The working class wasn't big enough. But this still applies. There still hasn't been industrialization on a scale nearly extensive enough to bring about any considerable increase in the size of the wage-earning class. UTUC simply hasn't the numbers and consequently hasn't the major economic resources to establish itself in opposition to Mweta's government. Under Shinza or anyone else. Shinza's been in the union movement since he was on the Boss Boys' committees as a youngster on the mines, remember. He's been around in other African states. Remember he's an old buddy of Ben Salah; he knows who came off worst in Tunisia in the clash between the trade union organization and the Neo-Destour gov-

ernment . . . it's the same sort of thing here. Shinza must know that
at this stage it can't be done."

"It can be tried. Anyway, if Shinza could bring off even a Ben
Salah here I've no doubt he'd consider himself lucky. If you can't beat
'em, join 'em. Perhaps he sees himself, the old union leader turning
the screw on the government so successfully that he ends up making
a gala appearance, *à la Salah,* as Minister of Planning and Finance a
few years from now. And perhaps Mweta sees that in one of his teetotal cups and wants to make sure it doesn't happen."

While their voices grew louder and cut across each other vehemently the bats of early evening were flitting about them, an embodi-
ment of things that went unsaid. In a pause—the air thickened quite
suddenly with darkness, he could no longer see Dando's small face
clearly and felt his own to be hidden—he thought how they talked of
Shinza as if he had been in another country, an interesting man in an
interesting political situation one read about, instead of a mile or two
away, in the Gomas' house in Old Town. It was from Dando that this
attitude imposed itself. He was an old man in an official position, and
all his fiery objectivity was academic; as he had said himself, once, he
worked for Mweta. Shinza could not enter into consideration, in his
personal life.

After dinner he excused himself without saying where he was going
and drove to Old Town. The approach had not been improved;
streets were still untarred and streetlights irregularly few. He passed
the bar in an old shop where he had gone with Bayley and the others, that time, during the Independence celebrations. It had been Rebecca's discovery, but she was not with them; he remembered waiting
in the car outside the shabby flat building where she lived, while Neil
Bayley threw pebbles at her windows. But the flat was in darkness;
another time, another Rebecca.

He made out Mrs. Okoi's dry-cleaning shop in this present darkness
and what must be the Goma house just opposite; there once had been
numbers painted on the brick but they were long worn off. This was
one of the more prosperous streets and there were no cooking bra-
ziers out, but children and gangs of youths occupied it with their
yells, laughter, and games, the smallest ones standing about asleep on
their feet like a donkey that stood quietly nearby. The core of the
standard two-room house had been built onto all round and there was

a strip of polished concrete leading to a front veranda; the gate was missing and a dog tied to a wire between two stakes that enabled it to run up and down, brought up with a strangling jerk at either limit, struggled like a hooked fish to get at him. He knocked a long time before someone came: a pretty small child in pyjamas. It looked at him and ran away. But he could hear voices, and Shinza's laugh, beyond the tiny room the door opened on to. Straight-backed chairs in the room, a refrigerator and a *Home Encyclopaedia,* an old sofa made up as a bed for two more small children who were asleep under the bright light. At last the inner door opened with a glimpse of faces and gesticulation through cooped-up heat and smoke. A woman looked at him and at once looked back into the room for direction, but Cyrus Goma appeared impatiently, and as soon as he saw who was there came forward and shut the front door behind Bray in welcome. "Come right in. My mother . . . My younger brother . . . Basil Nwanga . . . Linus Ogoto . . ." It was full house, with Congress in town. Shinza was on his feet and standing pleasedly about; he put an arm on Bray's shoulder. Two men were playing cards at the end of the table, oblivious, looking down at their hands and up at each other, not speaking. A lad was doing his homework in a corner he'd found for himself on the floor. The radio was playing. A young woman brought a pink glass with a gilt rim and Shinza poured Bray a beer. Cyrus Goma's mother, like a household god in its shrine, sat a little apart on a strange dark wood chair, a sort of small pew that clearly no one else would ever dare occupy. On a second look Bray realized that it was an old-fashioned commode that had been adapted for less private usage; whatever member of the Goma family had acquired it probably had had no idea of its original purpose. The old woman was large and black as only people from the part of the country that bordered on the Congo were. The features Cyrus had inherited were a pencil sketch of the central motif fully developed here; the head blocked out massively, the nostrils scrolled, the wide down-turned lips blue-tinged with age, the eyes bloodshot, one slightly bulging (a mild stroke, perhaps), the earlobes, now empty of the copper rings they had once held, hanging in self-ornament, contemptuous of all adornment, down to the thick shoulders. Under her long cotton dress her feet were bare. She did not speak, acknowledging Bray only with a deep breath and then, from that drawn-up height, a grand in-

clination of the head. Every now and then she hawked and took snuff
with a noise that everyone ignored. This was both sad and a sign of
respect commanded: she was not banished for the dirty habits of senility, but neither was she taken any notice of.

Shinza was in the mood that used to come to him on the eve of
elections when PIP first began to contest settler seats. He made self-
deprecating jokes, game rather than confident. A David rather than a
Goliath. The man who had been introduced as Linus Ogoto went
point by point through the resolution he was going to lead next day,
that the salaries of government personnel were too high. He was a
forceful man with a corrugated face and head—even the fleshy
shaven scalp was quilted with lines so that the intensity of the
changes in his expression were not confined to the face but ran over
the whole head. He lectured Bray in fluent, heavily accented English:
"You know what the estimated figure is? Forty-seven per cent of the
budget. Ministers and shop-front managing directors like Joshua
Ntshali—" "Careful, Ntshali's a neighbour of James's," Shinza put in.
"—They're getting three to ten thousand a year. —Our unskilled
workers earn between thirty pounds and seventy-two. —Wait a minute, I haven't finished. I've got a few other figures. Free house, basic
car allowance seventy-five pounds, special extra allowance of one
shilling a mile on official trips, and any day they like, cheap petrol
from the PWD pumps. Senior civil servants and officials of the corpo-
rations get very much the same privileges."

Cyrus Goma and Nwanga were both M.P.s and had a good salary
and some privileges themselves; but of course they were not cabinet
ministers. It seemed taken for granted by them that they would accept cuts in their salaries; this surely would not fail to be noticed
when they were lobbying among ordinary people. "I've got the figure
for the average earnings of Congress delegates. Seventy-three per cent
earn under six hundred a year, and of that seventy-three per cent
nearly three quarters earn between thirty and a hundred a year.
That's all."

"Cash earnings, of course—? Subsistence crops and so on don't
come into it, ay?" Under his levity Shinza was alert to holes into
which opposition would poke its way.

"Cash earnings. What a cabinet minister gets from his garden in
the land doesn't come into the reckoning for him, either."

Shinza nodded rapidly, satisfied.

Nwanga said to Bray, "The Dondo and Tananze crowd are going to back that up full strength. They want a freeze for all earnings above six hundred a year."

"Well, nearly everybody in that hall earns less than six hundred. They shouldn't feel like disagreeing." Ogoto looked as if he were staring them all out.

"That was some detective work, Linus," Shinza said aside. "How'd you do it?"—referring to the figures for delegates' earnings.

"I was on it for months, man. People don't answer letters, you know—you have to keep on at them. It's cost me a lot in stamps." Ogoto laughed suddenly, embarrassed, and his ears moved the hide of his scalp. Then once he had overcome the embarrassment of praise it went rather to his head; he couldn't stop talking, with intense enjoyment, of the trouble he had gone to. He told one anecdote after another; everyone laughed except the card players and the schoolboy, burrowing down in their concentration, and the old woman.

Bray talked to Cyrus Goma about a resolution concerning peasant workers. He had noticed it was to come from the Southern Province's regional council—Goma's seat was in the Eastern—but Goma knew its terms precisely. "The idea is farm workers should be recognized as the personnel of an agricultural industry, and they should be organized, just like any other sector of industry. Seventy-one per cent of workers in this country are still on the land. They haven't any proper representation, no properly laid-down conditions of employment, no minimum wage, nothing. Of course it's a tricky thing to work out— most of them aren't employed full time as cash wage-earners, as you know. They're employed seasonally by white farmers; part of the time they work their own or tribal land; or they're squatters allowed to work some of the white man's land in exchange for a share of the crop. . . ."

"Is there good support?"

Goma gave a short laugh. "In principle. Who'll get up and say he's against improving the life of nearly three quarters of the working population? But people can hold back for other reasons."

"Of course. Organize that seventy-one per cent of peasants and the trade unions increase their power out of all recognition."

Goma shrugged. Whenever Bray approached the definition of

policy behind the separate resolutions of Shinza's faction, Goma presented a bland front. Shinza was back in discussion with Linus Ogoto
and Nwanga, his cigarette waggling on his lip. ". . . In Guinea, I
mean, don't let's forget the issue of Africanization didn't arise . . . the
French pushed off as soon as Sékou opted out of the French Community, there were no more expatriate civil servants earning fat salaries
for local people to compare themselves with. They were on their own.
It was easy to introduce drastic salary cuts. But you must be very
careful how far it goes . . . if you get deteriorating wage scales and
fringe benefits at the level of, say, the teachers, it's a boomerang"—he
yawned, now and then, with excitement—"you get their union cam-
paigning for a review of salaries again—"

Shinza was disturbed at the fact that the question of Mweta taking
power to appoint the Secretary-General of UTUC was placed early
on the next afternoon's agenda. A man in a grey suit with tribal nicks
on his cheekbones said, "They want to get it out of the way." Shinza
ignored him, ignored Bray's eyes. He leaned his elbow on the table,
put his hand over his mouth and gave a heavy sigh through distended
nostrils: "Out of the way." Of course, he wanted to have time to make
an impression on Congress, to demonstrate over several days his return to active leadership and his claim to support before the issue
came up. He was half-forgotten and he must remind PIP of what he
still was and could be. Then whichever way it went—if the motion
were to be defeated and Mweta took to himself the right of appointing UTUC's Secretary-General and overlooked him, or if it succeeded
and UTUC's executive retained the right to elect him—Shinza's political stock would rise.

Cyrus Goma said something to Shinza about the time. The little
group took on the wariness, eyeing each other, of people expected
elsewhere. Shinza scorned the mystery. "If you feel like it, come
along . . . ? If you wanted to . . ." Goma with his hunched head
frowned down at himself; the others stood awkwardly. Shinza sensed
the pressure of disapproval and passed over the invitation as if Bray
had already refused, "I'm sorry . . . we're just pushing off to see
Dhlamini Okoi." So Okoi, Minister of Posts and Telegraphs, was in
the Shinza camp too, now. Shinza smiled lazily to see that conclusion
in Bray's face. But Goma looked sharply, gloomily annoyed. Bray
paid his respects to the old woman again. Now that Bray was on his
way out, Cyrus Goma was pleasant with relief, chatting to show that

there was nothing personal. ". . . after all these years. And how's Mrs. Bray? She's happy out there in England? When you write please give her my greetings, I don't know if she remembers me. . . ." He still had on the West African cotton robe that was his form of dress for public appearances. "Let's go." Shinza gave the word. He said to Bray, as if in confidential amusement at the attitude of the others— "Till tomorrow morning. Don't get into trouble in the big city."

It was not yet ten o'clock and the darkness was thickly hot. A flying cockroach got into the car and slid itself, flattened like a knife-edge, under the torn floor mat when he swatted at it. Well, there were probably tasty pickings beneath the seats and in crevices, left over from journeys with the children. They had made the car as homely with crumbs and broken toys as Rebecca's always was. He didn't feel like bed, or drinking with Roly; he thought he would go round by way of the Silver Rhino and say hello to the Wentzes. They would expect him some time and he didn't mean to linger in the capital after Congress was over. The Rhino was full; "Reduced rates for delegates—what can you do," Hjalmar said. "We have to pay the staff the same, no matter what the guests pay." Margot was in bed; "Not ill?" "Who knows, with Margot? She says she's tired; and she's ill. She says she's ill; and she's tired. I want her to go on a holiday. She says why don't I go away for a few days." He left the office unattended and they sat in the little private sitting-room with its round table under the cone of light from the low-hanging shade, the windows of this Vuillard interior pushed gasping-wide into the hot night smelling of red dust and grass fires. Hjalmar Wentz always generated the immediate intimacy of someone who has no one to talk to; he gave the impression, tonight, of a prisoner of whose cell Bray unknowingly had sprung the lock. The son Stephen had taken his A levels but there was no question of a university—it was the first time for as many generations they knew of in either his (Hjalmar's) family or Margot's that anyone simply left school and became one of the half-educated *petite bourgeoisie*. "He is a natural colonial—the adaptable kind who enjoys the sort of popularity you get when you run a bar and everybody calls you Steve—you know what I mean. There's nothing you can do about it. Everybody likes him. Margot finds it disgusting. Of course I don't exactly rejoice . . . but I see it as a solution to the problem of survival, nhh? We brought him here, in this world and this place, and that is how he's worked things out for himself. Not intellectually, you understand—he has only instincts. Margot in Europe never knew such people. Her father, the old professor —when they went to a spa, he took all his meals in a private room. They were taught that solitude and contemplation develop the human faculties and wasting time with stupid people prevents them from—inhibits them. He was a great Hegelian; they were made to turn every accepted idea round about and think the opposite before making up their minds—you know, negative thinking and all that. He had a great contempt for middlemen . . . well, who hasn't, specially if you have to become one. But he never did . . . he died before that might become necessary. Ah-ja-a-ah!"—it was not the German exclamation, but the unmistakable longer-vowelled Scandinavian one, with a rising cadence at the end—"All very Jewish-intellectual, although he hardly considered himself a Jew. If he'd been in Eastern Europe instead of Germany the old man would've been one of those Talmudic holy men who don't have anything to do with earning money—part of the rabbinical tradition that to him was a much worse kind of ghetto than the real ones."

Bray remembered the daughter was named after that remote and forbidding European. To distract Hjalmar from his son, he turned his attention to the girl he was much closer to. "And Emmanuelle? How's her musical career on the radio going?"

"She broadcasts regularly every Thursday evening." Hjalmar looked slightly taken aback; surely that was something everyone knew. But Bray never listened to anything except the news and was oblivious of his neglect.

"Oh, jolly good."

Hjalmar rejected his own easy pride in her as contemptible. "She should be at the conservatoire in Copenhagen. In Paris. Blowing little flutes made of sticks and pinging away at bits of tin over a calabash. Ahh, I can't talk about it. And now Margot with her ideas"—he took a breath and held it; let go hopelessly—"now Margot goes and brings her to the doctor, to fix her up. You take a pill and you take a man just like an aspirin, too." He was addressing the absent Margot. "Who are you to decide for her whether she's going to sleep with any man who comes along? She didn't ask for it; you decide. You decide that's how girls live these days." He turned away from himself. Accusations followed him. "And I'm the one who is out of touch with reality, I'm the one who lives in a dream world. Oh yes. Any man with five or six

children and a wife at home in the bush is all right for her, there's
nothing to worry about because Emmanuelle is protected. Against
what? Can you tell me? Are there no miseries and sorrows left once a
woman knows she will not risk a child?"

"We do what we can, that's all," Bray said.

"Your daughters are married."

"Yes. That's no form of immunity, either."

There was an easy pause; Hjalmar tugged the rim of his well-
shaped ear. "You know, often I've felt I'd like to come up to your
place for a couple of days—just a break, just to have a look. I've seen
nothing of the country."

"Well, why don't you."

"An idea to play with." He shrugged. "You can't get away half a
day, in this game. It's becoming more impossible to get staff, all the
time. Margot's just been back in the kitchen again—the cook was
stabbed in a fight. Well, what can I do? You can't call up cooks from
thin air. I've told her, what we should do is get someone out from Europe, an immigrant. Advertise in Italy or Germany."

Emmanuelle appeared, at once the expression on her face registering: on about that again. She held out her slender sallow hand, shaking it like a tambourine. "Keys, keys, please. —Hullo, Colonel Bray, I
didn't know you were here."

"Unfortunately he's snubbed us this time, he's with Mr. Dando.
We're deserted."

What did one say to girls of Emmanuelle's age? Not you've grown
. . . although it seemed she had. She looked taller than when he had
seen her last, and even more elegantly thin. They chatted a few moments; but she asserted an equality of adult status that, of course,
they had established last time. He had forgotten the talk in the garden. "Come and have a drink with us," she said, leaving the invitation open, as if he would know the company she had temporarily left.
She shook her hand for the keys again, standing legs planted apart,
before her father. "What do you want?" "Never you mind." He
smiled, giving in. "No, Emmanuelle, what is it?" "I'm going to unlock
all the family secrets and display before the jealous eyes of the populace all the family jewels, that's what." Her dark, narrow face was
still bare of any make-up but her hair was grown and hung forward
on either side of her long neck from the pointed peak of her skull,
straight, coarse and shiny. She looked at him with love and pity, a

strangely ruthless and devouring look. So one might make the decision to put down a faithful and beloved horse, when the time came. Then she was gone, with her sloppy stalk, very female in its disdain of femininity.

Hjalmar Wentz was another person when speaking of matters outside his private life. In a curious reverse, his public self was preserved as a retreat where he felt himself to be most himself, shored up against attrition. He leant intensely forward (he still wore espadrilles and rumpled linen trousers, as if he had been kidnapped on holiday from Denmark on the Costa Brava) while they talked of the strikes and disturbances of the last few months. "Behind every good man in the politics of reform, there is a gang of thugs. —No different for him. In a country of illiterate peasants they know the arguments to persuade where reason isn't understood." Mweta's opening address was in the evening paper; THIS DAY IS OURS—PRESIDENT MWETA. "What does it mean to people when he says the needs of economic development come before anything? What does it mean if he says work, and more work, and still more work? But when the Pioneer boys beat them up when they defy the unions and strike, *then* they understand. They know then that the union is the Party and the Party is the country. It's all one and anybody who squeals at what the union bosses decide is a traitor. Between ourselves, I hear the fact is the Pioneer hooligans are the only active link left between the Party and government in lots of places. The pity is that he's let Party organization in the bush go to pots"—Hjalmar didn't always get his English idioms right—"the branches are neglected . . . if the youths didn't kick up a row plenty of country branches would feel they had no connection with the PIP government at all. . . . It's a mistake. . . . But what can you do. He's had to centralize for efficiency. Well, these are teething troubles."

"The trouble is many of the Young Pioneers are already a bit long in the tooth."

"Yes, well, that's the paradox of these countries—a shortage of manpower and a surplus of unemployables."

"We'll need two and a half thousand school-certificate holders, alone, next year, and thirteen thousand in fifteen years' time. On a hopeful estimate, there won't be more than a thousand next year. But in fifteen years it should be possible to make it."

"That's what you're working on, eh?" Hjalmar acknowledged the comfort of figures, perhaps spurious. "You are right. I still believe education's the only hope. I still have to believe it, in spite of everything"—he meant Germany, the failure of the knowledge of human sciences to make people more humane; that axis his life had turned on. "Nowadays it's love, eh? Back to love. And not even Christ's formula. I don't trust it any more than I would hate."

Bray said, "In Europe we've talked from time to time of a lost generation, but in Africa there really is one. What's going to happen to them?"

"They help to make the coups, I suppose. Who knows? —They'll get old and go home to grow cassava somewhere. We won't be here to see."

"But even now you'd say things aren't going too badly?" Bray asked, curiously.

"No. No. On the whole. He's keeping his head."

"And his promises?"

Hjalmar took on the look of an old woman giving a confidence. "He made too many. Like everyone. But if they give him time. If they don't squeeze him from all sides, the British and Americans, the OAU."

"I'm afraid the involvement of the Young Pioneers is simply something on the side—a circumstantial phenomenon. They're there; they're idle; as you said, their very hooliganism has a certain function in being just about the only dynamic participation in the country's affairs left to some PIP branches. But forgetting about them for a moment—what happened in the rolling strikes at the gold mines, the dispute on overtime at the iron-ore mine, that affair at the Kasolo railway: they are all signs that the workers are losing confidence in the unions. They don't feel the unions speak for them any more. All the way from the smallest local matters right up to federation level decisions affecting them are being made over their heads. If the Secretary-General becomes a presidential appointment, UTUC will be more or less part of the Ministry of Labour. —It's no good bringing in PIP chaps to break the heads of people who strike against wage agreements and so on made without proper consultation. The split in the unions is the real issue."

"But is that a fact? The President would never encourage a fascist situation here. No one can tell me that. He would never allow it. He doesn't like totalitarianism of the left or the right, it's all the same to him. . . . But this man Edward Shinza—you used to know him?—people say he's behind the whole thing."

Bray had forgotten that he was the one who was asking questions. "But it's a real thing. He hasn't invented it. All these issues are coming up openly at the Congress. It'll be a great pity if they're fought down as a power bid."

Hjalmar Wentz wriggled confidentially in his chair. "Isn't that what it is?" His smile confirmed the shared experience of a generation. "Well, it's interesting to be there—you are lucky. Is that cinema all right? There was talk at the beginning they might want to hold it here, you know. . . ."—a twinge of amused pride—"but I suppose we've got enough troubles."

Emmanuelle, Ras Asahe, and a rumpled young white man were sitting in the residents' lounge. She hailed Bray as he left; he refused a drink but stood talking a moment. The young Englishman had the amiably dazed and slightly throttled look of one who has been sleeping in his clothes, in planes, for some weeks. He was from one of the weekly papers or perhaps a news agency correspondent (again, Bray was expected to know, from his name) and was on the usual tour of African states. Ras Asahe was briefing him on people he ought to see; stuffed in his pockets he had a great many scraps of paper from which he tried to identify various names recommended to him by other names: "Basil said not to miss this chap, wha'd'you-call-it. . . . Oh and do you know a fellow . . . Anthony said he's marvellous value. . . ." He said to Bray, "I'm sure someone gave me *your* name?"

"Oh yes, Colonel Bray is one of the well-known characters," Ras Asahe said.

Emmanuelle gave Bray one of her infrequent and surprisingly beautiful smiles, in acknowledgement of the slightly sharp imputation, due to Ras's equally slight misunderstanding of the nuance of the English phrase.

"You're the one who was imprisoned or something, with the President?"

"Just or something."

"Don't snub him." Emmanuelle put Bray in his place; it was perhaps her way of flirting with the journalist. She slumped in the deep sofa with the broken springs, her little breasts drooping sulkily and apparently naked under the high-necked cotton dress.

"Colonel Bray knew that crowd well—my father, old Shinza." Asahe, the man of affairs, turned to Bray with a flourish—"They ought to put Shinza inside, ay? The trouble is the President's too soft with these people."

The journalist was still matching identities. "You don't know a man called Carl Church? I think he was the one who mentioned you. Used to be with the *Guardian* . . . about forty-five, knows Africa backwards."

He did know Carl Church; but when he began to ask for news of him, it turned out that the young man didn't—they'd met for the first time in a bar in Libreville a few days before.

He said goodnight. "Why d'you want Edward Shinza imprisoned, Ras?"

"He ought to be expelled from the Party, at any rate. They say he's been to Peking with Somshetsi. . . . Anyway. Well, that's the story. But he was going round holding secret meetings with the gold miners, he gave them the blue-print for the rolling strike, masterminded the whole business. How could they've had the knowhow on their own? I had an idea to do a live documentary, interviews and such, talking to the strikers—but the new Ministry of Info' boss turned it down . . . it had to be played cool, so . . . If I'd've done it, Edward Shinza'd have been inside by now."

Ras Asahe had the particular laugh of complete self-confidence (as Bray remarked of him to the Bayleys) guaranteed not to dent, scratch, or fade. No wonder the Wentz girl, who loved her father, the natural victim, was attracted to one in whom the flair for survival was so plain. One ought perhaps to comfort Hjalmar by pointing out that Emmanuelle, too—not only her brother—displayed an unconscious instinct of self-preservation.

Linus Ogoto's branch resolution condemning the high salaries of government personnel turned up the pitch of Congress early on in the morning session. A wary silence stalked his first few sentences, but concentration and alarm pressed in as he went on, scaling the abstraction of figures and suddenly coming up face to face with a petrol pump doling out free petrol; arranging percentages like a handful of cards; on behalf of Congress, inviting himself to take one—any one—and producing the dimensions of the weekly cut of cheap meat a labourer could buy his family on his contribution of man-hours as compared with the man-hours that brought the official his chicken—sometimes deductible as entertainment allowance into the bargain.

A woman near Bray sounded to these revelations, very low, like a cello accidentally bowed. Men who belonged to the income group under attack showed the wry superior patience with which the rich everywhere remark the poor's ignorance of the bravely borne burdens of privilege. When the debate opened two or three of them rose to the chairman's eye wherever he rested it; eloquence swelled against fountainpen-armoured breast-pockets. It was asked again and again whether high-ranking government personnel would be expected to clock in the hours of sleep that were lost while problems affecting the life of the nation kept them up far into the night? The claims of these men to a "modest remuneration" for their knowledge and untiring

work—"what a lie to talk about man-hours because the truth is that
in a big position you can't knock off at five like any lucky workman"
—almost defeated the motion, but Ogoto's innocent revelation that
three-quarters of the delegates present themselves earned under six
hundred pounds a year was enough to tip the decision in his favour.
Ogoto's mouth was twitching; Bray saw he had to purse it to control
an impulse of triumph. He kept smiling uncertainly in this direction
and that like a short-sighted person who doesn't want to seem to ignore greetings. Up on the stage, Shinza smoked.

In a curious kind of contradiction of Ogoto's success, the Tananze
branch's call for a freeze of earnings above six hundred produced uncertainty in Congress. Jason Malenga, the Minister of Finance, did
not actually admit the whole basis of the political system might be
challenged by more equal distribution of money, but warned that a
wage freeze and levelling-off would endanger foreign investment; he
got the matter referred to a select committee.

The beginning of the rural branches' offensive, asking for the organization of agricultural workers, and the demand for a minimum
wage according to region with which it was linked, also took a little
time to get under way. The chairman had first to clear the debate of
speakers who wanted to ramble through local cases of the abuse of
farm labour rather than speak to the issue itself; there was restlessness, and the sense of conflicting preoccupations. Shinza, Goma,
looked stony. Then, emerging as though it had not been there all the
time, the particular pattern of this Congress, the disposition of human
forces present in the gathering, began to come clear. Bray knew the
moment from all the conferences, talks, discussions of his life: there
was always a time when what the gathering was really about came
out strongly and unmistakably as the smell of burning. No conventions, evasions or diplomacy could prevent it. Since many of the
Party officials and leaders were also in the government, there was always some member of the appropriate government department to
give—in the guise of his presence as a Party delegate—the government line on each issue. The Under-Minister for Agriculture had been
primed for this one. The seasonal nature of farm work, primitive
farming methods, and the predominance of unskilled labourers who
still keyed their efforts to subsistence rather than production, he said
with almost bored urbanity, made the organization of farm workers

totally impracticable and "ten years too soon." "The government's agricultural development schemes must first be allowed to make the
land more productive. He warmed to the common touch. "It's always
been traditional for people to hire themselves out for weeding or har-
vesting when the white farmers need them—are we going to say that
these women and children and old people who can't work regularly
must give up their chance to earn a little cash and help cultivate the
lands, because the organization of farm labourers along the lines of
factory workers will forbid it? You can't make a modern working
community out of the most backward part of the country, overnight;
not by a charter or any other bit of paper."

Cyrus Goma, his robe hitched up on his one high shoulder, agreed
that agricultural development schemes were essential—"Of course
most of them, too, are still bits of paper. But agrarian backwardness
can't be changed only by giving people dams and lending them tractors and sending out someone to teach contour ploughing. However
backward and unskilled people are they have to live now in a modern money economy, and the first step is to recognize that their labour must be assessed in terms of that economy. The money they
have to have to buy things with is the same as anyone else's; the
work they do to earn it must be valued in terms of that money, not as
what the white farmer thinks is enough for old women and children.
This principle will never be established until the farm workers are organized like any other worker. And the haphazard working of the
land—the persistence of the old ways of our grandfathers who
burned down enough trees for space to plant just enough crops to
feed themselves, and moved on to another place when that soil was
worked out—this won't become a high-production, modern agricultural industry until the farm worker is an organized worker. How can
there be an industry without proper wage scales, conditions of work,
social benefits? Without these things the farm worker remains a serf."
The deeper his accusations went the drier his voice became. "I want
to ask Congress whether the pledges that were made by the Party for
the whole population are now for the people in the towns alone?" He
paused but was rejected by silence. "—If you don't want to ask yourselves that, then perhaps you'll let me tell you that experts of very
different political opinions all agree on one thing: agrarian backwardness always slows and sometimes prevents entirely any possibility of

rapid economic expansion as a whole. In England the agricultural
revolution, the enclosures of the sixteenth to eighteenth centuries,
greatly facilitated the industrial revolution. In America, in Japan as
recently as a hundred years ago, it was rapid agricultural reform that
made the industrial miracles of these countries possible. In France,
the land tax of the movement known as the physiocrats . . ."—Bray
recognized a string of quotations from the fashionable agronomist
René Dumont.

"What a cruel thing, to come along to us on the farms with meetings and ask money to pay membership for union and tell us we will
get all sorts of things we will not get." A young man was on his feet;
whether he actually had caught the chairman's eye or not was too
late even for the chairman to decide—heads turned as if to track the
passage of a hornet among them. "What a cruel thing to make the
people on the lands think they can live like in town just because they
will have unions . . . we dig the mud and not the gold . . . we plant
in the time when others are in school . . . why tell us that can
change because we pay two-and-six and the United Congress of
Trade Unions will say so. . . ." People tried to interrupt and the
chairman's head bobbed on disorder. The speaker switched suddenly
from an illiterate eloquence to conventionally phrased committee-
room English, with the effect of sweeping up an advantage for himself from the consternation. "—The rural branches of PIP have been
misled into pressing for this motion. Agricultural workers' wages will
rise and their conditions of employment improve as a result of improved production through government assistance schemes and nothing else. The farm workers are being used, they stand to benefit nothing by their demand, because there's nothing in it for them. All there
is in it is the attempt of a certain section of the trade union movement to extend its influence and funds, for reasons of its own. —I
don't want to say anything about those reasons. . . . The unions can't
do anything for the farm workers that the department of agriculture
can't do. This Party started as a people's party, a peasants' party, because that's where we all come from, from the land"—applause, especially from those whose dress suggested they had moved furthest from
it—"and there is no need for this nonsense about the people on the
land being forgotten because there is still no difference between the
people on the land and the people in the towns. We are the same.

The idea of a different class of person in town, I don't know where any of our people get it from. It is not an African idea. It comes from somewhere else and we don't need it. Our Party was simply a people's party and our Party in power is simply a people's government."

Now Shinza spoke for the first time. He wore the same shirt as the day before, a cigarette pack outlined in the buttoned breast-pocket. Bray, who had heard him so many times, felt a bile of nerves turn in his belly, found himself alert for the silent reactions emanating from the mass, intent and yet moving with the calm tide of breathing around him. Shinza, like Mweta (Mweta had begun by modelling himself on him) let them wait a moment or two before he spoke, a trick of authority, not hesitancy. Then he opened his mouth once—the broken tooth was an ugly gap—and let it close slowly, without a sound. The voice when it came seemed to be in Bray's own head. "The People's Independence Party grew from bush villages and locations in white people's towns where villagers came to work. It grew from the workers' movements in the mines, where the mineworkers were also people from the bush." The voice was quiet and patient; a little too patient, perhaps—they might think it insinuated that they would be slow to follow. "It is true that it was a peasant movement and that we are all sons of peasants. But it is not true that this is enough to ensure for all time that the ruling party remains the people's party, and the government a people's government. Looking back to the face of our youth will not take away the scars and marks it has now." A hand absently over the beard that hid his own. "For some thousands—less than a quarter of the population—life has changed. They work in ministries, government departments, offices, shops and factories. Those at the top have cars and houses; even those at the bottom know they have a regular pay packet coming in every week and can make down payments on their stoves and radios, those things that are the quickest way to show a higher standard of living." A small shrug. "But for tens of thousands, very little has changed. Three-quarters of the population is still on the land, and although industrialization—provided it is something more than a growing foreign concession—will absorb a good percentage in time to come, tens of thousands will always remain—on the land. We are all the same people, in town and country, yet they have no cars and brick houses, no fridges and smart clothes. . . . We are all the same people, yet they have no regular pay coming in twelve months a year, no unemployment insurance, no maximum working hours, no compensation for injury, and no redress for dismissal. We are the same people? —The same but different? Yes—the same, but different. We must face the fact that big talk about un-African ideas is a stupid refusal to see the truth. Industrialization itself is an un-African idea—if by that you mean something new to Africa. A political party is an un-African idea. This beautiful cinema we're sitting in is an un-African idea, we ought to be out under a tree somewhere. . . . The recognition of the fact that we have developed an urban elite, that there is a fast-widening gap in terms of material satisfactions as well as other kinds of betterment between that elite and the people in the country, that the few are racing ahead and showing nothing but their dust to the many— this recognition isn't un-African or un-anything, it's a matter of looking at what's actually happening. If we were a classless people, we are now creating a dispossessed peasant proletariat of our own. The lives of the people in the rural areas are stagnant. If PIP as a ruling party is to remain the people's party it was through the Independence struggle it must recognize what it has allowed to happen. Just now we heard members of Congress opposing a motion that asks for elementary rights for farm labourers as a working force. Can we believe our ears? Is this the voice that PIP speaks with, now?" He paused to goad interjection; but again there was a sullen silence. His voice strode into power. "Well, we are here at the seventh Congress of PIP, the first since the Party formed a government; we must believe. Yesterday our women's organizations had to protest because they were shut out from Congress. We had to believe our ears then, too, when we heard that women who from the beginning worked for Independence alongside the men, our women who have always been full members in a party pledged not to discriminate against any human being on grounds of tribal affiliation or sex—our women have been left outside to make the tea while Congress debates decisions that will affect their lives and their children's lives. —We have heard, and what we have heard can mean only one thing: the lines of communication between Freedom Building in this town and Party branches in the villages and the bush are breaking down. That is why the Party discusses the position of farm workers as if they were strangers, people living somewhere else—men from the moon. That is why. The Party remains a people's party and the government remains a people's government only so long as the people know that the government and Party are at their service. There should be no forgotten districts, there should be no forgotten sections of the population. The task of the Party is to be the direct expression of the masses, not to act as an administration responsible for passing on government orders. The Party, whether ruling or not, exists to help the people set out their demands and become more aware of their needs, not to make itself into a screen between the masses and the leaders. If PIP is prepared to ignore the demand of the farm workers for organization as a recognized labour force with the right to negotiate its own . affairs, PIP is guilty of the contemptuous attitude that the masses are incapable of governing themselves—an attitude we thought we had got rid of forever when Government House became the President's Residence. This Congress must face the fact that the Party is in danger of becoming a party of cabinet ministers, civil servants, and businessmen."

Applause and dissent clashed like the two halves of a cymbal; many who applauded did so in the hunch-shouldered, half-defiant way of those who fear disapproval. Country people whose characteristics and clothes had not seemed prominent in the ranks of knees and faces suddenly emerged in a distinctive force of numbers. Faces with tribal marks, stretched ear-lobes hanging to frayed shirt-collars —they seemed to be everywhere. Bray felt oddly elated; yet for the moment he had hardly taken in what Shinza had said—he had been gauging the faces around him, the faces on the stage. Mweta kept his head turned away while Shinza was speaking; no reaction whatever, except perhaps—revealed to Bray's nervously heightened observation —a slight lift of the chin that showed he was listening, all right, after all. The motion was very narrowly defeated, and the defeat greeted with a grumbling groan of resentment; the collective presence is a strangely emotional entity, whose combined voice has a command of expressive noises—nonsyllabic cries, warnings, keenings—that the people who comprise it have forgotten how to produce, individually. Cyrus Goma moved restlessly in the restriction of his own defeat. Shinza met nobody's eye, looking straight ahead with what, from Bray's distance, looked like a faint, private smile, or a delicate lifting of the lips in endurance. While Bray's eyes were on him he suddenly scratched himself vigorously on the chest; a kind of comic signal, a sign of life.

He certainly had made an impression on Congress. If two sharply defined factions had never existed before, they did now. When those delegates hesitantly but irresistibly sounded their palms for Shinza, his support, his own popular following came into being once again for everyone present to see and hear. It existed now. Mweta must know that. He must have taken, too, the messages smoothly slipped into the speech that were meant for him; no turning away of the head could avoid them.

In the foyer Bray came out of the men's room and into Roly Dando and Shinza at exactly the moment they couldn't ignore each other. Dando said, "So that's your line now, Edward," just as if they had been meeting every day. "I have no line, Roly. I'll support any resolution that constitutes action based on the workers' productive role, against economic imperialism. That's my policy. Always been the same. You know that."

Dando's grin at the patness of it rearranged his wrinkles. "Oh yes, the party-within-the-party."

"Let's have lunch and you can expand what he knows," Bray said.

"You two can go off and enjoy your lunch. I've got work piling up in my bloody office. These circuses are just a waste of time for me."

People gathered around Shinza openly, now. Goma, Ogoto, and huge young Basil Nwanga were racing about, marshalling his attention tensely here and there, with eyes that deftly selected and rejected among the crowd of delegates. Mweta, who had not appeared before outside the sessions but gone off at once in the presidential car, moved through the foyer surrounded by Central Committee people. He saw Bray and steered towards him, bringing his encirclement with him as he could not duck beneath it. Past heads and faces he called, "I'll see you tonight?" Bray's look questioned. "Didn't the secretary telephone you?" "Might have, after I'd left the house." "Dinner. About eight o'clock. After the cocktail party. All right?"

It was awkward to go back to the orbit of Shinza after this singling out. Cyrus Goma had watched accusingly. Bray had to make a determined effort to overcome his own feeling of culpability and get Shinza aside for a moment, pushed to it by a mixture of excitement and anxiety over the motion condemning Mweta's power to appoint the Secretary-General of UTUC, that was due to come up in the after-noon session. Shinza was not too hopeful; yet it was difficult, in the rush of vigour that the evidence of real support in the people gather-ing round him brought, for him not to feel heady with the chance. Anyway, talking to Bray, it seemed suddenly to make him make up his mind about something. His face stiff as a drunk's, he brought out calmly, "You remember old Zachariah Semstu? He still says the word and all five branches in the Tisolo district bleat back. . . . Cyrus's been chatting him up for days, but you know how it is . . . no matter what he thinks, the idea of a vote against Mweta sticks in his throat . . . well, it's understandable. But he knows that you—that so far as you're concerned—I mean, he'd always trust what you'd say. If you'd just have a word with him, there'd be no trouble." And Bray said, so quickly that he heard his own voice, "All right. Where is he?"

"He's down in the carpark. Linus's just passed him. Near the fence at the back of the building. Just stroll down as if you're going to your car, and you'll see him."

Bray left the Luxurama unheeded and came out into the heat. He was walking over the humpy ground with the momentum of a push in the back. A hundred suns revolved at him from the cars he ap-proached and passed; every now and then his feet crunched over patches of clinker that had been used to fill up hollows. A single tree left standing was covered with a whole dry season's dust like a piece of furniture shrouded in an empty room. The little boys who hung about with dirty rags, pestering to clean windscreens, were gambling for pennies around its exposed roots.

He saw some men sitting half-in, half-out of an open-doored car. They were eating fish and chips and one of them crushed his paper packet in his fist and aimed it at the rest of the rubbish that had col-lected under the tree. The old man Zachariah Semstu was sitting neatly on an upturned fruit box, smoking a pipe with a little tin lid on a chain. As Bray came up the old man gestured at the children to point out where the packet had fallen, and, not recognizing Bray for a moment, said testily to the others, "Let them eat if you don't want to." Bray was greeting him formally in Gala, he called him "my old friend."

The old man's ears recognized what his eyes had not. A look of joy-ous amazement wakened his face. The business of greeting went on for five minutes. "But you have seen me in there," Bray said, with a tilt of the head. "Well, well . . . I had heard you were back in the country. I had heard it. But we thought you had left us forever . . . you stayed away so long."

"I had no choice. As you know, I wasn't allowed in, all those years."

"And I have grown an old man," Semstu said.

The others had the look of people who have heard it all before; they were inert under his authority. He introduced two of them, both apparently office-bearers in Tisolo Party branches, but presented the less important ones collectively, with an encompassing movement of a hand whose fingers, Bray saw, had the characteristic sideways slope away from an arthritically enlarged first knuckle. Ten years is a long time; depends which stage of life you were in at the start.

Both standing, they talked about Tisolo. There were brickfields there, good deposits of clay, the best in the country. For the rest, subsistence farming of the poorest kind. "Your brickfields must be expanding? So many government building projects coming up?" Yes, but the new clay deposits were in the eastern end of the district, and a rail link was needed before they could be worked to full capacity. "The Ministry of Public Works and the radio station building are going up with bricks from Kaunda's country," the old man said. "I wrote to Mweta. He's a very busy man. It's not so easy to see him these days. —But he answered. Yes, a very good letter in answer."

The man who had thrown away the packet of food spoke. "It told us what we know. Bricks will have to be imported until the railway is made."

"And the railway link is on the Number One list," Semstu said, saying "Number One" in English. They all laughed a little, Bray as well. Semstu said, "I think the Number One list is a very long one. I would like to know where the railway is, on that list."

"And was that the cause of the trouble," Bray said. There had been a strike at the brickfields the previous month. There was a second's pause of indecision: the implication that this was not a matter to be spoken of with an outsider. But Semstu had known Bray before he had known any of the others. "People were told either wages must stay the same, or some men must be put off work. The union said that. Then when trouble started, the government sent someone down from here to tell them: the new brickfields are losing, until the railway comes, they ought to put off men anyway. But they will keep them on in the meantime if they don't ask for more pay."

"But from what I read in the papers, the union itself was already negotiating for a wage increase when the trouble started?"

"Yes, yes—first the union was asking the company for a wage increase, then the union turned round, you see, turned round again—and told the men at the new brickfields they would be put off if the men at the old brickfields went on asking for increase—"

Bray nodded vehemently; none of the men looked at each other. The man who had spoken before identified himself as the one whose eyes were being avoided. "What else could we do. After we started talking with the company"—the brickfields were a subsidiary of the gold-mining consortium—"we got called up to the Ministry of Labour's place, we were told by the Secretary there, look here, boys . . ."

If someone could tell Mweta," old Semstu pressed. "If we could get the railway. When *you* are talking to him perhaps you can tell him, next time?"

Bray had seen working towards expression the realization that he was someone who might be able to be used. The old man said, "Of course you see him."

"Yes, I see him. But as you said, he's a very busy man. Everybody wants something."

Semstu considered, but his face remained closed to any attempt to put him off. He settled his old hat back on his head; he dressed still in the reverend's or schoolmaster's black suit with a watch chain looped across the stomach, the early robes and insignia of literacy. "Letters are no good. They are written on the machine by someone." His arthritic hand, holding the pipe, flourished a signature at the bottom.

The others were looking at Bray and him with eyes screwed up against the light. The union man jutted his bottom lip and blew a lung-full of cigarette smoke before his own face. Bray said to him, "Your union will have to press UTUC to bring up the business of the railway with the Development Plan people."

The man grimaced up the side of his face, as at one who doesn't know what he's talking about. He shook his head and laughed, wary to commit himself, even to a fool.

"But of course you've done that already."

"And then?" the man said.

Bray smiled. "Well, you tell me."

"UTUC doesn't say what we want, it tells us what the Company wants."

Silence. A deep inhalation of smoke drew both in together—company, development plan, all the same.

Now that the exact moment had presented itself, Bray almost took his opening as a casual question to the man he was already in conversation with, but turned in time to Semstu. "Well, I'm sorry to hear things are not going so well in your district, *Mukwayi*, my old friend — What do you think, anyway, of this idea of the S.-G., of the United Congress of Trade Unions being appointed instead of elected? It's a very important post—I mean, so far as troubles like yours are concerned, the S.-G., if he's the right man, he's the one to get the government to see—"

"Oh but it's Mweta who'll say who it is."

"We were just saying—Mweta's got so many decisions to make. Mweta has so many things to think about."

The old man said, "Mweta's not going to choose a fool or a bad one."

"No, of course not. But as we were saying, he can't keep in touch with what everybody thinks these days. He would have to take advice from someone, now, don't you think—"

"Yes, yes. But who?" The old man implied that it could only be the members of Mweta's own cabinet, people of his own choosing.

"People from the Ministry of Labour. Perhaps the Planning and Development people." Bray added, to the union man, "The ones you ran up against."

"And who can know better than Mweta which is the right man?"

The other men left the car and began to draw nearer, cautiously. Bray appealed to them all, simply, openly—"Well, I'd say the workers themselves. They must know whom they want to speak for them. That's what trade unions are for."

"The Secretary-General should go on being elected." The old man set out the statement in order to consider it.

"It's always been like that until now," Bray said. "Since Shinza and Mweta started the unions and got the colonial administration to recognize that the workers had rights. Ever since then."

The old man suddenly pulled back against the direction of the talk. He seemed to be warning himself. "Ah, now we have Independence. Mweta knows what to do. If he decides to choose the man, he knows why he wants to do that."

After a moment he cocked his head sideways under his hat at Bray, a man unsure of his hearing, and pointed the pipe at Bray's middle. "But you are a clever man. You went with Mweta and Shinza to get us Independence. We don't forget you. People will remember you as they remember our fathers. You are not saying it, but what you are saying now is that you don't think Mweta is right."

"I'm saying that whoever Mweta chooses, it's not right that he should choose. UTUC must elect its own Secretary-General."

"Yes, that too; but you are saying Mweta is wrong."

"Yes, I am saying Mweta is making a mistake. And I will tell him. Because he is a great man I always tell him when I think he is wrong."

The old man liked that; grinned. "Oh I see you are still strong. — When the British made him go away, we said here they will have to tie him down to their ship like a bull—" but the younger men were not interested in these legends of colonial times.

"I hear that Shinza wants to be the Secretary-General." Instinct told him to be bold; for the first time in his life he did not seem to have much else to go by.

He could not tell whether or not they knew about Shinza all along, whether it was the factor they balked at inwardly. "Shinza, eh?" the old man said. "And do you agree with that?"

Bray said offhand, "He was S.-G. before. If UTUC wants him. Nobody knows trade union work better than Shinza."

"I want to talk to you about something." The old man looked round at the others. They drifted off in a group, taking their time about it, holding their smart jackets over their shoulders. Bray and the old man got into the back seat of the car; although the doors were open it was no cooler than standing outside. There was a vase of wax roses in a holder beside the rear mirror. Semstu said, "Will it not be a bad thing . . ."

He might mean that it was bad to cross Mweta's will, or he might mean he did not like the idea of Shinza in office at this time. It would have made sense to have found out a bit more, from Shinza, about his more recent relations with the old man. "You want to know what I think? I think Mweta needs Shinza in a position like that. He needs Shinza"—Bray made a measuring gesture—" 'up there'. Shinza has become too far away."

"Down in the Bashi, yes. It's far. And Shinza understands the trouble—he was in the mines himself."

"Exactly. Shinza is another pair of eyes and ears for Mweta, and he knows what he sees and hears, too."

"The man they sent down to the brickfields"—Semstu's tongue-click cracked like a whip in disgust. "He had passed his school, yes—"

Bray let him alone to think a minute.

"Goma's been worrying me about the vote. All the time he comes to me."

"Well, it's important. The five Tisolo branches, you know."

"But I was worried it was a bad thing . . . because Mweta wants to choose."

"I don't think it's a bad thing." Even in Gala, he heard the English habit of authority and self-assurance in his voice; just as a whore turned respectable retains a professionalism in her manner towards men.

Semstu talked on, about Goma—"his head is pressed into his shoulder like a vulture, it's hard to trust a man who looks like that bird"; jealousy of Mweta, jealousy of Shinza—"someone must have talked between them"; the comfort of the Luxurama seats, the first Congress —did Bray remember?—when the police had seized the agenda. When all this preamble was over and he could do so with independence, he said, "You can tell Goma I will do it."

"All five branches?"

"All five."

That was all there was to it. He saw himself saying to Shinza, that was all there was to it. I have done my errand. As easy as that. He went to the café where he and Shinza had eaten sausages but was not hungry. His feet and hands had swelled, after the chill of the Luxurama, standing in the heat. His watch stuck to his wrist and gave way from wet flesh and hairs with a sucking pull as he shifted it. The artificial fruit juice was moving round and round in its container, bright and cloudy. The Greek proprietor and his wife were drinking Turkish coffee in tiny cups. "Could I have a cup of *that?*"

The little man had two dimples in his greenish-pale face as he smiled at the big Englishman. "Oh, we don't sell this kind of coffee, it's what we Greeks drink ourselves." "I know. I like it very much. Could I have a cup?" The man was amused. "Oh if you want. I'll give you." The pregnant wife, very young, with wisps of black hair showing in the white arches of her underarms, fetched a cup, unsmiling. In the cupola between the body and the arm he tasted always the sweety-scentedness of something smeared there to disguise sweat, and the slight gall, as of an orange pip bitten into, of the sweat itself, and his tongue, moving one way smoothly, felt the nap of shaven hair-roots when it moved the other. The coffee was boiling hot, thick and delicious. Rebecca had not been in his mind at all; only this one part of her, suddenly, claimed him with an overwhelming sense of reality of its own. Cunt-struck, they call it—never mind that it wasn't the right part—he thought deeply lovingly, not minding what they called it. He was at once swollen in the other way, too. He ordered a bottle of soda water because the man wouldn't take money for the coffee: it was he, Bray, who had done him the honour of appreciating the customs of the country—a country thousands of miles away.

Every day in October at this time a strange transformation of elements took place. The sky was no longer colour or space but weight of heat; it pressed down upon figures, trees, and buildings. The streets of two o'clock in the afternoon looked squat and beaten. He felt his height hammered towards the ground, where only the big red ants moved lightly and freely. He took a taxi the few blocks back to the Luxurama. The taxi drivers of the capital were in the euphoria of good business—Congress brought plenty of customers to town. The driver wore a white golfer's cap and sunglasses, and at the traffic light played the drums with flat palms on his thighs in time to loud music from his radio.

The foyer had almost emptied itself back into the auditorium already; Bray saw that he could slip in without seeing the Shinza contingent. He didn't want to talk about Semstu. But Shinza himself came out against the stream of delegates going in; he was hurrying somewhere with papers in his hand.

"Well, how did you get on with your old friend Semstu?"

"You will have the Tisolo branches."

A parody of his own thought, it came from Shinza: "Easy as that."

Bray said nothing. Shinza was in that state when the imminence of a decisive event becomes unbearable and the mind seizes upon some trivial detail to be completed, some half-phrase to be added, putting into the performance of these useless things all the urgency that is turned back by the event itself: here; now; carrying with it the oracle of its outcome. Whatever the bits of paper were, he held them as if they were his destiny, his eyes already impatiently past Bray, his lips clamped with a sort of smile on a dead cigarette. "I wish they'd trust me easily as they trust you."

"They trust me because I haven't got any power. That wouldn't be much good to you, would it." He took from his pocket the little gas lighter Rebecca had given him, and the tiny flame spurted with the roll of his thumb: "Here."

"You haven't got a box of matches for me?—I'm out." Mechanically, Shinza bent his dark fleecy head and relit the cigarette.

"Keep this." A few scribbles of white, like threads of white cotton you'd pick off woolly cloth, there on the crown. Bray had never had with Shinza the sense of affection he had with Mweta, the affection that of course meant a certain physical affinity, too, which is to say a tolerance for the other person's body, its essences and characteristics. That was partly what the girl meant when she said once that he "loved" Mweta; he would have used Mweta's razor or put on a garment of Mweta's (not that he could ever fit into anything Mweta wore!) as unthinkingly as he would use a towel streaked with the black stuff that washed off Rebecca's eyelashes. But with Shinza, who knew him so much better than Mweta did—Shinza, matched with him in mind, locked with him in generation—between Shinza and himself there was something of physical hostility. He remembered once more the moment the day he had first seen Shinza again, with the boy-child he had begotten on a young girl, feeble in his hand. A moment of pure sexual jealousy. And no woman involved; no individual woman, only woman as the symbol by which a child was fathered. Well, the genie was out of the bottle these days; his feelings, that whole flood of nervous responses, had somehow pushed forward into daily use, overwhelmingly available and alert, a kind of second intelligence. Looking down on Shinza's head for a second, he thought, was that when it began—when *he* was holding his son?

Someone had forgotten to turn up the houselights in the Luxurama

M*

and only the red exit lamps glowed. After the daylight he saw little in
the dimness and was aware of all the eyes there, turned not upon him
but in quiet tension upon what was to come. There was not much
talk. He felt his way to a seat. Then the lighting was corrected and
everyone was discovered by it in a kind of dreamy impatience, waiting for the Executive and Central Committees and the President to
file in.

Mweta had put on the robe he had worn for his investiture. It left
his neck free of collar and tie for the October heat—but that didn't
prevail in here. The robe made him look much taller and the muscles
running to a V at the base of his throat showed in a streak of shine
along the smooth black skin as he turned his head. Shinza was
hunched at the table, his raised shoulders keeping out his neighbours,
his two fists supporting his chin and covering the lower part of his
bearded face. Bray kept looking at him to see if he would look up; to
make him look up. He felt curiously anxious that Shinza should do so,
anxious about what the delegates were thinking of this image. Shinza
did not move. The familiar gesture with which he fished in his breast-
pocket for a cigarette was missing.

With the same conventions that carried it from any one piece of
business to another, Congress came to the motion: "That the People's
Independence Party Congress views with grave alarm the intention to
make the position of Secretary-General of the United Trades Union
Congress a personal appointment by the President of the State, instead of an appointment voted by election within the United Trades
Union Congress membership, as it has been since the birth of trade
unions in this country. The People's Independence Party moves that
the President be respectfully informed that such usurpation of democratic procedure is contrary to the spirit of the State and the principles of free labour upheld by the People's Independence Party and
the United Trades Union Congress, on which the State was founded;
and that the President be requested to affirm the unalienable right of
UTUC to elect its Secretary-General."

The legalistic jargon, the chairman controlling the order in which
voices might be heard, the people sitting with that bit of paper, the
agenda, token of the taming of their wildest and most urgent thoughts
translated into symbols on cheap white paper; this ancient form of
human discipline—frail cracked amphora, handed down by the

Greeks, that it was—held. All the festive *bonhomie* of the gathering at its first meetings had worn off by now. Suits were rumpled with sitting and the smokers went through pack after pack, enduring the alternation of boredom and tension. In spite of the air-conditioning, or rather, circulated coldly by it, there was the smell of the herd, man-herd, brought about not by physical exertion but the secretions of determination, resentment, apprehension, nervous excitement, coming, Bray thought, from myself and all the others. We don't speak, I don't know what they're thinking on either side of me, our arms touching on the chair-arms, but we give it off, this message that we no longer know how to read as animals do.

The first speaker to the motion had been carefully chosen: the trade unionist Sam Gaka was a man of the kind dubbed "painfully sincere" —that is, given a particular, insistent grasp of a certain set of facts without relating them to a hierarchy of other facts. In any society where it was possible, he would have been apolitical; here he simply failed to understand what his political position was. He was a believer (almost in the evangelical sense) in corporate trade unionism —the restriction of union activities purely to professional questions of the employer-employee relationship. And so, although corporate trade unionism was something that UTUC could never have practised, since from the beginning UTUC had been part of the nationalist political struggle, with the employer/white-colonial one and the same force against which the worker/black-subject had to assert his demands/rights, and although corporate trade unionism was something that UTUC could not practise now, because an underdeveloped country had to be able to "call upon" its workers in the old political sense to fight the State's struggle for economic emancipation—he was able to argue for the election of the Secretary-General from the "pure" position of corporatism. For those who recognized it, gave a name to it; to the majority he was simply saying that UTUC's members, representing the whole working force of the country, must always know the best person to speak for them to the government, that the whole idea of trade unionism was based on the workers' selection of their own spokesmen, etc.

Clever Shinza, Bray thought, to pick this man. But there were statements to be twisted from this politically unaligned context, too. Ndisi Shunungwa, present Secretary-General of UTUC, was able to speak from another advantage—everyone knew he himself had been elected to office, yet he was reminding Party members that the man to be appointed in future by the President would not be an outsider —there were provisions that this could not happen—he would be a member of the executive of UTUC, and therefore someone freely elected to speak for them by the union members themselves, else how would he be in UTUC at all?

Basil Nwanga's huge backside blocked the view of the men in the seats on either side of his as he rose. "Mr. Chairman, that's all right as the nice and tidy answer of an incumbent who maybe feels confident he'll stay where he sits if the Secretary-General is appointed instead of elected"—his sharply affable voice went on at once before the chairman could raise any objection—"Well, of course, personal views are not what interests us, we must decide on facts, hey, and the one that got left out here is that in UTUC itself there are people who represent different ideas in the trade union movement. It's only the majority of members of UTUC who have the right to decide which man, representing which ideas, will serve the workers best as S.-G. If the appointment comes from outside it can only be seen to favour one set of views above another. It must be like that. —There will be trouble in the unions. Let the workers elect their own man—it's the duty of the Party to support this right—" He spoke jerkily, in his heavily accented English that broke up sentences into unfamiliar stress-patterns, but he had a youthful bluntness that released spontaneity. Applause came like thrown pennies as he lowered his bulk out of the way again. Someone stood up to ask why the matter was being discussed at a PIP Congress at all—wasn't it something for the trade unions to argue?—but was at once ruled out of order, to triumphant applause meant not for him but as self-congratulation on the part of the supporters of the motion.

Shinza had come slowly out of his concentrated withdrawal; he had applauded Nwanga, but merely smiled a moment at this affirmation. As the debate quickened Bray had the impression that Shinza was all the time keyed to something that he was listening for, watching out for, behind the echoing voices of the speakers, even behind the rather disorderly background murmur that rose in spite of the chairman's censure. A sub-debate was going on among the delegates all over the tiers of seats; notes were being passed, people changed

places, backs were hunched confidentially and as ears were inclined
with bowed heads, eyes—eyes yellowish and veined with blood, eyes
clear and prominent showing white, eyes marbled with ageing—met
others with that gloss of inner-directed attention that gives away
nothing.

Mweta folded his arms across his robe; unfolded them and sat back
in his chair, hands loose upon the table. How few public gestures
there were—and even these governed by the same set of conventions
as, even if they were not actually set down by, the ancient form that
held the gathering. Did Mweta have doubts about the power that was
being questioned? Did he sit there, handsome little Roman emperor
in his robes, knowing himself in the wrong but believing himself justi-
fied in accepting the rigging for power that he thought he couldn't
hold any other way?

Someone—a picked member of the Shunungwa-Mweta faction—
was whipping up heat at the "insult to our great leader" shown by
those who opposed his right to choose the S.-G. "These people should
leave this Congress. This is a one-party state. We are one nation, we
have one leader, he is the leader of the members of the Trades Union
Congress and all the people—"

The uproar made the speaker inaudible though he went on bellowing. He was being applauded, shouted down—a great surge of opposing energies seemed literally to shift the cinema seats clamped to one
another and the floor, so that Bray felt the pressure heaving at him.
Roly Dando's little sliver of a white face was moving on his neck like
a roused bird's. Party stewards were reinforced by the sudden presence of white-helmeted policemen who appeared through the curtained exits where the Joshi brothers' smart mulatto usherettes usually
waited with torches and trays of sweets. There was a scuffle up on
the left of Bray somewhere, near the back of the cinema—a fight? —
"Old man's had a heart-attack," someone repeated—but the white-
helmeted men went up the aisle three steps at a time and swiftly
brought down a young man with fury bunched in his face at being
exhibited like this, and another man with the sleeve of his worn
jacket torn out of the armhole. As they were pushed through the
doors chanting of some sort came from out there, as if the dial of a
radio twirled briefly through the wavelength of a station—the women
again, no doubt—and a few red-sashed Young Pioneer "marshals" got

in. The police did not seem to know what to do about them; but the young men's self-styled authority wavered in the company of that more obviously vested in white helmets, leather boots, and holstered guns. They stood beside the police, their presence neither asserted nor rejected, looking sideways at each other.

There were calls for Mweta but he gave no sign that he would speak. Bray, putting himself in his place, wondered why he left it to Shunungwa and his other lieutenants to argue the case. —You don't want to be in at the kill? —He wouldn't hear the question from me, now, even if I could be there right next to him, asking it for his ear alone; wouldn't hear. And he was far away on the other side of this sounding-place vibrating as if they were all within a vast bell with the ringing of speakers' voices and the numberless thought-waves spreading, overlapping, looping among echoes: a single intention towards him drowned out before it got there; he became, to Bray, as Bray tried to hold him in sight, in mind, something that stood for Mweta—the familiar face, the robe. Justin Chekwe, Secretary-General of PIP as well as Minister of Justice, had apparently been chosen as big gun against the motion. He was an eloquent speaker (ex–Oxford Union, as a cocky black scholarship student) and while he didn't descend to emotional appeal, the very sight and sound of him, enhanced by the power of his portfolio since Independence in the way a woman is made more sexually attractive by her private knowledge that she is conducting a love affair, drew confidence. Every villager in his scraped-together best could see what—if it were too late for oneself —a son could become. There was no austerity in Chekwe's manner; he wore the white man's expensive clothes as he used the most expensive words, words that came only at the price of the most expensive education. And in this he remained African in a way that was recognized instantly without any need of explanation, such as was necessary to reassert a pride in things reinstated from Africa's own neglected scale of values. What he was saying, of course, was aimed directly at Shinza; it was based, for tactical reasons, on a deliberate misinterpretation of motives. Was Congress being urged to approve the adoption by African movements of a purely professional trade unionism? Supporters of this attitude refused to allow trade union participation in any form of governmental activity. The late Tom Mboya once argued the case for this and, indeed, in theory, it was admirable

. . . "for countries whose economies are sufficiently highly developed to afford it—though if we look at some of them, England, for example"—he allowed himself a sympathetic smile at the Labour government's troubles—"we wonder if anyone can afford it." . . . But even the most ardent supporters of this theory had come to realize through experience in Africa that the trade union movement could not concern itself solely with the defence of the workers' immediate interests, and "let the country go hang." Even the most ardent advocates of so-called "corporate" trade unionism today realized that the only way to further the interests of the workers was to assist the government in every way to achieve its economic goals. It was absolutely necessary for the trade union attitude to take into account long-term economic planning and ensure that this was carried out "with the closest possible trust and cooperation between the government and the unions. The President's appointment of the Secretary-General of UTUC is the most important recognition of this cooperation. It is the government's guarantee that this cooperation will take place on the highest level and will never be endangered by such petty internal dissensions as might arise from time to time within trade union movements themselves. . . ."

The arguments were being taken down at the press table, recorded on tape, but rising and falling decibels would not capture what was really happening. Beneath this graph was another, the shift back and forth of a balance between Shinza and Mweta. And beneath that, yet another: and of the nature of that, even Bray wasn't sure. All this afternoon's clamour and talk would become part of a small curve in the rise and fall of forces over the whole continent, would be swept up in the historian's half-sentence some day—"towards the end of the decade, there could be discerned a certain paradigm of alignment into which apparently dissimilar states. . . ." It isn't signifying nothing, this clamour, that's too easy, too. Its significance is something to be listened for, reached by parting a way through words, presences, the cramp in one's knees, and the compulsive distraction of lighting another and another cigarette.

Still Mweta made no sign. He could have spoken if he wanted, even if it had been agreed that he wouldn't. He had done it before; it was part of his impulsive naturalness, the political sense he had had that went beyond the stale concept of politics as a "game" in which all moves must be plotted and adhered to. Politics had always been concrete to him, a matter of bread, work, and shelter. He sat there in his robe; a piece of popular political art, Bray thought—just as there is popular religious art, plaster figures painted blue and gold.

The other faction had their plan of action, as well. Shinza was to have their last word. When he stood up he waited for silence and got it; but then those who had given it as a due exacted found that he was looking round as if he wanted to remember them all, everything; he lingered on the thugs and the policemen, awkward presences that had no dealing with words, in a gathering whose meaning depended on the binding validity of the word or was nothing—he looked at them with the beginnings of a dry, playfully pitying smile, the smile men give jailers. And then he began to speak. "In our country, as in most other African states, before independence nationalism was given priority in trade union activities because the economic and social situation of the African worker was a direct consequence of colonialism. Now that independence is gained, economic and social problems come to the fore again—look at them all around us in the strikes and riots on the mines, the fisheries, the railways. The African trade union movement has to reformulate its policies to deal with these problems. Now let us be clear about one thing. This reformulation can only take place within a framework limited by the legacy of the colonial system, the trade unions' role in the political growth of the State, and the size of the social and economic problems which face us. —That is what the Yema resolution is about; that is what the Honourable Minister Mr. Chekwe is talking about; that is what I'm talking about." All the mannerisms that his eager pupil (robed, shoulders back like a bust on a coin) had learned from him; but, in Shinza himself, without that concession known as charm: done with that. "The label of professional trade unionism, corporatism, won't stick on UTUC. Not even the 'enlightened' professional trade unionism that Mr. Chekwe is prepared to flatter it with . . . Because what he is saying in effect is that trade unions can support any government whose policy favours the workers, *no matter what that government's over-all policy is.* Well, we know where this reasoning can lead. In Europe it led to Mussolini, it led to Hitler—it led to fascism. Africa is making enough mistakes of her own; one of the last hopes of the world and ourselves is that at least she will not have to repeat all Europe's. In Africa, Mr.

Chekwe quotes the example of Mboya. Yes, the late Tom Mboya did
follow 'enlightened' corporatism as a union man and later as Minister of Economic Planning and Development, and we respect his memory as one of the great men of our continent; but there are people
who say he used this argument to justify his blind attachment to the
Western bloc, abandoning the principles of positive neutralism to
which the People's Independence Party and our country are committed; and at the time of his death foreign business interests were flourishing while the Kenyan people remained poor. . . . No, the label of
professional trade unionism, of an evasion of the realistic and proper
role of the unions in a developing state, won't stick on UTUC because
what UTUC has stood for since the days when our Party grew out of
the trade unions is the fullest participation of the worker in the formulation of the policies of the state. In 1959 when I came out of jail I
hardly had time to look for a clean shirt"—splendidly casual reminder that he had been in and out of prison for PIP—"before UTUC
sent me off to Conakry to the UGTAN conference—one of the first
important attempts to create pan-African trade unionism—with a
mandate to support trade union involvement in political action as the
only way to achieve social and economic progress. During the years,
later, when PIP was banned and for a time UTUC acted as our front
organization, the trade unions reaffirmed this conviction in actions"
—perhaps he said "louder than words"—his own were beaten out by
a swell of aggressive applause somewhere— "The trade unions saw
then that the workers' greatest need was the country's need to struggle against colonialism and imperialism. The reason why now their
Secretary-General should not be appointed over their heads is not because they think their role after independence is to be *less* involved
at government level, but on the contrary, because it is to be *more* involved, because the workers' greatest need *now* is to ensure that the
government continues the struggle against neo-colonialism and all
that it means to the workers. This thing neo-colonialism is not, as
some people would like to tell us, a catch-phrase, an honest investor
from Europe or America or wherever, dressed up by the Communists
in sheets and an evil spirit's face. It is with us now in the form of
'disinterested' help given by the great powers; in the domination of
our national resources by international companies; and in the perpe-
tuation of our economic inferiority as the eternal producers of raw

materials at low prices and customers for the finished product at high prices."

Two fingers went into the pocket of the rumpled shirt, as if, carried away in discussion with a friend, he were looking for the usual cigarette. But what he encountered there with the package was the realization that he was on a public platform, talking for his political life; Bray saw the hand become absent, withdraw. "After independence, *trade unionism is the population's means of defence against foreign capital.* You don't believe me? —We only hear about the need to attract foreign capital. But the fact is that we need a defence against it, too. We need to make sure it doesn't own us. . . . We have valuable resources in our country and of course we'll have to go on seeking money to develop those resources for some time to come. But the conditions under which that foreign capital is invested and the type of development for which it's used—these are matters where we need the active involvement of independent trade union opinion, not the rubber stamp of a government appointee"—and he brought down his fist so that the water carafes all along the table shook and this was visible right to the back of the cinema in the wobble of light off their contents. "—And it's not only as a watchdog that trade unions in a newly independent country defend the population against foreign capital. Julius Nyerere was speaking to his people in Tanzania, but it could have been meant for us when he said, 'We have made a mistake to choose money, something which we do not have, to be our major instrument of development . . . the development of a country is brought about by people, not by money.' Where a government admits vigorous cooperation with the trade unions, there are possibilities for types of development we haven't even touched on, here. I'm not talking of structural changes in the country's economy— nationalization of mining, banks, insurance companies and so on— though we mustn't forget, in our fear of frightening off the rich man from over the sea, that nationalization is, after all, a post-colonial measure to restore the national economy and give a democratic base to independence. . . . What I am saying is that it's possible, through cooperation at the highest level between government and trade unions to establish such things as a fishermen's cooperative on the lake, cooperatives among peasant farmers. —We could get help from the Histadrut, for example, the Israelis, with this, as other countries have done. And why don't we go into the possibility of the government purchase of the farms of departing white settlers for the benefit of the people who worked the land for the settlers? There's the *autogestion* scheme that was first started in Yugoslavia and then taken up in Algeria—the word means self-management, the idea that the land is handed over to the farm workers, the people who know how it was being made productive in the first place, and then the farms are run by committees of the farm workers themselves. A better idea than setting up big brand-new government plantations from scratch, as our agricultural services are busy borrowing money to do now; those plantations the experts find in the end they're unable to turn over to the management of inexperienced villagers. . . . The self-management system has a very important side effect, too. It helps the integration of the unemployed into a permanent work-force by discouraging the use of casual labour and putting all agricultural work on a permanent basis.

"And in the towns—in industry—where are the profit-sharing schemes for African workers? Many international companies operating here have stock purchase plans or profit-sharing plans for their employees in other countries, outside Africa. Why must Africa be the exception? These companies should develop appropriate schemes for our workers, incorporated in bargaining agreements with the trade unions. There are many other possibilities and they all need recognition of trade union initiative at government planning level. A workers' investment corporation could be set up as a prelude to other business activity, to get Africans into the sector of our economy at present dominated by expatriates. It makes more sense than throwing stones and looting foreign shops, as some Young Pioneers did last month at Temba. . . . Why shouldn't we have a people's bank, a state-aided bank to help our small farmers and shopkeepers who can't raise loans from ordinary banks? The self-management scheme can be adapted to small factories, too; you can set up in towns a system parallel to that of the rural areas. Factories, shops—a whole industrial unit can be controlled by the workers who run the management through their own board of administration, while managerial staff and engineers are appointed by the government. The foreign investor doesn't own those factories and shops. They may not run as efficiently as the foreign firm would have run them, the profits may not be as high as they would have been, but there are no shareholders in other countries waiting to take the profits away. I know a small foundry that's just closed down because it wasn't making enough money to satisfy the white man. But it was earning enough to satisfy the twenty-six men who worked for him. . . . They have now joined the unemployed . . .

"When we vote on this motion, there are two things to remember, and both show the state appointment of the Secretary-General of UTUC as something to be condemned by this Congress. One—whatever the avowed position of the trade unions in relation to political power, UTUC can't avoid fulfilling its main function, which is to convey the discontent of the workers it represents. No appointed S.-G. will get round that. Two—the role of the trade unions in an independent state is not to become purely functionary, a branch of the Ministry of Labour, but to see that the type of society being planned based on the people's labour is in accordance with the *aims* of the people. In the United Trades Union Congress constitution there is laid down as one of its aims 'the maintenance of the UTUC as one of the militant branches of the movement which will build the socialist state under the political leadership of the People's Independence Party.' I call upon Congress to defend that branch of the Party, or betray the Party itself."

Shinza's supporters battered the assembly with their hard-heeled acclaim. A flash of acknowledgement lit across his face, a taste of something; but the sort of sustained applause that comes strength after strength, from every corner and tier, and sweeps a man higher and higher above opposition, was not there. Instead there was a strange atmosphere of consternation. He sat down. The debate went on but there was the feeling that nobody listened; yet a crystallization was taking place in every creak of a seat, every uneasy shift of position, in the echoes stirred like bats when voices came from certain quarters, and even—Bray felt absurd portents press in—the boredom of the thugs from the Young Pioneers. Others were talking and now Shinza like Mweta said nothing. But Mweta's silence, his presence, was growing, spreading over the people who sighed, scribbled absently, avoided each other's eyes, sat forward tensely, or back, waiting. And before the vote was taken it was there: Mweta's silence had spoken to them. It was *that*, then, for which Shinza had been listening, from the beginning, behind the debate. Now Bray heard it, felt it—no word for how it was apprehended—as Shinza must be doing. The waverers were overcome with their hands, so to speak, in midair for Shinza. They voted for *him*, seated there asking nothing of them in his robe, because he expected it of them.

Shinza took the cigarette out of his pocket now. He stuck it in the corner of his mouth and was lighting it with Rebecca's present, that always worked first try.

So that's my man Bray thought; that's my man.

H

e found himself with Dando and Shinza in one of the bars of the Great Lakes Hotel; if it were true that anyone ever "found himself" anywhere: by haphazard more purposeful than would appear, the pull of a fascinated reluctance had brought them slowly from group to group at the cocktail party going on in the Golden Perch Room. He hadn't known whether to expect Shinza to turn up at all; Dando's was the first voice he heard—"What sort of sex symbol, without a between to its legs"—declaiming over the latest piece of redecoration, the huge stuffed lake perch that had given the room its name and now had the upper half of a woman's body, in gilded plaster, in place of its own fishy head.

Many of the delegates had never seen the inside of a place like the Great Lakes before. They stood about overcome by unfamiliarity with the required manner of eating and drinking in such surroundings and were ignored by waiters who disdained to initiate them, hurrying past with gins and whisky-sodas for those who knew how to appreciate these things. When Mweta (in a correct dark suit) moved among them lemonade in hand, and himself pressed them to the plates of tidbits and drinks, they sat down solemnly to the treat they were bidden and blindly ate the bits of shrimp on sticks; some even became roistering among themselves, as the drinks went down, while the professional politicians and the people who sat on company boards drank steadily and achieved nothing more than the glowing

self-importance associated with social drinking. The triumphs and resentments of all factions seemed to be contained this way, a feast following a funeral as it does a wedding.

Shinza was wearing the same crumpled holiday shirt, as if he had
come with the object of making his presence a jarring note. He was
seen with various knots of people, never in the vicinity of Mweta, apparently talking detachedly. Now he was surrounded by a few young
men like a dangerous object that may go off any moment. One, older
and a little drunk, was the leader in boldly taking him up—they were
asking questions about *autogestion*— "Was that the blacksmith's
place in Kinshasa Road you're talking about? —But one of my in-
laws worked there and he's got a job at a boiler-makers' place now."
"So what, man." Someone was ashamed of the level of the question.
"—But who owns these farms and factories, then—the government?"

Roly Dando had had a great deal to drink; his companions were
head-down, entranced over their glasses while poker-faced he talked
louder and louder until his voice reached out into the neighbouring
discussion—"of course, respect for trade union action's just a pious
hope in African states. You know that, for God's sake, don't you,
Shinza? —Of course he does. Knows it as well as I do."

Faces opened up to make way, gleaming. Shinza smiled slowly
with closed lips and ran his first finger along them in a parody of
apologetics. "Well, I'm learning—fast." They were pleased with him;
they laughed. Ras Asahe, who had dragged Bray off to the bar, addressed Shinza through Bray. "Oh yes, we believe you, my friend.
There's only one way to make you learn, though."

". . . talking into your beard, this business about the workers and
the government building the socialist state for the benefit of the workers," Dando was saying. "In African states the economy can only be
developed to the detriment of the workers. For a hell of a long time
to come. That's a fact. I don't care what political creed or economic
concepts you want to name, the realities of production and distribution of wealth remain the same, just the same, right through the continent. No, no—I know what's coming—don't trot out what happened
in Europe a hundred years ago, because you know the answer to that
one, too. The sacrifices squeezed out of the European working classes
in the nineteenth century enabled Western economies to reach a
point where they could acknowledge the demands of the poor bas-

tards who'd sweated their guts out. It was possible for one reason only: the point had been reached without disturbing the pattern of growth. Within limits, they'd come to a stage where increased consumption leads to greater investment."

Shinza and Dando were shoved into the cockpit by the smallness of the bar, the drink in their veins, the curiosity of their companions—and also something else, an awareness of each other in the same room. Shinza took up the exchange with the air of a man who has done with argument. "And why is that impossible?"

"Because, my dear Shinza, in Africa today internal saving's nonexistent. Nonexistent or unproductive. A few quid stuffed into a mattress along with the bugs. And consumption's so low it's impossible to restrict it any more to encourage increased investment, so your salary freezes won't help. Wealth is distributed in an irregular and morally unjustifiable way, but I'm damned if anyone knows what to do about it. Trade unionism's all trussed up because it's come on the scene long before complete industrialization has taken place."

"Spouting Marx to defend black capitalism! Remember who you're working for these days, Dando." Shinza pulled down his bearded mouth, half-humouring, half-patronizing. "—All you're saying's the workers won't feel the benefit right away—"

"—Not Right away or Left away or Middle-of-the-road away—you can talk till kingdom come. Have a drink, Edward. —Come on, man, look after the gentlemen," he berated the barman. The circle drew in closer. "Edward and I were talking about these things when you were all a lot of snotty-nosed kids . . . he knows what I'm saying."

"What's this rubbish about trade unionism being 'tied up.'" Shinza took a swallow of Dando's round of whiskies. "Listen—what it has to do is make a choice. For the sake of economic development, it can become an organ of the government's policy-making machinery—which means any criticism of government incompetence is out—finished. Then union activity's restricted to one thing—ensuring the allegiance of workers in productive industries. Now *that's* something that perpetuates your famous inequitable distribution of national income, all right. You hand out the big money to dignitaries, you foot the bill for a massive police force to keep everyone quiet. And all that represents unproductive expenditure, ay? So the trade unions'll be able to congratulate themselves on consolidating the political power of the elite. —But there's another way—"

Dando started shaking his head while Shinza was speaking. "—Defence-of-the-workers'-interests line. Tell me another one, do. *Inevitably* leads to a slowing of economic growth. All your ideas about activities based on the workers' productive role can have only a very limited effect. Either you get the workers to buckle down and shut up—"

Shinza was waving an arm at him—"That's what you've tried to do, that's what you've tried!"

"Oh nobody's denying there're plenty of doubts about the unions' ability to put their policies into practice. We know that." Bray, also on Dando's whisky, found himself borne into the argument. "Until now, the trade union leader's metamorphosis into a political's forced him to compromise . . . that's one of the principle causes of weakness here. But the fundamental weakness is a mixture of the two—industrial underdevelopment plus the political responsibility trade unionists have had to assume."

"Oh for Christ' sake. The only thing is, take that political responsibility properly—" Shinza's hands extended under something invisibly heavy— "No holds barred," Dando said. Bray turned on him—"You'd agree that a big say in the drafting of an economic development plan is one of the basic demands of most African trade unions, Roly?"

"Listen to it: demands, demands—" Dando began showing off, appealing to his audience.

But to them Bray was as much a part of the performance as he was. ". . . it's the only way to overcome the contradiction between demands that aim at short-term results, and measures you're going to have to take if you want to establish a real development policy. Of course the difficulties are enormous . . . it's risky . . ."

Every now and then Dando momentarily lost grip and talked out of some hazy response twitching through the alcohol in his brain—"Risking your life every time you cross the road, feller."

". . . the position of the unions and the government could become irreconcilable."

"Ha-ha, ha-ha-ha." Dando wasn't laughing; he shadow-boxed above the bar. "Tread lightly, Bray, eggs underfoot, y'know." His attention lashed back, drawn to Shinza. "You get your trade union membership largely from public administration, apart from the mines. If you start cracking down on bureaucracy, there'll be cutbacks. How're you going to get these people to agree without losing hundreds of members?"

"I couldn't care less about your few hundred bloody bureaucrats if we can gain thousands of peasants. Forget it, man—"

Two or three people had started singing PIP songs, at first raggedly, and then, with the African inability to sing out of tune even when drunk, in noisy harmony. Roly had become defiant without knowing what about; he looked very small and white, his thin greased hair standing up sparsely at the crown, his glasses turning on this target or that. "Better than the whole damn bunch of you, I can tell you that. More guts than some of you'll see in a lifetime . . . I don't trust him as far as the door, old bastard . . . but *you*, wet behind the ears, the lot of you, you won't see another one like him, not for *you* to start telling me—"

Bray felt an old affection for poor Dando, never standing on the dignity of his office but keeping for himself the exactions of personal response, no matter how battered or ridiculous he might emerge. Only an African state would employ a man like that; anywhere else, his professional ability would be lost against considerations of professional face.

Ras Asahe was talking of the strikes at the mines and Bray was only half-listening—"not such a push-over to stop production now that the Company's got the hardware to crack down on them!" The phrase was an arrow quivering: "Hardware?"

"Yes, they won't have to stand around biting their fingernails any more when the boys cut up rough. I saw it the other day, very hush-hush—but, man, it's all there! A nice little fleet of Ford trucks converted into armoured vehicles—"

"The Company police are being armed?"

"Well, what do you think? They're going to stand around waiting for the space men" (the regular police were called this because of their helmets) "to come? Or for the President to decide whether or not it's time to call in the army? Apparently the Company went along to him and said, look here, if *you* can't do it, you must let us. . . . And he gave them the green light."

"They've got guns?"

Ras spread his elegant hands. "The full riot-squad outfit. Tear gas, guns—helicopters so they can move a dozen or so men where they're needed, fast. It'll be a great help wherever there's trouble . . . even if it's not the mines . . . the Big Man knows they're there if he needs them."

At the same time there was some sort of sensation in the knot round Dando and Shinza. All Bray saw was Dando putting his arm round Shinza's shoulder in a flamboyant gesture, a lunge, and—distinctly—Shinza avoiding it quietly and swiftly as a cat slips from under a hand. Shinza wasn't looking at Dando, he was turned away talking to someone else at that particular moment; he must just have become conscious between one instant and the next of the arm claiming him. But Dando, already over-reached from the bar-stool, was unsteady, and the movement tipped his balance. He fell; there was a scuffle—people picked him up in the confusion that looks the same whether it represents hostility or concern.

Asahe said disgustedly, "That old man's the best argument for Africanization I know. They should let the two of them finish each other off; this place needs streamlining."

"What a prig you are, Ras. Perhaps you should send for some tear gas."

But Asahe was flattered to be thought tough; Bray was aware of being under the smile of a man who felt he could afford it. He went quickly to Roly Dando. Dando was on his feet again, somehow rather sobered. "Shall we go home?"

"Why the baby-talk, Bray. Anyhow, aren't you eating with Mweta?" He had the look of a fowl taken unharmed from the jaws of a dog.

"There's time to go home first."

"Good God no, I've got a date." He went off with two young men who had dusted him down, a cheerful, short-arsed little Mso—they were a dumpy people; Batwa blood trickled down from the Congo, there, in some forgotten migration—and a talkative, stooping man who, in addition to the Party tie, wore various insignia from colonial times—Boy Scout and Red Cross buttons.

He left behind him raised voices and exaggerated gestures; the confusion had released private antipathies and post-mortem tensions over the day's business in Congress. Shinza was surrounded solidly by his own men, now; Nwanga, Goma, Ogoto were drinking round a small table with an air of not being anywhere in particular, as if they were in a railway waiting room or on an airport. But Shinza said to Bray over his shoulder, "The old man's all right?"

He had dinner alone with Mweta, late; those guests at the Great Lakes who had not gathered in the bars took a long time to disperse from the Golden Perch Room. Mweta was troubled, as always, by the choice of a cocktail party as a way of entertaining people— "Specially Congress."

So Congress deserved something better. Yet he had sat there, in his robe that symbolized their coming into their own, and allowed himself to take from them consent to his rigging himself into a position of more power. Bray smiled. "Cocktail parties and democracy go together."

"Is that so?"

"In dictatorships, it's banquets."

Mweta grinned. "Do you want this, James—" There was a bottle of wine on the table.

"No, no, you're right, I've had enough—" They were served unceremoniously with steak and potatoes, and Mweta told the servant not to wait. The big dining-room had been air-conditioned since Bray was last in it and felt chill and airless. Mweta impatiently opened the windows and let in the thick warm night, like a signal of intimacy between them. He knew that Bray thought it a mistake for him to make the Trade Union S.-G. his appointee; he himself brought up the subject at once so that it should not seem an obstacle; they talked with Bray's attitude assumed. The cosy clink of fork on plate accompanied the emptiness of an agreement to differ. Mweta ate with unaccustomed greed, getting the steak down with a flourish.

"Of course one can't deny it, in many countries the trade union organization is subordinated to the government's policy. But these are countries whose economic development is slow, they have the greatest difficulties to face in overcoming their initial disadvantages . . . reasons that don't apply here."

Mweta took in what he was saying with each mouthful, nodding not in agreement but to show that he was attentive. "—Yes, but trade unions in the most advanced African countries must be careful not to become radical opposition movements as their position is consolidated—that's a serious danger to the success of any economic development policy."

Bray was aware of his own cold smile and shrug; he reached for the wine after all. "It depends where you draw the line—what does and what does not constitute opposition? There's a difference between a radical approach to labour problems and radical opposition to the government. That's where the confusion comes in. In the choice of economic priorities, can a government afford to take action without the support of the majority of an organized labour movement?"

Mweta smiled as a man does when dealing one by one with objections for which he is prepared. "We have the support."

"That's not borne out by what's been happening in the last few months."

Mweta didn't believe that was what he meant. He answered words put in Bray's mouth. "That business today was a perfect example—an attempt to push the unions into the position of political opposition. Well, as you saw for yourself, it failed. That answers the question whether or not we have the support."

He said dryly, kindly, "Edward failed. You won."

Mweta showed no signs of distress. He no longer said, trust me. He no longer urged to explain himself. "So you think it's between Shinza and me—never mind economic prosperity." He was half-joking, in his new confidence.

"I think that's the way you see it."

"Opposition—especially political opposition—from trade unions can only be allowed when it's clear the governing class is working to consolidate its own benefits rather than for the development of a progressive economy," Mweta said, confining himself to concern to be exact. "When it's only an attempt to discredit the government, the government has no choice except to break these people, ay?—even to use force, probably."

"—I wonder what it was you won."

But they both rendered the remark harmless by a kind of nostalgia, regretful, giving way to each other; what's-done-is-done.

He had held in himself the necessity ever since the mission was accomplished in the glare of the carpark that morning—"my old friend, Semstu"—that he would have to give an account of himself on that behalf this evening; here. Why?—now the whole intention was irrelevant. And by the same token it was not necessary for Mweta to admit to him that he was allowing the Company to equip a private army. The evening passed. Each had what he left unsaid. Yet they talked a great deal. Mweta was eager to discuss some mistakes he admitted, difficulties, some doubts—particularly about members of his cabinet.

The frankness was a substitute for a lack of frankness. It was perhaps not calculatedly ingratiating—an unconscious appeal (to loyalty? sympathy?) that did not yield an inch. The business of whether Bray was staying on in the country was not mentioned either; Mweta merely remarked that he supposed the work in Gala must be nearly finished? He did not ask why Olivia hadn't come. And if he had?— what answer, what hastily offered and hastily accepted lie?

Congress remained restlessly divided on everything it discussed. The margin of order at each session was very narrow. Shinza stared out over the auditorium, disdainfully unkempt. He looked more and more like a stranger who suddenly appears from the wilderness and takes up a place to the discomfiture of other men. Even his supporters seemed to approach him at the remove of Goma, the cheerful Basil Nwanga—men more like themselves. Bray wrote to England (he took advantage, these days, of having something objectively interesting, such as the Congress, to tell Olivia about, to make a long letter to her possible) describing Shinza as "an uncomfortable reminder that ideas are still on the prowl. Beyond the charmed circle of the capital's glow, the whole country . . ."

It was a letter that would be read aloud to the family or friends. "Interesting," and nothing in it that anybody couldn't read. What was happening between himself and Shinza, Mweta—there was no word of that; one confidence, like another, was not possible. Yet—reading it over (he sometimes read over his letters to her several times, now) —he saw that the remark about Shinza reflected some truth about his attitude towards him that had come unconsciously through the studied tone.

He was included in discussions at the Goma house in Old Town. Of course it was his talk to Semstu—using the claim "my old friend" that day sitting in that oven of an ancient car with the plastic rose at eye-level—that, to the rest, made him proven and acceptable; Shinza, no doubt, banked on things more durable and of longer standing. But maybe they were right: the smallest act can be more binding than the largest principles. Shinza's group themselves continued to attack, through every issue debated, what Goma called "the ossification of Party leadership," although, gathered in the Goma house, they knew that the defeat of the Secretary-General motion was their defeat at this Congress. They seemed determined that delegates should have in their ears, even as they voted this opposition down, demands for more initiative for the basic units of the Party and a transformation of antiquated social and economic institutions. They pressed the need for simple living, discipline and sacrifice, instead of what they called the careerism of the new ruling elite. Bray remarked privately to Shinza that they were beginning to show the symptoms of puritanism typical of a pressure group. Shinza smiled, picked at his broken tooth; "That's what's wrong with pressure groups in the end, ay—it's all they've got to do with themselves."

But in the closing day's debate on the President's opening address, he made a brilliant assault on Mweta's position without appearing to attack him personally, and pleaded passionately for a rejection of the "false meaning of democracy that sees it in the sense of guarding the rights of the great corporate interests and the preferential retainment of ties with the former colonial power." He summed up the "spirit of dissension" that had "sprung up everywhere at Congress, because it is in people's hearts and minds" by pronouncing with a turning from side to side of his bushy-maned head like a creature ambushed, "Independence is not enough. The political revolution must be followed by a social revolution, a new life for us all. . . ." And he quoted, his hands trembling, not quite resting on the table in front of him,

"Go to the people
Live among them
Learn from them
Love them
Serve them
Plan with them
Start with what they know
Build on what they have."

It was audacious; this Chinese proverb was, after all, the favourite quotation of Nkrumah, who had both professed socialism and set himself up as a god . . . but Shinza could hardly be reproached, through association, with similar aspirations, because Mweta, like Kaunda, had continued for some time to recognize the deposed Ghanaian head of state. Later, interviewed by a visiting English journalist and referred to as "the fiery political veteran whirled back like a dust-devil from the Bashi Flats," Shinza was quoted as asking, "When we have built our state, are we going to find the skeletons of opposition walled up in the building?" (Olivia sent the cutting at once.)

The man chosen for the closing address to Congress was traditionally a right-hand man of the Party leader; now that the Party leader was the President, the choice was generally taken to signify a coming man in the government. There was talk that John Nafuma, Secretary of Presidential Affairs, was going to be the one. But it was Ndisi Shunungwa, Secretary-General of UTUC, who gave the address.

On the Sunday there was a big Party rally; many delegates stayed on for it and people came by lorry and on foot for miles. The Independence Stadium, used for the first time since the Independence celebrations, had been tidied up for the occasion; the weeds, the damage done by the rains and by people who (it was said) had removed parts of the stands to use as building material—all this was cleared and made good, apparently by the generosity of the Company, using the gardeners and workmen who still maintained Company property with the green lawns and beds of cannas that had created a neat, neutral environment for white employees in colonial times. Bray was there with Hjalmar Wentz and his daughter Emmanuelle, and heard the Chairman thank the Company, among others that he referred to as "sponsors"—an international soft-drink firm had provided delivery trucks to transport old people and parties of school children.

Hjalmar had been so eager for the outing, and Emmanuelle was more or less in attendance on Ras Asahe, who was directing a recording and filming of the event for both radio and one of the rare locally made television programmes. The girl wore a brief tunic made of some beautiful cloth from farther up Africa, and, all legs, clambered about among the throng with Asahe, looking back now and then to where her father and Bray sat with a radiance that came from a presentation of herself to them as a special creature, much at ease among these black male shoulders showing through gauzy nylon shirts, these yelling women with faces whitened for joy. In her own way she was so exotic that she was part of the spectacle, as in the Northern Hemisphere a cheetah on a gilt chain does not seem out of context at a fashion show. Bray remarked on the fact that Ras Asahe was making films as well, now, and Hjalmar said, almost with grudging pride on his daughter's behalf—"Whatever he touches seems to go well." He spoke in a close, low voice; this was the sort of remark he would not pass in the presence of his wife, Margot.

Shinza had gone straight back to the Bashi—had left the capital, anyway: "—I'll see you at home, then," presumably meaning Gala. Without him, it was almost as if nothing had happened. All these people before Mweta, old men in leopard skins with seed-bracelets rattling on their ankles as they mimed an old battle-stride in flat-footed leaps that made the young people giggle, church choirs with folded hands, marching cadets, pennants, bands, dancers, ululating women, babies sucking breasts or chewing roasted corn cobs, men pa-rading under home-made Party banners—the white-hot sun, dust, smell of maize-beer, boiling pluck and high dried fish: the headiness of life. Bray felt it drench him with his own sweat. If he could have spoken to Mweta then (a gleaming, beaming face, refusing the respite of the palanquin, taking the full glory of sun and roaring crowd) he would have wanted to tell him, this is theirs always, it's an affirma-tion of life. They would give it to another if, like a flag, you were hauled down tomorrow and another put up in your place. It's not what should matter to you now. And he wondered if he would ever tell him anything again, anything that he believed himself. The other night was so easy; how was it possible that such things could be so easy. Suddenly, in the blotch of substituted images, dark and light, that came with the slight dizziness of heat and noise, there was Oliv-ia, an image of a split second. It was easy with her, too. She did not ask; he did not broach. It made him uneasy, though, that she and Mweta should be linked at some level in his mind. Of course, there was an obvious link; the past. But a line between the stolid walk down the carpark to lobby for Shinza ("Semstu, my old friend"), and the presence of the girl—always on him, the impress of a touch that doesn't wash off—could only be guilt-traced. And guilty of what? I have gone on living; I don't desire Olivia: something over which one hasn't any control; and the things I believe in were there in me before I knew Mweta and remain alive in me if he turns away from them.

He felt, with the friendly Hjalmar at his side and the amiable crowd around him, absolutely alone. He did not know how long it lasted; momentary, perhaps, but so intense it was timeless. Every-

N

thing retreated from him; the crowd was deep water. A breeze dried the sweat in a stiff varnish on his neck.

They went to the Bayleys' house for a drink afterwards. Roly was there, Margot Wentz, and a few others. "How've you survived?" Neil Bayley meant the tedium of Congress. Bayley was "worried about the Big Boss"; "But you should have been there,"—Hjalmar was comforted somewhere within himself by the contact with the crowd of simple people at the rally. "They love him, you know, they love him." An expression of impatience passed over Margot's face; it recurred like an involuntary nervous twitch, these days, when Hjalmar was talking. Bayley said Mweta was being "ridden hard" by Chekwe, his Minister of Justice, and others. They wanted Tola Tola out of Foreign Affairs, for one thing. "Well, I know Mweta wasn't too happy with him at the beginning—you remember that question in the House about his globe-trotting" —Bray smiled—"but he's done pretty well, in fact, I'd say—wouldn't you?"

"Yes—but those very people who accused him of spending too much time up in jets—they're the ones who're too friendly with him now, for Chekwe's liking. Chekwe says he's got contacts with Shinza's crowd."

Hjalmar deferred the company to Bray. "Is there anything in that?"

"We've seen this week what Shinza's support consists of."

Roly Dando waved his pipe. "Bray for one."

Neil said, "You found him impressive? —When I read what he says I think what a bright guy, he's right, most of the time. But if he's talking to me—I mean if he's there in the flesh and I'm listening—he makes me bristle. I don't like the chap."

Vivien's body had the collapsed-balloon look of a woman who has recently given birth. In its frame of neglected hair that lay stiff as if sculptured, a verdigris blonde—her beautiful face kept its eternal quality through the erosive noise of children and transient talk. "He's a very attractive man. I'm surprised none of us has taken him for a lover."

"You've never met him. Schoolgirl crush." Her husband did not let the remark pass.

"I have. I met him at a reception the first year we were here."

"—Once her passion is roused, she never forgets, my she-elephant —"

"And I talked to him three days ago. We met at Haffajee's Garage."
Everyone laughed, but she remained composed.

"Delightful rendezvous—"

"We were buying petrol. He remembered me at once."

"This positive neutralism is a very fine idea and all that, but we
have to be a little practical, nnh?" Hjalmar said. "Wherever it's attempted the Russians or the Chinese or the Cubans come in and
you're back in the cold war; it's like driving a car, nnh—if you stay
in neutral, you can't move. . . . He wouldn't be any more nonaligned
than Mweta. And as the West is frightened of ideas like his, the East
would be the ones to get him. It's between two sets of vultures."

"Ah well, that's the art of it. Keeping the flesh on your bones.
That's what our bonny black boys've got to master."

Bray said to Dando, "Do you think Mweta's having a try?"

Dando chewed on his pipe with bottom teeth worn to the bone.
"We've talked about it a hundred times. You know quite well what I
think; what you want is to confirm what you think. Because you've
woken up out of your bloody daydream at last . . . I don't know
what did it . . . now you don't like what you see. I'm in the stronger
position because I've never expected to see anything I'd like"—there
was laughter; even Margot smiled—"Mweta's not a man to take great
risks, he's not a radical in the smallest fibre of his body. To make
great changes here you've got to take the most stupendous risks; he's
chosen to play for half-safety for the simple reason he *isn't capable of
anything else* and in his bones he's the sense to know it. He's chosen
his set of vultures because he thinks he can gauge from experience
the length of their beaks; all right—now he's seeing how much flesh
he can keep from them."

He found himself speaking to Dando, to them all, looking at the
faces, one to the other. "Why are we so sure one set of beaks is so
much more dangerous than another? —Because of the prisons, the labour camps, the thousands of dead in the Soviet Union over the
years; because the Great Leap Forward's been overtaken by civil
wars in China; because of Hungary, because of Czechoslovakia,
Poland—yes, I know. But we're people who know what's wrong with
the West, too, the slavery it practised with sanctimony so long, the
contempt it showed to the people it exploited—and still shows, down
south on this continent. The mirror-image of itself that it sets up in

the privileged black suburbia that takes its place . . . The wars it perpetuates in the cause of the 'free world' . . . If positive neutralism is the ideal, but the third world boils down to Roly's art of living between two sets of vultures, why can we be so sure it mightn't conceivably be more worth while to see how much flesh one can save in an association with the East? Why? Because we 'belong' to the West? Express our views—hold them—by the permissiveness of the West? . . . tied to it by that permissiveness? Roly—myself—I don't think he'll say he's ever believed anything else—would you agree we've always accepted what Sartre once wrote, that socialism is the movement of man in the process of re-creating himself? —Is that or is that not what we believe?— Whatever the paroxysms of experiment along the way—whether it's Robespierre or Stalin or Mao Tse-tung or Castro—it's the only way there is to go, in the sense that every other way is a way back. What do you want to see here? Another China? Another America? If we have to admit that the pattern is likely to be based on one or the other, which should we choose?"

"You're saying socialism is the absolute?" Neil loved strong sentiments, as a form of entertainment. He at once took charge. "The standard of reference by which any political undertaking is to be judged?"

"Yes! Must be, if we believe, people like Roly and me, what we've been saying all our lives—the lawyer and the civil servant. Yes! What else?"

"But I am still a lawyer and you are no longer a civil servant," Dando said, looking at him. Their eyes engaged; and then he withdrew, under Dando's gaze of a man who stands watching another go out of sight.

The talk had gone back to Tola Tola, the Foreign Minister. "But what about the Msos," Hjalmar was insisting. "Neil—how will Mweta get him out without causing trouble for himself there?"

Neil Bayley stood about among his seated guests like a ringmaster, running his hands up through his bright curly aureole of beard and hair. "Ah, there's the advantage of the strange position of Tola Tola —although he's nominally Mso, it seems he actually comes from the Congo . . . someone's dug that up. It's clearly not an Mso name . . . is it, James? Tola Tola?"

"Probably not; you don't get the two-syllable repetition . . ."

"—So even though he's got an Mso seat, there's some"—he swivelled his hand right and left, fingers fanned stiffly—"ambiguity about the whole business. But Mweta'd have to put an Mso in his place, that's the snag. Apparently the Msos would want Msomane. Or rather Msomane would want to make sure he was the man. He's mad keen to get rid of Labour, which is hardly surprising."

Bray said, "Neil, would you say Mosmane was one of the people who're pushing Mweta?"

"Depends what way. It's always a tricky business to keep the Mso faction happy. Without making too much of them."

"I don't mean that. Would he have had enough influence with Mweta to get him to approve the Company setting up its private army?"

"Is that story true?"

"Hjalmar has to be told twenty times if it's something he doesn't want to believe," Margot said. "You'd have to run him over with a tank first."

"My source of information only mentioned armoured cars," Bray put in lightly to protect poor Hjalmar. And Vivien's clear commanding voice that stamped her origin as undeniably as any princely birthmark on the backside of a foundling: "Hjalmar, I'm just like you. I wouldn't have believed it if one of the Company mothers who picks up children at Eliza's school hadn't told me how much safer she feels now. —I told her how much less safe *I* feel."

Neil still held the floor. "Cyprian Kente's more likely to be the one who's done the pushing, and even Guka, maybe. If your Interior and Defence boys give advice, it's difficult not to take it."

"And no one's asked any questions in the House."

"It's been done so discreetly . . . the first anyone heard was when these men appeared out of the blue last month at Ngweshi Mine—the report was that 'police' reinforcements had come down from here. Then it leaked out that they were a new kind of police. . . . But when the House sits again"—his mind went back to the "worry" about Mweta he had begun with earlier. "Of course, it *looks* so sinister. I don't doubt that he's tough enough to keep it under control. But it would have been better to keep the Company in the background—could have been called a force of civilian reservists, some such. He's been badly advised to let the Company's name come in openly—I

wouldn't agree that he shouldn't use the resources of the Company if
he needs them, one may have to use existing resources—"

"It doesn't help me to talk about the Company as if it were a
natural phenomenon," Vivien said. "It still looks like the old days we
read about down in Zambia and Rhodesia, with the old Chartered
policing the place for the Great White Queen. . . . What sort of thugs
will the Company recruit, anyway? It's terrifying. All those mercenaries from the Congo wandering around Africa looking for a job . . ."

"I gather it's a black affair, mainly, no whites—" Neil dismissed
her.

"And the Company administrators are running an *army?* You believe that?" Vivien laughed at him.

"Well I suppose they've borrowed a few people from George Guka.
Anyway, you're exaggerating as usual."

Vivien's speckled blue eyes balanced the two men in a sceptical
challenge, inquiringly. "Tell Rebecca I'm keeping my riot bag packed.
. . . I *am* so glad that Gordon's disappeared again, everyone is always much more content without him." Perhaps Rebecca had made a
confidante of her; Bray didn't know. But she spoke so easily, linking
him naturally with Rebecca as a friend who lived in the same place;
it might have been—as this was Vivien—a way of showing him her
acceptance of his relationship and her calm and capable intention to
protect Rebecca and him from the others.

He said, "Oh the children didn't seem to think so. They loved having him around."

"Yes, exactly, Gordon rouses expectations and that's always exciting
—he makes people feel all sorts of things are going to be changed.
But if he stays, they aren't. So it's always better for him to move on,
you know. Now they'll see him in the school holidays, and that will
be fun for them without lasting long enough for any damage to be
done. Rebecca shouldn't worry about them. She's managed awfully
well. I really ought to send our young to my mother or somewhere for
a while; they've been too unrelievedly in my company. Neil objects
for some reason or other." He knew she didn't believe it; she was establishing, in this company, the ordinariness of Rebecca's situation.
But her husband said swaggeringly, "I'm *here*, my girl, not digging
some bloody dam for Vorster and Caetano at Cabora Bassa."

Ras Asahe and Emmanuelle burst in with a few of Ras's satellites.

One was a lecturer at the university, a young black man who caught
a pink end of tongue between his perfect teeth in amusement as Neil,
his registrar, mimicked the staff at a recent meeting, drawing him
into a professional privilege of burlesquing their institution. The gathering began to change character, with more drinks and disjointed
chatter. The subjects they had been talking about were dropped;
whether this was a matter of mood, or because it was not possible,
once again now, for black and white to talk in a general way of these
things without seeming to extract from the blacks secret loyalties and
alliances that might be dangerous for them. It had been like that before; before Independence, when the Governor's hospitality in detention camps and prisons waited at the other end of candour become
indiscretion. The ease in between—the ease of a few months ago—
belonged to a time when the people from Europe were neither in a
position of power on their own behalf, nor as witnesses of a situation
in which the Africans had something to fear from each other. He felt
a wave of impatience with the capital. While he was drinking and
lending himself to the air that it was "marvellous" to be back among
these friends again, he wanted to be off, driving alone through the
night for home, Gala.

Before he left he telephoned Rebecca at the *boma* and told her to
send him a letter granting him her power of attorney. She sounded
chastened, on the other end of a bad line, as people often do at the
idea of urgency. He prepared himself to be kept a few days, hanging
about in Roly's house. But she must have made some arrangement for
the letter to come up by air courier in the government bag—he
hoped she had not discussed the contents with Aleke—because it was
delivered to him at Roly's very promptly, by government messenger.
Folded as an afterthought round the formal letter whose wording he
had dictated, was a half-sheet of green copy-paper with a foolish
password of endearment scribbled on it; exclamation marks. She was
an awkward letter-writer; the things he got from her reminded him of
his daughters' letters from school. He carefully burned the half-sheet
and smiled, aware that the other document was the kind that would
be best burned, too.

But he took it to the bank and withdrew the money from the sale of
the house Rebecca's parents had built for her when she married Gordon, the man everyone was more content without. Half the sum

would have equalled the maximum amount exchange control regulations permitted to be taken out of the country, and then only by people leaving permanently. In breakfast table conversations with Roly
about foreign exchange, Roly was easily led to turn his tongue on the
officials who didn't seem able to put a stop to money going out of the
country illegally, just the same. He said it was well known how these
things were done; there was one crowd, a South African white man
and a couple of Congolese, who had agents in the capital and just
plain smuggled the cash over to Lubumbashi and thence wherever
the client wanted it, and there was a certain Indian down in Old
Town who was known to have more reliable ways and means—a relation of the people who had taken over the garage since old Haffajee
died. How was it done? Well, travel allowances for one thing; poor
students going off on scholarships to study abroad; they were allowed
a maximum allowance that was invariably in excess of the money
they had, so they were paid a small percentage to take out someone
else's money as their own. Businessmen; the wives of white Company
officials going "home" on leave; Moslems going on a pilgrimage to
Mecca—lots of people one wouldn't think it of were happy to earn
their profit on the side.

He thought it might easily be that the Congolese would turn out to
be Gordon's friends. It was not too difficult, through casual inquiry at
the garage, to find out where to go in Old Town. Again with the sun
on his head and purpose at his back he tramped over waste ground.
If the elderly gentleman in the grey persian lamb fez knew who he
was he showed no surprise; and perhaps he had long ceased to be
surprised at the people he recognized. It was all satisfactorily con-
cluded. Rebecca's name would never appear, in fact the elderly gentleman would never know it. The money, nearly four thousand
pounds in English currency, twice that figure in local currency,
would become Swiss francs in a numbered account. In due course Rebecca's signature would be lodged with the Swiss bank as the one required to draw on that account. He explained that delays in the
transfer of the money—a piecemeal transfer, for example—would not
do. This too, was accepted as a matter of routine practice: then the
commission rate would be higher, of course. The money would be de-
posited within two or three weeks at most.

After it was done he walked back to the empty lot where African and Indian children were playing together with hoops made of the tin strips off packing-cases. For the first time he could remember, the Volkswagen was reluctant to start, and they made a new game of helping him push it so that he could take advantage of a downward slope. As he got going and turned into the street a young man in the usual clerk's white shirt and sunglasses greeted him. He did not feel worried that he had been seen; such a worry had no reality for him because it had never seemed it could ever apply to him, have relevance to his way of life. He felt the commonplace peace of being on one plane of existence alone, for once: his mind was entirely occupied with practical matters to be ticked off one by one through a series of actions, before he could get away. The dentist; resoled shoes to be collected; wine as a present for his host.

On the way back to Dando's to pick up his things he was held up, as he had been once before, by the passing of the presidential car. The outriders on their motorcycles rode before and behind—the car was borne on the angry swarm of their noise.

He saw only the black profile of Mweta's face rushing away from his focus. The next time, next time they met—it was difficult to realize that it had ended like that, this time. But human affairs didn't come to clear-cut conclusions, a line drawn and a total added up. They appeared to resolve, dissolve, while they were only reforming, coming together in another combination. Even when we are dead, what we did goes on making these new combinations (he saw clouds, saw molecules); that's true for private history as well as the other kind. Next time we meet—yes, Mweta may even have to deport me. And even that would be a form of meeting.

PART FIVE

PART FIVE

Her car parked outside the Tlumes', Kalimo's washing on the bushes, the fig, like the trees over the main street, under a hide of coated dust, the quality of the silence that met him in his bedroom with the thin bright curtains and in the shabby living-room—he walked through the rooms with clenched hands, suddenly. All here; not a memory; life, now. He entered into it and took possession. Kalimo's welcome flowed over him like an expression of his own joy.

And soon she came, he heard her walking up the veranda steps and the squeak of the screen door that let her pass—in the rush of assurance that in a few seconds she would be standing there in the room, alive. There she was, herself. The self that couldn't be stored up even in the most painstaking effort of the mind and senses, the most exact recollection, never, never, the self that was only to be enjoyed while she was *there*. The moment he embraced her (slight awkwardness of disbelief that it was happening, taste of the inside of her mouth coming back to him, feel of the flesh on her back between his spread fingers) the sense of that self entered him and disappeared, a transparency, into familiarity. She wanted to hear "all the stories" with the amused eagerness of one who has been content, waiting behind—she hadn't envied him the capital or the company of her old friends. They ate their first meal: yes, that was exactly how she was, her way of considering, from under lowered eyelids, what she should help herself

389

to next. He kept pausing to look at her and she, every now and then, reached for his hand and turned it this way and that, squeezing the bones.

"You took the phone call very calmly."

She was hardly expectant. She said with tentative curiosity, "You were very calm yourself."

"Don't you want to know what I wanted the letter for? Aren't you concerned about what I did with it? Rebecca, I've taken your money out of the bank."

She searched him for the joke. "No, really."

"I did. The money from the house. I sent it away. It will be there for you in Switzerland whenever you need it. No one else can touch it, no one will block the account. You can use it wherever you are."

She became at once tense and helpless, an expression that flattened and widened her face across the cheekbones. "Why? I'm not going away."

"You must be safe. You and your children. Now I feel satisfied you are."

"I see."

"You don't see . . . you don't see . . ." He had to get up from the table and come over to her, enfold her awkwardly against his side. He took her arms away from her face; it was roused, red. A vein ran like a thickness of string down her forehead. He thought she was going to cry. He chivvied, humoured—"You're a very trusting girl, I could have run off with all your cash. You handed over without a murmur."

She squared her jaw back against her soft full neck for self-control. "The trouble is that you never try to deceive me. I know what you will do and what you would not do. I could never change it."

"At least I hope the money's in a Swiss bank. We'll know in a week or two whether it's there or whether I've been a gullible ass who's lost it for you."

Between the "stories," the unimportant news of friends, he talked a little of Congress: but it was massive in his mind, it could not be dealt with anecdotally, nor as an account of events, even an explanation. It broke, over the days, into the components most meaningful to him, and these took on their particular forms of expression and found their own times to emerge.

She said that night, "What you did—the money from the house—it's not allowed, is it?"

He had been asleep for a blank second and her voice brought him back. "No, it's illegal." He found his hand had opened away, slack, from her breast; in sleep you were returned to yourself, what you dreamed you held fast to was nothing, rictus on a dead man's face. She said, "It's more in Gordon's line. And if they find out?"

"What's left of the settlers who had me deported will say they knew all along what kind I was."

"And Mweta?"

Her nipple was slack for sleep, too. His hand could hardly make out the differentiation in texture between that area and the other surface of the breast; he dented the soft aureole with his forefinger until it nosed back. She shifted gently in protest at this preoccupation, evasion.

He was suddenly fully awake and his hand left her and went in the dark to feel for a cigarette on the one-legged Congo stool that was his bedside table. He smoked and began to talk about the day of the debate on the UTUC Secretary-General, told her how he had gone down to the carpark to persuade Semstu to support Shinza.

"You knew Semstu from before?"

"Oh yes, an old friend. That's how I could do it. I've known him as long as Mweta and Shinza."

"And Mweta?" she said again, at last.

"I had every intention of telling him. He knew anyway what I thought about the Secretary-General, so I don't suppose it would have been much of a surprise. . . . But it seemed to me after all it was my own affair."

"How d'you mean? You did it for Shinza."

"For myself, I'm beginning to think. Shinza's trying to do what I believe should be done here."

She said, "I'm afraid you'll get into trouble, Bray."

"You're the one who told me once that playing safe was impossible, to live one must go on and do the next thing. You proposed the paradox that playing safe was dangerous. I was very impressed. Very."

"I didn't know you then"—she always avoided the word "love," like a schoolboy who regards it fearfully, as something heard among jeers.

"He will think you're siding with Shinza," she said, out of her own silence. "—Won't he? What'll he do about that?"

"I don't think I can be regarded as a very dangerous opponent. Mweta's the President; he can always get rid of me."

"That's what I mean. You may not be dangerous, but his feelings will be hurt . . . that's dangerous."

"Then for his part he'll be able to say he threw me out because I was smuggling currency."

She sat upright in the narrow bed. In the dark he saw the denser dark of her black hair, grown to her shoulders by now. "Oh my God. You see! I wish you hadn't done it. It's all right for someone like Gordon—"

"My darling . . . just a joke! . . . nothing will happen." He drew her down, made a place for them again, told her all the things that neither of them, for different reasons, believed, but that both accepted for the lull before sleep. "I could see from the way it was managed, it's perfectly safe. . . . Everybody considers currency laws, like income tax laws, fair game—"

"You are not everybody."

They were overcome by the reassurance of being (in the sense of a state of being) so close together; something perfect and unreasonable, hopelessly transitory in its absolute security.

Aleke, to save himself the bother of deciding how to deal with any other situation, behaved as though of course everyone—Bray included—was satisfied to see Shinza put in his place. He asked questions about the "fireworks" with the knowing grin of a man who expects boys to be boys and politicians to be politicians. As he sent one of his children running to fetch cold beer and wrestled fondly with another who persistently climbed over the back of his chair onto his head, he kept prompting, "They let him have it, all right . . . he didn't get away with it. . . ." Bray was giving a matter-of-fact account of some of the main debates, summing up the different arguments and the points that emerged. He said, when the beer had arrived and they were drinking, "Your cynicism amazes me, Aleke."

"Well, that's the first time I've ever been called that."

"Exactly. That's why I'm surprised. You don't seem interested at all in the issues . . . they might just as well not exist. You see it as a contest. . . . They're not concrete to you, then?"

If it were possible for someone of Aleke's confidence to be embarrassed, he was. It took the form of a quick understanding that to accept the charge would be to decry his own intelligence, since he'd already refuted cynicism as an explanation, but to deny would bring
the necessity to discuss the issues themselves—and overcome a disin-
clination, half-laziness, half-apprehension, to find himself and Bray in
disagreement. He smiled. ". . . such a lot of talk. It's only when it
comes down to getting busy with administration that you c'n see how
things are really going to work out. Didn't you always find that? —
You get some decision to cull all cows with a crooked left horn because that's going to improve the stock in some way the brains up in
the veterinary department've discovered, but the result is some people won't pay taxes because it turns out that in Chief So-and-so's
area, *all* the cows've got damned corkscrew left horns—"

But the sidestep in itself was, Bray saw, a recognition of himself as
an opponent.

"Anyway, perhaps we'll get some peace and quiet now," Aleke said
sociably, to include his wife in the talk as she appeared shaking a
packet of peanuts onto a saucer.

"Then take a week off, please, let's have a holiday."

"I didn't say anything about a holiday—just that Edward Shinza
will be out of the way, that's all. —I've told you, you can go off to
your mother if you want to, I'll join James as a bachelor again—"

"I just hope he stays out of the way, then. I don't like these night
trips up to the iron mine and God knows where in the bush—and I'm
alone here with the children." She turned with her slightly sulky, flirtatious manner to Bray. "I'm scared."

"I heard the same complaint from a young woman when I was up
at the Congress. Only she's scared of the Company's private army.
She's afraid they've recruited Schramme and his out-of-work mercenaries."

"Oh *town*. What's there to be afraid of in town. It's not like here
with those bush-people from the lime works shouting in the streets,
poor Rebecca, you remember in the car that time—"

"Yes, yes—but now Shinza's back in the Bashi with his tail between his legs, the Party Congress is over, all that nonsense will stop
—"

"Not only cynical; also very optimistic, Aleke." For Agnes Aleke's sake, he changed the subject. "Have you seen the Malembas since he's been back? Sampson was a triumph with his resolution about the club, I'd no idea he was even contemplating it—"

"Malemba? Really?" Aleke murmured amusedly; and once he said as he drank his beer and gazed round with the preoccupied contemplative criticism of a man too busy to do what he felt he should, "Agnes, either fix up that place like you said or chop it down for firewood."

His wife and Bray looked up uncomprehendingly a moment, and saw that he meant the old summerhouse in the garden. She said, for Bray's benefit, "Oh no, we won't pull it down. I want to make it nice again."

Olivia had built it—or rather had it built, the prisoners coming over under guard to put up the mud-and-wattle walls and tie the thatch (tea and bread sent out to them from the D.C.'s kitchen). It had been for the children, the little girls, dressing up in their mother's clothes and playing in there with their English governess, that girl with hefty freckled calves luminous with ginger hairs who (Olivia said) had been in love with him. But to him now it was Aleke's house; as he walked up the fan of steep, uneven veranda steps or entered the rooms, he hardly remembered he had lived there.

Barely a month went by peacefully for Mweta. If he thought the rebels in the unions had been dealt with at the Congress, the most favoured workers, who had not made common cause with them, had received no such chastening. The "loyal" mineworkers began to renew the pay demands for parity with expatriate white miners that he had refused with his famous "empty hand" argument before. For the time being, he kept out of the dispute publicly, while first Ndisi Shunungwa—his "coming man"—then the Labour Minister's secretary, and finally Talisman Gwenzi, the Minister of Mines himself, intervened. Yesterday's newspaper arrived on Bray's and Aleke's desks each morning with the daily report of meetings and talks whose outcome—failure—was "not disclosed." Aleke remarked, "Mweta should tell them where to get off—he's the only one they'll listen to." Bray did not say, he can hardly show the necessity to do that, now. "That's what he's got Gwenzi for." But it was hard, for people who had long been ruled by a faceless power across the seas not to see authority solely in the face of the individual from among themselves who had taken over in their name. "The government" was so long the alien, abstract puissance; "the leader" their own flesh-and-blood man.

He wondered whether perhaps—for Shinza—one of those strange lulls would now come about; one of those apparently inexplicable breaks in African political life when someone turns away just as he seems about to close his grasp. He had contemplated (with strong unease) Shinza disappearing into the hiatus of that hut smelling of woodsmoke and sour baby, talking, smoking, while an old body slept in a bundle of rags outside in the yard waiting to die as Shinza waited—for what, sign or time, Bray did not know. But Shinza sent for him to come to Boxer's ranch. They had just spent the day at the lake, on their island—he and the girl. It was much too hot and she was in full war-paint of the sun; streaks of scarlet down her shins and calves, across nose, cheekbones and round high forehead. "I hope you're not in for heat stroke"; but she kissed him with burning swollen lips that suggested she was ready to make love. They were both rather exhausted and this seemed to put a fine edge of enervation on their nerves; since he had been back the urgency between them had been constant—sometimes he had to seize her hand and press it on his sex.

Under the rusty old shower she said between gasps and gulps, "I forgot to tell you—old Boxer turned up while you were away. Came to look for you at the *boma*."

"—Stay a bit longer, you may have a slight temperature."

Her hair conducted streams over her face, she pressed her thighs together and stood pigeon-toed in the cold water. She shouted, "He won't be at the ranch."

"How d'you know?" It was a good thing her eyes were closed; the shower belched forth a dead insect with long filaments of drenched legs, and he flicked it unnoticed off her belly. "Oh how could I forget —just let me tell you—" She stepped out blindly onto the soggy mat and felt to turn off the tap, forcing him to come out of the bath too— "That's enough hydrotherapy now, Bray. —Because he's in England. He's gone back to England! His wife died. So now he's gone back to England!" They both began to giggle. "Well what's so funny? I told you, his wife died!" But they laughed more than ever. "Is he coming back? Did he say for good?" "Of course not. He's coming back. He's just gone because she died . . . to see if she did, really, I suppose . . . I don't know . . ."

He made to kiss her on her sunburned eyelids, her neck, but suddenly she resisted with a kind of exasperated embarrassment even while she laughed. In just exactly that way her son, the little one, clenched his face, laughing or crying, and kicked to be free of her sometimes when she snatched him up. Bray fought her but her eyes flew open and he saw—accusation, complicity; an absent wife, a dead wife. "Come on. Pat yourself dry. I'm going to put some cream on your shoulders." They went quiet and purposeful over the small task.

In the morning she rested her face against his back while he was shaving, her sleep-slack arms round his middle. So pleasantly hampered, he cleared away in swathes of the razor the snowman's face in the mirror, and freed his own to meet him, talking at himself, while they gossiped about the capital. He told how Vivien had said it was surprising none of them had taken Shinza as a lover. "Was that what she said—'taken,' I mean? That's her upbringing coming out, dear old Vivien, when it comes to things like that she thinks she's back in one of the stories of her grandmother—or perhaps it's her great-grandmother?—she was a famous Edwardian beauty with a lord for a husband and she would *decide* on this man or that. Never mind what he thought about it."

"Have you told Vivien?"

He felt a wet felt tip draw a line up the groove of his spine: her tongue. "Not directly. But when I write of course it's always 'we did this, we did that.' "

"Because I had the impression she knows about us."

"She always knows about these things, Vivien. She knows but she never talks."

Of course Vivien has been discreet before; perhaps even when it came to her own husband and her friend. "And she's never wrong about people—her judgement," the mouth behind him was saying.

He wanted to say, "She doesn't like Gordon," but his half-closed eyes, directing the shaving of his neck in the mirror, shamed him out of it amusedly. Without glasses, with the blood drawn freshly to the surface of the skin, the younger man whom for some not very convincing reason every man thinks of as his definitive self was almost present in the heavy, strongly planed flesh of the face that he supposed represented him. He saw that face with calm equanimity, feeling her at his back.

When she left for the *boma* he promised to try and return that same night; gave a gentle, reassuring smile to reassert a certain perspective: "—And I'll find out whether Madame Boxer was dead or only shamming," but she busied herself with the heel of her shoe, which she said was loose, and rushed back to the house to change into a pair of red sandals. Red shoes Oriane de Guermantes had preoccupied herself with in order to evade the news that Swann was dying: but Rebecca wouldn't know who Oriane and Swann were, it was with Olivia that he had reread Proust one winter in Wiltshire. Exactly the sort of treat retirement promises to compatibility beyond passion. One (final?) kick of the prostate and so much for that.

Boxer's house appeared shut up; the servants' children were taking advantage of the luxury of playing on the veranda, Round the back, the kitchen was sociably full, with the cook and his friends among pap-encrusted pots soaking in water, jars of milk set to sour, the smell of meat burning on the stove and beer being drunk from jam tins. The cook gave Bray an hospitable tot of the sour thin stuff—in a white man's glass—and sent a young boy to direct him to Shinza. The heat shimmered up from the cattle camps all around but Bray, out in the bush without the crevices of evasion which the shelter of the town offered, had taken it into his lungs, now, his body learnt again to exist within it, drawing it in and sweating it out without resistance like some perfectly adapted organism that maintains the exact temperature of the environment it enters, at one with it.

Shinza and Basil Nwanga were in a little home-made house in European style that belonged to the teacher at the farm school. Shinza pressed upon him a leg of boiled fowl he had in his hand— "No, go on, go on." "But I can have something else—I'll help myself —" "Take it, man"—Nwanga grinned—"he's already helped himself to everything there was—" "Who ate the other leg?" Shinza challenged him.

"*You* man, there, look on the plate, what's that bone—"

Shinza held the bone up for the world to see: "What d'you mean, bone? That's the wing bone, eh?" Nwanga dug a big greasy finger at Shinza's plate. "*There, there*, what's that big one—don't show me any rubbish, just be straight, you hear—you take that leg, Colonel, take it, take it, you won't get it for nothing, don't worry—" Laughing, Shinza snatched up the bone the young man had singled out and threw it to a pale mongrel who caught it in mid-air. "He's destroyed the evidence against him!" Basil Nwanga yelled, beating his palms on the table.

"Send the boy up to the house for more beer." And to Bray, "Just mention booze, Nwanga drops everything. —And say we want a big pot this time, no bloody lemonade bottles— They make good beer at this place, the best I've had for years, since that very good beer— *very* good, eh?—my wife used to make, you know, my first wife, the tall one. A big pot, Nwanga—"

Making a pantomime of haste, fat Nwanga went over to the door to yell for a volunteer from among the children in the yard.

"You seem to be well established here."

"Oh sure. These are all my father-in-law's brethren. Their beer is mine to command."

Bray gestured round. "Not only their beer."

Shinza smiled at the unimportance of the place. "They'll do anything for me. You want to stay up at the house tonight?" He had forgotten that Bray was, anyway, a friend of the owner.

"Look, when you send a message, Edward, why the hell don't you make it a bit more precise. This is a huge estate. —Oh I realize everyone on it knows where you hide out—but then there's the matter of time as well as place. I never know if you're going to be here three days or one, I don't know how long it's safe to wait without missing you, and suppose for some reason I can't drop everything and come right away . . ."

"I'm here until you come, of course."

They laughed. Nwanga said, "What was the Sunday school treat like?" He was talking of the Party rally. "We heard you were there," Shinza said. "Asahe is the man who wants to have me arrested."

"Yes, I went with some friends—the daughter works with him."

"Oh everyone knows about Asahe's white girl. She pretty?" Nwanga was amiably disbelieving.

"Rather pretty."

"He should have seen the girls I used to have in London, ay, Bray? And my American—you remember how she brought me those pyjamas when I was in prison at Lembe—silk, man, Nwanga, with a red belt with a wha'd'you call it, a tassel."

"I've come into the political game too late; that's the trouble."

"Is Mweta happy?" Shinza said.

"Confident, yes, I should say, and that's usually a sign one has no doubts. Or has stifled them successfully. He doesn't seek any reassurance that he's right."

Shinza held a cigarette ready to draw but did not put it to his mouth while he listened; then said, "I see," and took a pull.

Bray saw that the "he doesn't seek any reassurance" gave itself away as admittance that Mweta had released him. Mweta has broken with my approval. He's cut loose; I'm free. So many different bonds, so many kinds of freedom. And each relative to another bond: the freedom to commit yourself to it. Free to make love with her and so become a petty currency swindler. Freed of Mweta—for Shinza.

He said, almost impatiently, "Well, what's happening?"

"Oh there are plenty of things to talk about . . . I want to discuss with you, quietly, you know? I wanted a chance to talk. . . ." Nwanga at once became studiedly attentive as Shinza began to speak; they must have settled it all beforehand. "There's no good to go over that whole business at Congress—a waste of breath, eh . . . I think along other lines now."

"Yes?"

Shinza looked at him almost exaggeratedly anxiously, perhaps, being Shinza, a hint of parody of the seeking for reassurance that Mweta no longer showed. His half-smile admitted it. "There's going to be all hell in the unions. And even if I were to die tomorrow, I'm telling you, it wouldn't make any difference, there'd still be hell—I mean some of what he's got coming to him I wouldn't have anything to do with, it's absolutely contrary to our policy. . . . The miners, now. Already they're better paid than anyone else in the country. But there you are. You'll see, by the end of the month they'll come out, there'll be the biggest row ever, and we'll see what he'll do then. That's the one crowd everyone's afraid of. He won't hold them down so easily this time. The authority of the unions is broken, the government begins to run them itself, and then it turns out even government stooges ask the price for keeping quiet the one industry they're scared to manhandle. What's he going to do? If the miners get more there'll be new demands everywhere. If he gets tough, it'll run like wildfire, there'll be a solidarity between those who've followed the government yes-men and been let down, and those who've refused to follow and are put down."

"And the rebels will have to be blamed for the whole thing."

"Of course. —So-called rebels," Shinza corrected automatically, with the politician's alertness never to be caught out in any semantic slip that could be construed to bely the legitimacy of one's position. "Agitators! Shinza and Goma and Nwanga were there!"

"A good excuse to put us all in jail." Nwanga had never been in one; spoken aloud casually, the subject of fear loses some of its potency.

Shinza had, many times; for him it was irrelevant to waste time contemplating eventualities in which one would be out of action. "The basis for whatever happens is the corruption in the unions, eh—?"

"Corruption?"

"Government interference. Same thing. That's why I've been thinking, why not bring someone—some authority—who can show this up? Without taking sides in the political sense. Some opinion that no one can turn round and say . . . Well, I thought, while we're going ahead here, you could take a little trip, James, go and see the family" —he stretched himself, gestured 'something like that'—"you could go by way of Switzerland, say; lots of planes make a stop there, don't they?"

For an idiotic moment to him the reference was to the money in a bank.

"Go on."

"Oh nothing very terrible, nothing very difficult . . . you could go to the ILO and see if they would send someone—an observer, commission of inquiry—someone to look into the state of the unions here . . . what d'you think?"

It was his way to look at practical aspects first, to withhold other reactions until these were considered. "If the ILO did agree, don't forget there's no guarantee such a delegation would be let in. If I remember, there was the same sort of thing—in Tunisia, wasn't it?— and the government refused. Of course it would be awkward for Mweta to say no, a man of his reputation for reasonableness, but . . . Then there would have to be a proper report to present to the ILO —"

"Oh Goma's got all the stuff for that," Basil Nwanga said, and Shinza added, "We'll knock that out, no problem."

"—And what would my authority be?" Logical considerations were nothing but playing for time; they were overtaken by others. "Ex-civil-servant busybody? Black Man's Best Friend?" And as they all laughed.—"Political mercenary?" Basil Nwanga's laugh became a deep delighted cluck and he hit his thighs. "—Yes, that's it, that's about the nearest definition we'd get for me—"

"Oh you'll be properly fitted out," Shinza said airily, sweepingly.

"I'd have to have credentials. At least show I'd come at the request of a pretty representative string of unions—even then, it'd be going over the head of UTUC—"

"It'll all be fixed up, we'll get to work on it," Shinza overrode. "That's nothing. That's easy. Nothing at all."

He had the curious impression that this was the thoughtless insistence of assurance on a matter that has served its purpose and is no longer of much interest or validity. He said to Shinza, rather hard, "You say you're going ahead here."

"Well, I want to talk to you about that." Shinza clapped at the flies that kept settling on his dainty African ears; caught one and looked at the spot of blood and mess on his hand with disgust. He tore a strip off the morning paper Bray had brought and wiped his palm clean as he spoke. "We know who our friends are in the Party as well as the unions now. We've got to keep up the contact and work together."

"Openly?"

Shinza slowly unbuttoned his shirt. "As far as you can expect."

"Which isn't very far, is it."

The creases under Shinza's breast were shiny lines of sweat, he passed one hand over the hair and nipples. "Oh I don't know. You can put a few union men in jail, you can't arrest the whole labour force." Again and again, the hand skimmed the flesh.

"But you and Goma and Nwanga won't last long."

Shinza caressed his bared, vulnerable chest. "Goma and Basil've got their seats in parliament to protect them a bit—I'll have to make myself hard to find."

"Until you surfaced at Congress, you were rather that way already weren't you. But no one was looking for you all that hard. I have the feeling it's all going to be different now. You'll be arrested the moment you move."

Shinza looked at the ceiling and smiled; turned to Bray. "Because he won't have to explain it to anyone any more?"

A small boy with the beer arrived skittering barefoot onto the veranda and stopped, dead-shy, panting in the doorway. Shinza got up and took from him the plastic container that had once held detergent for washing Boxer's dishes. He gave him a coin and teased him about the strength of his dusty little arms. "Why isn't he at school, James? You know that there's no place for him in the school? Put it in your report."

"It's all there, don't worry."

"Your last word," Shinza said.

"Possibly."

"I mean on the subject—there won't be anything left to say." Shinza was pouring the beer. "Which was yours, Basil?"

"Thanks I won't—I don't know, my bowels are not right today—"

"Come on. It's good stuff, this!"

Shinza filled Bray's glass. "Of course—needs money, to keep going. I don't suppose any of my old friends at the ILO would do anything about that, though . . . ? I'll have to see what I can find. Goma wants to print a paper . . . we need a couple of cars . . . everything takes money."

"Who's been providing it so far?" Bray said.

Shinza was eager to be frank. "We've been depending on my pa-in-law, Mpana. But that's a nothing. That old car of his is just about a write-off, ay, Basil?"

"Needs a new engine, to start with."

"It depends how far you want to go," Bray said. " 'Openly'—that mayn't take you there."

"You heard me." Shinza meant at Congress. "That's where I'm going. To see this country given back to our people. You know me. I've never wanted anything else. Yes, I think I know what's good for us"—his fingers knocked a response from his own breastbone, angrily —"just as he's decided what's good enough for 'them.' That's the big difference between him and me. I hope I'm stinking in the ground before I come to what he's settled for. Stinking in the ground. Only I was cunt enough to believe all those years that we'd taught him what independence was—cunt enough." Nwanga sat dead still. Bray saw with amazement Shinza's tears shining at him, holding him. "If this bloody country ends up belonging to the Company, the cabinet ministers, the blacks who sit on white men's boards, after all the years we've eaten manioc and presented our arses for the kicking and asked

and begged and had our heads cracked open and sat it out in jail"—
his voice reeled, saliva flew from his teeth—"then I blame myself—
myself. And you, Bray. I blame you, and you'll never get out of it,
never! So long as I'm alive, you'll know it, I don't care whether you
sit in England or the end of the world, I don't care if you're white. So
long as I'm alive!"

The room was a vacuum for a moment. Outside children must have
been playing with Chief Mpana's car; there was a blast on the hooter,
then shocked silence. Shinza stalked out. He could be heard chasing
the children. He came in again with his walk of an embattled tomcat.

Shinza was looking at him and slowly buttoning his shirt.

He said, "Shinza, what would you do with him?" There was the
strong feeling between them that Nwanga had no place in their presence; huge Nwanga, caught in this very current, was unable to leave.

"But I could not kill him," Shinza said.

"You will lock him up somewhere for years, or give him over to
some other state so that he can waste his life plotting to oust you."

". . . Oh God knows."

"But the others around him—they'd have to go?"

"They'd have to be locked up, certainly."

A feeling of distance, like faintness, came over him. Without pause,
he said matter-of-factly, "You are still seeing Somshetsi and the others. Am I right in thinking you have a deal—they would help you
with men and arms in return for some promise that, afterwards, you
would give them a base?"

"Along those lines. It need not be too—not cause too much—"
Shinza struggled, suddenly flashed, "Not much more damage than
he'll do whenever he lets his Company guerrillas loose among the
workers. It need not—if the time's right."

"You're going to try to make the time right."

Nwanga's presence had slowly become accepted again. Shinza was
silent while the young man, looking to Bray, nodded heavily.

"If I come through Gala one night and want to see you, that's all
right—you're alone at your house, h'm?" Shinza remarked.

"I'm not alone."

Shinza said, "Oh then I'd send a message, okay? Come let's move
—I want to take you to this fellow Phiti, disappeared after the iron-
mine case was dropped, been in detention all this time while those

bastards from PIP went scot free. —That's Chekwe and our old friend Dando."

The tall, protruding-eyed man's nose had been broken while he was under interrogation. He was at once listless and yet loose-tongued, the real misery he had suffered came out mixed with the obvious lies of self-dramatization. There were two hundred men in the prison camp—three hundred—five hundred. He had been kept in solitary confinement; he had been locked in a shed with fifteen, twenty others. They were half-starved, they had lived on cane rats from the sugar fields, their shoes were taken away. "Why the shoes?" said Shinza, cold at this poor showing before Bray. "Why? Why? —Look at this, they hit me with the leg of the chair that was broken." The man kept feeling the crooked saddle of his nose and looking round at them all to see if they were reacting properly.

Shinza need not have been embarrassed before Bray; as a magistrate he had come to know that suffering was not the noble thing that those who had never seen it thought it ought to be, but often something disgusting, from which one's instinct was to turn away. The man sat in a hut full of relations who had come to be there as if at a sick bed; more squatted among the chickens and dogs outside, the old and the children. A tiny girl crawled into the doorway in a rag of a garment that showed her plump little pubis with its divide; every time Phiti touched his nose her small hand went up with his and felt her own face.

Compassion was too soft a thing anyway. Anger came of disgust, and was of more use, most of the time.

The camp where Phiti was held was at Ford Howard; the old "place of safety" where the colonial government had "confined" Mweta. Shinza was alert to Bray all the time, intent to be one jump ahead of his mind. He said dramatically, "We'll plough that place over and plant it. It just mustn't be there, any more."

A tremendous dust-storm blew up on Boxer's ranch, coming through the pass from the Bashi Flats. Feathers, leaves, maize-husks, ash and rubbish from people's fires danced in the vortex of dust-devils that swayed toppling columns up into the sky. The wind was hot. In place of the sun an apocalyptic red intensity moved down the haze; people sniffed for rain in the turbulence, although it might not come for weeks yet. They sat tight in their huts. Bray stayed the night after all, sleeping naked in a stifling room closed against the wind with Shinza, Nwanga, and the schoolmaster. He could just as easily have driven home through the night, but he had a strange reluctance to step outside the concreteness of the atmosphere between himself and Shinza; these men. They talked until very late: the unions, Vietnam, the Nigerian war, the Arabs as Africans, Wilson's failures in Africa, and Nixon's cooling towards its white-dominated states; about the unions again. He had allowed himself to forget, for years, the superiority of Shinza's intellect. Lying there in the room that smelled of the sweat of all their bodies, the dregs of their beer, and the bitterness of cigarette ends, hearing the man snort, turn on the cheap iron bed uninhibited in acceptance of himself in sleep, as he was always, Bray thought how it was a remarkable man, there—like many of the other remarkable men on this continent who had ended up dead in a ditch. Then the blacks blamed the white men for manipulating power in a continent they had never really left; the whites blamed tribalism and the interference of the East (if they themselves were of the West) or the West (if they themselves were of the East). The remarkable men talked of socialism and the common man, or of glory and Messianic greatness, and died for copper, uranium, or oil. Mweta was one of them, too. Mweta and Shinza. For him—Bray—the killing had been made, for Mweta, already. The phrase in political jargon was "yielding to pressure"; it's finished him off, as I knew him. Couldn't say how Shinza would go, yielding to another kind of pressure (but I couldn't kill him, he lied; and I lied, accepting it?).

Neither away in England, nor the other end of the world . . .

He thought he didn't sleep but he must have, because the words hung there.

A man was sitting with Rebecca in the living-room. The room was dimmed against the heat.

But Hjalmar Wentz was in the Silver Rhino; in the capital!

Wentz and Rebecca sat deep in the sagging old morris chairs on either side of the empty fireplace, sunk in the silence of each being unable to explain his presence to the other. So great was the awkwardness that neither could get up.

"Well Hjalmar! What are you doing here!" He released them, Rebecca's eyes signalling a complicated anguish, warning, heaven knows what, Hjalmar saying with a painful smile, "Well, you did ask me, perhaps you remember . . . ?"

The fact that his platitude of greeting had been taken as a protest warned him more explicitly than Rebecca's eyes. "I just never thought I could get you up here no matter how hard I tried . . . this is splendid . . . when did you arrive . . . are you"—but the eyes, absolutely yellow now with intensity, signalled—". . . you drove up all the way?"

A shaky gesture—a smile that twitched faultily and an attempt at humour: "Don't ask—I got here. And Rebecca gave me a nice lunch."

"That's splendid. I simply gawked . . . couldn't believe it. I've been off trudging round some schools . . . just eating dust all day. I must have a shower—was there a terrible wind, here, last night?" They talked about the weather; "Well, some tea first and a bath later.

Wash the dust down instead of off . . . have you got your things in, did Kalimo look after you all right?"

"Yes, yes—Rebecca gave me a very good lunch, avocados fresh from the tree, everything, the service was first class!" The voice seemed to wind automatically out of the stiff blond face. Bray and the girl were standing round him as if at the scene of an accident. She said, "I must dash." "My best to Aleke," Bray said, but followed her to the garden by way of the kitchen on the pretext of ordering tea.

She was waiting for him. "Something ghastly—you didn't hear the radio?— Ras Asahe's fled the country. Emmanuelle went with him."

"Why should Asahe do that? Are you *sure*? Has he—"

"Only mentioned Emmanuelle. 'I suppose you know Emmanuelle's gone away,' he said to me, but I was afraid to ask, I was afraid he wouldn't stay calm. Oh my God, I thought you'd never come. I phoned the *boma* and said I couldn't come back, I was feeling ill or something. I couldn't leave him alone. I don't know what's happened . . . with them. He doesn't mention Margot. 'Emmanuelle's gone'— that's all. And then we just sat with nothing to say. I don't know what he thinks about finding me in the house as if I owned the place. Well—I don't think he notices anything at the moment. But why come *here*? Why to you?"

"Oh my darling . . . I'm sorry . . . don't worry." He looped her hair behind her ears—she was so pretty, now, with her hair grown. He wanted to kiss her, and doing so, not caring that Kalimo had come out to throw tea-leaves on the compost, felt the whole warm body fill the shape it had made for itself within him.

"How long will he stay?"

"My love, don't worry."

"Now I won't be able to come here tonight." She suddenly pressed her pelvis up against him in misery.

"Bloody hell. Oh come, why shouldn't you. We simply won't offer any explanation, that's all."

"Yes. Yes. —Oh why choose here, why couldn't he have gone some-where else."

"It's all right, it's all right." He stroked her hair as if it were some delightful new texture he had never had in his fingers before.

"Would you like to make love to me now?"

"Of course."

"Damn him," she said. They nursed each other against their resentment.

He went with her to her car, touching her hair. As she started the engine she turned to him a smile of pure happiness. "So I'm coming." He nodded vociferously. She lingered over him a moment longer: "You've got dust in every line of your face." He understood what she was saying. "I know, my darling."

And there was the man and his misery waiting.

Bray went in, to him.

He felt conscious of his own height, his heavy, healthy muscular bulk—his wholeness—as he stood there; it seemed to owe an apology, to be an affront. He took a packet of cigarettes from the pocket of his bush jacket and gestured it to Hjalmar before taking one.

"Anyone have any idea why Asahe should have done it?" he said.

The haggard blond face winced into life. "He was at the hotel on Wednesday evening—she rushed in and said she was going out for an hour. She came back very late—must have, I had already tidied up and gone to bed, and she wasn't home yet. Then on Thursday I understand she took some clothes to the cleaner and insisted they must be done the same day. Apparently she begged Timon—the head-waiter—you know—it was his day off and she asked him to pick them up when he came from town. She didn't want her mother to know about it, you see—so she must have already decided then. . . . Friday she was quite normal, quite normal, nothing . . . and in the afternoon she said she was going with a few friends for the weekend at Matinga, to the dam. She even came into the office and asked me to get her water skis out of the storeroom. Can you believe it?" The face went blank again. He got up suddenly, struggling slowly out of the chair so that Bray had to hold back the urge to put out his hands to help him, as from interference in a private act that should not be observed. The man walked across the room, his jacket peaked up crushed over his shoulders; faltered in sudden loss of purpose. "She was with me in the storeroom and we looked among the rubbish for the water skis. She said to me had I never tried, and I told her we didn't do it when I was a youngster, and she said but you used to ski properly in the snow and you use the same muscles—she said I must come one day and try. She said, you feel powerful, don't you, when everything is rushing past—you feel you can do anything you want."

He began to shake his head very hard in order to be able to go on. "She actually went with me to get the water skis."

Bray sat down on the stool with the ox-thong seat the boys at the carpenter's shop had made for him. There was nothing to offer but patience.

"I told her that was exactly the way I used to feel in Austria. Funnily enough, just what I used to think. And then she went to her room with the skis and I never saw her again. I had to go down to the cold storage in town and when I got back I was told she'd left for Matinga."

"Didn't see her again?"

He began to talk excitedly. "I mean we expected her Sunday night, sometime, that's all, we didn't think anything. . . . On Sunday I'm just seeing that the chairs are put out in the beer garden, and Timon comes up, there's a phone call. Well, you know . . . I said, let someone else take it, can't you. Then he said, it's from Dar-es-Salaam, it's Miss Emmanuelle. I told him, Dar-es-Salaam! It's Matinga! I wasn't worried, I thought, she wants to stay another night."

"She phoned you from Dar-es-Salaam?"

"She was on the airport. I didn't believe her. She kept on telling me, listen, Ras and I are in Dar-es-Salaam, we are leaving for London in a few minutes. She couldn't hear me well. I shouted to her, live with him here, Emmanuelle. You don't have to run away. She lost her temper. She said didn't I realize she wasn't 'playing the fool'—those were her exact words—she wasn't 'playing the fool,' Ras was in great danger and he couldn't have stayed. That's what she said."

"And the announcement on the radio?"

Hjalmar was sunk back in the chair. "Well, we were cut off then. I phoned, I tried to get a connection from here . . . by the time we got through to Dar-es-Salaam again they were gone. Margot wouldn't believe me, I had to repeat over and over again, everything, like I'm telling you . . . She went hysterical, why hadn't I called her to the phone. And then Stephen heard on the news that Asahe, with a white girl and so on—no name—had slipped out of the country. They must have been at our airport in the afternoon waiting for the plane just two miles from where we were sitting in the hotel. People say he was in some political trouble. Can you think why he should be in political trouble?"

o

He was eager to turn this mind to reasonable supposition. "Hjalmar, honestly, whenever we spoke together he gave me the impression of being a staunch supporter of whatever the government might choose to do. Perhaps some pressure of personalities, at work . . . ? But suppose someone were trying to jostle him out of his position at the radio, he wouldn't have to disappear out of the country, would he."

"I've been to the police." He shrugged. "I tried to get hold of Roly but he wasn't in town, I couldn't . . . all she says, I want to know word for word . . . why didn't you call me to the phone. Night and day." He leaned forward and whispered into Bray's face: "I don't know any more what Emmanuelle said on the phone. I don't know if perhaps she didn't say something else, I don't know if I talked to her at all."

Bray did what he would not have known how to do a year ago. He gripped Wentz's two hands, pinned them a moment on the chair arms. "What about Dando . . . ?"

Such bewilderment came into the face, such confusion that he dropped the question. The man obviously had fled without waiting for Dando to return; somehow let go, lost hold . . . No wonder Rebecca was uneasy to be with him.

"London's a good place for them to have gone. You will hear soon from her there. One can always arrange things in London—friends, money, and so on." Olivia. But quick on the thought, reluctance: to spin a new noose, draw this house and Wiltshire together, produce, in Emmanuelle, evidence that a life unknown to Wiltshire existed here. As if somehow the lines of the girl could be traced in Emmanuelle, so different!

It was not possible to give Hjalmar Wentz any relief. He could not be distracted. If one did try, there was blankness; what had happened had run rank over his whole mind and personality for the time being. It was destroying him but at the same time it was all that held him together: attempt to disentangle him and he would fall apart sickeningly.

So it was Emmanuelle; Emmanuelle and Ras Asahe; the Friday afternoon and the telephone call from Dar-es-Salaam on Sunday night. The three of them sat in the old Colonial Service chairs in Bray's living-room for the next few evenings while Hjalmar Wentz talked. His face had taken on a perpetually querulous expression and the middle finger of each hand, inert on either arm of the worn chair, twitched so that the tendons up to the wrist trembled under the skin.

"When she went with me to the storeroom, I wonder if she didn't want to talk to me . . . eh? Perhaps I said something . . . I put her off without knowing . . ."

"Oh I don't think so. You and she get on so well. If she'd meant to say anything, she'd've, well . . ."

The blue eyes continued to search inwardly. Bray took the glass away from the hand and topped up the whisky, but drink didn't help, you couldn't even make him drunk, he held the glass and forgot it was there. "Why say that about 'feeling you could do anything'? I should have said, what d'you mean, 'anything.' "

Rebecca had remarked to Bray, "It's better for him to drive us crazy about what he thinks he did wrong, poor soul—at least it keeps him from thinking how calculating she was—right down to the business of her skis."

But Bray could not help looking for some reassurance that would hold. "Hjalmar, was what she did so extraordinary to you—after all? You say she's really very attached to the man. Perhaps you even feel responsible in a way, for the loyalty she probably feels to him? Because you and Margot—well, your children grew up in an atmosphere where Africans were regarded as people in need of championing—you know what I'm getting at? —If something terrible threatened him (we have to believe her) and she helped him to get away, well . . . you yourself, in Germany when Margot . . ."

He didn't know what there was in this that was so destructive to Hjalmar. He saw the face of a man falling, falling, crashing from beam to beam through glass and dust and torn lianas of the shelter that this ritual of discussion built to contain him. Into the silence lying like an irredeemable act between the two men, came the sound of Rebecca singing to herself in the shower under the impression that she could not be heard above the noise of the water. Bray found himself, appallingly, smiling. In Hjalmar's face only the fine fair skin seemed intact, the bone structure seemed to have loosened and his mouth was always a little parted as if he lacked oxygen. Now something faintly stirred there, a kind of coordination in the eyes, an awareness of the existence of other people, as if his wild glance had fallen upon a scrap of undated newspaper picked up in the rubble.

Bray began to carry drinks and glasses into the garden. In his present state Wentz noticed neither abrupt changes of subject nor apparently aimless activities. He picked up a stool and newspaper, stood a moment, slowly put the paper down, then picked it up and followed slowly to the fig tree. The dust in the air at the time of the year made a chiffon sky after sunset, matt grey and pink, and the atmosphere was thickened with the same colours reflected on soft, invisible suspensions of dust. Bray lit the lamp; Hjalmar said, "I'm sorry I walked in on you like this."

"It's quite all right."

But his self-protective stiffness seemed curiously to succeed in helping Wentz as all his sympathetic responsiveness had not. "No, I shouldn't be here. You ought've been left alone. I know that."

"It doesn't matter, Hjalmar. In the end the only secrets one cares to keep are those one has with oneself—and even that's a mistake."

"I don't follow you."

He smiled. "I think I mean the doubts one has about repudiating aspects of oneself one can't live by any more."

"And if there's nothing left?—wha'd'you do then, kill yourself?" But the words were lost, they could be ignored in the appearance of Rebecca, smelling of the perfume he'd bought her in the capital, calling out, "Oh good idea, yes, let's eat outside tonight. Shall I ask Kalimo? Have you got cold beer there for me?"

There was a phone call next morning to Bray at the *boma*. Stephen Wentz—"Is my father there? —Yes, well he was seen by someone on the bus at Matoko, so we thought he must have made for your place." "He's all right," Bray said, although the son didn't ask. "My sister cabled." "London?" "Yes, she's staying there." Bray phoned his house at once. Kalimo took a long time to find Wentz. What did he do with himself all day: he was apparently sitting somewhere in the garden. He spoke at last, a hesitant croak, "Hullo . . . ?" "Emmanuelle's safely in London. She cabled—your son's just phoned." "To your office?" Wentz confirmed nervously.

"He doesn't want to speak to any of them," Bray reported to Rebecca, who happened to have slipped into the office while he was telephoning. She shrugged, pressing her chin back so that it doubled, half-comically, and he ran a finger along it to tease her. Lying in bed early that morning he had told her of Shinza's suggestion about the

ILO in Switzerland. She said, now, "If you go out, will you be let in again?" It was that she had come for.

"Why not . . . and if I do as he wants me to . . . say I'm going to England."

"You'll go to England." She was standing in the doorway.

"I may not go anywhere at all. I don't know how serious he is about it. I had the feeling . . ."

He had not told her anything more. He had always told Olivia everything. But in the end? Now he could tell Olivia nothing at all, nothing. So what was the answer, between men and women?

He had to go over to Malemba's house; Sampson wanted to talk to him, privately.

"I've been threatened." Malemba waited until his wife had put down two big cups of milky tea and left their small living-room again. He looked embarrassed, as if he had to confess to an infection caught in compromising circumstances. "I've been told if I don't stop the classes for the lime works people 'I won't come home one night.' "

"By whom?"

"A man, Mkade—he calls himself Commandant, the Young Pioneers. The same people who started a fight outside the Gandhi Hall while we were up in town." —He meant at the Congress.

"We're going to ask Commissioner Selufu for protection. We're going to go to him together. There must be a witness that you've been promised it."

The courses being given at present for the limeworkers were the most straightforward elementary education. "Who would want to put a stop to that?" Malemba repeated.

"It's the one I did earlier about workers' rights and the trade unions, I suppose. They don't want anything like that run again."

Selufu with his East Coast man's curved nose and eyes crinkled in a professional expression of decision listened without reaction. "I don't think you've got to worry about anything, Mr. Malemba, I would ignore the nonsense—"

"These people have shown themselves to be violent, Commissioner —you yourself know the police have had to intervene many times, where they're involved," he heard himself saying coldly.

"—But if you feel nervous"—a patronizing, very quick smile thrown towards Sampson Malemba—"I'll see there's somebody on duty around the Hall these nights. Of course, feelings run high in politics—feelings run high in our country, eh?—and if you start these lectures and clubs and then people—well, it's natural you run into trouble, and then we . . . we are obliged to protect you. What can we do?" He laughed with determined pleasantness, and as they made to leave remarked, "And you, Colonel? What was your complaint?"

"Malemba and I run the adult education scheme together, as you know, Mr. Selufu. I am concerned with whatever affects it—and him."

"Oh well I'm glad you are all right. No trouble in your trips around the country. You don't run into any of these trouble-makers, eh—that's good, that's good. I'm glad."

At dinner that evening the news came over the radio that Albert Tola Tola, Minister of Foreign Affairs, had been arrested as the leader of a plot to overthrow the President. Several "prominent people in public life" as well as two members of parliament were involved, and there had been at least five other arrests. Another conspirator, the broadcasting and television personality Mr. Erasmus Nomakile "Ras" Asahe, had apparently fled the country last week. Hjalmar Wentz listened like a prisoner brought up from the cells, dazed, to hear a sentence. Rebecca stared at Bray. He felt a nervous excitement that made him want to laugh. Tola Tola! Kalimo came in to take the soup plates and clicked his tongue in annoyance because they were not emptied. Hjalmar lifted his spoon and began to eat.

They all ate. Bray shook the bell for Kalimo. "So we know nothing, Hjalmar, we know nothing!"

"Tola Tola," Hjalmar said, clearing his throat. "Has he got something to do with Edward Shinza?"

"Apparently not! It must've been a right-wing coup they were trying!"

"I always found Asahe such a vain fellow," Hjalmar said. But it was the only reference he made to the political sensation. Emmanuelle had gone; public revelations neither added to nor subtracted from that. Rebecca made a shy offering—"At least they didn't drag her in." And Bray added, "No, that's good—it looks as though there won't be any difficulty," meaning that the Wentzes would not suffer from being suspected of implication in the Asahe affair. Surely Roly would look after that much, anyway. Hjalmar didn't suggest that he might telephone his wife, or that he would be going home. He drank a brandy with Bray after dinner and went to bed early; from under the fig tree they saw him pulling the curtains across the light from his room.

They walked round the garden—a thick hot night and no moon—and carried on, talking, close but scarcely able to see each other, through the bush. They found themselves in the rough of the golf course—but at night the tamed and trimmed colonialized landscape went back to the bush, was part of the blackness that made all but the centre of the small town (feeble light cupped in a huge dark hand) one with the savannah and forest that stretched away all round, closed over it with the surging din of a million insects in a million trees. Shinza, Mweta, and the two of them themselves, walking by feel among the shapes of bushes; Tola Tola, Ras Asahe.

"D'you think she was in it with Ras?" Rebecca said.

"Oh I doubt it."

"She's so clever. She used to make me feel she knew what you were thinking."

"What I'd like to know is whether this was an Mso attempt or whether Tola Tola was on his own, so to speak—I mean he's always been regarded as part of the Mso faction, Mweta gave him Foreign Affairs under the old electoral bargain with them. We'll only find out when they publish the names of the rest . . . Ras's family background's solid Gala, old-guard PIP—but he was disdainful about old man Asahe . . . she was clever, all right, if she always knew what *he* was thinking. Come to think of it, Neil was talking about Tola Tola not being Mso by birth."

"There'll be a proper old witch-hunt now. Nobody'll be able to move without being frisked." Sometimes her turn of phrase unconsciously echoed Gordon, the husband; somewhere away across two thousand miles of dark he was there, too, the consciously handsome little male in his silk scarf.

"I don't know about that. Nothing makes people feel safer than to have uncovered a plot and handed out retribution. Fear takes on a face and a name and is dealt with."

Maybe attention would be distracted from Shinza for a while; who knew? Moving along with her in the dark he was conscious of suppositions dissolving one into the other. They came to an eye of water, the sheen off black satin; something dived into it noisily—leguaan? The beasts persisted here, among the lost golf-balls, ungainly prehistoric survivors disguising their harmlessness in the appearance of an alligator—he had met one once, and idly remarking on it to Kalimo, Kalimo had captured the thing and eaten it.

"You mean you'll still go to Switzerland."

He felt beneath his hand the articulation of her hip as she walked. "Come with me. We'll try another lake."

"How'd I get back again."

Of course, they were not perfectly and secretly at large in the dark at all; if she stepped outside the accepted justification of her necessity for staying in the country, she could not return to this life. It existed only here.

The house where he lived with her was in darkness, far below the great tree. It looked deserted, already the forest was rooted beneath it. They went in, talking again of Tola Tola. He was too preoccupied to think of love-making, but while she moved quietly about the bathroom (not to disturb Hjalmar across the passage) his whole body, flung down upon the bed, of itself made ready for her; she saw when she came in. And so he entered again the fierce pleasure that was in her, while the bats from the fig pierced pinholes of sound in the thickness of dark.

He was clear-headedly awake for a few moments some time in the night. Why go to Selufu with Sampson? He and Sampson laid a complaint with the Commissioner of Police; the Commissioner detailed a man to the Gandhi Hall. A series of procedural gestures: what ought to be done had been done. According to what code? And if Malemba were really to be killed? He could be knifed in any of a dozen ambushes around the township; outside his own gate. . . . *It was still something they couldn't believe;* we—I am still acting within a set of conventions that don't apply. No more dangerous delusion than that. Selufu won't—can't—give the word to the Young Pioneers that will bind them. There is no word. A policeman outside the Gandhi Hall: it was the perfect symbol of a moral surety become meaningless. There was nowhere in the world now where *Satyagraha*—already polarized with violence the moment the term was translated as nonviolence—could find the compact of respect for human life on which its effectiveness depended.

Who can protect Malemba? Mweta, whirling about-face from Shinza only to defend himself against Tola Tola, could not offer anything better than Selufu's policeman walking round the Gandhi Hall. Shinza had no power to offer the kind of safety he promised—after . . .

Malemba needs a gun, he must carry a gun these nights.

But in the morning the urgency of that flash of wakefulness that had lit up his mind between dark and dark was pale in daylight. It was Saturday; Rebecca went into "town" early on some shopping errand, and he lingered at the breakfast table under the tree until she returned with mail and newspapers she'd called for at the *boma*—although the offices were closed, there was always someone who cleared the mail-box. There was more in one of the overseas newspapers about the Tola Tola affair than could be gleaned from the local papers; they were reading over a fresh pot of coffee when Hjalmar appeared, somnambulistic as he was in the mornings; he obviously took strong sleeping pills. They said nothing to him about Tola Tola; let him linger in that sleep-walking state in which he went measuredly back and forth between kitchen and breakfast table—as an unconscious sign, perhaps, of the awkwardness he felt at staying on, he had developed a kind of reluctance to be waited upon.

Bray had finished his breakfast; Rebecca ate with the guest. He had dreamt all night—"That's why I'm so tired this morning . . . there was a beetle on the floor, buzzing on its back."

"In the dream?" Because Rebecca resented Hjalmar's presence she was always particularly attentive to him.

"No . . . in the room, on the floor. I heard it when I turned out the light. And every time I fell asleep I woke up and heard it, still there, on its back. I kept thinking, it's on its back, it can't get up, I must turn it. Poor thing . . ." Bray smiled a moment, over the top of the paper, over the top of his glasses, and he directed himself at Bray—"And then I got up and turned on the light and found it and took the slipper and killed it." He looked intently first at Bray, then at the girl, as if for an explanation. They hesitated, Bray laughed mildly and so did she. "Finish the rest of the scrambled egg," she said. While they read, Hjalmar listlessly took up the review section of an English paper.

Rebecca went off to wash her hair, running her hand up through it in one of those ritual gestures connected with the care of their bodies that women have.

"So Wilhelm Reich is in fashion again with the students . . . I see his wife's written a book about him. When I was young in Germany he was our prophet . . . but while we were discussing the sexual revolution as the break with authoritarianism in the father-dominated family, others were already kissing the feet of Father Hitler and Father Stalin. —What about our ideas of democracy, when we know the majority will has been so many times self-destructive . . . ?"

"Of course you tend to see everything from the point of view of the place you are . . . so I find . . ." Bray said. "But what would Reich have thought of the authoritarianism of this continent, now—the sexual basis of authoritarianism according to his theory simply doesn't exist in African societies, their sexual life has always been ordered in a way that makes satisfaction available to everyone the moment he's physically ready?"

But Wentz's flicker of interest damped out; he turned pages dutifully and folded the paper aside.

"Poor thing. Only when I was in bed again, I realized I'd killed it," he said. "I squashed it under the slipper—you know those *Kaefer*, they have a hard case but it squashes in a minute. But I'd got out of bed just to stop the noise, to put it on its legs, to stop the useless struggle."

Along with the newspapers and other mail was a letter from Olivia. Bray had left it there though he had seen it at once when the girl put down the bundle—it lay under their eyes a moment while he was already tearing wrappers off the newspapers. He opened it now.

". . . I mean to be on your back, hour after hour on the floor."

The large well-formed, well-educated handwriting covered thin sheets without a word crossed out—the marriage of a son of some old friends, Venetia's new car, the Labour Party's Brighton conference—*I sat watching on TV while you were in the smoke and heat of Shinza's battle with Mweta. Joosab's cinema, of all places—do you remember when it was opened, just before we left, and little Indian girls garlanded all the white ladies with hibiscus full of ants, so we were scratching ourselves politely all through the speeches. . . .*

"A sign of weakness. It's fatal to show a sign of weakness. She accuses me of weakness. She says I had no authority over the children. But she also blames herself. D'you know why?" Hjalmar began to laugh weakly, unable to help himself. "D'you know what Margot said?"

His eye was following Olivia's letter as he listened to Hjalmar . . .
you are having a so much more interesting time . . . my poor dull
news . . . I sometimes worry. I wonder where we'll take up again. Of
course I should have come, but the fact that I didn't . . . shows that
it wasn't possible for us.

"She said, I blame myself. A Jewish father would have had some
authority over his daughter. He would have seen that she was provided with a proper musical education. He would have found somewhere better for his children to live than buried in this place. A Jew
would have done better."

In the appalled silence the weak giggle spilt over, again. "I know
I'm not well. But that's true—she said it." The terrible weak laughter
was suddenly a fiercely embarrassed apology—not for himself, but for
his wife.

"Poor Margot," Bray said.

"I left all the keys, I left the van outside the bar, and I walked to
the main road with my things. She was carrying a vase of flowers into
the entrance and she saw me putting the keys down."

I sometimes worry—he skipped the lines he had read before—*You*
may be bored, now, in Wiltshire. And the place is looking so beauti-
ful. I have come to love it more and more. It seems to me the only
home I ever had, not excepting Dargler's End. —Her father's house.
Olivia was one of those people who have had so happy a childhood
that they cannot be thrown back into a state of insecurity, whatever
else they may suffer.

"So you don't get rid of me."

"You stay, Hjalmar."

"You don't come out with a thing like that—just on the moment,"
Wentz said. "She had been thinking it for years, eh?"

Rebecca appeared with her wet hair combed as it had been the
first day she had come to the house, only now it was long. He got up
oddly ceremoniously, his wife's letter in his hand, and for the first
time touched Rebecca in Hjalmar Wentz's presence, lifting the wet
hair and kissing her on the cheek. "I'm going to Malemba's." She sat
down in the sun near Hjalmar with a bit of sewing; it was a dress for
her little daughter and it lay in her lap for a moment under her eyes
and Bray's as the letter had done.

Rebecca and Hjalmar waved; he drove off down the road. The eld-

est Malemba boy was cementing the cracks in the concrete veranda
of the Malemba house, and the younger children were standing about
waiting for an opportunity to dabble in the mess. Sampson was still
waiting for the house he had been promised when he became Provincial Education Officer; Bray had often remarked that the Malembas
ought to have the house *he* had been given, but Sampson, in whom
courtliness always took precedence over right, refused to hear of it.
Sampson took him into the little living-room with its framed school
certificates and palette-shaped, plastic-topped coffee table before the
sofa. He said, "Sampson, I think you ought to have a gun with you at
night. Something to frighten anyone off with."

Malemba said, "It's all right. I've got my cousin coming with me all
the time now."

"I'm glad. D'you think you can look after yourselves?"

"He's a man who carries a knife." Sampson sat with his hands dangling between his knees heavily, as if already he disowned them for
what they might do.

The streets of the township were lively as a market, on a Saturday
morning. Children, bicycles, slow-moving sociable people—the car
was carried along through this, rather than progressed. Bray bought a
newspaper-cornet filled with peanuts (for the Tlume children; he and
Rebecca were going there for lunch) and while he and the vender
completed the transaction a head popped in the car window on the
other side—a young man, Tojo Wanje, who had been attentive and
argumentative at Bray's night classes. They went to the King Cole
Bar on the corner. Tojo wore transparent moulded plastic sandals
with broken straps, azure sunglasses shaped like a car windscreen,
and used a folded newspaper to emphasize what he said. "This Tola
Tola, what's he want? What's he want?" He had a way of laughing,
head up, open-mouthed, vivacious. "I don't know—you think it's the
Msos?" "This paper! I don't learn nothing!" "No, well I think they're
not being given much information. Or they're told not to use what
they've got." "Then why must I pay sixpence? I'll rather buy myself a
beer." Bray bought two more bottles and the young man, who was a
foreman at the lime works, told him there had been a fight the day
before, pay-day. "These men, we call them the Big Backs—you know,
they work putting the bags on the trucks, and they're strong. Two
new men were just taken on this week and when we were waiting at

the pay office the Big Backs started kicking up a trouble, they told the new men to show their cards. So they show their union cards but they haven't got party cards. Well, they were beaten up. I don't know. Their money was gone, they were kicked on the ground. Then we made a complaint to the union—I myself, I said to them, who are these bulls, these shoulders without brains—oh, I think I better not open so wide in future!" And delighted, he roared with laughter. "But there is fighting, fighting all the time. —They don't care to raise production," he added, to show his tuition had not been wasted.

At first it looked as if Tola Tola would not be brought to trial immediately; he was, after all, being held under the Preventive Detention Act and in theory could be detained indefinitely—at least until the Act came up for yearly review as Dando had provided when it was framed. The pay dispute on the mines was not settled, and a two-week "cool-off" period which the unions managed to get the miners to agree to was broken by a wildcat strike. It was supposed to be a token one-day affair and restricted to the mine with the biggest production, but some categories of workers did not return to work the following day, and it dragged on sporadically, complicated by internal disputes not only between the mineworkers' unions and the miners, but also among groups of the miners themselves. "It's deteriorating into gang warfare," Bray remarked one night at the Tlumes'. "Another chance for the whites down South to say how blacks don't understand anything but tribalism."

"Well it's our own fault," Nongwaye said, frowning with reasonableness. "It *is* the Galas and Msos who are beating each other up."

"They're turning on themselves in frustration because the unions've lost control. The unions are strung up between the government and the miners. They've made promises to both they can't fulfil for either."

"So those idiot Galas take it out on the Msos." Nongwaye was Gala himself, and spoke as if of a family failing.

"Nobody understands anything but tribalism," said Hjalmar. He, Bray and the girl had become so close, in a parenthetic way, that she was able to fling out her bare arm half-comically, half-consolingly, and give his shoulder a squeeze. And wan though it was, the remark almost succeeded in being a joke against himself.

It was probably because of the strike position that Mweta and Justin Chekwe were in no hurry to have a political trial. If people were in a quarrelsome mood, a trial would bring out more dissension for them to identify themselves with, or the confirmation of other grievances, perhaps opposed to their own, that would nevertheless widen the reference of dissatisfaction and rebelliousness in general. But the strike grew and spread anyway, its two aspects somehow coexisting in a third: that whatever the miners did in place of work—strike or quarrel among themselves over it—the mines could not run without them. Hardly later than Shinza had said, all the gold mines were out, and the coal, iron-ore, and bauxite ones followed. At the gold mines near the capital the Company army used tear gas and baton charges to disperse a huge march of miners making for the President't Residence. The mine and capital hospitals were full of people suffering temporary blindness from tear gas, Vivien Bayley wrote; "bloody Albert Tola Tola can be thanked for all this. We know that he whipped up his little flop on the battle-cry that Mweta didn't have the strong arm to hold down the unions and Shinza. Now Mweta's showing the beastly kind of muscle they want. Why didn't he stand out on that balcony of his and talk to them? They didn't have so much as a stone. Even Neil says it was the last chance. They didn't come to kill him, they came to talk to him because they won't talk to Chekwe and his crowd. Hjalmar was right to flee from the wrath of Margot without waiting for the wrath of the Big Boss and the Company to fall upon this place (don't tell him I said so). My riot bag stands packed."

It was true that the day before the trial of Tola Tola and his co-accused opened (it was suddenly announced: Dando, perhaps, getting tough, standing out obstinately against Chekwe for his inch of the rule of law?) Mweta arrested twenty-three trade unionists. "That's the way to do it," Aleke sat back in his big office chair and dropped his chin to his chest with a grin. "Selufu says there were others, too. And now he expects he'll get the okay to put away a few people here we can do without at the moment."

"What was there to stop him? If there'd been any rioting at the iron mine, he'd have made arrests—but the strikers seem to be keeping their heads there better than most."

"These aren't actually strikers he's thinking of—some of the wise guys here in town. Prevention is better than cure. But ever since you caught Lebaliso on the wrong foot that time, everyone here is v-e-r-y careful." He laughed good-naturedly at Selufu's difficulty.

"Oh that."

"You've forgotten?" Aleke's was a reminder of the graceful removal of Lebaliso from the scene rather than of the boy whose back was scarred.

"No. But everyone else has. Selufu has nothing to worry about."

"Oh he's ambitious, Selufu. He's a bright fellow. No flies on that nose of his."

"I hope he'll use his zeal to deal with the people who've threatened Sampson."

At least Selufu was managing so far to prevent the Young Pioneers from Gala from "settling" in their own way, this time, the strike at the iron-ore mine; apparently he had set up police check-points that investigated all vehicles and people on foot approaching the mine or compound. Of course this would also make things difficult for Shinza —for any of his people from outside who were working with the strikers; but Shinza's men were obviously so well established in leadership among the workers themselves that this might not be important. And Shinza? His "headquarters" at Boxer's ranch were very near the mine. —Shinza was probably miles away in some other part of the country, if not over the border. Yet if he wanted to see Shinza now, their old agreed meeting place was out of the question.

Mweta made a vengeful speech on television; a fly crawled and lingered, bloated hairily out of focus by the cameras, round the marvellous smile become an aggressive mouth. In the Tlumes' hot dark living-room the sound failed a moment and the white teeth seemed to be snapping at the fly. . . . The voice came back: he was "finished with patience," he would "rub out the vermin," "burn the dirty rags that carry filthy subversion." He spoke of the Tola Tola affair openly although it was *sub judice*. A state of emergency was proclaimed over the whole country; there was a curfew in the capital. An interview with the Chairman of the Company—obviously a statement prepared in consultation between the Company and the government—was given a full page in the newspapers. The strike crisis had already "done untold damage" to the country's prospects of foreign aid and investment. The country should not be "misled into the belief that it was only private investment—which people were comfortingly told

was 'economic imperialism,' 'exploitation,' and other catchwords of
Communist propaganda—that would be lost." International financial
aid organizations, without which he would emphasize none—*none*—
of the major development projects could be achieved, depended
heavily on reports from industry for "stability collateral" when allot-
ting funds. (His voice in the ear of the World Bank?) . . . The Company, which had played a major part in making the country's economy one of the healthiest in Africa, would cooperate in every possible
way (recruiting more men for their private army, buying more
guns?) with President Mweta to restore industrial peace and prosperity.

They listened to every news broadcast in silent concentration. At
meals, not the clink of a spoon. In the stifling nights under the fig,
Bray and Hjalmar with their shirts off, only the pale blurs of their
chests giving away their presence with the girl. In the bathroom, with
the little transistor radio on the windowsill while he shaved and she
lay still in the bath (under-lake landscape, white rock of flesh, garden
of dark weed, clinging snails of nipples; he had floated up, face to
face with another man there); even in the bar of the Fisheagle Inn,
once, among the white men who cut off their talk and stared ahead
while the fan sent currents shivering across their sweating foreheads,
hearing the voice and waiting for it to be over. *Waiting for it to be
over.* In the white shops of the main street the shopkeepers and white
residents had this same air; a habit of mind saw what was happening
in the country in terms of "trouble among the natives" that, while it
made one uneasy, would be put down, dealt with, pass incomprehen-
sibly as it had come ("they" didn't know themselves what it was all
about, never knew what they wanted). Be dealt with by whom? Pass
into what? Their long isolation as settlers in this remote place under
the mahogany trees had not prepared them to take the proposition
further. With their reason they knew this was a foreign country now
(a colonial country belongs to the colonizers, not the colonized who
serve them), but their emotions refused to ratify reason. Someone in
the bar at the Fisheagle remarked of Mweta, "Sir Reginald'll have to
clear up the mess for him, as usual," and then they all went back to
their gin and cold beer and weekend golf scores. Bray, swallowing his
own beer, alone after a nod from one or two faces, felt no resentment
or real dislike; but rather the sort of half-interested disbelief, undeni-
able inner recognition, with which one goes back to an institution—

school, barracks—and smells again the smell of the corridors and sees
again the same curling notices on the baize. He had been here; he
was one of these people in the colour of his skin and the cast of his
face.

This dependence each day on the oracular announcements of the
radio displaced the normal divisions of decisions, moods, actions by
which, hand over hand, life is taken and left behind. Each midday,
you waited to hear what had happened that morning; each evening
you waited to hear what might have happened since then. And in the
town itself, in Gala, there had opened up again those moments of hiatus when anything might rush in, anything might be the explanation
—a truckful of police went shaking down the main street, past the bi-
cycle-mender's and the barber's and the venders with their little piles
of shoelaces, razor-blades and cold cream. Where were they going?
The limeworkers began to gather under the slave tree in their lunch
breaks; no one could find a reason to disperse them so long as they
were apparently simply hanging about in the shade, but other people,
trailing along the red dust road into town or out again with a loaf of
bread or a bottle or paraffin, gathered round loosely—what was it all
about? As if in unconscious response to an audience, one lunchtime a
scuffle broke out and there was a chase through the town: torn shirts,
heaving breasts, and a small boy with his little brother on his back
breaking into howls outside the post office. He had been knocked
down by the brawl; no, he hadn't, he was simply frightened by it—
but already there was another group around him: the crazy woman
who sang hymns, a few old men who lived out of dustbins and sat
most of the day on the post office steps, the young messengers who
gossiped there. (Rebecca, passing, bought the child an icecream; fat
Mrs. Maitland from the dry cleaner's stood shaking three white chins
and said to her, "It's terrible the way they neglect their children.
Most of them shouldn't be allowed to have any." Bray and Hjalmar
were delighted with the story.) Someone spray-painted HANG TOLA
TOLA on the wall of the Princess Mary Library. A house was set fire to
in the African township and neighbours said "Commandant Mkade"
had told them that the people in that house were "Tola Tola men."
Albert Tola Tola, spending his time as he did in London, Washing-
ton, and West Germany, had never been anywhere near the remote
north of his own country, and the Galas traditionally discounted the
importance of the Msos, so it was more than unlikely he would have

had any supporters in Gala. But whoever it was they were determined to harass, the Young Pioneers set fire to three more houses and
there was street-fighting in the township at night. Selufu had most of
his small force concentrated on keeping peace at the iron-ore mine,
a hundred and seventy miles away; Aleke imposed a curfew in Gala,
like the one in the capital. "Old Major Fielding's offered to get together a group of volunteers to help out, patrolling the centre of
town," he said to Bray; a piece of information that was in fact a request for advice.

"Oh my God. What a prospect—Commandant Mkade and Major
Fielding let loose among us with guns. Why can't you arrest Mkade?"

"Selufu says the trouble is the evidence is so vague. You can't prove
he was behind the burnings."

Bray found a cheap window-envelope under the lump of malachite
quartz (Rebecca's gift) he kept on his desk at the *boma*. A note, on a
sheet torn from an exercise book, written carefully along the lines in a
mission-school hand: "Have a drink at the Fisheagle Inn tonight
seven o'clock." The full stop dug deeply into the paper, apparently in
indecision about the correct form to be followed where there was to
be no signature. It was felt that "Yours faithfully" was essential, anyway. He thought of Shinza; but why the Fisheagle? —Perhaps he was
going to be invited to join the white vigilantes.

He had to find an excuse to slip away from Rebecca and Hjalmar;
they would be astonished if at this hour when they were usually all
sitting cooling off under the tree, he were to announce that he was
going for a drink at the Fisheagle Inn. He remarked that he would
have to see Sampson Malemba around seven; Hjalmar and Rebecca
were pacing out the area under the fig, Hjalmar with a metal tape
that shot forth like a chameleon's tongue, Rebecca with a notebook
and pencil. Hjalmar was beginning to busy himself quietly about the
house; first he had rigged up an insect-repellent yellow light so that
they could read outside at night, now he was going to make a paved
area under the fig tree. Rebecca had remembered the pile of bricks
left lying next door in the Tlumes' garden by the government build-
ers. Apparently, during the day, Hjalmar, Kalimo, Mahlope, and the
elder Tlume children carted them over in wheelbarrows. Rebecca and
Hjalmar were discussing whether they should be laid basket-weave
pattern or in contrasting horizontal and vertical blocks. "Will they be

cemented?" "No, no" Hjalmar demonstrated with his hands, "If bricks are laid properly, sunk up to the face in the ground and tightly together, they don't need anything. If you like you can leave a few open spaces to put a small shrub or so—plant something, that looks quite nice, eh? After the rains are over, when it won't get washed away, you can establish small plants." "Won't it be pretty by next year?" She turned enthusiastically to Bray.

He left them working on improvements for the house as if he, she, and Hjalmar were some sort of family making their home in a place where they expected to live undisturbed for the rest of their lives.

Dave, the black barman at the Fisheagle, was popular with the white men who went there to drink. He wore a midnight blue flunkey jacket and a bow-tie and had picked up many of their turns of phrase in his fluent English. "What'll it be, Colonel, sir? —You on your own, or you want to wait?" Grinning, flourishing a napkin across the counter, setting his little saucers of crisps scudding. Bray was thinking how ridiculously conspicuous any man of Shinza's would look here when he realized that it was the barman himself who was singling him out for attention. "Excuse me, Colonel, sir, but your car is blocking the way—could you please move it—" As he left the bar, the barman disappeared through another door and met him in the passage. "Just come this way, what a bother." It was for the benefit of anyone who might hear; he steered Bray past crates of empty bottles: "Go round behind that hedge by the garage, my room is there, there with the tall roof, you can see it. You got my letter okay, eh? Just open the door—he's inside . . ." Shinza had friends in some unexpected places. But that was because little Gala remained, on the surface, a white colonial town and one could make the mistake of seeing black men in white contexts—it was merely because he did his job well that the "character" Dave seemed to be a white black man who shared his customers' interests rather than any other concern; at the end of colonial times in many African states white clubmen had been shocked to find that the man they thought of as their favourite waiter or driver was in his private life a political militant.

The yard of the hotel was dark except for a single bulb above the Men's—the one that served the bar was out there so even if he were seen there would be nothing unusual about a white man wandering about near the servants' quarters. In the outhouse room Shinza sat on

a bed raised on bricks and covered with flowered cloth. "Look—
before we say another word—Selufu's got the go-ahead to pick up anyone he considers 'undesirable,' which means that he's got plenty of
informers about, so—"

Shinza was shaking his head, he pressed the point of his tongue up
to the broken tooth. "I don't go near the township, no worry about
that—and these people here are a hundred per cent. Basil's arrested
—you know? He was picked up at Lanje, the same day as the twenty-three."

Aleke had said that "there were a few others" in addition to the
trade union leaders. Lanje was a small village near the capital.
"Well"—Shinza cut himself short—"it had to be someone, I suppose.
Bad it was Basil. James, I've got to have a car. Basil was using the
old one, my father-in-law's."

"You were there too?"

Shinza dismissed it. "It was all right. They missed me. But none of
us can go back for the car. I need one badly, badly. I must get out of
here tonight."

"That's not easy. In Gala everyone knows everyone else's car."

"I know. But I've got to have one."

"All right. I'll try."

"Don't try, James; I must have it . . ."

The room was so small they seemed to be pushed too near each
other. He said to Shinza, "Did you know about Tola Tola?"

"What do you mean?"

"Was it unexpected?"

"Tola Tola was circling around us. Just before Congress he had a
talk with me. He said he could carry the Msos with him, and of
course, he knew a lot of people still believed in me . . ." Shinza
laughed. "Eh? He thought if we could perhaps work together . . . he
made it clear he could get the money—who for Christ's sake was prepared to give money to Tola Tola? Eh? Anyway—he offered me a junior partnership or he tried to get me to talk so he could denounce
me—I don't know which it was . . . I told him he knew I had retired
from politics. He said I was insulting him by treating him like a fool.
Of course, travelling around all over, he found someone to back him,
he could get his hands on things . . . look, James, I want you to go
for us. Now."

"To Switzerland."

"Anywhere. Everywhere."

Bray looked at him.

"Oh that ILO thing—well, it's too late. There's a chance now that may never come again. You know what I'm talking about. This mine strike wasn't my doing, I don't have to tell you that—but now that it's going this way, I'll have to move if I'm ever going to move at all. We must make use of it, you understand. It may still go on a long time, and if it becomes a general strike . . . if the whole country— James, what I want is you to go and get money for us. Quickly. Now. You know the right people in England. There are a few contacts of mine . . . there's Sweden, East Germany. We must take money where we can, at this stage. I've got some, already, I've had some, of course. Somshetsi must have money if he's going to help us and I need him. I need him, James. He's got trained people . . . you know. With a small force of trained people in the right places at the right time, you take over your radio station and telecommunications . . . airport . . . you can bring it off without . . . almost without a scratch. If Mweta can't hold this country together and we hang back, what're you going to get? You're going to get Tola Tola. You see that. Tola Tola or somebody like him. That's what you'll get. And the bribes'll be bigger in the capital and the prisons will be fuller, and when the rains are late, like now, people will have to scratch for roots to make a bit of porridge, just the way it's always been here."

Bray thought, he's saying all the right things to me; but then Shinza paused, and in this room that enclosed them as closely as a cell, there was the feeling, as often happened between them, that Shinza knew what he was thinking: was thinking the same of himself, and said, "I never thought I would ever do it. Now I have to."

He said. "What will I say to you? I'll think it over?"

Shinza gave a sympathetic snort.

"When I've 'thought it over' I'll only know what I know already: that I didn't think it would ever be expected of me. Not only by you. By myself."

Shinza smiled at him almost paternally. "I suppose we didn't know how lucky we were to get away without guns so far. Considering what we want. You don't expect to get that for nothing."

It will be such a very little token violence, Bray; and you won't feel a thing. It will happen to other people, just as the tear gas and the baton charges do.

"But you expect it of yourself?" Shinza was saying, detachedly interested.

"Yes."

"Good God, James, remember the old days when we used to come to your place starving hungry after meetings? After riding a bicycle fifteen miles in the rain from Mologushi Mission? And when the order came from the secretariat that I was to be "apprehended" and you decided it didn't say arrested so you could "apprehend" me to tell me about it—?" They laughed.

"I'll be back later if I can dig up a car. If I'm not here by say, eleven, don't count on it."

But Shinza seemed confident that he would be there. Perhaps he knows, too, that I have a woman, and that it will have to be her car because mine is too well known in this province.

He went back to the house and called to her from the bedroom so that he could speak to her alone. "You can use my car in the meantime, and we'll say yours is in the garage for repair. Hjalmar won't know you haven't taken it to work in the morning because you're always gone by the time he gets up—" "I only hope to God it goes," she said, her eyes moving about the room in the manner of someone who is not going to ask questions.

He said, "The only thing that worries me is what happens if he's arrested somewhere . . . it's your car he'll be driving. But with mine . . . if I were to be connected with him so obviously I wouldn't be much use any more—"

"No no, not yours." She held off any explanation, from both of them.

It was all practical as a discussion of what supplies they would take when they went on a little expedition to the lake at a weekend.

The night was big with humidity that could not find release—moisture could still be drawn up by the sun day after day, even in the drought, from the water and forests to the north-west. About half-past nine he said he had forgotten his briefcase at Malemba's; out of sight round the back of the house, he took Rebecca's car instead of his own. White men in shorts were playing darts among flying cockroaches on the lighted veranda of the Fisheagle; he remembered standing at the top of the steps there, when he had first come back to Gala, and thinking that he could make out the lake away over the glassy distance. If he had been able to see it, the girl was there ahead in that presence. He had the feeling that the area of uncertainty that surrounded him visually when he took off his glasses was the real circumstance in which he had lived his life; and his glasses were more than a means of correcting a physical shortcoming, they were his chosen way of rearranging the unknowable into a few outlines he had gone by.

He drove round to the backyard quarters. Shinza was lying on the bed, barefoot, smoking. There were two of the young men Bray had seen with him before. A radio was playing. Bray gave him the key, and he held out his yellow-palmed hand with its striations of dark, a fortune-teller's map. "Someone'll drive you back." "No, I can walk." "Hell, no, man. Really? I suppose it's better." Almost lazily. The young lieutenants sat, one on a chair, one on an upturned box, their feet planted, hunched forward in the manner of men who are used to using their hands, in the company of men who use words. Shinza flipped the key to one and told him in Gala to move the car down into the lane behind the Fisheagle property. He looked at the other with his impatient authoritative glance, rolling his beard between thumb and forefinger like a bread pellet. The man got up, stood a moment, and followed.

"You're going back there?" Bray was talking of the capital.

"The army doesn't worry me so much—" Shinza didn't bother to answer. Bray grinned, and Shinza sat up on the creaking bed and put his arms round his knees, raising his eyebrows at himself. "—No, wait a minute. With the army I can get somewhere. A white man's at the top. Mweta's man, the state's man. Brigadier Radcliffe works along with the Company's army—as a matter of fact a friend of his trained them, an old Sandhurst colleague he recommended. Oh yes. But Radcliffe's officers are Africans. At least two high-rankers don't love him very much and they're ambitious. And in any case he depends on all of them to carry out his orders. If one day they don't . . . There are only three thousand men, and Cyrus has very hopeful contacts among the officers. He's been working on it for some time."

"Good God."

Shinza swung his legs down over the side of the bed decisively. Bray couldn't escape him. He went on as if nothing would stop him; the more Bray knew the less risk there was in telling him, the more bound over he would be.

"Cyrus has been pretty successful, I don't mind saying, James. Dhlamini Okoi's useful too. His brother's in army area HQ. You can learn a lot from him. You know that the army was rejazzed a bit before Independence, decentralized so that almost every echelon is operational now. If you can take over control at almost any level, the orders you give will be obeyed at all levels below, because the various commanders aren't used to taking their orders direct from GHQ any longer, as they did before. You've got a pretty good chance to be effective at all levels—except division and battalion, of course, because that's GHQ. Brigadier Okoi went to Sandhurst too. He thinks he could count on the officers of the Sixth Brigade as well as his own, the Twenty-third. That's two brigades, out of a rather small army. The main worry there is the Company task force—that's what he calls it. It would depend how occupied that was . . . But the police, that's another story."

"Onabu as chief, but plenty of white officers who really run the show, under him."

"Exactly. Those whites are the real professionals who just want to do what they're paid. No chance of any of them being interested in us. And there are more police than soldiers."

"Onabu's not a fool, either. Roly wouldn't have advised Mweta to hand over to him if he had been. He knows how to rely on his white officers when it comes to a situation like this. He'll be thanking God for them."

"That's how it is, James. Too many policemen. And their organization is old-established, eh? People are used to listening to them. They were all we had for donkey's years, when all there was in the way of an army was a few kids from the U.K. doing their military training here. The police force's always been paramilitary. And they've got the Young Pioneers to do the things it wouldn't look nice to do themselves. I know all that. But there are a few signs that are not so bad . . . D'you know of any coup in the last fifteen years or so where a police force has defended its political masters? It's inclined to be essentially bureaucratic . . . And in a country this size, with a population still mostly agricultural, living in villages, the biggest numbers of policemen are in the country areas—can you see Selufu's local men rushing off to the capital to protect a government they've never seen?"

He listened but would not answer.

"We've got other friends, too. In a good place. The Special Branch. It isn't only a help to get information, it's also important sometimes to be able to do something about what's leaked. I mean, to have Tola Tola out of the way, that's something, you know?"

"So it's all very professional," Bray said.

Shinza looked at him appraisingly a moment. "Yes! If it's done properly, there should be no heads broken. Not a drop, not a scratch."

"What about Somshetsi?"

"He's been thinking about nothing but this sort of thing for years. We need portable equipment for communications, man—things like that. We go for the organizational centre, we don't look for battles in the street."

"When would you want me to go, Edward?"

"Now. As soon as you can. You'll get back the fare at the other end. I'm going to tell you the addresses because we don't write down anything, eh? I don't want you to be 'apprehended' . . ."

"I don't know how soon I can go. I'm not still playing for time. There are personal things to be arranged—thought out. I have to decide how best to do it."

"Fine. Fine. But I won't be here. People are always coming up and down, you can leave a message here at the bar, but it might not reach me right away. Best thing would be to make contact when you come down to get your plane. Go to Haffajee's Garage—you know?—ask for the panel beater, Thomas Pathlo."

"Haffajee's Garage again."

"Mmmh? Pathlo knows where I am. Or Goma, if I'm not there. — Well, so you'll see the family again in England, anyway. At least I'm doing Olivia a good turn."

"I may not be able to come back," Bray said. "Mweta may not let me in. He must know we are in touch. And if he let me in again he would have to arrest me."

Shinza suddenly spoke in Gala. "Perhaps he needs you to set his hand free for that, even now." The phrase 'to set the hand free' meant the lifting of the taboo against harming a member of the tribe, one of one's own.

"It's been done," said Bray.

They discussed exactly where he should go and what sort of support he should try to find; they arranged the contacts he should use to inform Shinza, both at home and through Somshetsi over the border. It was long after the curfew time when he began to walk home. The Fisheagle was in darkness, the main street still and shrill with crickets and the tiny anvil-ring of the tree frogs. He met only one police patrol and did not try to dodge it: a white man coming from the direction of the Fisheagle bar would hardly be regarded as a security risk. The policeman mumbled a hoarse good night in Gala and he mumbled back. Of course, in England too, he would be breaking the law; wasn't it an offence to plan the overthrow of a friendly state? Winter was beginning there, as it was last year, almost a year ago, when he left. Cold damp leaves deadening the pavements and the sweet mouldering grave-smell muffling up against the face. England. A deep reluctance spread through him, actually slowing his steps. England.

Hjalmar and Rebecca were still outside under the fig tree when he got back to the house. Mechanically, he had taken care to open and bang shut the door of his car, so that it would seem he had driven home in it; he could smell his own sweat as he flopped down into a chair and hoped Hjalmar wouldn't notice he'd obviously been walking. It was so hot that no one felt like going to bed. The moon had dispelled some of the haze, high in the sky, and seemed to give off reflected warmth as it did light. The strange domestic peace that had made its place among them these days, as if it could grow only in the shelter of all that made it impossible and absurd, contained them.

Later Rebecca said, "I can smell burning." Over towards the township, the sky showed a midnight sunrise.

H

ouses were fired that night, and fifteen people died.

"Holy" burnings began all over the country; Mweta's "burn the dirty rags" metaphor had been seized upon by the Young Pioneers for their text. Nothing he said now, angry or desperate, threat or appeal, was able to reach them in their fierce evangelism.

Many of the strikers from the iron-ore mine had families living in Gala. On the day of the joint funeral while the police were diverted from the mine back to town to deal with the arsonists (and people whose houses had been burned began to band together to retaliate with further burnings), these strikers suddenly swarmed upon Gala. They overpowered the small contingent of police left guarding the mine and commandeered mine trucks, travelling at night, and in the confusion managed to get to the town in the morning before the police could stop them. There they somehow split into two factions, the one making across the golf course for the African township, the other ending up in the streets of Gala itself. Bray and Rebecca watched from the *boma;* the men had been up all night and came singing, plodding along with big, dreamlike steps, a slow prance, some of them in their mine helmets, some carrying sticks more like staffs than weapons. Rebecca had tears in her eyes; he thought it was fear. She said, "Poor things."

Aleke sought him out, standing legs apart, holding a deep breath.

"Does he think parachutes are going to drop from the sky? He's mad. How can I get troops here now, this minute?" Selufu had knocked him up out of sleep early in the morning, and kept telephoning.

"Well, he's a worried man."

"Everyone's a worried man. I've spoken to Matoko, I've put through a call to the Ministry, I've asked for the Minister himself. Now what does he want? To hell with it."

He stood there looking out at the procession with a curious expression of sulky indecision. All his confident good nature seemed balanced like an avalanche that so much as a shout could cause to fall.

"Any help from Matoko?"

"Are you crazy too. There's all hell at the asbestos mine since last week. The Company's had to send riot breakers. They fired on the strikers yesterday, killed a woman who was somehow mixed up in it. God knows what's going on up there."

The singing grew cello-loud and wavering, bringing close under the windows the peculiar awe the human voice has in its power to produce. *Boma* clerks and messengers appeared on the patch of grass and flowers. Old Moses the gardener snaked the jet of his hose in the air and shouted in Gala, are you thirsty! The *boma* people laughed discreetly, expecting to be called back to work; one held a brown government folder to protect his eyes from the sun.

The strikers' destination was not clear; it existed within, where they knew themselves threatened over months now by many things: lack of trust in the people who spoke for them at the mine, the puzzling power of men who bullied them in the name of the President's Party, the failure of authority to protect them. They moved past the *boma* towards the market.

Aleke suddenly said, "Come on" and urged by an apprehension rather than clear about what they could do, Bray found himself with him, down the old wooden-balustraded stairs of the *boma*, out past the clerks, who, although Aleke didn't so much as look at them, were afraid to follow, and striding up the road after the men. Aleke's big muscular buttocks in well-pressed terylene shorts worked like an athlete's. He managed with superb instinct to turn to advantage the undignified aspect of the chase—instead of hurrying alongside the strikers he cut a swathe for his presence right in among them. He and Bray moved up with the will of sheep-dogs swiftly through a flock.

Bray felt the jogging bodies all round him and smelled the sweat and dust; more of the men recognized him than knew Aleke. Eyes on him: a contraction of inevitability, flash of exposure—as if his commitment to Shinza, his real place in all this instead of the image of himself as the neutral support of Aleke, were bared a moment for those who could see. But the habit of authority was instinctive. He and Aleke broke through the front ranks of the men just at the market and strode backwards a few paces, their hands raised in perfect accord. The singing died; the men in front stood, and those behind came on, closing. They spilled so that Aleke and Bray were surrounded, but in a clear space, among small piles of drought-wizened vegetables and dried fish. One old woman was trapped there with them at her pitch and sat without moving, horny legs drawn up under her cloth. Aleke began to speak. His arms were folded across his big chest. When the men pressed forward to hear he broke through them again and jumped on a home-made stall, standing among peanuts and manioc. It creaked but held; his strong good-humoured voice neither bullied nor pleaded. He said he knew why they had come: they were worried about their relations. But he promised that everything was being done to stop the burning and fighting. If they took it on themselves to try and stop it they would make things worse for their relations. If they would go back the way they came he would personally guarantee that they would not be arrested or molested. . . .

He knew and they knew that he could promise nothing of the sort. But they believed he would try; and their purpose, unsure of its proper expression, wavered, comforted, before his command. The tension dissolved as he moved talking among the men, and the people in the market broke into discussion, peering and pointing. Bray said, "Get them back to the golf course. Out of here as quickly as possible. But it would be safer to manage it in groups. And they must avoid the main street." There were about a hundred and fifty men; difficult not to alter by too obvious a taking over of the authority of the leaders, the atmosphere of consent rather compliance that Aleke had managed to create.

"Shall we go with them ourselves?" Aleke and he stood as if in a crowd coming out of a football match, sweat streaming down their faces, the market flies settling everywhere. Aleke wanted above all to avoid any encounter with the police. Then with a touch of old easy confidence: "I'm going to look a damn fool, stepping it out in front."

"If they divide into three groups, one can go back past the *boma*, another round behind the abattoir—no, no good, too near the lime works—round the old church hall, that's better, there's a path across the open ground. And then the third can follow the *boma* road about ten minutes behind the first. The great thing is to let it all fizzle out," Bray said.

"I'll just sort of stroll up to the *boma* with the first lot—it'll look as if I'm going back there, and then I can simply carry on with them after all."

"That's fine."

"But you stay here," Aleke asked of him. "Just stay put and keep your eyes on them. . . . I don't like the idea of this market, with all these people, eh?"

The men were beginning to disperse, eddying, become tired individuals rather than a crowd. One or two were even buying manioc to chew; it must have been many hours since they had eaten. Bray heard behind him at once the scud of tyres, yells, and turned full into a lorry-load of Young Pioneers bursting into the crowd. Something struck his shoulder savagely in passing, the old woman was leaning over her onions in protection, wailing—the Young Pioneers with their bits of black-and-red insignia flew past him like horses over an obstacle and battered their way in among the strikers. They hit out with knobbed clubs and bicycle chains. Aleke had stopped dead, thirty yards away, with the other strikers. Bray yelled at him to go on, but it was too late, the men were racing back to their mates. Vegetables rolled, a pile of fowls tied by the legs were being trampled upon, squawking horribly, feathers and blood mixed with ripped clothing and gaps of bare flesh. He saw with choking horror hands grab bright orange and green bottles from the cold drink stall, the coloured liquid pouring over the burst of broken glass, the jagged-edged necks of bottles plunged in among heads and arms. One of the strikers staggered towards him, the terrible astonishment of a blow turning to a gash of blood that opened the whole face, from forehead to chin. Blood of chickens and men was everywhere. Bray fought to hold back an arm that had raised a bottle-neck above another head; he twisted that arm and could not have let go even if he had heard the bone crack. When the bottle dropped into his other hand he thrust it deep into his trouser pocket, struggling at the same time with someone who had grabbed him round the neck from behind. People came running from the *boma* and the turn of the road that led to the centre of town. While he fought he was filled with anguish at the awareness of more and more people pressing into the bellowing, fighting crowd. He was trying to get to Aleke without having any idea where he was; suddenly he saw Aleke, bleeding from the ear, struggling towards him. They did not speak but together heaved a way through blows and raced behind the market lavatories, through the backyard of a group of stores, and to the back of the *boma*.

Rebecca's teeth showed clamped between parted lips, like someone who has been taken out of cold water. She stared at them with embarrassment. Godfrey Letanka, the elderly clerk in his neat alpaca jacket, grabbed the towel from beside the washbasin in Aleke's office and held it to the bleeding ear. "Is it from inside?" Bray asked. "Was it a knock on the head?" Aleke, his great chest heaving for breath, shook his head as if a fly were in his ear. They tried to wipe away the blood so as to see where it was coming from; and there Bray discovered a small, deep hole, right through the cartilage of the ear shell: so it was not a brain injury. Letanka found the first-aid box somewhere and Rebecca held the ear tightly between two pads of cottonwool to stop the bleeding. Aleke was no longer dazed. "Get hold of Selufu—try the phone, James—" "—The police are there," Rebecca said. "You didn't see—they were on the edge of the crowd, two jeeps arrived from Nairobi Street, that side. Godfrey and I saw them from the roof." "The roof?" "Yes, we found you can get up onto that little platform thing where the flag is."

With Aleke holding a wad of cottonwool to his ear, they rushed along the empty corridors ("Those bloody fools of mine, they've all gone to get their heads broken") and climbed through a window onto the curlicued wooden gable that had been built as a setting for the flagpole when the Union Jack had flown there. "Don't come up again, it may be too much weight," Bray said to Rebecca, and she stood there below, waiting. A car had been overturned and was burning, obscuring everything with smoke and fumes. But they could see the two police jeeps, the shining whips of their radio antennae.

They went back inside the *boma* and Aleke tried to telephone Selufu. While he questioned the constable on duty and they watched his face for his reaction to the replies, Rebecca whispered to Bray, "You're bleeding too." He looked down; there was dark blood on his shoe. "Chickens were killed." She shook her head; she pointed, not touching him before the others. "It's running, look." His hand went to his pocket and he took out the broken neck of the lemonade bottle. He looked around for somewhere to put it. She took it from him and laid it, bloody and dirty, in Aleke's big ashtray. The inside of the trouser pocket was sliced and in his groin Bray's fingers touched a mess of wet hair and beneath it, a cut. He shook his head; it was nothing.

"He's in the township. People have been killed there. They had to fire on them. There's nobody at the police station but the man on the phone. Nobody."

There was silence. She looked at the bloody shoe.

He said, "We could take the car and go back, if you like."

"What can the two of us do," said Aleke.

"You were doing fine. If only the Young Pioneers had kept out of it everything would have been all right. What you could do—we could make a quick whip round the lime works and so on—keep people inside and off the streets."

"What about Rebecca? Think it's okay for Godfrey and her here?"

Bray said, "We'll drive them up to my house."

"I can drive us. I'll keep away from these roads. Godfrey and I'll be all right."

Bray and Rebecca looked at each other for a moment. "Take the track past the cemetery. Don't go near the golf course."

Sitting beside Aleke he had a moment of deep premonitory gloom about Rebecca, as if something had already happened to her rather than that she was likely to run into trouble. The small wound hurt like a cigarette burn that produces a radius of pain out of all proportion to its surface injury. Aleke was very good down in the industrial quarter. There was some disruption of work there; rumours of what was happening in the township had made people take their bicycles and race home. He spoke to groups of men while they stared at his ear bound to his head by Rebecca with criss-crossed tape, and Bray saw them drawn to him, to the physical assurance of his person just as, at home, women, friends, children were attracted without effort on his part.

Aleke said, "D'you want to go into the township?"

It was one way of putting it. "I'll come with you."

Aleke suddenly yawned passionately, lifted his hands from the steering wheel and slapped them down on it again. "We'll go round by your house to see if they got back all right."

He said. "I wonder about town. There're a lot of people hurt."

"I can't cut myself in half. The police are there. The shopkeepers will have the sense to shut up shop."

The Tlumes were with Rebecca, Hjalmar, and Letanka at the house. The children were making a party of it; Kalimo chased them out of the kitchen and they ran squealing through the rooms. Rebecca and Kalimo were carrying round coffee. Aleke swallowed a cup in a certain aura of awkwardness—the unspoken questioning that builds up round someone in authority. Edna Tlume was on night duty and supposed to be sleeping during the day but she had gone back to the hospital and had rushed in now only to make sure Nongwaye had fetched the children from school. She offered to dress Aleke's ear but his wife, Agnes, had been telephoning Rebecca hysterically after getting no reply from his office—he dashed off to "shut her up" by showing himself to her for a moment. He had another reason, too: "Have you got a gun?" he asked Bray.

"For the birds. Six thousand miles away."

Godfrey Letanka was worried about his mother and they were trying to persuade him not to go to the township. Bray telephoned Sampson Malemba's house. Sampson's wife answered; she didn't know where Sampson was, there was trouble, trouble, she kept repeating. She had locked herself in. Cars and lorries of "those people" —she meant the Young Pioneers, but they might have been strikers, too—were going through the streets.

"What can Aleke do about it? Whether you're the P.O. or anybody —" Nongwaye Tlume said.

"He has certain gifts, you know."

"Rebecca says you have a leg injury, James? Let me examine it quickly." Little Edna had acquired her fluency in English while doing her nurse's training course, and she had the vocabulary of hospital reports. She insisted, and he had to go into the bathroom and take off his trousers. He stood there in his underpants while she cut away the hair and cleaned the cut. He smiled. "Self-inflicted." "It really needs a stitch. You should come up to the hospital. I could do it in a minute, but I'm not supposed to." "Oh come on. You'll do it better than the doctor." They went hurriedly over to the Tlume house —unfamiliar with locked doors and closed windows in the middle of the day—and she brought out her curved needle and plastic gut, "like a good shoemaker," he said. The needle stabbed quick-to-be-kind through the resistance of the tough skin, the thread was expertly drawn up, tied, and cut off. The pink palms and nails of the narrow black hands were beautiful markings. "What's going to happen, James? Why can't the President stop all this? A person doesn't know what to do. You should see the burn cases at the hospital. Rebecca is lucky she hasn't got to worry about the children."

She left him to dress; he pulled on his blood-stained trousers heavily. And Rebecca was still there, because of him. Events carried consciousness unreflectingly from one moment to the next, but this dragged on the mind.

Back at the house Rebecca was playing with the Tlume children with the ingratiating attention of a childless adult; Kalimo and two or three friends presented a deputation, backing up each other's words with nods and deep hums: Mahlope, the young gardener, had gone off to the golf course earlier "to look" and hadn't returned. "There are a lot of rubbish-people here," Kalimo pronounced. But his friends were trying to prevent him from going after the boy.

"If we all start looking for each other, we'll all be lost, Kalimo," Bray said. They were speaking in Gala.

An appreciative note went up from the chests of the others.

Kalimo said, "He's just got drunk somewhere. I know that. And there are always people ready to steal someone's pay while trouble is going on."

"You're worried about his pay?"

"*Mukwayi,* you know yourself you paid him yesterday night."

"I'll try and make inquiries about him later. You stay here. I need you, Kalimo." An empty promise, a little flattery; the old man went off reluctantly.

Bray was listening for Aleke's car; Hjalmar kept him, describing the men who had come across the golf course. ". . . singing, you know—it was just like the student days in Germany, we were singing the *Internationale* like schoolkids and it didn't seem true when they would come and beat us up." He was excited. "It's always the same, students and workers make mincemeat for police and thugs. — They've picked it up here like V.D. and measles. . . . Measles kills people who've never been exposed to the virus before. . . ."

Outside, the old fig wrinkled in its skin of dust was fixed as eternity. The midday peace of heat enclosed in the garden beneath it was un-reachable indifference: Bray stood amazed for a moment—the grunts and screams and desperate scuffle, the yellow guts of crushed chick-ens and the miner's face splitting into blood surrounded him in delu-sion. Over beyond the trees, an indefinable turmoil was apprehended through all the senses, atmospherically. The clamour in the township was too far away to be sorted out. There was only the roar of a sea-shell held to the ear.

Aleke hooted in the road on the other side of the house, and he went round and got into the government car beside him.

In the old part of the township, life was so dense that violence was obscured—in the mud houses, tangled palms, lean-tos of waste mate-rial, old vehicle chassis, piles of wood, paw-paws and lianas growing out of rubbish the distinction between dwelling and ruin disap-peared, the pattern of streets itself disappeared, and if doors were broken, posts uprooted, weapon-like objects littered the dust, that might easily be part of the constant course of decay and patching-up by which the place maintained its life. Only the burned-out houses were a statement of disruption; and even one or two of those had al-ready those signs—a bit of tin over the angle of standing walls, a packing-case door propped up—of habitation creeping back. The old township smelled of disaster and hid everything; the people were not to be seen, their cooking pots and fire tins left outside the houses to be taken up in the usual activity as soon as this threat to everyday life, like every other they had known, passed and left them once again to make a fire, to cook, to wash clothes in a tin bath. It also hid their partisanships, their sudden decisions to take the threat into their own hands. Bray and Aleke heard later that down here several people had been killed in street battles that morning, but they themselves met nothing but a sullen withdrawal and the faces and hands of chil-dren behind the flaps of sacking at window-holes.

The new housing-scheme area near the hostel had no such protec-

tion. The substance of life there was still too new and thin to withstand assault. The web was broken. The fact that there were panes in
the windows was enough; shattered glass lay everywhere among
bricks, twisted bicycles, wrecked food stalls, yelling clusters of people
—all this naked to the red-earth clearing bulldozed from the forest. It
was impossible to get into some streets. They backed up the car and
zigzagged. Knots of people meant hand-to-hand fighting or someone
wounded. A police van tore through filled with shouting faces behind
the wire cage; a miner's helmet lying on the ground was caught and
sent bowling like a severed head. A Gala woman with her dress
ripped down her breasts, her turban gone, and her plaited snakes of
hair standing up exposed, shrieked again and again.

They followed the trail of chaos to the hostel. A gang of screaming
youths ran into the car, clung to it, rocked it. As if they were a swarm
of flying ants Aleke kept going until they fell away. Outside the hostel
Selufu and some of his men were beleaguered in two open vans.
Stones and tins were lobbing out of the windows in a battle between
the strikers, and the Young Pioneers, whose "stronghold" the hostel
was. Selufu's men began to throw tear-gas bombs, not into the building but among the strikers. Bray opened the door of the car while it
was still moving and while Aleke continued to grind on through the
crowd, he hung outside, clinging to the roof and shouting in Gala for
the men to fall back. He was deafened to noise and chaos by the bellow of his own voice, brutally commanding, hard and ringing, a voice
dredged up from his racial past, disowning him in the name of sea-
captains and slavers between whose legs his genes had been hatched.
His sight became blurred by the pressure of blood in his neck. Still he
bellowed; raggedly they were turning back, making for the car, turning away from the building. He thought they were shouting, "Shinza!
Shinza!"—Aleke had put the car into reverse, whining and jerking
backwards through the fringe of the crowd, and the men were racing
after, calling at Bray, "Shinza! Shinza!" as if he had come to deliver
them. When Aleke must have judged they were out of range of the
tear-gas he came to a stop and leapt out. The look the faces had
turned on Bray, the name that they had called, were lost in the confusion. Aleke and Bray again formed an instinctive compact of discipline and moved urgently among the men, throwing an invisible cor-
don round the orgiastic excitement, shepherding them in the
advantage of the moment of hesitation that deflects mob will.

The immediate problem was to get the men from the iron mine out of the quarter. —Selufu couldn't arrest the lot and wouldn't have had anywhere to hold them if he had. It was obvious that every time the running battle that was going on between police, strikers and Young Pioneers died down, while the local men disappeared in their own streets, the "invaders" remained more or less collected, at least in bands, and were a target for both police and the next gang of Young Pioneers they might run into. One thing about Aleke, he was not bothered by protocol and it did not seem to occur to him that he was acting independently of the Police Commissioner. He had the idea of leading the miners away somewhere—where?—"Agricultural show-ground," Bray suddenly thought of—and keeping them there until they could be transported back to the mine. Bray took the car and raced off through the littered streets to try and find Malemba and comman-deer a couple of school buses. It was all absurd, as desperate meas-ures often have to be: Sampson and Bray and Aleke with busloads of battered men, fighting off the interference of mobs who no longer knew whether the spectacle enraged or threatened them. When the operation was successfully accomplished, Bray and Malemba drove wildly between the showground and the town to pick up Bray's car, fetch food and medical supplies and help. But at the house, Bray's car was gone; Rebecca, Hjalmar, and Nongwaye had been telephoned by Edna to help bring in wounded people who were still left lying at the market. Bray and Malemba got back to the showground: there Aleke was in angry argument with two white men, Mr. George Nye and Mr. Charles Aldiss, president and secretary of the settlers' agricultural so-ciety, who were demanding that he remove his "trespassers" from private property. An old dread, from the years when a black man and a. white man shouting at each other signified a break in the particular order of society he was paid to maintain, caught Bray off guard. It had no special significance now; Aleke was the man in charge and Nye was simply the uncooperative private citizen; being white was no help to him at all. But at the sight of Bray, Nye turned on him. "Of course! This is just the day you were waiting for! That's why we got rid of you once! You white bastard!"

It was a cry that mingled with all the others of the afternoon. At nightfall—two truckloads of soldiers had arrived and were patrolling the town with sten guns—they collected back at the house again, Re-becca, Hjalmar, Nongwaye, himself. He was still in his filthy trousers;

a dried bloodstain on the groin reminded him of something that might have happened days ago. Kalimo had been looking after the Tlume children the whole afternoon and the house had the roused and rumpled atmosphere of another kind of riot. Rebecca and Hjalmar shared the animation of having made themselves useful; the graining of her chin and cheeks showed coarsened by a glaze of sweat and self-forgetfulness. He said in a private voice, "Was it very bad?" and she answered breathily, vacant, "No, no. Luckily I didn't see any of the dead ones." He squeezed her hand.

Nongwaye went home with the children and the night was suddenly very quiet around their exhaustion. They drank beer and heard over the radio that the strike had spread to the railway workshops and docks, and that in the capital transport workers, post-office workers, and teachers were out. There were "reports of disturbances in the Gala district," the voice said with his own African accent but the BBC announcer's standard indifference. Hjalmar pulled a face and laughed silently.

Bray went out into the garden to have a look at the sky over the township but Rebecca called from behind the gauze of the veranda, "Aleke!" and he ran in to the telephone. The radio was turned up for news flashes, sending a can-can rhythm galloping through the house. Against it, covering his other ear, he heard Aleke's beguiling voice, resonant in that great body. He was talking about a plane—"What plane?" The twice-weekly service was not due for two or three days.

"Well, the thing from the department of agriculture . . . you know. Agnes is going down. To her mother, with the kids. I think she might as well. And she—well, you know. What about Rebecca? They can squeeze her in."

He was looking at her while Aleke spoke.

He said, "I'll try."

"It's the best thing for them, get them out from under our feet," Aleke said, with the carelessness which was his way of expressing embarrassment.

"When would it be?"

"In the morning. Tell her to stick a few dresses in a suitcase and come over. They want to take off about seven."

He stood a moment before Rebecca's and Hjalmar's expectancy. He turned down the radio. "Agnes and the children are going to her mother—getting a ride with the agricultural plane tomorrow morning. She wants you to come along, Rebecca—" her name stuck in his mouth awkwardly, it sounded like the name of someone neither of them knew—"you can spend a few days with Vivien and Neil. I think you must go."

Her eyes, on him, seemed to open up into her self, to force him to look there. "No."

"Just for a few days. Aleke agrees. It would be sensible."

She said, like a child shifting retribution, "And Edna?"

"Edna's a nurse." And of course Edna belonged here, it was her bit of country, her home and people, while Agnes and Rebecca—even Agnes, a town girl, from the capital—had no commitment to what might happen in Gala. If Gala were to be cut off, as it so easily could be, with its single road, no railway, and tiny airstrip, the Tlumes would be at home.

She walked past the two men and went out of the room into the bedroom. He had a very real sense of panic, as if he had done something he could not undo.

She was standing there between the ugly old wardrobe where her dresses hung and the bed where they had slept last night. These things had become the possessions of a stranger; he and she might never have been there before.

"If it were not for me . . . you understand, my darling . . . ? I feel I'm behaving like a lunatic, hanging on to you."

"I won't go."

He approached her as if they were in a hotel room, alone in a strange room. He stroked her hair and held her. "I stink. I shouldn't have you near me."

They said nothing. She scratched the nail of her forefinger down his shirt. She said at last, "How many stitches?"

"Four, I think. No, two—I was counting the four holes as a stitch each."

"Didn't hurt? She's good, isn't she."

"Here." He took her finger and showed her where to feel the little knots of plastic gut through the trousers.

She asked, "You phone Aleke," and he nodded. They went peacefully back to the living-room, where Hjalmar was slicing a leg of lamb. "Mahlope's back," Kalimo announced belligerently from the doorway.

Aleke was often in the house; he had no one at home and all their lives were thrown together by an hour-to-hour uncertainty in which Kalimo's hot meals—congealed, dried-up and indigestible—continued to be prepared with dogged regularity fixed as the passage of the sun, and eaten any time by whoever happened to be there. Kalimo apart, everybody else's functions were blurred and individual purpose and conviction were passed over in simply doing the next thing.

Harassed Selufu depended on Aleke and Aleke assumed that Bray and Sampson Malemba would arrange food supplies for the men sheltered at the showground. But when he and Sampson arrived the second day with meat and porridge commandeered from the hospital kitchen, mugs and urns from Malemba's Boy Scouts' equipment—whatever they could beg or borrow—they found the men herded into the arena in the blazing sun, surrounded by soldiers. The soldiers were Talefa from the west and had no common language with the strikers. At the sight of Bray the hail went up: Shinza, Shinza. Malemba argued with the soldiers to let Bray in among the strikers. He stood there absolutely still, tensely wary, holding off any reaction he might precipitate. Then he was let in; the men crowded round to claim him. They wanted to go home; they would walk it. But the police would not let anybody go; the police had taken away more than twenty of them and the rest had been told they were going to be kept in this "cattle place."

There was nothing to do but get on and distribute the food. He and Malemba addressed themselves to that and that only. He knew that Sampson (despite his firm indignation over the "dog-kennel" issue at Congress) had no doubts about Mweta and would always support Mweta however saddened and puzzled he might be about things that happened under the regime. At the same time, Sampson trusted *him;* so nothing was said about the way he had been hailed in Shinza's name. There could be no discussion between them of what they had just seen. The weight of circumstance was palpable in the burning heat that had collected in the old Volkswagen.

He dropped off Malemba; the market was closed, the Indian shops shuttered, but the supermarket had its doors open that morning. There were few people about and wherever they drifted together, even women with baskets on their heads and babies on their backs, they attracted the attention of slumping soldiers who came to life and moved them along roughly. He saw the Gala women swaying off, sweeping their *kangas* round their backsides, laughing rudely and shouting abuse the soldiers couldn't understand. Outside the *boma* Aleke was talking to Selufu through the window of a squad car. He signalled Bray over; the three were a conclave, representing law and order; Selufu greeted him with a businesslike smile. "Everything all right? That's a very good job you and Malemba're doing—I was just saying, I must keep that crowd isolated, and where can I put them?" "Nye's been told where to get off," Aleke said with satisfaction. And to Selufu—"You should have heard him swearing at Bray—what a character. If it'd been another time I'd have given him one on the jaw." "Oh, the Colonel isn't going to worry himself about a man like that one"—Selufu shaped the flattering estimate as one of a company of men who were peers.

"The men've been rounded up in the cattle arena without shelter from the sun."

"Now what nonsense is that—I'll go down myself and see about it. That sergeant doesn't know what he's doing. —How's the leg? It's not worrying you, eh?" And he drove off with a word or two to Aleke.

Aleke had brought Rebecca to the *boma* to try and keep some sort of routine going, but the place was under guard and hardly anyone

had turned up for work. Aleke himself had been called down to the
industrial quarter—there was fighting going on there sporadically between the fish-factory and lime-works men and bands of Young
Pioneers—he avoided naming them and always spoke of "the hooligans." A fire had broken out—"But it was only that old tree," he said.

"The slave tree?"

"The one the out-of-works used to sit around under—you know.
But it was all right, the fire didn't spread. The thing's still damp inside even though the leaves went up like paper."

"Bray's fond of that tree—aren't you," Rebecca smiled on him.

"Maybe it's an evil symbol—time it went. I just rather liked seeing
people eating chips so at ease there, after all."

Back at the house, he said to Aleke—"Look, the showground's been
made into a prison camp. What for? Those men ought to be got back
to their homes. But Selufu's arrested about twenty and he's treating
the rest as if they're under detention—they *are* under detention."

"He can't spare police transport to take them all that way—he
needs everything he's got."

"Let him commandeer the school buses. Good God, you did it."

"Yes, but that was an emergency."

"The whole thing's an emergency! We weren't collecting people together for the police to arrest."

Rebecca and Hjalmar did not look up from their plates. There was
a silence between Bray and Aleke.

Aleke said, "The business of coming into town like that—it wasn't
just an idea they got in their heads. Shinza's fellows are among them;
Selufu's trying to find out more. From the ones he took inside.
There're reports that there are camps in the Bashi just this side of the
border—arms hidden in the bush. People have said Somshetsi's
crowd have been filtering over." He lifted his shoulders and let them
fall. "I don't know. We've got enough troubles of our own."

When they were drinking coffee, Bray forced himself to say, "You'd
better check up that Selufu ordered to let the men go back to the
stand." The strikers had been camping out on the plank seats under
the shelter of the grandstand, before the new "arrangements."

"Yes, okay."

"Sampson will be going up there later—"

"Yes, I'll do it, don't worry. Oh, here's a surprise for you—" Aleke

handed over a packet of letters. Because of the transport-workers'
strike in the capital there was again no mail. "Someone had the
bright idea of giving the bag to the chap who flew the soldiers in—
but the officer only managed to remember to give it to me now." One
of the envelopes had a Swiss stamp. He opened the letter and read
rapidly under the conversation. When Aleke had gone, he handed it
to Rebecca. He said to Hjalmar and her, "I suppose I'd better go and
see for myself. I can hardly give orders to the Commissioner of Police, can I . . ." Her eyes followed quickly: *Dear Colonel Bray, Your
copy of* La Fille aux Yeux d'Or *has been reserved for you and we
await instructions at your convenience.* She folded it and gave it back
to him with a little shake of the head.

Hjalmar had a telephone message for Bray to get in touch with Mr.
Joosab. He tried to ring the shop but there was no reply; boarded up,
no doubt. Poor Joosab. He supposed he had better go and see him,
too. Rebecca said, "Not much point in my going back to the office, if
Aleke's not going to be around."

"No, stay here." He was thinking of the gangs and the attempted
fire so near the town, in the industrial area.

"Should we get on with the job in the garden?" Hjalmar said. "If
there's no use for you in one place, you have to try somewhere else."

As he left them and was driving off, she came running out the
kitchen door. He stopped and waited for her. "Was it from the Swiss
bank?" He nodded. "All safe and sound." "What was that about the
girl . . . ? Where'd you get that from?" He kept her waiting a second,
giving himself the pleasure of looking at those eyes with the fashionable black outline she had taken to giving them lately. "It means 'the
girl with the golden eyes,' it's the title of a novel. I once heard Roly
call you that. So you had a code name, all ready."

"Who wrote it?" —Though he felt the curiosity was directed more
towards herself, to the way he saw her.

"—An old French novel. Balzac."

Joosab's house backed his tailor's shop. There was a small grassless,
flowerless garden with an empty bird-bath held on the head of a concrete elephant. The façade of the house was painted bright blue. The
bell rang a long time before the door was opened by Ahmed, Joosab's
second son; he was led in silence over the linoleum into the best
room, filled with a large dining table and sideboard, both topped

with plate glass. Joosab must have been working somewhere within although the shop was closed, and appeared with silvery expanding bands holding up the sleeves of his very white shirt and his measuring tape round his neck as usual. He found it agonizing to get to the point, whatever that was to be; offered tea, a cold drink—all interspersed with flitting remarks about "things being as they are," the heat, the drought—ready to interpret the riots and burnings as some sort of seasonal act of nature, if that would be more tactful. "You are worried, my dear Joosab. But I don't know what would reassure you. Or myself. Cynical people will please themselves by saying independence solves nothing. People like us should always have known that independence only begins to solve anything. The moment it's achieved it's no longer an end."

"You are so right, Colonel, you are so wise. It's a pleasure to talk to someone like you. You can't imagine what I go through with some of these people. I say to them, no good comparing the old days. But they are nervous, you know? They say why attract attention. And the Gandhi Hall was built with contributions from the community. I say to them, change the name then, if you are afraid all the time something will happen to your investment. Gandhi didn't believe in investment. But they are nervous—you know what I mean?"

"Well, there aren't any classes going on there, now, of course—no one to teach, no one to come for the time being."

"That's true. But—Colonel—they want you to take away your things. The carpentry stuff and so on . . . they say if someone should get the idea to come in and smash it up . . ."

"You want us to clear out?"

"Colonel—"

"Oh don't be upset, Joosab; I'm just thinking—"

"Our community has made regular contributions to the Party, Colonel, and then with you being a good friend of the President, we thought we wouldn't have to worry. But now these people—who are they, they don't listen to anybody—"

"I just don't see how Malemba and I can manage it with only two pairs of hands. Right away, ay?"

Joosab held up his own hands in distressed admittance.

"Can you find some young men to help us? Your son's friends? — Never mind, they'd better stay out of it. I'll get hold of someone."

One of the anonymous females of the household appeared with ghostly shyness, placing a tea-tray so softly that not even a teaspoon clinked. "Oh have a cup, Colonel, look it's here," Joosab said, as if it had materialized of itself. "This is a terrible time for President Mweta, terrible, terrible. What do you think it is, Colonel, is it the Communists?"

Bray, Malemba, the elder Malemba sons, Hjalmar, Mahlope, Nongwaye Tlume and Rebecca lugged the adult education centre's equipment out of the Gandhi Hall that afternoon and evening. They had a jeep from the agricultural department and a vegetable lorry that Joosab managed to borrow from one of the Indian storekeepers. The stuff was dumped in Bray's lean-to garage, in the rondavel at the Tlume house that Rebecca and her children had occupied, and even at the *boma*.

In the middle of the night the telephone rang. Joosab's voice was at once faint and shrieking as if he were being borne away while he spoke. "Colonel, stop them, stop them, you must stop them. You know the President . . ." "Joosab, for God's sake what's happened to you?" "They're burning down the Hall—you must come and stop it—"

He dropped back the telephone and leaned there, against the wall in the dark living-room, come out of sleep to a return like nausea. His hand went wearily over his breast—Shinza's gesture. A mosquito's siren unfailingly found him out, singing round and round this daze. He telephoned Aleke. As he left the house with a pair of pants pulled over his pyjamas he was stopped by one of Major Fielding's men, who had rigged themselves out with red armbands and sporting rifles. "For God's sake don't argue—there's a fire."

Aleke and he saw the blaze from a long way off and felt it, a huge heat coming as if from the open door of a furnace. The Young Pioneers who had looted the place and set it alight were gone and the fire engine was there, its hoses sufficient only to wet the area round the building to prevent the fire spreading—in the middle of veils of water and smoke the hall and the school to which it was attached were just at the stage when a building on fire holds its shape in pure flame rather than matter; in a moment it would begin to collapse upon itself. Joosab and a few other men stood there, wearing coats over their nightclothes despite the heat of the night and the fire. The smell of wet and burning was choking; their black eyes ran with tears of irritation. They seemed unable to speak. They stared at Bray. The building must have been ablaze beyond remedy and the firemen already there when Joosab telephoned. Among the soaked and charred things that had been rescued Bray saw a chest neatly lettered in white, THE MAHATMA GANDHI NON-VIOLENCE STUDY KIT. One of the younger Indians said to him, "I don't suppose the insurance will pay out."

Rebecca had been so tired she had not heard the telephone, had not heard him leave the house. When he came back she sat up alarmed. "The Gandhi Hall's burned down." "Oh my God, all that effort for nothing." He lay down on top of the bed next to her. He smelled of wet burned wood and burned paint. "Get in," she said, tugging at the covers beneath him. He pushed the sandals off his feet and lay there unable to move, on his back. He heard himself giving great shuddering, snoring breaths as he was helplessly overcome by sleep.

Early in the morning, Dave the barman from the Fisheagle Inn was there to see him. Kalimo was polishing the living-room floor, all the furniture pushed to the middle, and kept his head turned away from the visitor as he showed him in. Then he went on his knees again, shifting about under Bray's and the other man's feet with the obvious intention of showing that this visitor would not be accorded a respectful withdrawal.

Rebecca was in the bathroom. He took the man into the bedroom and the presence of the unmade bed, the woman's shoes and his fire-pungent clothes lying on the floor. "Selufu's letting them have it. The ones he arrested."

"The twenty from the showground?"

"Fifteen or twenty—I don't know how many. They're being beaten and made to stand the whole night. A very bad time. They are beaten and those Young Pioneer bastards are let off. Selufu's even afraid to arrest them. Yes, it's true. You see yourself, all this burning and fighting keeps going on because he doesn't arrest them, he arrests the people they attack. That's why he doesn't like the soldiers—they grab anybody who makes trouble. He's scared, he's scared for his job."

"If I go to Selufu, and he asks me where I've got my information?"

The barman took his arm as if to confide a gin-inspired platitude. "Don't go near him."

"Oh I'm one of his willing helpers."

"Why I came, I knew you're taking the trip down. Tell Shinza. Some of them might say things that will make him change his plans. He'll know if they knew anything important. I've got the names."

"Well, I suppose there are all sorts of rumours . . . I could have heard from anywhere? D'you think anyone'll have noticed you've been to this house?"

"Perhaps someone has seen me, perhaps not. Everybody looks now, where you are going, when you go."

"Selufu can't just be left to do as he likes with people."

The barman ignored the appeal. "You don't want the names?"

"Yes, give them to me anyway. D'you know whether Shinza is all right?"

"He will be all right." Half reproof, half belligerent loyalty.

When the barman had gone Kalimo came into the kitchen, where Bray was fetching his freshly polished shoes from Mahlope. "I hope you didn't give that one money, *Mukwayi?*"

"Why should I do that?" He was guardedly amused.

"That's the man from the bar at the hotel, ay? I know. Everyone knows him. He borrows money, money. They say he even gets it from the white men who drink there." In English, "He *no good.*"

"Don't worry, Kalimo, I didn't give him anything."

All day he lapsed into periods when he could not think at all; when the opposing pressures exerted themselves equally, holding him in deadly balance between them. He was going to the police station at noon; and then simply stopped the car down the road under a tree and smoked a cigarette. By early in the afternoon he knew he would go at six, and if Selufu wasn't to be found, he would go to his house (Aleke had given him a pass, now, issued by the police, that allowed him out after curfew; another mark of grace and favour). If Selufu did find out that the informant was the barman at the Fisheagle, the man would probably be picked up and detained to see what *he* knew. If Selufu didn't find out, and had the ready-made advantage that Bray "admitted" the torture story had come as a rumour round Gala, Selufu would certainly deny it outright. All this was quite apart from any conclusions he might reach about himself—Bray. He thought, I could demand to see the men—again, in the name of whom, or what? Selufu was sent here by Mweta to replace Lebaliso because of the boy with the scarred back. So if I have the crazy authority to ask it, it's in the name of Mweta.

And at the same time, there was that remark of Selufu's, when he went to see him with Sampson Malemba: ". . . no trouble on your trips about the countryside, Colonel . . ."—vaguely taken as a reference to his contacts with Shinza, or to a suspicion about them. It could have been a warning hint: don't think I don't know.

He must know.

And yet I have been so cooperative in this mess. Acting out of common humanity. Keeping the peace. (In the name of whom; what sort of peace?) And maybe Mweta hesitated even yet to "set the hand free. . . ."

He scarcely spoke to Hjalmar or the girl when they ate together. When he and she found themselves alone he kissed her without desire. He and Malemba took the daily food supply up to the showgrounds; the men were back in the grandstand but still under heavy guard. The whole of Gala smelled burned out from the Gandhi Hall fire. There was news of riots and hut-burnings at the fish-freezing plant at the lake; roadblocks prevented the fish trucks from getting into Gala.

After dinner he sat under the fig in the dark smoking a stale cigar he had come across. He would get up and go to Selufu at any moment. He sat on. Rebecca came out and finding he did not speak, moved quiet as the bats blotching the old tree. Hjalmar brought a book and turned on the special insect-repellent light; in the garden, as well as the patriarchal fig there were jacaranda trees that one didn't notice outside their brief blooming-time—they had suddenly unfolded into it in the last few days and the light was caught in caves of lilac flowers. Mahlope was sent by Kalimo to fetch the coffee tray; the young man was singing to himself in a moth-soft voice.

He went into the house and stood a moment at the table where his unfinished report lay, some pages clipped together, some in folders, some loose sheets held down by an ashtray and even the little photograph frame with Venetia and the baby pressed into use—Kalimo's precaution against the dusty wind that often blew into the house. The paper was gritty to the touch. A hairy black fly lay dead on its back. She had sat on the floor against his legs at the fireplace—it was empty, except for the cigarette butts they all lazily threw there. It was weeks since he had sat at the table, had written a letter, even to his wife. He took a sheet of the typing paper Rebecca had used for his report and wrote out the details about the money in Switzerland: name of bank, address, account number, code name. He folded the sheet and flattened it with his thumbnail, cigar ash falling onto it, and then carefully tore off and folded once again the half he had written on, putting it into the pocket of his bush jacket.

He got up and called her from the dark veranda.

She found him in the bedroom, where they would be safe from Hjalmar. He was sitting on the bed. He said, "We're leaving tomorrow. We'll pack up tonight and go in the morning."

She came no farther into the room. "Why don't you believe me. I'm not going."

He put out his hand to her. "Come here. My darling, we're going together."

"You are taking me because I wouldn't go the other day."

"No, no. I'm not going to dump you anywhere. We're going. I can't stay here acting vigilante for Aleke, can I? How can I?"

She stood in front him where he sat, looking down at him, slightly drawn back. He slowly put out his hands and rested a palm on the shape of each hip.

"You are coming with me?"

"We'll go together."

"And then?"

"I'm not sure. We'll go to the hotel so's I won't compromise anybody by anything I do . . . we'll say I've had to come to bring you down because it was unsafe here. —It *is* unsafe."

"I was only afraid of one thing—not getting back."

"I know. But I'll be there."

"You won't come back here?"

He shook his head.

"Not at all?"

"Perhaps not."

"This funny house of yours," she said. She sat down on the bed beside him and took his hand.

She asked, "You mean you'll go to Switzerland?"

There was a ringing closeness in the room around them. Inside him was an experience exactly the reverse of the emptiness, the sense of all forces disengaged and fallen apart, that he had been having all day.

"Maybe. But it's too late for that. There's something else I have to do in Europe. I'll tell you tomorrow when we're out of here. But so far as everyone else is concerned, I'm just in town because of bringing you, hmm?"

"How can we go together. Overseas," she said slowly, using the colonial's term, loaded with distance and unattainableness.

"We'll see. Perhaps we can manage. We'll decide what to do. I can't stay here, my darling." He stroked her hair, it had grown, it was growing very long. She said, "What are you thinking?"

He smiled at her. "—What a pity, in a way."

It was she who thought of Hjalmar. They agreed, of course he would go down to the capital with them. "And it'll make it easy for him to make it up with the family. I mean it won't look as if he's come crawling back." He went to the garden to tell Hjalmar; the good-looking blond head was bent, skull asserting itself gradually now through the thinning hair and drawn bright skin, reading George Orwell's letters over the top of rather than through rimless lenses. Hjalmar took the glasses off and listened with detached reasonableness. Then he got up, closing the book, nodding in understanding. He asked a few factual questions about the journey—there were no roadblocks, no difficulty on that stretch of road, eh? Bray said he'd heard nothing like that. Hjalmar went purposefully indoors; there was his voice remarking something to Rebecca, and her laugh.

Bray turned off the light so that the colour shrank away into darkness as a piece of paper, swollen with the glow of flame, suddenly turns black and shrivels. In the dark he felt one or two of the big ants that journeyed ceaselessly over the fig crawl blunderingly over his foot. The multiple trunks of the tree, twisted together forty feet up, made the shape of a huge wigwam under the spread of its enormous, half-bald branches. How old was it? As old as the slave-tree? He had found thickened scars where at some point or other in its life there had been an attempt to hack it down. A reassuring object, supporting life even in the teeming parasites whose purpose of existence was to eat it out from within; an organism whose heart couldn't be got at because it was many trees, each great arterial trunk rotting away in the embrace of another that held still the form of sap and fibre; a thing at once gigantic and stunted, in senile fecundity endlessly putting out useless fruit on stumps and in crotches. But only for trees is it enough simply to endure; not for human beings. The black heat was stirred by small whirls of air currents, somewhere in its density the tree frogs clinked ceaselessly. He had known this night a thousand times.

He went into the house, stood looking at the table of papers, left it and went into the bedroom where Rebecca was already emptying drawers. The spear-fishing goggles and guns were dumped in a corner. "We can stick them in one of those big laundry baskets of Kalimo's. I would have liked to go one last time to the lake." He said, "They say the spear-fishing's wonderful in Sardinia." "Sardinia, here we come." She waved a blue snorkel. She stood as if she were momentarily giddy: "It doesn't seem real, does it?"

"No. It never does." Very far back in his mind, he had been putting these clothes in this suitcase in Wiltshire. A sentence came to him idiotically, like the line of a popular song: *Your waist measurement hasn't changed for ten years.* Now, as then, a decision became the progression of small practical tasks. He found a basket for the spear-fishing gear; in the end he did shuffle together all the papers and files from his table and look around for something to pack them in. There was a thin plywood box of the tea-chest kind that he thought would do, if he could clean it out a bit. He had turned it upside-down and was banging at the base; Hjalmar appeared and watched a moment with the tentative air of someone who doesn't know whether or not to help or give advice. "And how're you getting on? Finished already?"

Hjalmar sat down on the edge of an old veranda chair whose legs splayed under weight. He said shyly, "I think I'll stay and keep an eye on things in the house."

Bray was picking an old label off the box. A small cockroach flashed from beneath, fell to the floor and was caught by his sole. "I don't know when I'll be back, you know."

"That's okay. Maybe I'll come down soon. If I get lonely or so. Do you want to take the Orwell?"

"Good lord, keep the books. There's nowhere to put them."

Rebecca appeared with an armful of children's worn-out sandals. "What's this about?"

"Hjalmar's decided to hang on a bit."

"Oh. Have you?" she said, friendly, awkward, to make it seem neither unreasonable nor unexpected.

Hjalmar gave a short laugh—"It may sound crazy, but you know I want to finish the paving out there under the tree. I hate to leave it half-finished—you know? Then I'll be able to decide the . . . the next thing. Only I must do it first. It's such a mess there with the fruit dropping and the leaves on that uneven ground. When it's paved all you need to do is just sweep it off."

"That reminds me—money for Mahlope and Kalimo. If I give you a cheque could you pay them? And please—phone Aleke for me, tomorrow—tell him I decided to get Rebecca out." He wrote the cheque to the amount of three months' wages for each servant and enough left over to keep the house running for a while, but Hjalmar put it in his wallet without glancing at it. Bray looked at the chest with a sudden infirmity of purpose. "Hjalmar—if I leave this stuff, could you pack it away for me sometime? And then if you come down, either you could bring it or—?"

"Of course, no trouble. I'll see to everything."

While they fetched and carried and threw away, turning out the life of Bray's house as one turns out a drawer, Hjalmar busied himself making tea.

He said to the girl as the three of them drank it, "I like this house. I'm going through a bad time but just the same I like this house." She stood there strangely with the cup in her hand and Bray saw her looking, looking, eyes averted, round the ugly, shabby, impersonal furniture, the chairs they had talked in, the table they had eaten at. There was a moment's embarrassment, as if something too intimate had been spoken aloud. But most of that night she struck him as vividly animated—suppressing animation. The thought even crossed his mind once: perhaps she is elated without knowing it at moving towards her children again.

They went to the narrow bed in which somehow or other they had slept many nights, folded together or rolled away to the edges in the heat, always touching at some point, at shoulder or foot, or hair to hand, as if one sympathetic nervous system took over and controlled two bodies in a special tolerance. They had both had a shower and lay naked without covering and without having dried themselves properly—evaporation at least gave the sensation of coolness. She said, "I want to feel you in me but we won't make love."

"We'll have a big bed at the Great Lakes. They must have big beds."

"Will we get there in one day?"

"We'll just keep on driving, mmh?" He had his hand on her face and he felt her smile.

Sometime later the rain came. Thunder bore down grandly upon the roof, he half-woke and saw his foot coming down on the quick cockroach, a shiny almond. He had softened and fallen away from the warm tunnel of her. The forest of heavy rain hid them, and they slept.

In the morning there was a world that had cast its skin. All the green glistened like dragonfly wings drying in the sun. The jacarandas had shed their shape in fallen flowers on the ground. Glossy starlings flashed about; Hjalmar was out there, seeing how his brick mosaic had stood up to the wet.

Mahlope put the three suitcases and the basket with Gordon Edwards' spear-fishing equipment into the car. Kalimo trotted back and forth with his hands under his apron, watching. Bray had told him *Doña* was going to her friends in the capital. To him the capital was the two Poles and all the great cities and places of the earth: if you got there, you were near everywhere. "And bring my greetings to the children, please," he said in English to Rebecca, smiling and repeating in a comforting rumble, "Yes . . . yes . . . mm'h,. . ." When they said good-bye he handed over the basket they always took with them for picnics at the lake. "Is it eggs with small fish in, as well?" Bray said. The old man hunched with laughter—"Those eggs you like it, blead, litt'e bit cheese—"

"No roast chicken?" Rebecca said.

Kalimo's eyes were rheumy at the good old joke. "Well, *Mukwayi* he didn't tell me you driving today! I don't cook chicken for roaste' yesterday night—"

"As long as we've got those eggs, Kalimo."

Hjalmar kissed Rebecca. "Walking out on the job, eh? Where'm I going to get another bricklayer's assistant? You'll see when you come back, it'll all be finished for you."

Hjalmar and Kalimo were left, the one with hands on hips, the other's under his apron. Mahlope, chatting outside his room with a friend, waved cheerfully. Rebecca settled herself more comfortably, lit cigarettes. "I feel as if we *were* going off to the lake."

As the old Volkswagen left Gala behind they left the whole anger and disruption of the country behind there as well. The *boma* under

guard, the smashed stalls of the market, the scars and stains where
flies hung, marking the place of street battles, the dead smell of
charred buildings—all this that they lived among was undertow beneath their wheels: it seemed that the light screens of forest and bamboo around the firm wet road provided no surface to reflect turmoil,
to be seized by the violent charge and make it manifest; the current
was earthed.

He pointed out the track leading to Tippo Tib's Arab fort.

"We never ever managed to go—"

"I must take you one day. It's quite impressive."

The road ran empty for many miles. Now and then there were the
usual bags of charcoal waiting for custom; a barefoot man appeaɪed
from the forest. Where rain had fallen parties of women were out
with their hoes. The few villages looked lean and wispy after the
drought. In patches of scrub, one night's rain was enough to have
brought the wild lilies blooming straight from the sand. They had an
eye for everything; the past week became a prison from which they
suddenly found themselves let out. Talk rose and died down; sometimes they let the repetition of trees and giant bouquets of bamboo
flow over them dreamily. Thoughts broke up and formed like spume
on a sea. They laughed at the prospect of the household consisting of
Hjalmar and Kalimo quietly following their private obsessions. "But
Kalimo will be in charge." "Oh without question. He will play Margot to Hjalmar's Hjalmar."

"I can't help feeling sorry for Margot," Rebecca said. "A weak man
makes you into a bitch. Even I felt like beginning to bully poor old
Hjalmar a bit over that paving."

"Even you? You've always been able to smell out a weak man?"

"Mmm. If I'm attracted by one, there's still something that protects
me."

"When first I knew you—knew about you from other people—I
thought you were very much the type to be exploited. Emotionally
and in other ways; by everybody. And your friends gave that impression. Vivien was always anxious about you."

"Oh well, I got into a bad way down there. They didn't trust Gordon, any of them. Oh I mean, everybody always *likes* Gordon—but
they didn't think Gordon treated me properly. I knew they were sorry
for me. They persisted in being sorry for me. It made me behave fun-

nily; I can't explain, but when they made passes at me—Neil, the others—I saw that they felt they could do it because *to me* they could risk showing that things weren't so good for them, either. I felt sorry for them. I felt what did it matter . . ." She put a hand on his thigh. "You don't like to hear about it."

"Vanity, I suppose. Stupid male vanity, not much different from theirs. I ought to be ashamed of it. I've always believed in freedom in sex. Not that I've taken much of it. But on principle."

She laughed. "I'm glad. I don't want you to have made love to a lot of women."

"Although you've made love to a lot of men?"

"I'm not like you. It doesn't matter for me. But there's one thing that matters a lot—I'd decided I couldn't stay down there among my friends any longer, before it began with you and me. I came to Gala because I wanted to get away from that."

A moment later she said, "You're thinking about the first time, in your living-room."

"Yes."

"You're right. It did seem it was like the others."

"You wanted to show me I had a need of you before I could begin to feel sorry for you."

"You were, already. That poor girl with her kids. And where's the husband?"

"Yes. I ought to have offered you my house instead of letting you pay for those weeks at the Fisheagle."

"But after you went down to see Mweta and came back again you made it right. From the day we went to the lake it was all different. I was different."

"Were you?"

"You made me different."

"Have I reformed you, my darling, your paunchy old lover. You don't want other men any more." But he knew it made her sad to hear him refer to himself as getting old.

"Living with you is different from anything else."

"But it has been for me, too."

"Oh don't say that."

"Why not?"

"Not has been."

"My darling! I just mean the time at Gala, that's all. Kiss me." He turned to her quickly a moment.

She rested content, against his shoulder; she waved at a solitary figure at the roadside.

"You don't think Gordon has . . . well . . . presented you with a certain element of weakness?"

"How d'you mean?"

"Well you told me he would never dream of thinking you could be interested in men."

She gave a small chuckle. "That's because Gordon's so sure of himself in everything. Gordon can cope."

"But that's arrogance, pride. You've proved it a weakness in him, haven't you?"

"In a way. But you say you believe in sexual freedom."

"We're talking about Gordon—he doesn't see it as sexual freedom, it's quite the opposite—he doesn't even see the possibility of sexual freedom for you."

"Of course it wasn't sexual freedom. Just that the whole thing didn't mean much. Whether he thought me incapable of bothering about any man, or I thought it didn't matter whether I did or not—it all amounted to the same thing." Her weight was slack and warm against him. "I'm very jealous of Olivia. I suppose that's what it is: I have a horrible feeling when I think of her."

"Why do you think you're so jealous, since you're different from me, with my stupid sexual jealousy about the other men?"

"I don't know." She seemed to wait for the answer to come to her. "Because *you* don't separate sex and love. —Do you? If you slept with her again it would be because you love her."

What she had said did not conjure up for him Olivia, but Gordon —the red road was drawn away under his eyes through the windscreen already dirtied with insects, and it was Gordon he saw, talking away, coming across the strip of scrub between his house and the Tlumes'.

"I don't know why—I feel so marvellously sleepy. Keep sort of dropping off."

She slept for more than half an hour, thirty or forty miles. His mind was calm. It was not that he had no doubts about what he was doing, going to do; it seemed to him he had come to understand that one could never hope to be free of doubt, of contradictions within, that this was the state in which one lived—the state of life itself—and no action could be free of it. There was no finality, while one lived, and when one died it would always be, in a sense, an interruption. He went over and over in his mind the possibilities of raising money for Shinza quickly. Perhaps, the way things were going, Shinza would be dead before he could arrange anything; perhaps Shinza would go into exile over the border, and Mweta would hang on a while. Perhaps there would be many more burned houses, more blood running as easily as chickens' blood in fighting in which the real cause was not understood, in which the side-reactions of little groups of people battled out apparently uselessly the passions of the real struggle to which their situation—the years of slavery, isolation, colonization—committed them. There would be waste and confusion. He was party to it, part of it. The means, as always, would be dubious. He had no others to offer with any hope of achieving the end, and as he accepted the necessity of the end, he had no choice.

The instincts in himself that he had unconsciously regarded as the most civilized, unwilling to risk—as a fatal contradiction in terms—his own skin or that of others for the values of civilization, were outraged. He was aware (driving between the swish of tall grass stroked by the car's speed) of going against his own nature: something may be worth suffering for as a matter of individual conviction, but nothing is worth bringing about the suffering of others. If people kill in a cause that isn't mine, there's no blood on my shoes; therefore stand aside. But he had put aside instead this "own nature." It was either a tragic mistake or his salvation. He thought, I'll never know, although other people will tell me for the rest of my life. Rebecca's hair fluttered against his shoulder in the draught from the window. He passed a swampy *dambo* and there were the widow-birds hovering their long black tails. A snake lay coiled in the road and he avoided it; the next car would kill it. There was also in his mind the possibility that he would go and see Mweta one last time, in the capital. The preposterousness of the thing lay like a jewel that has fallen into a pool and rolled among the stones like any other pebble. If one could pick it out . . . and even now, since only audacity was possible, Mweta might seize upon Shinza, not the enemy but the only chance. . . . He saw himself actually walking up the steps to the red brick façade of that huge house; he supposed the image would fade out as the shape of an hallucination born of obsession fades, with health, into an empty wall.

His mind scarcely ran ahead to Shinza, because *that* he was being borne towards as surely as the road was the one to the capital. Haffa-jee's Garage. And if Shinza had moved off to another part of the country, it did not matter. He had the list. Shinza was not a man who depended on you; it was rather that he banked on what you would have to do, driven from within yourself. He knew one doesn't ask of a man what is not there already.

And if Hjalmar is attacked in the house? —Why should that be, there was no anti-white feeling as such in Gala's state of siege. But by hazard—someone with a petrol-soaked rag flaming on a stick turning down one street rather than another; one of Fielding's vigilantes losing his nerve at a shadow? But what Hjalmar had in him was survival. Hjalmar would not escape that. It was in his instinct for staying put, there in Gala; he fears nothing so much as the situation of his mar-riage. —I'll have to go and see Margot, he thought, feeling the girl give a shuddering sigh in her sleep; I can tell her quite honestly he's not making a bad recovery. Curiously, although the nervous break-down had had the effect of making Hjalmar lose interest in what was once his passion to talk politics, so that they had never talked of what was happening as anything more coherent than a series of sensational village events, he had the impression now that Hjalmar understood perfectly what his—Bray's—position in Gala had been these last weeks, as if the shattering of Hjalmar's own core had opened and laid twitching bare a heightened receptivity to the unspoken, to the inner reality that such talk itself buries. Hjalmar had made a remark, one of the nights when they had watched the township burning from the garden: "The fire's in the minds of men, not in the roofs of houses"— it came from somewhere in Dostoevski.

Rebecca woke up. Her cheek was marked with the folds of his bush jacket, her eyes were still dazed and darkened with sleep. He stopped the car a minute for her. She found herself a culvert and came back along the road in the sun, smiling, twirling a lily she had picked. She was wearing her old jeans and moved a little awkwardly, perhaps conscious that they showed her to be as she had always been, a bit heavy in the thigh. She looked so young when she woke up—like that every morning. Life seemed to breathe out of her skin as vapour does through the earth above a mineral spring; wherever he touched her neck or face there was a pulse beating.

They stopped late to eat Kalimo's lunch, sitting on the newspaper wrappings because the ground was richly damp. They felt lazy to talk about anything important, after all; it would carry away into the quiet and airy savannah forest as their voices must be doing, wandering, far. There was no sound of birds, in the middle of the day. But Rebecca did say to him, at last, pouring the coffee from the thermos, "If it's not going to be Switzerland, well, what?"

"I'll know in a few days. I'll tell you just a few facts for now, because I shouldn't talk about this at all. Not to anyone. Not even to you."

"Not even here?" She lifted a hand at the forest, half-joking.

"But when I know exactly, I'll tell you everything. Because you must know."

The dappled shade made a shawl on her arms, her eyes were on him. "So far it's just this—there may be something I can do—for Shinza. And I will do it. Whatever it is."

She did not say, what about me? She got up as if to begin tidying up the remains of the meal and then came over behind him where he squatted on his haunches and put her arms around his neck and pressed his head back against her belly.

He said, "I'll tell you everything."

"I know you will. This time."

She came and squatted in front of him and took off his glasses. She touched the skin round his eyes and played the old game, looking into the shortsighted opacity that she complained of. He said, "If I start kissing you we'll never get there." She picked up the thermos. "Shall I pour the rest away?"

"Well, we might still feel like some later."

"It won't be hot."

"Never mind, it'll be wet."

As they moved back to the car two children appeared out of the forest; or they had been there, behind the trees, patiently watching for the moment to come forward. She gave into their cupped hands the remains of the bread and cheese and the last of the eggs with small fish in them. Before the car had driven off the two frail figures had disappeared once more into the forest.

Not long after they came upon what was evidently a road-block that had been half cleared. Branches and stones had been dragged aside and there was just sufficient room for the car to pass. There was no-body about, but it was not far from the turn-off to the cattle-dipping station sixty miles from Matoko. No rain had fallen yet in this part of the country; towards three o'clock the heat and the monotonous rhythms of motion, of the hot current of air coming past the windows with the sound of someone whistling through his teeth, now made him drowsy. They changed over; Rebecca drove but he did not sleep, merely stretched himself as much as he could in the small car and rested his eyes away from the hypnotic path of the road. Now he was the one to light cigarettes for her. He had shut his eyes for a moment, when he heard her make a small sound of impatience beside him, and he roused himself and saw that up ahead, quite far, was another road-block. There was a heat-mirage that magnified the jumble of branches and green; they couldn't make out very well whether it stretched across the whole road or not. She slowed down and they kept their eyes strained on the obstacle. But of course she could see so much better than he. "Damn it, it *is* right across. Now wha'd'we do?"

"Just keep going slowly." He put his head out the window; the grass was very high, elephant grass, very dry, last season's grass still standing; a dead tree had been dragged into the road, roots and all, broken branches had been piled upon it. She stopped and turned off the engine.

"Let's have a look. You stay in, a minute."

He walked slowly to the barrier, climbed over to the other side, walked up and down it and climbed back. He came to the car, smil-ing. "How energetic are you feeling? We'll have to do some hard la-bour." She got out and they started with the easy stuff, the broken branches. But the tree trunk, with its dead roots clasping a great boulder of red earth with which it must have been uprooted in some storm, would not budge. She began to laugh helplessly at their grunt-ing efforts. "Wait a moment, my girl. What about trying the jack? If we get it under this hollow bit here, maybe we can get a little eleva-tion and then heave."

The jack wasn't kept in the boot, in the front, but under the back seat, because the clamp that held it in its proper place had been bro-ken ever since he bought the car. He got in and dumped the picnic basket on the front seat and jerked up the back one in a release of dust. At the same time something burst out of the grass, he felt himself grabbed by the leg, by the waist, and he was caught between the steering wheel and the driver's seat, somehow desperately hampered by the size and strength of his body. At once there were people all round and over and in the car, there had been no sound and now there was nothing but yells and shouts and his great, his lung-bursting, muscle-tearing effort and he did not know if they were yelling, the men who were upon him, or if Rebecca was screaming. Even greater than his effort to defend himself was his terrible effort to make himself heard by her, to reach her with his voice and make her run. They had his legs out of the car and the back of his neck hit the rim of the floor and he was deafened, his voice became a silent scream to him as pain felled him for a moment, but then a brute strength burst up in him and he got to his feet, he was aware of himself staggered gigantically to his feet among men smaller than he. Then he was below them, he was looking up at them and he saw the faces, he saw the sticks and stones and bits of farm implements, and sun behind. Something fell on him again and again and he knew himself convulsed, going in and out of pitch black, of black nausea, heaving to bend double where the blows were, where the breath had gone, and he thought he rose again, he thought he heard himself screaming, he wanted to speak to them in Gala but he did not know a word, not a word of it, and then something burst in his eyes, some wet flower covered them, and he thought, he knew: I've been interrupted, then—

PART SIX

She was a long time in the culvert by the road. Her nails were full of red earth. The red earth walls, staunched with tufts of dead grass, rose on either side of her. With her head pressed against them she waited for it to happen to her, too. There was earth and saliva in her mouth. She was gulping and howling like an animal. She heard the tearing of flames and saw the thick smoke.

And then there was silence. Behind the sound of burning, nothing. The burning died away and there was only the smell and the smoke.

She had run towards him at first when they started pulling him out of the car. He had got to his feet and looked straight at her without seeing her because of that shortsightedness. But in the same split second he was brought down beneath them and the sound of the blows on the resistance of his big body sent her crazedly hurling herself through the grass, fighting it. She was turning her ankles, running, her stumbling scramble led her off down a kind of slope cut into the ground. And she was there, deep in the ditch beyond the grass. But she was not twenty yards from them, from him, and she knew it would come to her, it was no use, she was held by the walls, waiting for them.

She was sure they must be there in the silence.

She did not move. The smoke no longer poured up; it was thin, hanging in stillness. She did not know how much time passed. But the silence was empty; above, in the tops of the long grasses between her and the road, scarlet weaver-birds flicked, swung, and chirped a question. More time passed. She got up and tried to climb out of the culvert but the walls were too high. She wandered along out the way she had been driven in, up the diagonal cutting made by the roads department. She pushed weakly through the heavy grass. The car was on its side, blackened, the seats still smouldering, the road full of glass.

He was clear of it. He was in the road unharmed by the fire. Unharmed. She began to sob with joy because he was not burned, she went concentratedly but not fast—she could not move fast—towards him, towards his legs rolled apart. She walked all round him, making some sort of noise she had never heard before. Round and round him. His body—the chest, the big torso above the still narrowish male waist that he kept, for all his weight—was something staved in under the dirtied bush jacket, out of shape, but he was still there. The whole of him was there. Strange, soft-looking patches of earth and blood; but the whole bulk of him, complete. A lot of dirt and blood on the face, a sort of grimace, lips slightly drawn back as when he was trying to unscrew something tight.

Suddenly she saw that his glasses were smashed into his cheekbones. The frame lay near his ear but glass was embedded there in the firm flesh just below that tender, slightly shiny area of skin that was always protected by his glasses. The glass was pressed in so hard that the flesh was whitened and had scarcely bled. She went down on her knees and with a shaking impatience in her fingers began to try to take out the broken glass. She was concerned only not to hurt him, it was difficult to do without hurting him.

After a little while she went and sat on the white-washed milestone at the side of the road. His eyes were not open but the lids were not quite closed and showed a line of glint. She broke off a stalk of dry grass and cleaned the earth from beneath her nails, carefully, one by one. It was very hot. Sweat ran down the sides of her face and under the hair, on her neck. She watched him all the time. She became aware of a strange and terrifying curiosity rising in her; it was somehow connected with his body. She got up and went over to this body again and looked at it: this was the same body that she had caressed last night, that she had had inside her when she fell asleep.

The basket and his briefcase had been flung out of the car and so were not burned. She picked them up and balanced the briefcase across the basket beside him, to keep the sun off his face.

And more time went by. She sat on in the road. Her shirt was wet with sweat and she could smell it. Sometimes she opened her mouth and panted a little; until she heard the sound, and stopped. She was beginning to feel something. She didn't know what it was, but it was some sort of physical inkling. And then she thought very clearly that the flask was still in the basket and got up firmly and fetched it and poured what was left of the coffee into the plastic cup. As she saw liquid there, it all came back to her with a rush, to the glands of her mouth, to her nerves, to her senses, to her flesh and bones—she was thirsty. She drank it down in one breath. Then for the first time she began to weep. She was thirsty, and had drunk, and so it had happened: she had left him. She had begun to live on. Desolation beat down red upon her eyelids with the sun and the tears streamed from her eyes and nose over her earth-stained hands.

Some people came down the road. An old man with safety-pins in his earlobes and a loin-cloth under an old jacket stopped short, saying the same half-syllable over and over. There were little children watching and no one sent them away. All she could do before the old man was shake her head, again, again, again, again, again at what they both saw. The women sent up a great sigh. Bray lay there in the middle of them all. They brought an old grey blanket of the kind she had seen all her life drying outside their huts, and an old door and they lifted him up and carried him away. They seemed to know him; he belonged to them. The old man with the safety-pins said to her in revelation, "It is the Colonel! It is the Colonel!"

She did not know him any more. She had left him. She was walking along the road between the cotton-covered, great soft hanging breasts of two women, she was alive.

They took them to an hotel that was closed or deserted. The building was boarded up and there was some sort of huge aviary outside but no birds in it, the wire doors open and a lot of burst mattresses and rubbish piled there. They took him to their own quarters, to one of their mud houses, and laid him on an iron bedstead in the cool dimness. It was the old man's bed and there was a pillow-case embroidered free-hand with yellow crosses, red birds with blue eyes, and blue flowers with red leaves. The women sat with him and clapped their hands together soundlessly and kept up a kind of archaic groan, perhaps it was praying, perhaps it was just another human sound she had never heard before. She rested her head against one of the big breasts on cloth that smelt of woodsmoke and snuff. The D.O. from the Matoko *boma* came and took her away in his landrover, and his little wife, looking rather like Edna Tlume, seemed afraid of her and put her to bed in what was obviously the marital bed. A white doctor in priest's robes came and gave her an injection; they put her to sleep because she was not dead. She understood; what else could they do with her? She slept the whole night and in the morning found herself in a big bed, after all those nights in the narrow one.

Neil and Vivien Bayley appeared to take her to the capital. She wore one of the D.O.'s wife's dresses and she had nothing but the picnic basket and the briefcase.

At the Bayleys' house the children were all over her, pulling at her, chattering, asking where Clive and Alan and Suzi were. Vivien used the adult formula: "You mustn't worry Rebecca, she's very, very tired," but to them she was the familiar Rebecca into whose car they used to be piled for entertainments and expeditions. All Vivien's children went through a stage of being rudely aggressive towards their mother; Eliza yelled, "It's not fair! Rebecca's nicer than you!" A scene swept through the house, banging doors, raising voices.

Neil's way was to say whenever he came into the house, "I think we all need a brandy." They did not seem able to talk to her without all three of them having a drink in their hands. She drank to make it possible for the Bayleys but she would not take the pills Vivien gave her because then she had to go and lie down and sleep, and when she woke there was a moment when she didn't know it had happened and she had to discover it again. Vivien said, "I think it'd be a good idea if we made you some dresses." The sewing machine was brought into the living-room and Vivien kept up a sort of monologue while she sewed, handing bits of the finishing over to her to be done. She was wearing Vivien's clothes, which fitted her better than the D.O.'s wife's dress had. She remembered and said to Vivien, "Did you send back the dress to Matoko?" Vivien said gently, "No, but I will when the transport starts running again, don't worry."

She was turning up a hem. The material was pale green cotton. She said, "What will they do with him?"

Vivien's hands were taken slowly from the machine, her face had an imploring look. "They've cabled his wife to see if she wants his body flown back."

The airport was closed, they had told her. He would be kept lying somewhere, there were refrigerators for that sort of thing. No one knew when planes would leave again. She had tried to make a joke about the airport, saying, "So your riot bag's just standing by," but Vivien had taken it as a reminder of something unspeakable and could not answer.

With the brandy glasses in their hands they talked about what had happened. Out of that day—yesterday, the day before yesterday, the day before that: slowly the succeeding days changed position round it—another version came into double exposure over what she knew. The men who had attacked were a roving gang made up of a remnant from the terrible riots that had gone on for a week centred round the asbestos mine. A Company riot squad led by white strangers—"*You see*," Vivien interrupted her husband, "I knew they'd get round to using those men from the Congo and Mweta wouldn't be able to stop them. I knew it would happen"—had opened machine-gun fire on strikers armed with sticks and stones. The white men dealt with them out of long experience of country people who needed a lesson in the name of whoever was paying—they burned down the village. The villagers and the strikers had made an unsuccessful raid on the old Pilchey's Hotel, where the mercenaries had quartered themselves. Someone had put up those road-blocks, probably with the idea of ambushing the white men (hopeless, they had left already, anyway). . . . It was said that the one who started the hut-burnings was a big German who didn't travel in the troop transports but in his own car.

Vivien said, "But this was a little Volkswagen, and there was a woman in it."

"To asbestos miners an army staff car's the same as any other kind. A car's a car." Neil spoke coldly to her. "Nobody knows anything, any more, when things get to the stage they are now. I don't suppose Mweta knew they would machine-gun people. Burn their houses over their heads. He just put it in the hands of the Company army, left it to their good sense . . . that's quite enough."

She offered the information, "The people who helped us knew Bray.

An old man with safety-pins in the holes in his ears. He knew him from before."

Neil had put the brandy on the floor. His hands were interlocked between his knees, his big, bright, bearded head (river-god's head, Bray had once called it) stared down through his legs so that the veins showed in his rosy neck. He said thickly, sternly, "Yes, they knew him. But it only takes a handful of strangers. Miners are recruited all over the country. God knows who *they* were. Nobody knows who the white men were. White men from somewhere. Perhaps they travel in Volkswagen cars, perhaps they cart women around with them. Putting up their road-blocks a mile from those people who'd known him for twenty years was a bunch of men who'd never seen him before. That's all."

Agnes Aleke came to see her. Agnes was wearing her smooth wig, she was smartly dressed, and she cried all the time. "If only you'd come in the plane with me, if you'd come when I went." Through Bray's death she seemed to experience in her plump voluptuous little body all that she had feared for it. Rebecca sat with her in the garden and held her hand to comfort her; Vivien carried out tea. "Come and stay with me, Rebecca, come to my mother's place. It's a nice house. Oh how I hated that place, that Gala, don't show me that place again, never—and how you must hate us—I said to my mother, she will hate us and why shouldn't she." They embraced, Rebecca patting her gently while she sobbed. Vivien said with firm kindness, "What do you think of our dressmaking, Mrs. Aleke? You know Rebecca and I made that dress she's wearing, ourselves."

Roly Dando came. It was in the late afternoon; they all drank. Thin little Roly had about him the air—taint, portent—of one who knows what is going on in a time of confusion and upheaval, when what official information there is ceases to be trustworthy. It was known that Mweta was not at the President's Residence; his messages to the people continued to be issued, but from some unknown retreat. His television appearances were, it was said, old films to which new taped statements were—not too well—matched. None of this was mentioned. But they talked. Dando seemed convinced that Shinza was over the border, planning a guerrilla insurrection. Dhlamini Okoi and the Minister of Health, Moses Phahle, had disappeared and were obviously with him. Goma was said to be in prison; there were so many people in prison that if someone wasn't seen for a few days it was presumed that that was where he must be. Neil said, "Roly, is it true that Mweta has asked for British troops?"

Roly sat there in the dusk with his sinewy shrunken neck pulled up very straight from his collar; he did not seem to hear. He rose to fetch another drink and hesitated on the way, where Rebecca sat. He put his hand on her head: "*La Fille aux Yeux d'Or, La Fille aux Yeux d'Or.*" He stalked awkwardly to the veranda table and poured himself something. He came back and sat on the arm of her chair, his arm round her, touching her neck as he talked, as he grew a little drunk, unable even now to resist the dismal opportunity to take advantage of his grief to fondle a woman. He was talking of Bray. "The thing is, of course, all our dear friends abroad will say he was killed by the people he loved and what else can you expect of them, and how ungrateful they are, and all that punishment-and-reward two-and-two-makes-four that passes for intelligent interpretation of events. That's the part of it that would rile him. Or maybe amuse him. I don't know."

Vivien's beautiful controlled voice came out of the dark. "I wish we could know that James himself knew it wasn't that, when it happened."

"Of course he knew!" Roly spoke with the unchallengeable authority of friendship on a plane none of the others had shared. "He's got nothing to do with that lot of spiritual bed-wetters finding a surrogate for their fears in his death! He knew what's meant by the forces of history, he knew how risky the energies released by social change are. But what's the good. They'll say 'his blacks' murdered him. They'll go one further: they'll come up with their guilts to be expiated and say, yes, he certainly died with Christian forgiveness for the people who killed him, into the bargain. Christ almighty. We'll never get it straight. They'll paw over everything with their sticky misconceptions." Roly spent the night because of the curfew. She heard him snoring in the room next to the one she had been given.

Vivien talked to her a lot about her children, about Clive and Alan and Suzi, but she herself was not thinking about them at all. She began to bleed although it was not the right time and it was then that she thought: so it never happened; there never will be a child. Vivien put small activities in her way as if driving some lost creature, out of kindness, along a track. "I think you ought to go and see Margot. If you feel like it. She's very down. She really would like to know about Hjalmar, though of course she wouldn't say it." So she took Vivien's car and drove to the Silver Rhino. It was the first time she had driven since that day. The car was the same kind—an old-model Volkswagen. Her feet and hands managed of themselves. It was only five days ago.

It had rained all night again and the morning was beautiful. (Put on the green dress, Vivien said.) There were soldiers on guard round the post office and broadcasting studios, people were cordoned off from the area where the newspaper offices had been stoned. Outside the railway station and bus depot hundreds of women, children, and old people sat in bright heaps among household goods and livestock in the strong sun high with the stink of urine and rotting vegetables; there were no trains or buses running.

And everywhere the rain and heat brought out flowers. The soldiers in their drab battledress stood under blossoming trees, poinsettia and hibiscus were crudely brilliant as carnival paper blooms in the driveway of the Presidential Residence that was said to be empty. In the old garden of the Silver Rhino an enormous American car was parked, with an older but scarcely lesser one behind it. There were nylon curtains in the balcony of windows round the rear of the new one, and ocelot-patterned seat covers. Some African men in pyjamas were sitting on the grass outside one of the bungalows—she did not really notice, on her way to the main building. But one of them got up and came forward with arms wide, a huge, fat man with a cigar in his mouth and a leopard-skin toque on his head: Loulou, Loulou Kamboya, Gordon's ex-partner from the Congo. "Madame Edouard —I say I know dat girl walking! What you make here?" "Loulou— and you?" He took her by the shoulders, beaming at her, an enormous grape-black face with thick ridges of flesh that pressed back against the ears and even up the forehead from the frontal ridge. "I make everywhere business. You know Loulou. But what this fighting, eh? They mad, eh? I sit here, I come yesterday one week wid my people, nothing for do, nothing. Sometime I think I go *faire une petite folie*—" He laughed hugely. She knew from Gordon that *"faire une petite folie"* meant to find a girl and make love; Loulou and Gordon spoke French together, the Congo French spoken by semiliterate

Africans, mixed with Lingala words and Belgian usage, but Loulou
had always been proud of being able to speak to her in English so
that she wouldn't feel left out. "*Et les bébés,* they grow okay? Where
Gordon? He making cash again or no? Ah Gordon, if he stay this
time now with me, you have plenty dresses! I make the big time—
that's right, I say the big time, eh?—I hear in *cinéma!* Oh business
continue to go good but now this damn war or what. *What? What?*
Eh? I here wid my people yesterday week already."

"Where are you making for?"

"I go for South. Down, down. Far for here. I have ticket but the
plane don't go. You see, I want to go for Jewburg. You remember?"

Yes, she remembered; he had always had a yearning to see Johannesburg. He had refused to be convinced that South Africa didn't let
in black men from other countries as a rule, and that if he did get in
he wouldn't be able to enjoy his habitual freedom of bars and girls.

"You know—I got business there now. I send goods already three
time—thirty thousand francs. Pay in Switzerland. Not Congo." He
roared with laughter at the old story. "But you sick, Madame
Edouard? What makes this—" He drew his ringed hands dolefully
down his face. "You short money?"

"No, nothing. I'm all right. —I'll see you again when I come out?
I've got to go and look for Mrs. Wentz."

"Anytime. Anytime. Look like I stay for Christmas."

Her fingers felt damp and twitchy. When he had drawn that face,
only succeeding in looking comic, she had felt tears coming back to
her suddenly again. At the Bayleys' she had gone dry: as you speak of
a cow going dry.

Margot Wentz had let her hair outgrow its dye. While they talked
she looked all the time at that inch or two of speckled white and gilt
at Margot's hairline. It was perhaps a sign of private mourning. They
sat in the little sitting-room at the round table with the fringed cloth.
Coffee was set out ready, with thin silver teaspoons and a silver
cream jug in the shape of a tulip. They discussed Hjalmar as if he
had had an illness and had been advised to go to Gala to recuperate.
Rebecca said he had been looking much better lately. The work he
was doing, pottering about the garden, seemed good for him. She
said, in a sort of final explanation for everything that was left unsaid:
"He offered to stay to look after the house," and a look of trapped dis-

tress came over Margot Wentz's face because now they had come up inevitably against what had happened: to that day when Rebecca and Bray left Gala. Every time Bray's name had occurred in Rebecca's account of Hjalmar's life in Gala, Margot's left cheek had moved a little as if a string jerked inside there, but now she could not avert herself any longer. She said something about that terrible business, about what a wonderful man he was; she stared at Rebecca, unable to go on. She looked magnificent; hers (unlike Loulou's) was a face made to express tragedy.

They drank more coffee and Rebecca asked about the hotel and the son, Stephen. "No one knows what will happen," Margot said, almost grandly. "I have no money to go, if I want to. And even if we want to, the airport is closed. I suppose the frontiers too. Hjalmar wouldn't be any better off here—" and then remembered that if he had not stayed to "look after the house" he might have been dead, and had again that look of dislocation that Rebecca saw her presence brought to people's faces. Rebecca asked about the daughter and that was better; she was settling down in London—"Of course, there are all the things Emmanuelle never had, all the concerts and recitals—music is her life, you know." When she got up to leave, Margot said to her, "Rebecca, if you should need anything. I don't know what—somewhere to stay, perhaps?" But she thanked her, there was nothing, she was staying with the Bayleys of course. "I see you've an old friend of ours in the hotel—the famous Loulou Kamboya."

"Oh him." Margot's voice was dry. "He's travelling with his own prostitutes, never mind his drivers and secretaries. It's a good thing for my licence the police've got other things to do, or I'd be in trouble for running a brothel."

Loulou was on the lookout for her and left his friends sitting drinking beer on the veranda of one of their rondavels. "You don't want have a little drink? No? Come I show you in my limousine my business I'm making nowdays—" He had dressed in pale blue linen trousers and, despite the heat, a brown mohair sweater with a gold thread in the knit. He wore it over his bare chest, where a gold chain followed the crease of fat round the base of his neck and ended in a big medallion with a red stone. The tail of some sort of civet hung from the leopard skin hat. The great rear bay of the car was filled with specially made cases, travelling-salesman style, but with the

Loulou touch—locks of scrolly gilt and red plastic crocodile covers. "From U.S., from U.S." He was selling the same old stuff—ivory paper knives and necklaces, crude copies of the famous seated figure of King Lukengu carved for him by the dozen in some Bakuba village up in the Kasai, masks decorated with cowrie shells and copper, made not for dancing but for the walls of white people's houses. "If I can't go Jewburg, I think now I like go over Portuguese side myself now tomorrow. I sell this; is not so bad place there . . . here, I make for you *petit cadeau* . . . yes, yes you take—" and she had to find a pair to fit her out of a bundle of gold-heeled sandals with thongs made of the skin of some poor beast. "Madame Edouard, but for why you sick, eh?" He stood back and shook his head over her, well aware that presents would not help. An African xylophone was being played up and down the Silver Rhino to announce lunch and his entourage rose with a screech of chairs, chattering and arguing, the girls laughing in their special careless, loose-shouldered way, waving about pretty black hands with painted fingernails like opalescent scales, breasts bobbing, earrings swinging, little black pigtails standing out all over their heads. He called some sarcastic-sounding remark, but all that happened was more giggles and one of the girls put her hands on her hips and stamped her foot so that her bracelets jiggled and so did her round backside in her tight *pagne.*

Rebecca was almost at the Bayleys' when she turned and drove back to the Silver Rhino. They were sitting at lunch, their chairs tipped this way and that, the waiters pounding and sweating round them, beer bottles being handed up and down, Loulou at the head. Wherever he went he carried with him the atmosphere of an open-air African nightclub. "Are you really going?" "To Portuguese? Yes, I tell you—this place is enough. And the plane—nothing. I go. —I go there one time already, is not bad. . . ."

She said, "Could I come with you, Loulou—would you take me."

"For sure I take you! For sure! *Demain? Sais-tu venir?* You plenty *bagage* and *biloko?*"

The Bayleys did not know what to say to her. "And when you get there? What will you do?"

"I can get a plane."

Vivien said, "You'll go to South Africa then."

She shook her head.

"Where will you go Rebecca?" Vivien spoke gently.

She told them about the money Bray had sent to Switzerland.

"Don't repeat that story to anyone else. Not even your friend Loulou," Neil Bayley said. Vivien was silent.

"I think I'll go and take the money."

They did not ask any more questions.

Vivien gave her a camel-hair coat she had brought from England:
"It's almost winter in Europe—you've got no warm clothes." She had
the two cotton dresses they had made, the old jeans and shirt
(washed, no trace of red earth), the picnic basket and Bray's briefcase. Neil had had to ask her to let him look in it for Bray's passport
and other papers but he had given it back to her.

Neil came into the bedroom where she and Vivien stood with the
coat. "What about the air ticket?"

"I'll borrow the money from Loulou."

Neil nodded: Loulou was her husband's associate, the matter of the
money would be easily arranged. She said at once, "He'll be pleased
to have me pay in Swiss francs."

When Neil had left the room, she said to Vivien, "I'll never live
with Gordon again," and Vivien stood there, looking at the coat without seeing it, pressing her thumbnail between her front teeth.

They gave her one of their suitcases. When she had packed, it was
still half-empty. Up to the moment she left they seemed to feel both
somehow responsible to stop her and yet unable to offer any reason
why she should not go. "I don't think he'll ever get through the border," Neil offered. "Specially him. It's probably known he's done some
gun-running in Katanga in his time."

"He'll get through all right. Gordon always says Loulou can do
anything."

He drove a day and a night with only a short nap two or three
times with the car come to rest at the roadside. It was dangerous for
anyone to drive so long and fast without rest but she knew nothing
would happen. She found it was not that you don't care if you live or
die but just that you know when you can't die. You have been left
alive. He had brought with him only one of the girls, and there was
plenty of room to stretch out and sleep. She and the girl had no com-

mon language, so their communication consisted of an occasional
smile and a wordless accord about the times they needed to go off
into the bushes together to pee. The heat was very great and with the
speed produced a daze: forest, savannah, scrub, a change in motion
winding down a pass. Loulou got on well with the officials at the border post and "forgot" two bottles of whisky left standing beside the
air-conditioner that sweated water in the humidity. On the other side
of the frontier was night, sudden bursts of cackling music as he tried
to pick up some station on the car radio, confused sleep, the fuzzy
bulk of him there in the sweater, the headlight beams cloudy with insects, dawn coming in as a smell of freshness before the light. They
were in a near-desert, hard yellow earth funnelled into antheaps fifteen feet high, dowdy thornbush draped in tattered webs, huge
baobab trees. They drove over wooden bridges above dry riverbeds.
Towards midday all growing things ceased to exist and there was
nothing but hard yellow cliffs, drifts of pollen-coloured dunes, more
cliffs runnelled and sheered away by exposure, and then behind the
yellow, a blue as bright and hard—the sea. Through the filthy villages, the escort of bicycles and chickens and overburdened buses
and lorries that are the first sign of every colonial town, they came to
factories with Portuguese names, cliffs clothed completely with the
pink and white walls and tiled roofs, the dark trees and brilliant
trails of bougainvillea of white men's houses, and below, the pale
cubes and rectangles of the commercial centre behind a curved cor-
niche and a harbour-jumble of ships and cranes. Loulou took her to
the Lisboa Hotel ("You like it—two bar for cocktail") and gave her
the equivalent of fifty pounds, partly in dollars, partly in sterling, in
addition to the price in *escudos* of a ticket for Europe. On one of
their trips to the bushes the girl had shown Rebecca packets of notes
in a calico bag on either hip under her *pagne*—she seemed to have
been brought along more as a piggybank than *une petite folie*. Loulou himself did not book into the hotel; he had his good friend in the
harbour customs to go and see, and then he had promised to buy the
girl a wig—she put her fingers on her shoulders and smiled demandingly to show that it must be long hair, really long—before they set
off again to drive down south to the other seaport.

When they had gone she sat on one of the beds in the room she
had been given, swaying slightly, still, from the motion of the car,

and telephoned the airways office. She was told she would have to wait two days for a connection to Zurich; there was a seat for her on the plane. They took her name and she said she would come to pay for the ticket later.

It was a double room with two beds separated by a little night-table holding the telephone, an ashtray, and a booklet entitled, in English, French, and Portuguese, *What to See and Where to Go*. There was a bathroom and behind thick curtains she found a little slice of balcony. She went out for a moment. A half-moon of flat bay, the palms moving away at regular spaces along the curve, and just opposite the hotel, a new block going up behind screens of matting. In a gap, workmen sat on the tightrope of steel girders eating their lunch. Down below, a tiny square that must have been the plaza when the town was a garrison outpost was divided by sand paths and ornamental plants, like the quarterings of a heraldic crest. A workman with a paper forage cap on his head waved at her. She came inside, pulled the curtains again, and stood looking at the two beds. She turned down the cover of the one she had sat on while telephoning, and lay on her back. Six fake candles of the chandelier had made six shaded brown circles on the ceiling. The glass drops giddied slowly in some current of air that she did not feel. There was nothing familiar in the room but the picnic basket and the briefcase. And herself. It was on this day, exactly one week ago, that they had been on the road from Gala.

One of the men at the reception desk of the Hotel Lisboa was short, with a large head of crimped hair, a tiny mouth blue-shaded all round no matter how closely shaven, and young brown eyes ringed like a marmoset's. This large head was not very high above the counter and was always inclined in one kind of service or another— he was either changing travellers' cheques, getting a number on the telephone for someone, or clicking the lead out of his little gilt pencil to draw a street-map. He spoke English fluently and it was he who told her how to get to the airline office. He would step out to prod at the button when the lift was slow to come; with a smile like the smile from a hospital bed he would take up the room-key dropped at the desk by a guest going out into the sun.

She could recall at will every detail about this man's face, it was a rubber stamp tried out on a blank page, whereas in Bray's face there were gaps that could not be filled in. Between the cheekbone and the angle of the jaw, on the left side. From the nose to the upper lip. She could not put him together. She caught certain expressions and certain angles but she could not find the steady image.

The promenade under the palm trees was much longer than it looked. It took more than half an hour, walking slowly, to reach the entrance to the docks. She would walk one way along the promenade and the other way on the opposite side of the wide boulevard, along the shops and buildings. Just before the docks there was a smelly place where the promenade was slippery with bits of fish and African women wholesalers bargained for catches and took them away, in the boots of the local taxis. On the town side was a new complex of banks and insurance companies, all mosaics and metal collage and the sort of monumental sculpture of black goddesses that white architects tend to commission in colonies where the local population is particularly malnourished. There were shops crammed with transistor radios, tape-recorders, and electric grills with well-browned plaster chickens stuck on their spits. There were older buildings, storerooms and warehouses shuttered blind, and others with peeling pastel façades, trompe-l'oeil pillars and garlands painted faintly round the doors and windows. At the pavement cafés men read newspapers; the white ones lowered them a moment when a woman passed. She sat in the street at one or other of the little tables for long stretches, drinking her black coffee well sweetened and watching the big birds that stood all day in the shallow water of the bay, looking stranded on the mud when the tide was out, and locked to their mirror-image, upside down in the calm pale surface, when the tide was in. Once she walked down to the edge of the sloppy mud but the birds did not move. There were concrete benches on the promenade. She sat for a while pestered by child beggars selling lottery tickets, and young Portuguese soldiers; perhaps the benches were the traditional place for picking up girls, although prostitutes in that town were hardly likely to be white. The young soldiers came from an ancient fort on one of the yellow hills above the bay; if she turned left instead of right, along the promenade, when she came out of the Hotel Lisboa, she passed beneath it. It was solid and worn as the crown of an old molar; the Portuguese had built it five hundred years ago and were

there still—army jeeps went up and down the steep road to the bat-
tlements and sentries' huts stood among the very old fig trees, rooted
in the walls, that had never let go, either. At night it was floodlit; one
of the sights mentioned in the trilingual guide beside the bed.

The plane did not leave until six in the evening on the second day.
She bought a bottle of shampoo and washed her hair and went to the
little square to dry it in the morning sun. A ragged old black man in
a cap with the coat-of-arms of the town was splattering a hose on the
coarse leaves of the shrubs. There were no English newspapers but
the reception desk at the hotel displayed a wire stand with *Time* and
Newsweek for the foreign businessmen who sat at all times of day
under the neon lights of the bar lounge, exchanging handshakes and
the misunderstandings of language difficulties with local businessmen
and their hangers-on. She had bought *Time* and turned the pages in
the square while the workmen whistled at her from the scaffolding.
Married, divorced, dead—actresses, members of deposed royalty,
American politicians she'd never heard of. Pictures of a group of nude
students burning an effigy on a towering bridge; of a Vietnamese
child with her arm blown off at the elbow. Near the bottom of a
page, the photograph, the name—EENY MEENY MWETA MO—WILL HE
BE THE NEXT TO GO? *This has been the year of the coup in Africa—
half-a-dozen governments toppled since January. Good-looking good
boy of the Western nations, Adamson Mweta (40) is the latest of the
continent's moderate leaders to find himself hanging on to the presidential seat-belt while riots rock his country. His prisons are full but
even then he can't be sure who, among those at large, Left or Right,
is friend or foe. His Minister of Foreign Affairs, urbane anti-Commu-
nist Albert Tola Tola, is inside after rumours of an attempted take-
over last month. His trusted White Man Friday, Africa expert Colonel
Evelyn James Bray (54), who helped him negotiate independence,
has been murdered in mysterious circumstances on the road to the
capital. His one-time comrade in arms, Leftist Edward Shinza, has
succeeded in stirring up an insurrection in the trade unions that has
escalated from general strike to countrywide chaos. As if to prove this
old friend's taunts that he is no more than "the black watchman
standing guard outside the white man's enterprise," Adamson Mweta
has had to call upon Britain to send troops to his country. Will the
invasion-by-invitation of the former colonial master keep him in his*

seat and the country's gold and other valuable mineral resources in the hands of British and U.S. interests?

Quite short; the last of the columns under the general heading of Africa. It was Mweta's face that she had seen—Bray's name was come upon in the middle of the text. She read the whole thing over several times. She walked down to the promenade and back along the shops and sat down again at one of the pavement tables. Other people had their newspapers and she had the magazine lying there beside the bowl full of paper sachets of sugar. The tide was coming in round the birds' legs. A few empty tables away a man and a small boy were concentrating on something the man was drawing. The child had his head cocked sideways, smiling in admiration, anticipation and self-importance—the drawing was being done for him. The man was ageing, one of those extremely handsome men who might have a third or fourth wife the same age as a daughter. Every now and then he lifted his head and took a look under a raised, wrinkled brow at the sea for some point of reference. It was a very dark Mediterranean face, all the beautiful planes deeply scored in now, as if age were redrawing it in a sharper, darker pencil. Brilliantly black eyes were deep-set in a contemplative, amused crinkle that suggested disappointed scholarship—a scientist, someone who saw life as a pattern of gyrations in a drop under a microscope. But he was shabbily dressed and poor looking. Perhaps an intellectual who'd got into political trouble in Portugal. The little boy hung on his arm in eagerness, hampering him. At last the picture was finished and he held it out at arm's length against the sea and the little boy clambered down from his chair to see it properly. She could see, too—a picture of great happiness, past happiness, choppy waves frilling along, a gay ship with flags and triumphant smoke, birds sprinkled about the air like kisses on a letter. The child looked at it smiling but still in anticipation, looking for the—*something*—the secret marvel that exists only in children's expectation. It was the man himself who laughed at his work in enjoyment. Then the little boy took the cue and eagerly laughed, to be with him. The child had a final pull at the straw of his orangeade and then the pair crossed the boulevard hand and hand, taking the drawing along. The man steered the child in a special kind of alert protectiveness that suggested the charge was temporary, or new; a divorced father who has abducted the child from the custody of a former wife. —But no, he was really too old to be the father; more likely a grandfather who found himself alone with a child; she had the strong impression that this was *the last thing* in that man's life, all he had left.

They were gone. For ten minutes she had felt a deep interest in those two human beings. One of the birds opened its wings—she had not seen them move before—and flapped slowly away over the bay.

The plane came in late from stops farther south in Africa and by the time it took off the town was a scimitar of sparkle along the bay, a bowl of greenish light that was the sports stadium, a tilting stage-set that was the fort, and then a few glows dying out like matches on the ground. She saw nothing of the forests and deserts of the continent she was leaving for the first time, although the man in the seat beside her kept turning on his reading-light to look at the map stuffed in along with the sick-bag in the seat-pocket. Brownish shaded areas, green areas: drops of moisture shimmied outside the double window and she could not even see the darkness—only her own face. The hostess brought along a trolley of papers and there was the cover of that same number of the magazine there, and when the trolley was steered back, it was gone: somewhere along the rows of seat-backs, someone was reading it. The man who was her neighbour drank individual bottles of champagne with the air of doing so on principle rather than with any enjoyment and at an hour when at last there was no food being served and the lights had been dimmed he pressed the red button for the hostess and asked for seltzer. Since he was awake she took out of the briefcase (beside her, between her legs and the wall of the plane) the half-sheet of typing paper on which, in Bray's handwriting, there was the name of the bank, the number of the account, and *La Fille aux Yeux d'Or*. She had looked at it a number of times since she had got into the plane. It was probably the last thing he had written. The cheque for Hjalmar? No, that must have been before. But she could not be sure; she did not know when he had decided to put down on that piece of paper the particulars about the account. She wouldn't ever know if it really was the last time he was to write when he wrote: *La Fille aux Yeux d'Or*. There was nothing but the facts, the address, the code name. What could one find in the shape of the letters, the spacing? She searched it as the child had searched the man's drawing.

She put the paper away in the briefcase again. Beside her there were suppressed belches.

If he had copied out (from some notebook? from memory?) the details of the account, of course, it must have been to give to her. So that she would know where to go. But if they were to be together there would be no need for her to have the piece of paper. He had put it in the briefcase, he had not given it to her. When was he going to give it to her?

But perhaps it had been in the briefcase a long time. No notebook, no commitment to memory: kept in the briefcase for the record, and automatically taken along with them when they left as part of the personal papers, his and hers, they would need together. The man at her side fell asleep and she felt her mind begin to slide, too; there was a jerky snatch of dream with Bray walking about in it, but she drew back fearfully into wakefulness. And in hours or a little while, looking out into the blue-black that was clear now, she saw a burning crust along the edge of a darker mass. She thought of a veld fire but then was aware of a narrow reflection of the fire mirrored along its shape. It was a coastline down there—the seashore and little harbours lit up all night into the early dawn while the land mass behind was asleep. Now she saw blackly glittering swells of darkness: the sea.

The man beside her was craning his neck at a polite distance over her shoulder. He said, "The coast of Italy."

She had never been out of Africa before. A feeling of intense strangeness came over her. It was day, up in the air. Down below, the people of Europe slept on. Soon there were the Alps in the cold sun, shining and elegant. Passengers revived to look at them, spread like a display for watches in a jeweller's window.

A black Mercedes taxi took her from the glass and black airport into the city. Gentle humps of fields were still green, or stubbled after harvest. A chill breath misted them over. All the new buildings were the same heavy black frames squaring-off glass that was the same sheeny grey as the lake reflecting the sky. A high jet spouted out of the lake as if a whale were kept in captivity there. The hotel the girl at the airport information desk sent her to was an old villa above the lake and she had to walk down the street to get a tramcar into town.

The houses had little spires, balconies, towers, and were closed away behind double windows; along a wall, an espaliered pear tree held still a single pear, ruddy and wizened. She wore the camel-hair coat and her legs were cold. The tram faltered and teetered steeply down and she got off with everyone else at a terminus in the main street. She had, not in her bag but in her hand clenched in the pocket of the coat, the piece of paper: apparently the bank was in this main street. She began to walk along looking at the way the numbers ran, and she crossed because the evens were on the other side, and walked on and on, gaining the impression that everyone was making straight for her as if she were not there. Then she realized that here people kept to the right, not the left. The street was very long and wide and busy but she was not conscious of shops or people, only of numbers. There was a bank with a satiny façade with tiny show-cases where a beaming puppet in a blonde wig held up her savings, but that was not the one. She showed someone the name on the piece of paper and was directed a few yards on to a pillared portico and huge double doors. Inside she was in an echoing hall with a black-and-white tiled floor and a few mahogany and brass-railed booths pushed far back round the walls. A porter intercepted her on the way to one of them. He couldn't understand her and took her to a pale clerk who spoke perfect English. They sent her in a mahogany lift up through the great vault of the building. The feeling of strangeness that had begun in the plane grew stronger and stronger.

There was another echoing hall in which footsteps were a long-drawn-out approach or retreat. But here there was a corner with a thick carpet and leather-and-velvet chairs. She sat and looked at banking journals in French and German full of pictures of black frame-and-glass factory buildings and people skiing with wings of snow. An Indian man and woman were waiting, too—the woman in a gauzy sari with a cardigan over it—a stranger from another climate, like herself.

She did not believe, now, that anyone in this place would know about the account, or that the account or the money, spoken about so far away, existed at all. An impostor in bare legs and borrowed coat went along corridors, past troughs of plants, a wooden bear with hats and umbrellas on its arms, into a large stuffy, muffled room unlike any office she had ever been in. Another wooden bear. A glass-fronted bookcase. Table held up by a satyr caryatid. A desk too, but with its functional aspect so softened by tooled leather, photographs, and a pot of African violets in a gilt basket that it was just another piece of furniture.

Herr Weber introduced himself like a doctor ready to hear any intimacy as blandly as he might ask about regular bowel action. He had a neat kind face and an old-fashioned paunch with a watch-chain. *La Fille aux Yeux d'Or* might have been Schmidt or Jones; he wrote something with his silver pencil, rang a bell, sent for some papers. While they waited he made conversation. Bray had teased her that Goebbels and Goering as well as Tshombe had put away their millions in Swiss banks. Herr Weber was an old man—"Already forty years in this bank," he told her, smiling. Where did she live? "Oh Africa must be interesting, yes? I have always wanted to visit—but that is so far. My wife likes to go to Italy. It is beautiful. And we have been once in Greece. That is beautiful. But Africa is beautiful too, neh?" Perhaps he had had this same conversation with Tshombe and would have it with the woman in the cardigan and sari—"Oh India must be interesting, yes?"—while all through the years he had sat safe among his family photographs.

When the papers came he read through them at the odd angle of people who wear bifocal lenses and asked how much money she wanted to draw. She said she thought all of it.

He made the fatherly suggestion: "Don't you want rather to transfer it wherever you're going? Where do you go?"

She had thought only of coming here: that was where she had been going. She said, "England."

His short soft forefinger was a pendulum. "You know if you take your money to England, you don't get it out again? You have it here in Switzerland, you can write to us from anywhere in the world, we send money to you. It's better you take now only what you need, and I transfer to England what you are going to need there—where it is? London? —Whatever bank you say."

"Any bank—I don't know any."

She signed some papers. He wrote down the particulars of the sum to be paid into the account of Jean-Louis Kamboya, of Lubumbashi. "Congo Kinshasa, no?" He was proud to know the difference. "With this Congo and that Congo—" He gave her a slip for the teller and shook hands, "I wish you a pleasant stay, dear lady. Unfortunately this is not the best time. You should come in springtime, neh?"

Downstairs white male hands with a gold wedding ring counted out fifteen hundred Swiss francs in notes and clipped them together. She was like Loulou's girl, now, with a variety of currencies about her.

And now it was done. Her own footsteps died away behind her as she came out through the great doors and she was confronted with figures in raincoats and overcoats hurrying all round her, the sound of children's inquiring voices in German. Now she had no purpose at all and bewilderedly she met the shops full of suède coats and crocodile-skin luggage (real, not like Loulou's), the splendid toyshops, shops with rosy salami and horseshoe-shaped sausages, showcases of steel and gold and diamond watches, shops with fur boots. A constant waterfall streamed down the inside of a window filled with bowls of roses, lilies and orchids, magnifying them and somehow setting them out of reach as the lenses of goggles did the wild gardens under water in that other lake that was left behind. In a confectioner's women bought cakes and ate them at the counter. A blast of heat at the door kept the chill out and while she drank a cup of coffee in the vanilla-scented room where everybody was eating sweet things she watched fingers pointed at this cake or that and felt her legs warmed by the central heating. Out in the street she wandered on past a tiny buried square with a lichened statue deep in hand-shaped leaves cast like old chamois gloves. She had never seen a chestnut tree before but she recognized the conkers children played games with in the English storybooks of her childhood. It began to rain; an old fat woman sold roast chestnuts from a brazier kept aglow under an umbrella. In the tram going back up the hill she sat among the housewives going home with their morning's shopping, already equipped in full dress against the coming of winter—coats, boots, umbrellas, gloves; even the little children with their gumboots and duffles zipped up tubbily. They seemed so placid, matter-of-factly prepared for hazards all foreseen in an environment of their own where all risks were known ones. But of course, it was never really like that: even these damp pink noses (even Herr Weber) could be invaded in their lawful feather-beds by the violence of sudden love or death.

She felt so cold and bloodless that she ordered a glass of red wine in the hotel lounge. It was furnished with rickety antiques and family portraits and ended in a little conservatory where the common plants that grew everywhere at home, in Africa, were warmed by central heating and trained up the glass from pots. A young couple were sitting there, stirring the cream on their coffee and slowly finishing bowls of berries sprinkled with sugar. They murmured to each other in German—something like, "Good . . . ?" "Oh very good"—and went on dreamily licking the spoons. The girl wore trousers and a sweater with a string of pearls, she was tall and narrow-footed and remote. The man, shorter than she, looked not quite at home in rather smart casual clothes and had a worried little double chin already beginning beneath his soft face. The girl yawned and he smiled. It was the stalemate of conversation, the listlessness of a newly married couple who have never previously been lovers. "Very good," he said again, putting his bowl on the tray.

The wine rose to her head in a singing sensation and she thought of them sitting on politely round a coffee table for ever, he slipping down into fatness and greyness, she never released from her remoteness, while their children grew, waiting to take their places there. She became aware of an ornamental clock ticking away the silence in the room between herself and the couple.

And so she came to England, flying over a grey sea with scum floating like spit, a sea into which the sewers of Europe emptied; over European cities made up of grey blocks like printers' lugs.

Her parents were living there. But the fact was just an address to which she had written letters and not a place probably within an hour's journey of the streets she knew now, in London, where people walked off into a thickening of mist as if off the end of the world. She made no attempt to get in touch with her family. She wandered the streets and rode the buses going to see all the things that stood for this city. If there was a lane that said "To Samuel Johnson's House," she took it; if there was a brochure, she bought it. She waited on the steepening stairways of tube stations, descending into darkness. She crossed bridges and smelled the musk of churches. She passed the pubs full of beer-coloured light where people stood close-packed, touching. She was among them in trains where they stood close-packed, not touching. She read the messages: in the tube, a girl dropping paper panties from between forefinger and thumb—Give Your Dirty Washing To the Dustman; in the Soho chemists', Pregnancy Test—24-Hour Service. She went along the titles of second-hand books on a barrow off Old Compton Street; the faces of old men under the yoke of sandwich-boards; the look-out of touts standing like shopwalkers outside strip clubs.

She crossed between the puddles from the fountain and the legs of the people who sat all day with their packs and guitars, marooned on that traffic island that was Piccadilly Circus. A young Jesus in dirty white robes had a ring of frizzy-maned disciples. Girls in Red Indian fringes rested on boys in fur-trappers' jackets. They streamed past, around, behind her in Shaftesbury Avenue, cowboys with belts as wide as corsets, pale girls with long tangled hair, long bedraggled coats and broken boots like the waifs in illustrations to school-prize editions of Dickens; gipsies, Eastern mendicants, handsome bandits with mustachios, a bullfighter in green velvet pants and bolero, coming full on at her. What did this cold fiesta know of the reality of hot sun on a burning car? Of the load of mauve flowers carried by the trees in the village where chickens tied by the leg were mashed into blood and guts under men's feet—a moment of sudden displacement came to her like the dazzling dark brightness that follows a blow. She went unrecognized here; she was the figure with the scythe.

Yet this was where Bray came from: there were faces in which she could trace him. An elderly man in a taxi outside a restaurant; even a young actor with sideburns and locks. He might have once been, or become, any of these who were living so differently from the way he did. It was as if she forayed into a past that he had left long ago and a future that he would never inhabit. She wandered the bypasses of his life that he had not taken, meeting the possibility of his presence. It came to her as a kind of wonder, an explanation. Of what? His life? His death? Her experience of living with him? Something of all three. She had started off with the knowledge that she would not live with Gordon again. It was the first positive thing she knew after the moment, on the road, when she had become conscious of thirst; she had said to Vivien, "I will never live with Gordon again." Now she began to have an inkling of why she knew this. This place where Bray had come from was full of faces that he was not, that he had chosen not to be. He had made his life in accordance with some conscious choice—beliefs, she supposed, that she also supposed she didn't properly understand. It didn't have much to do with being what her father would have called a nigger-lover. But it had something to do with life itself. Gordon was always trying to outwit; Bray lived not as an adversary but a participant. She had never lived with anyone like that before. And once you did, you couldn't live again with a Gordon, who wanted only to "make his pile and get out"— always to the next country just like the last and the next "opportunity" just like the last: to make his pile and get out. Bray's way had ended on the road as if he hadn't mattered any more than a bunch of chickens tied by the leg—yes, the explanation given by the people in the capital was nothing to her, meaningless against the fact of his death as she had heard it and seen and felt it in flesh as she picked glass from his cheek. Whoever they were, they had killed him like a chicken, a snake hacked in the road, a bug mashed on a wall, and what they had done was pure faceless horror to her, the madness of waiting in the ditch, the earth under her fingernails. But she was sure he would have known who they were. He would have known why it had happened to him. Old lecherous Dando, trying to feel the beginning of her breast from over her shoulder, was right about that.

She kept still the piece of paper with the particulars of the Swiss account in his handwriting; she carried it around with her in the pocket of the new coat she had bought herself in one of the shops full of lights flashing on and off to nasal music. He had smuggled the money out because he loved her, that she also knew. But this did not please her as proof, because (taking the paper out in tubes, buses, on park benches) it meant at the same time that he accepted they would part, that there was a life for her to live without him. And—cracking the code further—at the time when it was written, that meant he would go back one day to Olivia; not that he would be dead.

She thought of Olivia as an empty perfume bottle in which a scent still faintly remains. She had found one on one of the shelves in the wardrobe of her hotel room: left there by some anonymous English woman, an Olivia. She knew nobody in the city of eight millions. She had nothing in common with anyone; except his wife.

At times she was strongly attracted by the idea of going to see Olivia and his daughters. But the thought that they would receive her, accept her in their supremely civilized tolerance—*his* tolerance—this filled her with resentment. She wanted to bare her suffering, to live it and thrust it, disgusting, torn live from her under their noses, not to make it "acceptable" to others.

She had bought herself warm clothes and now looked like anyone else, as she went about. After an exchange with the Irish maid in the

hotel on the subject of the ages, temperaments, and proclivity to illness of their respective children, she thought of how she would send
for her children and perhaps live in London with them. It was not so
much a plan as a daydream—walking with them over the piles of
fallen leaves in the parks. The Irish maid was the only person she
talked to and the conversation began the moment the woman opened
the door with her pass key every day and went on, impossible to
stem, until a final burst of the Hoover drowned parting remarks. The
answers to questions about children were factual but it was Bray she
was speaking of when husbands were discussed, and he was alive,
waiting for her to come back to whatever part of Africa it was they
lived. The maid was satisfied without any precise definition: she referred to Africa as "out there" and looked sympathetic. "I had to
leave me job down in the men's university hostel after twelve years
becaz the coloureds was needlin' each other in the bathroom—I saw
the pots of vaseline. I went straight down to the superintendent, I
said, all those coloureds the government's lettin' in, I'm not used to
things like that, I said, my husband wouldn't let me stay another day
—I won't stand for *that*, I said, thank you very much."

Although there was the half-sheet of paper in the coat pocket, there
was also what Bray had said the night before they left Gala. She had
told him—not in so many words—the only thing she feared about
Gala was being sent away, and he said, I know; but I'll be there. And
when she had said, how can we go together, and he knew England
was in her mind, he had said, perhaps we can manage. He had said:
we'll decide what to do. (Sitting one afternoon in something called
the Ceylon Tea Shop, she suddenly remembered that precisely.) We'll
decide what to do. Perhaps the code of the paper didn't read that he
was going to set her down somewhere, gently, regretfully. It might
have meant they were going to Sardinia, where the spear-fishing was
so good. No, not really that . . . but somewhere together outside
Gala; they had never had any existence, outside Gala.

In the teashop with the blown-up photographs of tea-estates and
the framed quiz *How Much Do You Know about Tea?* facing her, she
came back again to the fact that on that last night they had not made
love properly. It was she who had decided, because they were both
so tired and had to get up early, that they wouldn't finish it. He fell
asleep inside her body and there was the thought, like a treat, that

they would make love in a big bed for the first time the next night, in the capital. So he had never come to her, she had never come to him; it had never been reached, that particular compact of fulfilment. She passed through days now when she was racked by an obsession of regret about this. Of all the deprivation, the loss, the silence, the emptiness, the finality, this became the most urgent, and the cruellest, because urgency itself was a form of mockery thrown back at her from the blank of death: there was nothing for it to be directed at. She told herself that they had made love a hundred times, the compact was made—what did one more time matter? But she hungered for that one last time. It had been given up, for nothing, lost along with the rest, for no reason. She asked herself again and again what difference it would have made. But the answer was fiercely that she wanted it. It was hers. Before death came. It had belonged to her; it was not death that had taken it—what death took was unarguable—it had been forgone. She thought about it so much that she produced in herself the physical manifestations of the unfinished act. The lips of her body swelled and she knew with horror the desire of that night that now would never be satisfied.

She felt afraid of herself.

The smell of stale cigarettes in ashtrays was the smell of Gala after burnings.

Walking round the shivering ponds, down the avenues of leaves sodden as old newspaper under the trees of parks, she saw the nodules of next year's buds on the stripped branches, the callousness of the earth endlessly renewing itself. Would she, too, seek again—she tried to reduce it to the baldest fact—that coming up of one flesh against another until like a little stone breaking at last the surface of a still pool, sensation in ring after ring flows out from that little stone, that pip fructifying from its hiding place, the plumb centre of her being . . . she thought: that's all it is. She grew afraid. It would come back, commonplace desire. Everything else would come round again; be renewed. She sat in the bus and felt the threat of ordinary bodies around her.

There were days when hammering fists of anguish ceased for no more reason than they would begin again. Then she cried. She had begun to do exercises on the floor of the hotel room every morning because she had read in some newspaper that you could get through long periods simply by going through the motions of some routine, and she lay there on the maid's Hoovered carpet and the tears ran from the outer corners of her eyes. She wept because the sense of Bray had come back to her so strongly, as if he had never been dead on that road and it had never happened. What was she doing in the hotel room? The sense of him was restored to her and she did not have to look for signs of him or question him, because he was gone and there was nothing more to find. And so he died, for her, again. The Irish maid came to clean and the marks of weeping could not be hidden from those hen-sharp eyes beneath the hackle-like fringe; she said that she'd just heard how her children were missing her. The lie became a tenderness towards them and a longing to see them; and the fantasy of walking with them in London changed to an intention. In a few days she would work out what sort of letter to write to Gordon about them. She did not know how or why she expected Gordon to hand the children over to her. She supposed everything might even seem to go on as before, with Gordon satisfied that he had a wife and children somewhere, only just a little more remote than they had always been.

One afternoon she was coming out of the supermarket in the suburban shopping street near the hotel when somebody said her name. It came like a heavy hand on her shoulder. She turned. A tall, very slender girl with a narrow, sallow face curtained in straight black hair was leaning casually on a wheeled shopping basket. It was Emmanuelle. "I thought it was you but it couldn't be—are you over on holiday?"

"My family live in England. I've been here about two weeks." She held tightly closed her packet containing one pear and one orange; evidence of her solitariness. "And you—you live round about?"

Emmanuelle's hair wrapped itself across her neck like a scarf, in the wind. "We're just down the road. Beastly basement flat. But we're getting a big studio next month—if we don't go back, instead."

"Back? Could Ras go back?"

"It's someone else."

"I'm sorry—I just thought—"

They stood there talking, two women who had never liked one another much. Emmanuelle's elegant hands mimed a sort of trill of inconsequence along the handle of her basket. "That's all right. No drama. We're friends and all that. I'm living with Kofi Ahuma—he's just published his first novel, but now his father's in favour again in Ghana, and he can indulge his homesickness. So we may go to Ghana. Are your children with you? We're producing a children's play together—he wrote it and I did the music. It's on at the Theatre Club for the next three days, they might enjoy it."

"No, they're not here."

Emmanuelle gave the quick nod of someone who reminds herself of something that hasn't interested her very much. "Oh my God—you were in that awful accident, weren't you?" She was mildly curious. "What happened to Colonel Bray—he was beaten up?"

"He was killed."

"How ghastly." She might have left Ras but she was still armed with his opinions. "Of course, he was with Shinza and that crowd. Poor devil. These nice white liberals getting mixed up in things they don't understand. What did he expect?"

The two airlifts of troops who were flown in at Mweta's request for help from Britain succeeded in bringing order to the country for the time being. It was the same order of things that had led to disorder in the first place. But Mweta was back in his big house and Shinza was in exile in Algiers and Cyrus Goma, Basil Nwanga, Dhlamini Okoi and many others were kept in detention somewhere and—for the time being—forgotten.

Hjalmar Wentz was unharmed in the house in Gala and it was he who packed up Bray's things after Bray's death and sent them to his wife, Olivia.

No one could say for certain whether, when Bray was killed on the way to the capital, he was going to Mweta or to buy arms for Shinza. To some, as his friend Dando had predicted, he was a martyr to savages; to others, one of those madmen like Geoffrey Bing or Conor Cruise O'Brien who had only got what he deserved. In a number devoted to "The Decline of Liberalism" in an English monthly journal he was discussed as an interesting case in point: a man who had "passed over from the scepticism and resignation of empirical liberalism to become one of those who are so haunted by the stupidities and evils in human affairs that they are prepared to accept apocalyptic solutions, wade through blood if need be, to bring real change."

Hjalmar Wentz also put together Bray's box of papers and gave them over to Dando, who might know what to do with them. Eventually they must have reached the hands of Mweta. He, apparently, chose to believe that Bray was a conciliator; a year later he published a blueprint for the country's new education scheme, the Bray Report.